Ingram Brothers Series

ROZ LEE

DEDICATION

To my wonderful, devoted readers.
You inspire me every day.

TABLE OF CONTENTS

Ingram
Brothers #1
WILL
TODAY BESTSELLING AUTHOR
ROZLEE

AUTHOR'S NOTE

Thank you so much for purchasing *Will – The Ingram Brothers #1*. If the town of Willowbrook, Texas and some of the characters seem familiar, then I'll assume you've also read *Lost Melody* by my alter ego, Dolores W. Maroney. If you haven't, then Melody, Hank, and a few other characters will be new to you. No worries. I loved the town of Willowbrook and its residents so much I had to go back there to see what they were up to. I hope you'll love them as much as I do, and if you haven't read *Lost Melody*, will choose do so when you've finished reading Will's story.

Thanks again. I hope you enjoy the read.

Roz

CHAPTER ONE

William Ingram stared at the drink he held loosely between his thumb and middle finger. Was this going to be his only drink today or the first of many? In the last six months, he'd gone from mildly successful to virtually broke. So, the decision was a no-brainer. It would be the first of many—or at least the first of as many as he could afford.

The boarding pass in his jacket pocket and the drink in front of him represented the majority of the funds he had left to his name. The few art supplies he hadn't sold at rock-bottom prices to fund his return home had been checked as luggage which, an airline employee by the name of Brandy had assured him, would be transferred to the new plane as soon it arrived to take him and the rest of the passengers aboard their aborted flight on to their destination.

Just his luck. He'd admitted defeat and then his flight from New York made an emergency landing in Philadelphia. It seemed the universe wasn't done with him.

The airline had booked as many of the stranded passengers onto existing flights as possible, starting with the ones who were making a connection in Dallas. He wished he was one of them, but the truth was, once he got to Texas, he was there to stay. He'd ventured out into the world, had followed his dream until it had turned into a nightmare. When things had gone to shit, he'd raged and fought back, convinced the police would eventually find the people responsible and return his property to him. After several months with no break in the case, his confidence had eroded until he'd lost hope and slid down the slippery slope into despair. His girlfriend/agent had stolen more than his livelihood, she'd stolen his will to create, leaving him one option — cut his losses and return home to Willowbrook, Texas.

What he'd do once he got there was anyone's guess. Maybe he could get a job painting houses. It was honest work and required the one thing he still had — an able body. He'd never been one to do much physical labor, avoiding it at all costs, but in New York, he'd seen the necessity of keeping in shape and had been a regular at the local gym until he'd had to cancel his membership due to lack of funds. He'd never painted a structure before, but he knew how to hold a paintbrush. It wasn't like anyone would be asking his opinion on the color or anything else. He'd be hired muscle to get the mindless job done.

He gave himself two, maybe three weeks before the mind-numbing physical exertion pushed him to the edge of his sanity.

Great. Just fucking great.

He took a healthy sip, closing his eyes as the cheap bourbon ate away at the lining of his throat and nibbled at the ragged edges of his mood.

A knee to his hip almost knocked him off his seat and caused the liquor in his glass to slosh over the side onto the back of his hand. Grabbing the bar to steady himself, he groaned at the waste of alcohol he'd been counting on. "Shit! Watch what you're doing!"

"Sorry."

The feminine voice slid through him like fifty-year-old whiskey, setting fire to parts of him that had suffered Jessica's betrayal perhaps more than any other. It was good to know the physical damage wasn't permanent even if he had no intention of taking any part of himself out for a test run. Determined not to engage, he sucked the liquid from his skin. The bartender hustled over with a rag, drawing Will's attention upward. His gaze locked on the reflection in the mirror behind the bar, and he damn near bit his hand as he recognized the woman sitting next to him.

He didn't know her name, but he'd seen her before. More importantly, he'd seen her type before. Beautiful, sexy, and high maintenance. Everything from her clothes to her hairstyle to the perfect application of makeup on her clear complexion screamed *rich girl*.

She'd been on his flight — in first class while he'd been lucky to be in the cheap seats. If not for the cute flight attendant who'd taken pity on him and offered to let him change seats, free of charge, to an open bulkhead seat, he never would have seen this woman. She'd come breezing in at the last minute like she owned the plane, and taken her seat next to the aisle in the last row. Just feet from where he sat trying not to notice anything about her. Of course he'd noticed everything, from the color of her hair — auburn — to the shape of her body — a perfect hourglass — to the slight sheen of perspiration on her forehead as she shoved her Louis Vuitton carry-on into the overhead bin. He'd looked her over as a man then and liked what he saw, but now, with only her face visible in the mirror, the artist in him took over.

She wore makeup, but it was artfully applied, so, at first glance, it appeared she wore none at all. Strategically placed streaks of — whatever-the-hell-women-called-it — highlighted already distinct cheekbones. Some sort of dark magic applied to her eyelids showcased the most beautiful blue irises he'd ever seen. Shades of blue paint swirled through his mind as his brain automatically tried to replicate the color in his preferred medium — oils.

Coupling what he'd already seen of her body with what he now knew about her face, he realized he had to paint her. Only he didn't paint anymore. The sharpness of the realization had him reaching for the glass the bartender had so kindly refilled at no cost. Forcing his gaze from the mirror, Will gulped the last of his whiskey. Placing the cheap highball glass on the bar, he contemplated his next move. He couldn't paint her, but there was something else he could do to her, and he wanted to do the *something else* even more than he wanted to commit her likeness to canvas. Just because he'd sworn off relationships didn't register in his thinking. This was a one-time deal. Nothing more. They were two passengers on a one-way trip to Hell. Well, that was *his* story, but they were passengers on the same cursed flight. What would a little fuck between strangers hurt?

The barkeep arrived with the woman's order, and Will signaled for a refill of his own. He'd expected to see something pink with an umbrella or maybe a cutesy martini glass rimmed with sugar and swirled with chocolate sauce. Instead, her drink looked suspiciously like his. No-nonsense. No ice. Just two fingers of amber liquid—probably the good stuff. She surprised him by knocking the contents back with one swallow. She didn't even gasp for air afterward, confirming his suspicions about the quality of the whiskey. It was either good whiskey or there was more to her than he'd thought.

He couldn't wait to find out. He turned to face her. "Hi. Looks like we're going to be here for a while. Know someplace we can go to kill some time?"

"That's the worst pickup line I've ever heard." And MacKenzie had heard plenty. However, none had tempted her the way this one had from the Hot Guy she'd spied earlier in the boarding area at JFK. Tall, dark, and handsome despite his grim countenance. And despite her recent vow to abstain from anything with a Y chromosome, his voice ignited something inside her she'd almost hoped was dead for good. Men were trouble. It was a lesson well learned from her latest failed relationship. Men thought with their little head more often than not, and it tended to lead them astray.

Like the guy on the barstool next to her.

Yes, after determining she wasn't going anywhere anytime soon, she'd made a quick stop at the ladies' room then gone in search of him. He'd been easy to find. Their gate was at the far end of the terminal, and he'd stopped at the first bar he'd run across.

She couldn't blame him. She needed a drink in the worst way possible, as clearly did he. Travel could tempt a person to drink, especially when things went awry, as they had today. She didn't know anything about how planes worked, but she figured if the pilot decided he needed to set the thing down as quickly as possible, then whatever had gone wrong must have been major. The way she saw it, she was lucky to be alive, even if her life was a shitstorm.

If today's events didn't call for a couple of fingers of Macallan and a good fuck to celebrate surviving a near-death experience, then nothing did. She'd save the recriminations for later—like when she got to Texas and started her new job. From what she'd heard of the small town where she'd be living, she'd have plenty of time to visit past regrets and beat herself up over her poor decisions in regard to men. It didn't appear there was anything else to do there.

Her savings were dwindling fast. Thankfully, her new employer had sprung for the plane ticket—first class—much to her surprise, leaving the remains of her nest egg untouched. She'd need most of it to get settled. She had no idea what a place rented for in off-the-grid Texas, but she assumed it was considerably less than what it would have cost her to rent a place of her own in Manhattan. After her boyfriend/boss had gone missing, she'd had no choice but to move out of his modern high-rise and into a friend's closet. It hadn't actually been a closet, but Bethany had been using it as one and probably was again since MacKenzie had cleared out.

She'd calculated and recalculated her financial situation enough times the grim figures were etched on her brain. Pocket change was short, but she still had room on her American Express card. With a bit of luck, she'd be able to pay it down once she was receiving regular paychecks again.

The guy sitting next to her didn't need to know her hard-luck story. Today was about celebrating life and maybe just a little about celebrating her *new* life, and that was on her. Today, she wasn't the loser who'd been duped and dumped. Today, she was a strong woman with a future. A woman who saw what she wanted and went after it.

And she wanted…him.

She dug the well-worn card from her wallet and waved it at the bartender. He hustled over. Making a sweeping motion with her hand to indicate Hot Guy's drink and hers, she said, "Close out our tabs, please."

Hot Guy's head jerked up. "I can pay my own way."

"I'm sure you can but allow me." Before he could argue further, she thrust her card at the bartender who snatched it like it was platinum instead of green plastic, smirked at Hot Guy then took off to process the sale.

"No, really," Hot Guy protested.

MacKenzie signaled him to stop. Fantasy was about all she had left and she'd be damned if he was going to ruin this one. "I've got it." She slid off the stool, deliberately letting her breasts brush his arm. The bartender returned with the charge slip which she signed and slid back to him. Grabbing the extended handle on her carry-on, she made eye contact with Hot Guy. "You coming? Or not?"

It was all she could do not to look over her shoulder to see if he followed her. Once she'd made it out to the crowded concourse, he caught up to her. "Where are we going?"

"Someplace private."

He said nothing, just matched his stride to hers and used his broad shoulders to clear a path for her. If she hadn't been as nervous as a cat in a room full of rocking chairs, she would have admired the little bit of chivalry from a man who didn't have a clue where they were headed. Now, if she could only remember where the article she'd read in the magazine she'd found in the seat-back pocket had said the micro suites were located. She hadn't paid much attention since she'd never in a million years envisioned being in a situation where she'd actually use one. She'd been impressed at the number of airports where the mini-hotels had been installed and wondered if they'd been selected because they had the highest number of stranded passengers, or if there'd been another reason. What did it matter? She was horny and they had one here—somewhere. She scanned the directional signs posted overhead for a hint then, there it was! On the wall, sandwiched between the ladies' room and an automated candy dispenser hung a giant illuminated advertisement for the fancy no-tell motel. Noting the location, she made a quick assessment of their whereabouts then pointed. "That way. It isn't far now." She hoped.

A right turn sent them down another wide concourse lined with stores selling souvenirs and survival gear for weary travelers. Nestled in their midst was an oasis of calm. MacKenzie stopped. The check-in desk reminded her of a mid-range hotel chain with its faux wood counter and cheap artwork.

"Whoa. Wait a minute."

She whipped her head around to glare at Hot Guy. "What? You've changed your mind?"

His head swiveled from side to side. "No. I haven't changed my mind, but I was thinking of something a little less expensive—like a janitor's closet or something."

"I'm going to pretend you didn't just say that and get us a room. Will an hour be enough?"

"Sure."

"Wait here. I'll be right back." The disinterested employee behind the counter walked her through the check-in process with all the enthusiasm of a turnip. Under other circumstances, she'd be annoyed, but none of it mattered in this instance. She held the key up for Hot Guy to see then, heart pounding, she strode past the desk to the short hall, dragging her carry-on behind.

She waved the keycard in front of the electronic lock mechanism and clasped the telescopic handle on her suitcase. "Allow me." Hot Guy's body pressed against her from behind. A long arm reached around her to push and hold the door open for her. It wasn't much, another one of those chivalrous acts she'd grown unaccustomed to in New York, but it did unexpected things to her insides.

"Thank…thank you," she said as she stumbled over the threshold, the sight of his hand, purely masculine, with long fingers and strong knuckles making her clumsy, and for the first time since she'd decided to take him up on his offer, nervous. *What the hell am I doing?* She didn't know this guy from Adam. He could be a serial killer or…or…something. But damn, he smelled good—like the Catskills on a warm summer day. If he'd been a tree, she'd hug the shit out of him.

The door swooshed shut, the sound of a dead bolt sliding into place sounding like the final nail in her coffin. Whirling around, she gasped at the sight of him leaning against the door, his arms behind his back and his ankles crossed. His eyes blazed with a heat she'd only read about in romance novels as he slowly undressed her with his gaze. The tiniest hint of a smile as he completed his inspection told her how much he liked what he'd seen. Turnabout was fair play. She released her tight grip on her luggage then kicked off her shoes before returning the favor.

Her first impression of him at JFK was that he was a man who took care of himself, and, at closer inspection, she'd been right. She'd bet the available balance on her last credit card there was a sculpted body beneath his expensively cut suit coat and tailored dress shirt. His tight-fitting jeans, worn nearly white in all the right places, left little to the imagination. She checked him out all the way down to the Italian leather loafers on his feet before letting her gaze slide up again to caress what promised to be a very generous package barely contained behind a button fly. Whoever he was, he had style. In fact, he reminded her of a guy she'd seen on the cover of a magazine once. She'd gotten herself off to the cover, and, after the magazine had gone missing, to the memory of it, more times than she dared recall.

Finished with her perusal, she dragged her eyes back up to his. "Thanks for getting us a room, but you don't have to do this."

And he's too fucking nice. She didn't want nice. She wanted wild-monkey sex. The kind where words weren't necessary. Where both parties took what they wanted without regard to the needs of the other. There was only one thing she wanted to know. "Do you have protection?"

"I do." The timbre of his voice nearly melted her panties off.

MacKenzie dipped her chin once to acknowledge his answer then reached for the top button on her blouse.

CHAPTER TWO

Holy, fuckin' shit.

Will could hardly believe his eyes. Maybe his luck was changing. How else could he explain the goddess doing a striptease before him?

Maybe she was a siren sent by the Fates to finish him off. If so, she was doing an excellent job of incinerating him. Fists clenched behind him, he forced himself to remain glued to the door as she slowly revealed herself to him, one inch of creamy skin at a time.

Like any piece of exquisite art, she deserved to be admired, to be studied, and knowing this would be his one and only chance to do so, he took in the sight before him with both his artist's vision and the appreciation of a human male who had seen his fair share of nude females.

He'd recognized her beauty from the beginning, but even his artist's eye couldn't have imagined the gentle swell of her breasts or the sweet curve of her hips or, god help him, the enticing pillow of a belly that drove him insane with lust. That part of the female anatomy seemed so womanly to him. He was glad to see she hadn't tried to diet it away like most women did these days.

As a teenager, he'd fallen in love with the paintings of voluptuous nudes by the old masters. While his brothers and friends had studied purloined centerfolds, he'd studied Rubens and Bouguereau. A woman's body was a thing of beauty to be admired and, in this instance, coveted. Any man would be fortunate if they could claim her as theirs, but it wasn't in the cards for him. He had this one opportunity, and, as much as his fingers itched for a piece of charcoal and a pad of paper, he needed the physical release more—needed this reminder he was still alive.

Mustering as much restraint as he could, he lifted his right hand and, with his index finger, signaled for her to turn around. Her lips curved into a seductive smile then she did a graceful about-face, peeking over her shoulder to gauge his reaction which was immediate. Will pushed away from the door with one thing on his mind, taking what she so freely offered.

Fully clothed, he pressed his front to her back. The need to touch her, to commit every inch of her body to tactile memory was almost more than he could bear, but to touch her the way he wanted to would make this encounter too personal. There was nothing personal about it. She wanted to be fucked, and by god, he wanted to oblige her. No names. No more physical contact than was absolutely necessary to get the job done. An anonymous encounter they'd both, hopefully, recall fondly years from now. Hell, if it went no further, he'd be eternally grateful to this woman, though she'd never know what she'd done for him. He hadn't looked forward to anything in months.

Hoping he didn't need words to get his message across, he nestled the hard ridge of his erection in the cleft of her cheeks and, with a subtle nudge of his hips, silently demanded she move closer to the sofa. God bless her, she took the hint and shuffled her feet in the right direction.

"Stop," he growled in her ear. "Bend over."

She bent at the waist and braced herself on the edge of the pleather sleeper/sofa. A tap with his foot against hers and she spread her legs, offering her priceless treasure for him to plunder.

Will removed his wallet, extracted his in-case-of-an-emergency condom, clenched the packet between his teeth then returned his wallet to his pocket. There was precious little in the billfold, but he couldn't afford to leave it behind, and god knew if he'd have any brain cells left when he was done. Better to pack it away now.

Valuables stowed, he slipped the top button on his fly through the well-worn buttonhole with ease. Then he did the next one and the next. He didn't bother with the last one. Hooking his thumbs in the waistband, he shoved the denim until it bunched at his hips.

From there, it was a simple thing to maneuver the front of his briefs out of the way.

Shit. He nearly came at the sight of his dick, engorged and throbbing, laying heavy on the curve of her creamy smooth backside. He was fucking ready, but was she? He'd always been careful to make sure his partner was prepared, and had just enough courtesy left in him to do the same for her. A two-finger swipe between her legs brought a groan to both their lips. He'd never donned a raincoat as fast as he did then.

Positioning the head of his cock at her entrance, with the last vestiges of his control, he growled out, "Tell me to stop now or hold the fuck on."

Spontaneous. Human. Combustion. The words crystallized in her brain. Pseudo-scientific bullshit—or so she'd thought up until this moment. Naked and spread wide, waiting for this stranger to fuck her senseless, she was perilously close to going up in flames. He hadn't removed a stitch of clothing, and god, wasn't that hot? No sweet talk unless she considered his warning to *hold the fuck on* sweet, but damn if her insides hadn't turned to liquid at his gruff command. She'd never done anything like this in her life and had to wonder why the fuck not as she gave him the consent he demanded. With a shift of her weight, she pushed her hips back and drove herself onto his cock.

Sweet mother of god.

He was thick and hard, and as he flexed his hips and filled her the rest of the way, her toes curled into the industrial-grade carpet, and her fingers instinctively dug into the upholstery. A groan of pure pleasure escaped her lips. He gripped her hips with hands so hot she was certain he'd branded her with his touch. He pulled all the way out of her then slammed back in. If not for him holding her, she would have collapsed from the force of his thrust.

This is what it feels like to be taken.

This wasn't love. It was pure lust unleashed without restraint, and she loved it.

She'd been desired before, but it had always been tempered with civility and/or consideration, but there had *always* been caution. There was no caution here. Hot Guy took her as if he owned her. Like it was his right, and only his, to fuck her. And as he rode her like a cowboy on the run from the law, she thought for a moment, it wasn't an illusion. He was running from something and he was taking her with him.

I'm his. No one will ever do it for me the way he does. It was a crazy thought, driven from her mind as his balls slapped an age-old rhythm against her clit, and the delicious pain of tender tissues stretching to take all of him coalesced into a dizzying need to come.

As if he'd read her body, he tightened his hold on her hips and said the magic words. "Take it, baby. Suck me dry."

Dear. God.

His words were filthy and raunchy and the sexiest thing she'd ever heard. The image they created in her brain, of bringing this powerful man to his knees, was all it took. The tremors began in her thighs and spread upward where they detonated charges in her womb. Her clit throbbed; her nipples tingled. When her pussy spasmed around the steel pole reaming her, Hot Guy let out a primal groan and lost control. His thrusts became short. His groin ground against her as if he was trying to burrow deep inside her and never come out, and, in some way, he had. With a string of profanities directed at a supreme being, he came, filling the tip of the condom with scalding cum.

The moment he let go of her, MacKenzie's knees gave out and she tumbled face-first onto the sofa bed. Breathless and feeling like a rag doll, she must look a sight, but she couldn't find it within herself to care. She'd move—eventually—then she'd thank Hot Guy. Maybe offer to buy him another drink. It was the least she could do for his stellar performance. She hadn't been with many men, but she'd been with enough to know what she'd felt, what she'd experienced today was beyond compare. Hot Guy was a sex god, and he had the equipment to match his status. It was a shame they'd never see each other again. She could get used to his style of sex on a regular basis.

The sound of the door opening spurred MacKenzie to action. Bolting upright, she crossed her arms over her breasts and winced as the pleather upholstery snagged her bare ass as she tried to scoot into a sitting position. By the time she peeled her abused flesh off the sofa and resettled, she opened her mouth. "Wait!" hovered in the air, a second too late as the door closed. Hot Guy was gone.

"Asshole." MacKenzie tucked an errant strand of hair behind her ear. Maybe he'd just gone out to get something from the vending machine. She could use a snack herself. Glancing around the room, her gaze fell on the small desk on the opposite wall. The keycard she'd used to open the door lay right where she'd dropped it when they first entered. Her lungs deflated as she spied the used condom lying like a testament to her folly in the bottom of the waste basket. Hot Guy, aka Asshole, wasn't coming back.

Gathering her clothes, she dressed then curled her legs beneath her on the sofa. She'd paid for an hour, might as well take advantage of the privacy to get her head on straight. She didn't think her lady parts were going to stop humming a satisfied tune anytime soon, but she could hope. There was a good chance she'd see Hot Guy again at the gate and she didn't want him to see how his abrupt departure had affected her. Would it have killed him to hang around another minute, perhaps inquire as to her well-being?

He's a love 'em and leave 'em — no — a fuck 'em and flee type.

"What did you expect?" she mumbled to herself. "You picked him up in an airport bar for cryin' out loud." If the situation didn't have pathetic loser written all over it, she didn't know what did. The biggest problem was, she didn't know which of them the label applied to. Her for encouraging Hot Guy or him for taking her up on the offer. It could go either way, but no doubt about it, he was an asshole. If she never saw him again, it would be too soon.

CHAPTER THREE

"Thanks for coming to get me." Will embraced his older brother, Jake, in the baggage claim area.

"We couldn't let you hitchhike to Willowbrook," his younger brother, Rick, said as he engulfed William in a tight hug. His brother felt solid, more like the soldier he'd been, up until the war on terrorism had chewed him up and spit him out nearly a year ago. Over Rick's shoulder, Will's gaze locked with Jake's. The brothers shared a meaningful look. Now was not the time for them to discuss Rick's recovery or his future. There'd be plenty of time to dissect each other's lives once they were all home. "Glad you're back, bro."

"Thanks." He just wished his homecoming was under different circumstances, but like Rick, only a catastrophe could have convinced him to return to Willowbrook for anything more than a visit. Unless pigs sprouted wings, he was here to stay. He wasn't so sure about Rick. Something else they needed to talk about.

"Would you look at that," Jake murmured. William turned to see what had caught his brother's attention.

After he left her, he'd tucked his balled fists into his pockets and walked until he'd found what was possibly the only deserted place in the terminal and leaned against the wall to catch his breath. Only then did he bring the fingers he'd swiped through her juices up to his nose. Inhaling deep, he let her scent take him back to their rented room, to the woman he'd never forget.

It had taken some work on his part, but he'd managed to avoid seeing her in the Philadelphia airport until they'd called his flight. He'd boarded earlier than most and been satisfied with his seat as far from first class as possible. Heck, he didn't know for certain they'd been on the same plane. She could have been waiting on a connecting flight to anywhere for all he knew. They'd exchanged orgasms, not itineraries. But there she was, on the other side of the baggage carousel, a shit-ton of expensive luggage piled on a cart being pushed by a man in the livery of a chauffeur. He hated the way his body responded to her presence. He'd taken what she offered, thinking it would be more than enough, but as the plane had made its way across the country, he'd been surprised to find out it hadn't been nearly enough. Her orgasm had done something to him he couldn't name then she'd collapsed onto the sofa, and he'd had visions of her sprawled across a velvet chaise, looking like she'd just been fucked. He'd wanted to put a just-fucked expression on her face then paint her more than he'd wanted his next breath. He'd had no choice but to leave.

"Seeing *her* is worth the trip, Billy boy."

Will cringed at Jake's use of the nickname he hated with a passion.

"Hey, is that yours?" Rick pointed to a beat-up cardboard box coming around the bend in the carousel. It appeared a band of gorillas had ripped it apart then patched it back together with tape bearing the TSA logo.

"Yeah." Will stepped toward the luggage conveyor, but Rick's hand on his shoulder stopped him.

"I'll get it."

He opened his mouth to protest, but Jake's elbow dug into his ribs. "Let him. He seems to feel a need to be useful these days."

A lump the size of Texas formed in Will's throat. He nodded, silently acknowledging what his brother was saying. Of the three of them, Rick had always been the one to offer a helping hand — thus his desire to enter the military. When he'd first come home, he wouldn't even help himself, much less someone else. He was glad to see this small indication his younger brother still lived inside the shell of a man who had returned to them. Maybe there was hope for Rick after all.

Rick joined them a few minutes later with the battered box tucked under one arm and the strap of Will's giant duffel slung over the opposite shoulder. "Is this everything?"

"Yeah." Not much to show for nearly a decade of life. He reached for the duffel.

Rick shrugged him off. "I've got it."

Jake fell into step beside Will as they followed their younger brother out into the Texas heat. As they crossed the busy roadway to the parking garage, Will caught himself scanning the people loading luggage into cars at the curb, wanting one last look at her — for posterity's sake, he told himself. It wasn't like he was ever going to see her again. He knew for a fact he didn't frequent the kinds of places she did. Everything about her screamed money and class — two things he most certainly didn't have and wouldn't find where he was going. The only thing they had in common was a shared air-travel experience and good sex. Hell, maybe the best sex he'd ever had, if he was being honest with himself. Best to put her out of his mind and get on with his life — whatever that was going to entail.

MacKenzie smiled at the driver who'd been sent to pick her up. She'd expected someone in a pickup truck, not a limo. From what she'd heard about her new employer, he didn't flaunt his wealth or celebrity status. By all accounts, he was a humble, yet incredibly talented man. She appreciated the first-class treatment while reminding herself not to get used to it. He was just trying to make her transition from New York to Texas easier. She couldn't expect to be pampered once she was settled. She doubted the small town where she'd be living had cab service, much less limo service. Besides, a car came with the job — something she'd need since her employer lived outside of town. He'd converted an old barn on his property into state-of-the-art workspace. She'd have an office there, but live in town.

She forced her brain to focus on reining in her expectations of the place instead of obsessing over Hot Guy. She'd managed to avoid him in the Philly airport, wasn't even certain they would be on the same flight to Dallas. He could have been waiting in the bar for a completely different flight. She hadn't asked, and he hadn't offered. What he had offered, she'd accepted way too easily. He'd given her what she wanted then sprinted out of there like the TSA was after him for a strip search.

She couldn't blame him. She'd been two seconds away from breaking her own hastily adopted airport hookup rules. Rule number one being—under no circumstances exchange personal information, i.e. name, phone number, destination—and god forbid—relationship status. Rule number two—under no circumstances beg him for a repeat. One and done. It was the only way.

Then she'd spied him at baggage claim. If not for Bernie? Bennie? *Her driver,* she might have hurdled the carousel like a crazed fan at a rock concert and broken all of her rules for the chance at one more time with him.

He'd seemed more relaxed than he'd been in Philly. Maybe it was the warm greeting from the sexy as hell guys who met him, or maybe he was happy to see his friends? Family? It was difficult to tell from across the carousel. They were all tall with dark hair. If they were related, they each had a distinctive style. The tallest one wore work boots, jeans, and a ragged T-shirt. She wouldn't be surprised to find out he could bench-press a horse. The idea gained momentum when he gathered Hot Guy's baggage, lifting the tattered box and duffel as if they weighed nothing. The other one was the polar opposite of Buff Guy. His suit branded him a professional of some kind—banker, lawyer, corporate exec. His attire fit him well, but she preferred the sexy, sophisticated style Hot Guy sported. There was something about a guy in jeans topped with a smart blazer that did it for her. Especially when she knew what those jeans held.

Perfection.

Yeah, it was a good thing the chauffeur found her when he did. He'd saved her from making a complete fool of herself. It was time to look forward, not back. Her mistakes were behind her, her future a blank slate waiting for her to write a new chapter. Pulling her attention away from the trio of sexy men, she counted the bags stacked on her cart, came up with the correct number, and waved the driver on. It took every bit of self-control she could muster to raise her chin and follow him out the door, without glancing over her shoulder.

"It's about an hour's drive, ma'am." The car pulled away from the curb and accelerated into traffic. "There's water in the mini-fridge on your left."

"Thanks—"

His gaze caught hers in the rearview mirror. There was a smile in his voice when he said, "Bernie, ma'am. No problem. You just relax. Leave the traffic worries to me."

It had been a long time since she'd met with such kindness. Courtesy wasn't a required trait for drivers in Manhattan. Mad driving skills were. If they got you there in one piece, they were good. If you also arrived on time, they were fabulous.

She thanked him again before he raised the glass partition sealing her into a cocoon of silence. God, it felt good to close her eyes and let the rhythm of the road lull her to sleep. She'd done nothing but run at full blast since she'd accepted the job offer in Texas. She'd pared her belongings down to the bare necessities, packed her bags, said goodbye to her friends and colleagues, promising to keep in touch. Her client had an apartment in New York City he co-owned with his partners. She'd been given the go-ahead to use it as needed whenever her new job dictated a trip to the Big Apple, which it occasionally would. He'd also mentioned his agent lived in the city. She'd be expected to work with him on certain projects, too. But her main job would be here, managing publicity for her new boss—Hank Travis.

How in heaven's name she'd ended up working for a rock star—scratch that—a superstar rock band, she'd never understand. She'd been a fan of BlackWing for as long as she could remember. Now, she was going to work for them! She'd been even more surprised to find out her friend Sunny Sheldon knew Hank and his wife, Melody. She'd called on her friends to get MacKenzie this job. The jury was still out on whether she could live in a small Texas town without losing her mind, but what choice did she have? After things had gone south with her previous job, she'd tapped everyone in the PR industry she knew and had come up with zip. Sunny had come through for her. She owed it to her friend to give this her best effort, even if it felt like she was being shipped off to another planet.

They'd left civilization behind almost the minute they departed the airport. MacKenzie gazed out the window at the passing scenery. Trees. Fields of…were those crops? God, she was in over her head. Visions of scruffy men in overalls and women in dowdy paisley dresses down to their ankles flashed across her brain. She was going to die out here in the wilderness. These…farmers probably ate people like her for lunch.

Maybe she could talk Hank into letting her work from home. She could rent a place in Dallas. Video conferencing was practically as good as talking in person. She could do her job remotely. She was certain of it.

The car slowed as they passed through a town. MacKenzie prayed it wasn't her destination. This was worse than she'd imagined. Empty storefronts. Weed-infested sidewalks. Pickup trucks with gun racks in the back window. She'd never survive in a place like this. She didn't relax until the driver turned a corner and she saw a sign indicating her new home was another twenty miles down the road.

Please. Please don't let it be the same. Please.

She remained on edge, surveying the vast empty spaces punctuated by the occasional house, some with barns, some without. When she spied the city limit sign declaring the population of her new home to just over two thousand, she had to hold back her tears. This was going to be awful. Two thousand people? That was…nothing!

"Welcome to Willowbrook, miss." The driver's voice made her sit up and take a deep breath. "Mr. Travis suggested I give you a short tour of the town before heading out to his place."

She couldn't imagine what Hank's reasoning was, but the more information she had about her situation, the better she'd be able to negotiate a move to Dallas. "Thank you, Bernie."

"My pleasure, miss. My mother grew up here. It's a nice place."

The affection in his voice eased the tightness in her shoulders just a little bit. Bernie drove slowly, stopping where it was convenient to give her a better look at a particular location. He pointed out several churches, the schools, the post office and municipal building then circled the park at one end of town. MacKenzie gasped at the heart of the town. Disney's Main Street had nothing on this one. The buildings were quaint and well maintained. The storefronts vibrant with sparkling glass to display their wares.

"Most people around here don't have much, but they take care of what they do have," Bernie said, taking a left off the busy downtown street. "This is my favorite part of town. All the streets are named for trees. Oak. Maple. Pecan. You get the idea. My grandmother lived on Walnut." He made another turn, and MacKenzie powered the window down to get a better view.

Air fragrant with the scent of fresh-cut grass rushed in. It was as different from Manhattan as a place could be, but as she filled her lungs, she thought perhaps it wouldn't be the worst place to live. She scanned the street. The houses were mostly post-war bungalows, painted white with various color shutters, but that was where the similarity ended. Yards were lovingly tended, planted with flowers and shrubs to match the owner's personality. And lining the street were the most magnificent old-growth trees she'd ever seen.

"It's beautiful."

"Yes, ma'am. It is. All the streets in this neighborhood are like this. If you're hunting for a place to live, this would be my choice. It's hard to get in though. Most of these people have owned their houses since they were built after World War II. They've been passed down to kids and grandkids. It's rare to see one go on the market."

"Guess I won't be living here, then," she said, powering the window up.

"Do you have a place?"

"My employer said they'd arranged something for me."

"I'm sure you'll like it." Bernie steered them back out onto Main Street then on to the outskirts of town. "We're almost there." He pointed out the window. "See the big barn with the wings painted on it?"

MacKenzie craned her neck to get a glimpse of her new place of employment. The giant barn rose up from the expanse of crops, its black wings making it stand out from the others she'd seen along the road. She swallowed hard, willing the nerves fluttering like a flock of ravens in her stomach to settle. I can do this. I *can* do this. So what if the job was in the middle of nowhere? A job was a job. BlackWing needed a PR guru, so here she was.

~~

"Welcome home," Rick said as they made the last turn and headed into Willowbrook. Will nodded and mentally added one to the tally displayed on the population sign marking the official boundary. "Lot of people gonna be glad to see you."

"Like who?" He'd never been particularly popular in school and hadn't wasted a minute longer than necessary leaving after graduation.

"Hank, for one," Jake offered. "I saw him the other day at the diner. He asked about you, and I told him you were moving back."

Will closed his eyes and took a deep breath, letting his frustration out with it. He'd been so caught up in his misery, he hadn't given much thought to what it would actually be like living here again. In the same graduating class, they'd known each other since they were in diapers. Hank had lived a few blocks down on the same street. They'd played together as toddlers and stuck beside each other as teenagers when their interests went beyond Friday night football. Hank had been into music and opted to lead the drumline in the high school band, while Will had contributed to the gridiron insanity by painting the team mascot on the paper banner the team demolished by running through it at the beginning of every game. To this day, he could draw a wildcat with his eyes closed. He wondered if Hank could still play his solo riff from memory.

Will chuckled to himself and felt a smile tug at his lips.

"Something funny?" Rick asked.

"Nah." Will shook his head. "Just thinking about Hank and me as kids. We did some stupid stuff."

Jake glanced at him then back at the road. "I thought Dad was going to blow a gasket the time the two of you rode your bikes through half the flower beds in the neighborhood."

"He did blow a gasket." He'd never forget how angry his father had been when one neighbor after another called to demand he do something about his unruly kid. "He took my bike away for the rest of the summer and made me replant every flower we'd run over."

"Hank was right beside you, as I recall," Rick said.

"He was. His parents weren't any happier than Dad was."

"That wasn't all Dad did." Jake twisted his hand on the steering wheel.

"No, it wasn't." Will had missed riding his bike the rest of the summer, but he'd missed his art supplies more. If there was one thing his dad knew how to do, it was punishing his kids. He knew their weaknesses and went right for them. Thankfully, he had his brothers. They'd stuck together—a united front against what had sometimes been cruel treatment. A lump formed in his throat as he recalled how he'd made it through those months. Rick and Jake had risked punishment and smuggled their own art supplies to him. They hadn't had much—colored pencils and crayons—but it had been better than nothing, and they'd known it. Here they were, saving his ass once again.

"Did I say thank you?" he asked, knowing it didn't matter if he had or not. His brothers didn't expect thanks, but he couldn't say it enough. No matter what, they had his back just as he had theirs.

"Yeah, you did." Rick who'd taken the rear seat so Will could ride shotgun nudged him in the shoulder. "So, don't mention it again."

He wasn't promising anything.

They pulled into the driveway of their childhood home. His neck muscles tightened. The place looked the same on the outside, but the inside had recently undergone a complete restoration—thanks to Rick's hard work. "Needs paint," he said past the lump in his throat as his crushed dreams pressed heavy on his shoulders.

"I was saving the job for you." Rick opened his door and piled out as soon as the car came to a stop.

Will took a deep breath before joining him. He'd had such big dreams when he left here all those years ago, and those dreams had taken him to places he hadn't known existed until he'd left small-town life behind. "White, as usual, with black shutters."

"Blue shutters, asshole." Jake joined them in front of the house.

"Black," Rick reiterated.

Will studied the familiar sight. "Does it matter? It's a fucking house."

"It matters if we're going to sell it." Jake had been advocating liquidation since they'd inherited the place. "It needs to stand out from the others."

A quick glance at the houses on either side supported Jake's vision. "He's right. Blue or green or something shocking like red will make the house stand out on the street." Will smiled at Rick's stunned expression.

"Standing out is not necessarily a good thing," his younger brother said as he returned to the car for Will's luggage.

Jake caught Will's gaze, and with a shrug, the two parted—Jake to unlock the front door and Will to help with his worldly goods.

Rick was putting on a good face, but something wasn't sitting right with him, and Will thought he knew what it was. Jake wanted to sell the house and Rick didn't. Will didn't give a shit what they did with it. Jake had never returned to live in the house after he'd left for college, opting to buy a place of his own on the other side of town when he'd returned to take over their father's law practice following the old man's death. Will had only spent a handful of nights in the house since he'd gone off to New York to pursue a career in the art world. Of the three of them, Rick was the only one who had any kind of attachment to the place. On the rare occasions Rick had come home to visit, he'd stayed with their dad, sleeping in the room the three brothers had shared growing up. When Rick had returned home for good, a silent and sullen man with no direction and even less ambition, his older brothers had seized on the sorry state of the house Rick insisted on living in as a form of therapy for him. They'd supplied him with paint, tools, and a modest budget to fix the place up. To their surprise, he'd thrown himself wholeheartedly into the project—or so it seemed from the pictures Jake had sent over the last few months.

"I can't wait to see what you've done inside." Will shoulder-nudged Rick out of the way and reached for his duffel.

"It's looking good if I do say so myself." Rick hefted Will's box of art supplies from the trunk then shut the lid. "You can have our old room. I've been sleeping in Dad's old room since I got it fixed up."

"Please tell me you got rid of the bunk beds in our room." He'd had a king-sized bed all to himself for years. Just thinking about folding himself into a small bunk bed for the foreseeable future made his back hurt. Or maybe it was the heavy bag he'd slung over his shoulder.

"Gone. The room wasn't big enough for anything but a full-size though. Sorry."

Will stifled a groan. None of this was Rick's fault so no need griping about his circumstances. He'd take what he could get and be happy about it. "I'm sure it'll be fine."

"*Fine* might be stretching the truth," Rick teased, "but it's better than the bunk beds we used to have." He held the front door open for Will. "It's a miracle I'm still alive. Those beds were cheap to begin with and we weren't gentle on them. I'm surprised you didn't crash down on me at some point and smoosh me."

Will smiled. "It wasn't for lack of trying. There were times I dreamed of ways to end your life."

"Like the time you put paprika on my toast instead of cinnamon?"

"It wouldn't have killed you," Jake said, taking the box from Rick's arms and placing it on the floor of the hall closet.

"You were in on it, too?" Rick placed his fists on his hips and glared at Jake.

"What can I say?" Jake straightened. "You were a brat. Always up in my and Will's business."

"Was not."

"Yes, you were." Will dropped his bag on the floor and slowly took in the new decor. Rick had refinished the hardwood floors, giving them a darker stain to contrast the light wall color. He kicked off his shoes and dug his toes into the soft pile of the new contemporary rug Rick had used to define the seating area. He ran a hand over the back of the mid-century sofa that fit the clean lines of the house better than the old Early American furniture ever had. A trio of his early paintings hung on the far wall above a couple of chairs that matched the sofa. He recalled sending the paintings to Rick for his birthday in lieu of a real present. It had been Will's first year at college in New York. He'd been full of himself and short on cash. He couldn't believe his brother had kept them, much less displayed them in his home, and this was very much Rick's home now. No wonder he didn't want to sell the place. "Wow, little brother. This is awesome. Who would have thought?"

"I know, right?" Rick waved him on. "Come see what I did to the kitchen."

"You aren't going to believe this," Jake said, trailing behind his younger brothers.

Will stopped cold, blocking the door to the kitchen. If he hadn't seen the outside, he wouldn't have believed he was in the same house.

"I thought about knocking the wall out to create an open floor plan, but I didn't want to change the architecture of the house, so I settled for changing the layout. What do you think?"

"This is…incredible." Will took in the Shaker-style cabinets, new appliances, and countertops. "You did good, bro. Real good."

Jake shoved past him. "Want to see the best part of this room?" Before Will could answer, his older brother yanked on a cabinet handle. A large panel opened to reveal a refrigerator stocked with the essentials. "Who wants a beer?" he said, grabbing three bottles.

Will had dreaded returning to this house, dreaded the memories, but as he sat around the sleek new table in the eat-in kitchen, sipping ice-cold brews with his brothers, he was surprised to find they didn't come. Yeah, there were memories, but most of them were good ones. He wondered if his brother had weaved some sort of magic, throwing out the bad along with the old décor. If so, he was a genius. Will hadn't thought there was a chance in hell he'd feel comfortable in this house, but he was. And so was Rick. Only Jake looked like a prisoner eyeing the door, ready to escape any minute.

It was no wonder. Jake had taken the brunt of their father's abuse. No one had called it abuse back then. They'd called it *stern parenting. Making men out of boys.* Everyone knew better nowadays. Somehow, they'd all survived to varying degrees. Jake, if not ecstatically happy, seemed settled even though he was basically living their father's life—carrying on his law practice in the same offices in the same town with the same clients. Then there was Rick. He'd served his country with distinction and come home with wounds no one could see or touch. In rebuilding this house, he'd rebuilt himself. It was good to see him smile and joke again, particularly in this house that hadn't seen much of either since their mother had passed away. As far as Will knew, Rick hadn't dated since he returned home, and he hadn't mentioned anyone special in all the years he'd been serving the country.

"There's something I wanted to talk to you guys about," Rick said, drawing the brother's attention.

Will finished his beer, tossed the empty in the new built-in recycle bin then got them all fresh bottles. "This sounds serious. What's up?"

"As you can tell, I'm almost done here. Unless we add a second floor, there isn't anything left to do."

"Do you want to add a second floor?" Jake asked.

"Hell, no! Are you insane?" Rick glanced at his feet then lifted his eyes to his brothers. "Don't think I'm not grateful for all the two of you have done for me. I didn't know what to do with myself when I came home. This remodel gave me something to do with my hands while my head caught up." He stood and propped his hip against the counter, arms crossed over his chest. "But it's time for me to move on."

Will's heart jumped into his throat. His brother was leaving? What the hell? "To where?"

Rick cocked his head to one side. "Down the street. Henry Travis contracted me to remodel his kitchen."

"He did?" God, he could barely hear himself speak over the blood pounding in his ears. "When did this happen?"

Rick shrugged. "Couple of weeks ago. He's been stopping in a few days a week ever since I started working on the house. He'd talk while I worked. I think he's lonely. Hank got married. The old lady next door to him—"

"Miriam Wallingford," Jake supplied.

"Yeah, she's the one. She married Jonathan Youngblood and is living in England most of the year now. Anyway, Henry's going to travel some. See the world. He's renting the house out, and he asked if I'd be interested in remodeling the kitchen. It won't be anything as elaborate as this, I'll be staying within the existing footprint, but it's a complete remodel."

"Don't you have to have a contractor's license to do remodeling?" Leave it to Jake to ask the practical questions.

Rick's face turned red. "I have one. Been studying in the evenings. I took the exam a couple of weeks ago and passed."

Will couldn't hide his surprise or his happiness. He smiled and lifted his beer in a toast. "Way to go, bro! That's awesome."

"I didn't want to tell you guys—in case I lost my nerve or failed. I'll have to sub the electrical and plumbing work, but I'll do everything else myself. I gave him a really good price, seeing as he's my first customer. You know, see how this goes. If it works out, maybe I'll look for another job."

He was ecstatic about Rick's newfound ambition, but worrying about his little brother had become ingrained in his DNA. "Are you sure you're up to this? A few months ago—"

"I was a mess. I know." He ran his fingers through his overly long hair. "I don't know if I'll ever be the same person I was before, but I'm coping. Taking one day at a time. I know I can do the work. I don't know how I'll handle the stress of being in business for myself, but I managed to get through the contractor's exam without having a meltdown."

Will nodded. He could imagine the guts it had taken for Rick to step out of his comfort zone and take the test. His brother was slowly working his way back to a normal existence. He wished he had some of his brother's fortitude. "Okay, then."

"Wait a second." Jake had a propensity to beat every subject with a hammer until it was dead. "Who's Mr. Travis renting his place to? Are they going to be a problem?"

"She's the new PR person for BlackWing. I haven't met her yet. Gonna live in it during the remodel, too."

"You okay working around a tenant?"

Rick shuffled his feet. "Don't have a choice."

"You could say you changed your mind about doing the job."

"No. I need to do this. Need to see if I can. Besides, it's not like she'll be watching over my shoulder. She'll be at work when I'm at the house."

Will nodded his acceptance. His brother had made up his mind, and who was he to throw a monkey wrench into Rick's plans? Rick making plans was a monumental step in the right direction. "Well, I'm glad you have something to look forward to. When do you start?"

"Couple of weeks. Thought I'd let the new tenant settle in a bit before I start ripping things out."

"Have you drawn up a business plan? Filed for a DBA?" Jake went into full-lawyer mode, peppering Rick with questions. Will expected his younger brother to be upset by the detailed questioning, but he took it all in stride. His little brother was getting his shit together which made his own lack of planning seem worse in comparison.

CHAPTER FOUR

"MacKenzie, this is my wife, Melody Ravenswood Travis." Hank Travis smiled at the gorgeous brunette who'd just joined them in the recording studio. "Mel, this is our new PR guru, MacKenzie Carlysle."

Melody extended a slim hand. "So nice to finally meet you," she said as Kenzie took her hand. "Please, call me Mel. Sunny has nothing but good things to say about you."

"Thanks. Please, both of you, call me Kenzie, and Sunny filled my ear about the two of you and all the band members. I can't believe she didn't tell me she knew you until I cried on her shoulder about needing a job."

"Sunny was just honoring our wishes. Despite Hank's high-profile career and my not-so-secret background, we're pretty private people—as you can tell by the way we live. The middle of nowhere suits us, and we hope it will suit you, too."

Kenzie wasn't so sure about being suited to this kind of life, but if there was a paycheck involved, she was all for it…for now. Sunny had been right, Hank and Melody were lovely people who just happened to be famous, much like Sunny who was the daughter of one of Hollywood's favorite sons. "I grew up in D.C., moved to Manhattan for college then stayed there to work. I've never lived in a small town before. I'm looking forward to it."

"I speak for the entire band," Hank said. "We're glad to have you on board. Our agent has been filling in since Jason retired. With the new album dropping in a few months, we need someone who knows what they're doing."

"I've never worked in the music industry, but I'll give it all I've got. You won't be disappointed."

"Excellent. We couldn't ask for more. Jason left a ton of files for you." He indicated the file cabinets behind her new desk. "You'll find a lot of answers there, and Jase is only a phone call away. Feel free to ask us anything. Now, if you'll excuse me, I've got a song to write. Melody will bring you up to speed on the rest." With a kiss for his wife and a wave to Kenzie, Hank Travis left the women alone to talk.

"Wow." Kenzie let out a nervous breath as she turned to survey her new office space. It wasn't much, but it had all the necessities, including a window with a view of…crops. What kind, she didn't know or care. "I'm really here."

"Yes, you are." Melody waved Kenzie to her place behind the desk then took one of the visitors' chairs facing the desk. "How does it feel?"

Kenzie frowned.

"The chair?" Mel clarified. "It was Jason's. If it doesn't fit you, we'll get a new one. In fact, make a list of things you need and we'll get them for you. We want you to be comfortable."

"Thanks." The chair squeaked, and Jason's butt print didn't match her own. A new chair would top her list of needs. Other than proper seating, she couldn't think of a single thing she needed.

"Oh, and we ordered a new cell phone for you. It should be here tomorrow. It will have unlimited everything, so feel free to use it for your personal calls, too. The computer system here is state-of-the-art, but if there are any programs you need, put them on your new company credit card. We need to stop by the bank and pick your card up. Your new company car should be delivered to your house today."

"House?" Kenzie's head reeled with all the information coming in.

Mel's smile lit up her face. "I found a place for you to rent. Well, I didn't exactly find it. It sort of dropped in my lap. It's the perfect place. Not too big, not too small."

She had all Kenzie's attention. "I can't wait to see it. Where is it? When can I move in?"

"It's Hank's dad's house. It's in an older neighborhood, but all the houses are so cute and well-kept. You can move in today."

"Wait. What about Mr. Travis?"

"He's decided to do some traveling. He said he wants to see the world while he still can. He's starting out in England. He's going to stay at Ravenswood with Jonathan and Miriam for a little while."

Kenzie had heard all about Ravenswood, the ancient stone monstrosity Melody had inherited from her father. Since Earl Ravenswood's death, his best friend and former band-mate, Sir Jonathan Youngblood, had managed the singer's estate from his ancestral home. The place was high on Kenzie's list of places to visit if she ever got the chance.

"Is he coming back?" Kenzie wasn't sure she was going to stay here long, but she didn't want to bounce around like a rubber ball, either.

"Of course he is. His only child and his granddaughter are here. But don't worry." She waved her hand. "He'll either stay at Miriam's place, which is next door, or he'll stay with us."

"Sunny mentioned Mr. Travis' next-door neighbor married Jonathan Youngblood."

Mel nodded. "Miriam still has her house here. She and Uncle Jonathan split their time between Ravenswood and Willowbrook; otherwise, you could have rented her house."

"What about furniture?"

"Truthfully, it was all pretty old. I don't think he's bought so much as a new chair after his wife died. Hank convinced him to donate most of it and store the few pieces he couldn't part with."

"I doubt I'll have overnight guests, but I will need a bedroom set for myself, a kitchen table, and some living room furniture."

"No worries. Put it all on your company credit card. Pick whatever you like and consider it a signing bonus from the band. We're so glad to have you, Kenzie. You can't imagine what a burden you're lifting from Hank's shoulders."

"That's really generous." She didn't know what else to say. Her last employer had bought her a new blotter for her desk. She'd had to supply her own pens and staples. Cecil's penny-pinching ways should have been her first clue to his character.

"Oh," Melody said, "Henry—Hank's dad—said you could paint the walls. Even said he'd pay to have any work done you want to do. He'd already had plans drawn up to refurbish the kitchen and the bathroom before the travel bug bit him. If you'll supervise the remodel, he'll cut your rent in half until it's completed."

"What's the rent?"

Melody named a figure. "Half during the remodel."

"That's nothing, practically. Are you sure you got the amount right?"

"Positive. Henry doesn't need the money. He just wants someone to take care of the place and be there to keep an eye on the progress. With Miriam's house next door being unoccupied half the year, he's afraid to leave his empty, too."

"Makes sense, though I don't know about living next to an empty house. Does someone keep up with the maintenance?"

"Yep. Uncle Jonathan had a security system installed and hired a local company to take care of the landscaping year-round. Oh, and we have a key in case we need to use the house for overflow."

"Overflow?"

"When BlackWing is recording, there's not enough room at our place for the band, their families, and all the extra musicians and technical people who come in. We used to send them to Henry's house, but with you living there…well, we didn't think you'd appreciate the company."

"Depends on who you send over," Kenzie said, with a grin. Her spirits were lifting higher with each new revelation from her new employer's mouth. "If they're hot and single, I wouldn't mind."

Melody shook her head. "You're going to fit right in with BlackWing, I can tell."

"Thanks. I'm excited about being part of the team." She was. Really. It was the move and getting used to small-town life…and leaving behind everything leading up to her departure from New York. Once she got past it all, she was sure she'd find her footing in Willowbrook. Or maybe Dallas. She still held out hope she could convince Hank to let her work from home.

"Oh, good. Your car's here." Melody pulled to the curb in front of a small white bungalow on Pecan Street.

Kenzie couldn't believe her eyes. This was going to be her home? She'd fallen a little in love with this neighborhood when her limo driver had given her a tour of the town, but never in her wildest dreams had she thought she would live here. A city girl all her life, the tree-lined streets with their quietly unassuming houses were reminiscent of another time, a simpler life she'd never known would appeal to her — until now.

Kenzie stepped from Mel's Jeep to the shaded walkway and stared at her new home.

The house itself appeared much like all the others on the street, white with black shutters on the windows. Pots and hanging baskets filled with flowering plants adorned the wide front porch. An old-fashioned screened door was flanked by rocking chairs on one side and a swing on the other. Flower beds skirted the front of the house, providing vibrant color against the backdrop of the house and the perfect green lawn. Like a movie set — it was almost too good to be true.

She focused on the neatly edged grass. She couldn't wait to take her shoes off and walk barefoot across it. "I've never had a lawn."

"Don't worry. We hired the same landscape company Miriam and Jonathan use to do yours, too. I think they come on Friday, but don't quote me on that. I have their card somewhere. I'll hunt it up for you. If you need to change the date or time they're here or need something specific done, give them a call."

"Thanks." She'd be grateful for the help, but, seeing the neat flower beds, she thought she might like to give gardening a try.

As if she'd read Kenzie's mind, Mel added, "There's a little garden in the back where Hank's mother used to grow a few vegetables. Henry has kept the weeds and grass out, but it's been years since anyone planted anything there. Feel free to try your hand at some flowers or veggies."

She'd fallen down a rabbit hole. It was the only explanation for all of this. The job. The house. The car. A garden for crying out loud! What was happening to her? First, she'd hooked up with a stranger in the airport — something she should regret but couldn't bring herself to — now she was thinking about gardening. Next, she'd be carrying on a conversation with a cat and attending a tea party.

"Come on." Mel started up the walk to the porch. "Let's see what Henry left in the way of kitchen stuff." She paused on the porch and dug around in her giant purse, eventually coming up with a leather-bound notepad and a pen. "We'll make a list then we'll go shopping."

CHAPTER FIVE

"I've got a bed, a sofa, and a TV. What else do I need?" Kenzie never thought she'd complain about shopping, but she couldn't stop the words from spewing past her lips. She and Mel had done nothing but shop for the last three days. Hank insisted there was plenty of time, but Kenzie was dying to dive headfirst into her new job. Apparently, it wasn't happening today. Currently, they were on their way to the local diner to have lunch with Mel and Hank's friend, Cathy, who owned The Donut Hole on Main Street. Mel had been in there every morning so far and was quickly becoming addicted to their chocolate croissants and dark-roast coffee.

"Curtains, for one thing, and we need to choose paint colors for all the rooms." Mel set a brisk pace any New Yorker would be proud of. "You said yourself the wall colors were dingy."

She had commented on the wall paint, but she was beginning to regret opening her mouth. If she'd known Mel was going to drag her all over North Texas, looking for furnishings, and now, paint, she would have kept her mouth shut and lived with the dull interior finishes. A few cheap prints on the walls would brighten the place up enough for now. She'd already ordered a few from an online art catalog and charged them to her personal charge card. She'd admired the artist's work for years, but when she'd just started out on her own in New York, she hadn't been able to afford even a small print. Once she'd had the funds to purchase whatever she wanted, she'd had no place to hang one. She'd lived in her former boyfriend's loft, and, as an art dealer, every available space had been covered with originals from the artists he admired. There'd been no room for her favorites. She should have realized then what a bastard Cecil was, but she'd been in love—stupid blind love. Until his deceit had restored her vision to 20/20.

She could see clearly now. No more relationships. Just sex. Visions of Hot Airport Guy popped into her brain, making her heart trip all over itself. Why, oh why, did he keep coming to mind? It had been quick, hot, and extremely satisfying sex. Nothing more. End of interlude. End of discussion. So why couldn't she move past it? It wasn't like she was ever going to see him again. He'd gone his way. She'd gone hers. Their paths would never cross again.

"Cathy's good with colors. I'd never dream of choosing a paint color without her input." Mel tugged the door to the diner open. Kenzie followed her inside.

Heavenly aromas greeted the women. Mel may have been immune, but Kenzie inhaled deeply, sure she'd gain several pounds just from the smell of deep-fried everything and home-baked desserts. Her stomach growled, reminding her how long it had been since she'd last eaten.

"There she is!" Mel waved at the woman leaning out of one of the window-front booths. "Come on. You'll love Cathy. She's the greatest."

Like everything else in Willowbrook, the place could double as a set for a 1950s era movie. They crossed the black-and-white checkered floor, weaving through a maze of four-top tables with mismatched chairs and tabletop jukeboxes. So far, everyone Kenzie had met in town had been warm and friendly despite her being a Yankee. She didn't doubt Cathy would live up to Mel's hype.

Mel made the introductions then the two of them slid into the opposite side of the booth from the donut shop owner. Kenzie had expected someone as big as a barn, but Cathy was slim and absolutely gorgeous with a smile to put anyone instantly at ease.

"It's nice to officially meet you," Kenzie said. "I've been in your shop nearly every day this week."

"Really?" Cathy's smile grew brighter. "I hope you're addicted." She directed her next comment to Mel. "I hear I've lost one of my best customers."

Melody adjusted her purse on the seat between them. "If you're talking about Henry, it's temporary. He wants to see a little bit of the world while he still can." She passed out menus from the holder next to the window. "Hank's worried about his dad traveling alone, but nothing we said was enough to convince him to stay."

Cathy opened her menu. "I understand where Henry's coming from. If I were in his shoes, I'd do the same thing. I'm sure glad he found me a replacement for the lost business though." She winked at Kenzie.

"I don't know how many donuts Mr. Travis bought, but I'll do my best to keep up." It wouldn't be difficult. Everything she'd tried at The Donut Hole had been to die for. She needed to find a gym soon, or she'd be a dumpling in no time.

"Well, well, well. Would you look at that?"

Kenzie glanced up from her menu to see what Cathy was talking about. A trio of sexy men walked single file past the counter seating complete with a view of the kitchen pass-through to the circular booth in the back corner of the café. Tall, dark, and brooding, they each had a distinctive style, yet they moved as one cohesive unit. Any woman who didn't sit up and take notice of such a fine display of manhood needed hormone supplements. Her lady parts were doing just fine—thank you very much. No assistance needed. Especially where the one in the middle was concerned. *Lord have mercy. It's* him.

Even from this distance, she could see flecks of white paint in his hair. His tattered, paint-splattered T-shirt and equally ratty jeans hugged and defined every muscle of his lean body. Not exactly the urban chic guy she'd hooked up with in the Philly airport—but it *was* him. No doubt about it. Her core melted as the visceral memories of what she'd done with the man incinerated the mental box she'd placed them in, scorching her from the inside out. Heart hammering, Kenzie ducked back behind her menu, hoping against hope he hadn't seen her. *What is he doing here anyway?* The city girl in her immediately wondered if he'd followed her, but she immediately swatted the thought away like she would a pesky fly. A covert peek told her the guys he was with today were the same ones he'd met at the airport. What were the odds they were just passing through Willowbrook today and stopped for a bite to eat? Her gut told her it wasn't the case, and Mel confirmed it.

"It's the brothers Grim."

Kenzie's gaze snapped to her friend. "Grimm? As in the fairy tales?"

"Their real last name is Ingram," Melody clarified.

"Grim as in ghastly, gloomy, and glum," Cathy offered.

"They live here?" *Please don't say yes.*

"'Fraid so." Cathy closed her menu, set it back in the holder then drummed her fingers on the table's red Formica surface. "They haven't always been grim."

"You know them?" Of course Cathy knew them. If there was one thing she'd figured out in the week or so she'd been a resident of Willowbrook, it was that everyone knew everyone else. She didn't know how long she was going to live here, but if it was longer than another seven days, her path was going to cross with his. Best to know what she was up against, so she could avoid running into him as much as possible.

"Do they have names?" She couldn't go on calling him Hot Guy from the airport.

Mel set her menu aside. "Jake, Will, and Rick. Jake's the oldest and Rick's the youngest."

Instinct, or something more, made Kenzie glance toward the brothers. Her breath caught in her throat. The brothers were looking their way. The one on the far left of the semicircle booth clenched his jaw before returning his gaze to the menu he held open in front of him. Opposite him, another Grim brother shook his head slightly then flipped his menu open. Kenzie's gaze fell on the one sandwiched between the other two. His dark gaze met hers, and, instantly, she knew he knew. Just like in the airport, her brain registered danger, but her body responded like she'd stuck her finger in a light socket while standing in a puddle of murky water.

Oh, he was a dangerous one all right. It was there, in those dark orbs that both threatened and promised with a single look. His broad shoulders filled the space allotted him by his brothers. Was his hair longer, or was it her imagination? She clenched her hands into fists as her fingers itched to see if the dark strands were as soft as they appeared. He'd had a bit of scruff on his jaw when she last saw him, but she was beginning to think he didn't own a razor. The style was sexy as hell on him. Damn. She had it bad if she didn't care he'd gone from GQ model to blue-collar heathen. She still wanted him more than she should. More than was prudent. More than was sane.

Mel waved a hand in front of Kenzie's face, forcing her to break contact. "Earth to MacKenzie. Earth to MacKenzie. Come in, Kenzie."

Another quick glance told her the game was over. Hot Guy hid behind his menu. With a silent sigh, she focused on her lunch companions. "What? Can't a girl look?"

Cathy leaned across the table. "You won't get anywhere with those guys. No one ever does."

Kenzie raised one eyebrow. "Do you speak from experience?" *Please don't tell me she's been with him.* Kenzie didn't want him. She really didn't, no matter what her lower body was telling her. But the idea of any woman having him, especially one she'd just met, unleashed something primal and possessive within. What was it about him that made her go cavewoman?

"No," Cathy insisted. "But I know others who have tried to put a smile on one of those faces. Every single one ended in disaster."

Recalling the intensity of her recent Grim stare-down, she thought smiles might be overrated. There was something to be said for determination and commitment to a goal. Hot Guy had both in spades. He'd proved as much in Philly. "How so? Details, please."

Uttering a long sigh, Cathy sat back. "The stories aren't mine to tell, but I can say any attempts to reform Jake and Rick have been unsuccessful. It's as if they don't want to be happy. And from what I hear, since Will returned last week, he fits right into the family mold."

A waitress wearing a pink-polyester dress, complete with a white collar and the pointed tips of a fake handkerchief poking from a breast pocket, stopped at their table, pencil and green order pad at the ready. A white oval name tag said, "Penny."

"Hey, Mel," Penny said.

"Hi, Pen." Mel gestured across the table. "This is the new PR person we hired for BlackWing. MacKenzie Carlysle, Penny Michaels."

Penny's gaze swung to Kenzie. "Nice to meet you." Tossing her head to indicate the brothers Grim, she waggled her eyebrows. "Saw you checking them out. They're our version of Mt. Rushmore. Bigger than life but cold and hard as stone."

She could see the hard-as-stone bit—and personally testify to the accuracy of the statement in regard to one of them—but cold? No way. She recalled the feel of Will gripping her hips as he drove into her over and over again. After he'd left, she'd checked to see if he'd branded her and been somewhat sad to see he hadn't. Not in any physical way, but he'd imprinted on her brain. As much as she'd tried, she hadn't been able to get him out of her mind. She fanned herself with the menu as she smiled up at the waitress. "And not easily accessible?"

"Many have tried. None have succeeded."

"Told you so," Cathy smirked.

Kenzie laughed. There wasn't a thing she could do about her present situation, so it was time to change the subject. "I'll have a cheeseburger, fries, and a diet soda." She placed her menu back in the rack.

"Excellent choice." Penny asked the requisite questions to complete the order then turned to Kenzie's lunch companions. "The usual?"

"Chicken Caesar salad and sweet tea," Mel confirmed.

Cathy took one last look at the menu then, with a sigh, slapped it shut. "Who am I kidding? I'll have the usual—the cheddar bacon burger and sweet potato fries."

"Diet soda?"

"Yep," Cathy said.

Penny scribbled on her pad then tucked her pencil behind her ear before nodding discreetly at the table across the way. "They weren't always grim," she said. "Cathy can tell you. She dated Rick in high school." Penny cruised over to take the brothers' orders as if she hadn't just tossed a flash/bang grenade in the middle of their table.

Once Kenzie picked her jaw up off the floor, she narrowed her eyes at the woman who'd, moments ago, denied any intimate knowledge of the brothers.

"You dated Rick in high school?" She leaned in closer.

"Yes, I dated Rick Ingram," she said, sounding anything but happy about it. "I went out with Hank Travis a couple of times, too." She flashed an apologetic smile in Melody's direction.

Mel patted Cathy's hand. "I thank you for not sleeping with my future husband when you had the chance."

"You're welcome, though if the offer had included better accommodations and/or a ring, I might have made a different decision."

Mel leaned over and half-whispered to Kenzie. "He offered her a romp in the bed of his pickup." She rolled her eyes. "Can't imagine why she passed on the offer. Can you?"

"Nope." Squelching an urge to laugh out loud, Kenzie shook her head. "Sounds like a pretty good offer, knowing the source." Melody's husband, Hank Travis, besides being Kenzie's new boss, was sexy as hell. Not to mention he was the drummer for BlackWing, one of the hottest rock bands in the country.

"You didn't know Hank then," Cathy said. "Who knew he'd turn out to be a rock star?"

Melody relaxed in the booth. "He asks the same question all the time. But it's what he was meant to do."

Kenzie had to agree with Mel's assessment. Hank Travis was crazy talented. "Enough about Hank." She cocked her head toward the table full of single hunks. "Which one of those is Rick?"

"The one on the right," Cathy said without turning to check.

Kenzie could just see him past Penny's polyester-clad hips. Broad shoulders like his brothers. Hair way too long for convention. His clean-shaven jaw resembled the stone monument Penny had referenced. Thanks to the way the waitress held her arms while she wrote on her order pad, Kenzie couldn't see Rick's eyes, but she could see his hand, clenched in a tight fist, sitting atop a tree-trunk thigh. *Damn.*

"You let *him* get away?"

"I didn't *let* him do anything," she said. "It was his dream to go to the Naval Academy. When he got in, he left and never looked back."

Oh, there was a story there, one she fully intended to hear — in great detail — later on. For now, she'd settle for the broader picture.

"So tell me," Kenzie said. "What happened to make the brothers so glum?"

"Don't know, exactly." Cathy slipped her flatware from its napkin cocoon. Smoothing the white embossed paper over her lap, she continued. "Jake is the oldest. He was a few years ahead of me. William graduated a year ahead of me in Hank's class. Rick's my age, and the youngest of the bunch. There's little more than a year between each of them. Stairsteps, as my mom would say.

"Their mom passed away, cancer, I think, when Rick and I were in middle school. No. Wait. It was our last year of elementary school. I remember because he missed a lot of classes and had to go to summer school to make up the time. My mom was the teacher that summer. She'd come home with a story to tell almost every day about something Rick had done or said."

"He was acting out?"

"I don't know. Maybe." Cathy moved the cheap knife and fork from the left of her placemat to the right.

Kenzie and Melody shared a look, reaching an unspoken agreement to pry the rest of the story out of the woman with a bottle of wine and chocolate later on. Right then, Kenzie wanted all the intelligence she could get on the other two brothers, particularly the one in the middle.

Penny arrived with their food, temporarily distracting them from the subject of the Ingram brothers. Kenzie groaned as she chewed and swallowed her first bite. "Oh. My. God. This has got to be the best cheeseburger I've ever eaten," she said, wiping greasy drippings off her chin.

Melody laughed. "Keep it down, girlfriend. People are going to wonder what's going on over here!"

Kenzie swirled a thick French fry in a puddle of ketchup and brought it to her lips, painting them with the sauce before opening her mouth to take the fried spud in. "Mmm. This is good, too. Soooo good," she crooned.

"Stop it." Mel blushed at the same time she kicked Kenzie under the table. "People are staring."

"What people?" Glancing around, her gaze met and locked with eyes belonging to Hot Guy.

Oh god. Staring wasn't even close to the right word for the way he was watching her. Involuntarily licking her lips, she swallowed hard past her heart which had lodged itself in her throat and forced her attention back to the plate of food she no longer wanted. Yes, she was hungry, but not for food. Everything she wanted was on the other side of the restaurant, and if looks could convey a message, he wanted her, too.

Trying her best to appear unaffected by his gaze, Kenzie popped another fry into her mouth and washed it past the now-massive obstruction in her throat with a swig of her soda. She turned to Cathy. "You were telling me about the brothers Grim. Did the other two go into the military as well?"

Cathy took a quick sip from her glass. "Nope. Jake, he's the one on the left, is a lawyer. Took over their dad's practice here in town a couple of years ago after their dad passed away. William—the one in the middle—went to college in New York to study art. He'd always been the quiet one of the bunch, but at least he used to smile. I thought he was doing well, selling paintings left and right." She shrugged. "Don't know what happened, but word on the street is he's back to stay."

Kenzie froze, the straw sticking out of her soda just a few centimeters from her lips. A hodge-podge of memories flashed through her brain. Paintings. Ingram. The sexy guy on the cover of the New Yorker magazine. Her vision clouded, and she forced herself to breathe as the impossible became highly likely. Her hand shook as she placed her beverage back on the table. "Wait just one minute."

She fought for enough breath to voice what she was almost certain was the truth. It defied explanation but was undoubtedly another chapter in the shit-show her life had become. Leaning in, she whispered, "You're telling me, the man sitting over there—William Ingram—is W.H. Ingram? The artist?"

Before either woman could answer, the images flitting around in her brain coalesced into one.

Oh. My. God.

I had airport sex with W. H. Ingram.

Did he know who I was when he accepted my offer? Suddenly, it all made sense. He was way out of her league when it came to sexual partners. She'd known it then and hoped for the best—and been somewhat stunned when he'd agreed to a hookup. *And why wouldn't he? I fucked him over, and he'd returned the favor. Those glorious moments in the Philly airport were a revenge fuck.*

Thanks to the giant lump still in her throat, Kenzie was able to stifle the groan of misery bubbling up from her gut.

Could my life get any more fucked-up?

"I seem to recall he signs his paintings as W. H.," Mel said. "I can ask him if you want?"

Apparently, it could. "No!" Kenzie recoiled at the sound of her voice raised beyond the acceptable level.

"Or, better yet, I'll look at the one in Hank's office."

Kenzie forced wind past her vocal chords. "Hank has a W.H. Ingram painting in his office?"

Mel nodded, her expression one of concern. "Yes," she replied cautiously. "I bought it from Sunny's gallery in New York a few years ago. That's how we met. I saw a painting in the window and bought it for Hank."

"Did you buy it because Will Ingram painted it?"

"I didn't know anything about the artist when I purchased it. I was walking down the sidewalk and saw it in the window of her gallery. It reminded me of Willowbrook, so I bought it for Hank, and a few others for myself. It wasn't until much later we realized it *was* Willowbrook and Will had painted it. Hank was impressed. He's been trying to buy another of Will's paintings but hasn't had any luck."

No. He wouldn't have any luck finding one unless the man had a secret stash of paintings no one knew about. *Like the ones that have gone missing?* She mentally shook her head. He hadn't taken his own paintings. She was 99 percent certain. He'd been a victim of two ruthless people, just as she had been, for reasons she still didn't understand and might never know. She recalled the paint splatters she'd seen on his clothes when he walked in. Had he resumed painting? The art world would be a better place if he had, but she'd heard he'd vowed he'd never lift a brush again. That kind of hurt was something she could relate to. As much as she loved the art world, she didn't want to go back there. She had this opportunity to work in the music industry, and she was going to give it everything she had.

The part she'd played in the demise of Will's career was a small one, but it weighed heavy on her shoulders. She owed him an apology, but, after the revenge fuck, she doubted he'd be interested in anything she had to say.

She could at least explain why Hank couldn't find another W.H. Ingram to purchase. "He quit painting."

"I didn't know. Hank will be disappointed. Will is a talented artist."

"I agree." Cathy ate another of her fries. "I've seen the painting you're talking about. It's absolutely gorgeous. It should be in a museum."

"It probably should be." Sorrow laced Kenzie's words. "He's really good. Hang on to the painting, Mel. It's probably worth a lot more than what you paid for it, and when your daughter is grown, it will be worth a fortune."

"I don't care what its monetary value is. It's special to Hank and to me. We'll never part with it."

Kenzie pushed her plate away. "As delicious as this is, I can't eat another bite."

Cathy gaped at her. "You hardly touched it."

"I know. My eyes were bigger than my stomach, I guess." She took a couple of bills out of her wallet and placed them on the table. "I need to get a few things from the drugstore. Take your time." She scooted out of the booth and stood, grateful her legs held. "Meet me in front of the hardware store when you're through?"

Both women seemed perplexed at the abrupt change in her demeanor, but readily agreed to meet at the prescribed location midway between the diner and the drugstore. Kenzie squared her shoulders and bolted for the door as fast as she could without making a scene. With every step, she felt William H. Ingram's gaze burning a hole through her.

She'd deserved the revenge fuck. She deserved his hatred. She just wished there was some way to make up to him for what she'd done.

CHAPTER SIX

Will sensed *something* from the moment he'd stepped into the diner with his brothers. Once he'd located the source of the feeling, he couldn't take his eyes off the woman. *What the hell is she doing here? Is she following me? Is she a reporter?* The possibility punched him in the chest and stole his breath. But what would she be doing with those two?

He knew the ladies sitting across the booth from her. Cathy owned The Donut Hole a few doors down from here, and had been in Rick's graduating class, a year behind him. He'd known her most of his life. The other woman had moved to Willowbrook a couple of years ago. She'd been Melody Harper then, just a reporter for the local newspaper. The whole town had been stunned to find out she was the only child of Rock and Roll legend Earl Ravenswood. Her father's music as lead guitarist for RavensBlood had been the soundtrack for his youth and inspiration for Hank Travis, the man Melody had married. *Melody used to be a reporter. Is that how she knew the woman from the airport?*

Shit.

He hadn't told anyone except the police where he was going when he left New York. Had they leaked the information to one of the investigative reporters who'd sniffed around the case at the beginning—or worse—to one of the tabloids?

His brain cycled back to the airport bar and the way she'd approached him. Not the other way around. God, she must have thought he was an easy mark, and he had been. Fortunately for him, all he'd wanted was a quick fuck, a way to release some tension, and, yes, make sure the important parts were still in working order. For the last several months, desire had been in short supply. He hadn't hung around for pillow talk—something she'd probably counted on.

Bitch.

He had no desire to tell his story to anyone, though eventually he would tell Jake. There were things only a lawyer should ask interested parties, and Will had plenty of questions. Too bad he didn't know who had the answers. Maybe Jake could find out. The NYPD had done all they were going to do. Unless someone walked into a precinct with a stack of paintings and confessed to stealing them, they weren't going to spend another minute hunting for his property or the people responsible.

Jake's voice dragged Will out of the well of depression he'd fallen into. "Hey, Rick. Who's the looker sitting with your old girlfriend?"

"Dunno. Don't care," his younger brother replied. Opening his menu, Rick studied it like it held the secret code to happiness. Lord knew Rick needed the code. Hell, they all did. Life had served Rick a shitty hand. It had dumped a lifetime of bad luck on Will's head, and he didn't know what had crawled up his oldest brother's butt.

"Maybe you should care," Jake said. "She's checking us out."

Only she wasn't looking at Jake or Rick. Her focus was entirely on him. From across the crowded diner, he could tell her eyes were blue, the kind a man could get lost in, drown in. He should know. He'd almost drowned in them at an airport bar in Philly. His reaction to her gaze had been one of the motivating factors in the way he'd taken her later on. Eyes didn't lie. They didn't say I love you when they meant otherwise. He hadn't wanted to read her emotions, and he damn sure hadn't wanted her to read his. Though he was now questioning her motivations, all he'd wanted was emotionless sex, and the best way to ensure it remained strictly physical was to fuck her from behind. No eye contact. No words whispered in an ear. No kissing. Served her right for trying to weasel a story out of him. But he wasn't stupid. Not anymore, anyway. He'd learned his lesson about trusting women. It would take more than a good fuck to make him talk.

Will redirected his attention to the only people in his life who mattered—his brothers. Rick didn't need any shit from either of them. He was getting his life together in his own way. Pushing him toward a relationship he didn't want wasn't any way to help. "Mind your own business, big brother."

Not taking his gaze off his menu, Jake countered, "Both of you *are* my business."

"Like hell we are."

Jake's head jerked up, his gaze locking with Will's. Will continued, "When are you going to get it through your thick skull? We're grown men, Jake. Rick and I are no longer your responsibility. We never were."

Jake glared across the table, and his lips formed a thin white line across his flushed face. "If you're so grown up, why don't you act like it?"

What the hell was I thinking coming back here? This was the same argument they had nearly every time the brothers got together, and one seemingly with no resolution. Jake thought his position in the family gave him the right to boss his younger siblings around. Will and Rick thought otherwise.

"Hey," Rick said. "Can't we have lunch without you two arguing?"

Will forced his grip to loosen on the menu. One of these days, he was going to force Jake to loosen his grip on him and Rick, even if he had to beat him to a pulp to get his message across. This was not the time or the place to hang their dirty laundry out though. "Fine by me."

Jake held his gaze for a long moment then, with a sigh, focused on the lunch offerings. "Fine."

Will glanced at Rick. His little brother had been through hell and brought some of the demons home with him. He was doing a lot better than when he first got home, but he hated conflict. Even the harmless kind between siblings put shadows in his eyes. "Sorry," Will said.

"No problem." Rick pretended to read his menu.

Will kicked Jake under the table. His older brother jerked and turned on him. Before Jake could say a thing, Will cocked his head toward Rick and raised one brow. Thankfully, his oldest brother got the message.

"Sorry, Rick."

"No problem. Anybody else want a milkshake?"

"I'll have one," Will said.

"Me, too." Jake set his menu aside. "The bacon cheeseburger sounds good with sweet potato fries."

While Will kept cautious watch on the table across the way, the brothers discussed the merits of their lunch choices like normal folks. The way Penny stood while she took the ladies' orders blocked his view of the newcomer, but he could hear the lilt of her voice, as she conversed with the waitress. Definitely the woman from the airport. He could practically feel her soft skin beneath his hands and, if he closed his eyes, recall her scent on his fingers.

Fuck! He shouldn't be thinking of her, but there was no hope for it. He couldn't get her out of his mind.

His jeans grew uncomfortably tight, and he considered starting another argument with Jake to ease the unwanted pressure. One glance at Rick convinced him to come up with another way to deal with his problem. It was so rare to see his younger brother's face devoid of tension, he couldn't bring himself to wreck the moment.

How did we get to this point? Three angry men unable to have a meal together without cutting each other to shreds?

They'd been normal kids, once upon a time. They each had their reasons for the way they were now, reasons they hoarded like favorite toys, unwilling to share. Rick was short on specifics, but it didn't take a genius to see his years in the Navy had changed him. Jake apparently had taken himself on as a client and refused to divulge anything about his life to anyone. Will didn't need a shrink to tell him what had gone wrong in his life. He'd trusted a woman and gotten burned. Seared to the soul was more like it. It would be a cold day in hell before he'd make the same mistake again.

They'd barely gotten their plates when he saw her slide out of the booth and head for the door. Will looked at his cheeseburger then to the woman weaving her way through the scattering of tables, and made a snap decision.

Tossing his napkin on the table, he shoved Rick in the shoulder. "Move it, asshole. I need to get out."

"Hey, who you calling asshole?" Despite his irritation, Rick stood, allowing Will to slide out of the middle seat. "You sick or something?"

"Nah. I'll be back. Give me a minute."

He didn't want to explain to his brothers where he was going, or why, but he'd have to tell them something. Neither one was stupid. They'd see her walking out with him trailing behind, and there was nothing in the world to keep them from reaching conclusions. None of which would be correct, thus the reason he'd have to tell them something when he returned. For now, all he could think about was catching up to her and letting her know he wasn't the story she was looking for. The sooner she left for New York, the better.

He hit the glass door at a sprint, shoving it open with his shoulder as he craned his head both ways, searching for her. She wasn't difficult to find. She leaned against the wall of the hardware store next door, her face turned in his direction.

Damn. He'd fallen right into her trap. Followed her out like a puppy on a leash. And he'd thought he knew better.

Will closed the distance between them, his anger growing with each step. He'd left everything behind in New York, except, apparently, this one reporter. The sooner she left, the sooner he could get on with his new life — whatever his life was going to be.

He stopped, his toes inches from hers. Up close, his artist's eye took in the perfect structure of her features. His fingers itched to touch, to add a tactile memory to the visual one imprinted on his brain. To prevent the involuntarily motion, he stuffed his hands in his front pockets.

Any artist worth his salt would give anything to paint her. Anyone but him. He wasn't an artist any longer. Now he painted houses. He'd started with his childhood home and, thanks to Rick, now had another one down the street waiting for his brush. Nothing artistic about swabbing white paint on tired wood. It was all muscle and sweat. No brain power needed. It was exactly the kind of job he wanted from now on.

But, god, she made him want things he had no business wanting. Like in the airport. He'd wanted to fuck her. Hard. Had wanted to prove something to himself, and maybe to her for having the audacity to proposition him, a perfect stranger, in an airport bar.

Ah, but he hadn't been a stranger after all, had he? She'd known who he was all along. Had planned the whole thing in an attempt to get his side of the story. It would be a cold day in Hades before he told her anything.

He inhaled deeply. Her intoxicating scent filled his nostrils and damn near disintegrated his resolve to send her packing. Sunshine and flowers. It somehow suited her, and when he painted her, both would be represented. A vision of her naked, a shaft of morning light revealing her perfect features, soft and replete from a man's attentions, burst across his consciousness. His dick responded, hardening against his fly, wanting to be the man to put a satisfied look on her face. He wouldn't be, and the realization felt like a rusty knife had been thrust between his ribs.

Will stepped away, hoping some fresh air would clear his big brain of its stupid ideas. Before he lost control and followed through on one of his crazy thoughts, he forced the words he'd come to say past his lips. "I don't know who the hell you think you are, but I've got some advice for you. Go back to New York where you belong. There's nothing for you here."

"But—"

"No buts. I said all I was going to say in New York. I'm done talking. W.H. Ingram no longer exists. End of story. Tell that to your readers."

"But...I'm not a reporter. I swear."

Already halfway to the diner's door, her words stopped him cold. He turned. "Then who the hell are you?"

"No one you want to know, but I swear, I didn't follow you. I didn't even know who you were until Melody told me a few minutes ago."

"How do you know Melody Travis?" He stepped closer but stayed out of range of her scent. Whatever was going on here, he needed all his brain cells engaged.

"I don't, really. She's a new friend. She's helping me shop for furniture. I work for her husband, Hank. Well, technically, I work for BlackWing. I'm MacKenzie, their new public relations person."

"You're telling me you didn't recognize me in the Philly airport?"

Her long hair swirled around her shoulders as she shook her head. "No. I swear. Our meeting was...spontaneous."

Well, shit. Will ran the fingers of one hand through his hair, murmuring a curse when they snagged on a clump of dried paint. *What a clusterfuck.* "Why did you hightail it out of the diner?"

"Uh." She bit her bottom lip and looked up at him through long lashes. "I don't know. Mel had just dropped the bomb about who you were, and, all of a sudden, it hit me—what I'd done in the airport. I couldn't just sit there and eat my burger like nothing had happened, and I couldn't *tell* them what happened, so I made up an excuse and left."

If she was lying, she deserved an Academy Award for her performance. But, then again, he'd fallen for another woman's lies and was still paying the price for his mistake. Time would tell if she was who she said she was. He backed toward the diner's door. "Tell Hank I said hello."

"Will do."

The moment he stepped inside the diner, he knew he'd made a tactical error. His brothers glanced up from their meals with expressions he should have predicted. Concern graced Rick's face. He always expected trouble, and, in this case, he was right. MacKenzie—he realized she hadn't given him her last name—was going to be trouble with a capital T. He could feel it in his bones. On the other side of their table, Jake's face radiated disapproval, reminding him so much of his father when Will had failed to live up to his expectations, he had the urge to turn around and leave. Fuck lunch. He could find something to snack on at the house.

"You want me to box your meal up for you?"

Will snapped his attention to Penny who had snuck up on him. Jake and Rick were almost finished eating. His would be cold, but what the hell? "No, but thanks. I'll finish it here." With a little luck, his brothers would go back to work and leave him in peace.

"No need to wait on me," he said as Rick stood to let him slide to his spot in the middle of the horseshoe-shaped booth. "I'll finish up and be along in a few."

"Fuck you." Rick settled into his seat. "What was that all about? You know her?"

The lyrics of an old country song came to mind. *If it weren't for bad luck, I'd have no luck at all.*

I should have it tattooed on my ass.

"No. She looked familiar though." It wasn't exactly a lie. He didn't know her. Hell, he still didn't know her last name. He knew plenty of other things about her, but he wasn't going to share those with anyone, especially his brothers.

Will popped a cold fry into his mouth and when he tried to find the ketchup container, his gaze locked with Jake's. *Shit.* The old Rick Ingram never would have let him off so easily, but this new version of his brother wasn't into confrontation. But Jake, the fucking lawyer, wasn't buying the mistaken identity excuse.

"Let it go, big brother." He glanced at his little brother. Rick was checking sports scores on his phone. Will caught Jake's gaze and mouthed, *later.* He wasn't happy about the delay, but Jake dipped his chin, acknowledging receipt of the message.

Every bite Will took felt like wet concrete sliding down his throat, but he didn't dare leave a scrap on his plate. Loss of appetite wouldn't go unnoticed by either brother. Rick didn't need the worry, and Jake didn't need any more ammunition. He'd heard a little about what had happened to Will. Both brothers had, but neither had the whole story. The police in New York had strongly advised him to have someone do some digging on his behalf. No one was dead—as far as they knew—so they weren't going to expend much manpower on the investigation. After a few weeks, all trails had gone cold and the file had been buried beneath a slew of new ones. Will simply hadn't had the funds to hire an investigator. He still didn't, but he had Jake. A call from a lawyer could loosen tongues and jog memories. It was the only shot he had at recovering any part of his career. Hell, he'd settle for getting some of his cash back. Fuck the paintings.

CHAPTER SEVEN

Kenzie's knees shook like limbs in a nor'easter as she watched William H. Ingram walk back inside the diner.

William. H. Ingram. Holy shit.

She still couldn't wrap her head around the fact he lived in Willowbrook or how she'd propositioned him in an airport. Not just propositioned. She'd provided the room and stripped naked in hopes he wouldn't walk out the door before he fucked her.

What were the odds she'd end up working in the town he lived in, or he'd fuck her over in a much more pleasant way than she'd fucked him?

She hadn't actually done anything to him back in New York, but she'd worked for one of the people who had screwed him over. She'd been screwed, too, in a manner of speaking. She'd followed her boss/boyfriend's orders like a good little minion, all the way up until the day he and his secret lover disappeared with most of William Ingram's money and all the paintings he'd entrusted them with for a gallery showing.

Cecil hadn't even liked Ingram's paintings, but the woman he'd run off with, Will's agent and girlfriend, Jessica, had done nothing but gush about how wonderful her client's work was. All while she had apparently been planning to end his career.

Kenzie had expected the paintings to start showing up on the black market, but it hadn't been the case. Months went by without a single one of them surfacing. There was no evidence they'd been destroyed. Surely, they would have left the debris where it could be found. Wouldn't they? Why haul them off if you planned to destroy them?

It was all such a fucked-up mess, she couldn't wrap her head around it. All she knew for sure was one day she had a boyfriend, a job, and a place to live. And the next, she'd had none of those things. She'd been questioned by the police several times. Her life had been taken apart at the seams and haphazardly put back together. They found nothing because she knew nothing. She'd thought Cecil had been faithful, as she had, to their relationship. After going over every minute of the six months leading up to the heist and disappearance, she had come up with nothing. Not a single clue to what the pair had planned. They'd simply disappeared. Poof! Now you see them. Now you don't.

Kenzie blew out a frustrated breath, blinked back the tears threatening to spill over, and focused on her surroundings. Will Ingram was going to find out who she really was. In fact, she was surprised he hadn't put it together in his head already. MacKenzie wasn't a common name, and she was from New York. She hadn't even pretended not to know what had happened to him. Everyone in New York talked about nothing else for months. The story had been on all the local and national news stations and made the front page of every newspaper and news magazine there was. She'd only been referred to as Cecil's girlfriend and gallery employee in all the news reports. However, her full name was in the official police files multiple times. Surely, he'd seen it.

Well, she wasn't going to look a gift horse in the mouth. As long as he didn't know, she wasn't going to tell him.

Mel and Cathy would come searching for her soon. Pushing away from the wall, she hustled two doors down to the drugstore and walked the aisles. She didn't really need anything, but as she heard the bell over the front door jingle, and glanced over her shoulder to see her companions enter the store, she blindly grabbed a couple of items from the nearest shelf and made her way to the checkout. She dropped her purchases onto the counter and dug in her purse for her wallet as the older woman at the register began to ring up the sale.

"Think you're going to need all those?" Cathy's humor-laced question prompted Kenzie to examine the boxes she'd snatched from the aisle.

Oh, god! Her fingers tightened around the plastic card in her hand as a wave of embarrassment heated her skin.

On the counter sat three boxes of condoms and a tube of lube.

"Credit or debit?"

"Uh."

"The brothers Grim are made of granite, but not in a good way," Cathy said. "But good luck to you." She gestured to the counter. "I hope you need all those and more."

The cashier sighed and pointed to a card reader. "Slide it in the slot, or insert it if it has a chip."

Behind her, Mel and Cathy dissolved into a fit of giggles they did a poor job of hiding. There was only one way out of this mess. She turned the card to match the picture on the device and inserted it into the chip reader. She shook her head and, over her shoulder, commented, "Next time we need balloons for a bridal shower, the two of you have to buy them. I'm done." She smiled at the unforgiving face across the counter. The card reader beeped. She removed the card, held out her hand for her receipt as she snatched the bag containing her purchases. "Sorry about my friends. They're usually more mature."

"No problem," the woman said without cracking a smile. "Have fun at the shower."

Cathy bumped shoulders with Kenzie once they were out on the sidewalk again. "Are you going to tell us the real reason you just bought enough condoms to supply an entire football team after the homecoming dance?"

Kenzie sighed. "No. I'm not." Nothing she could make up would be any less embarrassing than the truth—she'd been thinking about Will Ingram—and maybe, subconsciously, had ended up in that particular aisle.

"Leave her alone," Mel said. "It's none of our business. MacKenzie is a grown woman."

"Okay, okay," Cathy sulked. "But do me one favor?"

Kenzie glanced at her new friend.

"If you get the opportunity to use some of those, I'll need details."

Kenzie smiled. "Not unless you provide details first. Mel and I want to hear all about you and Rick."

They stopped in front of the hardware store, where Mel assured her they could find the paint she needed. Cathy paused with her hand on the old-fashioned doorknob. "Fine. But you're going to be disappointed."

"I seriously doubt it," Mel said and followed Cathy inside the store.

~ ~ ~

Cathy's house reflected the woman's personality with its cozy furniture and brightly colored accoutrements. Kenzie immediately felt at home, which was why she was in the kitchen, opening the bottle of wine she'd brought to share for their girls' night out while Mel and Cathy relaxed in the family room. She wasn't at all surprised when Mel's raised voice met her ears.

"Kenzie! When are we going to be able to invade your house?"

The two of them had been alternating between their houses for their biweekly evenings out and were "chomping at the bit," whatever *that* meant, to add her place to the rotation.

Strolling in, open bottle in hand, Kenzie refilled Cathy's glass then Mel's before pouring herself a generous amount. "I'm working on it." After settling in the big overstuffed chair across from the sofa where her friends sat, she took a sip from her glass. "Some of the furniture I ordered online is arriving later this week. I've got a few key pieces—a bed, a table and chairs in the kitchen, and a television. All the things Mel and I bought are supposed to arrive tomorrow. And don't forget, Rick Ingram is supposed to start the kitchen remodel next week. I have no idea how long it will take, but I'm thinking of asking him to paint some walls for me before he starts tearing things out."

"Rick is going to remodel your kitchen?" Cathy asked.

"So it seems." Kenzie wiggled to get more comfortable in the big chair. "He called me at the office yesterday. He's starting his own contracting business, and, apparently, I'm his first customer. Well, technically, Henry Travis is his customer. I'm just there to supervise and answer questions as they come up."

"I didn't know he was starting his own business." Cathy sipped from her glass. "Good for him."

Mel cradled her wineglass in both hands. "So, are you going to tell us what happened between you and Rick?"

Cathy gulped half the liquid in her glass then set it on the coffee table and tucked her legs underneath her. "Okay. I can see the two of you aren't going to let this go, so I'll tell you. Then I don't want to hear another thing about it. Are we clear?"

Mel and Kenzie both nodded. "Not another word," Kenzie said.

"What she said, now spill."

Cathy took a deep breath then let it out. "I've known the brothers all my life. This is a small town, was even smaller when we were kids. The Ingram's lived on the next street over—a few houses down from Hank. We all played together…rode our bikes all over the neighborhood…built lemonade stands together…roller-skated on the sidewalks. Stuff kids do.

"Then we grew up, and the boys started noticing other girls, except for Rick. He was my first date. We were thirteen."

"Thirteen?" Mel sat up straighter. "Kinda young, don't you think?"

"Maybe," Cathy conceded. "But my parents knew him and trusted him. He was a good kid. Didn't get into trouble."

"Go on," Kenzie urged. "Where did you go on your first date?"

"We walked into town—all of three blocks—to the soda fountain at Harrington's Pharmacy. I had a root beer float and he had a purple cow."

"Yuck!" Mel made a face. "A purple cow?"

"Yep. It was his favorite." Silence filled the air as Cathy decided on her next words. "As you can guess, there wasn't much for teenagers to do in Willowbrook back then. We spent a lot of time at the soda fountain, went to the movies, and studied together at the library. At least that was what we told our parents when we wanted to be alone."

"Where *did* you go?" Mel asked.

"There are some secluded places in the park. Make-out places. Rick had two older brothers, so he knew them all. Jake wouldn't take us anywhere, but when Will got his driver's license, he'd take us places. The drive-in was a favorite. We'd take the front seat so Will and his date could have the back."

Mel massaged her temples with the fingers of one hand while holding her wineglass with the other. "Geez, Cathy."

"Yeah, we were young. And stupid. I loved him, and he loved me." She grabbed her glass and drained it. Kenzie refilled it then sat back, waiting for the rest of the story. "We didn't go all the way until we were sixteen. It was his birthday and he'd just gotten his driver's license. Jake was away at college, and we took his old junker car to the drive-in. Rick said he loved me, and we'd already done everything except *you know*, so we did it in the back seat."

"How romantic." Kenzie shifted in her seat.

Cathy shrugged. "I said we were young and stupid."

"How was it?" Mel asked.

"Awkward. Beautiful. I loved him. Was glad to give him what he wanted. We were together for another year, screwing our brains out at every opportunity then we had a fight."

"Over what?"

"I thought I might be pregnant. We were careful—always used protection. Remember, Rick has older brothers. Four males living in one house. I suspect they bought condoms by the case. Anyway, I was late and I told Rick. He went ballistic. We broke up for a while." Cathy looked at Mel. "That's when I dated Hank. I was still in love with Rick and Hank knew it, I suspect. At any rate, Rick and I got back together before our senior year. I knew he wanted to go into the military, but I never thought he would actually do it. He had the grades to get into any college he wanted. He went off the rails a bit the year his mom died, but he was a straight-A student the rest of the time. I underestimated how badly Rick wanted out of Willowbrook, I guess. He enlisted in the Marines the day before graduation. I was going to junior college, and he was going god knew where."

"I'm so sorry." Mel set her glass on the coffee table then scooted down the sofa to hug Cathy.

When they parted, Cathy continued, "He said he loved me but he had to go. It wasn't me; it was him. Yada, yada. I'd been a fool. I gave Rick everything, thinking we'd be together forever, but he discarded me like I was no more important than those stupid paper caps and gowns we wore for graduation."

Kenzie grabbed a tissue box from the end table and handed it to her crying hostess. She was getting a clearer picture of what had happened, though she felt there were still pieces of the puzzle missing. Cathy had been dreaming of marriage and white picket fences while Rick had been dreaming of escape. From what, was the question. "He didn't write or call?"

Cathy shook her head and yanked a couple of tissues from the box. "No."

"Have you spoken to him since he came home?"

"No."

"Maybe he's waiting for you to make the first move?"

Cathy's grunt said it all. "He'll be waiting until Hell freezes over."

Mel picked up the bottle and refilled her glass. "Are you still in love with him?"

"No! God, no." Cathy blew her nose, clutching the used tissues in a tight fist. "He's obviously not the same person he was in high school."

"Are you the same person you were then?" Kenzie asked.

Cathy sipped from her glass. "I don't suppose I am."

"Maybe you should contact him," Mel said, settling against the arm of the sofa. "It's been a long time. I bet he doesn't know how to approach you."

Their friend drained her glass, refilled it from the rapidly emptying bottle, and sat back.

"What do you know about Will?" Kenzie asked.

"I think I told you all I know. He went to New York to study art—against his father's wishes, as I recall. Rick and I were done shortly after Will left town. I have no idea what happened to make him as grim as his brothers."

Kenzie knew, but she had no intention of telling anyone. It had all been big news in New York, but not so much here, she thought. She would have expected everyone in Will's hometown to have followed his career, but it didn't seem to be the case. Maybe that was why he came back here instead of staying in New York. She could sure relate to the need for a change, and Willowbrook was as different from the Big Apple as any place could be.

"I wonder if he's here to stay?" Mel set her glass on the coffee table. "Hank and his other friends would like it if he stayed."

"That group was thick as thieves," Cathy said. "Hank, Will, Randy, and Chris."

"Who are Randy and Chris?" Kenzie couldn't recall hearing them mentioned before.

"You'll meet Randy soon enough. He's the only other lawyer in town, and he handles all Hank's legal stuff. Chris runs the farm for Hank as well as his own family's farm. He's a busy guy, but you'll probably see him around from time to time."

"I wondered who was taking care of the crops. It looks like a big responsibility."

Mel stretched her legs out straight and wiggled her bare toes. "Hank helps when he can, but he can't count on being around when things need to get done, so it's easier to put Chris in charge. At least he knows what he's doing. Can't say Hank does."

"Guess he can't be good at everything." Kenzie carried her glass to the kitchen. "I better get home," she said as she slipped her sandals back on her feet for the walk home. "Tomorrow's a big day—my busiest yet at BlackWing."

"Really?" Mel stood, too. "What's going on?"

"I've arranged a bunch of remote radio interviews for Hank. We'll be in the studio for most of the day answering the same boring questions for talk show hosts across the country."

She wasn't looking forward to the long day, but as Hank said, it beat the heck out of traveling to all those cities for five minutes of work.

"He mentioned you'd set those up. I can't tell you how happy he was you'd arranged it so he could stay home. He really does hate to travel, especially when it doesn't include a performance."

"I'm working on some of those, too. If all goes as planned, BlackWing will be one of the featured performers for the morning show's concert in the park series later this year."

"Oh. My. God. Seriously?" Mel bounced on the balls of her feet. "The guys will bust a gut! They've wanted to be a part of that series for years."

"Well, don't get their hopes up too high. I'm still negotiating with the network and the show's producers. There's lots of competition and only so many Fridays in the summer." It would be a huge accomplishment if she scored them a spot on the roster. Lucky for her, an old friend from her days at NYU worked in the network's offices now and had a bit of pull when it came to booking the slots. She was going to owe Avery big-time if BlackWing made the list.

Kenzie was glad she'd decided to walk the few blocks from her house to Cathy's. Used to walking everywhere in New York, she missed the daily exercise. Maybe she'd have to take up running to keep the pounds off. As far as she could tell, salad was something Texans fed to rabbits. When she did find it on a menu, it was topped with fried chicken or steak and smothered in a creamy dressing. Neither was doing anything for her figure—except making it expand.

CHAPTER EIGHT

The night air felt good on her skin, and the moonlight playing peek-a-boo through the leaves of the trees lining the street was more than enough to show the way. The occasional porch light left on provided additional illumination.

Kenzie turned the corner onto her street and stopped beneath the streetlamp to admire the tranquil scene. Old-growth trees between the street and sidewalk acted as sentinels at night and provided shade during the day. Other than a car passing now and then, there was no traffic to speak of. Insects she couldn't identify provided a nocturnal symphony she'd come to appreciate in the absence of city noise. Treading the uneven walkway at a pace that would get her runover in New York, she let her mind wander to the one subject she couldn't seem to eradicate from her mind — William Ingram.

Having the memory of their close encounter in the Philly airport was bad enough, but now she had the memory of him in front of the hardware store, so close his unique scent swirled around her, through her. So close she could feel the heat radiating off his body. So close she could see the depth of pain in his dark eyes. So close all she had to do was reach out to touch him. But she hadn't. Couldn't. He wasn't an anonymous hookup in an airport any longer. He was W. H. Ingram. A man she couldn't have, no matter what her traitorous body said.

She'd felt sorry for him when everything hit the fan back in New York, but since she'd seen the pain etched deep on his face and swirling in his eyes, guilt for the small part she'd played in his demise ate at her.

The pain had been there in Philly. Maybe it was what drew her to him in the first place. Misery loves company. Had she known who he was then, she wouldn't have gone anywhere near him. But she hadn't known, and when her pain had collided with his, they'd combusted. Sparks had flown. It was a wonder they hadn't burned the place down.

Sex had never been stupendous for her. Good, yes. Good enough she hadn't wanted to give it up, but since their encounter in Philly, she *craved* it. Not just any sex. She wanted more of what she'd had with Hot Guy, a.k.a. W.H. Ingram.

Only it wasn't going to happen. He'd made it perfectly clear the other day he wanted nothing to do with her. *Yeah, he'd want even less to do with you if he knew who you really were.*

If she had any brains at all, she'd get the heck out of Willowbrook before he found out. People in this town loved him. They didn't know her. She'd lose any popularity contest between them.

Lost in thought, she jumped when a shadowy figure moved on a nearby porch. Hand on her throat, she took a step back before she realized this was Willowbrook not New York. It was one of her neighbors in a town where a rash of toilet-papered trees constituted a crime spree.

"Didn't mean to startle you."

She recognized his voice. Her heart raced. She'd been wrong. So very wrong. This man was dangerous in so many ways. Yet, instead of running toward the safety of her new home, her feet remained planted on the sidewalk, as the figure stepped from the shadows.

"Out a little late, aren't you?"

"What are you? My mother?"

"Nope. Just a concerned citizen looking out for the welfare of our newest resident."

"It's none of your business, but I was at a friend's house."

"Did you have a nice time at Cathy's?"

"How?" she squeaked as her mind raced to figure out how he'd known where she was. "Are you following me?"

"Nope." He tapped his temple. "I have excellent powers of deduction. You're new to town, and I doubt you've had time to make many friends. You know Cathy. I saw you with her at the diner, remember? She lives on the next street over. Thus, it's logical to deduce you were at her place."

She latched on to the subject like it was a lifeline. Anything to keep from doing what she really wanted to do—drag him into the bushes for a repeat. "You know Cathy?"

He strolled closer, hands stuffed in the front pockets of his jeans. "Yep. All my life."

"That's…uh…nice." Damn, why couldn't she string two words together without stumbling over them? Maybe it was because of the way he was looking at her. Suddenly, she felt like the adult version of Red Riding Hood. And W.H. Ingram was her personal big, bad wolf. The feeble grandma in the deepest recesses of her brain urged her to run, but her overactive libido wouldn't let her move.

"She mentioned you the other day when I went in to pick up some donuts. She seemed glad to have you here."

It was good to know she was making friends in Willowbrook, but there was someone else's opinion she was more interested in. "And what about you?"

He drew closer and leaned against the corner post of the white picket fence surrounding his yard. "I hate having you in the same town."

"Oh. Well." She looked down at her feet and silently willed them to move.

"I hate that I want you even more than the first time I saw you."

Kenzie jerked her chin up. "What?"

"I said, I hate that I still want you." His gaze swept the surrounding area then landed on hers. "I can't stop thinking about you—or all the things I want to do to you."

"L-like what?"

"For starters, I want to turn your naked ass over my knee and spank you until your skin is red and your pussy is dripping wet. Then I want to fuck you six ways to Sunday." He paused, shook his head as if to clear it then his gaze met hers again. "I don't want a relationship. Just sex. Raw. Nasty. Sex."

She forced air into her lungs, struggling to comprehend his words.

"You up for a purely physical arrangement, Kenzie?"

~ ~

Lord, when did I become such a prick?

Will knew the answer to the question but refused to think about it right then. MacKenzie was from New York. She understood the game. She'd proven it when she propositioned him in the airport. He'd been a prick then, too, but she'd gotten what she'd asked for. Since he was doing the propositioning, he hoped she didn't expect anything more than what he'd given her in their rented room. If she did, she was in for a rude awakening. *If* she said yes. And that was a big if.

Against his conscious will, he committed her shocked face to memory, filing the image away with the others he couldn't seem to get out of his head. In the dark of night, they came to him, waking him from what little sleep he got these days, torturing him, tormenting him until he did something about the fire raging inside him. He was damn sick of his right hand. Had even tried to do it left-handed just to mix things up a bit.

He hadn't considered propositioning her until he'd seen her turn the corner a few houses down and felt his body come alive with need. Willowbrook had grown some since he'd been gone. He could probably find companionship somewhere else if he wanted to, but he didn't want anyone else. For whatever reason, it was this woman, and only her, who stirred his cock to life.

She closed her mouth, glanced around him to the porch where he'd been sitting, contemplating the next chapter of his life. "Where?"

Every nerve ending in his body stood up and took notice. *Holy crap!* He should have thought this through, but he'd been certain she would say no. What were his options? The house was out. Rick was home, and there was nothing but a thin wall between the two bedrooms. There was the garage…fuck, no. He wasn't *that* desperate. *Think. Think.*

"My place." Her fingers closed around his right wrist, dragging his hand from his pocket as she started walking. "Hurry the fuck up."

Yes, ma'am!

The walk was painful as hell. He'd been hard since the moment he laid eyes on her, but that one little word from her lips—"Where?"—and he'd gone hard as stone. He knew the street well. Knew every crack in the sidewalk, every house and its inhabitants. Not much had changed in the years he'd been gone.

"Careful," he said, lacing his fingers with hers to guide her over a spot where tree roots had raised the walkway, leaving a crack wide enough to catch a foot.

"Thanks." She squeezed his hand then pulled hers free.

They turned up the walk leading to her front door. Will blocked out the memory of this being Hank's house—a place he'd spent many a day and night—and concentrated on the woman opening the front door. He didn't want to take his eyes off of her, but the minute he stepped inside, a wave of nostalgia swept over him. The living room was empty except for a new sofa and a flat-screen television resting on the floor. He could still see the furniture Hank's mom, Gloria, had taken such pride in—and the easy chair his dad, Henry, had claimed as his own. Blinking, he forced the memories away. The previous occupants of the house had moved on, and so had he. The house down the street where he'd grown up wasn't home any more, either.

"Sorry. I don't have much furniture yet."

"No problem. We don't need much." He strode toward the kitchen, hoping she at least had the basics in there. He wasn't disappointed. A small table sat in the exact same spot as the one he remembered. He pulled out a chair, turned it around, and sat. "This will do fine."

"You want to do it in here?"

"You have a problem with kitchen sex?"

"No." Her brows knit. "I have a bed."

"Don't need one." He made himself comfortable on the chair. "Come here."

She approached, one cautious step at a time. He pointed to a spot beside his right thigh and saw the moment comprehension dawned on her expressive face. In the span of a second, she went from confused to aroused as she relocated to the spot he'd indicated.

"Push your pants and panties to your knees then lay across my lap."

With a slight nod, she eased shaking hands beneath her loose pullover top to the waistband of her yoga pants. Will swallowed hard as she wiggled out of the tight garment, her oversized shirt falling to cover much of her exposed skin. No matter. He had a vivid memory. An artist's memory. He could still recall the gentle swell of her belly and the neatly trimmed curls on the crest of her womanhood.

"Help me?"

He jerked his attention to the present and the bare thighs pressed against his denim-clad leg. "Put your hands behind you and bend over. I won't let you fall."

God, he was going to die right here if he didn't get his heart rate under control. The damn organ was working overtime to pump blood to his dick. He needed a little of it to remain above his neck long enough for him to get through this portion of the night's entertainment without actually hurting her. Yes, he was going to spank the hell out of her ass, but he wouldn't cause actual harm. No way. Not his style.

He eased her into place then brushed the hem of her shirt up to the small of her back before he clamped her wrists in his left hand. "Don't want you to get hurt," he explained. "If you want me to stop, say red. If you need a break, say yellow. Otherwise, I'm in control here. Understood?"

"Yes."

"So we're clear, this spanking is not a punishment. It's because I can't get you out of my head." Yeah, the statement didn't even make sense to him, but he wasn't going to stop unless she put the brakes on. He'd honor her wishes, but, judging from the heightened scent of her arousal, she wanted this as much as he did. "Tell me you understand. Tell me you want me to spank you."

"I want this. Please, spank me."

Without warning, he brought his palm down hard on her right ass cheek, leaving a clear imprint. She cried out, but her cry quickly morphed into a groan. Shit, she was going to be the death of him.

He repeated the process on her left cheek then gently massaged the twin red handprints until she was groaning and writhing on his lap. "God, I love seeing my mark on you." He squeezed the plump globes before stroking them again, firm but soft. "I wanted to leave my mark on you before—"

He landed two more strikes slightly off center from the others. Her skin flamed red where the two overlapped. Christ, he wanted to paint her like this. His stupid brain was already mixing colors to achieve the perfect shade. Angry with himself, he landed four more blows, not as hard as before—he didn't dare in his state of mind—but hard enough to have her trying to jerk out of his grasp.

Breathing hard, he laid his palm on her ass. "Too much?"

"No."

He could hear the tears in her voice and instantly felt like a shit. "Want me to stop? Just say the word."

"Please, Will. I need—"

"What, baby?" He knew, but the perverse person he was, he wanted to hear her say it. To beg for it.

"I need to come. Please, Will."

He parted her ass cheeks with his middle finger, sliding lower until he found her drenched center. Her pants, bunched at her knees, held her legs together, and though he would have loved to have been able to see more, the position was good for her. Her thighs held him snug as he pushed two fingers inside her tight entrance then found her clit with his little finger. "You want it, baby? Ride my hand. Make it happen."

God, I really am a bastard. But, Heaven help him, watching her ass buck and wiggle, hearing her cries of frustration as she sought the release she so desperately needed was possibly the most erotic thing he'd ever witnessed in his life. "That's it, baby. Make yourself come then I'm going to fuck you so hard. I'm going to ram my cock in you over and over. Take what I want and leave you wet and sore."

"Fuck. You!" Her body tensed. He smiled as she screamed out her pleasure. He'd been right not to take her to his house. They'd be lucky if her neighbors didn't call the cops.

He released her wrists then stroked her ass and beneath her shirt as far as he could easily reach until her breathing evened out and she tried to sit up.

"Fuck you, Will Ingram." The weak smile on her flushed face made a lie out of her curse.

"You're welcome." He stood. "My turn now." He held out a hand to help her stand. "Kick those pants off and grip the edge of the table. You know the drill."

Legs still trembling from one of the most intense orgasms she'd ever had, Kenzie did as Will said so she stood before him naked from the waist down. Following the silent signal of his spinning index finger, she turned and stretched over the table, gripping the far edge with her fingers. The cold wood on her heated skin was a shock to her senses. Pain from pressing her breasts, tight with arousal, against the table was an unexpected aphrodisiac. Without being told, she spread her feet wide, presenting her pussy to him. How was it possible she still needed to feel him inside her, stretching her, filling her? She'd had enough solo orgasms to know once was usually enough, but not with him.

She'd wanted him again at the airport, and nothing had changed. She still wanted him. Feared she'd always want him. But from the position he'd chosen, then and now, he didn't want more. Just a hard fuck. A release.

No kissing. No tender caresses, unless you could count the way he'd massaged the sting of his handprints into a slow burn that had ignited a conflagration within. Those gentle touches had been a surprise, but as she listened to the sound of a zipper being lowered and plastic ripping, she understood there'd be no conciliatory gestures this time.

Internal muscles clamped tight then released. She was wet in anticipation of his entry.

"Red is your only word; otherwise, I'm not stopping until I'm finished. Come if you want to. Won't make a difference to me." He drew the head of his cock along her slit then fitted himself to her opening and dug his fingers into her hips. "Tell me you want me to fuck you."

Hell, yes! "Please, fuck me, Will. Fuck me hard."

His first hard thrust rocked her pelvis against the edge of the table and drove her lungs up into her throat. She gasped for air and held on for what she was certain would be the ride of her life.

She wasn't disappointed. His cock was every bit as big and hard as she remembered, his grip as tight, his stamina impressive. She was going to be sore tomorrow in places she'd never been sore before, but she wouldn't stop him. It felt too damn good. He took and took and took, and god, it felt glorious to be the one he lost control with. Kenzie gave and gave and gave, but it wasn't unselfish. He took his pleasure, and in doing so, gave her more.

"Ride the edge of the table. Fuck it, baby."

God, she loved his dirty talk. She groaned and moved her hips as best she could, grinding her clit against the unforgiving wood while Will continued to pound his pelvis against the abused flesh of her ass. He eased his grip on her hips, allowing her more movement. She rode toward her release, felt the coil inside her tightening. Then he slipped a thumb between her cheeks, found her most secret place, and pushed brutally inside.

Pain and embarrassment melded into a solid wedge jettisoning her into a place she'd never been before where pleasure and pain were one and the same. A place where the thick cock pummeling was all she needed. All she wanted. She convulsed, over and over again, clamping down on his shaft, and she knew, in an instant of clarity and awareness, this man had been made for her. There would be no other. Ever.

"Fuck me! You feel good." His curses made their way past the blood rushing in her ears. "God, woman, you're killing me."

Kenzie found the willpower to order her internal muscles to grip him tight one more time. Her effort was rewarded as his thrusts became erratic and his curses garbled. Then, with a series of short, brutal thrusts, he came, his dick pulsing inside her, filling the condom and making her heart ache, wanting to feel his hot seed bathe her inner walls, knowing she never would. Tears spilled from her eyes. Tears of regret for what they could never have together. He didn't know who she really was. Didn't know what part she'd played in his downfall. He would find out, and when he did, all she'd have left would be the memory of these perfect moments when they'd shared an intimacy, a bond beyond the physical.

It was impossible, but her heart belonged to W.H. Ingram.

CHAPTER NINE

I'm an ass.

Hands tucked into his front pockets, shoulders slumped, Will's feet carried him down Main Street to the park where he'd be alone at this time of night. He'd done it again, fucked her then left without a word.

Shit.

He'd never been a coward before, but he was now. How else could he explain his behavior? Fuckin' afraid to look her in the eye. What was with him?

He knew. It was the pain he'd seen in those eyes—twice. Once when she sat down next to him in the airport bar then just the other day when he'd confronted her outside the diner. She hurt inside just like he did. If he hung around, inevitably, they'd talk. It was how relationships worked. The last thing he wanted to do was share his pain with anyone. The humiliation went too deep, the wound too fresh. And if he was being truthful, he flat out didn't want to carry anyone else's burden. His was heavy enough.

Yep. A cowardly ass. That's me.

This can't go on.

But as long as he continued to feel like a victim, he'd never have a chance at a normal relationship again. Hell, he didn't have a chance at a normal life of any kind. It was time to get his shit together. Time to own his circumstances. Time to fight. Maybe, if he knew he'd done everything he could to get his paintings back—never mind the money—he'd be able to move forward.

He wanted to paint. He just couldn't see the point in it anymore. The situation had to change because, without his paints, he didn't know who he was.

And not knowing fucking sucked.

~ ~

Jake opened his front door, wearing sweatpants bearing the Yale logo and a T-shirt Will suspected dated to his brother's days as quarterback for the Willowbrook Wildcats. Though it was late, he didn't look at all surprised to see Will on his doorstep. "It's about time."

Refusing to be baited, Will pushed past him in the entryway of the ultra-modern home his brother had built on the outskirts of town and marched straight for the kitchen where he'd find a cold beer in the refrigerator. He might need something more bracing before this conversation was over, but, for now, a beer would do. He popped a top on one, handed it to Jake who'd followed him through the house then opened one for himself. He closed the refrigerator and leaned against the fancy quartz countertop. "The last thing I want to do is talk about this, but I need help."

Jake opened his mouth to say something, but Will cut him off.

"Don't say it, Jake. I know I've been a jerk. I should have asked for your help months ago, but I didn't. Can't change the past. I'm here now. That should count for something."

Jake nodded and took a sip of his drink. "I was going to ask if you would like to sit down." He pointed with the hand holding the bottle. "Den or out by the pool?"

"Pool." Will followed his brother who stopped in his home office to grab a yellow pad and a pen before proceeding to the back of the house where an expansive patio looked out on a vanishing-edge pool and several acres of lakefront property. Jake wouldn't have suggested they talk outdoors if he thought there was a chance in hell someone would overhear. He hadn't gotten to be the successful attorney he was by doing stupid things.

Will, too agitated to completely relax, straddled a lounge chair, while his brother stretched out on the adjacent chaise. Between the underwater lighting and a nearby lamppost, there was just enough light for Jake to take notes. Though the setting was casual, Will sensed his brother slip into lawyer mode—silent and predatory.

He'd hear every word Will had to say and note every word he didn't say. There'd be no hiding from the truth tonight.

Will took a long pull on his beer then, gaze focused on the dark horizon, told his story. Starting from the moment he'd met his agent, Jessica Blackwell, to the evening he'd shown up at Cecil Hawthorne's gallery to find the doors locked and his paintings gone. He left nothing out, including the fact he'd been sleeping with Jessica since he'd met her at another opening, also held at Hawthorne's gallery.

The more he talked, the stupider he sounded. He'd been in love, or so he thought, but in retrospect, his relationship with Jess had been a sham from the outset.

"You think they targeted you from the beginning?"

Leave it to Jake to get right to the heart of the matter. "I think it's possible. I didn't then. Never saw it coming. I thought we were in love. We made plans." Plans he didn't want to think about ever again. He'd given his heart to a thief and wouldn't make the same mistake again.

"What kind of plans? Was anything in writing? Did you buy property together?"

Will shook his head. "No. Nothing like that. We talked about buying a place upstate. Something with an outbuilding I could use as a studio. Even rented a car and took a few trips up there to scout areas."

"Did you talk to a real estate agent?"

"Once. We stopped to eat at a local diner. The agent was next door. Had some flyers in the window. One of them looked promising, so we went in to ask about it."

"Did you go look at the property?"

"No. It had already been sold. He just hadn't taken the flyers down."

Jake scribbled furiously on his pad. "Tell me everything you remember about the visit."

"Why? We didn't do anything but talk to the guy."

"Humor me, okay?"

Will sat up, his legs splayed on either side of the lounger. Shoulders slumped, he bowed his head and closed his eyes, searching for memories he'd tried desperately to erase from his mind. He couldn't imagine any of this would matter, but he trusted

Jake. If anyone could find a thread to pull in this case, it was his brother. "We'd been together for almost a year," he began.

Even the crickets had called it a night by the time Jake finished his interrogation. They'd been down roads Will hadn't dared explore and through doors he hadn't even known were there. His brother was good. Really good. Though he was rung out from all the talking and soul-baring, he felt better for having told his story to someone who really listened. The police had heard him out, but he never felt as if they'd listened.

Jake returned from the house with two cups of coffee and a plastic bag. He set the cups of steaming liquid on the small table between them then set about filling the bag with empty beer bottles. They'd consumed more than Will realized over the last few hours.

"Thanks." He picked up one of the mugs.

"You should spend what's left of the night here."

Will nodded. "Might be a good idea. I'll call Rick." After leaving the park, he'd gone home and helped himself to his younger brother's pickup. "Let him know I'll bring his truck back early."

"I called him. He said if you weren't back in time, he'd walk down to Henry's house in the morning. It's just a walk-through with the new tenant to get a feel for what has to be done and establish a schedule."

Mention of Henry Travis' new tenant did more than any cup of coffee could do to sober him up. He stifled a groan as he recalled the way he'd treated her. Getting to his feet, he followed his brother inside the house. He'd been there enough times to know his way around. The common rooms, kitchen, living room, and den were in the center of the sprawling ranch-style structure. The master suite and Jake's office took up one end of the house. Will sauntered in the opposite direction, toward a selection of guest rooms to choose from.

"Wait a second." Jake disappeared into his office. A few seconds later, he emerged with a yellow tablet and pen in hand. "Here. Take these. If you remember anything at all, write it down. And when I say anything, I mean even the smallest detail. Even if you don't think it's significant." Jake grinned. "You never know. It could be the key we're looking for."

Will nodded. Just as he'd taken another step, Jake's voice stopped him again. "Oh, and I need a list of every gallery where your paintings were sold. Names, addresses, any—"

"Anything. I get it." He waved the pad of paper in a goodnight gesture then resumed walking. He'd been looking forward to a good night's sleep, unburdened as he was after spilling his guts to his brother, but Jake's last comments had jump-started his brain again. There'd be precious little sleep, if any, tonight.

CHAPTER TEN

Kenzie placed her palms flat on the table and pushed herself upright. Her knees buckled under her weight, and she grabbed for the nearest chair, the one Will had sat in only a few minutes ago, and crumpled onto the seat, the sound of his footsteps walking away still echoing in her ears.

Hell and damnation. He'd told her up front what he wanted. Raw, nasty sex. And he'd delivered. Nothing more.

So, why did her heart hurt so damn bad?

You knew the score. You agreed to his terms.

At least she was pretty sure the airport encounter hadn't been a revenge fuck as she'd thought. Those were a one-and-done. He'd come back for more—admitted he wanted her—but wished he didn't.

Welcome to the crowd.

She needed to stay far away from Will Ingram. Far. Far. Away. He'd eventually find out who she was. He apparently hadn't linked her name to his scandal yet, but he would. And when he did, god help her. He'd destroy her.

She hated he held that kind of power over her, but there wasn't a thing she could do about it. If only she'd met him in New York before things had gotten so screwed up. Maybe things would have been different for both of them. Would he have given her a second look back then? Probably not. According to the news reports, he'd been involved with his agent up until the night Jessica and Cecil betrayed him.

Had he been in love with her? Was losing her more of a blow than the loss of his money and paintings? Was lost love the pain she saw in his eyes?

She didn't want to think what a lost love, if it was true, made her relationship with Will.

Whoa! Hold the fuck right up! There is no relationship. None. Nada. Zip.

They were….

Absolutely nothing came to mind. Not friends with benefits. Not fuck buddies, but not exactly enemies, either. Though they would be as soon as he realized who she was.

Kenzie closed her eyes and did the deep breathing exercises she'd learned during her short stint in a yoga class a few years ago. She'd been horrible at the exercises, but she'd found the breathing techniques useful on occasion. Tonight was no exception. After a few minutes, her heart rate calmed and her mind cleared enough for her to take stock of her circumstances.

Her ass hurt sitting on the hard wooden chair. The sensations coming from between her legs were a mix of satisfaction and a hollow ache tied to her heart with invisible strings. With effort she found hard to come by, she rose, picked up the small pile of her clothes, and trudged to her bedroom.

Not even a hot bath had eased the ache between her legs, so she'd tossed and turned most of the night, determined not to give in to the need to touch herself. The few minutes she'd slept, she hadn't been alone. Will Ingram had invaded her dreams, fulfilling them one second then dissolving into nightmares the next when her truth came to light.

Groaning, she dropped her forehead into one upturned palm while the other held tight to the mug of hot caffeine she hoped would obliterate last night from her memories—if she could find the energy to lift the cup to her lips and drink. Every muscle in her body ached. Some from the vigorous workout they'd had right there on her kitchen table, and others from a night fraught with tension, both real and imagined.

She'd taken a few hours off this morning to meet with the contractor Mr. Travis had hired to do the kitchen remodel. He'd be here any minute with plans and schedules.

Kenzie was pouring herself a second cup of coffee when the doorbell rang. Setting the mug aside, she took a deep breath and double-checked to make sure she'd actually dressed this morning. Any and everything was in question, given the state of her mind and body. Assured she'd put on clean clothes and was indeed presentable, she opened the front door — and gasped at the two men standing on her porch.

"MacKenzie Carlysle? I'm Rick Ingram. He hitched a thumb over his shoulder. And this is my brother, Will."

Shit. Shit. Shit. What was *he* doing here? Her hands clenched into fists, her nails digging painfully into her flesh as she stared at W.H. Ingram. His lips rose on one corner as he wiggled his fingers in a half-hearted wave. She wasn't sure which it was, the almost smile or the sight of his fingers doing *that*, that made her insides turn to liquid.

Rick held up a notebook. "We're here to go over the plans for the kitchen remodel. Mr. Travis has authorized a few more items he'd like done."

There was no hope for it, she had to let them in or try explaining why she didn't want Will Ingram in her house. She unlatched the screened door, giving it a slight push toward the two men. Rick grabbed the handle and stepped inside with his brother on his heels.

"Nice to meet you," Will said as if he hadn't ever seen her before.

Were they going to pretend they hadn't talked in front of the diner? Or had sex in her kitchen a few short hours ago? Apparently so. "Uh. Yeah. I mean, yes. It's nice to meet you, too." She turned, as much to avoid looking at him as to decide what to do with the two of them. "Won't you have a seat?" She motioned to the lone sofa in the front room.

"Perhaps the kitchen would be a better place to talk," Rick said, "since the bulk of the work will be in there."

The kitchen. Visions of what had gone on in there less than twelve hours ago flashed through her brain. "Ri-right." It made sense. It did. But dear god, why did *he* have to be here? Calling upon every bit of manners she'd ever possessed, she led the way to the rear of the house. "I've got coffee —"

"Coffee would be great," Rick said, pulling out a chair at the table. Thank god it wasn't *the* chair. Kenzie found a couple of mugs her landlord had left and filled them. Turning around, she almost dropped them when she saw Will Ingram's hand on the back of a chair. The one he'd sat in the night before. The one she'd planted her bare ass on as he'd closed the front door, leaving her well fucked and more confused than she'd ever been in her life.

"Here. I'll take those." Will took the mugs from her and set them on the table. "Why don't you sit here so you can see the plans?" He indicated *the* chair without any hint it meant anything to him.

"Th-thanks." *Crap.* She really had to stop stammering. She sounded like an idiot. *Get a grip.*

What is he doing here?

"Is this yours?" He set the cup she'd abandoned earlier in front of her.

"Yes. Thank you." She gripped it with both hands like it was an anchor.

"My pleasure," he said as he slid into the chair on the other side of his brother.

She'd fire Rick if she could, but she wasn't the one paying him. Her landlord was. In exchange for overseeing the remodel, she was getting a significant discount on her rent until the project was done. She had no choice but to see this through, which meant she'd have to put on her big girl panties and deal.

Crap. She glanced at the floor where she'd dropped her panties last night so *her contractor's* brother could screw her brains out right here on the kitchen table. The tiny hairs on the back of her neck tingled like she was having an orgasm or someone was watching her. Absolutely certain it was the latter, she glanced up. Across the table where Rick was busy sorting papers for her to look at, her gaze met *his*. There wasn't a doubt in her mind he was thinking about last night, too.

Was that a smirk?

W.H. Ingram had a reputation for being arrogant, sometimes to the point of rudeness. He'd been famous for it in the New York art world. He didn't attend parties—just the occasional gallery showing for a friend. The magazine article and cover photo had been an anomaly, and had launched his fledgling career into the stratosphere where it had stayed until earlier this year.

He understood exactly what he did to her, and had done to her. How dare he sit there with a silly smirk on his face? Because he'd been inside her twice, he thought he had the upper hand. Thought he knew what she liked. He wasn't exactly wrong, but he didn't know everything. She liked a bit of cuddling after, but she'd never have that level of intimacy with Will. A bit of touch and kiss and maybe, if both parties weren't dead, another round — slower, with more feeling.

Shit. There she went again, hoping for something she would never find with Will Ingram. He didn't do relationships. He'd said so in plain English, and she'd acknowledged such. Kenzie squared her shoulders and dropped her gaze to a drawing Rick had placed in front of her. She didn't know what game Will was playing, but she was through.

"What's this?" She pointed to a big square on the meticulous layout.

"The refrigerator." Rick nodded toward the current one. "Mr. Travis agreed to a set amount to replace all the appliances. The one you have isn't too old. If you want, we can move it to the garage and you can continue to use it as an extra."

"Whatever would I need an extra refrigerator for?"

Rick shrugged. "Some people like to have them for overflow during the holidays. These kitchens are too small for a wine fridge, so you could fill it with your extra beverages."

"Did Mr. Travis want to keep it? Because I don't think I'll need it."

"Nope. He said to leave it up to you." Rick wrote something in his notebook. "Okay. I'll leave this one in place as long as possible then move it out to the garage until we're done. I'll have the delivery people haul it off when they bring the new appliances. Don't worry. I'll give you plenty of notice so you can get your stuff out."

"Oh. Thank you."

Rick was nice. The exact opposite of his brother who continued to stare at her while Rick walked her through his proposed timeline.

"That's about it," he said, "except for deciding on paint colors."

"Paint colors?"

"Mr. Travis authorized us to paint the interior and exterior of the house. White for the outside, but he said you could do whatever you wanted, within reason, inside."

"Mr. Travis is being exceptionally nice, but I can do the painting myself."

"Why would you want to?"

Truth was, she didn't know squat about painting, but she could learn. Mel and Cathy had promised to help when they'd taken her shopping for color swatches. "Won't interior painting slow down your remodel schedule?"

"Nope. Not a bit. Will has agreed to help me out. He'll do the outside while I'm demo-ing the old kitchen. As soon as he's finished outside, he'll get to work on the inside. All you have to do is choose the colors."

W.H. Ingram was going to paint her house. Paint. Her. House. "But—"

"Don't worry. He knows his way around a paintbrush. In fact, he just finished painting the outside of our house."

It was so absurd it was almost laughable. Kenzie choked back a nervous laugh. Did Rick not know? Of course he did, but for whatever reason, he was trying to protect his brother. If only he knew his brother didn't need protecting. W.H. Ingram could take care of himself. She turned her attention to her new paint contractor. "When can you get started, Mr. Ingram?"

"Tomorrow? I need to pick up paint and supplies today for the outside. Do you have any idea what color you want to paint the inside?"

Cathy had done a fantastic job of selecting colors for her, but W.H. Ingram didn't have to know she'd already made her decisions. She had a pretty good idea what his game was now. She made a snap decision to play along. "Nope. Why don't you pick up some paint chips while you're getting the things for the outside? Maybe you could bring them by this evening?"

Yep. He'd been waiting for her to issue an invitation. His lips lifted on one corner in a satisfied smirk. *Fuck you, Will Ingram.*

"Around seven?"

"Perfect." She'd have almost ten hours to find her dignity and the backbone she'd need to tell him his game was over. No matter how much she wanted him in her bed, or anywhere else, she needed to put an end to whatever it was they were doing. To continue on their present road would lead to nothing but heartache for her. Him? She was nothing but a warm body to him. She'd proven twice to be an easy conquest, so he had no reason to expect her to turn him down now.

CHAPTER ELEVEN

This is such a fuckin' bad idea.

The thought didn't stop Will from putting on a clean shirt, checking to make sure he had a condom tucked into his wallet, and walking down the sidewalk to what had once been the home of one of his best friends. Knowing a woman he had no reason to trust now lived there should have stopped him. But it didn't.

He couldn't get MacKenzie out of his head. She haunted his dreams and crept into his thoughts throughout the day. He wanted her — the physical desire being something of a miracle in itself. But it was more than physical desire. For the few minutes he'd been with her, he'd forgotten the shit-storm his life had become. He'd felt like a man in charge of his kingdom — something he hadn't experienced in a very long time. Truth be told, he'd lost his edge even before his career had come tumbling down around him.

Looking back, he should have realized how wrong his relationship with Jessica had been. The desire he'd felt for her at first had diminished a little more each time they'd been together, until it had all but disappeared, leaving an empty shell of a relationship. The last few months they'd been together, he hadn't touched her and she hadn't pushed for more. She'd turned to Cecil Hawthorne by then. Or had they been together all along?

This thing with MacKenzie felt different than any other relationship he'd ever been in. He'd expected the desire to taper off after their first encounter in the airport, but it hadn't. He'd wanted her again as soon as he'd had her, and nothing had changed since he'd had her again. He wanted more. Didn't think he could get enough of her, no matter how many times he went back to the well to drink her in.

So, against his better judgement, he stood on her front porch, one hand curled around the color palette he'd borrowed from the hardware store, the other flexing open then closed in a nervous gesture he found impossible to control.

She'd seen through his charade this morning and played along. He supposed a single woman living alone didn't need everyone in town knowing she was sleeping with her house painter. He didn't have a clue how he would hide an affair from his brothers, particularly Rick, who he was working for and living with. In the past, the brothers hadn't had any secrets between them. If one scored, they all knew it. For reasons he didn't want to think about, he wanted to keep this to himself. Maybe it was because of the way his last relationship had imploded. He didn't trust his judgement, and his brothers would be quick to concur. He had no business starting anything with anyone at this point in his life. Distance provided clarity. The more time he put between him and what had happened with Jessica, the better his decision-making process would be.

Yet…he couldn't do it. He couldn't stay away from her.

Why the fuck did she have to end up in Willowbrook? Life would have been so much easier if he'd never seen her again.

He lifted his hand, knocked on the screened door. He was just about to knock again when the inner door swung open and every rational thought he'd ever had fled.

"You coming in?" She pushed the screened door open, inviting him in.

"Yeah, sure." He gave his head a little shake to clear it as he followed her inside. He'd never found sweatpants sexy, but on her—holy crap! He couldn't stop his gaze from raking over her from head to toe. *Shit.* He imagined taking her from behind, her damn hoodie thing wrapped around his hand. As his gaze traveled south, he licked his lips at the thought of pushing the T-shirt visible beneath the unzipped jacket up to her armpits, exposing the perfect breasts he remembered from the airport. He'd wanted to taste them then, but knew better. He'd been too close to the edge of his control.

Anything more, and neither one of them would have made their next flight.

Pushing thoughts of her tits aside, he imagined how easy it would be to yank those elastic-waist pants down to her ankles—then off completely. He'd lay her back, spread her wide, and bury his face between her thighs.

"You brought the paint chips?"

The sound of her voice jolted him out of his daydream. "Yeah." He held the palette up, fanning it out. Did she really want to talk paint? He'd been pretty sure they'd been on the same page this morning. She could damn well go down to the hardware store and pick out her own paint colors. The palette had been an excuse for him to come back tonight for other things. The expression on her face told him he might have been mistaken.

"The light's better in the kitchen." She led the way, and he followed.

Was she expecting a repeat of last night? And here he'd been thinking about actually taking her to a real bed tonight. Something he hadn't considered before. It was darn near impossible to do it in bed without at least some face-to-face contact. Up until he'd unburdened himself to Jake, he'd been content with the less intimate position of taking her from behind. No eye contact involved. No kissing.

Now, he wanted more, and it appeared she'd changed her mind. Though he found the sweatpants sexy as hell, he doubted she did.

Fuck me. As she pulled two glasses from the cabinet and filled them with ice, he realized he wasn't going to get any tonight. Perhaps never again from this woman, and, presently, she was the only female his body wanted.

"Sweet tea or soda?" She pulled a pitcher of dark liquid from the refrigerator. "I won't vouch for this stuff. I'm just learning to make it."

What the hell? He'd welcome some hemlock right about now. Anything to put him out of his misery. "Sweet tea will be fine."

What am I doing? Kenzie poured two glasses of sweet tea, minus the sweet, and set them on the table. Tonight was about taking back control of this situation with Will Ingram. The arrogance she'd seen in his expression earlier had set her teeth on edge. It was one thing for him to know how much she wanted him and quite another for him to rub her face in it. She couldn't let him see how much she craved the raw sex she was afraid she'd only get with him. When he sank inside her, she forgot all about her practically empty bank account and her former boss/lover's betrayal. She almost forgot Will Ingram would never want to see her again once he found out who she was.

She should tell him, but she was such a chicken she might as well have sprouted feathers. The best she could do was put the brakes on their relationship, and the only way to do so was to make it clear she didn't want any more mind-blowing sex. What said "Not tonight, buster," better than a ratty old sweat suit she saved for rainy days when she had cramps? There was nothing like sitting around in cozy clothes, eating double-chocolate fudge ice cream, and watching sappy movies on cable to make a girl feel better.

However, she had the distinct impression she'd underestimated the man currently sitting across from her. Her trusty sweatpants and hoody might as well have been a sheer negligee for all the good they'd done her. She could still feel the heat of his gaze on her skin as he'd undressed her with his eyes. Oh, and the naughty things she imagined he would do to her once he'd gotten down to her bare skin. Will raised his glass to his lips. Kenzie did the same, downing a healthy swig of the brew she'd made three times as strong as recommended and deliberately left the simple syrup out of. It was all she could do not to gag on the bitter drink.

To his credit, Will smacked his lips and set the glass cautiously on the table. Then his gaze met hers and once again—they were playing his game, not hers. "What's going on?" he asked.

"I—"

"Are you trying to poison me? Because if you are, there are less obvious ways to do it."

"No. I. Oh hell. I don't know." She snatched both glasses and dumped the contents down the sink. Needing to keep her distance in order to think, she propped her hips against the cabinet and grabbed the countertop for support. "You said it last night. You don't want to want me. I feel the exact same way, and I don't know what to do about it."

Will raised one brow and slouched in his chair, his gaze more thoughtful than heated this time. "So, your solution is to fry my eyeballs with the ugliest garment you could find then poison me for good measure?"

"No. Well, yes. About the clothes," she hurried to add. "Not the poison. It's just very strong unsweetened tea. Harmless. Really."

"Let me explain a couple of things to you, Kenzie." Will stood then closed the distance between them. Kenzie sighed and her lids dropped as he placed his hands on her hips. "First, leave the making of sweet tea to the experts." His thumbs found the hem of her T-shirt, delving beneath it to stroke the skin at the edge of the waistband of her pants.

Kenzie fought for control. "And second?"

He dipped his head. His lips grazed her neck right below her ear then teased their way up to nibble at the lobe. Hot breath raised bumps on her flesh right before his voice sent a shiver down her spine. "These are the sexiest goddamn clothes I've ever seen, and I'm going to peel them off of you very, very slowly."

Kenzie groaned. She couldn't help it. She wasn't sure if his words were a threat or a promise, and she didn't care as long as he followed through.

"Should I take your groan as consent?"

He was big on consent, had asked every time they were together, and she appreciated his thoughtfulness even though every cell she possessed screamed for him to get on with it. Needing to feel his solid body, she let go of the countertop and gripped his shoulders. "How long is this going to take? I need to choose paint colors."

He nibbled his way across her jaw to the corner of her mouth. He raised his head then and, with one hand, tilted her face up to his. She hadn't been this close to his eyes since she'd sat down next to him in the airport bar. For a split second, she felt as if he could see her soul, every secret want and desire. Before she could decide what it was she saw in his, he broke the connection, his gaze going to her lips, parted in blatant invitation.

"You can choose paint colors in the morning." Then his lips were on hers in the hottest, wildest kiss she'd ever experienced. His lips were magic, taking, giving, coaxing hers to try and match what he was doing to her. When his tongue thrust past her teeth to stroke the roof of her mouth, her tongue entered into a duel, as eager to taste him as he was her. When he took her head in his hands, positioning her to his advantage, she gripped two fists full of his hair, joining the struggle for supremacy.

His lips abruptly left hers, but he didn't relinquish control of her head. His words were urgent, and she felt them rumble up from his chest now pressed hard against hers. "God, I love the way you take what you want."

Then he dove back in for more, and she did the same. She didn't know how long they stood there kissing each other like starved animals, and she didn't care. As far as foreplay went, it was the best she'd ever had, and they were still fully clothed. God help her when they got naked together. She'd probably die from the sheer pleasure of feeling his skin against hers.

He moved like lightning. Suddenly, her feet left the ground and her butt hit the counter. In a flash, she was naked from the waist up, her nipples hard. She didn't wait, couldn't. Hands cradling his head, she urged him forward as she arched her back. He took the hint. Taking both breasts in his hands, he palmed her left while he squeezed her right to the point of delicious pain. Then he took the distended point into his mouth.

"Oh, god!" Kenzie almost rocketed off the countertop as a bolt of white-hot heat shot from her nipple to her core. The tender tissues between her legs tingled then began to throb with an urgency she'd never experienced before. She worked her hips in an age-old rhythm meant to bring satisfaction, but only brought frustration at Will's slow pace.

Her nails dug into his scalp. "Please." *Please. Please. Please.*

The audible *pop* when he released her breast was as erotic as any sexy talk she'd ever heard. Cool air from the window air conditioner brushed the wet tip, making her shiver with need. Her mind scrambled to make sense of too many things happening at once—to grasp some scrap of sanity before she lost all touch with reality. Will squeezed her left breast hard enough to make her gasp. Then his mouth closed over the tip, and she was once again at his mercy.

Pleasure. God, what pleasure. And pain. And need. Desperate, aching need to see him, to touch him, to feel him moving inside her. It consumed her. Devastated her.

"Please." It was a weak plea from lips gone numb.

Another *pop!* and his face was in front of hers, his hands still doing wicked things to her breasts which made it difficult to think. "Please, what?"

"Please." It was the best she could manage, and inadequate in the purest sense of the word.

"Tell me what you want, Kenzie. Your pleasure is my pleasure."

God, he was too perfect for words. He couldn't be real. She skimmed her hands from the back of his head to his shoulders and down to his chest. "Strip."

His face turned to stone, every sharp plane and angle frozen. Had she asked for more than he was willing to give? The two times they'd been together before, he'd never fully removed any clothing.

Eyes burning into her, his lips barely moved. "God, I love a woman who knows what she wants."

He stepped back. In one smooth motion, he pulled his shirt over his head and tossed it aside. He threw his wallet on the counter beside her then shed his jeans and boxers at the same time as he toed off his shoes. No socks. God, so New York.

"What now?"

His voice jerked her attention from his strong, bare feet to his crotch where his cock stood erect and proud. Nothing to complain about there. Her gaze followed his treasure trail up and over his defined abs to his chest. Her nipples tingled as she imagined the way the light mat of hair there would feel against them.

He hadn't moved an inch during her perusal—a testament to his control. "I want to touch you."

CHAPTER TWELVE

Will clenched his jaw tight and took a step forward, putting himself within her reach. Giving her what she wanted.

Her fingertips brushed his bare shoulders. So soft, yet the bold way she explored his upper body set him on fire. He closed his eyes, hoping to retain control as long as possible as she learned every plane and valley of his torso. He had to be crazy. No sane man would endure this kind of torture.

After what Jessica had done to him, he'd vowed to avoid this level of intimacy at all costs, but he'd also vowed to avoid this woman. MacKenzie Carlysle was a force he couldn't resist. The way things were going, he might not ever have his entire life back, so why not take the parts of it he could? Beginning with this. And, lord, how he wanted this part of his life again.

His dick pulsed with need, his blood pumping through him like molten lava. As she explored south, he shifted incrementally closer, and bent to grip the countertop on either side of her hips. The move brought him close enough to nuzzle the spot on her neck where her pulse beat strong and rapid. She was as turned on as he was. Then she closed her fingers around his shaft. Control became a rope dangled just beyond his reach. He couldn't remain still when every fiber of his being screamed, *Fuck her!*

He acted on pure instinct. Flexing his hips, he thrust into the cradle of her palm then retreated and did it again.

Easy. Easy. Don't want it to be over before it even starts.

On the next withdrawal, she used her thumb to swipe a bead of pre-cum over the sensitive head. Will groaned and wrapped his left hand around her nape. He tilted her head to allow him maximum access then buried his face in the crook of her neck where he gave in to the primal urge to mark her as his. Clamping his mouth on her neck, he sucked her sweet-smelling flesh into his mouth.

Her left hand slid from his shoulder to the back of his head while the fingers of her right tightened around his erection. He wasn't sure who was in control, and he didn't care, as long as the pleasure continued. He'd had hand jobs before, but with her gripping him tight, he couldn't recall a single one. One thing was certain, none had felt this good.

Needing to put an end to this before it went too far, he peeled his hand off the countertop and wrapped it around hers, guiding her as he pumped into the circle of her fingers, slowly shortening his thrusts until he was barely moving. Only then did he lift his mouth from her neck to admire the red circle that would become his mark of possession within the hour.

A sense of pride filled his chest as he straightened and glanced between them. Their hands, entwined around his dick, had to be the most erotic thing he'd ever seen in his life.

"Fuck, woman. I've got to have you. Now."

"I need you, too." She tugged, urging him forward.

He could take her right there on the countertop. Fuck her senseless, but this time, he wanted more. He wanted to feel her beneath him. Wanted to take his time. Explore every curve of her delectable body. Bring her to the peak over and over until she begged him to let her come. "Grab my wallet." He dipped his head, directing her attention to the item he'd dropped on the countertop earlier. She picked it up then he dragged her to the edge of the countertop and off. She wrapped her arms around his shoulders and her legs around his waist. It was all he could do to keep from dropping to the floor and taking her right there, but, somehow, he managed to hold her tightly to his chest. "Bedroom?"

"First door."

He didn't need more direction. Her house was the mirror image of the one he'd grown up in. A few steps brought them to the door. Two more to the edge of the bed—a giant four-poster occupying most of the floor space. It could have been a futon and he wouldn't have cared. He dropped her. She bounced once then raised her arms above her head and lifted her hips.

It was all the invitation he needed. He hooked his thumbs in the waistband of her sweatpants and tugged them to her ankles then off. He looked at her bare pussy then at the clothes still in his hands. No panties. "Christ almighty," he growled. Tossing her pants aside, he spread her legs and went to his knees between them.

His heart skipped a beat as he realized what he was about to do. He'd wanted to taste her ever since he'd swept his fingers through her drenched folds at the airport. From then on, he'd wondered what she would taste like. She brought her heels up to the edge of the bed and dropped her knees, opening herself to him. Will placed his hands on the back of her thighs, pressed her knees up and wide open. Like a man lost in the desert for days without water, he dove headfirst into her wellspring.

At the first swipe of his tongue, she screamed and bucked her hips. Will wrapped his arms around her thighs, pinning her in place then he buried his face in her pussy.

She tasted even better than he'd imagined. Salty and sweet, and god, she was so fucking wet. He drank his fill then turned his attention to her pleasure. He explored her folds, taking time to fuck her with his tongue until she begged for his cock. Then he focused on her clit. A teasing nip here. A slow lick there. He smiled at the curse words flowing freely from her mouth as he took her to the peak then backed off, over and over again. When he couldn't stand another minute not being inside her, he fixed his lips on her clit and sucked gently. He felt the muscles in her thighs grow taut then he thrust two fingers into her channel, crooking the ends up until he found the tiny pad of flesh that would send her over the edge. Two light taps coupled with the gentle sucking on her clit was all it took. Her inner walls clenched around his fingers as he continued to work her clit with his tongue and lips. She rode his mouth like a rodeo queen determined to make the eight-second buzzer. He would never tire of hearing her shout his name in the same breath as the Almighty's. Every spasm was a trophy to be treasured forever.

As her orgasm waned, he gently withdrew to place a line of kisses on the inside of her thigh. She shivered and tried to clamp his head between her trembling legs, but he easily pushed them apart and rose up to cover her.

She felt better than good beneath him. Perfect. He wouldn't trade what he'd just done for anything, but nothing could compare with being inside her. Raising up on his elbows, he searched the bed for his wallet.

Kenzie felt as satisfied as she'd ever been, but she needed more. She needed to feel Will's cock inside her, stretching her. Filling her. It was as if there was a part of her missing, and somehow, only the man currently searching for a condom in his wallet could fill the emptiness inside her.

It was crazy. She barely knew him, and he didn't know her at all. But there was chemistry between them neither one of them could ignore.

She should tell him who she was, but as soon as he found out her role in the demise of his career, he'd hate her. Call her selfish, but she needed the human connection she found with him. When he filled her, she felt whole. When he moved inside her, she felt alive. When he made her body sing, she felt like a woman. And when he lost control, pulsing inside her, she felt invincible.

I can't give him up. Not yet.

Will settled on his knees between her legs. God, he was beautiful. Broad shoulders tapered to a narrow waist, and in between, every muscle group was present and accounted for beneath taut skin. A light pelt of dark hair covered his chest then narrowed, drawing her gaze down. Her pussy clenched with need at the sight of his imposing erection straining toward her. He'd found a condom somewhere and was in the process of rolling it on. Even his hands were beautiful. Artist's hands. She could imagine his long fingers holding a paintbrush, commanding the paint to bring his visions to life. Much the way he had brought her back to life in a dingy airport mini-hotel. "You have beautiful hands."

His eyes met hers. His lips lifted in a smirk. "That's what you see?" He fisted his sheathed erection, waving it to draw her attention.

"Your equipment is um…impressive." She licked her lips. "But your hands are…I don't know…sexy, I guess. I love to feel them on me."

"What else do you like?" He leaned forward, bracing himself above her on one arm while he guided his cock through her damp folds, notching it at her entrance.

"This." She lifted her hips in invitation as he teased her sensitive flesh. "God, you're big." She needed to feel him inside her. Stretching her. Filling her.

Braced above her on both arms, the tendons in his neck standing out with the strain of denying himself, he took her breath away. He flexed his hips, driving her farther up the bed with one smooth thrust. "You're so fucking tight."

Kenzie grabbed her thighs and pulled her legs up, spreading herself wide. "Fuck me, Will. Fuck me hard." *Fuck me hard enough to make me forget.*

Will groaned and, with an expression of utter concentration on his face, did as he'd been told. He pounded into her over and over again. The sound of flesh slapping against flesh filled the room along with the grunts and groans forced from their throats as his movement took them both to the highest peak and over.

Her orgasm began with a burst of something so sharp she wasn't sure if it was pain or pleasure. Then the blissful waves took over, coming one after the other as her inner muscles clenched and released around his invading member. Kenzie cried out and, letting her legs fall, gripped his locked arms like anchors while he continued to ride her.

"Fuck, you feel so good." Without breaking his rhythm, he managed to bring her legs up again, holding them over his shoulders. Seconds later, his thrusts became erratic then short and hard, as his orgasm tore through him. His roar rent the air. His cock pulsed as his hot seed flooded the end of the condom. He towered over her, a man destroyed by passion, devastated and beautiful at the same time.

With a long groan, he released her legs and collapsed on top of her, his face buried in the crook of her neck, his cock perfectly filling all her empty places. She wrapped her arms around him, holding him as she'd longed to do since the first time he'd walked away without a word. He wasn't walking away now. Their hearts beat the same wild rhythm against each other. Blunted pain, in no way associated with his weight pinning her to the mattress, radiated out from Kenzie's heart and infused every cell in her body.

Love.

How is it possible for something to feel so perfect and hurt so bad at the same time?

Long minutes later, Will withdrew and rolled off of her. While he disposed of the condom in the bathroom across the hall, she dove under the covers, hoping he would come back to her. As the minutes ticked by and he didn't return, she refused to let the tears stinging the backs of her eyes fall. At the sound of footsteps, booted ones, she sat up, clutching the covers to her chest like a shield. Will Ingram, fully dressed, leaned on the doorjamb, his legs and arms crossed. Faint light from the kitchen illuminated one side of his face, revealing his hardened features. Had it only been a few minutes ago since she'd witnessed pleasure written in every line of his face? Kenzie's heart hurt again—this time for a man who was so broken he refused to believe happiness could last longer than a few seconds.

"I've got to go. I'll be here in the morning to start work on the outside paint."

Kenzie nodded. "Okay."

She waited until she heard the front door close before she pulled the covers over her head and let the tears flow.

CHAPTER THIRTEEN

"Jake called looking for you."

Will toed his shoes off and kicked them beneath the table next to the front door. These old houses didn't have an entryway, much less a hall closet, and Rick had worked too hard restoring the old hardwood floors to have them scratched up by hitchhiking pebbles caught in the waffle-weave soles of his boots. "Did he say what he wanted?"

Rick's gaze remained on the show playing on the TV. "Nope. And I didn't ask. Figured if he wanted me to know, he'd leave a message."

Anyone who knew Rick couldn't miss the hurt contained in those few words. *Shit.* He hadn't wanted to add his problems to whatever else his little brother had going on in his head. Damn Jake for not making up a bullshit reason for wanting to talk to him. "Give me a minute to shower and we'll talk. Okay?"

"Whatever."

Will hated to leave Rick hanging, but he needed a clear head before he could talk about what had happened in New York, and he damn sure couldn't think straight with Kenzie's scent clinging to his skin. The woman got to him on a level he hadn't expected. He couldn't stay away from her and he'd made up his mind tonight not to even try. It was a battle he wasn't going to win. Hell, if he'd stayed in her bed another minute, he might have stayed all night, and waking up in the morning with a woman bordered on relationship status.

Still, as he stripped and stepped under the stream of hot water, his chest felt tight and he couldn't shake the feeling he'd screwed up. Again. Leaving her had been harder than it should have been. God, the sex tonight had been off-the-charts hot. When it came to passion, she was his equal in every way. He'd had rough, raw sex before, but with her it was…more. More intense. More intimate. He fucking couldn't get enough of her. When he was deep inside her, he wanted to be deeper. And he never wanted to leave. This evening, when he'd collapsed on top of her, he'd been amazed at how hard his dick remained as long as he stayed inside her, only going limp once he'd left her bed. The reprieve had lasted as long as it took to find his clothes and pull them on because the second he laid eyes on her again—laying naked beneath the covers of her bed—his dick jumped to attention. It took every bit of control he could muster to walk away from her. Even then, he'd walked around the block twice before he'd been decent enough to go home and face his brother.

Rick. *Shit.* Will regretfully washed Kenzie's scent off his skin then toweled dry and put on clean jeans and a T-shirt before heading down the hall. He stopped in the kitchen for a beer, needing something to do with his hands, and perhaps a little liquid courage. Telling Jake had been one thing. As a lawyer, he'd heard it all and didn't judge. Rick? Well, he wasn't a lawyer.

He grabbed his cell phone where he'd left it charging on the kitchen counter and pulled up the missed calls. As he strolled into the living room, he pressed callback for Jake's number. While it rang, he put it on speakerphone and tossed it on the coffee table. Rick muted the television and straightened in the new easy chair he'd bought to replace the old recliner they'd had as long as either of them could recall.

"You sure you want to do this?" Rick asked. "You don't have to."

Will sat on the sofa and kicked his heels up on the coffee table—another new purchase. "I don't want to, but I'm living with you. You have a right to know why."

"No, I don't." He made to stand just as Jake's voice came over the speaker.

"Will. Where the hell have you been?"

Will gestured for Rick to stay put. "I was out. What did you want?"

"Am I on speakerphone?"

"Yeah." Will ran the fingers of one hand through his hair. "Rick is here. He knows something is up. Might as well tell him."

"Your call, Will. It's always your call."

"I know. I'm tired of hiding my stupidity. Go ahead, tell me what's up."

"I'm going to put a private investigator on this up in New York. I read the file the NYPD sent, and there are several people on your list they didn't interview. Or if they did, the notes aren't in the file. Once he locates some of these people, I'll go up there and talk to them. I don't mind telling you, this whole thing stinks. They did a shoddy job of investigating. Plus, I want to talk to the officials at your bank. The signature on those withdrawals aren't anything like yours, yet they let Jessica withdraw a shit-ton of money without making any attempt to verify with the only signatory on the account. That's on them. Not you. At the very least, I should be able to get your funds replaced. But, it's the kind of strong negotiation best done in person."

"She fucking cleaned out your bank accounts?" Rick's heated question reminded Will of the boy his brother had been before he joined the Marines.

"They have her on security camera at three different branches the day before she disappeared." Will filled in the blanks for Rick. "She left me enough to cover my purchases for a few days. She was supposedly busy getting my gallery showing up and running, and I had my head buried in a canvas. Our paths didn't cross for those intervening days. I didn't know she was gone until I showed up at the gallery for the opening and found the place locked up tight. Not a painting in sight."

"Fuck. That. Bitch."

"What he said," Jake added.

"Apparently, she and the gallery owner, Cecil Hawthorne, targeted me from the get-go. It was an elaborate setup, months in the making. The two of them disappeared off the radar with my savings and all my assets." Will paused to take a long draw from his beer. "I still don't understand why they took the paintings. They haven't shown up on the black market anywhere. I have enough friends in the art world, someone would have noticed and called me."

"It doesn't make sense to me, either," Jake said. "It almost seems like this is personal."

"How can it be? Jessica was my agent. She made money off every painting I sold." He stared at the bottle in his hands. "I was sleeping with the bitch, too. What else could she want from me?"

"Whoa!" Rick sat forward. "Wait a minute here. You were sleeping with her? For how long?"

"Since the night we met. A couple of years. Hell, she practically lived in my loft."

"Were you in love with her?"

He'd thought he was, but, as an image of MacKenzie Carlysle popped into his head, he knew his feelings for Jessica had never equaled what he felt for Kenzie and he'd only known her for a few weeks. "No. I don't guess I was. Hell, I never gave it any thought. We were fuck buddies."

"Did *she* know you were just fuck buddies?"

"What? Yeah. No." He ran his fingers through his hair again. "Fuck. I don't know."

"Hell hath no fury," Rick said.

"Like a woman scorned," Jake added. "This is starting to make sense now."

"Man, you are dumber than a box of rocks." Rick stood and sauntered into the kitchen.

Will spoke to the phone on the table. "You think she did this because I didn't…what? Propose?"

"Maybe," Jake said. "Women are inexplicable creatures. Let me ask you this. Do you think she loved you?"

Will let the question sink in as he drained the remainder of his beer. "I don't know. Maybe. We were a lot closer the first year or so we were together. I wasn't working as much. When she booked the gallery showing with Hawthorne for me, the pressure was on to produce enough paintings to fill the place. I was in the studio night and day for months. I guess we sort of drifted apart."

Rick sauntered back in with two fresh beers. He handed one to Will then resumed his seat. "Jake?"

"Yeah?"

"You have to find this bitch. She's holed up somewhere with Hawthorne. You find her, you'll find the paintings."

"Yeah, I suspect you're right."

"How much money did they take?" Rick asked.

Will named a figure. Rick whistled.

"That's a shit-ton of money, bro, but unless they're living on a shoestring, they'll blow through it sooner or later. Then what are they going to do? They'll have to come up for air."

"Hawthorne had money, too. Hell, they could be living it up on a beach in some third-world country for all we know."

Jake cleared his throat. "As far as I'm concerned, they can keep the money. The bank let the funds slip through their hands and they need to make it right. It's the paintings I want to recover. They're one of a kind—original W.H. Ingram's. I don't want them showing up when we're all dead and gone, selling for millions a piece at auction."

"I can paint more," Will lied. He hadn't picked up a paintbrush since the day he'd found out about Jessica's betrayal.

"You're missing the point, William."

Rick raised an eyebrow at their older brother's use of Will's given name. Will shook his head as he shared a silent laugh with his younger brother. Jake always did have a pompous way about him. "What is the point, Jacob?"

"I hear you snickering, Richard. Don't think I don't know when the two of you are laughing at me."

Will tried to wipe the smile off his face. "Go on, Jake. What were you saying?"

"I was saying, I'm going to get your fucking paintings for you then I'm going to kick your sorry ass if you so much as look at another woman for the rest of your life."

Another image of Kenzie popped into his mind. Will sobered immediately. Jake was right. He needed to stay the hell away from women.

They spoke for a few more minutes before Jake signed off. Will kicked back, relaxing now that the conversation was over and Rick knew everything. A few months ago, he couldn't contemplate telling his family what had happened. Since he'd spilled his guts to his brothers, he felt better about his future. If Jake wasn't able to recover the paintings or the money, he'd live. Maybe even paint again. Unbidden images of MacKenzie came to mind. He'd start with her eyes —

"So, you gonna tell him you're fucking BlackWing's new PR lady?"

Shit.

"Hell, no. And you aren't, either."

Rick shrugged. "Not my news to tell."

"Damn right it isn't." Will stood and stretched, the evening's activities suddenly taking their toll. "I'm turning in. Need to get an early start in the morning."

"Me, too. I put the ladders and the paint supplies in the truck earlier. We can drive down together if you want."

"Sure." They agreed on a time then Will shuffled off to his room, leaving Rick to finish the show he'd been watching.

As soon as the door closed behind him, Will went straight to the closet and dug out the box of art supplies he'd brought from New York. His hand trembled as he reached for the nearly empty sketchbook and his favorite set of pencils sitting on top of the expensive brushes and other items he hadn't been able to part with.

Sitting on the floor and using the bed as a backrest, pencil in hand, he stared at a blank page. His gut churned with anxiety. *You can do this. Just like his first drawing class at The Cooper Union. One line at a time. The first one's always the hardest.*

This was so much different than his first semester class though. Then, he'd doubted his abilities in relation to the other students, many of whom had come from fancy prep schools and charter schools devoted to the arts. He'd had a public school education in a small, rural Texas town where art classes were considered minor electives, not career preparation. He still considered it sheer luck he'd gotten in, and with a full scholarship to boot. Angels had been looking out for him then, and maybe they still were. Will placed the tip of the pencil on the paper and closing his eyes, sketched the first line, and the next, and the next. Only after he'd nearly completed the drawing did he open his eyes to see what he'd done. There, staring back at him was a reasonable likeness of the woman who captivated his every thought.

CHAPTER FOURTEEN

I'm so screwed. And she wasn't talking about what she'd done with Will Ingram the night before. The way they'd come together had been…special. More than just another good fuck. She'd bet her last dollar it had meant more to Will, too. She'd seen it in his eyes when he came, and felt it when his heart beat next to hers. He'd run this time, too, but he'd allowed her to hold him first. Those few minutes of silence had said more than any words could have. He cared for her. Probably not as much as she cared for him, but he did care.

Which was the reason she felt like shit.

I have to tell him.

This morning.

She put the finishing touches on her makeup then stood back to take a look. There wasn't enough concealer in the world to completely hide the dark circles under her bloodshot eyes. "That's what you get for crying half the night," she told her reflection. She applied her lipstick, a shade she hoped wouldn't clash with her eyes then once again examined the overall effect. *Not bad if you like zombies.*

"Promise me you'll tell him today."

Kenzie pressed her lips together, smoothing the glossy color. "I promise."

"And now I'm talking to myself. Great. Just great." With a sigh, she stepped into her heels and checked the buttons again on her blouse to make sure she'd fastened them right. Satisfied her second attempt had done the trick, she trudged to the kitchen to fill her travel mug. Tomorrow, she'd be getting her coffee at The Donut Hole since Rick Ingram was scheduled to begin demolition later today.

She filled her mug, washed the pot then moved the coffee maker to the kitchen table where Rick had said her few kitchen items would be fine for the time being. She'd just finished covering everything with the plastic sheeting he'd left for her when a loud clatter outside almost made her jump out of her shoes. Risking a peek through the window over the sink, she saw the source of the noise—a ladder had been placed against the side of the house. Will Ingram stepped into her line of sight. Her heart did a Vaudeville-worthy tap dance.

He'd been hot in his metro-sexual getup when she'd first seen him at JFK airport, but dressed in a paint-splattered T-shirt and jeans ready for the trash bin, he was hot with a capital H.

You promised to tell him, she reminded herself. *So, go do it. Now.* Kenzie wiped her sweaty palms on her skirt and forced her feet to move. Opening the back door, she stepped out onto the small concrete porch. "Hi."

Will paused two steps up the ladder. "Hi." His gaze raked over her business suit—one she'd paid too much for when she actually had money to spend on such things. It had been tailored specifically for her and fit like the proverbial glove. She'd chosen it this morning because she'd always felt more confident wearing it. Under his scrutiny, her body heated, and she felt her resolve to do the right thing evaporating. "You're…stunning."

"You, too." Kenzie ducked her head, hoping he didn't notice the flush she was sure had stained her cheeks bright red. "I mean…you look…" She waved up and down to indicate his person. "Good."

Christ. She sounded like an idiot. She wiped her palms on her skirt again then raised her chin, determined to get the words out before she did something really stupid like jump his bones. "Look, Will—"

"Hey, you forgot the paint scraper."

Kenzie jerked her gaze from the sexy man on the ladder as Rick came around the corner of the house, a tool in his outstretched hand. "Oh, hi, Ms. Carlysle."

She nodded and cleared her throat. "Mr. Ingram."

Will took the scraper from his brother then continued up the ladder. A second later, a screeching, scraping sound reminiscent of fingernails on a blackboard, sent a shiver up her spine. Flakes of white paint drifted down, creating a summer snowstorm. Kenzie stepped back to avoid having it land in her hair.

Rick joined her on the porch. "You heading out? I'm going to get the cabinets out this morning then. If I have time, I'll start to work on removing the old linoleum flooring."

"Oh. Okay." Rick followed her into the kitchen. Kenzie grabbed the mug of coffee she'd left on the counter. "I'll get out of your way, then."

"No problem. Figured we'd get an early start. Take your time."

"Not a problem. I was just leaving." Shit. She couldn't talk to Will with his brother around. She'd tell him tonight—if he came around. Would he? She had no idea, and she couldn't very well ask him. Theirs was a no-strings, no-obligations kind of relationship. Who was she kidding? They didn't have a relationship. They were fuck buddies—at best. There were no guarantees between them. No promises. No expectations.

"What time do you think you'll be finished today?" She slung the strap of her purse over her shoulder and snagged her keys off the hanger by the back door.

"I'll probably knock off around four o'clock. I suspect my brother will stop earlier. It gets awfully hot in the afternoon."

Kenzie nodded. "Okay. Call me if you need anything."

"Will do." Rick waved to her as she went out through the back door. She didn't look up at the man scraping old paint off her house as she made her way to her car parked in the driveway, but her awareness of him made her body hum and her heart ache. She couldn't imagine what his reaction would be when he found out who she was. One thing was certain, she'd never see him again. *How will I survive?*

She needn't have worried about Will's reaction because she didn't get a chance to tell him that night or the next or the next. After their first work day, he and Rick had arrived after she'd left and were both gone when she got home. They'd been there because the work was progressing and then there was the occasional note from Rick informing her where he'd moved something to, or asking her a question about her preferences.

At night, she ached for Will's touch, but he didn't come. So maybe the connection they'd made had all been in her head after all.

~~ ~

Even though Will's actions were hurting Kenzie, he couldn't help himself. He wanted to be with her every night. He wanted to tell her what she meant to him. But each night after he and Rick left her house, something else took hold of him and wouldn't let go.

So, he waited for his brother to go to bed then crept out to the garage where he'd cleared a space big enough for an easel and a stool. He'd found an old unused canvas in the closet of his room, a relic leftover from his high school art classes, and dusted it off. It was cheap, but he didn't care. It saved him from having to buy one. He didn't want people, meaning Rick and Jake, to assume he was painting again. He was dabbling. Trying to work a woman out of his system by putting her likeness on canvas.

It wasn't working.

If anything, he wanted her more than he had before. His fingers itched to feel her soft skin. His hands ached to trace her curves and his entire body ached to possess her. Staring at her likeness every evening until he forced himself to go to bed didn't help, either. She'd somehow gotten past the roadblocks he'd put up when his life had gone to shit. From the moment he first saw her, he'd wanted her. A few months earlier, it wouldn't have surprised him. He'd always had a healthy libido. But Jessica's betrayal had affected him on a molecular level. He'd lost the need to paint. Food, sleep, exercise, hell, even the desire for sex of any kind had disappeared. He'd become a shell of a man—until he saw Kenzie.

The painting was stunning, if he did say so himself, but the familiar ritual of applying paint to canvas had done nothing to push MacKenzie Carlysle out of his head. Instead, he stood before the completed work and cursed himself for being a fool. He had no business getting involved with a woman at this point in his life. He had little to offer other than his body, and after the last time they'd been together, a purely physical relationship would never be enough. Not for her. Or for him.

He lifted his brush again to add a hint of rose to her skin tone then thought better of it and let his hand drop to his side. Stepping back from the easel, he studied his work. This one was done. Finished. Perfect.

Reclining on a bed, her auburn hair spread wantonly across a pillow, an expression part pain part pleasure on her face, she looked gorgeous and feminine and powerful in the throes of her orgasm. As he stared at it, he thought it might be the most honest thing he'd ever painted. The bold brushstrokes said this wasn't her story. It was her unseen lover's story. "*I did this to her,*" it said. "*I made her feel this way.*" Yet she held something back from her lover. He hadn't consciously put it there, but he could see it. Eyes clouded with pleasure hinted at a secret she held close. *What is she not telling her lover?*

God, he couldn't look at the painting and not want to fuck MacKenzie again and again. And he doubted there was a man on the planet who wouldn't feel the same way.

Sighing, he forced his gaze to the floor now covered with splatters of paint. He hadn't intended to paint Kenzie at such a vulnerable moment, but he'd had little say in the matter. In the past, he'd tried to explain his process to inquisitive gallery owners and reporters, and felt he'd only convinced them he was either a liar or outright crazy. Or maybe a little of both. The truth was, he didn't plan his paintings. They formed in his subconscious and somehow ended up on canvas. It was as if his hands were nothing more than tools his mind used to bring the images to life.

He painted because he was compelled to.

The compulsion had quieted for a few months, but it was back with a vengeance.

He tightened his fingers on the brush he still held and prayed the need would go away again. Life would be so much simpler if it did. He could go on painting houses. Maybe even get Rick to show him how to use a few power tools so he could help him with the inside work, too. Millions of people lived their lives in control of every little thing they did each day. They decided when to wake. When to sleep. When to eat. When to work. When to rest.

Not so with him. The need to paint ruled him. He woke, slept, ate, worked, and rested when the creative urge let him. And if it demanded only work? He worked.

When he'd lived alone, he'd learned to set alarms to remind him to stop and eat or sleep. Then he'd met Jessica, and she'd managed his life for him so he didn't have to remember to set alarms.

Maybe his art *was* a madness of sorts.

Van Gogh had been crazy. The guy chopped off his own ear, for crying out loud. Will didn't think of himself in terms of the old masters. He wasn't in their league, and he knew it. But he was good. Anyone with an eye for art could see it. He could paint landscapes as easily as he could do a portrait. It didn't matter to him. He painted what his subconscious wanted him to paint. And right now, it wanted more of *her*.

He glanced around the garage, looking for something suitable to use since he didn't have another canvas. Coming up empty, he rubbed the back of his neck and paced the confines of his tiny workspace. *Shit!* There was no way around it. He was going to have to buy more canvases or take to painting murals on the garage walls. He wasn't against the idea. In fact, he wouldn't mind having a life-sized nude of Kenzie, but he doubted she'd think it was so great, and he sure as hell didn't want his brother seeing it.

His gaze landed on the completed painting again. Damn it all to hell. He couldn't—no, wouldn't—show it to anyone, much less sell it.

Fuck me. Leave it to his muse to get him started painting again but make sure he couldn't make a living off it at the same time.

Will dropped his brush in an open jar of turpentine then grabbed a smaller one from the assortment awaiting him in the same old soup can he'd used as a stand since he was a kid. Loading the brush with black paint, he carefully drew the stylized *W* he'd adopted for his signature on the bottom right corner of the painting then stopped. W. H. Ingram was dead. Blowing out a pent-up breath, he continued until the signature read, *William Ingram.*

Straightening, he added the smaller brush to the jar of cleaning fluid then stepped back. Deep inside, the pain of the last few months raged inside him still. Probably always would. But it defined another man, not the one who'd painted this woman whose pleasure made a man feel like a god.

The signature, much like the painting itself, symbolized a new beginning for the artist and for the man.

Maybe it was time to take another crack at living.

CHAPTER FIFTEEN

The bell on the door jingled as Jake Ingram entered the boutique gallery on the lower east side of Manhattan. Sunnyside Gallery, the sign outside said. The private investigator he'd hired had indicated the owner, one Sunny Sheldon, had been interviewed by the police and dismissed as irrelevant to the case.

He'd check her out first. Absolutely nothing was irrelevant until he said it was. Someone, or several someones, had screwed his brother over, and he wasn't going to quit until he found them.

"Just a minute," a feminine voice called out from somewhere in the back of the long, narrow shop. "Make yourself at home. I'll be right out."

Make myself at home. Hmph! Maybe it was because his brother was so damn good at what he did, or maybe it was because Jake didn't have an eye for art, but as he strolled around checking out the eclectic selection of paintings and sculptures occupying the small space, he came to the conclusion they were all crap. Maybe he was wasting his time coming here.

"Can I help you?"

Jake turned around, his elbow sending a bronze sculpture — subject unknown — teetering on its pedestal. The woman reached around him, grabbing the piece before it hit the floor.

"Good catch."

She held the item rather than put it back while he was still standing there, he guessed. "Not your style?"

Jake shook his head. "Nope. Not even sure what it's supposed to be."

She, however, was very much his style. Dressed in a suit obviously tailored to fit her trim, petite body, her yellow-blonde hair twisted into a fancy knot and secured with a tasteful gold hair ornament he'd glimpsed when she bent to catch the sculpture, she exuded class and confidence. Two things guaranteed to turn him on. Unless she'd discovered some miracle youth serum, she was close to his age. Maybe a bit younger.

"Not sure what your style is, or not sure what this is?" She held the item up so he could get a good look at it. He took the opportunity to check for a ring on her finger instead.

"Both, I guess."

She flipped the item over, examining it from all sides. "Hmm. I don't know what it is, either. Perhaps it was the artist's intention? Let each person see what they want to see?"

He didn't know about the artist's intentions, but he liked what *he* was seeing. Her. "Then I know it's not my style. I like my art straightforward. What you see is what you get."

"You're a realist, then."

He let his expression convey his lack of understanding.

"You like realistic paintings. Still lifes. Portraits. Landscapes. You like to look at a piece of art and know the artist intended to paint a bowl of apples or a tree-lined river bank. There's a photography exhibit going on right now at the Metropolitan Museum of Art you'd probably enjoy."

"I don't know. I might need someone to explain the photos to me. Interested?"

He almost forgot to breathe as she walked away from him, her pert ass swaying side to side in a dark-green pencil skirt he'd give anything to see her take off. She halted at an empty pedestal on the other side of the room. Setting the art object down, she spun on the toes of the sexiest shoes he'd ever seen on a woman. "Maybe. I don't go anywhere with strangers though."

Her comment jolted him back to the reason he was there in the first place. "Jake, ma'am. At your service."

"Sunny Sheldon. What brings you in today, Jake?" She swept her hand toward the relocated sculpture. "I know it isn't the interpretive art on display."

Sunny Sheldon lived up to her name. She dazzled from her blonde roots to her sparkling eyes to the tips of her shiny shoes. Sunny, indeed. She had a cheerful demeanor, but it was the sassy, sexy undertones of intellect making his dick stand up and take notice. Jake shook his head. "No, it's not. I'm looking for anything by W.H. Ingram."

She straightened her spine, her gaze taking him in from head to toe. "You aren't NYPD. FBI?"

"Why would you automatically think I'm law enforcement?"

"Because anyone who knows anything about the local art world is aware of what happened to W.H. Ingram's paintings. Is this some kind of sting operation?"

"No. I'm simply looking for my brother's paintings."

"Your brother?"

"William Ingram is my younger brother. I'm here on his behalf."

Anger poured off her in waves. "What makes you think I would know anything about the missing paintings?"

"Will said you sold a few of his a while back."

"Those were legal sales, and he was paid promptly, according to our standard contract. I'm sure I can locate the payment records, but I won't divulge the names of the customers who made those purchases. Shortly after I sold the ones he'd consigned with me, he acquired a new agent. I tried to get more of his work—they were very popular—but was turned down. I believe the words his agent used were, 'I've got bigger things in store for him.'"

Years as a trial lawyer had honed his ability to tell when a person was lying and when they weren't. In his opinion, Ms. Sheldon was telling the truth. "I'm sorry. I didn't mean to insult you. Will said you didn't have anything to do with the disappearance of his paintings."

His apology took most of the starch out of her, but he still had a ways to go before he was in her good graces again.

"I've never had anything but the utmost respect for your brother. He has an extraordinary talent."

"I agree." He hoped his smile was reassuring. "I'll be sure to pass on your regards to him."

"Oh. My. God. You know where he is! He's all right, isn't he? Please tell me he is."

"He's fine. He's moved back to Texas."

"Thank goodness. I've been so worried about him. I tried to contact him after things settled down, but no one seemed to know where he was."

"I'd like to ask you a few questions, if I may?"

"Sure. Sure." She fidgeted with the hem of her suit jacket, getting her emotions under control. He'd seen witnesses and clients do it before. He wondered why she was so emotional about his brother. Did she know more than she'd told the police? "Let me close up then if you don't mind, we can talk in my office? I'll fix us some tea."

He didn't want any damn tea. He wanted answers, and he wanted her. She turned the open sign around and threw the dead bolt on the front door. Jake followed her through a maze of angled walls and display pedestals, past an ornate desk with a computer terminal and a stack of business cards in a glass holder. "I only use this desk to finalize sales." She waved him on. "My real office is in the back."

She paused at a closed door. "Please. No comments about the clutter." He barely had time to process the comment when she opened the door and stepped inside.

The place looked like a tornado had hit it. Magazines were piled on every horizontal surface. She grabbed a stack off a leather armchair facing the desk and dropped them on top of another haphazard bunch sitting on the floor. Jake held his breath, waiting for the tower to topple, but after a few seconds of wobbling, it came to an unsteady stop.

"Have a seat." She indicated the now-empty chair as she slid between the end of her desk and a bookcase crowded with framed pictures and what he supposed were small pieces of art. But what did he know? He'd told her the truth. He liked the stuff Will painted and that was about it. The stuff on her shelves could have been priceless pieces and he wouldn't have had a clue. "I don't know about you, but I could use a cup of tea."

She shoved a mountain of books to one side of the credenza behind the desk to reveal an electric kettle. A couple of feminine-looking teacups, complete with matching saucers, sat nearby. He preferred coffee, but aware he'd already been rude to her, he answered in the affirmative. She set the pot then picked a couple of tea bags from a wooden chest she pulled from a shelf just above her head.

Fascinated, he watched as she prepared the very civilized drinks with a grace and economy of movement he couldn't ignore. He shifted in his seat to relieve the pressure building behind his fly. He forced his gaze away from her perfectly plump rear to the photos on the bookcase. Some were snapshots—the kind everybody had—of happy times. Her, he assumed, dressed head to toe in a puffy ski outfit, a ski lift clear in the background. Then there were the professional ones. One in particular piqued his interest. He rose to get a better look. "Is that you and Curtis Sheldon? The actor?"

She answered without turning. "On the red carpet? Yes. I think I was ten. Maybe twelve. It was the first time he took me as his plus-one to the Oscars."

"Wait. Curtis Sheldon is—"

"My father." She stood beside him holding a filled teacup out. "It's not a secret." He took the cup she offered. Relieved of the burden, she indicated several other photos he hadn't looked at yet. "I've been to nearly every one of his red carpet events since. Some of the photos turn out good, others not so much. These are my favorites."

Jake resumed his seat. "You're close to your father."

"I am. My parents divorced when I was young, but I've remained close to both of them." She sat behind her desk and stirred her tea with a dainty little spoon before taking a sip. "What about you? Your brother never talked about his family."

He wasn't there to talk about his family, but he reminded himself, he was on a mission. If telling her a few things would loosen her up a bit, he was game. "I'm the oldest of three boys. Then there's Will and the baby, Rick. Our mother passed when we were young, and none of us were close to our father."

"I'm sorry about your mother…and your father. You're lucky to have your brothers though. I'm an only child."

"Neither of your parents remarried?"

"Nope. They both claim the other was the love of their life. They just couldn't live together."

"Huh."

"Yeah. It's hard to comprehend, but if you saw them together, you would understand."

"You didn't go into show business?"

"No way." She gave a little shudder. "I was never any good at pretending. Both my parents could always tell when I was lying about something. What about you, Jake Ingram?"

"I'm a lawyer, just like my dad. Will and Rick escaped the family obligation gene."

"Speaking of William…is he painting? I'd heard rumors he'd given it up."

Jake shrugged. "I don't know. I don't think so. He will though. It's who he is."

"Please tell him I'd be happy to showcase anything he wants to send me. Given what's happened to him, I'd even pay him up front with a guarantee to split anything I make above my purchase price with him 50/50."

"You're sure you could sell his work?"

"Positive. You aren't the first person to ask about his paintings, and you won't be the last."

"Which brings me to the reason I'm here. Will wants his paintings back, and I aim to find them for him."

"What can I do to help?"

Jake pulled Will's handwritten list from his pocket and slid it across her desk. "Do you know any of these people?"

CHAPTER SIXTEEN

It had been nearly a week since she'd seen or heard from Will. After the night they'd shared the most incredible sex ever, he'd dropped off the planet. If she didn't know better, she'd think she'd dreamed him up—from the first moment she'd spied him in the airport, to the moment he'd held her and looked into her eyes as if they held the answer to every question he'd ever asked. But she hadn't imagined him. He was very real. And even if he never returned to her bed, he deserved to know the part she'd played in bringing down his career.

How he'd missed it, she didn't know. The attorney her father had hired for her had advised her to keep her mouth shut. She didn't actually have a hand in the crime committed against W.H. Ingram, but she'd worked for one of the people who had pulled off the crime of the century. No matter how she justified her innocence, it still came back to her being naïve. Stupid. Blinded by what she'd thought was love.

With her attorney at her side, she'd told the police everything she knew about her boyfriend/employer. In hindsight, it was pathetic how little she'd been able to tell them. Still, any relationship, good or bad, she might have with Will Ingram could only happen if she told him everything. Her father's lawyers could take their advice and shove it. She was done hiding things from Will. He deserved more from her. Unlike others, she hadn't set out to hurt him, but withholding her ties to the people who had undermined his career would hurt him. She could only hope, after the initial shock wore off, he'd come to see what they had together was strong enough to overcome the past.

She was still telling herself the fairy tale long after she'd deposited the take-out containers from dinner in the trash and snuggled in bed with a glass of wine and a romance book Melody had loaned her from her extensive collection. Three chapters in, she gave up hope Will would come over, and decided to wait for him to arrive for work in the morning. She'd tell him everything then. If it was the last time she saw him, so be it. At least she'd have cleared the air and maybe, just maybe, absolved herself of the guilt she felt for reducing one of the country's best artists to painting houses for a living.

After setting the book aside, she reached to turn off the bedside lamp when an insistent knock sounded at her front door. Startled, she glanced at the clock. Too late to be a neighbor wanting to chat. She grabbed her robe off the hook on the back of the bedroom door, jabbing her hands through the tangled arms as she hurried to the front of the house, her nose in the air, vigilant for any signs of fire. Why else would someone be banging on her door so late?

A quick glance through the peephole gave her the answer. Will Ingram stood on her porch, looking impatient and too sexy for words. Hand on the doorknob, her heart in her throat, she mentally ran through the short speech she'd practiced at least a million times over the last week. But as soon as she opened the door, he swung the screen door open and stepped into her space. He took her in his arms, pulling her tightly against him. His lips crashed down on hers, swallowing the words on the tip of her tongue and obliterating every thought from her head save one. Him.

She'd thought she'd known how much she missed him, but, surrounded by his strength, his scent filling her nostrils, his lips and tongue promising magic he could bring, she understood how desolate her life would be once he was gone. She craved his touch. Would never be the same without it. What could one more night in his arms matter? He'd still be gone in the morning, but she'd have one last memory of being his, if only for a short time, to sustain her through all the lonely days ahead. Because there would never be another man who made her feel the way he did. He was *the one*. The *only* one for her. But he could never be hers. Not when he learned who she was. What she'd done.

Kenzie melted against his hard body, gave herself over to the pleasure he alone could give her. He kicked the door shut behind him, and lips never leaving hers, walked her down the hall to her bedroom, undressing her with his hands as they went so when the back of her thighs met the mattress, she was completely naked, her heart in her eyes silently begging him to forgive her for not telling him before she'd fallen too far down the slippery slope of love.

I love him.

Had loved him since she'd first seen him in the airport in New York. Loved him before she knew who he was. Before she understood how completely he would own her.

Heart aching for the inevitable loss of something so special, she lay back on the bed and opened herself to him, inviting him to take what he wanted. Inviting him to give her what she needed more than she needed air to breathe.

As if he sensed her desire for actions, not words, with his hungry gaze raking over her, he stripped his clothes away. With equal hunger, she watched as he sheathed himself then climbed on the bed, his knees spreading her even wider. Then he was above her, the muscles in his arms and shoulders carrying the strain of his weight as he worked his hips until the head of his cock found her secret entrance.

His gaze locked with hers, dragging her into twin pools of swirling emotions. There was lust, for sure. And pain. Heartache so deep and dark she doubted a love, even as strong as hers, would be enough to repair the damage. He needed her. Needed to lose himself in her. Needed to feel the physical connection with another human being. Needed to feel alive. She knew the feeling too well. She'd needed him just as much back in Philly. Would always need him. Only him.

He flexed his hips, entering her, filling her, completing her with one powerful thrust. Hands on his biceps, she dug her fingers into his tight muscles and held on as he claimed her with a steady rhythm she matched, taking him as deep as possible on each stroke. She nearly wept as the now-familiar tightening began. God, it hurt so good. She never wanted it to end, but the pleasure on the other side of the pain beckoned to her, and too soon her body reached its limit. She threw her head back and dug her fingernails into his arms, dragging him down on top of her, an anchor as she crested the mountaintop and plummeted down the other side, clenching around his solid presence inside her, never wanting to let go.

Will's hands molded to her ass, tilting her hips to just the right angle, and sealing their bodies together from shoulder to groin. He rode her hard, prolonging her orgasm as he chased his own. He came with a roar of satisfaction she felt all the way to her toes. His cock pulsed inside her, his hot essence spilling into the condom. She'd never felt so much like a woman…or so broken.

This was what she would never have again if she told him the truth. Call her selfish, but as he lay atop her, still joined as intimately as two could be, his hot, ragged breath in the crook of her neck, she couldn't bring herself to tell him. Not tonight. Not tomorrow.

Someday in the future. Hopefully the very distant future when she was certain his love for her would overrule the pain her truth would bring him.

In the back of her mind, another truth she refused to acknowledge lingered. The future she envisioned might never come.

Their heartbeats slowly returned to normal, and though she welcomed his weight on her, he eventually rolled off her and padded across the hall to the bathroom. When he returned, she hoped he'd slide in the bed with her. Instead, he began to dress. Eyes closed against the pain of his leaving, she startled when something landed over her face. She swatted the clothes away—the ones she'd worn earlier and left on the floor in front of the closet.

"Get dressed."

"Why?"

"I want to show you something."

"What in the world? It's late." Kenzie tossed the bra he'd dumped on her head onto the floor. No way was she putting one of those on at this hour.

"I know, but this can't wait."

Curiosity got the better of her. Hurrying out of bed, she found a pair of sweat pants and a sweatshirt she liked to wear on a rare day off when she had nothing to do and pulled them on, forgoing her underwear altogether. Who would know? She stepped into a pair of canvas shoes, checked herself in the mirror over the dresser.

Yep. She looked like she'd just been doing what she'd been doing. "Where are we going?"

"Don't worry. You're fine. No one is going to see you but me, and I like the way you look."

Knowing full well what he meant, she asked anyway. "How do I look?"

"Womanly."

Though she'd been teasing him, the way his heated gaze traveled over her and the gravity with which he'd delivered the single word made her heart skip a beat. A spark of warmth ignited deep in her womb and spread throughout her body. She felt powerful and more beautiful than she could ever recall feeling. Any thoughts she'd entertained about refusing to go with him evaporated like mist under the morning sun. "Oh."

He held his hand out, and when she took it, he tugged her forward until he could grip her waist. "Oh? That's all you've got to say?"

She nodded.

Then he fingered her waistband. Worked beneath it until his fingers brushed her trimmed curls. With a groan, she dropped her forehead to his shoulder and spread her legs, giving him access to her still-sensitive pussy. Two blunt fingers forced her open, making her knees weak and freezing her breath in her lungs. "You have no idea how beautiful you are when I'm inside you. Or when you come. Do you?"

She could barely think with him doing wicked things between her legs. If he didn't stop soon, she was going to come. "Please." *Please stop? Please let me come?*

He withdrew his fingers—cupped her swollen flesh in his palm and held her there—captive. His wanton sex slave. "Don't come yet. Not until I show you…."

"Show me what?"

"You'll see. Come with me?"

"Yes." Anywhere. If he planned to strip her naked in town square and fuck her senseless for all to see, she didn't have the will to refuse him.

He removed his hand from her sweatpants, patted her tender crotch then tugged her out of the house and down the street. Within minutes, he was unlocking the pedestrian door to his brother's garage. "Watch your step." He led her through the darkened space, eventually coming to a stop. "Stand right there. Don't move."

Will shifted to stand behind her, his talented hands on her hips, holding her flush against him. The unmistakable ridge of his arousal pressed into the small of her back, evidence of the power she held over him. "Close your eyes and don't open them until I tell you to."

"If you're going to show me a car or a truck, I'm going to kill you."

His laughter rumbled through his chest as he pulled her tighter against him. "Nothing so mundane, sweetheart." She felt his breath on her cheek. "Are you ready? Eyes closed?"

"Yes. Can we get on with this?"

He moved slightly, his arm still tight around her held her firm. Then there was a click and the room beyond her lids brightened. Anchoring her hips again, he leaned in and whispered in her ear. "You can look now."

Kenzie opened her eyes—blinked. Blinked again. Her mouth flew open, words trapped in her throat by her heart. A single lamp illuminated a canvas propped on a paint-spattered easel. It was the most erotic painting she'd ever seen—and it was her. Naked. Open. Vulnerable. One fisted hand on the pillow next to her head, the other clenched tight against her stomach just above her mons. Her nipples were hard buds, her breasts chafed from her lover's chest hair. And—most shocking of all—her facial features contorted, yet radiant. Kissed from within by passion and lust and…a love so pure no one could mistake her expression for anything else. This was what Will saw when she came for him. It took her breath away.

"What do you think?"

She worked her jaw, trying to force the words forming in her brain past her lips.

"This is how you look when you come." He fingered her waistband again. Then he touched her, begging for entrance. Without conscious thought, she opened for him.

Two fingers. Then three spread her wide. Worked in and out while his thumb caressed her clit. "Look at yourself. See what I see when you're beneath me." His fingers worked their magic on her. "Come for me, baby. Come, just like you are in the painting."

She shattered. Clamped her thighs as she rode his hand mercilessly, crying out his name between ragged breaths until her knees gave out and she slumped forward over the strong arm banding her waist.

Then she was on the tarp-covered floor. Will dragged her pants off—tossed them aside. Seconds later he was over her and in her. Fucking her. Hard. As merciless as she'd been moments ago. Staring up into his beautiful, shadowed face as he gazed up at her likeness—the one he'd painted from memory. She saw what she needed to see. *Love.* As tormented as her love was for him. He needed her as much as she needed him. She found the hem of his T-shirt. Ran her fingers beneath, over his taut skin until he shivered and cursed.

Power surged through her. She reached between them until her fingers found his shaft—felt his slick, engorged flesh filling her then retreating, over and over. When he hissed in a breath and drove into her harder, faster, she found her clit—worked it in tandem with his thrusts until she teetered on the edge of sanity. Only then did she throw her head back and gaze up at the painting.

Her inner muscles convulsed, gripping his girth, blinding her to everything but the feel of him inside her, the rightness of their joining, the beauty of being completed by the one man put on the planet for her.

As the muscle spasms eased, her vision returned, and, with it, the need to see him as he saw her. She framed his cheeks between her palms. "Look at me. Look at me when you come."

His gaze locked with hers. "Come for me, Will. Come for me."

His cock swelled, grew impossibly harder inside her. She saw the brief bite of pain cross his face, his clenched jaw, at the same moment he lost all rhythm and began to savage her with short, powerful strokes. His hot seed bathed her inner walls—all the while his gaze remained locked with hers.

If she could paint, she'd paint him just like this. Savage. Primal. Undone. But she was no painter, so she committed his beautiful, pained face to memory. An image to treasure at some unnamed point in the future when he would no longer be hers. When he'd find his muse in some other woman's bed.

~ ~ ~

Kenzie sat in one of the old folding lawn chairs Will had found and set up facing the easel. He was painting again. Guilt was a living, breathing thing inside her. *I should have told him the moment I found out who he was.* It was too late now. He was painting again! He had a rare talent, and the world would be a better place if he continued to paint. She'd been part of the reason he'd stopped in the first place. If he knew…. "I don't know what to say."

"You don't have to say anything. I just wanted you to see it."

It was surreal to see a nude painting of herself — in a garage — in Texas. Even more surreal was the fact W.H. Ingram had painted it. "I thought you'd stopped painting."

"You mean, W.H. Ingram?" He didn't wait for her answer. "He did." He pointed to the lower right corner.

Kenzie leaned in to get a better glimpse at the artist's signature. "William Ingram," she muttered. Straightening, she locked her gaze with his. "Why?"

"I'm not the same person I was before. When it got down to it, I couldn't put my old name on it. Didn't seem right."

She'd seen portraits he'd done, but none of them conveyed the emotion this one did. It was stunning and maybe the most erotic painting she'd ever seen. "I can see why. I always knew you were good, but this is beyond good. It's—"

"Yours."

Kenzie gasped. "No! I mean, I can't let you give me the painting. Even with the new signature on it, you could sell it for a small fortune." She hated the thought of some anonymous person owning the painting, she couldn't deprive Will of the money he'd make if he sold it. He was too brilliant of an artist to be painting houses.

"I'm not interested in selling it, and I can't keep it here." He waved his hand around the darkened garage. "I'd put it in my room, but I'd never get any sleep looking at it."

Imagining why he wouldn't get any sleep with this painting in his room had Kenzie placing cool fingers on her heated cheeks. "Still, I don't feel right about taking it. Besides, where would I put it?"

Will continued as if he hadn't heard a thing she'd said. "I think I captured your expression well."

God, it was a good thing the only light in the detached garage was the one trained on the painting. Kenzie felt her cheeks glowing. "I wouldn't know."

"You know I got it right. What I want to know, what everyone who sees this will ask, is, what is she thinking?"

They'll think I'm a low-down, lying, weasel. She closed her eyes and pressed her lips together to keep the truth from spewing out. He didn't deserve what had happened to him, and she didn't deserve to be his muse. She was going to burn in Hell for what she was about to do, but she couldn't tell him—couldn't hurt him anymore than she had already.

Kenzie took in a deep breath, let it out. While focused on the painting, she took his hand in hers and laced their fingers together, and told him the other truth he probably wasn't ready to hear. "She's thinking how much she loves the man who put that expression on her face."

CHAPTER SEVENTEEN

Will stood and threw a tarp over the painting then, hands fisted on his hips, he stared at the cobweb-covered ceiling and tried to process what Kenzie had just said. She couldn't love him. It was the sex talking. All those orgasms, like the one he'd captured on the shrouded canvas, had muddled her mind. His fault. He'd take 100 percent of the blame. He should have stayed away from her. Should have painted a fucking landscape when the urge to paint had come upon him.

Yet, he couldn't deny he felt something for her, too. Was it love? Hell, no. But it was more than lust and more than like. How could he not feel something? She'd given him things he'd thought lost forever—physical desire and perhaps, the desire to live since painting was his life.

He owed her, but he wouldn't lie to her.

Shuffling behind him alerted him moments before she came to stand beside him.

"Too soon, I know." Her voice cracked a little, making him feel like a total ass. He did manage not to flinch when she lightly touched his arm. "I'll be going now." He took her hand, intending to offer to walk her home, but she shook her head and withdrew from him. "I'm a big girl. I can walk a few blocks by myself."

He couldn't find a single word to say, so he nodded. She held her ground as he leaned down to place a platonic kiss on her cheek. Hearing the door close behind her, he sat and stared straight ahead, silently cursing himself for being such an idiot. He'd let love blind him before. He wouldn't do it again. He'd thought Kenzie was in it for the sex, just as he was. Women were inexplicable creatures, and his track record confirmed he knew nothing about them.

He'd never intended to hurt her. Use her, yes, but she'd known the score. Hell, he never would have approached her in the Philadelphia airport—not in the state his mind had been in at the time. She'd initiated their first encounter, and he'd used her boldness to justify the way he'd taken what she'd offered and left without a word. Shitty behavior, but she'd had no right to expect more.

By some stroke of Fate or maybe karma had a hand in it, they ended up in the same small town where it was virtually impossible to not run into each other. He'd given her no reason to think anything had changed between them. They were two adults engaging in adult activities for the sheer pleasure of it. Nothing more. Until the other night.

He'd had an insane desire to see her face when she came. It wasn't supposed to mean anything, but it had. From the moment she'd touched him, he'd been lost to the swirl of pleasure he'd thought his ex-girlfriend's betrayal had taken from him forever. The fire in his blood had felt so damned good, and to see his desire mirrored in her gaze had broken through the wall of ice around his heart. He'd taken everything she offered, and he'd given a part of himself in return.

In the end, she'd given him more than he'd given her. The painting hidden behind his brother's discarded tarp was proof. He was painting again. W.H. Ingram no longer existed, but in his place, someone else had arisen. William Ingram. W.H. had a narrow vision of the world, influenced by what could be seen by the naked eye. William didn't live within those constraints. He exposed the hidden emotion, the secrets behind the surface beauty.

He'd been shocked by Kenzie's response to his question. Closing his eyes, he brought the painting to mind. She'd been correct, but love wasn't the only thing he'd brought to light through her expression. Had she seen the guarded secret and chosen to keep it to herself—as all good secrets were. Or had she simply not seen it?

The mystery was more obvious to him than the love and was why he'd asked the question, "What is she thinking?"

What are you hiding, MacKenzie Carlysle?

"Hey, Will!"

The sound of his brother's voice startled Will awake. It took all of a second to realize he'd fallen asleep sitting upright in an ancient lawn chair. In the garage! *Shit!* Heart pounding, his gaze flew to the painting. Thank God he'd left it covered.

"What the hell are you doing out here?"

Will stood, stretching muscles he wasn't sure would ever be the same. "I couldn't sleep."

Rick flipped on the overhead lights. Will's eyes protested the glare, but the sound of his brother's approaching footsteps cleared his vision like nothing else could.

"You're painting again."

The evidence, brushes, paints, and a recently used palette scattered on his dad's old work table, not to mention the tarp-covered easel, made it impossible for him to deny his brother's observation. "Maybe. Thought I'd give it a try."

"That's fantastic, bro!" Rick pointed to the giant white elephant in the room. "Can I see?"

Will shook his head. No fucking way was he going to let anyone see this painting other than the subject. It was too personal. And, he'd painted it without her knowledge or consent. In his mind, the portrait belonged to her. "Not this one. Maybe the next one. I'm still feeling my way around the painter I am now."

Rick stuck his hands in the front pockets of his work jeans and nodded. "Okay. I don't have a clue what you mean, but I can wait. I'm just glad you're painting again."

Will forced a smile. "Don't worry. You haven't lost your house painter. I'm getting used to the physical work. It's good for me, I think."

"Not if you stay up all night creating masterpieces. You can't do both, Will."

"I know. I need to find a balance." He turned away from the canvas. "And I will. I promise. I won't let you down."

"Well, if you need to take today off, go ahead. You're almost done on the outside of Ms. Carlysle's house, and I don't want you falling off a ladder or something."

The brothers walked toward the pedestrian door single file. Will flicked off the lights and locked the door behind them. "No worries. I could use some coffee and a shower though."

Rick jiggled his truck keys in his hand. "Take your time." He took a step toward his pickup then turned around. "Oh, and give Jake a call? He's been looking for you."

"Left my phone in my room." He shrugged. "No distractions."

With a slight lift of his chin to acknowledge the excuse, his brother resumed his course. "I get it." He climbed into the cab and leaned out the window. "See you in a few."

Will gave him a thumbs-up then climbed the stairs to the porch. He fixed himself a cup of coffee then made a beeline to the shower. Whatever Jake wanted could wait until he'd cleared his head. Unburdening himself to his brother had helped him get on the road to a new normal, but, as good a lawyer as Jake was, Will doubted he'd be able to recover any of the material things he'd lost. For months, he'd deluded himself thinking having the money back, or the paintings, or both, would solve his problems. The painting hidden in the garage was proof none of those things mattered. Losing them had broken him in some fundamental way, but being with Kenzie had put the shattered pieces together again, albeit in a totally different configuration.

As he soaped and rinsed, he tried to see the bad side in the changes he saw within himself and came up empty. He'd lost a small fortune, but he'd gained new insight. And it showed in his new painting. Artists were known to go through phases as they experimented and grew with their craft. Look at Picasso. He'd gone through over half-a-dozen phases in a span of less than thirty years. He wasn't a Picasso or anything close, but like the famous artist, his life had changed, and with it, his art.

He'd be fooling himself if he thought being with Kenzie had nothing to do with the change in him. She had everything to do with it. What it meant, he didn't know and wasn't in any hurry to figure out.

His phone rang again as he pulled the front door closed behind him. Jake. The man had something to say and, as usual, he wasn't going to give up until Will answered. Tenacity was probably a good trait for a lawyer to possess, but it was damn irritating in an older brother. Will leaned against the porch railing. "I'm here. What do you want?"

"Where the fuck have you been? I've called at least a dozen times and left messages. I even called Rick to make sure you were still alive."

"I left my phone in my room overnight."

"I ask again, where the fuck were you if you weren't in your room all night?"

"I was in the garage."

"Doing what? Or do I even want to know?"

"It's none of your business."

"You always were the weird one."

Having acquired what little sleep he'd had in a busted lawn chair, Will was tired and short on patience. "What do you want? I'm late for work."

"I've got good news and maybe not-so good news. Which do you want first?"

"Give me the good news first." He'd had so little of it lately, he craved it.

"Good news is, the bank has agreed to restore your funds."

Will grabbed the railing with his free hand to steady himself. "What? How the fuck did you manage that?"

"I had a little talk with the president. Explained to him how one of his tellers had let an unauthorized person have access to your accounts without even so much as a phone call to verify it with you, and how the teller's actions could result in legal action against the bank if the funds weren't replaced immediately. It didn't take long for him to investigate and come up with the truth. Jessica signed her own name to the withdrawal slips and yours was the only authorized signature on both accounts. They were liable, and he knew it."

"Christ, Jake." Will took a deep breath and let it out. "Does this mean I'm not a pauper anymore?"

"Depends on how much you had in the accounts but I'd say you're flush."

He'd had too much in both his checking and savings accounts. He should have moved some of it or invested it or something, but finances weren't his thing. As long as he could pay his bills and eat, he was good. Maybe it was time to hire someone who knew their way around a financial portfolio. "Thanks, Jake. I mean it man. I owe you."

"You don't owe me anything. You're my brother."

"Still. I owe you. I swear I told the bank manager the same thing and got nowhere. I don't know how you did it, but I'm grateful."

A loud sigh came across the line. "Hold onto your gratitude until you hear my other news."

"Seriously? You could tell me Jessica burned all my paintings right now and it wouldn't phase me."

"No sign of the paintings yet, burned or otherwise. However, you know the new PR person Hank hired? MacKenzie Carlysle?"

Every muscle in Will's body tensed. He gripped the top rail until his fingers screamed. He forced his jaw to unclench. "Yeah. What about her?"

"She wasn't on the list of people you knew in New York."

"Because I didn't know her in New York. I met her in the airport in Philly when our plane made an emergency landing."

"The police interviewed her. In fact, she was one of the first people on the scene the night of your gallery opening."

"I don't understand. Who is she?"

"She was Cecil Hawthorne's girlfriend and did PR for his gallery."

Will's legs gave out. He sank to the porch and cradled his forehead in his free hand. His gaze landed on the garage where the first thing he'd painted in nearly a year rested beneath a filthy tarp. MacKenzie Carlysle. Nude. With love and secrets in her eyes. Secrets no longer hidden.

Fuck it all.

Fuck her.

Shit.

This couldn't be happening. What kind of game was she playing?

"Apparently, she arrived at the gallery early to supervise the caterers and found the place locked up and empty. Instead of calling 9-1-1, she went home and tried to locate her boyfriend. According to the police report, when he was still missing the next morning, she went to the station to file a report. I don't know who put the missing person case together with the heist of your paintings, but someone did. They interviewed her and quickly came to the conclusion she didn't know anything. I don't have any way of determining if they were right or wrong, but I thought you should know."

"Thanks, man." What else could he say? His brother was doing him a solid no matter how devastating the news was. "How did you find all this out?"

"Remember the gallery owner you had on your list, Sunny Sheldon?"

"Yeah. Nice lady. She sold several paintings for me and was always trying to get more." He massaged his temple where a massive headache was forming. "Should have let her have them all." Hindsight was 20/20.

"It might have been a wise thing to do, but too late now. Anyway, I asked her to check a list of names and see if she recognized any of them. She knew several and vouched for all of them. Seems the Carlysle woman did some work for her when she first moved to New York. They kept in touch. When Hawthorne was a no-show after a couple of weeks, she approached Ms. Sheldon, looking for work. Sunny didn't need her services, but here's the interesting part—some of those paintings Sunny sold for you?"

"Yeah, what about them?"

"She sold them to Melody Ravenswood."

"Hank's wife?"

"She wasn't his wife then, but she bought one of the paintings for him and a couple of others for gifts to family members. Anyway, the two of them became friends and still are. Every time RavensBlood comes to New York, they all get together. Hank mentioned he needed a new PR person the last time he was here."

"She hooked them up?"

"Yep. So, as much as I distrust coincidences, I have to concede this is a genuine one."

"No chance Sunny Sheldon was involved in this somehow?"

"Not a chance."

"How can you be so sure?"

"Trust me, Will. She didn't have anything to do with your paintings going missing."

Sunny Sheldon had been one of the first people to take a chance on him when he first started out. When he was in college, she sold a few of his early works for enough to keep him from having to wait tables in order to eat. He'd repaid her kindness by giving her a more than generous commission on several of his later works. He didn't want to believe she'd be a part of what had happened to him, but what did he know? He'd trusted Jessica and look where his naivete had gotten him. Still, Jake sounded certain. The ability to ferret out liars made for a good attorney. Jake was as good as they came. If he said Sunny didn't have anything to do with the crime, then Will believed him. "I believe you." Then it hit him. "Where the hell are you? New York?"

"Where else would I be, asshat? I did all I could do over the phone. It was time to meet face-to-face with some of these people. I'm glad I did. You're getting your funds back, and I hope to at least pick up a scent regarding your stolen paintings."

"I hear a but in there."

Jake's laughter helped lighten Will's mood. Dredging all this up again was twisting him up in knots. "But," he dragged the word out. "I need you to help me out."

"I'm not going back to New York. You're on your own, big brother."

"No. Don't need you here. I need you to ask MacKenzie Carlysle a couple of questions."

Well, shit. "I'd rather go to New York."

Silence stretched over the miles until it became uncomfortable. Then Jake spoke. "Jesus, Will. Tell me you aren't fucking her?"

"It's none of your business, Jake. Just tell me what you want me to ask her."

"This isn't good, little brother."

"I won't disagree with you, but it's nothing. Just hooking up." His stomach revolted at the lie. "What do you need from her?"

"You know we talked about the trip you and Jessica made upstate?"

"Yeah, what about it?"

"Ask Ms. Carlysle if she ever heard Hawthorne talk about any place upstate. Did he take any trips out of town? If so, does she have a clue where he went? She might have seen something or read something in his office or an email. Anything along those lines. Think you can handle that?"

The dull thud in his temple now felt like a rock band was practicing inside his skull. "Yeah, I can handle it. When do you need to know?"

"ASAP, dickhead. I'm in New York. This is costing me a fortune. The sooner I get home, the better."

"Okay, okay. I'll borrow Rick's truck and drive out to Hank's place in a few. Catch her at work."

"Don't accuse her of anything, Will. We have absolutely no proof she's done anything wrong. The police believed her, and Sunny vouched for her, too. She's most likely a victim of all this, same as you."

He wasn't convinced. Not by a long shot. "I'll call you later." He ended the call and dropped both his hands to the porch floor. What a clusterfuck.

CHAPTER EIGHTEEN

Will sat on the porch until his ass hurt as much as his head, before going inside to take a couple of over-the-counter painkillers. After splashing his face with cold water, he resumed his walk down the street to where his brother was working.

"I've got to run an errand for Jake. Can I borrow your truck?"

Rick tossed him the keys. "When will you be back?"

"Don't know. Couple of hours?"

"Let me get my shit out of there, then." They walked outside together, and Will waited while his brother gathered up the tools he'd need for the rest of the day. "I'm good." Rick hefted an overflowing toolbox out of the bed of the truck and slammed the tailgate.

Will nodded. "Thanks. I'll finish the outside painting tomorrow." Then Rick would expect him to start on the inside walls. *Shit.*

"No worries. I've got a couple more weeks of work. It won't take as long to paint the rooms she wants done."

He put the truck in reverse. "See you later."

The drive out to the house Hank had inherited from his maternal grandparents took forever. As he followed the familiar road, he couldn't help but remember the times he'd run wild there along with Hank, Randy, and Chris. Life had been simple then. Go to school. Eat. Sleep. Play as hard as you could. It had all gotten complicated somewhere around the time he hit puberty and began

136

to notice girls. Here he was, pushing the thirty year mark and women were still complicating his life.

His fault. He had a knack for choosing the most deceitful females on the planet. Which brought his thoughts around to the reason he was driving this nostalgic road in the first place. MacKenzie Carlysle.

Was she playing him? Again? Had they ended up on the same flight by coincidence? Or could it all be some elaborate scheme to…what? Finish him off? Make sure he never painted again? He didn't want to believe Sunny Sheldon had anything to do with stealing his paintings, but the link between her and MacKenzie and Cecil was awfully convenient. Still, coincidences did happen, and just because you knew someone who turned out to be a scumbag didn't make you one. If it did, he was guilty by association, too. He'd known Cecil and Jessica, two of the biggest scumbags on earth.

He couldn't dismiss the fact Kenzie had lied to him. When he'd followed her out of the diner and accused her of being a reporter, she'd claimed to have just discovered his identity and had been quick to tell him she wasn't looking for a story. If she'd mentioned her former association with Cecil Hawthorne then, he wouldn't have touched her. Ever. Hell, he probably would have borrowed money from Jake and got the hell out of town. Left her there to her new life and moved on. Starting over someplace else wouldn't have been easy, but it would have been preferable to getting caught up in her web of lies.

The road curved, and the big white barn with the black wings painted on the side came into view. Too bad all the good memories he had of the place, before and after Hank had converted the old barn into headquarters for BlackWing, would be tainted by seeing her there.

Hank had made a few improvements since the last time Will visited. What was once a gravel parking lot dotted with weeds was now a sleek blacktopped area, complete with striped slots wrapping around the back of the barn, out of sight from the house. The first few were marked for visitors. Will chose one, swung the old truck in, and cut the engine. Heart pounding, he stepped out. As he approached the new pedestrian door Hank had added to this side of the barn, he paused to take in his surroundings. The house and barn were a nod to civilization in an otherwise pristine landscape he'd always loved. Cotton fields stretched out in every direction as far as he could see. Off to his left, if he walked long enough, he'd run into a branch of the small river Willowbrook had been named for. God, how many hours had he and his friends spent there fishing, swimming, just laying around in the shade of a tree, talking about nothing and everything? Will smiled at the memory. Many of his early paintings had been of that very spot. Had he ever told Hank? He couldn't remember. He should someday. Hell, he should have sent one to his friend as a thank-you for the inspiration the trips out to this farm had provided.

Will glanced up at the restored barn, now offices and a recording studio for a world renown rock band. Who would have thought it? Hank had done well for himself but had stayed true to who he was—a small town guy who loved the land and honored the past. Will wished he could say the same for himself. He'd gone to New York, determined to let the grit of the city scrape away his small-town veneer. It had done a good job, scraping him down to the bone and spitting him out. Here he was, in Willowbrook, wearing skin he didn't recognize.

The city had fundamentally changed him, made him a great painter in some ways, an idiot in others. It had given him a life, an identity, and it had taken it away as soon as he let his guard down.

No more. He was home and he planned to stay here. The woman he'd come to see could get the hell out of his town. Move the fuck back to New York. Find some other sucker to play, to grind into the pavement.

But first, he wanted answers. What did she know? How involved had she been in Hawthorne's business? Where the fuck were his paintings? Most of all, he wanted to know, why him? What had he done to deserve what they'd done to him, to his career?

Then, muse be damned, he never wanted to see her again. If it meant he'd never paint again, so be it. He'd deal. He was starting to like house painting. It was good, honest work and kept him in shape. Hell, maybe he'd go into the remodel business with Rick. It wasn't the worst idea he'd ever had.

Forcing his feet forward, he stepped inside. Having never entered through the new door, it took a second to get his bearings. The sound of high-pitched squeals and disjointed banging drew him down the long center hall to an open office door. Hank's office. Standing in the doorway, Will took in the scene. What had once been an office fit for a rock and roll king looked like a cross between an executive office and a daycare center. His friend's beloved Ludwig drum kit still occupied most of the back wall, with a desk and electronic keyboard off to one side. Will noted the fancy computer monitors and what appeared to be about a million bucks worth of high-tech gizmos on top of the desk. Childhood artwork was haphazardly taped to the free spaces between framed platinum and gold albums and pictures of Hank with celebrities and dignitaries from around the globe. A pink toy stroller, complete with baby doll, sat to one side of Hank's desk. Smack in the center of the room sat a tiny drum set. A pixie with wild curls and bright-blue eyes held court behind the miniature kit, banging away with gleeful abandon while her foot-tapping dad indulgently looked on from a giant beanbag chair taking up most of the remaining free space in the room.

Will crossed his arms and leaned against the doorjamb to watch the concert. The more he listened, the clearer everything became. What at first had sounded like noise was indeed a simplified version of one of BlackWing's most famous songs. Damn if the kid wasn't half bad, at what, three years old? A perfectionist, too, like her dad, he determined when the child missed a beat, and a pout marred her adorably cute face as she paused then tried the bridge to the chorus again. Nailing it the second time around.

"Perfect, Gloria. You've got it, girl!"

The pride and love in Hank's voice twisted something deep in Will's gut. He'd never given much thought to having kids, but seeing this pint-sized version of Hank brought a lump of longing to his throat. What would it be like to find the right woman and have a couple of rug rats? Maybe one would inherit his talent with a paintbrush. Or not. He wasn't sure passing the creative gene on was such a good idea. It was hard as hell to make a living putting paint on canvas. Practically impossible, yet he'd done it for a number of years. Still, he wasn't sure he would wish the creative angst onto anyone, especially his own son or daughter. He'd do nearly anything to spare his child from the pain of ripping emotions from their chest in order to put them on display for the world to see.

He'd done it countless times, though if he was honest, not so much toward the end of his career. He'd still been driven by the need to paint, but there at the last, he'd done so with a voice in his head telling him to paint what people wanted to buy instead of what his gut told him to paint. It was Jessica who had convinced him to do the more commercially viable paintings. He'd argued, but eventually given in and painted what she wanted. She'd been right. They sold well and for prices he still couldn't fathom. He told himself he was happy, practically mass-producing art for living room walls. The truth was, he'd been in a rut of his own making. It had taken another woman to shake him out of it.

Closing his eyes, he brought to mind the painting in his brother's garage. Just thinking about it made his heart rate accelerate and his fingers itch to grab a brush. To try again. To dig deeper. To expose her every emotion. Her every secret. Every lie she'd ever told. To put it all on canvas in paint tinted with his sweat. His tears. His blood.

No matter what she'd done to him in New York, she'd cut him to the core in Willowbrook. There wasn't a drop of blood on the painting, nevertheless, he'd bled over it. He'd turned himself inside out to expose what he'd seen in her eyes, and, knowing her secrets, he hated her. He hated who she was, what she'd done. Hated every breath she took. Yet…he loved her with a fierce pain no amount of paint on canvas could cure.

He was so fucking screwed.

CHAPTER NINETEEN

The solo concert came to an end, shocking Will back to the here and now. As his friend sprang from his front row seat to envelope his daughter in a bear hug and pepper her with praise, Will began to clap. Startled eyes turned his way and, when recognition dawned, became soft and welcoming.

"Damn. Will Ingram." Hank scooped his daughter up, resting her on his left hip as he waved Will into his office. "It's good to see you, man." They shook hands. "Gloria, baby, this is one of my oldest and best friends. He paints pretty pictures."

Up close, he could see the child's resemblance to her mother was dominant, but her eyes were all Hank.

"Will, this is Gloria."

Will brought her tiny hand to his lips and placed a smacking kiss on her knuckles. She jerked her fingers out of his grasp, tucking them in close while she made up her mind about him. "Pleased to meet you." He nodded at her drum kit. "You put on quite the concert. Are you getting ready to go on the road?"

Hank laughed. "Don't give her ideas, buddy." He hugged his daughter tight. "She's got more talent in her little finger than I have in my entire body. If she wants to, she'll take the music world by storm one of these days."

Did he detect a bit of wariness in Hank's declaration? "Do you want her to go into the family business?"

"Heck, no! But Mel insists we let her explore her interests and talents. Not surprising, given the way she was raised."

"Oh?"

"Yeah. Long story best told by Mel herself. Come for dinner sometime and she'll fill you in." Hank addressed his daughter. "What do you say, Glo? Want Will to have dinner with us sometime?" Shaking her head, the child tucked her face against her father's shoulder, giving Will the side eye.

"Hey, pumpkin." He jostled her. "Better get all the facts before you make a decision." He pointed to the wall behind Will. Will turned. Christ. It was one of the paintings he'd consigned with Sunny Sheldon. It depicted a man and woman walking along a worn trail toward a copse of trees. A black dog ambled along behind them. It was Willowbrook, and the couple could easily pass for Hank and Melody Travis. "That's one of your favorite pictures in the whole world, isn't it?" Dark curls bobbed. "Know who painted it?"

Gloria shook her head. Hank pointed to Will. "He did." The child's face lit with interest. "Know what else he painted?"

"What?"

"The picture in Mommy and Daddy's bedroom. The one of the river?"

Shit. Will recalled the painting. At least Sunny Sheldon had been telling the truth about selling his paintings to Melody.

Gloria straightened in her dad's arms. "Really?"

"Really. If you don't believe me, ask him."

Will's heart melted when the child shifted her blue gaze to him. "Really?"

"Cross my heart." He made an x across his chest with his index finger. "You like them?" When she nodded, he smiled. Leaning in close, he whispered, "Don't tell your mom, but she paid too much for them."

Hank's brows rose in question.

"Another long story best told over a bottle of cheap wine."

"You're on. Maybe this weekend? We've got a bunch of people coming in the following week to record. I could use a quiet night before all hell breaks loose."

"Hell!" Gloria chimed in.

"Shh!" Hank rolled his eyes. "Don't let your mom hear you say that word or I'll be sleeping in my office for a month."

"I won't, Daddy. Promise."

Hank shared a conspiratorial smile with Gloria. "That's my girl." He set her down. "Practice time is over. Which means?" he prompted.

"Snack time!" She took off like a flash, stopping in the doorway long enough to tell her daddy goodbye and blow him a kiss. Will was smitten.

"You're a lucky SOB."

Hank smiled. "Don't I know it." He motioned to the couch situated beneath Will's painting. "Have a seat?"

Will shook his head. "Nah. I actually came here to see your new PR person."

Hank frowned. "If you think you're going to steal her away, you better think again. She's doing a fantastic job for us, and we won't let her go without a fight."

Hand up like a stop sign, Will was quick to shut down his train of thought. "Hell, no. Just need to talk to her for a few minutes." Hoping Hank wouldn't ask him to elaborate, he went on. "Heard the drums and couldn't pass up the opportunity to see a musical genius at work."

"Takes after her grandpa Ravenswood." Hank's smile almost made it to his eyes. "It's a bit frightening, to tell you the truth."

"I bet." He could only imagine the responsibility Hank carried on his shoulders. By all accounts, Earl Ravenswood had been a musical prodigy. If Gloria inherited even half his talent, nurturing it without letting it consume her would be difficult. "Add her remarkable talent to our list of things to talk about over dinner."

Hank's smile was genuine this time. "You bet." He extended his hand, and the two shook again. "It's good to have you back, man. We missed you."

Will dipped his chin in acknowledgment. "It's good to be home."

MacKenzie's office was a few doors down from Hank's on the opposite side of the hallway. Her door was open, and light spilled out into the hall. Will recalled the soundproofed rooms, like Hank's office, didn't have windows. Which meant, the walls in her office were nothing more than studs and drywall. If he was going to maintain any privacy, he'd have to make sure they kept their voices down. Not an easy feat when he wanted to get right in her face and vent his frustrations at the top of his lungs.

Jake would be so much better at this, but his brother wasn't here, so it was up to him to get the answers. Raging at her probably wasn't the best way to go about it. He stopped, fisted his hands at his sides, took a deep breath then let it out, easing his fingers open at the same time. When he felt as calm as he was going to get, he stepped into the doorway and leaned against the frame. His stance said casual, but he'd no doubt the expression on his face said otherwise.

She was on the phone, but as soon as she saw him, she ended the conversation. After replacing the handset in its cradle, she tossed the pen she'd been holding onto the blotter, rocked back in her desk chair, and sighed. "You know."

It wasn't a question.

"I know." Why did she have to be so damn beautiful? Memories of what it felt like to be inside her, the little sounds she made when he hit the right spots, his name on her lips when she came—the emotion in her eyes the one time he'd allowed himself that intimacy. Her lies. It all twisted up in his gut, made him see red.

"I'm sorry—"

He straightened but kept his arms crossed over his chest, his fists curled into his armpits. He didn't want her platitudes. Couldn't care less about the answers Jake wanted. The hell with the paintings. They were crap anyway. He'd always known it, but faced with another betrayal, he could see the last few years with new clarity. The money didn't matter. The paintings mattered even less. There was only one question burning in his gut. "Cut the bullshit, Kenzie."

Her lips snapped shut. Her gaze dropped to the top of her desk. He advanced so he towered over her. "All I want to know is why? Why me? What the fuck did I ever do to deserve this?"

A single tear tracked down her cheek. "How did you find out?"

"Doesn't matter." He dropped his fists to her desk, leaned in so his voice wouldn't carry. This was between them. No one else. "Why, Kenzie?"

"I don't know." She looked up then. Her watery eyes did nothing to ease the rage inside him, threatening to erupt like a volcano. "I swear, I don't know."

"He didn't tell you anything?"

"No."

"Never said a word about his plans? Never dropped a hint about stealing a million dollars' worth of art?"

"No." She pressed those goddamn kissable lips of hers into a fine line.

"And I'm supposed to believe you? You were running PR for the gallery opening. You were sleeping with the bastard for Christ's sake. How could you not know?"

She snatched a tissue from a box tucked behind her computer monitor then dabbed at the corner of her eyes. It was no more than a moment, but she pulled herself together, squared her shoulders, and stared him down. "How could *you* not know? *You* were sleeping with Jessica, or had she gotten tired of being treated like a whore and moved on?"

Before Will could close his mouth and straighten, she'd pushed her chair back and run for the door. He caught a glimpse of her shoulder as she cleared the doorway, headed god only knew where.

Will collapsed onto her desk, his fingers digging into the edge of the wood surface. Dammit all to hell. The verbal barb she'd slung at him had hit dead center. He should have known what his girlfriend/agent was up to. Should have treated Jessica better than he had. She'd encouraged him to paint more, to become an assembly line, but he was the one who had thrown himself into the work until there was no time for anything else. He'd eaten sporadically, washed even less, and when she'd forced him to step away from his studio, he'd used her in much the same way he'd used MacKenzie those first few times they'd been together.

Fuck, MacKenzie was right. He'd brought it all on himself. Did his bad behavior make what Jessica and Cecil had done okay? Hell, no. But he was starting to understand why they'd done it.

Why?

He had his answer, and it wasn't a pretty one.

Because you're a dick.

The knowledge felt like smoldering cinders in his belly and fueled a new rage aimed at himself. There had only ever been one way to deal with his emotions. He needed to paint.

Shoving off her desk, he stalked out of the barn to his brother's truck. By the time he pulled into the driveway of his childhood home, his fingers ached from clenching the steering wheel like a lifeline.

It took him almost an hour to hang the new tarps he dragged from the back of his brother's truck and cover the floor with newspaper he'd found in a string-bound stack next to a garbage can. Only then did he squeeze paint onto his palette and pick up a brush.

He started with red. Bold, angry slashes he made no attempt to temper. When he ran out of red, he moved to black then bruising shades of blue, purple, and magenta.

He didn't have a plan. No idea what he was painting. His rage, his self-hatred had no shape, no physical form, yet it expressed itself nonetheless as a tangible, visual incarnation of himself. Broken. Miserable. Fucked.

When the paint ran out, he threw the palette at the tarp he'd desecrated then sank to his knees on the unforgiving concrete floor. Holding his head between his hands in a vise-like grip, the rage poured from his body in the form of tears.

He didn't know how long he'd sat there, but when Rick wrapped his arms around him and dragged him to his feet, his eyes were dry and his soul empty. He'd put it all on the cheap canvas tarps. Every last bit of himself.

"Come on, brother. You need to eat and sleep. Then you can tell me what the fuck you did to my new tarps."

He didn't argue. Let Rick help him into the house. He ate because his brother told him to, but the food had no taste. Later, he slept because he had no choice.

CHAPTER TWENTY

Kenzie cursed her choice of shoes for the day as she stalked across Hank and Melody's back yard. Damn spike heels. Who was she trying to impress anyway? No one around here dressed the way she did. This was fucking Texas, not New York. If she stayed here, she'd have to invest in a new shoe wardrobe. Maybe even a pair of cowboy boots. She imagined a pair she'd seen a few days ago. The embroidered yellow roses on them had caught her eye as she'd strolled past the store window. "Should have bought them then," she muttered to herself. If she'd been wearing them a few minutes ago she would have driven their pointed toe into Will Ingram's shin on her way out the door.

"Should have bought what?"

The feminine voice stopped Kenzie in her tracks. Where the hell had it come from? A quick glance around Hank and Melody's backyard provided her answer. Her boss's wife, book in hand, sat in a lawn chair beneath an ancient oak tree. Dressed in jeans and a BlackWing T-shirt Kenzie estimated to be as old as the tree, feet bare, the woman looked as if she didn't have a care in the world.

"Kick-ass cowgirl boots." She wobbled over to the cluster of lawn furniture. Bracing herself on the back of the nearest chair, she slipped her shoes off, sighing as her bare feet met the soft green lawn.

"They'd be more comfortable than those, but I'll warn you, they're hot as hell in the summer. Maybe you could compromise on some sandals?"

She envisioned kicking Will while wearing sandals. "Nope. Need something with some grit."

Mel's right eyebrow rose. "For?"

"Kicking someone?"

At the sound of a vehicle accelerating up the driveway, both women turned to look. "Would your someone be William Ingram?"

Kenzie closed her eyes and shook her head. When she opened them, the man and his truck were out of sight. "How did you guess?"

Mel shrugged. Marking her page with a scrap of paper, she set her book aside. "I can add two and two." She waved to the chair Kenzie was using to hold herself upright. "Have a seat."

Kenzie sat.

"Hank called to let me know he'd invited Will over for dinner later this week. He mentioned Will was here to see you. Seeing you huffing it across the lawn like a pack of hounds were on your heels, no pun intended then seeing Will drag racing up the drive—well, the conclusion was pretty easy."

"No woolgathering on your brain."

"Want to talk about it?"

"No. Not really." But it didn't stop her from telling Melody everything, starting with first seeing Will at JFK in New York and being attracted to him, to the accusations he'd thrown her way a few minutes ago. She left out a lot of details, but anyone with ears could have filled in the blanks, and Mel had two perfectly good ones.

"Does he know you're in love with him?"

Love. The word made her heart ache and her stomach churn.

"I told him. Sort of." *She's thinking how much she loves the man who put that expression on her face.* "But I don't think he believed me."

"Does he love you?"

"No!" She could still feel the heat of his anger as he accused her of lying. But maybe he had loved her, at least for a while. She'd seen it in his eyes, felt it in the way he claimed her the last few times they'd been together. What she'd seen and felt had been enough to make her rethink telling him everything. Another mistake to add to her mounting tally. "I think he hates me."

"Why would he hate you?"

"It's another long story, and I'm sure you've got things you need to be doing."

Mel shook her head. "Nope. Gloria is sound asleep. I brought the monitor out with me. If she wakes up, we'll hear her." She held up the romance novel she'd been reading. "And this can wait. I'd much rather hear about a real romance."

Kenzie's laugh held no mirth. "If you want romance, better stick to your book. Will hates me, and in his mind, he has good cause. Heck, I don't even blame him. I should have told him who I was as soon as I figured out who he was."

"And who are you, MacKenzie Carlysle?"

"I was involved in what happened to him in New York."

Mel adjusted in her seat. "There were a few articles about him in the local paper when it happened, but they were vague. Nothing since. I assumed it had all been resolved. How were you involved?"

She filled her new friend in on the particulars. No matter how she tried to spin it, the situation sounded bad.

"You're right. You should have told him."

"And you and Hank, too. Will is your friend. I don't want my employment to come between you."

"We knew some of your story. Sunny told us, but she didn't go into a lot of detail. She's a good friend, and we trust her judgement. However, I'll talk to Hank. See what he says. He's known the Ingram brothers his entire life. If you really didn't have anything to do with what happened to Will, then you working for BlackWing shouldn't be an issue."

"I swear I didn't know a thing about what Cecil and Jessica were up to. I was as surprised as anyone when I got to the gallery and found it empty."

Melody shifted in her seat. "I can't believe they stole the money *and* all the paintings. Who does something like that?"

Kenzie shook her head. "I can't tell you how many times I've asked myself the same question. How could I have been so stupid? I never saw it coming. I was working my ass off, doing PR for Will's showing and another one Cecil had scheduled a few months out. He never did or said anything to make me suspicious. It was business as usual, though, in hindsight, I can see how far he and I had drifted apart."

"It happens if you don't work at a relationship."

Nodding, Kenzie said, "Our relationship had broken down long before Cecil disappeared." She pressed her fingertips to her temples as old, painful memories came roaring to the forefront. "We argued a lot, mostly about him going out without me and coming home later than a guy with a woman waiting at home should. I know now he was with Jessica." Kenzie sighed and dropped her hands to her lap. "I was so stupid."

"You didn't want to see what was happening."

"No, I suppose I didn't. It was easier to pretend things weren't as they seemed. Deep down, I knew he was cheating on me, but I didn't know if it was one woman or a different one every night. I didn't *want* to know. So, I worked night and day and refused to look too closely at my personal life."

"Then he disappeared."

"Yeah. I had my own bank account where I kept my paychecks. Thankfully, he wasn't able to touch those funds—or maybe he didn't try—I didn't have much. But he cleaned out his personal accounts and the business accounts."

"Crazy things happen in the music and entertainment industries all the time, but your story beats anything I've ever heard."

"I landed on my feet, thanks to you guys and Sunny Sheldon. I was down to my last few dollars when I got here. I still had a credit card with some room on it, so I was able to survive." Just how she'd used some of her dwindling credit in the Philly airport warmed her blood. She'd been impetuous and more than a little stupid. If she'd known who the sexy stranger was, she never would have approached him, much less propositioned him. If she'd found an ounce of restraint, she wouldn't be in the predicament she was. She wouldn't be 100 percent, irrevocably in love with a man who hated her.

"What are you thinking?"

"Me?" Kenzie raised a hand to her cheek, felt the heat of her skin. "Nothing."

"Come on, girlfriend. You're blushing. What's going on?"

There was no use trying to argue the point. Her flaming cheeks had given her away. "Just remembering what it was like to be with him."

"Good, I take it?"

"Better than good. The best. He gets me. Did from the very first. It's not his fault I fell hard and he didn't."

"What makes you think he didn't fall, too?"

"You saw him spewing gravel to get away from here. He hates me."

Melody tapped her fingertips on the arm of her chair. "Haven't you heard? Love and hate are two sides of the same coin."

Kenzie's heart thumped hard. "You think he loves me?"

"I don't know, but I think it's highly likely. The deeper his feelings are for you, the bigger your betrayal would seem. Maybe he's trying to find a way to cope with the way he feels about you and the way he *thinks* he should feel about you."

Kenzie leaned back in the Adirondack chair and let her lids drop shut. "Betrayal." She mulled the word over in her mind. "I didn't betray him, but I can see how he would think I had. Not telling him about my involvement with Cecil was a mistake, but I did plan to tell him. I'd made my mind up to do it several times, but then we'd…well, let's just say we didn't do a lot of talking." She opened her eyes, studied the dappled light filtering through the leaves of the shade tree. "The time just never seemed right."

"Words aren't always necessary between two people."

Kenzie's laugh held no mirth. "Yeah, but trust is, and he doesn't trust me."

"I can't tell you what to do, but I know what it's like to love someone and be afraid to fight for him." Kenzie raised an eyebrow brow, and Mel continued. "I was stupid in love with Hank and because of my own fears, I almost let him get away. Be brave, Kenzie. If you love him, put on your big girl panties and go after him. Tell him what's in your heart. Beg him to listen to your side of the story. If he loves you, he'll find his way past the pain, and if he doesn't, maybe you can find peace in knowing you tried."

Leaning forward, Kenzie took Mel's hands in hers. "Thank you so much for listening to me today. You're right. Will is worth fighting for. I think we have a chance at something good, if I haven't ruined it."

Mel stood, and Kenzie rose with her. "I'm always here if you need someone to talk to, but now, if you'll excuse me, I should check on Gloria."

"Please, don't let me keep you."

"You haven't. I've enjoyed our talk. Feel free to stay a while. No one will bother you out here."

"Thanks. I think I will sit for a while. I know I need to face Will, but not before I figure out what I'm going to say."

"Take your time." When Mel reached the steps, she glanced over her shoulder. "My advice? Be direct. Men don't always understand subtlety."

With a wave and a genuine laugh, Kenzie dropped into her chair. She owed Will an apology, at the very least. Suggesting he in any way was responsible for what happened to him was beyond wrong. If Jessica felt like she'd been shorted in their relationship, she should have confronted him instead of conspiring with another man to destroy Will's career. She should have been direct.

Like I need to be. No more secrets. No more hiding my feelings or letting Will hide his. If he hates me, he needs to say so. Then we'll both know where we stand, and where we go from here.

CHAPTER TWENTY-ONE

Will cracked one eye open. Soft light spilled through the cheap vinyl blinds covering the single window in the small room. It was too early to be awake, especially since he didn't have a clue how long he'd been asleep. He vaguely recalled Rick helping him to stand. And he remembered the paint. So much goddamn paint.

The low rumble of voices coming from somewhere down the hall was what he needed to force his feet to the floor. Rick had called in reinforcements. A sure sign he'd fucked up—bad.

Will stumbled to the bathroom. Necessities first. Inquisition later.

After washing his hands, he dared a glance in the mirror over the vanity. He looked like he'd been to Hell and back. He splashed some cold water on his face which did nothing for his bloodshot eyes, but helped clear his head. He'd need his wits about him to face his brothers.

They knew he was up. The house was too small to conceal his movements. They could wait. After pulling on a T-shirt and sweats, he made his way to the kitchen, made a cup of coffee in Rick's fancy new one-cup brewer, and drank down half of it before heading to the living room to face the music.

"Thought you were in New York." He dropped into the only unoccupied chair in the room.

Jake adjusted the seams on his immaculate dress slacks. "I was. Rick called and said you had some sort of breakdown and I needed to get here ASAP."

Will sipped his coffee then stared at the remaining brew. "You should have stayed there."

"You aren't denying you had a breakdown."

"Nope. I hit bottom yesterday." Truth. He'd seen the depths of the pit and come back from it. Sort of. "I'm fine though." An enormous lie. He was far from fine, but his brothers would never leave him alone if they thought otherwise. "Just needed to work the toxins out of my system." If they believed his story, he should take up acting.

"Is that what we saw out there?" Rick gestured toward the garage. "Toxins?"

"You always were a Neanderthal when it came to art. That's a self-portrait, asshole."

"What the fuck?" Jake scooted to the edge of the sofa cushion. "Have you seen what you did? It looks like we let a madman loose in the garage."

Will held his older brother's gaze. "Fuck you."

"Look, Will," Rick appeased. "We're concerned about you. What you did out there yesterday isn't your normal technique."

"No, it's not. But it is the most honest thing I've ever painted." He jerked upright. "You didn't move anything, did you?"

"No. Jake just got here a few minutes ago. We weren't sure if we should leave it or throw it away before you woke up."

"Don't fucking touch it. You hear me?"

Jake held his hand up, palm out. "Okay. Calm the fuck down. We haven't, and we won't. It obviously means something to you."

He loved his brothers. He really did. But they would never understand what drove him to paint. Or not to paint. Just like he'd never understand how Jake could be happy wearing a suit and tie all day long, or how Rick could have joined the military. They physically resembled each other, but under their skin, they were as different as any three humans could be. "It means everything. Every. Fucking. Thing." He stood. "Come on. I'll show you."

The grass was cool under his bare feet as he led the way to the garage. He didn't expect them to truly understand, but he needed to convince them he hadn't lost his mind. Yeah, he'd been blind with rage and a host of other emotions he wasn't ready to pull out and examine in the light of day just yet, but he'd known what he was doing.

He thought he was ready to see it again, but standing there with the three huge canvases strung from the ceiling, reflecting his likeness back at him like a macabre three-sided mirror, was enough to freeze the breath in his lungs. His gaze swung from one panel to the next, assessing the technique, the message.

"Fuck, I'm good."

Jake stood to his left and just a little behind him. "If you say so. Looks like a mess to me."

"Me, too." Rick took up the same spot on his right side. "Explain, brother, before Jake and I have you committed."

He laughed, deep and loud. "It's a self-portrait. See." He pointed to the panel on the left. "Red. My life. My blood." He waved his hand to indicate the center panel. "Black. My soul."

"What about this one?" Rick faced the last tarp. "What the hell is this supposed to be?"

"My body. Purple for my heart, no disrespect to the military. Magenta, etcetera, for the rest of my organs."

"This is how you felt yesterday?" Jake stepped closer to look at the last panel. "Like you were a bunch of separate parts?"

Will nodded. "Yeah." He ran both palms over his face. "I'm surprised you picked up on it."

"I get more than you give me credit for, little brother. But this"—he got in Will's face and motioned to the walls of paint-splattered canvas—"is a bit frightening."

"I can see how you'd think so. Especially this one." He pointed to the first tarp. "It kind of resembles a crime scene."

"It's violent as fuck." Rick stared up at the slashes of red on beige backdrop. "What the hell were you thinking?"

"I wasn't suicidal or homicidal, if that's what you're asking."

"Good to know," Jake said.

"Have you ever looked at yourself and wished you could start completely over? New skin. New soul. New blood. New life?"

"Yeah." Rick's voice was a mere whisper, but there was truth behind the single syllable. Will should have been surprised, but he wasn't. He'd known Rick was hiding something from them, but he'd been too wrapped up in his own little world to question his brother. He made a mental note to let Rick know he was there for him if he needed anything. Anything at all. It was the least he could do for him, given how much Rick had done for him in the last few weeks.

"Then you might eventually understand. This is me." He swept his arm out to encompass the giant painting. "Bleeding out. Baring my soul. Hari-kari on canvas." He turned his back to the painting, held his arms out wide. "This is the new me. Starting over from scratch."

"What do you mean by starting over?"

Leave it to Jake to grab for something concrete. "I realized yesterday I've been a total shit for most of my life. I've thought of nothing but myself. I separated myself from my family and friends and let people who claimed to be friends but weren't rule my life. This"—he motioned to the still-wet tarps—"is the old me. Gone. I'm starting over. I'm going to paint what I want to paint, not what I think will sell. If I have to paint houses for a living, then so be it." He flashed a half-smile at Rick. "Maybe I can learn a few more things if you're willing to teach me. I'll work for apprentice wages—if you'll have me."

"Fuck, Will." Rick slapped him on the back. "You know I'll be more than happy to have you work with me. You've got a good eye." He pointed at Will's latest art work. "This, notwithstanding. I could use you, especially when it comes to design work."

"You're going to work construction?" Jake didn't even try to keep the skepticism out of his voice. "Seriously?"

"What? You're afraid you're going to have to support me?"

"No. You've got the money back they stole from you. You don't have to work manual labor if you don't want to."

"I want to. I thought I would hate it, but I don't."

Rick stepped between them. "Can we discuss something really important now?"

He'd snagged their attention. "My life isn't important?" Will asked.

"Not saying it isn't. I am wondering what the fuck I'm supposed to do with your self-portrait though. It can't hang here forever. I do use this garage, you know?"

"I was thinking about that. Can you make some big stretchers for me?"

Rick whistled low. "You're going to keep these?"

"Hell, yeah. I need to get them stretched before the paint completely dries. Otherwise, it's going to crack and peel off."

"*Then* what are you going to do with them?"

Will had wanted to do something like this for years, had thought Jessica would be the partner to help him make it happen. Yesterday, he'd realized he didn't need a partner. All he needed was himself. "I went out to Hank's place yesterday. You know how he converted the old barn into offices and a recording studio? I've wanted to do something similar for a long time. I told you about hunting for a place in upstate New York. Since I'm here to stay and I can't live with my baby brother forever, I was thinking of trying to find a farm for sale around here. Something with a barn I can convert to an art studio. I'll hang these on the walls for inspiration."

"Your own place isn't a bad idea." Jake smiled. "I think I might know a place, too."

"You're moving out?"

"Thought you wanted to get rid of me, little brother."

"Not you, just these scary as fuck paintings."

"I promise I'll take them with me." He turned his attention to Jake. "You know a place?"

"I handle a lot of estate work for people around these parts. Remember Bobby Hanover?"

Will searched his memory for the connection. "He was in your grade, right?"

"A year ahead of me. Anyway, his parents are both gone, left the family farm to him. He works for some big hotel chain, travels a lot. Wants nothing to do with the place. He's out of the country right now but said he was going to put it on the market as soon as he gets back. I could contact him, see what he wants for it. Bonus — it's next to my property. We'd be neighbors."

Will dug his phone out and pulled the property up on a popular real estate app. It had everything he wanted, a small house and a big barn that didn't appear too far gone in the photos. They discussed the particulars for a few more minutes then Jake left with a promise to contact the owner. Will was still exhausted, but he felt better than ever. The self-portrait had taken everything he had, mentally and physically, but it had been worth it. He was ready to put New York behind him and start his new life. One with more balance. One where he listened to his muse instead of telling it what to do.

"You ready to talk about the other painting?" Rick nodded at the draped easel stuffed in the corner. Jake hadn't seen it or he would have asked about it, too. The man couldn't help himself. He had to know everything.

Will shrugged. "What about it?"

"Are you going to show it to me? Or is it just going to take up space in my garage?"

He didn't know what he was going to do with it. He couldn't sell it, and the rightful owner didn't want it. "I'll take it with me when I go. Until then, it stays as is."

"What is it, a nude?"

Will's gaze snapped to his little brother.

"What?" Rick raised both eyebrows. "Really? And you aren't going to let me see?"

"Nobody sees it." He found the *I'll pound you into sand* voice he'd used on Rick when they were kids. "No. One. You got it?"

"Okay. Okay. I get it. No peeking."

Will stomped toward the door. "Got any food in this place? I'm starving."

CHAPTER TWENTY-TWO

For the second time in one week, Kenzie looked up from her desk to see one of the Ingram brothers standing in her doorway. She'd never met Jake Ingram, but the familial resemblance was unmistakable. This brother was perhaps a little taller than the other two, but, from the top of his head to his polished dress shoes, this one stood out. Jake's dark suit fit like it had been custom tailored to his broad shoulders and slim hips, physical attributions his brothers shared, but where Rick wore his mahogany hair in a military high-and-tight style, and Will went the other way, wearing his just a tad longer than the current fashion, this Ingram brother wore his hair neatly trimmed in a courtroom-appropriate style, as her father would say. And, like his brother before him, Jake Ingram didn't look particularly pleased to be there.

What now? She sighed and rocked back in her chair.

"A few minutes of your time." One long stride brought him in front of her desk. "I'm Jake Ingram."

"I know who you are." Throwing him out was beyond her abilities. She could call Hank or one of the tech guys working down the hall to assist her, but doing so would only draw attention to a situation she'd rather stay buried. Resigned to hearing him out, Kenzie waved to the chair in front of him. "Have a seat." Before his butt hit the chair, she repeated, "What do you want?"

Jake took his time adjusting his six-foot-plus frame into the tiny chair she'd inherited along with the office. Delay tactics designed to put the opponent on edge. Every lawyer had them. She should know. Her father stood at the top of the lawyer food chain, and he'd gotten there via his superior intimidation skills. Jake was good, but she'd faced down the best. *Get on with it.* She eyed the stack of press releases she still needed to edit and send out. The sooner he had his say, the sooner she could get back to work.

He made a show of straightening the creases in his suit pants then turned his *I'm in charge so don't even think of lying to me* expression on her. Oh, he was good, but compared to Sherman Carlysle, Jake Ingram was a teddy bear. "I'm here on behalf of my brother, William, who also happens to be my client."

"Is your brother planning to sue me?"

"No." He frowned. "Why would he sue you?"

"I don't have any idea." She leaned forward, picked up her discarded pen, and twirled it between her fingers. "But it's the only reason I can think of for you to be here."

Jake cleared his throat. "Well, actually, I came to ask you a few questions."

Though she knew the answer, she asked anyway—couldn't be too careful around lawyer types. She'd learned early on to understand exactly what was being asked and make sure her answer gave nothing else away. "About what?"

"About your relationship with Cecil Hawthorne and your possible involvement in the theft of my brother's paintings."

"My relationship with Cecil Hawthorne is none of your business, and I did not have anything to do with the theft of Mr. Ingram's paintings."

"Will said as much—about the paintings. But I beg to differ on the subject of your relationship with the man who did steal the artwork."

Will told him she didn't steal his paintings? Something inside her broke at his admission. Maybe he didn't hate her after all. *Not* hate wasn't love, but it was *something*. As much as she wanted to help recover the stolen art, she didn't see how anything she knew could be of help. Still…. She owed Will her complete cooperation. It wouldn't change anything between them, but she could answer a few questions. "I told the police everything I knew. I'm afraid it wasn't much. I was as shocked as anyone when I arrived to find the gallery empty." As the words spilled from her mouth, she wondered how many times she was going to have to say them in her lifetime. Would people still be talking about this case when she was old and gray?

"The police weren't overly concerned with locating the paintings. No one even filed missing person reports on Mr. Hawthorne or Ms. Blackwell. They're listed as persons of interest in the reports, so no effort was made to actually locate them."

"No one reported either of them missing?" She'd been so furious and hurt, she hadn't cared where the two of them had gone, but surely a family member had reported them missing by now. "Oh. Are you saying someone knows where they are?"

"I'm thinking it's highly likely someone does. Otherwise, missing person reports would have been filed on them by now, wouldn't you think?"

There was no mistaking the accusation in his voice. Kenzie straightened her shoulders. "Are you insinuating *I* know where they are? Because, if you are, you can get the hell out of my office right now."

"Simmer down, Ms. Carlysle. I'm not insinuating you know anything. I am saying, it's highly likely one or more of their family members know where they are."

"Yet, you're here asking me about them. Why aren't you asking their relatives?"

"Because it's also highly unlikely a relative would give them up."

"I told you, I don't know where Cecil went."

Jake nodded. "I believe you. However, I think you might have information that could lead me to them."

Kenzie shook her head. "I told you. I don't know anything. Cecil and I hardly saw each other for weeks before he disappeared. We talked even less."

"You were handling his business affairs."

"Yes. I was. To an extent. I didn't have access to any of the financial accounts. I could deposit, but not withdraw funds. I sorted his mail. Answered inquiries about the gallery and upcoming openings. It was my job. I did PR for the gallery."

"I don't expect you to remember anything right away, but think back, if you will? Did you see anything come for him from a Realtor or take a phone message from one? Maybe an email you saw or deleted thinking it was spam?"

"You think he's still in the country?"

"I don't know. Perhaps. Unless they stole money from someone other than my brother, they didn't get enough to start a new life abroad, at least not a comfortable one. Even if they did leave the country, I doubt they would have taken the paintings with them. Better to let them cool off for a while then ship them a few at a time. Did Mr. Hawthorne have a storage unit?"

"He did, but I had a key to it. The police checked. It was empty."

"What did he store there?"

"Stuff for the gallery. Pedestals, chairs, tables, tools for hanging paintings. Paint cans. The usual stuff."

"Was it cleaned out, or were those things still there?"

"It was cleaned out. Completely empty."

"Didn't it strike you as odd that he would dispose of mundane items such as you described?"

Had she thought it odd? "I don't recall thinking about it at all. I was in shock, Mr. Ingram. I'm sure I wasn't thinking clearly at the time."

"Which is exactly why I want you to think about it now. Don't force the memories, just let them come. Please, write down anything you remember, even if you don't think it's important. Odd phone calls, emails, letters. Did he take any trips out of town? Or disappear for any length of time you couldn't account for?"

Kenzie scoffed. "He was gone a lot. I couldn't possibly account for his whereabouts with any certainty."

"All I'm asking you to do is try to remember. Any tidbit of information, no matter how insignificant it might seem, could lead me in the right direction."

She didn't want to think about Cecil or what he'd done, but she would. For Will. Before she could think better of it, she asked, "How's your brother?"

Jake's left eyebrow arched. "Why do you ask?"

Damn lawyer. They were all nosy as hell. "Because he was pretty angry when he left here yesterday." She paused, swallowing her pride hard. "I didn't mean to upset him."

Will's brother stared at her until she began to fidget in her seat. "He's been better. He painted all night long."

Kenzie jerked her gaze to his. "He painted?"

"If you could call what he did painting. Looks like mayhem with a paintbrush to me, but he claims it's a self-portrait."

Kenzie felt her heart sink to her toes. "I might have said some things to him…."

"You think?" Jake stood. "I don't know what is going on between you two, but it's got him tied up in knots."

"I'm sorry."

"Don't be. As scary as his latest painting is, at least he's showing emotion. I don't know if getting the stolen art back will help or not, but I'm going to try."

"I'll think about those last few months. If I come up with anything, I'll let you know."

Jake reached into his pocket, drew out a leather card case. He tossed a business card on her desk. "Call me anytime. My cell number is on there as well as my office number."

"Jake."

At the sound of her voice, he turned, his hand on the doorjamb. "What?"

She didn't know why, but, suddenly, she felt the need to come clean with Will's brother. Before she could talk herself out of it, she blurted, "I'm in love with your brother."

With a faint nod to acknowledge her words, Jake continued on his way.

The sound of her desk phone ringing made her nearly jump out of her skin. After a quick deep breath, she picked up the handset. "MacKenzie Carlysle. How may I help you?"

Thanks to the phone call from the tour organizer, Kenzie didn't have a single minute to think about anything but work for the remainder of the day. Adding an extra show at five of their locations required immediate attention to ensure ticket sales wouldn't disappoint. She'd spent the rest of the day working to get the word out. By the time she pulled into her driveway, she wanted nothing more than to crawl under the covers and forget the day had ever happened, but as soon as she saw the work Rick had completed while she was at work, the visit from Jake Ingram popped into her mind and refused to go away.

The rain that had kept Will from working outside was the perfect backdrop for an evening revisiting one of the darkest periods of her life. Curled up on the sofa with a microwaved dinner and a bottle of wine, Kenzie let her thoughts roam to her time with Cecil.

Things had been good at first. He'd been a good boss, and soon after starting to work for him, he'd become an attentive lover. She'd been too shocked by his betrayal to examine the breakdown of their relationship too closely. She'd told the police they'd drifted apart, but was there more to the story?

The job at the gallery had been her first real job, and she'd worked hard to prove she was up to the task of promoting an established art gallery. She'd never once wondered why Cecil had hired her instead of one of the more qualified applicants, of which there had been many. She'd seen for herself when he'd left the applications for her to file. Several had experience with even larger galleries than Hawthorne's. The job should have gone to one of them. But he'd hired her. Then wooed her into his bed a few weeks later.

Sipping her wine and listening to the rain patter on the roof, she tried to look at the broader picture. Had Cecil been planning something even then? Had he hired her because of her inexperience? Because he knew she wouldn't question his actions or realize something was wrong? It was a possibility she hadn't considered before.

Had she been the perfect pawn in a crazy scheme to take W.H. Ingram down? Had she unwittingly played right into Cecil's plans? Had she been stupid, naïve, or just plain snookered?

All of the above.

She'd been played. When she'd asked about her predecessor, Cecil had told her the man had decided to retire outside the city to be close to his grandkids. He'd apparently worked for Cecil for almost a decade. What was his name? Kenzie clutched her wineglass to her breast and closed her eyes, willing the name to come back to her. She'd seen it dozens of times her first few months on the job as she slowly took up the PR reins he'd dropped.

What was it? What was it? Robert. Ronald. Roland. Ross. "Ross something." *It was something Scottish, like MacKenzie.* "McClelland! Ross McClelland!" He'd moved upstate somewhere. She searched her brain for any scrap of memory regarding his new location and came up empty. There had to be a record though. Cecil's accountant would have sent tax information to the man.

It wasn't much, but it was a lead. Ross had worked for Cecil a lot longer than she had. Maybe he knew things. Maybe it was the reason he'd retired.

I need to call Jake.

Kenzie grabbed her cell phone from the coffee table then stopped. Where was the card Jake had given her? *Fuck.* It was on her desk. Buried beneath a week's worth of work still waiting for her. Refusing defeat, she opened an Internet browser. Within seconds, she had a number for Jake Ingram, Attorney at Law. If he was anything like her father, he put in ridiculous hours at the office. She might just catch him there.

After three rings, she got his voicemail. She listened to the usual list—office hours—leave a message. She was about to hang up when the recorded voice added, "If this is an emergency, call 555-1619."

Was it an emergency? No. She didn't need someone to bail her out of jail, but she did want Jake to know she was taking her assignment seriously. Hanging up, she dialed his emergency number.

"Jake Ingram."

"Jake, this is MacKenzie Carlysle. I hope I'm not disturbing you."

CHAPTER TWENTY-THREE

He should get an acting award. He'd snowed his brothers good. They actually thought he'd gotten his shit together. Truth? He was knee-deep in excrement of his own making. Rick had ordered lumber to build the giant stretchers for his self-portrait, the one thing he hadn't lied about, and Jake was looking into property for him to purchase. So, maybe he hadn't lied about spending his money on real estate, either. A house was as good a place as any to invest the funds Jake had recovered. If he'd invested the money he'd made early on when he'd been putting his heart and soul into his paintings instead of squirreling the money away in a standard savings account, Jessica wouldn't have been able to get her hands on every dime. After all this time, he still couldn't believe the amount some of his paintings had sold for. Enough to establish him as a major player in the art world.

Then he'd met Jessica and let her persuade him to paint for the masses. The paintings were good, but, unlike his early work, he hadn't put an ounce of himself into any of them. They sold like snow cones on a summer day, and he'd painted more. The canvases destined for the gallery showing had been worth a small fortune in terms of money, but in art terms, they were emotionless, lifeless crap. Admitting he'd painted crap to feed his bank account hurt like hell, but it was a truth he needed to learn to live with. He'd put more of himself into the nude hidden in the garage and the self-portrait than anything else he'd painted in years. Hell, he'd put more of himself into painting Kenzie's house than he'd put into all the paintings her boss and his girlfriend had stolen.

He'd been motivated by greed. If future art historians even recalled his name, they'd probably dub his time with Jessica as his commercial period. He'd forever think of it as his asshole period. Take that Van Gogh!

Nevermore. If he couldn't make a living selling genuine paintings, he'd slap paint on houses during the day and indulge his muse at night. From now on, he planned to be one thing—authentic. He'd go back to his roots and paint from his heart. Dig down deep in his soul and put his emotions on canvas.

Thanks to a Texas-sized rainstorm, he'd had nothing but time on his hands for the last few days. Rick had offered to show him a few building techniques indoors, but Will had begged off. The last place he wanted to be right now was inside Kenzie's house. He'd borrowed Rick's truck again and made a trip into Dallas for art supplies. He brought a few canvases home with him and arranged for more to be delivered. There was nothing worse than needing to sling paint and having nowhere for it to go. Witness his self-portrait done on paint tarps.

Standing in the garage, listening to the rain on the roof and staring at a blank canvas, Will didn't know what he'd been thinking when he bought the new easel and stack of canvases. He only had one image in his head and it was one he couldn't shake.

MacKenzie Carlysle.

Every time he picked up a paintbrush, all he wanted to paint was her. When he tried to sleep, he dreamed of her. Scorching-hot dreams he feared were actual memories he had no hope of erasing from his mind. Waking from one such dream, Will kicked the sheet aside but refused to take himself in hand to ease the never-ending ache for her. Instead, he did what he always did—thought of the last time he'd seen her.

He'd accused her of all manner of things. Found her guilty by association alone. He'd hurt her with his words, but not nearly as much as he'd hurt her with his actions. Recalling her words as she'd left him standing in her office was enough to extinguish the fire burning inside him every time.

"How could you not know? You were sleeping with Jessica, or had she gotten tired of being treated like a whore and moved on?"

He owed MacKenzie about a dozen apologies. One for every time he'd fucked her then left as if she didn't matter in the least. Several more for thinking then accusing her of any involvement in what Jessica and Cecil had done to him. He owed her an apology for dismissing the love she'd all but confessed when he'd shown her the painting. The love he, himself, had captured for all time when he'd painted her.

Suddenly, he realized what he needed to paint. No need to sketch it first. He knew every line, every shadow, every curve of her face.

"Hey."

Will jerked his hand away from the canvas and spun toward the source of the interruption. Rick stood in the open doorway, rain dripping from the eaves behind him. Seeing it was only his brother, he raised his brush again and contemplated the exact spot where it should touch down. "What? Aren't you supposed to be at the jobsite?"

His brother's gaze darted from the rafters to the floor to his hand gripping the doorframe. "I'm taking the rest of the day off." He swallowed hard. "Friend of mine is going to be in town. Dallas. I'm going to go see him."

Will lowered the brush again and looked at his brother. As far as he knew, Rick hadn't left Willowbrook since the day he'd returned home from his stint in the Marines. He hadn't socialized with any of his old friends and never mentioned any he'd made during his enlistment. He looked nervous as a teenager caught skipping class and…he was taking a day off work. "A Marine buddy?"

"Yeah. Haven't seen him in a while."

"How long's he going to be in town?"

"Just passing through. Flight delay."

Will chuckled. "Know all about them. I'm sure he'll be glad for the distraction." He side-eyed the painting-in-progress. *Best airport distraction ever*. Not everybody could be as lucky as him — like the poor Marine who would have Rick for company. His brother never was much of a talker. These days he rarely said anything.

"I-I'll probably just spend the night."

"Okay. Don't worry about me. I'll be fine."

"If you get a chance, Ms. Carlysle asked if you could start painting the inside of her house since this rain doesn't look like it's going to stop anytime soon."

Will closed his eyes against the jolt of awareness shooting through him at the mention of her name. If he timed it right, he could get the work done while she was at her office. He wasn't ready to see her yet. But Rick had agreed to the job, and Will worked for Rick now. He'd just have to suck it up and do what he needed to do. "Yeah. Did she decide on paint colors?" His dick hardened, recalling the night he'd taken the color palette over to her house. They'd gotten a lot done, but it had nothing to do with paint selections.

"Yep. Bought some, too. Paint cans are in the rooms they go in. Everything else you'll need is in the kitchen. Wants you to start on her bedroom."

Shit. She was trying to torture him. Made perfect sense, given the things they'd said to each other the last time he'd seen her. "Got it. Start in the bedroom." He dropped his brush into a jar of cleaner. "I'll go over after lunch and get started."

"Should be home before lunch tomorrow."

Will kicked the leg of his dad's old workbench. "Fuck." By the time he'd cleaned up and eaten a sandwich on stale bread, he'd forgotten all about Rick's strange behavior. Foremost on his mind was screwing up the courage to walk down the street. *She's at work. Just go in. Do the work and get the heck out before she comes home.*

He knew her usual schedule — set an alarm on his phone for a half hour earlier than she'd ever returned home while he'd been working on her house — then set out to paint. Walls.

Honest work, he reminded himself.

She'd chosen a pale blue for her bedroom. As he moved furniture to the center of the room and covered it with plastic sheeting, he thought she'd done a good job of coordinating her bedding and window treatments with the wall color. The blue would anchor the white comforter and pick up the pattern in the curtains still in their packaging. The completed room would have a classic look. Like the way she dressed.

Did she want the inside of the closet painted, too? He peeked at the interior. The white walls had yellowed with age and were scuffed where shoes and such as had been tossed inside over the years. Yeah, she'd want the closet painted. Which meant her clothes had to go.

It was mostly work clothes, he decided, as he hauled armloads of sexy-as-hell suits to the adjacent bedroom and dropped them on the bed. Resting on the top of the last bundle was the suit she'd had on the day he confronted her in her office. He'd been furious. Beyond seeing straight, but he'd noticed her clothes. Noticed everything about her. She'd worn a soft, cream-colored blouse beneath the hunter-green jacket with a matching pencil skirt. He could still see her ass, perfectly delineated by the fabric as she'd stormed out of the office. Her calves, elongated by the fuck-me heels she'd had on were permanently etched in his brain.

Body parts. He loved body parts. Particularly women's. Calves. Breasts. Fingers. Shoulders. Loved how they all fit together to make a unique work of art. No two were alike, but in his eyes, they were all beautiful. MacKenzie Carlysle, however, put all the others to shame.

His fingers itched for a pencil or charcoal. Anything to record the image playing through his mind like the best porn ever. Running his fingers over the expensive fabric one more time, committing the texture to memory, he went in search of pencil and paper. Fuck the walls. They could wait.

CHAPTER TWENTY-FOUR

As soon as Rick Ingram called to say he was taking the rest of the day off to visit a friend, casually mentioning his brother had promised to get started on the inside painting this afternoon, Kenzie had begun to plan. She'd put in extra hours the last few days and was caught up enough to take a few hours off.

Fortunate to work for a boss who didn't care if she took time off as long as the work got done, she powered down her computer and recorded a *how to reach me in an emergency* message for her office phone. There were rarely emergencies in her line of work, but when one came up, it had to be dealt with posthaste or things could go sideways. She'd put too much work into BlackWing's upcoming tour promo to let something muck it all up. No matter what she had planned for the next twelve hours or so, she would only be a phone call away if disaster happened.

There was no one to save her if things went sideways at her house, which was highly likely. She was starting at rock bottom with William H. Ingram. Their relationship had begun at a crisis point for both of them, sped headlong into entanglement before it hit the median dividing their lives.

She'd said awful things to him the day he'd come to her office wearing his heart on his sleeve, not blaming her, only asking, why? She didn't have an answer for him, so she'd struck back, put the burden for everything their former lovers had done to him square on his shoulders.

It wasn't one of her better moments. She had a lot to answer for.

The house was silent as a tomb. Accustomed to hearing the music Rick kept on while he worked, she'd expected Will to do the same. Which meant the bastard hadn't shown up to paint the way he'd said he would. Frustrated, she stood just inside the front door, wondering if she should go to the office or stay home. Everything she needed to paint the walls was here, and she could search the Internet for instructions. Despite her decision not to pursue a law degree the way her dad had wanted, she wasn't a dummy. She could learn to paint.

Fuck Will Ingram. I'll do it myself.

Kenzie dropped her briefcase and purse on the sofa, stuffed her cell phone in the back pocket of her new jeans then went in search of old clothes to paint in. Determination or not, she wasn't stupid enough to believe she could paint without getting as much on her as she put on the walls.

Nearing the first, and smallest, of the two bedrooms, a slight sound caught her attention. Mice? God, she hoped not. Stopping to listen, she heard it again. Not mice then, which meant someone else was in the house. Creeping as much as her new western boots allowed, she made her way down the hall and peeked around the corner. Will Ingram sat on the floor in her spare room, a crude board against his raised knees, sheets of paper he'd no doubt lifted from the stack she kept next to the home printer on the living room shelf. The floor surrounding him was littered with discarded drawings. Next to his right hip sat the earthenware coffee cup holding the pencil collection she'd started as a child. If she wasn't mistaken, the writing implement currently in Will's hand bore the name and address of Sunny Sheldon's gallery in Manhattan. Her friend would be pleased to see the inexpensive advertising had made it all the way to Texas. Even more pleased to know an artist of Will's caliber was using it to draw…what, exactly?

He didn't seem to know she was there. Brow crinkled in concentration, Will focused entirely on whatever he was drawing at the time. Kenzie edged around the corner, leaned against the jamb, arms and legs crossed in a casual pose. How many people could say they'd watched the process of a world famous artist? Not many. She was one of the lucky ones, luckier still to be the subject of all his concentration, for, as she focused in on some of the discarded sheets of computer paper, his subject matter became clear. They were all drawings of her. Sitting behind her desk. Walking out her office door. Bent over the table in her kitchen. Looking up at him on the ladder outside her house. They were crude, mostly just lines to suggest a pose, but with enough detail to be unmistakable to someone who had been in those positions.

What the hell is he doing? She was about to ask when he tossed another drawing onto the floor and reached for another blank page. "Don't fucking move."

Then the pencil was flying across the page. "Where'd you get the jeans?" He didn't so much as pause as he flung the question at her.

"Um. There's a store in Fort Worth. Cathy told me about it." She'd stocked up on jeans and dressy-but-practical cotton blouses to go with the boots she'd purchased at the store over on Main Street. In New York, suits had been the attire of choice for women in the workplace. Not so much here, and, after a few days wearing casual clothes to the office, she was beginning to see the benefit of dressing down. Suits required rigid posture, which, in turn, required energy to maintain. The last few days, she'd come home less fatigued than ever before. Then there was the dry cleaning bill she wouldn't miss.

Kenzie glanced at the pile of clothes on the bed Will leaned against. She'd keep some of the suits for business meetings and those rare trips to New York Hank had warned her about. She'd find a place to donate the remainder. Maybe one of those places where they helped women dress for job interviews and new careers. Her mother had supported one in D.C. for years.

"Unbutton the jeans."

Her gaze snapped back to Will. "What?"

"Do it. Now. Unbutton your jeans. Slide the zipper down."

He was insane, but she did it anyway.

"Fold the sides back. Let me see your panties then put your hands behind you. Yeah, perfect. Don't move."

Another drawing joined the stack on the floor as he grabbed another sheet of paper and began to draw. "What are you doing?"

"Drawing, what does it look like?"

"You were supposed to be painting my bedroom."

"And you're supposed to be at work."

She shrugged. "I came home early to talk to you."

Silence broken only by the scratch of pencil on paper stretched between them. Her fingers were going numb pressed between her ass and the doorjamb. After what seemed like a lifetime, he tossed another drawing aside and reached for another sheet of paper.

"Keep your left hand behind you. Slide your right one inside your panties. Not too far. Perfect."

Yep. I'm insane, she thought as his gaze roamed over her before he bent to his task. She'd never seen him like this, and she had to admit, Will Ingram in full-artist mode was sexy as hell. Trying to forget her fingers were brushing her bare mound, she focused on him instead. His hair was longer than when she'd first seen him, and it had been longer than current fashion then. A couple days stubble covered his jaw, and he'd clearly not spent any time shaping it up. No, he'd simply forgotten, or chose not to shave. God, how she'd love to feel his scruff against her skin. *Don't go there.* Just because she was posing for him didn't mean they'd settled anything. She'd come to talk to him, so talk she would.

"I'm sorry about what I said to you the other day."

"No need," he said, his hand still flying across the page. "You were right."

"No, I wasn't. None of this was your fault. You were the victim. It wasn't right to blame you."

"Forget it, Kenzie. It's done. Jessica and Cecil can go fuck themselves."

"I can't help feeling responsible. I should have known something was up. I was too caught up in my own misery at the time to think clearly."

"Didn't help that the police hardly asked you anything."

"No, it didn't. My dad might have had something to do with the light interrogation."

"Your dad, the attorney general?"

"You know?"

He nodded. "Jake told me."

She should have known his brother would want to know why the police had dismissed her involvement almost from the get-go. She'd made the mistake of calling her mother, the only parent who had encouraged her to find her own way in the world. Within minutes, her dad, the attorney general of the United States had spoken with someone in New York. A heartbeat later she'd been cleared of any involvement. The questions had stopped immediately. "Did he also tell you I gave him a name to chase down? Cecil's former PR guy?"

"He told me." *Skritch. Scratch.* "He's on his way to New York as we speak." *Skritch. Scratch.* "Doesn't matter though. I don't want the paintings back."

She gasped. "What? Why?"

"They're crap. I hope they burned them. Save me the trouble."

"You don't mean that."

"I do." Another drawing slid across the floor. A clean sheet of paper took its place on his crude lap board. "Use your left hand to unbutton your blouse. Just a couple of buttons. Yes. Perfect. Now slide your fingers inside your bra. Make your nipple hard."

"Will."

"Just do it, Kenzie."

She did.

"Slide your right hand down more. Find your heat and stay there. Chin down. Drop your eyelids. Not too much, slumberous. Yes, perfect. Lips parted. Damn, you're so natural. Perfect."

Skritch. Scratch.

She'd been naked with the man, but standing like this, fully clothed, she felt more exposed than ever. Her heart beat like a hammer behind her left palm, and the fingers of her right hand were wet. So damn wet. Her clit throbbed. Will barely spared her a glance then bent to his work. All focused concentration while she was dying a slow death against a doorjamb in sore need of a fresh coat of paint. In an effort to distract her thoughts from the sorry state of her body, the need pulsing through her, she forced her mind to think of something else.

This had been her boss's room when he was a boy. Some of the grimy handprints on the jamb were probably his. And some could be Will's. They'd been boyhood friends. Had spent time in each other's houses. They weren't boys anymore. They were full-grown men, and my, hadn't they turned out well? Hank was gorgeous. Talented beyond belief, but he did nothing for her. Not even a twinge of interest there.

But Will? He was another story altogether. She'd wanted him from the first moment she'd laid eyes on him. She hadn't known who he was. Didn't care. She'd simply known she had to have him, even if it was just one time. It should have been enough. But it wasn't. She'd never get enough.

"Just a little longer. Now, touch yourself. Make it feel good. But don't come. Not yet."

She didn't think about what she was doing as she uncrossed her ankles, spread her legs, and shoved her hand deeper between her legs to do as he said. One finger wasn't enough. She pushed a second then a third inside her tight channel. Her thumb brushed her clit. Again. And again.

"Don't fucking come." *Skritch. Scratch.* "Not until I tell you to."

"Will. Please."

CHAPTER TWENTY-FIVE

She was fucking killing him. He'd thought her sexy in her fancy business suits. But those jeans. And those fucking boots. When she'd leaned against the doorframe, it had been all he could do to remain where he was and not go to her.

They needed to talk. He had been avoiding her for days because he couldn't keep his hands off her. Sketching turned out to be his salvation. He could talk and sketch. And look his fill while doing so.

He'd never sketched so fast, but he needed to record the basics of what he was seeing. He'd never forget the way she was right that minute—leaning against a doorjamb, busy getting herself off for him. Goddamn, the image would be in his brain for the rest of his life. It was the fine details—the way her blouse draped around the hand inserted inside it. The folds of her jeans where she'd inadvertently pushed them lower on her hips to accommodate her other hand. The angle of her legs, spread to allow access to her core. He might get those right from memory, but he couldn't be certain he would, not when every molecule of his being was focused on the expression on her face and the little moans and breathless gasps coming from her mouth. Her very kissable, fuckable mouth.

The woman was his Kryptonite. She destroyed him with a look. With his name on her lips. With her very being.

Fuck the sketch. He'd have to rely on his memory.

Tossing aside the slab of plywood he'd found in the trash pile Rick had yet to remove from the kitchen, Will got to his feet. A second later, he stood before her, his fingers gripping her waist. "Don't stop."

"Will."

He didn't miss the plea in her voice. He understood her need all too well. He was hurting, too.

"Ken. Baby." Then his mouth was on hers, his lips moving, devouring hers, his tongue tasting, promising as he matched her fingers below, thrust for thrust. Touching her was pure heaven. Her body was a perfect match to his. Her need, her desire equal to his.

The need to dominate, to have her submit to him, to claim her, had been there from the beginning.

Skimming the outside of her blouse, he brushed his thumbs over the gentle swells of her breasts. He covered the one she hadn't been able to reach and squeezed. She broke their kiss, a groan escaping her lips. So fucking perfect. He couldn't take it another second.

As he tugged her hands from their duties, her eyes popped open, a question and a protest written in their depths. Gazes locked, he brought her wet fingertips up to his mouth, sucked her essence from them. "Turn around." The vulnerability in her gaze nearly broke him. "I won't leave you this time. Promise. I just need to do this to you. With you."

Every breath she took brought her breasts in contact with his chest as she looked into his eyes, searching for the words she needed from him. Words she deserved.

"After, Ken. Give me this then I'll give you what you want."

To his everlasting relief, she spun in his arms to face the doorjamb. He pressed his front to her back until there was no place for her to go. Skimming his hands from her shoulders to her wrists, he threaded his fingers through hers, stretching their arms above her head on either side of the jamb. With a flex of his hips, he drove hers up against the unforgiving wood.

He ducked his head, flicked out his tongue to taste a drop of sweat trickling from behind her ear down her neck. The salty flavor melded well with the lingering sweetness of her juices on his tongue. She smelled like sunshine, inexplicable on this cloudy, rainy day. *She'll always be my sunshine. The light at the end of my tunnel.*

He sucked in another lungful of her then brushed his lips over the shell of her ear and breathed out. "Fuck the doorjamb, Ken. Make yourself come right here. Right now."

She tensed for the span of a heartbeat then her hips began to move. "Perfect, baby. Fuck it. Get yourself off." His words were nasty, just the way she liked them. Finding her rhythm, he flexed his hips against her ass, driving her up and hard, making sure she found the contact, the pressure she needed to get off. "God, baby, you're fucking making me jealous of a piece of wood. Fuck it good, baby. Grind it."

Her fingers tightened in his grip. Her movements became erratic as she chased her orgasm. When it hit, a sob broke from her lips as she shamelessly rode the doorframe into ecstasy. He held her pinned there until spent, she sagged in his arms.

"So fucking beautiful, Ken. I've got to have you."

"Yes."

His arms full of woman, Will stood looking down at the only bed in the house he had any intention of using. The one in the other room wasn't near big enough for what he had in mind. "Fuck." He didn't want to put Kenzie down, but the plastic he'd thrown over her bed had to go.

"I've got it. Dip me down."

He bent his knees until she was able to grab a corner of the plastic. Walking backwards while she tugged, they managed to uncover the mattress.

"We're good together."

"No argument there." He tossed her to the center of the bed then grabbed one of her feet. "Nice boots but they've got to go." Yanking on the heel, he pulled until her foot popped free. After repeating the process with her other foot, he reached for the waistband of her jeans then stopped.

"Turn over. Let me see your ass in these jeans." She rolled over without argument. Propped on her elbows, she glanced over her shoulder. "Like what you see?"

He'd thought her ass perfect in those pencil skirts she favored, but that was before he saw her in a pair of jeans. She'd tempt a saint to sin, and he was far from sainthood. "Fucking hell, woman. You aren't going out in public in these, are you?"

"Of course I am, why?"

"Because I'm going to have to murder a hell of a lot of people for looking at what's mine."

"Yours?"

He raised one eyebrow.

"Okay, yours, but I'm still wearing them to work. They're comfortable."

He growled. Actually growled, which made the damn woman laugh as she flipped onto her back. They'd discuss her wardrobe choices another time.

"As spectacular as your ass is in these, they have to go, too."

"Then, by all means." She planted her bare feet on the mattress and lifted her hips. Hooking his fingers in the waistband, he tugged them past her hips then grabbed the hem of both legs to pull them the rest of the way off, leaving her bare from the waist down except for a fucking pair of white, lace-trimmed boy-short style panties he'd only caught a glimpse of before.

"Fuck, Ken."

A single finger traced the lace spanning her hips. "Like these, too?"

"You know I fucking do. But they've got to go. I need to see all of you."

"Not until you tell me."

Will ducked his head. Hands on his hips, he studied the toes of his shoes. He'd promised to give her the words she needed. Hell, he needed to say them. He just didn't know if he could, not with barriers between them. "Not like this." He kicked off his shoes then grabbed his T-shirt and yanked it over his head. His pants were next, along with his socks and underwear. "Naked. Nothing between us, Ken."

She looked at him like he was a piece of candy and she'd been on a decade-long diet. "Okay. But you promised. You aren't trying to distract me, are you?" She licked her bottom lip, and his dick throbbed.

Will groaned. "No. Trust me. I need to be inside you. And you need to feel me, too. There's nothing but truth when we're together."

Without further argument, she wiggled out of her panties then sat up to remove her blouse and bra. He stood, watching her practiced movements, not meant to tease but driving him insane anyway. Then she scooted up to the headboard, lay back, and spread her legs in invitation.

"Christ, Ken."

He was on her, in her before he drew his next breath. Her legs closed around his hips, anchoring him in place while her arms encircled his neck. Will lowered himself until they were pressed together from chest to groin. One.

Keeping as much weight as possible on his forearms, he cradled her face in his palms, brushed her cheekbones with his thumbs. He'd never felt this kind of connection with another human being. Never felt like he'd come home when he'd coupled with a woman. Never wanted to stay right where he was for the rest of his life. The thought was daunting, but there it was. She made him want to be the man she thought he was. He gazed into her eyes, and the words he feared he'd never be able to say tumbled from his lips.

"I've been an ass. A friggin' moron. I said things I didn't mean. I used you. Hurt you. I can't tell you how sorry I am for all of it. Not for fucking you blind at the airport. I'll never regret being with you, only the way I left you. I wasn't ready for a relationship, and what I felt with you scared the bejesus out of me. I walked. No, I ran, as fast and as far as I could. But you found me. And there was no way I could keep my hands off you. I needed you. And every time we were together, the need for you grew stronger and I ran faster in the other direction."

He moved inside her because he had to. Couldn't hold the need at bay any longer. "Then one night, the need overcame the fear, and, instead of coming to you, telling you what was going on in my head, I painted you. I didn't realize the secrets you held until I saw them in the painting. I was willing to ignore them, have you, no matter what you were hiding. Then I found out, and god, I lost it."

Flexing his hips, he pulled out then joined with her again, slowly filling her so both of them felt the connection being made. "I lashed out. Blamed you for everything wrong in my life, but you set me straight. I didn't see it at first, but when I did, I had to paint you again. Had to paint what I see when I look at you."

"What do you see?"

"Perfection. My heart." He pulled out once more and drove back in, more forceful this time. "I love you, MacKenzie Carlysle. I think I fell in love with you the minute you propositioned me at the airport bar."

Her eyes misted over. "Oh, Will. I fell in love with you when you asked me if I knew a place we could go. I needed to feel alive, to be desired. You gave me exactly what I asked for then broke my heart."

"I'm so sorry, Kenzie, baby." He retreated then advanced again. "I was in over my head in so many ways. I was afraid to stay. Afraid I'd follow you wherever you were going and I'd never find myself again."

"I guess it's lucky we were going to the same place."

"Fate."

This time, when he moved, she moved with him.

"I love you, MacKenzie."

"I love you, too."

THE END

Ingram
Brothers #
JAKE
USA TODAY BESTSELLING AUTHOR
ROZLEE

CHAPTER ONE

Jake Ingram paced the confines of his office. He'd changed nothing, not the ugly carpet, not the heavy oak desk, not a picture or a book on the massive library shelves taking up one entire wall, since the day he'd stepped in to take over his father's mediocre law practice nearly a decade ago.

He wanted out. Not only out of the office. Out of the stagnant life he'd made for himself. Despite never wanting to be a lawyer, he was good at what he did. He helped people and made a decent living at it. But, on days like today, these four walls were a prison he couldn't escape. The large picture window looking out on a well-maintained courtyard behind the building should have provided solace, but, instead, it reminded him of a zoo enclosure, but he was on the wrong side of the glass.

He stopped his pacing to watch a squirrel dart around the lawn, grabbing up whatever it could find in the way of food. He understood the rodent's anxiety. Jake's belly was full, but he couldn't shake the emptiness inside.

These feelings weren't new. He'd recognized them long ago and successfully shoved them aside—until now. Ever since he'd laid eyes on the self-portrait his brother Will painted, the hollow pit in his gut had grown wider and deeper.

He closed his eyes against the hot sun beating down on the courtyard, and Will's painting immediately came to mind. It consisted of three enormous canvases he'd hung from the joists in their other brother, Rick's, garage. Each panel, covered with splashes of color, represented different facets of his brother—or so Will claimed. Will Ingram was a broken man, evidenced by the violent way he'd slung the paint—as if he'd dug into his soul with his bare hands and flung the ugliness away.

He'd pretended confusion at what Rick deemed a mess in his garage, but Jake instantly recognized the pain behind the painting. Staring at the slashes of black and red had been like looking in a mirror. He didn't know what hurt more, seeing his own unhappiness, his lack of fulfillment hanging there for all to see, or discovering the depth of his brother's despair matched his own.

He swallowed a groan then rubbed his palms over his face and turned toward his desk and the note his admin left for him. The private investigator he'd hired to look for the lowlifes who'd stolen Will's paintings had called. He closed the mental door on his own misery and focused on his brother's case. Since baring his soul in the painting, Will was in a better frame of mind these days. He'd opened up about his ordeal in New York, how he'd been duped by Jessica Blackwell, his fiancée/agent, and the gallery owner, Cecil Hawthorne, she'd secretly been sleeping with. Between the two of them, they'd emptied his bank accounts and made off with close to a million dollars' worth of Will's canvases.

Jake managed to recover most of his brother's cash by convincing the banker his employee had made a huge mistake by turning the funds over to someone who wasn't signatory on the account. Faced with the facts, he'd opted to replace the lost money. His brother said the paintings didn't matter, and maybe they didn't to the new Will Ingram, but Jake knew in his gut, sooner or later, the canvases would surface in the future. He wanted to find them and the people who'd snatched them before the culprits struck again. His brothers were all the family he had left, and he'd do anything to protect them.

Still too agitated to sit, he picked up the phone and dialed the private detective's number.

***

Jake waved and smiled at the TSA agent guarding the funnel from the gates to baggage claim at New York's JFK airport. The guy probably was calling for backup now, but he didn't care. He wasn't in Willowbrook, and he was going to take full advantage of this rare opportunity to breathe.

He loved his hometown, and he loved his brothers, Will and Rick, but he'd never planned on spending his entire adult life living in someone else's shoes.

He located the car and driver he'd hired waiting for him outside baggage claim and followed the man out into the humidity. Texas could be a bitch in the summer, but New York won the misery contest, hands down. He aimed to be in the city for a day or two then he was heading upstate where he hoped the hunting and the weather would be better. His prey had long since left town. Manhattan was big, but it was also expensive. Plus, why risk being seen by friends or old associates? It made more sense for the thieves to skedaddle, to lie low until their trail grew cold and it was safe to put the next phase of their plan into action. He suspected the culprits planned to ransom Will's paintings back to him—otherwise, why not destroy them at the gallery?

Which brought up another question. How did they transport all those canvases? It was a question he'd asked his private investigator to look into and hoped the answer would provide a solid lead.

Jake checked into his hotel then walked the few blocks to the private detective's midtown office. The small office occupied space in a century-old building but was, nonetheless, neat and well-kept. While he waited for his appointment, he studied the colorful nature photographs adorning the reception area walls. He'd hired Philip Holland on the recommendation of a friend from law school, and, so far, he hadn't been disappointed. His work was thorough and often went beyond Jake's expectations, and though he'd talked with the investigator on multiple occasions, he was looking forward to meeting him in person.

At the sound of heavy footsteps approaching, he turned. Philip Holland looked exactly as Jake had pictured him. Standing just under six feet with a slight paunch, the former NYPD detective who'd put in his twenty years before retiring to open his own business wore a brown, off-the-rack suit, a beige dress shirt, and a patterned tie Jake estimated to be older than he was. Lines deeply engraved around his eyes and lips spoke of years of cigarette use and things seen but not forgotten. With his thinning hair and scuffed brown dress shoes he'd blend into any crowd. "Mr. Ingram, I presume."

"Jake, please. You must be Mr. Holland." He extended his arm and they shook hands.

"You can call me Philip. It's a pleasure to meet you." He spoke to his receptionist. "If Sanderson calls, put him through. Otherwise, take a message."

Holland's office was as neat and stylish as the public space. Where the reception area had hardwood flooring, the boss's office boasted plush carpeting and a wall of windows overlooking the busy street below. The investigator took a seat behind his contemporary, industrial-chic style desk, waving Jake to a worn leather chair facing him.

They discussed Jake's trip and complained about the weather before the PI opened a file and got down to business. "You asked me to look into several things for you. Have you changed your mind about any of them?"

He appreciated the man's discretion, but he'd made up his mind. "No. This is my brother's livelihood, and possibly his life, we're talking about. I can't afford to assume anything about anyone involved."

"Okay, then." He sat forward and put on a pair of black-rimmed reading glasses. "I don't think there's anything new to report on Cecil Hawthorne's former PR woman, MacKenzie Carlysle. She never lied about who she was, and any cover-up of her involvement appears to have been her father's doing, not hers. Everyone I spoke with said the same thing—she's honest and hardworking. She's never used her father's influence to obtain a job or social status. What little she has, she's worked for."

"Her ending up in Willowbrook was coincidence?"

"As far as I can see, yes. When she left New York, she was practically penniless. Her bank account didn't have enough in it to pay the monthly service fee, and she was charging everything to a credit card she'd had for years and rarely used. She'd been living in a friend's apartment, sleeping on a cot in the closet, until another friend, Sunny Sheldon, helped her find the job in Texas. Her current employer paid for her plane ticket to Dallas; otherwise, she would have been hitchhiking."

"She didn't go to her father for help?"

"I couldn't find any evidence she asked him for assistance. Her roommate said MacKenzie and her father had an ongoing disagreement about her decision not to go to law school. According to her, they hadn't spoken in years."

"But he intervened on her behalf with the NYPD."

"The lead investigator, Detective Reeves, mentioned her father made some calls. In the detective's defense, he said the girl was so squeaky clean he saw no reason to look any closer at her."

After what his brother told him about the way he and MacKenzie met, the way she ended up in Willowbrook at the same time had raised questions in Jake's mind—and Will's, too. It was a relief to know she'd been telling the truth about her lack of involvement in the theft. "When I talked to her, she seemed genuine in her desire to help. She was the one who gave me the lead about Ross McClelland."

"Speaking of." He shuffled the papers in the file. "I think we've located him. My associate, Mike Sanderson, is checking into it as we speak. If it is him, he lives in Callicoon, a tiny little community up in the Catskills. I can have Sanderson question him if you like."

Jake shook his head. "I'd prefer to do it myself, unless you think he's dangerous?"

"I doubt it. He's seventy-five years old and in failing health."

"I'll go talk to him, see if he knows anything we can use to track down Hawthorne."

Holland turned the McClelland report facedown then picked up another one. "We also located the real estate agent your brother and his former fiancée, Jessica Blackwell spoke to. Sanderson didn't question the woman, per your request."

"I'll talk to her, too."

"Let me remind you, these individuals could be dangerous. If you get too close, no telling what they might do to protect their secrets."

"I understand. If I find Hawthorne and Blackwell, or get even the slightest hint of danger, I'll get the police involved."

"Sanderson is available if you want company."

"I don't plan to go alone." Unless the PI's final report changed his mind.

"Good to know." He set aside the real estate agent's file and picked up another. "That brings us to your final inquiry, Sunny Sheldon."

At the mention of the gallery owner, Jake's entire body responded. He'd met her briefly the last time he'd come to the city. There'd been a spark between them, but, at the time, she'd been on his list of suspects, potential accomplices in the disappearance of his brother's paintings. He'd had plenty of experience with liars and knew you couldn't always rely on your ability to ferret one out. Sometimes, you needed to dig deeper to locate the deceit. So, he'd added Sunny to the investigator's list. He nodded for the man to continue.

"Most everything about Ms. Sheldon is public knowledge. Her father is Curtis Sheldon, the actor. She grew up in the public eye, at her father's side for most of the major accomplishments in his life. Her parents divorced when she was a baby, but they shared custody. Her mother is from a well-known New York family and currently resides in Los Angeles. Ms. Sheldon inherited a great deal of money from her maternal grandmother, as well as a historic brownstone here in the city. She's lived independently since she was eighteen. Bought what is now Sunnyside Gallery, when she was twenty-one. Never been married. Dates occasionally but has never been involved in any kind of scandal, celebrity or otherwise. Never done drugs. Doesn't drink to excess. Stays to herself, except for attending gallery openings and charity events. She still does the occasional red-carpet event with her father. When she is confronted by paparazzi, she lets them take a few photos then moves on. Therefore, there are lots of pictures of her which makes them virtually worthless to someone who makes a living selling celeb photos."

"Any hint of a relationship with Cecil Hawthorne or Jessica Blackwell?"

"None. She knows them. Everyone in the art world does, but like everybody else we talked to, they were acquaintances, not friends."

"Cecil and Jessica didn't have any friends in the industry?"

"I didn't find any. They kept to themselves. It's not unheard of in this city. Acquaintances and associates are easy to come by. Friends, not so much. MacKenzie Carlysle and Sunny Sheldon are exceptions to the rule. They both have a lot of friends who sing their praises."

Jake nodded. "Got anything else?"

"Not at this time. Sanderson hasn't called. I'll let you know when I hear from him. I'm 99 percent certain the guy in Callicoon is our man, but there's no use going all the way out there if it turns out he's not." He arranged all the papers back in the folder then slid it across the desk. "These are your copies."

He took the folder and stood. The two men shook hands. "Thanks for all your hard work."

"All in a day's work."

The heat out on the sidewalk made him wish he'd called the car service again, but the walk to his hotel was a short one. Entering the lobby, he made a beeline for the bar where he ordered a cold beer and drank it while reading through the reports Philip had compiled. He skimmed the ones on top, eager to get to the last one.

Sunny Sheldon had occupied his thoughts and his dreams since the first moment he'd seen her. On his previous trip to the Big Apple to straighten out Will's finances, he'd stopped by her gallery to ask her some questions. If he'd been a celebrity follower, he probably would have recognized her. But he didn't have time for frivolous things, hardly watched TV, and couldn't recall the last time he'd been to a movie theater. When she'd invited him to her office for tea, the photos of her and her father scattered around her private space revealed her identity.

He'd been attracted to her from the start, but her celebrity status and her friendship with MacKenzie Carlysle made him reluctant to ask her out. Thus, the report. He didn't desire fame, or infamy, and he sure didn't need to complicate his brother's situation by getting involved with a potential suspect.

Will had assured him the gallery owner wasn't involved, and Jake had thought the same after talking to her. The inquiry was a safety measure because she tripped wires in his brain, and he didn't trust himself to make a rational decision where she was concerned. If he was seriously considering asking her to accompany him on his trip upstate, then it had been way too long since he'd been with a woman.

CHAPTER TWO

Sunny paced the gallery floor, devoid of customers on this hot, sticky summer day. She should have closed shop and gone out to the Hamptons like every other New Yorker and left the steamy streets to the tourists. She'd put off the trip because *he* might come back. Jake Ingram.

Only an idiot spent her days wishing a man would call, and her nights wishing she'd tried harder to get the sexy Texan in her bed when she'd had the chance.

She hadn't seen or heard from him in a month.

If his disappearing act didn't scream not interested, nothing did.

Yet, here she sat, bored and pining for someone who probably forgot she existed the minute he walked out the door of her gallery.

He'd said he would return.

And like a fool, she'd believed him. She'd waited for a call saying he was on the way.

He'd pledged to return, but his eyes vowed so much more. The unspoken promise of sex hot enough to set off the fire alarm kept her awake at night, wondering what his hands and lips would feel like on her skin. Wondering if making love with a man like him would live up to her imagination. There wasn't anything metrosexual about him. No fancy hair gel. No manicures, and she guessed, no manscaping. He made no excuses for being a man.

The long, tall Texan wasn't anything like the men she met in New York. They were all so polite, so afraid they'd be accused of sexual harassment if they showed any genuine interest. They'd never look at her like a starving man with her the last pastry on the planet. Only Jake Ingram had ever done so.

No, there was nothing wishy-washy about Jake. The man exuded alpha-male confidence from the crown of his dark head to the tips of his western boots.

He'd be the kind to take control in the bedroom, like he did in the courtroom. Yeah, sue her. She'd googled him, all the while hoping he hadn't done the same to her. He already knew about her famous father, and perhaps her minor celebrity status had scared him away. No guy wanted to end up on the cover of a tabloid because they dated the wrong woman. If he'd given her a chance, she could have explained. The paparazzi didn't care about her unless she did something with her dad or for a charity. Boring didn't sell papers, and her life defined boredom. He had nothing to fear.

But he'd never given her the chance to tell him. He'd gone home to Texas, leaving her with more fantasies than she knew what to do with. She spent way too much time daydreaming about a man who, despite his promise to return, had probably forgotten all about her the second he'd left .

"Enough!" Sunny verbally scolded herself then stomped off to her office. It was time to stop acting like a lovesick teenager and get on with her life. Jake went home where he probably had a stable of fillies eager to give him a ride whenever the mood struck. The Texan wasn't the kind of man who did without or who saw to his own needs.

She took a minute to call the garage where she stored her car then powered the computer system down and grabbed her purse. She'd go home, pack a bag, and go to the beach. She checked the lock on the back door then turned out lights as she made her way to the front of the shop. What remained of the daylight and the spotlights trained on the window display provided ample illumination. She stopped for a moment to turn off the lamp on the front desk when movement outside the front window caught her attention.

A customer, perhaps. Her only one today and reason to wait a few moments to see. Edging closer, she peeked out the window. Her heart skipped a beat.

She blinked then took another peek. Her mind wasn't playing tricks on her. Jake Ingram had returned. Deferring to the heat, he'd left off his suit coat and rolled up the sleeves of his dress shirt to reveal muscular forearms as he stood on the sidewalk, eyes downcast, hands stuffed in the pockets of his light-gray dress slacks. He looked good enough to eat.

Her heart tumbled. Was this a business call and he was choosing his words carefully to catch her in a lie? She had nothing more to add to her statement. She'd told him everything. She'd done her best to help him and his brother. She genuinely liked Will Ingram and hoped he was painting again. She'd take anything he wanted to sell. His older brother, however, was another story. He seemed to be the opposite of the well-known painter, yet she was drawn to him. Wanted to get to know him better.

Gritting her teeth against the bitter disappointment brewing in her gut, she crossed to the door and jerked it open. "Are you going to stand here all day, or are you coming in?"

Jake's chin rose, and the expressive eyes etched into her memory from a month ago met hers. The smile breaking across his face incinerated her anger. "I was waiting for you. I saw the lights go out, figured you were closing early, so I waited." He took a step forward. "Didn't want to spook you by coming in."

"Spook me?" New Yorkers didn't spook people. They scared the shit out of them, but spook? No. "Is that Texan for give me a heart attack?"

"You know it, darlin'." His gaze swept past her to the darkened and deserted shop. "Everyone gone for the day?"

"It's just me today. It's too hot for people to be out shopping."

"I won't argue with you. It is hot out here. Looks cooler in there." He nodded to the interior of the shop.

"Would you like to come in?"

"Don't mind if I do."

She turned the Open sign to Closed and threw the dead bolt. They stood facing each other, ambient light from the street and the window spotlights casting shadows over their features.

"Give me a second. I'll turn on some lights."

"No need. I didn't come to see the artwork."

"What did you come for, Jake?"

He gave the place a cursory glance then his gaze landed on her, and, with a little huff of breath, he confessed, "I don't have the faintest idea." He gave her his back. One strong hand kneaded the nape of his neck. This wasn't the same confident, bordering-on-arrogant man she'd met months ago. What had made him this indecisive?

"Are you here on business?" she prompted. "Did you find your brother's paintings?" If he'd recovered them, she'd do whatever it took to consign some. W.H. Ingram's paintings always sold well in her shop.

At her questions, Jake faced her, shaking his head. "I haven't found the paintings, but I have a couple of leads. I need to go upstate, chase a few people down who might have answers." He glanced at the floor then lifted his gaze to hers. "I could use some company." His lips quirked up on one corner. "Want to ride along?"

Sunny's jaw dropped. Surely, she'd misheard. "You want me to go with you?"

He nodded, and she glimpsed the banked heat in his eyes. So maybe all the sexy dreams she'd had about him weren't as one-sided as she'd thought. Upstate could be as miserable, weather-wise, as the city, but if the company was good, a woman might overlook a few inconveniences. "How long will you be gone?"

"Don't know. A few days? A week?"

She could call Ginger. Ask her to open the shop a few hours a day while she was gone. "Where're you going?"

"Not a clue."

"Then you'll need a guide." She hadn't spent much time upstate, but her dad owned a house in Westchester. Getting there and back without getting lost wouldn't be a problem.

"Yeah. I guess I will. You up for the job?"

Her heart raced as she pretended to consider his offer, when she didn't care where he was going as long as he wanted her along. It had been way too long since she'd experienced the intense attraction Jake inspired. She'd watched him walk away once. She had no intention of letting it happen again. "I'm in." She picked up her purse from where she'd left it on the desk. "When do we leave?"

Jake followed her. "Tomorrow?"

Sunny opened the door, ushered Jake to the sidewalk, then locked the door. "How about tonight? I can be ready in an hour."

***

Sunny studied the man behind the Jeep's wheel. She'd never seen Jake in anything but a suit and took in his "casual" attire—worn jeans, a crisp white button-down shirt, sleeves rolled up to reveal strongly muscled forearms. The man was gorgeous. The cowboy boots were sexy as hell, too.

"Where are we going?"

"New Castle. Will and Jessica stopped there once, inquired about some land for sale."

"You think Jessica and Cecil are in the area?"

"I don't know. Maybe. It's a place to start."

Sunny took in the passing scenery. She rarely left Manhattan. When she did, she usually went to her dad's house in the Hamptons. He used the retreat a few weeks in the summer, schedule permitting. The rest of the year, the place sat vacant. Sunny loved it, would live there year-round if the commute wasn't horrendous. The trees lining the parkway were beautiful, but having grown up in Southern California, she was more of a beach girl.

She glanced at him. "What do you think?"

"About?"

She waved her hand to indicate the scenery. "The trees. The area. Is this your kind of place?"

She caught the rise and fall of his shoulders out of the corner of her eye. "It's okay. Sort of makes me claustrophobic. Things are more open in Texas. I can see for miles from my backyard."

"Your brother wanted to buy land up here?"

"Will was looking for studio space. When he's working, it doesn't matter what's outside. Trees, fields, skyscrapers. Hell, he'd probably be happy in a lighthouse perched on a rock in the middle of the ocean."

"He's that focused?"

"He used to be. After…this, I'm not so sure. He hasn't painted much since he came home."

"But he is painting?" She'd really hate to think one of the country's best talents walked away.

"Yeah. Some." Jake's fingers gripped the steering wheel until his knuckles shown white.

Sensing his reluctance to discuss his brother's work, she changed the subject. "I prefer the beach. I grew up in Los Angeles. Water is my thing. Pools. Lakes. Oceans."

He relaxed his hold on the wheel. "My home is on a lake. And I have a pool."

"My dad has a beach house on Long Island."

"You go there often?"

"Not as much as I would like." She shifted on the seat so she faced him. "Is it a big lake?"

"Haven't you heard? Everything in Texas is big." His sexy grin made her smile and warmed parts of her body she'd almost forgotten existed.

He'd been the perfect gentleman since he stepped into her gallery yesterday, and though she appreciated it, she wanted more. She wanted what his eyes promised. If it meant stripping his gentlemanly veneer away, she was up to the task. She dropped her gaze to his crotch. "Everything?" she asked, infusing the single word with as much faux innocence as she could muster. She'd learned a few things about acting from her dad.

He caught her watching him and adjusted his position in the bucket seat. "You aren't playing fair, Ms. Sheldon. Keep it up and we'll be pulling off, looking for a quiet place in the woods."

Teasing Jake was fun. She liked this new, more casual side of the staid lawyer. She glanced out at the passing scenery. "I'm beginning to appreciate the benefit of all this green stuff. However…" She faced forward again. "We're on a mission here. We need to focus."

"You're right, though, you could easily distract me if you wanted to."

Their gazes met for a brief second. "Is that a challenge?" she asked before Jake shifted his attention to the road.

"Maybe." They passed a semi then he checked the side-view mirror and moved back into the right-hand lane. "Did I thank you for coming with me?"

"Did I thank you for inviting me along?"

"You might have."

She swiveled her head, caught him grinning at her. The heat remained in his gaze, but he'd banked it. She silently vowed to nibble away at his control every chance she got. She smiled at him. "Well, thank you. I enjoy being with you. This is a pleasant change from the city."

His smile vanished, ending the playful moment as he reminded her why they were here. "We're probably wasting our time. There's zero evidence the culprits who stole Will's paintings came this way. For all we know, they've destroyed them."

"If they wanted to destroy them, they easily could have done so in the gallery. Slashed them. Tossed paint or turpentine on them. They didn't, so I'd wager they have other plans for them. Maybe they hope to ransom them at a later date."

"When they run out of the money they stole from him?"

"Who knows? But as a member of the same art world they inhabited, I'm confident they didn't take the paintings so they could destroy them later. They plan to sell them on the black market or ransom them back to Will. Those are the only scenarios that make sense."

He nodded. "This way, they draw the torture out," he surmised. "Steal the money and the artwork. Crush the gallery opening. Pull the rug out from under the artist then wait until he's moved on, put the incident behind him then hit him again. Ransom one or two at a time. Drag the pain out over decades."

"It's vengeance at its best, don't you think?"

"It's sadistic." Jake checked the mirrors then moved into the left lane to pass another slow-moving truck. "What could Will have ever done to warrant this kind of revenge?"

"I have no idea. I've only met your brother a few times, but he seemed like a nice guy. You remind me of him. Not just your looks, you're remarkably similar there, but in your mannerisms. You're good people, both of you."

"Which brings me back to my question. Why Will?"

"I think he ran afoul of the wrong person."

"Jessica Blackwell?"

"I met her a time or two. I'm from Hollywood, remember? Her kind were all over the place. Everything is about them. They need to be the center of attention. I can't speak to Will's relationship with her, but he'd become extremely popular in the New York art world. Like I said, he's a friendly guy. People liked him, and he has an extraordinary talent."

"I know what you mean. I came to visit him once before he met Jessica. He took me to a couple of shindigs he'd been invited to. I might as well have been wallpaper. Everyone gravitated to him. Fawned over him."

She cocked her head. "I didn't realize you'd been to parties in New York."

Jake shrugged. "It was a few years ago, and nobody paid me any mind. They came to see Will, not his no-talent brother."

"Shame I wasn't at any of those events."

"How do you know you weren't?"

"Because I would have noticed you."

His gaze swept over her, lingering on her lips, then her breasts. "I damn sure would have noticed you, too."

His heated assessment warmed her from the inside out. She needed to keep this light or, like he'd said, they'd end up shagging in the forest. "Really? What makes you think so?"

"Fuck, Sunny." His grip tightened on the steering wheel. "You're beautiful, and the sexiest woman I've ever seen. I was a goner the moment I laid eyes on you."

And there it was, the acknowledgment she wasn't imagining the attraction between them. Her blood pressure spiked, and her skin tingled. "You aren't the first man to tell me those things, but when you say them, I believe you're being truthful. You see me as sexy and beautiful."

"The others weren't sincere?"

"Nope. Flattery comes with the territory in the entertainment industry. Men have been trying to weasel their way into my panties since I sprouted breasts. You'd be surprised what guys will say to convince a woman to part her legs." She suppressed a shudder as unpleasant memories rushed forward.

"I must be doing something wrong if those things didn't sound like flattery to you." He cut his eyes toward her. "I intended them to."

"Watch where you're going, Romeo." She waited until he focused on the road again. "I know you were flattering me, but it's not only the words. It's the speaker's inflection, and the way they look at you, too."

"Are you saying my flattery is different from other's?"

She considered the many glib lines tossed her way over the years. Only one other rang true — a testament to the man's acting skills. It had all been a lie wrapped up in pretty but meaningless words. Thankfully, she'd learned the truth before the tabloids found out about their brief relationship. One thing she liked best about Jake was that he wasn't an actor. She glanced at his strong profile, admired the air of competence about him that came from knowing exactly who he was. Actors, it seemed, were always trying to find a piece of themselves in each role they played. "All I'm saying is, some of the best actors in the world have said similar things to me. With you, it's different."

CHAPTER THREE

He was swimming in some deep waters. The more Sunny talked, the more he understood how lucky he was to be in her company and how bad he would hurt her. She trusted him. Let him in when she should have slammed the door in his face. As much as he enjoyed being with her, they only had a few days together. He knew it, but he wasn't sure she did.

He risked a glance her way. Eyes closed, head tossed back to catch the breeze through the open window, she was every man's fantasy. Way out of his league, yet they were good together. Easy. Relaxed. She'd been open and honest about her feelings and her life, and he'd planned to repay her with sex and a self-serving road trip. She deserved better — yet the thought of another man touching her made him want to kill someone.

There couldn't be two more different people on the planet — yet something about her drew him. It wasn't only her looks, though he wouldn't deny her beauty. Her golden hair matched her name, and her blue eyes reminded him of the Texas sky on a summer day. He loved the snappy business suits she wore to work. They showed off her womanly figure while still retaining a prim-and-proper appearance that made him want to do decidedly improper things to her. Today's outfit — shorts and a sleeveless blouse with buttons down the front—reminded him of a teenage girl out for a day at the lake, but the clothes were no less sexy than her business suits. His fingers itched to pop those buttons, tasting every inch of her skin as it appeared.

What future could they possibly have? He lived his boring life in Texas, and she had a vibrant life here. She attended black-tie affairs with movie stars, and he ate take-out barbeque all alone while he watched rented movies starring those same people. Beauty aside, behind the face she showed the world lurked something he saw in himself. Loneliness. Restlessness? Her life seemed exciting to him, but was it as unfulfilling as his? She didn't speak of close friends or relatives. Spoke only of large, media circus events.

"I'm not keeping you from doing something with your friends this weekend, am I?" They'd driven north with plans to rent two rooms for the night then visit the real estate office his private investigator located the next day.

"No. I didn't have any plans, and if I did, I would have cancelled them." She smiled at him. "I'd rather be with you."

"What would you be doing if I hadn't shown up?"

"Laundry?" She turned to the passing scenery. "Actually, I thought about closing the gallery for a few days and getting out of town. Then I found you on the sidewalk and changed my mind."

"Where would you have gone?"

"To my dad's beach house. He's filming in L.A. for the summer, so I'd have the place to myself."

"You wouldn't have been alone for long."

"What makes you say so?"

Jake shrugged. "I don't know. A beautiful woman like you? I'm sure you attract people like flowers attract bees."

"Dad's place is pretty isolated. No one would know I was there unless I told them, and trust me, I wouldn't tell anyone."

She didn't deny the bees-to-flowers comparison. "Why not?"

"Because." She straightened in the seat. "I'm not a social butterfly."

He was being a dick, pressing her for answers, but he wanted to know the mysterious woman accompanying him. He'd met no one like her, except maybe himself. "I bet you go out with friends in the city every weekend."

"You'd lose your bet, cowboy. I couldn't tell you the last time I went out with friends."

***

Yes, she could tell him about her last date. But she didn't want to talk about Ian with Jake. She'd met Ian Reynolds when his mother and her dad starred in a Broadway production together. She'd been six or seven and Ian a year older. During the summer months, they'd spent nearly every minute backstage under the watchful eye of a hired babysitter. After that summer, they didn't see each other for years. When they met again, Ian had become an accomplished actor in his own right, and she'd recently graduated from college. They'd dated in secret for a few months. He'd said all the perfect words, and the sex, though not spectacular, filled a need. He'd convinced her to take the relationship public, albeit quietly. Dinner at an exclusive restaurant where paparazzi weren't welcome, making it a favorite for the Hollywood crowd. They'd be spotted but only by friends. People they could trust. Like the woman who approached their table, her pregnant belly leading the way, to confront Ian.

The evidence he'd been sleeping with her and the starlet at the same time was right there at eye level. Worst of all, Ian didn't deny anything. He'd known about the baby for months and had been dragging his feet on the custody and support agreement. Sunny excused herself from the conversation, hailed a cab, and decided being alone was underrated. It suited her fine, until she met Jake.

From the very first, she'd been attracted to the Texas lawyer in a way she'd never experienced with anyone else.

Part of it was physical. Pheromones or some such. But the interest went deeper, for her, at least. She'd felt an unexplainable connection with him. Maybe it was his devotion to his brother or the way he'd looked at her, like she was a puzzle he wanted desperately to solve—one piece at a time. Whatever it was, the intervening weeks when she'd heard nothing from him hadn't diminished the attraction one bit. She wanted to be with this man. Wanted to feel his body pressing hers into a mattress. Wanted to feel him inside her. Wanted to trust him.

Jake was a handsome man. Not Hollywood Heartthrob handsome or rich, but those weren't qualities she valued. He did well for himself. She'd take a hardworking man any day over one who pretended to be something he wasn't. Actors made lousy spouses. As much as she loved her father, he was a perfect example to prove her point. He loved her mother, and her mother loved him. But their love, no matter how strong, couldn't hold their marriage together. According to her mom, Curtis Sheldon was impossible to live with. She often said she never knew who to expect when he walked in the door—Curtis or the character he portrayed on set. She'd warned Sunny of the duplicity she thought inherent in entertainers. Remembering her time with Ian, she realized how right her mother had been.

She shook off the unwanted memories of her failed love affair. "What about you? What do you do for fun?"

He glanced at her then back to the road. "I spend my weekends at the local honky-tonk. Line dancing and flirting with every female in sight."

Sunny laughed. "You do not."

"No. I don't." The smile he directed her way hit like a bolt of lightning, striking her at her core. "Would you believe I moonlight as a dancer in an all-male review?"

"Not in a million years." She grinned at him. With a few words, he'd chased her off the gloomy path her thoughts had taken her down and onto a now-familiar one where only the two of them existed. "Tell me the truth, Jake."

"I spend most nights and weekends alone. I get together with my brothers occasionally now that they're both home."

"What do you and your siblings do?"

Sunny relaxed, content to let the wind whip at her hair and Jake's drawl smooth away the ragged edges of her mood. She would not let her past intrude on what little time she had with him. As soon as he wrapped up his brother's case, he'd go home to Texas for good. It's where he belonged. *And I'll stay in New York. It's where I belong.*

The unwanted reminder cut like a sharp blade.

Focus on the here and now.

The situation reminded her of several other times in her life when she'd been forced to make the most of circumstances she wished she could change. Her parents' divorce, Ian's betrayal, and the decision to move to New York and make a fresh start in the brownstone she'd inherited from her grandmother.

She'd known from the beginning Jake wouldn't be staying. Whatever this was between them, it was temporary. A good time. Friendly conversation. A much-needed road trip and great sex—she hoped. She'd be wise to remember that was all it was and not let the perfection of the moment lull her into believing it could be more.

"Sunny? You awake over there?"

"Huh?" She sat up, suddenly aware her eyes had drifted shut. "What?"

Jake chuckled. "Didn't mean to bore you to sleep."

Sunny rubbed her hands over her face. A quick glance told her they were coming into a town. Signs touting local businesses dotted the side of the road. Rows of mailboxes marked the entrance to dirt paths. She couldn't imagine living in such a remote place. "You didn't bore me. I guess I was more tired than I thought."

"I anticipated getting to know each other a little more tonight, but you need your sleep."

Was he suggesting what she thought he was? God, she hoped so. Heat rose in her cheeks. "I'm fine. Honestly. It must be all this fresh air. I'm a city girl, not used to this much oxygen." *I can sleep when you're gone.* "Besides, we have so little time together. I don't want to waste it sleeping."

His gaze left the road, locking with hers for a second. All kinds of things swirled in the depth of his gaze — heat, desire, acknowledgment, regret. The therapist she'd seen after the breakup with Ian would question if she was projecting her feelings into the moment. Even if she *was* seeing things she wanted to see, she'd never regret the time spent with Jake. Every minute was an experience to cherish, including falling asleep to the sound of his voice.

Jake returned his attention to the road. A muscle clenched in his jaw, and he shifted in his seat. "Dammit, woman. You can't say things like that and expect me to behave. I'm only human."

Sunny smiled at his discomfort. The feeling was mutual. One glance her way and she wanted to get naked with him. "How far to our destination?"

"We're staying here tonight. I booked us two rooms at a B&B."

"Is it too early to check in?"

CHAPTER FOUR

She would be the death of him. He'd never wanted, needed, a woman as much as he did Sunny Sheldon.

He checked the GPS and the dashboard clock. Too early to check into their room. He'd planned to spend the early part of the afternoon scoping out the town and getting a look at the real estate office where Will and Jessica inquired about the property for sale. Now all he wanted to do was find a secluded place where he could rip Sunny's clothes off and fuck her senseless.

This wasn't like him. He'd always been able to compartmentalize his life. Women and sex in one drawer. Work in another. Family in still another walled-off room. Sunny breached all his walls. This was supposed to be a working trip, but it crossed the family/work line from the beginning. Then he'd added Sunny into the mix and turned his ordered world upside down.

At the moment, he didn't give a flying fuck about Will's case. All he could think about was seeing Sunny's skin in the soft light filtered through the leaves of the surrounding trees, her legs spread for him, her cries of ecstasy echoing on a breeze.

Fuck. He needed to get a grip on reality. The closer they got to town, the less he wanted to get there. Searching the passing landscape, he prayed he'd find what he was looking for. Then it was there, a slight break in the tree line up ahead. No signs. No mailboxes. A logging road, if he had to guess. He slowed, eyeing the well-worn track. Nothing indicated recent use. *Perfect.*

Jake cut the wheel, turning down the lane.

"Where are we going?"

"Some place private." His voice sounded like it had been wrenched from his throat with a rusty coat hanger. Need outweighed everything else in his mind. He hoped she felt the same way.

"Oh. Well." Her head swiveled as she took in the scenery bouncing by. "This looks like it fits the bill."

"Yes, it does." From the condition of the road, he guessed no one had been down it in years. When the road widened enough to pull off to the side, he did. Bending to look out the passenger side window, he spied a foot trail leading off into the dense woods. His hand was on the door latch as he spoke. "Come on. Let's see where that goes."

"You're kidding, right?"

He paused, took a deep breath, and let it out. "Do I look like I'm kidding?" He didn't even try to hide the raw need coursing through his system as his gaze met hers.

"No. You look like a man on a mission."

Maybe it was his libido talking, but she wasn't giving off the *I'm in the woods with a serial killer* vibe. He chalked her amiable attitude up to good fortune and said what was on his mind. "I am. You're my mission. I've tried to be a gentleman. Keep my needs under control. But I'm losing the battle. Honestly? I didn't ask you along on this trip to force you into anything. I'd never do that to a woman. I've wanted you since the first time I laid eyes on you, Sunny. You're all I think about. I know you were teasing earlier—about the size of everything in Texas, but I've never wanted to prove the point more than I do right now. I need you. Right. This. Fucking. Minute." In the courtroom, patience was a virtue. Thank god, this wasn't a courtroom because he was fresh out of patience and restraint. Unless she had other ideas, then he'd find some. Enough to honor her wishes. "I got the impression you wouldn't be averse to checking out your premise yourself. Tell me if I'm wrong and I'll turn this rig around and get back on the road."

"What, exactly, did you have in mind?"

"Fucking. In the woods. Horizontal if we can find a suitable place. If not…"

His dick throbbed, aching to be inside her, to claim her here in this forest like a wild animal. He'd never felt so close to the edge. When her lips parted on a breath, he focused on her mouth, hoping he could hear her response over the blood rushing past his ears on its way south.

"I packed a pashmina."

He shook his head, trying to make sense of her words.

"A shawl," she clarified. "We can put down on the ground."

He was out of the vehicle in seconds, opening the back hatch where they'd stowed their luggage. She met him at the rear of the vehicle.

"Here." She grabbed her bag. "It's right on top, I think."

She rummaged around, pulled a brightly colored item out. Jake closed the liftgate, fingered the lock button then reached for her free hand. "Let's go."

They were barely out of sight of the Jeep when they came upon a small clearing. A few stumps formed a rough circle and decaying logs established a perimeter. The field had probably been used as a staging area for the loggers a decade or more ago. When the workers cleared out, they'd left the area to nature. Several trees had grown up inside the ring. Jake stalked over to a shady spot. He kicked leaves and fallen twigs away until he could inspect the ground beneath. Kneeling carefully so as not to break his engorged dick in half, he bent to remove a couple of rocks then held his hand out. Sunny handed over the fabric thing she'd brought. As he spread it out, it pleased him to see it was bigger than he'd thought and would easily shield Sunny's petite frame from the dirty ground. It wasn't the Victorian bed-and-breakfast where he'd made reservations, but it would have to do. He needed her too much to wait for niceties.

Rising to his feet, he vowed to make it up to her later, with a fancy dinner, candlelight, and soft linens. A mattress fit for a queen.

The city reminded him how far man had come from their cave-dweller days, but out here? He was anything but civilized.

"Take your shorts and panties off," he ordered. "Leave your shirt on."

Her eyes lit with a fire from within then, with a nod, she did as he said. When she stood before him, naked from the waist down, a primal urge hit him so hard, his knees threatened to buckle. He pointed to the pallet. "Lay down. Hands above your head. Legs spread."

Silent, she complied.

He stood over her, looking his fill. *Fuck*, she was beautiful, her surrender complete. Moisture glistened on her folds. She was wet for him, and he hadn't touched her yet. He'd been with his share of women, some he'd tapped more than once, but never, ever, had a woman tempted him the way Sunny did. Tonight, in their soft bed, he'd bring her to the brink with his mouth before he gave in and filled her. But nightfall was hours away. This afternoon, in these woods, he'd take. And take. And take.

His hands shook as he fished a condom out of his wallet and freed his dick from its prison. He stroked himself, once, twice, never taking his eyes off the woman in front of him. She lay still, watching him, her hips rising in invitation as he sheathed himself then dropped to his knees between her legs. He shoved his jeans down his thighs then shimmied closer, lifting her ass into the air, fitting the head of his cock to her entrance.

"I've changed my mind. I want to see your tits."

She nodded, giving him permission. Slowly, he unbuttoned her blouse, pushing it open to reveal a plain bra that was sexier in its innocence than any lace gizmo he'd ever seen. He closed his hands over the twin cotton-clad mounds, squeezing. His dick jerked, begging him to get on with it. Instead, he sat back on his heels, taking in the view.

Sunny Sheldon in a state of dishabille, in the woods, on the brink of being fucked by a caveman, was radiant. Her skin glowed with life, and desire lit her eyes. Her nipples were hard pebbles beneath their modest covering. The scent of her arousal wafted on the warm breeze, taunting him to take what was his. What she freely gave to him.

He wanted it more than he wanted his next breath. He wanted her. Not for today. Not for this trip. Forever.

For. Fucking. Ever.

The thought barreled through him like a freight train out of control. He couldn't stop it. Didn't want to stop it.

Rising to his knees again, he fingered her sex, lined his cock up with her entrance, then, arms wrapped around her thighs to hold her in place, he drove into her hard. His balls slapped against her ass.

Mine.

Again.

Mine.

Again.

Mine.

He was close to coming. A scrap of civility broke through his caveman thoughts. She would come before he did. Always.

He fingered her clit. Her eyes flew open, burning him with her gaze. Then her hand was on his wrist, her hips moving with him, taking him impossibly deeper into her core. He stroked her nub until the first fluttering of her internal muscles hinted of her impending release.

Her body tensed then, on a cry loud enough to startle birds from the trees, she fell apart for him.

Jake released his hold on her thighs and pinned her beneath him. He drove into her repeatedly. Claiming her orgasm as his. Taking, taking, taking. Until her sweet, responsive body wrenched control. Taking. Taking. Taking.

***

Her body hummed with satisfaction. Jake's weight atop her felt like a security blanket protecting her from the world.

She recalled the moment she'd realized he was serious about doing it in the woods. The closest she'd ever come to outdoor sex was doing it with the window open. She'd worried the whole time someone would hear her and Ian. She'd experienced similar worries today. What if someone came along? What if they were in someone's backyard and didn't even know it? Jake ordered her to take her shorts and panties off, and as she'd stood before him naked from the waist down, exposed and vulnerable, her worries evaporated under his heated gaze.

A thought popped into her head, and she chuckled.

Jake nuzzled her neck. "What's so funny?"

"You never got to see my tits."

He growled and nipped at the skin below her ear. "Damned sexiest bra I've ever seen—bar none."

"I thought men preferred lace."

"Lace is good. Cotton is better." Pushing to one elbow, he cupped her breast with his free hand. "You weren't trying to seduce me, and that's what did it for me. You were just being you."

"You should have seen the panties I wore. They weren't sexy, either."

"Wear them for me later?" He pushed one cup up to expose her breast. Her nipple tightened as the soft air wafted across it. "Damn, you're going to be the death of me."

His cock twitched inside her, growing hard again. He flexed his hips, drawing a pained groan from his lips. "What are the chances this condom has one more round in it? 'Cause if it doesn't, I'll have to dig one out of my luggage."

"I'm on the pill."

"I'm clean. My right hand is the only partner I've been with for god knows how long.

You sure it's okay, baby?"

Needing to touch him, she grabbed his ass with both hands. "I'm sure. You can take it off if you want."

As he stared into her eyes, his cock swelled inside her. "Next time." He kissed the tip of her nose. "I'm so hard I'd probably come if I tried to get the damn thing off."

"Next time, then." She dug her nails into his taut cheeks, urging him to go deeper.

He took the hint, moving slowly in and out of her sensitive channel like time didn't matter. She supposed it didn't, unless a hiker or homeowner or some form of wildlife ran across them. As he bent and took her nipple into his mouth, every thought but one flew out of her head. She needed more of his skin against hers.

Running her hands up under his T-shirt, she shoved the fabric up around his shoulders. He took the hint, releasing her breast long enough to grab the back of his shirt and yank it over his head. He pulled his arms free then the garment sent up a plume of dust as it landed behind her head. She couldn't have cared less as he pushed the other side of her bra up and resumed his task of driving her crazy.

Cradling his head in one hand, she urged him on while her other hand explored every inch of taut skin within reach. There seemed to be miles of it stretched over firm muscles that shifted and rippled as he moved above and inside her. She loved his strength, held in check as he took her gently, but she'd loved it even more when need overruled civility. The two sides of Jake Ingram. The civilized attorney, negotiating a satisfactory outcome for both parties, and the Philistine, taking what he wanted with little concern for niceties. Both intrigued her beyond reason.

CHAPTER FIVE

What the hell was he doing?

Jake reached down, gathered up the shawl thingy Sunny had provided, enabling his moment of insanity. With his back to her, he folded the colorful swath of fabric while she dressed. She'd been 100 percent complicit in what they'd done, but since his blood supply was feeding more than one piece of his anatomy, he recognized how impulsive and selfish he'd been.

This wasn't him. He lived a measured, regimented, planned-to-the-maximum life. He controlled his needs. Never let them overrule his common sense or his ingrained sense of decency. But he'd done so today. He'd let his desire for Sunny off the leash. Let it run rampant.

Shit. He owed her an apology. He gave up trying to fold the fabric into a neat bundle and turned, prepared to beg her forgiveness and promise anything for a chance to make it up to her. Her timid smile made his knees weak and his heart stammer. Standing in this wild place with her mussed hair and skin flushed from a recent orgasm, she looked like a goddess. Despite his remorse for taking her in such a primitive way, he had the urge to beat his chest and shout like a crazed caveman. He'd done that to her. And god, he wanted to do it again. And again. And again. Ad infinitum.

He held out the ball of fabric. "I'm sorry."

She took the offering and shook it, dislodging a shower of grass and twigs. "It's washable. Don't worry about it."

It took a second for his brain to catch up. When it did, he laughed. "I wasn't apologizing for ruining your…what did you call it?"

"Pashmina."

He nodded, not even trying to push the unfamiliar word past his lips. "I meant, I'm sorry for losing control. For taking you here." He swept his hand out to indicate the clearing. "You deserve better."

"I don't know, Jake. If it got any better, I might not survive it. But I sure hope we can try."

The spark of humor in her eyes and the slight quirk of her lips hit him at the same time his brain registered what she'd said. "You aren't mad?"

"Why would I be? If I'd said no, we would have stopped, wouldn't we?" She didn't give him time to answer. "I wanted this as much as you. Back in the truck, you said you wanted me from the first minute you saw me. I wanted you just as much. After you went home, I hoped you would call me or come back. I can't tell you how many nights I lay in bed, wishing I'd had just one night with you before you left. I understand why you kept your distance then. You needed to make sure I had nothing to do with stealing your brother's paintings. I'm glad that's been cleared up because I can tell you, once will not be enough, Jake."

He closed the distance between them, took her in his arms. She lifted her face, and he bent to crush his lips to hers. A moan escaped as her lips parted, allowing him entrance. He tasted her, letting his lips and tongue promise all manner of wicked things he intended to do to her. Breaking away while he still had the presence of mind to do so, he met her gaze. "I still maintain you deserve better than a tumble in the woods, and you sure as hell deserve better than me."

"You could be right," she countered. "I'll need more data to come to a firm conclusion."

He rocked against her, showing her what she did to him. "Tell me one thing."

"What?" She stroked his nape.

"Do you have enough data to support the saying everything is bigger in Texas?"

Her face flushed a becoming shade of pink. She reached between them, cupped his growing erection. "God, yes. You've got a cannon, Jake. Impressive." She tightened her grip on him. "You've ruined me for other men."

At the mention of other men, Jake's caveman instincts reared to life again. Digging his fingers into her ass cheeks, he lifted her, brought her flush against him. In a move he recognized as macho bullshit but was unable to curb, he took her mouth with his — kissing the evil words from her lips. The same mantra he'd heard as he'd claimed her on the hard-packed ground came back to him, echoing in the recesses of his brain. *Mine. Mine. Mine.*

She shimmied in his arms, bringing him to his senses. He let her go, expecting her to put as much distance between them as possible. Instead, she pushed her shorts and panties to her ankles, and as she stepped out of them, reached for the button on his jeans. "Hurry, Jake. I need you. Now."

He didn't need to be told twice. He brushed her hands away then made short work of the fastenings. As soon as he'd pushed his jeans and boxers past his hips, she wrapped her arms around his neck. She hopped. He caught her in his arms, lifted her so the tip of his cock notched into her wet, heated entrance.

Resting her elbows on his shoulders, she fisted her hands in his hair, dragging his head back. "Fuck me, Jake. Hard. Fast. Now."

This time it was her lips crushing his as he lowered her onto his aching shaft. She felt so damned good, he was in danger of passing out from the sheer pleasure of being inside her. He fought to stay in the moment, unwilling to miss a second of the best sex he'd ever experienced. And recent drought aside, he'd been with more than his share of women, and he'd never taken one without a barrier between them. Never wanted to until now. As he helped her move on him, something shifted inside him. A key piece of who he was, who he wanted to be, tumbled, and fell into place.

***

She could ride him like this forever, she mused as she took what she wanted. Him. Inside her. Stretching her. Filling her. Skin-to-skin for the first time. As much as she loved his Texas-sized cock, she wanted to experience the rush of his hot cum shooting against her womb when he lost control. Nothing would come of it, but she wanted to be his. Wanted him to mark her. Claim her in a way no one else ever had.

It was very cave woman of her, but he brought something primal out in her. Or maybe it was this place, this magical place they'd stumbled upon. There'd be time to test her theory later — if they survived. The way her heart raced, she wasn't sure she'd make it, but if death was the price for these few minutes of bliss, she'd pay up and die with a smile on her face.

Was it possible he was even harder this time than he'd been before? She wrenched her lips away from his, raised her face to the sun, and bowed her back, supporting herself by digging her fingers into his shoulders. He buried his face between her breasts, his teeth working at the buttons of her blouse. His hot breath through the layers of shirt and bra nearly sent her over the edge as she silently vowed the next time, they'd be naked. Completely naked.

"Feels so good," she ground out as he moved inside her. "Don't stop."

Jake growled into the cleavage he'd exposed. Then his lips latched on to the top of her left breast, and he sucked at the tender skin. Marking her. There wasn't anything gentle about his assault, and she wouldn't have it any other way. The bite of pain tripped every nerve ending, sent an electric jolt to the spot where their bodies became one. She dropped her head to his shoulder, biting down on the corded muscles as she came in a rush of pain and pleasure so intense, she teetered on the edge of consciousness. Jake thrust into her until he, too, couldn't hold out any longer. He threw his head back and roared his pleasure for the world to hear.

Arms wrapped tight around his neck, Sunny collapsed against his chest. They stood there, connected in the most intimate way possible, clinging to each other as their breathing slowly evened out. Sunny'd never been more content. Jake's cock remained impressively hard even as the evidence of their mingled pleasure trickled from her channel. A smile broke across her face as she raised her head enough to flick his earlobe with the tip of her tongue. Then she whispered in his ear. "We made a mess, Counselor."

His laughter vibrated through her body then his hands squeezed her bare ass cheeks. "Give me a minute. I'm having a little trouble remembering which planet we're on."

Sunny found the energy to raise up. Their gazes met. "Does that happen often?"

"Never. You sent me into orbit, woman." He leaned in for a kiss, and she met him halfway. His lips were hot and firm, and she wanted to feel them on another part of her body. Jake Ingram knew how to make a woman feel like a goddess.

They parted when, by silent mutual agreement, they came up for air. Sunny's legs trembled, and she wasn't sure she'd be able to stand, but they couldn't remain where they were indefinitely. "We should go," she said.

"My knees are shaking," he admitted.

"Better put me down before you fall."

"No danger of me falling, but I don't want to drop you." He lifted her, and his cock slid free.

Sunny fought the urge to cling to him like a barnacle and beg him to never let her go. With a sigh, she unlocked her legs and he lowered her until her feet met the ground. She wobbled slightly, but Jake was there, holding her close until she pushed away and stood on her own. He righted his clothes then gathered hers from where they'd fallen, shook them free of dirt. She refused the panties, so he knelt in front of her, offering his assistance. Hand on his shoulder, she put one foot into her shorts.

"Hold on to me. I can't leave you like this."

Before she knew what was happening, he lifted her left leg and buried his face between her thighs. Sunny dug her fingers into his scalp and held on for dear life as his tongue swept between her folds. It wasn't her first go-round at oral sex, but in the past, it had been an appetizer before the main course. Jake lapped up their mingled juices like he couldn't get enough. And, lord, she was grateful for his thoroughness. Soon, she directed his movements. Rocking her hips to make all the right parts meet up. He brought her to the brink of a total meltdown then he abruptly changed things up. His lips latched on to her clit and sucked while he drove two fingers into her dripping channel where they instantaneously found some magical button previously unknown to her.

The orgasm took her by surprise. The clench of muscles sharp and painful yet, oddly, cathartic. Her cries of pleasure echoed off the trees ringing the clearing as her body convulsed, purging itself of tension and anxiety. Her leg gave out on her, and Jake was there to scoop her into his arms. She snuggled against his big, powerful chest as he carried her to the Jeep. He propped her against the passenger side and knelt to help her into her shorts. Then he lifted her onto the seat, fastened the seat belt, and closed the door. She was asleep before they made it back to the road.

CHAPTER SIX

Jake drove with one hand on the wheel. Elbow propped on the door, he ran his free hand over his face, reliving every glorious second he'd spent between her legs. He'd gone down on women before, lots of times, but never standing up. He'd intended to help her into her shorts, but their co-mingled scent caught his attention. Then he'd glanced up and saw a trickle of wetness running down her inner thigh—and the urge to taste her, to taste *them*, took over. The next thing he knew, he'd buried his face between her legs. Not only tasting. Eating. Like a goddamn caveman.

She'd tasted so damn good. He couldn't stop. Not until he'd made her come one more time.

He glanced at her slumped against the passenger side door, asleep. Or passed out? He'd behaved like a savage today. Her shirt gaped open where he'd gnawed a button off to get to her skin. The gap revealed the dark bruise rising where he'd marked her.

Christ. He'd done everything but drag her around by the hair while beating his chest to warn all the other cavemen to stay the fuck away from his woman.

He shifted his focus where it belonged—on the road—and reminded himself she wasn't his woman. And as soon as she woke, she'd probably kick his ass to drive the message home. He wouldn't blame her. He deserved her wrath. They hardly knew one another. Yeah, there'd been an attraction right from the start, but he was a grown-ass man. He could control his urges. Except where she was concerned. It had been bad enough before he came back to New York, when he'd jacked off countless times with nothing but his imagination to go on. Now that he'd been inside her—tasted her, tasted them—he didn't know how he'd ever keep his hands off her or his dick out of her.

"Won't be a problem," he mumbled to himself. He might as well turn the Jeep around and take her home. No way was she going to want to spend the next week or two with him.

At a faint moan from the other seat, he put both hands on the wheel and risked another glance at her. Eyes closed, her swollen lips slightly parted in sleep, her skin flushed, and her hair mussed, she looked thoroughly fucked. He chided himself for the lightning bolt of pride stiffening his dick. If she gave any indication she wanted to do it again, he'd pull over and fuck her brains out on the side of the road.

"Get a grip, Ingram." He tore his gaze to the road. The bed-and-breakfast he'd booked was up the road a ways. They were both tired. Maybe he could convince her to spend the night if he promised to take her home first thing in the morning. "Fat chance," he mumbled.

Beside him, she stirred. He caught a glimpse of her arm as she stretched just as they passed a sign for their accommodations. He stopped at the end of the long driveway. "We're here."

She blinked and sat up, taking in their surroundings. The instant she spied the house, her eyes grew round, and she bounced in her seat. "Oh. My. God. Have you ever seen anything like it?"

A three-story Victorian stood in the distance—a relic of another time when big families were the norm and porches connected communities. He'd seen a few in Texas but none as whimsical as this. "It's…interesting."

"It's like something out of a storybook." She pulled the visor down. When she slid the cover off the built-in mirror, a light came on. One glance at her reflection and she turned to him—a big smile on her face. "I look like I've been ravaged by a big, strapping Texan."

Jake sighed. "I'm sorry, Sunny." He glanced at the pastel house at the end of the lane, imagining a hot meal and a comfortable bed. Maybe a shower, though he wasn't in any hurry to wash her scent off his body. "If you want, we can find a drive-thru for dinner then I can drive you home."

"What?" Her expression shifted from confusion to anger in the blink of an eye. "Are you trying to get rid of me? Did I do something wrong? Oh wait. I jumped you. Is that it? You don't like women who know what they want and go for it? Well, let me set you straight, Mr. Macho Man. This is the twenty-first century and women have needs, too!" With a huff, she sat back and, staring straight ahead, crossed her arms over her midsection. The move made her blouse gape even more.

Jake fixated on the bruise he'd put on her. There was something about the mark. It wasn't all enormous, but to anyone with half a brain, it sent a message. Walk away. This one is taken.

Not for the first time, his shoulder ached. He reached up to rub the spot where she'd nearly taken a chunk out of his hide. She'd been the one to initiate their vertical encounter, and he'd been either an ass or a gentleman to take her up on the offer. If he were to believe her words, she was mad because he'd offered to take her home, not because he'd gone caveman on her. A glimmer of hope crept in, lifting his spirits. Time to test the waters.

"You can jump me anytime you want." He shifted the transmission into Park and took his hands off the wheel. "Right now is good."

He was a beast where she was concerned. He'd been hard since he'd inhaled their mingled scent. It was a wonder he'd managed to drive, with his groin commanding most of his blood supply.

She turned a haughty glare on him then her gaze dropped to his lap and the obvious bulge behind his zipper. "We can't do it here. We're blocking their driveway."

She had to be kidding, but the expression on her face said otherwise. He chuckled. "No, I don't suppose right this minute would be appropriate. How about we check in, get cleaned up and find some dinner. If you're going to jump me again, I'm going to need some sustenance."

The wicked intent in her smile made his dick twitch. "What are you waiting for? Let's get this show on the road."

"Yes, ma'am." Jake shifted in his seat and put the car back in Drive.

***

Jake insisted they keep both rooms he'd reserved despite Sunny's protests. No one this far from the city knew who she was, and she didn't care who found out she and the Texan were sleeping together, though there'd yet to be any actual sleep.

Still wearing the clothes she'd arrived in, she sprawled across the comfy bed in her room, arms stretched over her head, reliving every moment they'd spent in the woods. If she closed her eyes, she could smell the pine and hear the birds in the trees. She smiled, recalling the way Jake apologized for having sex in such a primitive place. Always the gentleman, except when it came to shagging her. Then his enthusiasm overrode his manners in a way she genuinely appreciated. He didn't seem to believe her when she said she wasn't the least bit offended by their impromptu sexathon. She'd have to work on convincing him because the sex today was by far the best ever.

A glance at the clock on the bedside table reminded her she needed to get a move on. The proprietor of the B&B recommended a restaurant a few miles down the road. She and Jake parted ways, agreeing to meet in the lobby in an hour, which meant she needed to hustle, or she'd be late.

Both of their rooms boasted private bathrooms, a luxury she appreciated as she eyed the ancient claw-foot tub and its equally antiquated shower system. It all looked to be in working order, but it didn't lend itself to a shared experience. If Jake's room boasted a similar setup, his head would probably stick out above the curved shower curtain rod, and he'd have to stand sideways in the tub to keep his broad shoulders from touching the wraparound curtain. She chuckled to herself, imagining the scene.

As she adjusted the temperature, she took in the depth and width of the old slipper-style tub and decided it could easily seat two in tandem. She pulled the curtain closed, flipped the valve to send the water up to the showerhead, then stepped into the tub. A quick rinse would do for now, and, with a little luck, she could talk Jake into a nice, long bath after dinner, followed by some very uncivilized sex on an actual mattress.

With her new goal in mind, she hurried through her routine and dressed in clean capri pants and a lightweight blouse; she arrived in the lobby one minute early to find Jake waiting for her. He'd changed into dark jeans and a dress shirt in a lighter shade of blue that matched his eyes. As a nod to the heat, he'd left the top two buttons undone and rolled the sleeves up to expose his muscular forearms. "I see you figured out the shower."

His gaze raked her from head to toe. An appreciative smile broke across his face. "It wasn't easy, but I can tell you, I have something in mind for that tub later."

Perhaps it wouldn't be hard to talk him into a bath after all. "I had a similar thought. Maybe we could discuss your plans and mine over a thick steak and a baked potato? Perhaps we can merge our visions into one?"

"Mergers are my specialty," he said as he reached for her hand and steered her toward the door.

Suddenly, she wanted to get the dinner portion of the evening over with as soon as possible. She'd yet to see all of Jake Ingram at one time, and her imagination was working overtime to fill the gap. Their activities earlier in the day provided a lot of data to inform her fantasies, but being able to explore every inch of his wet, slippery body was high on her list of priorities. On the front porch, she waited until he'd shut the door then she tugged him down the steps and across the yard to where they'd parked the Jeep.

"In a hurry?" he asked as he climbed into the driver's seat and pressed the ignition button.

"I'm not going to lie, Counselor. I see a merger in my future and I'm a tad bit impatient to get started."

"Are you, now?"

She almost swooned at the way he'd exaggerated his Southern drawl. God, could he be sexier? "And you aren't?"

"Didn't say that, sweetheart. Just didn't want to assume a merger was a given tonight. After what we did earlier…"

She sighed. He'd done the perfect gentleman thing again. "I'm fine, Jake. Except for the ache in a certain location I can't reach. I need your help, if you get my meaning?"

He braked at an intersection, waited his turn to proceed, then pressed the accelerator. Only then did he glance her way. "You sure it's only an ache? You aren't sore?"

"Not sore. But I will be sorely pissed if you don't do something about this aching as soon as we get back to the B&B."

His lips quirked up on one side. "I think I've got another merger in me." He glanced down at his lap, drawing her gaze there. He would cause a stir if he walked into the restaurant with a huge bulge leading the way.

Sunny licked her lips. She'd given a few blow jobs in the past, but they'd always been for the guy's benefit, not hers. Biting her bottom lip, she examined the thought running through her brain. Jake would enjoy the gesture but so would she. He'd tasted her earlier. It was her turn, wasn't it?

He pulled into the parking area. It was a large lot, testament to the popularity of the restaurant, but tonight there were only a handful of cars all occupying the front row of marked slots. Jake steered the Jeep toward an open one. Before he could shift into Park, Sunny covered his hand with hers.

"Maybe we could park over there?" She pointed to a row of empty slots on the fringe of the main lot. By day, the towering trees nearby probably provided great shade. This late in the evening, they cast a deep shadow. Not a suitable place if you were scared of the dark, but perfect if you wanted a bit of privacy.

Jake eyed the remote area then his gaze met hers. "I'm not fucking you in a parking lot."

"I have something else in mind." She moved her hand to cup his impressive erection. "You can't walk in like that."

His eyes searched hers for a long, silent moment. "I planned to let you go in first. Give myself a few minutes to get it under control."

"Let me help. Please?" To sweeten the offer, she licked her lips in what she hoped was a salacious manner. She'd never needed to convince a man to let her suck his dick. They were usually whipping it out, begging. Just another way Jake differed from the jerks she'd dated in the past.

"You're sure? I can master it myself. You know, think of puppies in a kennel or my fifth-grade math teacher."

"Not necessary. I want to do this. Please?"

He scrubbed both hands over his face then returned them to the steering wheel. He took his foot off the brake. "I must be losing my mind."

Once he'd parked, scooted his seat as far from the steering wheel as possible and reclined the seatback, she considered the logistics. The stationary console would be an obstacle, but one she'd manage.

"I'd recline more, but I want to watch. Do you mind?"

"Not if you don't mind me doing the best I can. I knew you were big, but…"

"You'll do fine, sweetheart. Just open your mouth and I'll do the rest."

She wrapped her fingers around the base, took over the slow stroke he'd been doing for himself. "You're beautiful, Jake. If I could, I'd paint you, just like this." She placed her free hand on his belly, slid it upward, taking his shirttails with it. "I can't wait to get you naked so I can see all of you."

"Which reminds me. I still haven't seen your tits. Mind if I touch while you, you know?"

"Not at all. Be my guest." She bent over the console and flicked her tongue out, taking her first taste of Jake Ingram at the same time his giant hand clamped down on her breast. His rough touch triggered a gush of liquid heat between her legs. If he kept it up, she'd have her own embarrassment to contend with when they entered the restaurant. But that was a worry for another time. Jake Ingram was right where she wanted him. Opening her mouth wide, she took him as deep as she could then lifted her head, letting his length slide through her lips.

"Fuuuuck."

Jake's hips rose then settled back against the seat as she dove again, taking him even deeper the second time. This time when she pulled up, she applied pressure to his stomach, urging him to stay still. He abandoned her breast, using both hands to grip the headrest as she repeated the process. This time, she took almost all of him, which brought her nose close enough to inhale his intoxicating male scent. If they were anywhere but a parking lot, she'd take the time to nuzzle him right there, lick his balls, familiarize herself with every inch of him. But if his profanity-laced commentary was any sign, he wouldn't last long.

The thought filled her with pride. She didn't think for a minute her technique was perfect, but she congratulated herself on making Jake want her so much. She did this to him.

Reduced him to swear words and made him throw out the rule book to have sex in the woods and chance a blow job in a parking lot. He made her just as crazy. One word from him and she'd shimmy out of her pants and climb on top of him, right here. Right now.

The ache between her legs was becoming more insistent with every sloppy repetition. She'd drooled all over his shaft, her hand, and even his boxers tucked beneath his balls were growing damp. This was messy and amateurish, but Jake didn't seem to mind.

In the woods, he'd held so much power over her, but here, he was at her mercy. It was a heady thought, and she took full advantage, pulling off him to stroke him slowly with her hand. The move wrenched a frustrated groan from him, followed by a plea for her to put him out of his misery.

"I won't last, baby. Thirty seconds, tops. My balls are halfway up my throat, ready to detonate. Please, baby."

She knew exactly how he felt. She was about two seconds from exploding as well. "Put your hand down my pants. Touch me," she said, shifting a little more to allow him access.

When he slid his hand in, found her wet folds, she closed her eyes, savored his touch for a couple heartbeats before returning her focus to his pleasure. A pearly bead of pre-cum formed on the tip of his cock. A swipe of her tongue took care of it before she took him deep again. His taste lingered in her mouth, and for the first time ever, she wanted to swallow every drop. But this was Jake, and he wasn't asking her to do anything. This entire crazy episode had been her idea, and she wanted to see it through to the very end, hoping it would be a satisfying one for him.

His fingers felt so good on her. Stroking, plunging inside her channel, teasing her to the brink then retreating. His other hand maintained a tight grip on the headrest as he tried to control his body's instinct to thrust. He was slowly losing the battle, his movements becoming more pronounced with each bob of her head until he surrendered. Moving his hand to grip her head, he held her down while he rocked into her, the swollen head of his cock hitting the back of her throat repeatedly until he lost the battle. He came with a shout she feared would bring people running from the restaurant to see what was going on. Sunny held on to his cock with one hand and his shirt with the other, determined to ride it out, to take everything he gave.

When he'd spent his load, his entire body relaxed, except for the hand down her pants. She released his cock, and he guided her head to his lap. "Let me make you come," he said. "You're close."

Sunny shifted enough to enable her to slide her hand alongside his. She gripped his wrist and hung on as he worked her up fast and hard. In a matter of minutes, she buried her face in his lap and screamed as her body reached its limit and she tumbled headlong into pleasure.

She didn't know how long they lay there, both wrung out and satisfied, before another type of hunger took over and propelled them to straighten their clothes. Jake raised his seatback and powered the seat to its original position while Sunny did the best she could to clean herself with a tissue from her purse. She didn't dare look at her hair. It had to be a mess. "Do we have to go in there? A drive-thru sounds mighty good right now."

"You're looking mighty good," Jake said as he started the engine and put the Jeep in gear. "The just-fucked look suits you."

"You're looking relaxed yourself, cowboy. Did you have an enjoyable ride?"

"The best." He checked the back-up camera for obstacles then glanced her way. "You can suck my dick anytime you want. Just give me a little notice if I'm driving so I can pull off the road. I think I went blind there for a few seconds."

"If you're trying to say thank you, then you're welcome. You have some wicked hand skills yourself. Thank you for taking care of my needs."

He nodded acceptance of her words. "I think there's a Mickey D's a little farther down the road. I'd hoped to feed you a little better, but I don't think either of us is up to sitting in a fancy restaurant right now."

"Can we get the food to go? I'm okay with eating in the car."

"Or, we can take it back to my room and eat it naked."

Sunny smiled. "I like your idea better than mine."

CHAPTER SEVEN

They ended up in Sunny's room because it had the larger bed and a small table perfect for two to share a quick meal. Once inside, their stomachs dictated they keep their clothes on long enough to fuel up, but once they'd satisfied one hunger, another took precedent.

"Now for dessert." Jake stood, offered his hand to her. When they stood toe-to-toe, he wrapped his arm around her waist, bringing her even closer. "I'm going to undress you and taste every inch of you as I go. Any objections?"

Sunny shook her head. "Not a one, Counselor, but I reserve the right to do the same to you. Later."

"I don't have a problem with allowing you the same rights. Your conditions will be duly recorded in the transcript."

With Jake nibbling on her neck and working the buttons on her blouse, she found it difficult to think, much less speak. "Oh, I like it when you speak lawyer. It's sexy."

"No one has ever said that to me before." He kissed his way down her chest to the top of her bra. "My profession usually turns women off."

Sunny clasped his head with both hands as he nuzzled her cleavage. Suddenly, he stopped, drew back. He cupped her breast; his thumb brushed a spot above her bra. "What have we here?" he asked before tasting the bruise he'd left on her earlier in the day. "Looks like someone has marked you as his." He kissed the spot again. "Enter this into the record as evidence."

"Evidence of what?" she breathed, holding him tight as he got up close and personal with the mark.

"Evidence that you belong to me."

The possession in his voice made her knees weak and her insides melt. No one had ever claimed her the way Jake Ingram did, and she couldn't find a single reason to object. He yanked her bra cup down, exposing one breast. "Who do you belong to, Sunny?" His tongue laved at her nipple, drawing a moan from her. When he took the hardened bud into his mouth and sucked, she would have crumpled to the floor, but he caught her, tumbled her to the bed, and came down on top of her, held her captive with her arms above her head, their fingers intertwined. "Consider yourself under oath. Tell me the truth, or you'll be held in contempt and punished." His eyes glittered with mischief and a smoldering lust.

"What's your question, Counselor?"

"Who marked you? Who do you belong to?"

He rocked his hips against hers, pressing his hard cock into her belly. She gave a fleeting thought to being on the receiving end of his punishment but decided they could circle back to the discussion when she wasn't desperate to feel him inside her. Sunny tilted her hips and spread her legs wider, inviting him to take what he wanted. "You. I belong to y—"

Jake's mouth came down on hers, swallowing the rest of her declaration with a kiss that cemented his claim on her body and incinerated his vow to go slow. She added going slow to her list of things they could explore later then went to work on the buttons of his shirt. In a blur of motion and acrobatics, her blouse joined his shirt and jeans on the floor, followed by her bra, shorts, and panties.

"These have to go, too." She slipped her hands beneath the waistband of his boxers.

Jake flashed her a smile filled with wicked intent. "No objection whatsoever."

He shimmied out of the confining garment then sat back on his heels, allowing her to look her fill. She'd seen her share of nude men, but Jake put them all to shame. A light dusting of hair across his pecs accented his broad chest. The taut skin across his defined abs she'd briefly touched earlier when she'd tried to keep him from interrupting her exploration of his other endowments. Her gaze traveled south, following an arrow of hair that merged with a thatch of curls at the base of his cock. A rush of possessiveness washed over her at the sight of his erection standing hard and proud. For her.

"I don't manscape." He didn't sound the least bit apologetic for not bowing to what she considered a ridiculous practice. She'd never seen the appeal of the Ken doll look. Jake was all man, and she loved it.

"And I hope you never do." She sat up. "Can I touch?"

"I'm not sure how long I can hold out once you put your hands on me, but go ahead."

***

Jake promised himself he'd take it slow with her this time, but the second she ran her fingers through the light patch of hair on his right pec, his resolve faltered. She was his Kryptonite. Her touch shredded the control he'd always prided himself on. He didn't use women. Didn't take them like a caveman. He'd always been a considerate lover, making sure his partner found her pleasure before he sought his own. One touch from Sunny Sheldon and he was in danger of going off like a Roman candle, and her hand wasn't anywhere near his cock.

When it came to her, he was a different person. Crazy. Out of control. Insatiable. Since his college days, he could count on one hand the women he'd been with more than once. One and done. It had always been enough for him. There were too many available women to get hung up on one. Of the ones he'd gone back to for more, he'd quickly grown tired of and ended it after a few weeks.

Sunny was different. They'd only been hooking up for a day, but he couldn't keep his hands off the woman. All he had to do was look at her and his blood supply rushed to his dick. Seeing the mark he'd put on her earlier in the day, he swallowed hard. He hadn't marked a woman since high school when he'd put a hickey on Jane Hansen's neck. She'd slapped him silly the next day when she'd been obliged to wear a turtleneck to school on one of the hottest days of the year. He'd learned his lesson. Girls, women, didn't appreciate the possessive gesture. Or maybe Jane was the only one. Didn't matter. Her wrath cured him of the need to mark a woman. Until Sunny. To distract himself from what her hands were doing, he reached out, brushed his finger over the purple bruise on her breast. "I'm sorry. I shouldn't have done this to you."

Her hands stilled. "Don't be. I like it." She placed her hand over his, pressing his palm over the spot. "It makes me horny every time I see it."

"You aren't just saying so to please me?"

"Why would I? I like the way you lose control—like you've got to have me."

"I want to do it again." He mentally palm-slapped his forehead even as he pushed her backward, used his superior weight to anchor her to the mattress. He caught her hands in his, stretched them above her head, then buried his face in the crook of her neck. "Right here. For everyone to see."

"Do it. Mark me, Jake. Please."

He couldn't deny her anything, so he drew her delicate skin between his lips and sucked until she writhed beneath him and spread her legs, inviting him in. Flexing his hips, he took her in one, brutal thrust, forcing a gasp from her. When she rocked her hips upward, he sank deeper. Determined to last as long as possible, or at least until she came, he forced himself to remain still. Sunny wiggled beneath him. He released his hold on her neck to look into her eyes. "Don't. I won't last."

Her eyes were dark with lust, her expression desperate. "I'm not going to last, either. I'm hurting, Jake."

"A good hurt?" He'd die if he'd caused her unwanted pain.

"It will be as soon as you start moving."

His gaze dropped to the fresh mark forming on her neck. "I marked you again. This one will be harder to hide."

Her head thrashed on the pillow as she used her hips to force him to get on with it. Her moan was the sexiest thing he'd ever heard. Her gaze met his head-on with a look of determination that made his heart stutter then slam against his chest. "Fuck me, Jake. Hard and fast."

***

They were late for breakfast the next morning, but Sunny couldn't have cared less about missing out on the hot meal. Passionate sex won out over food anytime. The fast food they'd consumed the night before fueled multiple sexy sessions but had more than worn off. As they packed their bags and left the cozy accommodations, Sunny's stomach rumbled. "Do we have time to grab some breakfast?" she asked as she handed her bag off to Jake.

He tossed the carry-on sized suitcase into the Jeep, slammed the liftgate shut, and turned to her, took her in his arms. "I wouldn't change a thing about last night or this morning, but I wish we'd booked a place with room service. I'm starving. How about we try the diner we saw on Main Street? It's only about a block from the real estate office. We can walk there after we get some food in us."

"Sounds good to me." After a brief kiss that promised a more heated session later, they parted and climbed into the vehicle. Sunny buckled her seat belt. "I could eat the south end of a northbound horse."

Jake chuckled. "You sound like a Texan."

"Really?" She beamed at him. "I think I might like Texas."

"You might."

A sign inside the door instructed them to seat themselves, and the smell of bacon and coffee encouraged them to seek out the last empty table against the wall next to the bathrooms. Like all the other tables, the chairs were mismatched. Photographs encompassing everything from high school graduation and wedding pics to birthday celebrations rested beneath thick glass on the tabletop. A condiment rack held laminated menus and a supply of flatware tightly wrapped in paper napkins. As they perused the menus, their server sauntered over, turned the mugs right-side up, and filled them from a steaming carafe.

"What can I get 'cha?" the woman asked, setting the pot on the table so she could extract an order pad and pencil from her apron.

Sunny ordered the Farmer's Breakfast, an enormous platter filled with breakfast meats, eggs, and biscuits. "Can I also get a large orange juice, please?"

"No problem, hon." She turned her attention to Jake. "What about you?"

"I'll have what she's having but with a side of pancakes. Ditto on the orange juice, too."

The waitress retrieved the coffee carafe then departed with a promise to return with their juice glasses.

Sunny's gaze met Jake's. "Do you think we ordered too much food?"

"I didn't see the south end of a northbound horse on the menu, so I improvised." His lips curved up on the ends, and his eyes twinkled. He lifted the white ceramic mug to his lips and took a sip. "I worked up an appetite, too, you know."

"Oh, I know. And, I meant to tell you how much I appreciated the effort you put out last night. And this morning," she added.

"You're welcome. I need to take care of myself today so I can do it again tonight. And tomorrow morning." He winked. "If you want to."

Sunny sighed. "I don't see myself ever turning down a night with you." She sipped her coffee, which smelled a lot better than it tasted. She grabbed two thimble-sized packets of cream and stirred them in before taking another sip. "If I think too much about what we did, I'll end up jumping you right here in the diner. I don't think the other patrons would appreciate the show, so why don't you tell me why we're here?"

They sat back as their server placed two enormous glasses of orange juice on the table. "Food's coming up soon," she said then left them alone again.

Jake picked up the conversation. "We're here because Will and Jessica stopped to inquire about buying a house in the area. I want to find out if Jessica came back later with someone else to look at the property — or another one."

"You think Jessica and Cecil might be nearby?" She couldn't help scanning the other diners to see if anyone looked familiar.

"Relax. Neither one of them has ever met me, and you said you've only met them a few times. I suspect you weren't wearing shorts, and you probably wore your hair up in a fancy do for the occasion."

She mentally willed her shoulders to relax. "You're right. I think the only time I met either of them was at a gallery opening. I usually wear a cocktail dress to those events. Lots of makeup and my hair up."

"What kind of cocktail dress?"

She brought her mug to her lips, looking at him over the rim. "Why do you want to know?"

"I want to picture you in it."

His eyes gave away his wicked thoughts. "Stop. We can't do this here." She glanced around to see if anyone was watching them. "Besides, we need food. Remember?" It was time to change the subject. "What will you do if you find Jessica and Cecil?"

"When. When I find them."

"Okay. When you find them. You aren't going to confront them yourself, are you?"

"I'm not stupid. I'll enlist the help of the local law enforcement, but I will have a word with them. They have a lot to answer for."

Sunny nodded. "No argument from me. Their duplicity rocked the art world. Especially in New York. Artists are wary about who they trust."

"Has your business suffered because of it?"

She shrugged. "Maybe. A couple of young, new artists did come in, asked a lot of questions, then decided not to consign anything with me."

The server returned with their food then, a short time later, came back to refill their coffee mugs. They abandoned conversation to dive into the plates heaped with delicious-smelling food.

At long last, Jake reopened their last conversation. "What kind of questions did the artists ask?"

She slathered blackberry jam on a biscuit. "They wanted to know if I'd known the people involved. Ours is a small world. I knew if I denied knowing any of the parties involved, the lie would come back to bite me in the ass, so I told the truth." When he didn't reply, she glanced up from her plate. His smile promised many things, none of which were appropriate for where they were. "What?"

"I'd like to bite your ass."

A rush of heat flooded her system. She ducked her head, reached for her juice, and took a long, cooling drink. "You have a one-track mind, Counselor."

"Not true. I can process several things at once. For example, are you sure the people who asked those questions were really artists? Could they have been looking for these two, same as we are?"

She mulled his question over while she chewed a slice of bacon. "You could be right. I didn't know either of the two I recall coming in. And I don't remember hearing about their work going on display in any of the usual places. Which means absolutely nothing. If they ended up consigning at one of the smaller galleries, I probably wouldn't hear about it. It's impossible to keep up with every gallery in the city."

"Makes me wonder though. I've always found it hard to believe Will was their first and only target."

"You think they've been scamming other artists all along?"

"Maybe." He shrugged and sat back to drink his coffee. "The attack on Will's livelihood could be a personal vendetta. A crime of passion—of sorts. No murder involved, thankfully."

"That we know of," Sunny corrected. "After what they pulled, I wouldn't put anything past them. How far would they go to protect their secret? That's why I asked what your intentions were when you find them. I don't want you getting yourself killed."

Jake sat forward, placed his hand over the rim of his juice glass, and turned the container in circles. "Two days ago, I would have said it didn't matter if I died." His gaze speared hers. "Now, I'm thinking I have something to live for."

Sunny was still processing his statement when their server returned with the coffeepot. They both waived her off, so she left the ticket with instructions to pay up front. Jake glanced at his watch. "The office should be open."

He tossed a generous tip on the table then stood and made his way to the register. Sunny followed in a daze. She didn't know which part of Jake's statement she wanted clarified most. The part about it not mattering if he died or the part about having something to live for now. Both made her palms sweat and her heart race. Jake Ingram was an enigma.

CHAPTER EIGHT

Jake silently cursed himself for saying the things he'd said. He'd broken the lawyer code and his own personal code—the one about keeping your damn mouth shut. What was it about Sunny Sheldon that made him act like a caveman one minute and a lovesick idiot the next? He should tell her to cover up the hickey he'd given her last night. The damn thing was distracting. It was a visual reminder of how she felt under him, her body taking him in, moving with him, coming apart around him. It was a wonder he could function at all under the circumstances.

As he handed over his credit card to pay the breakfast tab, he inhaled deep then let the breath out slow, hoping the oxygen, followed by a lung cleanse, would help him get his head on straight. He'd revealed too much about his state of mind before he came to New York and how this trip changed his outlook on life. Hustling out to the sidewalk, he didn't give Sunny an opportunity to question his statements. Her falling into a quiet step beside him told him she was thinking up ways to ask what he'd meant.

He'd have to distract her. Their teasing banter over a jam-covered biscuit came to mind. Yeah, he'd bite her ass tonight. Leave his mark there, too. Maybe he'd spank her. See how she liked a little punishment. She'd seemed to like it last night when he held her hands above her head and took her.

Jake stopped at the corner. He had a goddamn hard-on—again. He couldn't go in the real estate office looking like this. He glanced around at the shop windows for anything to help him focus. His gaze landed on a drugstore display of geriatric supplies. Someone had tied a giant ribbon across an elevated toilet seat. It was both absurd and sobering. Who would think that an appropriate gift, even if the recipient needed it? *Christ. Give the poor person a card or some flowers. Something cheerful. Not a toilet seat!* Though his brother Rick did have a milestone birthday coming up. He'd be thirty in a few weeks and acted like an old man sometimes. Maybe he'd get him one of those. See if it cheered him up or shook him out of whatever doldrums had a hold on him.

By the time the light changed, Jake's erection was well on the way to deflating. He crossed the street, Sunny on his heels. The Open sign hung in the window of the real estate office. He held the door, let Sunny precede him inside.

An older woman with frizzy, graying black hair sat behind a scarred wooden desk. She looked up from her computer monitor, a smile on her bright-red lips. "Good morning! Name's Ruth Winslow. What can I do for you?"

Jake placed his hand on the small of Sunny's back, directed her to one of the visitor chairs facing the desk. He shook hands with Ruth, taking a seat. "I'm Jake and this is Sunny. We were hoping you could help us. My brother and his fiancée stopped in here about six months ago, looking for a place to buy. Maybe you remember them?"

Sunny handed over the photos she'd stashed in her purse. "Do they look familiar?"

Ms. Winslow studied the pictures for a minute. "They asked about a farm listing. Sometimes when I have a lot of inventory, I print the listings out and tape them in the window, hoping someone passing by might see something they like, even if they aren't interested in buying. I can't tell you how many properties I've sold because of those postings." She returned the photos. "I saw them looking. Waved them in." She shifted a few things around on her already neat desk. "What's this about?"

Jake ignored her question. "Did you show them a property?"

"No. They said they were passing through and weren't ready to buy yet." She stiffened her spine. "I repeat. What is this about?"

"My brother was a victim of a crime perpetrated by his fiancée and another man. The two of them have gone missing. We're trying to locate them." Jake paused, deciding how to phrase his story. "They took everything my brother owned. I promised him I'd find them and get his stuff back."

"What kind of things did they take?"

Sunny jumped into the conversation. "They cleaned out his bank accounts and stole several paintings. Jake's brother is a well-known painter. The canvases are worth a small fortune."

"I see, but isn't this a matter for the police?"

"It is," Sunny agreed. "They're looking into it, but it's a nonviolent crime and the leads have gone cold. We're trying to help."

Jake added, "By any chance, did his fiancée come back later on to look at the property, or another one?"

The woman shook her head. "Not that I know of. I'm the only agent in town. I handle most every listing in this area."

"Did the farm they looked at sell?"

Ruth nodded. "It did. I believe it sold to a couple from the city. An agent out of the next county brought the buyer in. I never saw them myself, but they paid cash and planned to turn it into a free-range chicken farm. Craziest thing I've ever heard of." She huffed out a laugh. "The things these city people think up. I guarantee the place will be on the market within the year. Is your brother still looking to move to the country?"

He smiled at her attempt to sell the not-yet-for-sale property to Will. "No, ma'am. He went home to Texas."

Sunny sat on the edge of her seat. "Can you bring up the listing? I'd like to see the place." She glanced at Jake. He raised an eyebrow at her. "What? I've been thinking of moving someplace quiet. Maybe if I like the looks of it, Ruth can call me when it comes on the market again."

Ms. Winslow typed for a bit before swinging the computer monitor around to show them the pictures of the farm in question. "The house is in great shape for being over a hundred years old. Your brother was most interested in the barn though." She tapped a key, and a montage of photos filled the screen. "It's nearly as ancient as the house, but someone converted the hayloft into an apartment. Lots of light, which makes sense now that I know he's a painter. The barn apartment would be a nice studio."

Jake silently noted the address on the listing. The place would have been perfect for Will, except for being in New York. He hated what happened to Will, vowed he'd make it right, but he wasn't sad the incident brought his brother home.

Sunny asked a few more questions then left the woman her card. "Call me if the property comes back on the market. I'd like to see it."

Hopeful for a future sale, Ruth Winslow escorted them to the door with a smile on her face, not once realizing they'd played her.

"You're going out there, aren't you?"

"Yep. You don't have to go. You can wait at the diner, or I'll drop you at the library or something. They don't know me. I'll pretend I'm lost, ask for directions. See if it's them. If not, no harm done. If it is Cecil and Jessica, I'll come back and visit the local law enforcement, whoever they are. Does a town this size have a police force?"

"Probably not. Most of these small communities rely on the county sheriff's office."

"Perfect for a couple of fugitives."

"I'm going with you. You might not recognize them. All you've ever seen are promotional photos of them from their websites."

"Your choice, but don't get out of the car. They might recognize you."

***

"Plug the address into the navigation system." Jake rattled off the one he'd memorized from the real estate listing. Sunny tapped the keys on the virtual keyboard.

While the device searched for a route, Sunny rummaged in her purse, came up with a tube of lip balm. She pulled the sun visor down, flipped the cover open to reveal a mirror. As she swiped the soothing goo on her lips, she mumbled, "I hope it's not too far."

The GPS's recorded voice chimed in, "In 300 yards, turn right on Maple Street."

Jake put the Jeep in gear and backed out of the parking space. "If the GPS is correct, it's less than five miles. We'll know if it's them soon."

Sunny was torn. If it was Jessica and Cecil, Jake's business in New York would be done. She had no illusions about him staying there with her. He'd go home when he located the people who'd stolen from his brother or, at the very least, found the paintings. He'd mentioned another lead to follow if this one didn't pan out. "If it's not them, where do we go from here?"

"Callicoon. Cecil Hawthorne's former PR person, a guy by the name of Ross McClelland lives out there. MacKenzie Carlysle took over for him when he retired a few years ago. He worked for Hawthorne a long time. If anyone knows where the man might have gone to hide, McClelland is the man."

"And if he doesn't have information? What will you do then?"

"I don't know. Go home, I guess, and wait for something else to come up. I'm certain they have the paintings and plan to use them, even if it's selling them back to Will, one at a time, to keep them in funds."

"Can he afford to pay them?"

"Depends on what kind of money they want, but, last time I talked to my brother, he said if he saw the paintings again, he'd destroy them himself."

Sunny gasped. "What? Why would he do such a thing?"

"Says they no longer represent him as a painter. He talked about how Jessica convinced him to paint more commercial subjects—things she could sell easily. I guess he went along for a while, and those are the paintings she stole."

"I haven't seen his latest work, but the ones I sold for him were beautiful and appealed to a wide audience. He has a rare talent."

As instructed by the navigation system, Jake made another turn onto a narrow, two-lane road flanked by tall trees on both sides. Mailboxes on posts showed homes existed, but none were visible from the road. "I agree with you. Will is talented. I think he lost his way or, more likely, let Jessica lead him off his path. This entire thing has hit him hard, but he's finding his way out and will be a better person for what he's gone through. Maybe even a better painter, if possible."

"It's possible if he's more in tune with the creative force within himself. If I had any criticism of his early work, it was it lacked a measure of depth. That being said, he has an eye for esthetics few artists possess. I'm sure he's matured as an artist. I hope I get a chance to see what he's working on now. I bet it's spectacular."

"You've got a lot of confidence in a man you hardly know." He slowed the Jeep to take a better look at the number on a mailbox. "This is it." He checked the rearview mirror then stopped in the road as the GPS announced they'd reached their destination. "You still want to go with me? I can take you back to town."

"W.H. Ingram isn't the first artist to reinvent him or herself after a life-altering event, and I can't think of a single one who didn't come out on the other side as a better artist." She glanced at the narrow lane leading off the main road. "Cecil Hawthorne and Jessica Blackwell didn't only damage one artist's career. Their dishonesty hurt the entire art community. So yeah, I'm in. Let's do this."

"Okay." Jake accelerated, made the turn onto the rutted roadway. "It's a good thing I rented a Jeep. Don't think a car would make it."

"These people must value their privacy."

"Fugitives usually do."

"And free-range chicken farmers," she countered as they came around a curve in the drive. A bunch of fowl pecked away in fenced pastureland as far as the eye could see.

"And free-range chicken farmers," Jake agreed. "Looks like the house and barn are up there." He pointed to the hint of a roofline in the distance.

"I'm sorry, but I don't see Cecil or Jessica as chicken farmers. Not even as a cover for whatever else they may be up to. I never knew them well, but they didn't strike me as the farmer type."

"You're probably right," he said, disappointment clear in his tone. "Just in case, we need to get a look at the owners." He drove on at a slow pace.

"Agreed."

As they made the last curve and the residence and barn came into view, a couple came out of the house. "What do you think? Could that be them?"

Sunny didn't need to get any closer. "No. Jessica is almost as tall as Cecil. That woman is shorter than me, and Cecil would have given anything to grow hair like that man has. He was very vocal about going bald early in life."

"He didn't shave his head?"

"Nope. Completely bald, naturally."

"Huh."

There was no place to turn around, so it was back down the drive or continue to the parking area between the house and barn. "You stay in the car. I'll play the lost tourist, and then we'll get out of here."

Sunny studied the young couple as Jake got out, asked them directions to the town where they'd spent the night. The farmers graciously set him on the right path. She smiled as he tipped his imaginary hat to them and returned to the Jeep.

He turned the vehicle around, waved goodbye, then they were headed toward the road once again. He propped an elbow on the door, rubbing his temple and forehead with his raised hand. "Not them," he said, his voice laced with disappointment.

"No. Not them."

He'd been off in his own world since leaving the farm, driving by rote. If not for Sunny's helpful reminders of where to turn, heaven only knew where they would have ended up. Arriving in town, they sat at the stop sign at the corner of Main and Maple until another motorist pulled up behind them and honked.

"Shit." Jake punched the gas, turned onto Main Street. He parked in front of the diner and they both got out. "I need a minute. Some caffeine and a sweet roll wouldn't be amiss, either. How about you?"

"I'll pass on the sweet roll. I'm still pretty full from breakfast, but coffee sounds good."

They sat at the counter. A different server from the one they'd seen earlier approached. "Morning, folks." Her smile seemed genuine and friendly. "New in town or passing through?"

"Passing through," Sunny responded. "I guess you know everyone in these parts?"

The woman nodded then reached for the coffee carafe behind her on the warmer. She held it up. "Regular?"

Jake flipped his mug over. Sunny followed suit and watched as the waitress filled both cups. "Not many new people around here. Mostly the old folks. They raise their kids. The kids move off to the city as soon as they can. Most don't come back."

Sunny fished the photos of Cecil and Jessica out of her purse. She held them out to the woman. She talked as she stirred creamer into her coffee. "We're trying to find some friends of ours who we lost touch with. Last I heard, they were looking for property in this area. We got to thinking about them a few weeks ago and took some vacation time. Thought we'd see some scenery and maybe locate them."

CHAPTER NINE

Jake guzzled his coffee while Sunny did her thing. He had to hand it to her. She proved to be a first-rate actor. Marge, their server, bought her stupid story, hook, line, and sinker. She studied the photos before handing them back.

"The woman looks familiar, but I never seen the guy before. I'd remember his bald head, but I guess he could have been wearing a cap. Lots do around here. No manners, if you get my drift. Just sit there with their hat on like this is a barn." She topped off their mugs. "I could be mistaken about the woman. Is she a model or something?"

"No." Sunny tucked the photos away then added another thimble of cream to her mug before taking a sip. "She's an agent. Works mostly with artists. Or she did. Don't know what either of them are doing now. I think they'd both reached their burnout point, needed to try something different."

"We get a lot of city slickers out this way. Think they want to be farmers until they figure out how much work it is then they hightail it back to civilization. Some farms around here have changed hands a half dozen times in the last decade."

It occurred to Jake they were looking for the needle in the proverbial haystack. This close to the city, people came and went as if the freeway exit were a revolving door. People like

Marge kept track of all the comings and goings. If a person, or persons, needed a place to hide out, this wasn't it. He drained his mug, tossed a twenty-dollar bill on the counter, and stood. "You ready to hit the road, sweetheart?"

Sunny stood, smiled at Marge. "Thanks for everything. It's been nice talking to you."

The older woman scooped their dirty coffee mugs into a tub beneath the counter then picked up the twenty. "You're welcome. Wish I could have helped you find your friends." She waved the currency in the air. "I'll get your change."

Jake hurried toward the door, Sunny on his heels. "Keep it." He pushed open the door. Heat and humidity smacked them in the face, making him wish he could stay indoors the rest of the day.

"You left a generous tip for two cups of coffee and a lot of talk."

Jake popped the door locks. They climbed in. Jake cranked the engine and set the air conditioner to full blast before fastening his seat belt. "She has the gift of gab, but it was probably the most enlightening conversation ever."

"How do you figure?" Sunny adjusted air vents to blow right on her then snapped her seat belt in place. "She didn't recognize Cecil or Jessica."

"She might have remembered Jessica from when she was here with Will, but that's irrelevant. The woman knows everyone here. She's a walking, talking history of every person who's moved in or out of this area for decades."

"I don't understand how her busybody tendencies are relevant at all."

Jake programmed the GPS for Callicoon before backing out of the parking space. "Listening to her, it occurred to me if someone was trying to disappear, this wasn't the place to do it. Too many people like Marge. Busybodies who have no problem sticking their nose in other people's business. Wherever Jessica and Cecil are, it's someplace where they could settle in with no one paying them much mind."

"Based on your assumption, they're probably still in the city. People move all the time. No one pays them any mind. You can live next door to someone for years and never have a conversation with them. You might not even see them. Ever."

"Exactly. I've been thinking like a guy from a small town. Thinking they'd go someplace remote. Marge changed my way of thinking."

"Then why are we going to Raccoon?"

Jake laughed. "We're going to *Callicoon* because New York City is the largest city in the nation. If Cecil and Jessica are there, we'll never find them without help. Our best hope is Mr. McClelland. I got the impression he didn't leave Hawthorne's employ under the best of circumstances. He might know something. A connection we don't know about. A friend. Relative. Someone or someplace Cecil might go to hole up. And he might be willing to talk."

"You have a knack for this."

"Detective work?" Jake shook his head. "I'm a rank amateur."

"Don't sell yourself short. You're thinking this through, examining all angles. You're probably right about them being in the city, though I never would have reached the same conclusion based on what Marge told us. I guess that's what makes you an excellent lawyer."

"I'm an excellent lawyer because I hate to lose. No other reason."

***

The bitterness in his voice rocked her back. "I sense a story here. Don't you enjoy what you do?" Silence sat between them like a mute hitchhiker, but Sunny refused to let the subject rest. "Well, tell me this. If you weren't a lawyer, what would you be?"

More silence. According to the GPS, a long stretch of road lay ahead before their next turn.

She tried a different tact. "I wanted to be a teacher."

Jake's gaze landed on her for a brief second then switched to the road again. "How did you end up owning a gallery instead?"

"This isn't about me, Jake Ingram. Answer my question and I'll tell you my sob story."

"What was your question again?"

"I sensed you don't want to be a lawyer, so I asked what you would be if you could be anything you wanted."

"You promise you won't laugh?"

"Promise."

"I wanted to be a writer. A novelist."

"So, why aren't you?"

He sighed, buying time to gather his thoughts. He'd told no one about his dream to become a writer. What would have been the point? His dad had mapped out his life for him, and Jake hadn't been able to say no to his plans. "My dad was a lawyer. He wanted—no—expected me to follow in his footsteps. I wasn't given a choice in the matter. I won't say I was opposed to becoming a lawyer. I figured it would provide me a decent living and allow me to get out from under my dad's thumb until the day came when I could break out of the mold and do what I wanted. That day never came."

"Why not? I don't understand what's keeping you from writing. Most of the writers I know—remember, I grew up in L.A. where everyone and their landlord thinks they can write a screenplay—have a regular job and write at night or in the morning before work. Where there's a will, there's a way."

Jake's derisive laugh filled the vehicle. "I guess you nailed the real problem. I lost the will."

"How did you end up with your own practice in your hometown?"

"I inherited it from my dad. There wasn't enough business for me to work with him right out of law school, so I got on with a firm in Houston. Learned a lot there. Found out I'm a decent litigator. I thought about writing, as you say, at night or weekends. Then Dad died, and I stepped into his shoes. Took over right where he left off. Lived in the same house I grew up in for years until I finally realized I wasn't going anywhere anytime soon. I bought a piece of land out on the lake and built myself a house. Big one with an office and a pool. I even built a pool house I imagined would become my writing cave."

"What happened?"

"Will was in New York. Rick was in the service. He spent a lot of time in the Middle East. My head wasn't in the right place, I guess. I worried about both of them, constantly. Instead of a novel, I was writing wills and handling divorces day in and day out. I'd get home at night, and the worry would creep in. Between worrying all night long and the boring-as-hell day job, whatever creativity I once possessed vanished. Sucked right out of me."

***

Jake clamped his jaw tight. What the hell came over him? Telling a virtual stranger his deepest, darkest secret?

The thought gave him pause. Was Sunny a stranger? He'd experienced his share of hookups with casual acquaintances and women he'd met at functions and bars. He'd never, not once, been inclined to tell them anything personal, much less reveal his most closely held secret. Even his brothers didn't know he'd always wanted to be a writer, and they knew him better than anyone on the planet. Except, perhaps, Sunny Sheldon.

He'd felt a connection to the pseudo-celebrity/gallery owner from the first moment he'd met her. A connection like no other. He'd thought it was a physical response to a beautiful woman, but if that was all it was, distance should have put an end to it. Two thousand miles and weeks later, he still woke in the middle of the night with a raging hard-on and memories of her fresh in his mind.

Those wake-up calls were the reason he returned to New York. He could have paid the private investigator to follow up on every lead. Doing it himself was nothing more than an excuse to see Sunny again—to find out if his dreams could somehow become reality.

He risked a glance at the woman in the passenger seat. She'd grown silent following his latest confession. Sitting there in her summer blouse and shorts, her hair pulled back in a high ponytail, her makeup the barest minimum, she took his breath away.

He wished he could say he was sorry the chicken farmers weren't the lowlifes who swindled Will out of a fortune, but he'd be lying if he did. As soon as he found Cecil and Jessica, he'd have no reason to stay in New York. His time with Sunny would end, and he wasn't ready to let her go. Not yet. The craving for her would go away sometime. Wouldn't it?

Desire would run its natural course in a few more days. The sex would lose its spark. It always did. No woman held his attention for long. He ignored the part of his brain reminding him he'd thought time and distance would help. Sunny was an anomaly. One his logical mind would eventually figure out and tire of.

"I'm sorry you didn't get to follow your own path in life."

Her words startled him out of his musings. He glanced her way. Their gazes met. Something in the depth of her eyes made him grip the steering wheel until his knuckles ached. It was either hang on tight or reach for her. The need to touch her, to ease the pain he sensed lurking below the surface was as real as his next breath.

Jerking his attention to the road ahead, he ground out, "Well, thanks, but shit happens." They rode in silence for a while then he asked, "So, you wanted to be a teacher? What happened to your dream?

Gaze focused on the road ahead, she chuckled. "You've forgotten who my dad is?"

She said it like her dad's fame explained everything. Jake risked a glance her way. "No, but I don't see what his celebrity has to do with you not becoming a teacher."

She rolled her eyes at him. "I double majored in college—art history and secondary education, got my degree, but to get a teaching credential, you have to complete a semester of student-teaching. Basically, an internship under an experienced educator. I got my assignment, showed up to the school for my first day, and ran into a wall of reporters. The principal asked me to leave and not come back." She shrugged. "It was a wake-up call for me. My grandmother left me her brownstone in New York. I knew celebrities who'd moved there, and they sang its praises. They could walk the sidewalks, eat in restaurants, do as they pleased without being harassed all the time by paparazzi. So, I packed up and relocated to New York."

"Why didn't you complete your student-teaching in New York?"

"Like you, I guess I lost my will to teach. Instead, I put my art history education to use and opened Sunnyside Gallery. I'm sure you've guessed; I don't need an income. Besides the brownstone, my grandmother left me a sizeable trust fund. My dad set one up for me, too. Dealing in art is something to do. Keeps me from going nuts, and I like to think I help up-and-coming artists."

"Like my brother."

"Yes. I've seen a lot of talent come through my gallery. Some are more talented than others. Your brother hit the top of my list early on and remains there. He's really good. I hope you realize how special he is."

"I do. I'm not an expert or art history major, but I know when something moves me. I'm excited to see what he comes up with once he gets past what they did to him. He seems…" Jake thought for a moment. "He seems older. Wiser. If that makes any sense?"

"It does. He has more emotions, more depth of character to draw upon. He's experienced more of life—albeit a sad and sorry side of life—but life nonetheless."

"I think it forced him to look inside himself for the first time. See who he really is. I hope the insight comes out in his new works because the world needs to see what an amazing person he is."

"I agree."

Silence filled the cab, except for the hum of the tires and the occasional road hazard warning from the navigation app. Jake appreciated the time to absorb what Sunny had revealed about herself. There were layers to her personality he hadn't expected. She was a giver, and she possessed a kind heart. He'd seen her acting ability at the diner and knew she could put on a performance when she wanted to, but he didn't think she was pretending now. Maybe she was a better actor than she claimed. He couldn't know for sure, but his gut told him the woman who'd given up her dream of teaching was as genuine as they came. A rare thing in his book.

"You getting hungry? I'm thinking we should try to find some grub."

Sunny's laughter filled the cab and lit a match to Jake's libido. He was coming to realize it didn't take much where she was concerned to get him stirred up. "Grub? Don't look now, but your hillbilly is showing, Counselor."

"Just be glad I left my camo at home."

"Seriously? You have camo gear? The real kind, not the stuff people buy in high-priced boutiques and think they look cool?"

"You don't?" he asked, deadpan.

"No! Why would I?"

"I don't know. For all I know, you hunt your own meat and have a basement full of vegetables you canned yourself."

God, he loved to hear her laugh. Would keep up the silly banter forever just to see her smile. He fought the urge to pull off the road and make her smile for a different reason.

"Never been hunting, and, other than an experiment I did for the science fair in second grade, I've never grown anything in my life. I don't even have house plants." She held out both hands. "Two brown thumbs."

"Confession. I don't own any camo. My brother, Rick, used to have a complete wardrobe of the stuff. Liked to go hunting. That was before he joined the Navy. Since he's been home, I haven't seen him wear anything but jeans and T-shirts."

"Lost his taste for hunting?"

"I don't know. He's not much of a talker. Never was."

"You're an interesting family. A lawyer/wannabe writer, an artist, and a warrior."

"I don't know about interesting, but we are a family. We look out for each other."

"Must be nice."

Jake picked up on the wistful tone in her voice. "You don't enjoy being an only child?"

"I loved it when I was a kid, but as an adult I think it would be fun to have someone close to my age to share things with, to talk to."

He often thought having siblings was overrated, but, looking at it from her perspective, he had to admit he never felt alone. Not even when his brothers were off leading their own lives. He'd always known they were there. A phone call away, most of the time, and they had his back, no matter what. "I've got two brothers. I can loan you one."

Her smile and soft laughter wrecked him.

"Thanks, but I'm okay. I've got friends, and my parents."

CHAPTER TEN

Jake's silly offer to loan one of his brothers was sweet, but she didn't want Will or Rick. She wanted Jake. She tried to tell herself this was a physical thing. Great sex clouding her mind. But it was more than just sex. Jake Ingram was getting under her skin a little more with each thing he revealed about himself. No doubt he'd make a fabulous writer once he pursued his dream. He was an excellent storyteller, captivating her with his tales of growing up in a small Texas town as they put the Manhattan skyline farther behind them. And with each mile, she fell a little harder for him.

This would not end well for her. Jake would probably go on his merry way. Put a few extra notches—okay—a lot of extra notches in his bedpost when he got home in. He'd move on to some other woman and forget all about her. A man like him wouldn't be lonely for long. But the thought of being with anyone else creeped Sunny out. Maybe in a few months? Perhaps the memories would fade, and she'd see the flaws in the man. Realize how silly she'd been to put him on a pedestal and slap a label on him—*the one*. He couldn't be. He lived a different life from hers in another state, for crying out loud!

It was the sex. She'd never had better. Which, admittedly, wasn't saying much, given her lack of partners recently.

If it wasn't the sex, it had to be his Southern drawl. Always present but more so when passion ruled him, as if he had better things to do than modulate his voice. Oh, and the things he could do. Which brought her right back to the superb sex.

Ugh! Didn't she just prove her own point. She wasn't falling in love with the man. She was in a sex stupor. Once he went home, the pheromone fog would lift, and she'd be back to normal.

Translation: she'd be alone.

"Hey."

She plastered a smile on her face then turned to the man who occupied all her thoughts these days. "Hey, yourself."

"I'm starving. Want to check the mapping app for a place to eat?"

"Sure." She grabbed her phone from the cup holder. After an exhaustive search, she grimaced. "There's not much to choose from. No fast food of any kind. A few mom-and-pop places. There's one in Narrowsburg that sounds okay. Want to try it?"

"I should have had a piece of pie with my coffee back there to tide me over." His stomach growled as if agreeing with his assessment. "Plug in the address so we don't waste time getting lost."

Sunny chuckled then keyed the information into the navigation system. "Do we have a place to spend the night?"

Jake tapped the steering wheel with his index finger, his gaze fixed on the road and the enormous travel trailer trudging along ahead of them. "Uh. That would be a no. Want to see what you can find?"

"Where are we going, again? Calhoun?"

"Callicoon. I think it's close to Narrowsburg."

"Never heard of it."

"They have a post office."

"That's reassuring."

Following the automated directions, they eventually pulled into the parking lot of the eating establishment which turned out to be connected to a gas station via a convenience store. Potholes and weeds warred for top billing with gravel. An abandoned rail line ran behind the structure.

"I think that's a grocery store." Sunny pointed to a metal building across the street. "If this doesn't work out, we can see if they have a deli."

Jake stretched his arms above his head. She watched, her body heating as memories of the way he looked beneath his clothes came to mind. He propped one foot then the other on the bumper for some leg stretches. "I'm thinking it might be wise to have a stash of snacks and some water bottles in the car. The scarcity of services in this area reminds me of parts of Texas. I didn't expect this area to be so remote."

Together, they approached the diner. A server wearing jeans and a T-shirt, an apron tied around her waist, and a towel draped over one shoulder waved to them. "Take any seat you want. I'll be right with you."

The only other patron, a man wearing dirt-streaked jeans and a sweat-soaked shirt attacked a burger and fries at the Formica-topped breakfast counter. They chose a booth next to the plate-glass window overlooking the parking lot. The hard wooden seats didn't invite patrons to linger over endless cups of coffee, though an assortment of pies in a refrigerated case on the wall behind the counter suggested dessert might be in order. After checking out the ads from local businesses printed on the paper placemats, they examined the menus from the condiment rack. By the time the lone waitress came around to take their order, they'd made their selections.

"I'll have the cheeseburger and fries." Sunny returned her menu to the rack next to the wall. "And a diet soda, please."

The woman didn't bother to write the order down. "How you want your burger cooked, hon?"

"Medium-well, please."

She turned her attention to Jake. He ordered the same but went with iced tea. "Be right back with your drinks." True to her word, she plunked the plastic glasses and paper-wrapped straws on the table before disappearing through the swinging door leading to the kitchen.

Jake dumped a packet of artificial sweetener in his glass then stirred it with a straw. He took a sip and grimaced. "It's times like this I really miss Texas."

Sunny smiled. "That bad?"

"Tastes like horse piss."

"You don't really know what horse piss tastes like, do you?"

He shoved the offending beverage as far away as possible on the small table. "No, but I can imagine. Want to try it? See what you think?"

"Nope." She took a long draw on her straw. "I'll stick with my soda." She held the glass out. "Want some?"

"Nah. I'll have her bring me one when she comes back." He returned his attention to the placemat ads. "We need to find a hotel for tonight."

"Good luck finding a room." They both straightened to allow the server to set plates on the table. "There's a festival in town this weekend. Even the campgrounds are full."

"What about Callicoon?" Jake adjusted the plate in front of him to suit him. "That's close to here, isn't it?"

"It's north of here a few miles. There's a small, historic hotel there, but I wouldn't count on finding a room. If you're looking for one of those chain hotels, you'll be driving to Scranton for the night."

"Pennsylvania?" Sunny couldn't keep the horror out of her voice.

The woman rolled her eyes. "Hon, Pennsylvania is just across the river. Scranton is about an hour's drive unless you get behind a sightseer then it could take longer."

"You get many sightseers?" Jake asked.

"Plenty. People come up to fish the Delaware River. See the bald eagles. Camp. Lots of summer communities in these parts. Like I said, RiverFest is this weekend. Lots of people in town for the event. Craft vendors. Tourists. Figured you were here for the festivities."

"No, though I wish I'd known about the festival beforehand. I would have planned to stay awhile." Jake graced her with a hundred-megawatt smile. "Appreciate the info."

"Visitor information is on the house. You two enjoy your burgers. Is there anything else I can get you?"

"Nope. We're good."

Sunny glanced at Jake's untouched beverage then back to him as the waitress sauntered off. "What about your iced tea?"

Stuffing a french fry in his mouth, Jake shrugged. "I'll grab a water bottle later. I doubt it's her fault the tea tastes like horse piss." He grabbed the ketchup container, squirted the stuff all over his fries.

Sunny reached for the dispenser. When he handed it over, she carefully moved things around on her plate then filled the space with the sweet condiment. "Is that a Texas thing?" She motioned to his doused fries. "Drowning your potatoes before you eat them?"

He swirled another crispy slice through the sauce then popped it in his mouth. He pointed to the tidy dot of the sweet condiment nestled off to the side of her plate. "Is that a New York thing? Isn't the idea to get the ketchup on the fries?"

"Yes, but they get all soggy if you dump it on top of them."

He held up a limp fry coated with red goo. "Don't see what's wrong with my method." He opened his mouth, crammed the potato in, chewing with obvious satisfaction. "Mm-mm. Good stuff."

Shaking her head, she abandoned the argument over french fry etiquette for their previous topic. "I don't know about you, but I don't want to spend the night in your Jeep."

"I wasn't planning on driving to Scranton, but if we have to, we will." He took a big bite of his burger. Grabbing a napkin from the dispenser on the table, he dabbed the corners of his mouth as he swallowed. "Let's see if we can locate McClelland first. If he has a lead, we might want to head in a different direction before we call it a night."

"Sounds like a plan. How far are we from his house?"

"Half an hour? That's my best guess. Every road we've been on since we left the interstate has been narrow and winding. Not to mention full of potholes."

"So I've noticed." She pushed her plate away. "Why don't we get gas then go across the street to the grocery store? We can stock up on snacks and drinks for the road."

"Sounds like a plan to me. I'd bet they have a Styrofoam cooler for sale. That and a bag of ice and we're good."

Jake paid the bill. While he pumped the gas, she plugged their next destination into the navigation system. "You were right. We're only about a half hour from his house," she said as he climbed into the driver's seat.

"Best news I've heard all day." He pulled away from the pump. Traffic, mostly giant pickups towing even bigger campers, made it difficult to cross to the grocery store, but patience won out. The outside of the store didn't look like much, but the inside was brightly lit. The floors were clean and the shelves well stocked. Jake spied a stack of Styrofoam coolers near the registers. He tossed one in their cart. "Get whatever you think we need. I don't want to be stuck on one of these roads after dark with no place to sleep and nothing to eat. If we have grub, we can power through until we get someplace that has accommodations."

"I really, really don't want to sleep in the car."

"Me, either." He walked beside her, pushing the cart. "I'm holding out for a safe, clean room with a giant tub and a king-sized bed."

Sunny moaned. "A nice long soak sounds like heaven."

"Then let's get a move on. The sooner we find McClelland, the sooner we both get what we want."

CHAPTER ELEVEN

With their new cooler stocked with water bottles and snacks, they resumed the drive. Jake liked trees as much as the next guy, but as they wound back and forth through the forested Catskill mountains, he longed for the wide-open spaces of North Texas. If it weren't for the opportunity to spend time with Sunny, he would have gladly handed this part of the investigation over to the private investigator. He hoped Hawthorne's former PR guru was at home and would willingly give up any information he had so they could get out of the mountains before it got dark.

According to the GPS, they were less than five miles from their destination when they came upon a construction crew doing road repairs. One of the two lanes was closed. A stout woman wearing a reflective vest and holding a stop sign stood in the roadway, stopping their progress while oncoming traffic streamed by at a crawl. Jake put the Jeep in Park and took his foot off the brake. "Wonder how many potholes this stretch of road had if it gets repaired while the others we've been on don't warrant any attention."

"It must have been one giant pothole," Sunny agreed. "But at least they're repairing something."

Jake tapped the steering wheel. Something had been bothering him since they'd left the chicken farmer's place earlier that morning. The closer they got to McClelland's house, the more it bugged him. Changing the subject in the middle of a conversation was a cheap lawyer trick to catch a witness off guard. He hated pulling it out now, but he wanted an honest answer or, at the very least, an honest response. "Do you know Ross McClelland?"

Sunny snapped her head around to meet his gaze. "No. I think I may have talked with him on the phone once several years ago, but he worked behind the scenes as most PR people do. Like my PR person does."

At her vehement denial, a weight lifted from his chest. Everything he'd learned about Sunny Sheldon pointed to her being squeaky clean and honest in her business dealings. The lawyer in him found it hard to believe anyone could be as perfect as she seemed, but the more time he spent with her, the more he trusted her. And the more he wanted her. He couldn't seem to keep his hands off her. Reaching across the console, he took her hand, squeezed it gently. "Just wanted to know if you'd recognize him," he lied.

Sunny returned the hand squeeze. "I doubt I would. If I ever saw him, I didn't know who he was. It's possible we were in the same place at the same time. Some gallery openings are enormous affairs. Others, not so much."

"So, he might recognize you?"

She shrugged. "It's possible. Probably more likely than me recognizing him. I am a public figure—albeit a minor one. Couple that with owning a gallery, and you can see how the two might make me more visible than your average person in the art world."

The traffic controller turned their stop sign around so it read, *proceed with caution* then waved them to the open lane. He fell in behind the line of cars ahead of them. Once past the construction, he swerved back into the right lane, and they continued to their destination. "I think this is it." Jake put on his turn signal and slowed to make the left turn.

"Wow! What a house!" Sunny gawked at the Victorian set atop a gentle slope.

Jake concurred. According to the private investigator, the house sat on close to 100 acres of mixed-use property. About half had been cleared for farming over a century ago, while they'd left the rest untouched. The house and acreage had been in the McClelland family for four generations. Ross was the last living descendant of the original settlers. "It seems like a lot for a single guy. Especially one as old as he is."

"How old is he?"

"According to the investigator I hired, he's 72 and in failing health."

"Someone must help him keep all this up. A lawn this size doesn't mow itself, and the house looks to be in remarkable shape." She pointed to an outbuilding revealed as they got closer. "You don't see barns like that every day. This place is gorgeous!"

Jake followed the paved drive around to the back of the house where a late-model Lexus sat next to an older GMC pickup with more rust than paint. He pulled up short of the vehicles and cut the engine. Before they could exit the car, an old gentleman appeared on the porch, pushed the screen door open. He pointed a double-barreled shotgun at them like he knew what to do with it.

"Not the greeting I expected," Jake said.

Sunny's voice shook. "Let's leave before he shoots us."

"Give me a minute." Jake opened his door and stepped out, hands raised. "Name's Jake Ingram. Came all the way from Texas to talk to Ross McClelland." He stepped toward the man. "Would that be you, sir? I promise, I just want a minute of your time."

"State your business."

"My brother is W. H. Ingram. Does the name ring any bells?"

"You should have led with that." The gun barrel dipped slightly. Jake took it as a friendly sign and approached with caution. "Still don't see what you want with me."

"I'm hoping you can help me locate your former employer, Cecil Hawthorne. He stole a year's worth of my brother's work. I'm trying to get the paintings back."

"Goddamnit. Hawthorne always was a piece of shit." McClelland rested the weapon next to him inside the screened porch. He squinted at the Jeep. "Who's with you?"

"Sunny Sheldon. She owns Sunnyside Gallery."

"I know who she is. You two come in and tell me what this is all about." The door banged shut behind him as he retreated into the house.

Jake returned to the Jeep, leaned in. "Doesn't sound like he much cares for Hawthorne."

"No, it doesn't." Sunny released her seat belt. "You think it's safe to go in?"

"Yeah. Can't blame the old guy for being cautious."

"Guess not, but at the first sign of trouble, I'm calling 9-1-1." She held up her cell phone.

Jake smiled at her feisty attitude. "I don't think you'll need to call reinforcements, but if having a phone in your hand makes you feel safer, by all means…" He waited for her to join him before following McClelland into the house.

He found the old man in the kitchen, pouring hot water from an ancient kettle into three generous sized mugs. He handed one to Jake then carried the other two to a scarred oak table in the center of the eat-in kitchen. There was nothing modern about this farmhouse kitchen. Everything from the dated appliances to the worn linoleum and scarred Formica countertops screamed authenticity circa 1950. The cabinets themselves were probably original to the house, judging from the way the white paint on them had aged. Jake instantly thought of his friend, Hank Travis, and the exorbitant amount of money he'd spent to hide a modern kitchen behind a similar façade. Given a choice, Jake would take the warmth of this one over sleek and modern anytime.

"Have a seat." He set the extra cup in front of Sunny then sat across from her. Jake sat next to her. "Pick your poison." McClelland opened an intricately carved wooden box in the center of the table. "Got any kind of tea you can imagine in there. Sugar is on the table. Milk's in the fridge."

Jake preferred his tea sweet and iced, but he wasn't about to decline the man's offer. He'd drink the horse-piss from the diner before he'd insult the old man. He waited for Sunny to choose from the well-stocked supply then grabbed the same. Following her lead, he opened the small packet and dunked the tea bag into his mug. Their host made his selection, adding a generous scoop of sugar to his mug.

"Sorry about the greeting. I don't get many visitors."

"Don't blame you for being cautious. You live here alone?" Jake asked.

"I do. I grew up in this house. It was a different world then. You could trust your neighbors. Used to, you could trust your employer, too." He dunked his tea bag several times then brought the mug to his lips for a taste. "Cecil Hawthorne used to be an honest man. He changed once he met that woman. After she got her hooks in him, he lost every scrap of integrity he ever possessed. I decided it was time to retire shortly after they got together. Sold everything but my art collection and moved out here to spend my golden years in peace."

"You have a lovely home," Sunny said, glancing around at the clean but outdated kitchen. "I'd love to see the rest of the house."

Humor flashed in the old man's eyes. "You want to see my art collection," he stated, flatly. "Don't worry. I'll let you see it before you go."

Jake raised an eyebrow at Sunny. "What? He spent a lifetime in the New York art world. He worked with the best up-and-coming artists in the world. I'd be a fool to pass up the chance to see what he collected."

"She's right." Ross raised his mug, took a sip. "I bought as much as I could afford. Lived in a crappy fifth-floor walkup so I could afford to buy what I liked. I have two of your brother's paintings. His early stuff."

"I'd love to see them," Jake said, honestly. He'd missed a lot during the years his brother lived in the city. Missed seeing him grow as an artist. "But first, what can you tell us about Cecil Hawthorne?"

"I've been out of touch with the art scene for several years now. What did he do?"

Jake filled him in on the crime his former employer perpetrated against Will. "I'm not only Will's brother, I'm his attorney," he concluded. "The bank made good on the funds they let slip through their hands. Now, I'm trying to get the paintings back."

"You don't think Hawthorne destroyed them?"

Sunny jumped in, regaling the older gentleman with the reasons they believed Cecil and Jessica still had the paintings.

McClelland got up, refilled his mug from the still-warm kettle. Jake and Sunny waited for him to respond. After a few minutes, he looked up from stirring sugar into his tea. "I'm sorry to hear William has suffered so at the hands of a man I once thought of as a friend." The older man locked gazes with Jake. "Your brother has a rare talent. I don't know if it helps, but I think Cecil was jealous of his talent."

"What makes you say so?"

"Most people involved in the art world fall into one of two categories. Either they create art, or they wish they could. The wishers work behind the scenes. They own or work in galleries"—he nodded at Sunny who acknowledged his guess with a nod of her own—"or they become patrons. I fell into both. I worked in public relations for several galleries over the years, and I did what I could to support artists I believed in by purchasing their work whenever I could. I sacrificed to save enough to buy the pieces I admired the most. Cecil was too fond of keeping up appearances to be a patron. Most of the commissions he made from sales went to feeding his taste for expensive things. The trendiest loft apartment. Tailored suits. Lavish parties. Expensive vacations. His bank accounts were always scraping bottom because of it, so it doesn't surprise me he tapped into someone else's accounts."

"Why would he steal the paintings though?" Jake asked. "He has to know selling them will put him at risk."

"I wouldn't put it past him to sell them at some point. Your brother acquired quite a few loyal patrons, and anyone with an appreciation for fine art could see the value in owning one of his canvases." He took a sip of his tea. "But I think the theft goes back to my first statement."

"Jealousy," Sunny supplied.

McClelland tipped his head to her. "He hid it well, but sometimes, in private, he'd let it slip. He wouldn't come out and say he was jealous, but he'd pick an artist's work apart with a bitterness you couldn't mistake for anything else."

"He did that to Will's work?"

"Oh yes. He was harsh when it came to anything by W.H. Ingram." Ross cleared his throat and stood. "I want to show you something."

They followed him down a long hallway lined with paintings on both walls. Most were what Jake thought of as modern. Blocks of color, distorted images, swirls of paint he couldn't make heads or tails of. McClelland led them past a magnificent stairway at the front of the house to what Jake's grandma would have called a parlor. Landscapes of every size and description lined the walls. Hanging in a place of honor above the fireplace mantel was a painting Jake immediately recognized as his brother's work.

Ross flicked a switch, illuminating the painting in a soft light. The familiar scene took Jake back over a dozen years. He swallowed past the lump in his throat and willed the moisture in his eyes to stay put.

Beside him, Sunny squeezed his hand. "It's the three of you, isn't it?"

"Yeah. Down by the creek." Will captured the moment perfectly. Three boys, staggered in age, dressed in their Sunday best, sat on the bank of the creek, their backs to the artist, their heads and shoulders dipped in sorrow. "That was right after our mother's funeral. We got in trouble later for leaving the house, but we needed to get away from all the people and process. We sat there for hours. Didn't speak a word, if I recall correctly. Eventually, Rick stood up. Will and I got up and followed him home. We never discussed it. Never mentioned those stolen hours again, but I remember it like it was yesterday."

"I fell in love with the painting the moment I saw it." Ross's face tilted up at the artwork. "It's full of emotion. From the set of the boy's shoulders to the stillness of the willow trees and the ominous clouds on the horizon. I didn't know who the subjects were, but I related to them immediately. We've all known sorrow. The kind that reaches down to the marrow of our bones."

"He captured the day exactly how I remember it." Jake pointed to a clump of flowers off to one side. "The bluebonnets were starting to bloom. My mother loved them. She'd take us walking along the riverbank every year to see them. We went back when they'd gone to seed and collected as many seeds as we could fit in our pockets. The three of us planted them over her grave."

"What a beautiful story." Sunny squeezed his hand so hard he winced.

Jake took a deep breath, let it out. "If you ever want to sell it, call me."

The old man nodded. "I won't tell you the things Cecil said about the painting, but none of it was good. Where he resented your brother's talent, I rejoiced in it. There isn't a soul on the planet who wouldn't be moved by that painting. Unfortunately, it moved Cecil too much, in a bad way."

"Do you have any idea where he and Jessica could be?"

"I might." He led them to the dining room where another of Will's paintings hung in a place of honor. This one captured the spirit of the Fourth of July holiday in downtown Willowbrook from the patriotic bunting on the gazebo in the park to the families beneath the ancient oak trees, playing, picnicking. He captured the details down to scraps of busted balloons lying discarded in the grass, a little boy standing over it, tears streaking down his cheeks at the loss of his toy.

Jake studied the painting for a minute before he spoke, his voice thick with emotion. "That's Rick. Our baby brother. He was almost two then." He pointed to a couple on a plaid picnic blanket. "Those are our parents. And see" — he pointed out two older boys making their way through the crowd with a shiny red balloon in tow — "that's me and Will. Rick cried at the drop of a hat when he was little. His balloon popped. Will and I couldn't stand it, so we got him another one from the vendor. I'd forgotten all about that."

"Thanks for telling me the story. I'd never connected the two boys in the background with the crying baby in the foreground. It reminded me of my childhood. Callicoon used to have a big Fourth of July celebration. Now, not so much. All the young people have moved away. Nothing but old folks living here these days."

"Thanks for showing me the paintings. It makes me more determined to get the others back."

Sunny was eager to see the rest of the man's collection, so they wandered the rooms and hallways for an hour or more before returning to the kitchen where they sat around the table. "Cecil, despite his expensive tastes, grew up in a working-class neighborhood in Scranton. His grandfather was a coal miner. His dad worked for the railroad, as I recall. The work was above ground, and a step in the right direction for the family, but it wasn't the life Cecil wanted for himself. He's an only child, so when his parents passed, he inherited their house in Scranton. Or maybe it was Wilkes-Barre." He waved the memory lapse away. "Anyway, he held on to the house. Why, I never knew. Maybe it was security in case everything went to shit, which it did if he resorted to stealing from an artist."

Jake drummed his fingers on the table. "Why hasn't anyone mentioned this before? I've had a private investigator looking for Hawthorne ever since Will told me what happened. The police are investigating, too. No one has mentioned a house in Pennsylvania."

"Probably because Hawthorne isn't his actual name." Ross shook his head. "I'm sorry. I assumed you already knew."

Sunny recovered from the shock first and asked, "What is his real name?"

"Obediah Shupp, Jr. Named after his father. Don't know how that got overlooked. Everything was in his legal name — including the lease on the gallery."

Jake stood, pulled his cell phone from his pocket. "Excuse me. I need to make some phone calls. This changes everything."

CHAPTER TWELVE

Sunny shook her head. "I can't believe no one connected the dots."

"I can." Pushing away from the table, Ross got to his feet. "It's getting late. You should stay here tonight." He opened the vintage refrigerator. "I'll fix us something to eat."

"That's nice of you, but we should be going." She stood.

"Nonsense. Sit yourself down. I'll scare up something to eat then, if you really want to drive these back roads in the dark, you can go. Besides, it will take your fancy investigator a while to generate a report on Shupp. For all I know, Cecil could have sold the house in Pennsylvania years ago. He wouldn't have told me if he had."

Resolved to stay a little longer, Sunny resumed her seat. "You weren't close?"

"No. I was good at my job, so he kept me around, and I have an excellent eye for quality art, something he claimed to have but didn't, really. His lack of education was a detriment to his chosen profession. Like I said, he was a wannabe painter. His parents needed him to work, contribute to the household income, and he did until he graduated from high school. Then he took off for New York. He adopted his new name and worked his way up in the art world—all the way from gopher to gallery owner. Not bad for a guy with no formal instruction."

"No, not bad at all." Sunny finger traced the carvings on the antique tea chest as Ross chopped onions and tossed them on top of a lump of ground meat he'd dumped into a mixing bowl. "Why did you leave?"

"Hamburgers okay?" he asked. "We can grill 'em up pretty fast. Don't want to keep you two any longer than necessary if you're bent on getting out of here tonight."

Jake returned in time to hear the last part. "Are you fixing dinner?"

"We gotta eat, and in case you didn't notice, there aren't many restaurants out this way."

"Thanks." He leaned against the doorframe, his arms crossed over his chest. "Philip said he'd get right on it. We should have an address by morning."

"Jake, Mr. McClelland suggested we spend the night here. What do you think?"

"I think it sounds like a fantastic idea. I wasn't looking forward to driving the roads up here after dark." He turned his attention to the former public relations guru. "Are you sure we won't be an imposition?"

Ross waved a wooden spoon in the air. "Not at all. Stay as long as you want. Besides"—he glanced Sunny's way—"I'd like to catch up on what's been going on since I left."

Sunny smiled at the old man. "Hawthorne's actions rocked the industry. That's what's been going on. You didn't tell me why you quit when you did. What happened?"

Jake pulled out the chair next to Sunny and sat. Ross washed his hands then scooped up a handful of the meat mixture and squashed it into a rough patty then went to work on another one. Setting the finished patties aside, he sighed and wiped his hands on the dishrag he'd tucked into his waistband. With a sigh, he leaned against the counter facing them. "My life partner died. Frank and I were together for thirty-five years."

"I'm so sorry," Sunny said. "I didn't know."

"Thanks." He studied his shoes for a moment; when he lifted his gaze to the two sitting at his table, the sheen of unshed tears glistened in his eyes. "Few knew about Frank. We led a quiet life. He worked on Wall Street but, like me, preferred to keep to himself. No parties for him. I only went to the ones necessary for my job. Frank knew less about art than Cecil, but he never discouraged me from collecting."

"I wondered how you afforded to amass a collection the size of yours." Jake sat back, drumming his fingers on the table. "I didn't buy your story about scraping by, saving to purchase art."

Ross returned to the meal preparation. "It was mostly true. Frank and I lived in a fifth-floor walkup. I lived there for over a decade before we met. When he moved in, he started paying most of our expenses which were nothing for him and a burden for me. His generosity allowed me to splurge on art. So, it wasn't actually a lie."

"Then he died," Sunny prompted.

Ross nodded. "Heart attack at the office. He was gone before I got to the hospital." He added the final patty to the plate with the others then scrubbed his hands at the sink. "He left me everything, which was quite a lot. He was good. Knew when to buy. When to sell. Said it was instinct. Anyway, I was in a bad place after he died. My heart wasn't in my work any longer. Then that Jessica woman started hanging around with Cecil. She hated me, and I hated her. So I retired. Came out here where there's room to hang all the paintings I've collected. What good's a collection if you can't enjoy it, right?"

Ross opened a drawer, pulled out a metal spatula. "I figure a Texan knows his way around a grill." He handed the long-handled tool off to Jake. "Mind doing the honors while I come up with side dishes?"

"Not at all." Jake took the plate of meat and the utensil. "How do you like yours?"

"Well-done. I'm old. Last thing I need is to catch E. coli from a burger."

"I hear you. Two well-done patties coming up. Sunny? How do you like yours?"

"Medium-well?"

"Grill's that way." Ross pointed to the door they'd used when they first arrived. "Fancy one. Has a self-starter and a light so you can see what you're doing at night."

Jake disappeared out the back door. Sunny stood. "What can I do?"

"Set the table?" He ducked his head into the refrigerator, came out with a gigantic bowl covered in plastic wrap. "I made a macaroni salad yesterday. Never figured out how to make a single serving of the stuff." He placed the serving dish in the middle of the table, yanked the cover off, and stuck a big spoon in. "You'll be doing me a favor if you eat it all up."

Sunny got plates from the cabinet and silverware from a drawer. "I live alone, too. It's harder than it looks to cook for one person."

"Tell me about it. I don't mind leftovers, but after several days eating the same thing, I give up and toss it out."

"Do you ever think about moving back to the city?"

"Every time a stranger drives up and I have to get out the shotgun."

"Does that happen often?"

"Thankfully, no." Ross produced a bag of potato chips from a cabinet. After removing the clothes pin he'd used to secure the opening, he placed it beside the bowl of macaroni salad. "It's quiet out here. Exactly what I needed after losing Frank."

"Well, if you ever have the urge to visit some galleries, you're welcome to stay at my house. I have a brownstone on the Upper East Side. My grandmother left it to me," she added.

"Sounds swanky."

Sunny laughed. "Not hardly. It was a mess when I got it. I did some remodeling before I moved in, but it's far from fancy."

"I thought, with all the money your father has, you'd live in one of the modern high-rises."

"You know about my dad?"

"Doesn't everyone?" Ross snatched a chip from the bag. "It was common knowledge in the art community."

A sigh escaped her lips. "I suppose it is, though I try to keep my parentage quiet."

"You didn't want to go into acting?"

Sunny shook her head. "Nope. Plenty of opportunities came my way, but acting isn't my thing."

"I bet you could have any part you wanted." Ross abruptly stood. "Forgot the buns." He lifted the lid on an old-fashioned bread box. "Knew I had some." They joined the salad and chips on the table. He added a plate of lettuce leaves and tomato slices. Bottles of mustard and ketchup completed the meal.

"You're right about the divide in the art world." Sunny helped herself to a chip. "I dabble at painting. Never had the nerve to show the paintings to anyone. I've got enough of an eye to recognize my talent lies in identifying artistic talent in others."

"I'd like to see your work sometime."

She shook her head. "Oh, no, you wouldn't. Trust me. I've seen paint-by-numbers that were better."

"I'm sure it's not as bad as you think. It's the artist who thinks they're the best thing since Rembrandt that you have to watch out for. They have no self-awareness and don't appreciate being told their work stinks. The critical ones usually can't see their own talent. It takes a while to convince them otherwise."

She was still thinking about McClelland's statement when Jake came in bearing perfectly grilled hamburger patties. They took a minute to add lettuce, tomato, and pickles to their burgers then piled their plates with chips and homemade salad.

They chowed down for a few minutes then the old man broke the silence. "How's your brother doing? He's still painting, isn't he?"

Jake wiped grease from his lips with a paper napkin. "Will is doing better. This whole thing spun him out for a while." He sipped the beer Ross provided. "Did you ever meet your replacement?"

"MacKenzie something or other? No, but I talked to her several times when she first took over. She was green but eager. Why?"

"Just wondering." Jake took another bite of his burger, chewed, and swallowed. "Thanks to Sunny, MacKenzie got a job in our town, working for our resident rock star who also is a friend of Sunny's. MacKenzie and Will are…dating, I guess you could say."

"Really? That's the definition of a small world."

Jake nodded. "She's the one who gave us your name."

"Did I get it wrong? I thought she was involved with Cecil. She never said as much, but I got that impression."

"You weren't wrong. Apparently, she knew nothing about his relationship with Jessica. She'd moved in with him. Thought they would get married. He left her high and dry, too. No job. No money to pay the rent on his loft. She was fortunate Sunny knew Hank was looking for a new PR person."

"She and your brother are a thing now. Huh." He sat back, popped a chip in his mouth. "Funny how things work out sometimes," he said, eyeing Jake and Sunny who spoke at once.

"Oh no. We aren't…"

"We're not…"

"Don't try to fool an old man. I saw you holding hands. Saw the way you look at each other. If I'm wrong, tell me and I'll direct you to separate rooms for the night. Otherwise, the guest room at the back of the house is yours. It has a private bath."

"It's new," Sunny said.

Ross gathered his plate and took it to the sink. "I'm just sayin'…something good might have come of this whole sordid affair."

Sunny offered another protest, but the old man was having none of it. He waved off her comments before they got past her lips.

"I'm sure you kids are tired," Ross said, drying his hands. "You've had a long day. Let me show you to your room. I can clean this up later."

In the privacy of their room, Jake mulled over the possibility something lasting could come from the few days he'd spent with Sunny. No matter how he tried, he couldn't get past the fact they lived in two different states, far, far apart. She had her life in New York, and he had his in Texas. Even if he were willing to pick up and move halfway across the country, it wouldn't change the discontent weighing him down. He'd still need to make a living, and the law met those needs. Other than being with Sunny, which was a huge plus, he'd still be living a life he didn't want.

When she came out of the bathroom, wearing nothing but barely there panties and a slinky top that ended a couple of inches above her belly button, every thought but one flew out of his head. *Mine.* Need gripped him. Sunny Sheldon was quickly becoming an addiction he couldn't afford but had no intention of giving up. Not now, at least. Advancing on her, he framed her face in his hands, tilted her at the perfect angle, then crushed her lips with his.

Instinct drove them. They shed clothes in record time and came together like a summer storm, fast and anything but gentle. Moving over her, inside her, Jake knew he should take more care with her, but the primal urge to claim, to possess overrode everything else. Through every driving thrust, every savage nip, every possessive grip, Sunny was right there with him, her body moving against his, giving, taking, in equal measure. When she threw her head back, screamed his name, her inner walls grasping, Jake released the tether he held on his own pleasure. Jaw clamped tight, his entire being focused on their joined bodies, the orgasm began as a fireball in the small of his back and burned its way through his abdomen to spew from him in gut-wrenching spurts that stole his breath and all but stopped his heart.

He didn't know how long he'd lain on her, crushing her into the mattress with his sweaty weight. Rousing, he rolled off to the side. Arms thrown over his head, legs spread, he concentrated on bringing air into his lungs. "Are you okay?"

The answering affirmative hum eased his all-too familiar guilt at having taken her so hard. He really knew how to finesse a woman. He'd perfected the art of making love over the years, but with Sunny, everything he knew about what a woman liked vanished like smoke signals on a windy day.

He blew out a sharp breath. "We should have opened a window. I think I'm having a heat stroke."

Beside him, Sunny rolled to her side to face him. She rested a hand on his chest, her fingers tangling in the light mat of hair across his pecs. "I need another shower."

Jake reached for her, dragging her against him again. "Don't put images in my head. Please. I don't think I can take it." But it was too late. He could imagine her in the tiny enclosure, her body slick with soap, water cascading over her luscious curves. Desire stirred within. Jake groaned and, with one hand behind his head, reached for his cock with the other. "You're killing me, woman."

When her hand joined his, stroking his quickly hardening shaft, he cursed under his breath and rocked his hips in concert with their joint ministrations. Much more stimulation and he'd blow like a teenager in the movie theatre balcony.

"I've never been with someone like you," she said, a hint of uncertainty in her voice. "No one has ever wanted me the way you do. I like it. Especially the way you take control but seem to lose it at the same time."

Jake hissed in a breath, stilled her hand with his. "I do lose control. It's not something I'm proud of."

"Don't you dare apologize again." She squeezed his dick until he winced. "I love it when you take me hard and fast. It's exhilarating. And I liked feeling you inside me without the barrier, and I especially enjoyed feeling you come. It's…sensual…intimate. Rather primal. It makes me horny thinking about you leaving part of yourself inside me."

"Fuck, woman." Jake dragged her atop him. "You know how to drive me insane."

***

Sunny straddled his hips, fitting her wet slit to his steel length. His strength was a turn-on, she just wished he'd stop apologizing for making her feel like a goddess. No one ever worshipped her body the way he did.

Placing her palms over his pecs, she explored the hard planes of his torso, committing as much to memory as possible. In a few days, he'd be gone, and her memories would be all she'd have to get her through the lonely nights of the rest of her life. Maybe she'd get over him, eventually, but she didn't see it happening soon. If it were only the sex, the memory would fade, replaced by the pleasure of another lover—eventually. But it wasn't only the sex. Somewhere along the way, he'd burrowed under her skin, straight into her heart.

"You're a wonderful man, Jake Ingram." She leaned down, placed a kiss over his heart. "Will and Rick are lucky to have a brother like you."

"What makes you say so?" He returned the favor by skimming his hands over her breasts, massaging, awakening.

"Few would do what you're doing. You've put everything on hold to chase down leads, to help Will get his life back on track."

"Would you hate me if I told you I had another reason for coming to New York? One that's as selfish as they come?"

"No. You can't change my mind. You're a generous man. Admit it."

"I won't. You can't make me."

"Maybe I can't make you see yourself as others see you." She rocked her hips, slipping easily along his length. "Tell me what selfish endeavor brought you here."

He dropped his hands to the curve of her waist, guiding her to move against him again and again. "You. I came for you. To see if you were as sexy as I remembered. I thought if I could have you once, I'd get you out of my system."

"How did that work out for you, Counselor?"

"Not worth a shit. I want you all the goddamn time." As if to prove it, he lifted her like she weighed nothing then eased her down onto the tip of his shaft. He held her there, poised to take all of him, until her gaze met his. "Ride me, sweetheart. I need to be inside you. Now." He raised his hips while simultaneously applying pressure to her hips, filling her with the proof of his desire.

Sunny cried out. She'd never get enough of him. Never tire of feeling him inside her. He made her feel whole, like he was a piece of her she hadn't known was missing until he filled the empty space inside her. Looking down into his incredible blue eyes, she poured her heart out to him through her gaze and through their intimate connection. She moved over and above him, raising and lowering herself on his shaft, rocking her pelvis against his on every downstroke until he couldn't take it any longer.

He flipped them, easily placing her on her back, then positioning her for maximum penetration. Legs hooked over his shoulders, he braced himself above her by holding her hands above her head. Nose to nose, he powered into her, filling the room with the sound of damp skin slapping against damp skin, and the sound of lungs desperate for air. The old bed creaked beneath them, but both were too far gone to care who they disturbed.

He thrust and thrust. She reveled in each powerful stroke until the friction ignited a flame that grew into a conflagration. Shards of pain morphed into tightly wound coils of pleasure. Meeting his gaze head-on, Sunny greeted each challenge with one of her own until surrender filled his eyes.

"Fuuuuck!" he cried out as his cock swelled, stretching her impossibly wider. He came with a beautiful grimace and a string of curses. The feel of his hot cum bathing her inner walls was the catalyst for her own orgasm. She closed her eyes against the raw pain of muscles seizing and releasing around the hard shaft buried balls-deep inside her.

Tears streamed from her eyes unchecked as she gave herself over to the glory of the moment. He hadn't just pierced her core; he'd tunneled his way into her heart and taken up permanent residence. The tears were happy tears. Tears of joy. Tears of heartache. She was his, but he'd never be hers. Not in the way she wanted. And oh, how she wanted. Everything. His body. His heart. His forever.

Jake dropped his forehead to hers then placed a tiny kiss to her lips. Out of breath, he nuzzled her ear, discovered the tears. "Fuck, Sunny, sweetheart. I fucking hurt you."

She reclaimed one of her hands to cover his mouth before he uttered yet another unwanted apology. "Don't ruin the moment, Jake. I'm fine. Just a little emotional. You have to admit, that was intense."

A smile broke out beneath her fingers, so she dropped her hand to get a better look. "Intense? I guess that's one word for it."

"What would you call it?" she teased, returning his smile.

"Earth-shattering. I think my toes are numb."

***

Ross insisted they stay for a hearty breakfast before embarking on the next leg of their journey. Assured Scranton was, at most, a two-hour drive away, and since he hadn't heard from his private investigator, they didn't know exactly where they were going anyway, Jake accepted the old man's generosity. The meal of fresh eggs and bacon sourced from a nearby farm beat anything they could have found along the way, and, as he expected from McClelland, the conversation proved interesting.

Ross refilled their coffee mugs. "What if they aren't in Scranton? What are you going to do then?"

Jake reached for another slice of bacon. "We'll be back at square one. Cecil's hometown is our last lead."

Resuming his seat, the older man picked up the thread. "Have you considered the possibility Cecil and Jessica went to someplace she knew about? Does she have family she could have called upon to shelter them? Or like, Cecil, a property they could take advantage of?"

Jake straightened his spine. "No. I've been focused on Hawthorne. Figured he'd call the shots."

Ross pointed a finger at him. "That right there might be where you went wrong. Jessica Blackwell is a manipulator. Cecil was no saint, but when he got caught in Jessica's web, he changed. He did whatever she wanted, even if it wasn't in the best interest of the gallery."

"How do you mean?" Sunny buttered a slice of toast.

"We had a full slate, booked solid a year in advance when she got her hooks into Cecil. Suddenly, we were cancelling showings and filling those dates with artists she brought in. Some were good, like your brother," he said, nodding toward Jake. "Most were mediocre. The gallery was losing money right and left when I retired."

Jake sipped his coffee, letting their host's words roll around in his mind. They ate in silence for a few minutes then something Will said popped into his head. "Will told me if he gets the paintings back, he's going to have a giant bonfire with them."

McClelland's head jerked up. "Why in the world would he do a thing like that?"

Jake raised a hand to ward off more questions. "Hear me out, okay? He says the paintings are crap. In retrospect, he says they shouldn't be part of his portfolio. They don't represent him as an artist, so he wants them destroyed. He said Jessica convinced him to paint what he called more commercial subjects. He argued with her for a while, but, in the end, he followed along. What artist doesn't want easy money, right?" He didn't wait for an answer. "So, what if my brother wasn't the only artist she scammed? What if she manipulated others the way she did him and Cecil?"

"I'm still reeling at the thought of burning one of your brother's paintings, but I see where you're going with this line of thought." His eyebrows furrowed as he sipped at his coffee. "Give me a few minutes to think and I can probably come up with some names for you—artists Jessica brought to Cecil before I left. Maybe the new girl, MacKenzie, could add a few more. I'm not sure what kind of scam Jessica could have been running, but I know she is capable of running one."

Jake wiped his mouth with a paper napkin then stood to take his plate to the sink. "We still need to check out Cecil's home in Scranton, but you may be on to something. I'll let my PI know we want to look in another direction. If you can get me a name, anything to go on, I'd appreciate it."

Ross stood, scraped the scraps from his plate into the trash bin, then placed the plate in the sink. "You two go on, get your stuff together and I'll do the dishes. Nothing like menial chores for thinking. I'll get you a name or two. I promise."

"Thanks." Jake clapped him on the shoulder. "No matter what happens, I owe you. You've been more than generous with your time. And thanks for sharing your art collection with us. I'm glad two of Will's paintings found such a wonderful home."

"Jake's right. We can't thank you enough, on multiple levels." She hugged the old man. "I'd like to stay in touch. Maybe I can rent a car, drive out occasionally to see you?"

"I'd like that. I love it here. Moving was the right thing to do, but sometimes, I miss the art world."

"Anytime you want to talk art, or anything else, call me, okay?"

"Deal." Ross squirted dish soap in the sink. "Now, go on. I know you're eager to get on the road, and I've got some thinking to do."

***

They were halfway to Scranton when Jake's cell phone rang. Seeing Ross's name on the caller ID, he pressed the accept call button on the steering wheel, allowing the call to play through the Jeep's speaker system.

"Hey, Jake, it's me, Ross McClelland. Sorry to bother you, but I've got some names for you."

"You could never be a bother," Sunny said. "We've got you on speaker. Give me a second to get something to write on." She grabbed her purse from the floorboard.

"You guys make it to Scranton yet?"

While Sunny searched for pen and paper, Jake answered, "Not hardly. We ran into road work in three separate places and stopped at a scenic overlook because Sunny wanted to see the bald eagles."

Ross's laughter filled the cab. "Did you see any eagles? They're easier to spot in the winter when the leaves are off the trees."

"We saw one flying over the river, looking for his next meal. It was awesome. They're beautiful birds."

Sunny rejoined the conversation. "He didn't want to stop, but I insisted. The way he talks about it now you'd think it was his idea." She shot Jake a mischievous smile. "I found something to write on. Go ahead with the names." She jotted them down as he rattled off three possible leads.

"Did you talk to your PI yet?" Ross asked.

Jake pointed to a sign advertising another possible stop for them then picked up the conversation. "No. Why?"

"Because I thought of something else. Jessica claimed to be a New Yorker, but I overheard her on the phone one day. She'd slipped into a pure Maine accent. At the time, I chalked it up to something fun, you know, playing around, the way people do with accents. Frank and I used to try out our British accents on each other. It was harmless fun, but I remember thinking the conversation sounded serious. I'm thinking now she might have been talking to a relative or an old friend. You might have your PI check records in Maine."

"I wouldn't know a Maine accent if it bit me," Jake supplied.

"They're distinctive," Sunny added. "Hard to fake."

Jake raised an eyebrow. "And you would know this, how?"

"My dad has tried to mimic every accent on the planet at one time or another. Maine gave him a lot of trouble."

"She's right," Ross said. "Anyway, thought I'd mention it."

"Appreciate it." Jake nodded at the mileage sign showing they were getting closer to their destination. "We'll be in Scranton soon. If you think of anything else, no matter how trivial, call. We're grasping at straws here."

"Will do. You two be careful, now. I'll be in touch."

"What do you think?" Sunny asked after Ross hung up. "Could they be in Maine?"

"Anything is possible." He hit the call button on the steering wheel, directed the onboard computer to place a call to his private investigator. While the connection rang through, he added, "I'll get Philip to check it out."

CHAPTER FOURTEEN

Sunny took one look at the house bearing the address the PI gave them for Cecil Hawthorne's childhood home and refused to leave the car. "They aren't here. From the looks of it, no one has been here for decades."

Jake couldn't argue with her assessment since he agreed with her. The place looked like a crack house with its graffiti-embellished plywood-covered windows and door. The landscaping resembled an urban jungle complete with trash art. He counted six old tires in the front yard alone. From his perch, he had a view down an equally neglected ribbon driveway running the length of the house on one side to another structure. His best guess, a garage. It looked slightly less shabby than the house, making him wonder if Cecil used it for something—like to store stolen paintings.

Leaving the engine running, he grabbed the door handle. "I'll look around. If you see anyone, anyone at all, dial 9-1-1." His feet hit the faded asphalt roadway. "Stay in the Jeep and lock the doors. If there's trouble"—he tossed her the key fob for the keyless ignition—"get the hell out of here."

"Can't we call the cops? Have them come out here and look around?"

"We could, but this isn't an emergency, so it might be days before they could spare a patrolman." The worry lines marring her beautiful visage coaxed him to add, "The place is abandoned. I'll be okay."

"Famous last words."

He smiled though he shared some of her apprehension. For all he knew, someone was cooking meth in the kitchen—or the garage. He wouldn't know until he looked. Leaning in, he beckoned her to meet him halfway. When they were nose to nose, he placed a gentle kiss on her lips. "Lock the doors."

As he trudged along the driveway, he scanned the immediate area. He didn't believe he was in any actual danger. If someone was dealing drugs or cooking meth on the premises, there'd be some signs of life. Trampled grass, trash that wasn't bleached out from long-term exposure to the sun. Everything about the place screamed abandoned property. Except the almost-shiny lock on the garage door. Accounting for weathering, the padlock was maybe a few months old.

He glanced around at the side of the building, noted a grime-encrusted window no one had bothered to board up. He picked his way through thigh-high weeds, being careful where he placed his foot. The last thing he needed was to step on a rusty nail or god knew what else and end up at the emergency room. Reaching the portal, he pressed his face against the glass, blocking outside light with his cupped hands as shields.

Letting out a pent-up breath, he stepped back and shook his head. Nothing. The place was empty save for some old boxes on shelves, none of which were large enough to hide a canvas the size of the ones he was looking for. The entire trip had been a bust.

Shoulders drooping, he returned to the Jeep. The door locks disengaged as he approached. He climbed into the driver's seat, fastened his seat belt, then shifted the transmission into Drive. Not having any idea where he was going, he pulled away from the curb.

"Well?"

She'd waited until he stopped at the first intersection. He gave her credit for restraint. "Well, what?" He turned left, hoping to find his way out of the unfamiliar neighborhood.

"What was in the garage? Were there signs anyone had been there recently?"

"Nothing other than a fairly new lock on the garage door, but I peeked inside. It's empty. We're back to square one."

"Not completely. We still have the Jessica angle to consider. Maybe your PI can come up with some leads in that direction."

They came to a larger road. Jake made an executive decision and turned right. "I need some coffee and we better get gas. Keep your eyes peeled for anything that fits the bill."

Sunny fiddled with her phone. "There's a Dunkin's two miles from here." She pointed out where he should turn. "And where there's a Dunkin's, there's civilization. We should be able to find a gas station nearby."

Jake applauded her navigation skills as she guided him to the promised coffee and donuts across the street from a gas station. "Coffee first." He parked, and they got out and sauntered inside. Taking their steaming cups, they sat at a booth by the window overlooking the parking lot. Jake took a sip, savored the first jolt of caffeine. He rubbed his eyes. "Man, I needed this. Is it me, or does it seem like we ate breakfast a week ago?"

Sunny laughed. "No. I feel the same way. A lot has happened since we ate breakfast with Ross McClelland this morning."

Jake took another sip of the high-octane brew. He didn't realize how much hope he'd assigned to McClelland's lead until he'd looked in the Shupp's garage and saw nothing. The hopelessness of his investigation felt like a load of bricks weighing on his shoulders.

"I'm sorry, Jake." She blew across the top of her cup then took a sip. "I know you were counting on finding the paintings here."

He shrugged. "It's one in a long string of dead ends. I'll get over it." More than anything, he'd wanted to call his brother today with good news.

A church bus pulled up by the front door. A dozen or more kids of varying ages, wearing light-blue T-shirts bearing a summer camp logo, piled out of the conveyance and into the store. Jake's phone vibrated in his pocket. He glanced at the screen. Will. He stood. "I've got to take this." He found a place next to the building where he could hear and speak freely and monitor Sunny through the window.

"Will. What's up?"

"Where are you?"

"Scranton. Why?"

"I got a call from NYPD. One of my paintings turned up at Sotheby's."

"They're sure it's one of the stolen ones?"

"Positive. I have a code I write on the back of every canvas for authentication. I gave them a list of the ones those bastards took. It's definitely one of them."

"Someone waltzed into Sotheby's and consigned it for auction?" Every auction house in the country had been alerted to the theft and instructed to contact NYPD if any of Will's paintings were brought in. Looks like the move paid off.

"Yeah." He could practically see his brother rubbing the back of his neck to ease the tension. "It was a woman. Gave her name and contact info. Turns out she's legit. Has a sales receipt and everything."

"From where?"

"You won't believe it."

"Try me."

"She bought it from Sunnyside Gallery."

Jake's blood ran cold. He glanced at the woman he'd spent the last few days with. Sunny sipped her coffee like she didn't have a care in the world. Anger spiked. He turned, walked to the end of the building where there'd be no chance of being overheard. "When? Who signed the receipt?"

"It's dated two months ago. The receipt is signed by Sunny Sheldon. They questioned the woman who bought the painting. The description she gave of the person who sold it to her matches Sunny to a T. The detective who called me said they were working on search warrants for the gallery and her house."

"Did he leave a number where you could reach him?"

"Yeah. Why?"

"Call him back. Tell him Sunny will be home in three hours."

"How—"

Jake ended the call then turned the device off. No doubt Will would try to call him back to demand an explanation, and he didn't have one to give. Admitting he'd been taken in by a devious woman wasn't high on his list of confessions to make. He'd tell the police everything, let them sort it out. Then he'd go home and figure out how to tell his brother what he'd done.

Leaning against the building, Jake took a few minutes to compose himself. He'd have to continue the charade all the way back to Manhattan. Make small talk. Pretend he wasn't hauling her ass home so the police could question her. Pretend his heart hadn't taken a near-fatal blow.

"Just goes to show, you never really know a person," he mumbled to himself as he opened the door. He held it while the rowdy campers, amped up on sugar, streamed out to their bus.

Pasting a smile on his face, he approached the table where Sunny sat. He picked up his now-cold cup, tossed it in the nearest trash. "You ready? We need to get back to the city."

Sunny stood, tossed her cup in the receptacle. He gassed up across the street then they hit the freeway. If they didn't run across construction delays or major traffic getting into the city, he'd have Sunny home within the time frame he'd given his brother.

***

"Who was that on the phone?" Sunny waited until Jake navigated the complex streets to get to the freeway to question the tension she'd sensed in him since he'd returned from taking the call.

"Work. I need to go home sooner than I'd planned."

Sunny nodded. "Okay." She turned her attention to the road. He wasn't in the mood to talk. She understood, or thought she did. She didn't know much about his life in Texas, but she sort of understood lawyers. If a client needed him, he'd have to go. "If your PI comes up with anything on Jessica, let me know. I can follow up if you need me to."

"No need. If he finds something, I'll have him do the legwork. I wouldn't want to put you in danger."

She didn't know what changed, but something sure had. This wasn't the Jake Ingram she knew. That man was warm and funny and didn't snap a person's head off for offering to help. She snapped back. "I'm not stupid. I wouldn't put myself in danger, but I can drive by an address or… I don't know…something."

"No need for you to be involved. You've done enough."

"What do you mean I've done enough?" She couldn't keep the scorn out of her voice.

"It means, you've done plenty. This is a wild-goose chase. Will doesn't even want the paintings back. I've wasted too much time already on this. I've got to get home. I have other clients who need my attention."

Something was wrong, but she had no clue what it could be. And Jake wasn't talking. She'd been a fool to think there could be anything between them other than passionate sex. She'd miss the sex, no doubt about it, but as the miles sped by, her heart told her she'd miss the man even more. She already missed him. The person who'd left the donut shop to take a phone call wasn't the same one who'd walked back in. "That must have been some phone call," she muttered.

"You don't know the half of it."

"Are we going to have lunch? Or do I need to crawl over the seat and get the cooler we stocked? I'm hungry."

"There's got to be a drive-thru out here somewhere. We'll get something to eat on the road."

A half hour later, they picked up sandwiches and sodas at a fast-food chain then got right back on the highway. They'd left Pennsylvania behind and were well into New Jersey when he spoke to her again. "I'll drop you at your house then I'm going to the airport. See if I can catch a flight this afternoon."

She reached for her phone. "I can book you a flight."

"Don't bother. I have a return ticket, so it's just a matter of changing it."

She put her phone away. "Okay. I was only trying to help."

"I don't need your help. I can manage on my own."

Sunny bit her bottom lip to keep from saying something she'd regret later. When he took the Lincoln Tunnel instead of the George Washington Bridge, she kept her mouth shut. Let him slog through midtown traffic to get uptown. He didn't want her help. She wouldn't give it.

A stalled car in the tunnel and the usual heavy afternoon Manhattan traffic added almost an hour to what would have been a simple drive from the bridge to her brownstone. Sunny inwardly snickered at the typical tourist mistake. If the obstinate man couldn't admit he needed help, then who was she to offer it? It was his car, his gas, his time. She'd already decided the summer was too hot to stay in the city. She'd do some laundry then pack up and go to her dad's beach house for a week or two. Let Ginger run the gallery. Maybe she'd drag her painting supplies out of storage and take them with her. Talking with Ross McClelland opened her eyes to her discontent. Helping artists find homes for their work was satisfying, but deep down, she wanted to create. She'd let doubts about her talent get in her way.

No one was stopping her now. Even if her work stank up the entire Hamptons, she didn't care. She'd take the emotions crowding her chest, making her eyes water with tears she refused to shed, and pour them all onto canvas. What did it matter if it came out a colossal mess? And if painting wasn't enough of an outlet, there were plenty of outdoor activities like running, biking, and swimming she could indulge in to help get Jake Ingram out of her system. In a few weeks, she'd be good as new. Ready to come back to the city and her solitary life.

The atmosphere in the car grew colder with each block. By the time Jake turned down her street, she wouldn't have been surprised to find icicles hanging off his nose. When she glanced his way, the hard set of his jaw and the white-knuckle grip he had on the steering wheel spoke volumes. He'd shut her out completely.

She pointed out her house. "No need to hunt a parking spot. I'll grab my bag, and you can get on with whatever's turned you into a man I don't know." She opened the door, dropped to the street. Before she slammed the back hatch down, she volleyed her parting shot. "Have a nice life, Jake Ingram."

She'd muscled her suitcase inside and shut the door when her doorbell rang. Figuring she must have left something, and Jake brought it, she didn't bother looking through the peephole. She gasped at the man standing there, his NYPD gold shield held up for her inspection. "Are you Sunny Sheldon?"

"Yes. What's this about?"

He produced a folded sheet of paper from his jacket pocket. "I'm Detective Antonio Reeves, NYPD, and this is a warrant to search the premises." He slapped the document into her hand then brushed past her. Before she could catch her breath, four uniformed officers and a woman in plain-clothes followed him inside.

The female detective ushered Sunny over to the sofa and insisted she have a seat. She needn't have. It was all Sunny could do to take the few steps without her knees buckling.

"I don't understand." She could hear drawers opening and closing upstairs, and someone was in the kitchen from the sound of the cabinet doors slamming. "What's this about?"

"It's all in the warrant. You can contact your lawyer. In fact, I'd advise you to do so sooner rather than later."

It took a moment for the woman's words to register. "Am I under arrest?"

"Not yet. But you will need to answer some questions. You can answer them here or down at the station."

"But I haven't done anything."

"That's what they all say."

Hands shaking, Sunny unfolded the document. One line stood out—suspected of the possession and sale of stolen goods."

She looked up. "I've never stolen a thing in my life!"

"We believe otherwise, thus the warrant."

"But..." She couldn't think of anything else to say. The fog cleared. She took a longer look at the official document, looking for something to explain what they were doing to her house. What she found turned her blood to ice and went a long way to explaining Jake's sudden shift from friend to cold enemy. But it still didn't explain why? Why her? She'd cooperated with the police, and she'd spent the last few days helping Jake chase down leads.

When she'd read the entire thing, she pulled her phone from her pocket. Her dad answered on the second ring.

"Sunny! To what do I owe this pleasure?"

"You can thank the NYPD, Dad. I need a lawyer. Can you get me one?"

The conversation became stilted. She didn't want to say anything in front of the detective he could misconstrue, so she kept her comments to a minimum while still trying to convey to her father what kind of mess she was in. "I'm sorry, Dad," she said, winding down. "The media will have a field day with this."

"I'll call my lawyer, get him over to your place ASAP then I'll call my publicist and sick him on the story. He'll get out ahead of this thing. This is all an enormous mistake, Sunshine. Don't you worry about a thing."

Talking to her dad helped, but once the lead detective finished tearing her house apart and came to sit on the opposite sofa, a wide pit opened in her stomach, threatening to swallow her whole. Shock had long since been replaced by anger. She possessed infinite respect for the NYPD, but they'd gotten this all wrong. "I didn't steal anything from anyone, and I don't know the whereabouts of the paintings you're looking for. I do know they're too big to hide in my kitchen cabinets or any drawer in this house."

Detective Reeves flipped to a fresh page in his notebook. "I'm aware of the size of the paintings. I have photos of them, but you never know what you'll find in someone's house."

"What's that supposed to mean?"

"It means, would you like to explain why three of the paintings you claim you don't know the whereabouts of are in your basement?"

"What?" Sunny's heart felt like it would pound right out of her chest. "That's not possible."

"Can you explain this sales receipt from your gallery for one of the stolen paintings?" He held up a photocopy of a receipt bearing the Sunnyside Gallery logo. It looked legitimate, but she was quickly learning looks could be deceiving.

"It has to be a forgery. I'm not a thief, and even if I was, I wouldn't be stupid enough to sell stolen paintings out of my gallery."

"Yet, that's exactly what happened."

The detective stood. Reflexively, Sunny followed suit. "Sunny Sheldon, you're under arrest for possession of stolen goods and for the sale of stolen property."

CHAPTER FIFTEEN

Jake took the phone call minutes before boarding his flight from JFK to Dallas. "You found some of the paintings in her home?"

"Three, to be exact. She maintains she didn't know they were there and claims no knowledge of the rest. As soon as we book her, I'll serve the search warrant on the gallery."

"I don't mean to sound like I don't trust you, but you're certain they're originals?"

"I'm no expert, but they match the photographs your brother provided, and the inventory codes on the back match up."

Jake pinched the bridge of his nose. He'd developed a headache shortly after receiving Will's phone call, and it had only gotten worse with time. He looked forward to several hours in first class and a couple of stiff drinks. "I appreciate all you've done, Detective, and Will sends his thanks for all your hard work. I'm about to get on a plane, but please, call or text me with any updates to the situation."

He sat, elbows on his knees, his hands clasped, head bowed, trying to reconcile the woman he knew with the one he now suspected her of being. The ache in his chest was real. Probably the only genuine thing to come out of these last few days. He'd fallen in love with a woman only to find out she wasn't who he thought she was. As a lawyer, he understood people lied—all the time—and he'd developed a radar for deceit. Not once did Sunny set his radar off.

He didn't know what the oversight said about him, but he vowed never to let anyone snooker him the way she had. If they found Will's paintings at her gallery, what kind of idiot would he be? He'd been there a few days ago and never thought to look around. He'd blindly taken everyone's word regarding Sunny's character.

Jake waited until the last call before boarding. Seated in the plush first-class seat, drink in hand, he closed his eyes and painstakingly relived every minute he'd spent with the woman, from the time she noticed him standing on the sidewalk outside her gallery until she sat across from him in the Scranton donut shop. Several drinks and thousands of painful memories later, he still couldn't find any link between Sunny, the self-aware pseudo-celebrity/businessperson he'd fallen for and the heartless criminal she now appeared to be.

Yet, the evidence was there. Will's paintings were in her home. The detective forwarded him a copy of the gallery receipt as well. Nothing about it looked fake. Which only proved she was more of an actor than anyone gave her credit for. What did they say about being a chip off the old block?

Waving the flight attendant down, he ordered another drink and downed it in one gulp. He'd surpassed his self-imposed limit long ago, but if there was ever a day to self-medicate with alcohol, this was it. Back in Scranton, when he'd leaned into the Jeep to remind her to lock the doors, he'd been on the verge of telling her he loved her. Just in case something happened to him, since he hadn't known if the place was empty or a paranoid neighbor would shoot first and ask questions later.

"Bad day?" the lady in the window seat next to him asked.

He wasn't in the mood to talk. He grunted out, "I've had better," then closed his eyes, hoping to discourage anymore conversation. His attitude worked because she left him alone the rest of the flight.

Will and Rick waited for him at the baggage carousel. Rick had his own fledgling home remodeling business, and their middle brother helped him when he could. They'd both hopped in the car without bothering to change out of their work clothes. He hugged them anyway.

"Have you looked at your phone lately?" Will asked as he and Jake trailed Rick across several lanes of traffic to the parking garage.

"No. I turned it off for the flight."

"You probably have a dozen messages from Detective Reeves."

He was still feeling the effects of over imbibing, not to mention he'd be happy if he never heard a certain woman's name again for the rest of his life. "I gather you've been talking to him, so why don't you fill me in?"

They'd driven his car to the airport. Will had yet to purchase wheels, and Rick's old construction truck sounded like it was on its last legs. Even if he would need to have the interior detailed after they sat their dirty asses in it, he was grateful they'd both shown up for him. He let Rick play chauffeur, while Will rode shotgun. Once they'd navigated off the airport grounds, Will filled him in on what he'd missed over the last few hours.

"Reeves called a while ago. They arrested Sunny Sheldon."

"Yeah, that happened before I boarded."

"The rest of my paintings were in a storage room at her gallery. All but the one she sold."

Jake pinched his temples between his thumb and forefinger. "Shit."

"She claims she's innocent." Will's voice remained flat, noncommittal.

He glared at the back of Will's head. "All evidence to the contrary."

"As you say."

They drove straight into the setting sun. Jake didn't know which was worse, the harsh light driving nails into his skull or the way the world spun when he closed his eyes, waiting for his brother to drop the next bomb on his head.

"She also said she spent the last few days driving around upstate with you."

He hadn't planned on telling anyone about the time he'd spent with Sunny, but that ship had sailed, and apparently sunk, thank you, NYPD. As if Jake wasn't already the biggest ass this side of the Mississippi, Will verbally kicked him one more time. "I take it she didn't lie about her whereabouts?"

"Fuck off." If anyone deserved an explanation, it was his brother. But he couldn't think of anything to say that wouldn't make him look like an incompetent jerk who let the wrong head do his thinking.

As if he'd heard Jake's thoughts, Will said, "You don't owe me an explanation, but Detective Reeves is going to want one."

"Fuck." The last thing he wanted to do was explain why he'd spent the better part of a week, traveling with and screwing a prime suspect in the theft of his brother's art. Especially when he'd been acting as Will's attorney. It didn't sound any better in his mind than it would to Detective Reeves's ears. He'd fucked, literally, with the investigation. Convincing the detective he hadn't known would be the trick.

Will shifted in his seat, graced Jake with a smile. "Don't sweat it, Bro. None of us suspected Sunny, and she's a beautiful woman. If she'd looked at me the way she looked at my paintings, I would have tried harder to get her into my bed." His brows furrowed. "Never would have suspected her." He swung around, leaving Jake with the vision of his brother flirting with Sunny.

The image shouldn't have affected him. It wasn't the first time the brothers had been attracted to the same woman. They were too close in age not to have friends in common.

Over the years, they'd each lost a conquest to one or the other brother, but thinking about Sunny with Will made him want to beat his brother to a pulp. Sunny was his. For a few days. Nothing more. She'd betrayed Will then used Jake to deflect the investigation as far away from her as possible. Whatever feelings he'd developed for her were dead. Had to be.

The media storm hit the next day in New York. Interest in the crime dwindled quickly when it went unsolved for so many months. Now that a minor celebrity had been arrested and brought up on charges, it was headline news again. Everyone was looking for an angle.

Will wasn't answering his phone. He sent every call to voicemail where a recording declared he had no comment. It was only a matter of time before Jake's name became part of the narrative.

"You need to get yourself a new lawyer," he informed his brother that evening. "I've already talked to Randy. He's willing to take you on as a client." Randy Wallace was the other attorney in town. He was closer to Will's age than Jake's, and they shared a close friendship with another local, Hank Travis, who'd made it big as a rock star. Randy handled all of Hank's legal needs and was probably better equipped to deal with the media frenzy headed Will's way. Jake was considering hiring him to handle with the shitstorm he'd created for himself.

Will paced Jake's office. "Do we have to drag Randy into this? Why can't you handle it?" He stopped, and, hands on his hips, he faced Jake. "I'm the victim here. I don't see why I should need a lawyer, but since I do, I'd prefer you."

Jake stared his brother down. "You need someone to protect your rights and your reputation. Not every reporter or blogger or whatever has scruples. Some of them make shit up rather than admit they know nothing."

"I get it, but I still want you to handle it. Not that I don't trust Randy, I do. He'd never screw me over, but you're family."

"All the more reason to hire someone else. Anything I dispute will look suspicious because we're related. And have you forgotten? I've got my own storm brewing on the horizon. It's only a matter of time before some reporter finds out I was screwing a witness all over upstate New York, and it was me who returned her to her home the day they arrested her." He rocked back in his chair. "I'm considering retaining Randy myself."

"Go right ahead," Will said. "I think you should, but I'll stick with you."

"Why?"

His brother flashed him a shit-eating smile. "Because I'd have to pay Randy."

Jake sat forward, propped his elbows on his desk, and dropped his head into his upturned hands. "Fuck you."

Will sank into one of the ancient visitor's chairs. All humor leached from his voice. "Seriously, man. I know you have your own troubles, and if you need Randy in your corner, I'll pay for his services, but there's no reason my shit has to fall on you. I've already asked MacKenzie to draft a press release for me. I'll make a public statement, say what I want to say, and tell them to leave me the fuck alone."

Jake raised his head. Will sat sprawled out like he hadn't a care in the world. It was all an act. He knew his brother well. Of the three of them, he was the best at hiding his feelings. That was why when Will came home from New York, broke and broken, Jake jumped in to do whatever he could. Getting the funds restored to Will's bank accounts helped his brother move on, but Will did the real work himself through self-reflection and painting. Art had always been Will's outlet of choice, and he did it better than anyone Jake had ever known. He wished he had something as productive to help him deal with the guilt and failure he felt in relation to Will's case.

"The press release is a good idea," he conceded. "Probably won't shut them up for long, but it might buy you a few weeks."

"That's all I need. You know how it is. Something else will happen, and the media will drop my story faster than you can say polish my dick. I'll drop from front-page news to the back page of the Sunday Arts section overnight."

"I hope you're right." He hoped some celebrity would do something stupid today or tomorrow. Anything to deflect attention from their story.

"You know I am. That's the way the media works." Will pushed to his feet. "Are we good? You hire Randy if you think you need the distance, but you're still my attorney?"

Jake stood, rounded the desk, and grabbed his brother in a bear hug. None of that bro hug shit between blood brothers. He clapped Will on the back. "I'm still your attorney, but I'm sending you a big, fat bill when this is over."

Will shoved him in the shoulder. "You bill me, asshole, and I'll tell everyone about the half-done manuscripts you keep hidden under your bed."

His brother was driving away before Jake recovered enough to make his feet move. Standing in the doorway watching Will take off in Rick's old truck, Jake shook his head. He should have known. There wasn't anything sacred between brothers.

"Shit." He slammed the door then turned to see Jean, his secretary/paralegal, smiling at him.

"Family," she said. "Can't live with them. Can't kill them."

***

Jake spent the better part of an hour that afternoon on a video chat with Detective Reeves and his partner, a female detective he'd met on the sidewalk outside Sunny's brownstone. It was a typical good cop, bad cop interview designed to scare the truth out of a suspect. Only Jake wasn't a suspect, and no cop was going to intimidate him into revealing anything he didn't want to.

He told his story, concisely, leaving out intimate details that weren't anybody's business but his and Sunny's. No matter what she'd done, they were consenting adults.

"We appreciate your time, Mr. Ingram," Detective Reeves wound up the questioning.

"I wish I could help you, but she gave no indication she knew anything about the paintings. Just the opposite, in fact."

"She's still maintaining her innocence. Says she doesn't have a clue how they got in the basement of her home or in the storeroom at her gallery. She's convincing."

"I guess the acting genes run in the family after all," he said.

"We'll see. She's agreed to a lie detector test."

"Let me know how the test turns out."

"Sure thing. Oh, and you can tell your brother we'll ship the recovered paintings to him in a week or two. We're getting an art expert to authenticate them for the record first. The DA assures us photos and the documentation from the expert will be enough in court."

"I'll tell Will to be on the lookout for them. Speaking of being on the lookout… Any sign of Cecil Hawthorne and Jessica Blackwell?"

"None. Ms. Sheldon swears she barely knows them and has no idea where they went."

Jake recalled the conversation he'd had with Sunny right before he'd taken Will's call. "I have another thought. We'd reached a brick wall trying to track down Hawthorne. Then it hit me. Maybe we should take a harder look at Jessica Blackwell. We've been under the assumption Cecil was calling the shots, but what if it was Jessica? When we were talking to Ross McClelland, he mentioned overhearing her on the phone one day, and she'd slipped into an accent he associated with people from Maine. I asked the private investigator I hired to do a little digging."

"McClelland thought the accent was real?"

"He said she claimed to be a New Yorker, but it seemed to him she'd lapsed into the accent without realizing it, which suggests it might be something she's worked to get rid of."

"Ever tried to get rid of your Texas twang, Mr. Ingram?"

"Once, in law school. My professors at Harvard said I needed to lose it if I wanted to be successful outside my home state. After a few weeks working with a Ph.D. candidate from the speech lab at the university, I gave up. Too much work."

"You're right about one thing. Changing your speech patterns is hard, and there aren't many reasons people go to all the trouble."

"Actors do it all the time. Lots of Aussies and Brits playing American's in films and on TV these days."

"And criminals trying to blend in. A distinct accent makes a person memorable."

"It might be nothing, but I thought I'd mention it."

"If you think of anything else, or if your PI comes up with a lead, let us know."

They ended the call not exactly as a team, but Jake felt like he was no longer under the microscope. He called Will, filled him in on the conversation. "I came clean. Told the detectives I'd literally fucked up and apologized for any harm my actions might have done to the investigation."

"You couldn't have known, Jake. Forget about it."

"I'll try." He didn't think he'd ever forget the way Sunny felt in his arms, moving beneath him, on top of him. For a few days, he'd known the magic of being with the right person. Only Sunny wasn't the right person. Her betrayal cut deep, and he wasn't sure the wound to his heart would ever heal. Shaking off those thoughts, he related what the detective said about Will's paintings.

"I need to have a bonfire. I was thinking down by the lake at your house."

"Works for me. I've been wanting to build a firepit close to the shoreline. Maybe we can work on it together?"

"Sure thing. I'll see if Rick wants to help. You pick out the stone, and I'll pay. It's the least I can do since I'm not going to pay you for your actual work."

Even though his asshole brother couldn't see him over the phone, Jake shook his head. "I should have drowned you when you were a baby."

"Nah. You love me; you just won't admit it."

Damn straight. He loved both his brothers. "If you say so." He hung up without saying goodbye. As predicted, a text came through within seconds. Jake opened it, laughed at the obscene emoji, and fired one back. "Asshole," he muttered before muting his phone and getting back to work.

CHAPTER SIXTEEN

Jake handed Will another brick then returned to the pallet that had been delivered earlier in the week. Because all three brothers were swamped with work, they'd put off building Jake's new fire pit until the weekend. It was the first time they'd been together in ages and longer since they'd worked on anything together.

"Last time we built something had to be the treehouse," he mused out loud. "Remember that?"

Rick chuckled. "By treehouse, you mean a couple of rotted boards nailed into the fork of that old oak behind the house." He held his hand out for another brick. "I think the rusty nails are still there but the wood disintegrated years ago."

Rick would know, he still lived in the house they'd grown up in and the oak he spoke of still shaded most of the backyard. "It was more than a few boards, and they weren't rotten when we put them up there."

Will tossed a pebble at Jake's head. "You know what they say, your memory is the first thing to go."

Jake picked up the pebble and tossed it, hitting Will square in the back. "Eyesight, asshole. Your eyesight is the first thing to go." God, he missed hanging out with his brothers.

"We need to do this more often," he said, unloading an armload of bricks where either brother could reach them.

"Fuck off," Rick said, adding another row to the rapidly growing ring. "You just want the free labor."

"Not true. Besides, I'm paying you with food and all the beer you can drink." With the toe of his boot, he nudged a brick closer to Will.

His middle brother sat back on his heels and used his T-shirt to wipe sweat from his brow. "Tell me again why you didn't hire someone to build this thing?"

"Because you said you'd do it, asswipe. As I recall, our verbal contract included your labor in lieu of my billable hours on your behalf."

Rick grabbed a water bottle he kept nearby, took a drink, then poured the rest over his head. "I didn't agree to do anything, so why am I here?"

Will threw a clod of dirt at the youngest Ingram brother. "You're here because you're too stupid to say no."

"Hey!" Rick used his forearm to shield his eyes from the missile. "Who gave you a job when you came home with your tail tucked between your legs?" He launched his own attack, hitting Will square in the chest with a lump of soil.

"Fuck you!"

Jake snagged himself another beer from the cooler then dropped into the folding lawn chair he'd brought to the build site earlier and watched his younger brothers have at each other. "Just like old times," he mumbled to himself then took a long pull from the bottle.

The two of them tussled like idiots since they were kids. When they were little, it usually ended when one of them got hurt. It had been years since he'd seen either of them smile the way they were, so he figured he'd let it go on for a while longer before he broke it up.

They were winding down when a distinctly female voice cut through the heat like a sharp knife. "William Ingram! Stop that. Right now!"

All three brothers turned toward the source and froze. MacKenzie Carlysle stopped behind Jake's chair, a frown marring her beautiful face. Will was the first to recover. He shoved Rick off him and stood, dusting his clothes off as he approached the woman he'd fallen for. "Kenzie! What brings you out here?"

She held up a hand to keep him from getting too close. "I came out to check on the project." Her gaze cut from Will to Rick to Jake then back to Will. "Looks like I arrived in the nick of time. What were you two fighting about?"

"I don't know." Will glanced at Rick. "You remember?"

Rick stood, used the hem of his T-shirt to clean his face. "Nope."

Jake opened the lid of the cooler sitting next to his chair, a silent invitation for everyone to have something cool to drink. "They used to tussle all the time when they were kids. Drove Mom nuts."

Kenzie pulled a soda from the ice, popped the top. "And you didn't stop them?"

"Why would I? Seeing them get in trouble was one of the few perks of being the oldest."

Rick limped over, helped himself to another water bottle. "I don't remember hurting this bad when we were kids."

Will smiled. "Me, either." He rubbed the small of his back. "No fair using your military training."

"Like grinding a fistful of dirt in my face was fair? Asshole. You're lucky I didn't fuck you up for real."

MacKenzie huffed and stomped her foot on the hardpacked lawn. She glared at Will. "Really? You shoved dirt in your brother's face?"

"Hey, you should have seen what he did to me."

It was time to step in. Jake kicked out at Will then Rick, missing both with his big boots. "Enough. Playtime is over. If Mom were here, she'd make you kiss and make up, but I'll settle for a handshake."

The brother's complied then they both sat to finish their drinks. Jake stood, offering Mac the only seat in the house for the construction show. She declined, choosing to sit on the grass a safe distance from her smelly boyfriend.

"The fire pit looks like it's coming along," she said.

"A couple more hours then we'll be done, except for hauling the landscape rock over"—Jake pointed to the pile of stones next to the pallet of bricks—"and spreading it out."

"You can do that yourself," Rick complained.

"Got some day laborers coming tomorrow to finish up," Jake admitted. "They'll put in a path from the pool deck, too. Make it easier to get to the lake from the house."

"Then we need to finish this." Will climbed to his feet. He kicked Rick's foot. "Come on, jerk wad. I want to have time for a dip in the pool while Jake grills the steaks, so let's get busy."

"Okay, okay." Rick rolled to his hands and knees then boosted himself up. "You'd think I'd be in better shape," he groused as he followed Will back to the work site where a fire pit was slowly taking shape.

"I'm surprised they've gotten as much done as they have," MacKenzie remarked.

"They've been working hard. They were having fun. I didn't have the heart to make them stop."

"Did Will tell you the paintings are on the way? They're supposed to arrive on Tuesday. He had them shipped to your house."

Jake finished his beer. "No. He didn't mention it, but that's okay."

"You think he'll really burn them?"

"Yep. I do."

"Aren't you going to talk him out of it?"

He reached for a water bottle, twisted the cap off, and downed half the bottle. He stood. "They're his. If he says they're crap, then I'll take his word for it." He walked to the pile of bricks, grabbed another armload. Thinking about Will's paintings brought things better forgotten to mind.

It had been weeks since he'd heard from his PI or the detectives in charge of Will's case. The last phone call from Detective Reeves was to let him know Sunny made bail and passed the polygraph test. The tests were so unreliable they weren't allowed in court, so passing one meant nothing. Especially for someone with acting in their blood. Sunny was wasting her talent, Jake decided. He considered himself an excellent judge of character, but she'd reeled him in, hook, line, and sinker. His heart still ached where her barbs had sunk into the vulnerable muscle. At night, he lay awake, the memory of their numerous bouts of sex taking possession of his body. At the time, he'd been sure the sex had been more, but now he refused to believe it was anything more than a physical release for both of them.

***

The following Saturday, the brothers gathered around the firepit. Will invited some witnesses—MacKenzie and an old friend of the Ingram brother's, Hank Travis and his wife, Melody. He handed Jake his cell phone. "I want this on video. Every step. I don't want anyone to question what happened to these paintings. No chance copies can be passed off as the originals."

Following Will's instructions, Jake documented the removal of each canvas from the stack, getting a clear shot of the coding on the back and the actual painting before the artist himself, then added it to the firepit. By the time he'd added the last one to the pit, the pyramid was shoulder high and multiple canvases deep.

Before he lit the kindling they'd placed around the base of the structure, Will stood in front of the camera. "I, W.H. Ingram, solemnly swear the paintings you see here are the originals, and, to my knowledge, no copies exist. These paintings never represented who I was as an artist at the time I painted them, and they don't represent who I am now. Call me temperamental or insane, I don't care. They're mine, and I'll do with them as I please. This is what I please."

He touched a propane lighter to the lighter fluid-soaked kindling. Flames shot up, catching the oil paints on the nearest canvas. Within seconds, the entire pyramid erupted.

Will stepped back. Jake put a hand on one of his shoulders, and Rick did the same on the other, offering their support, a wall of solidarity. The three of them, along with the witnesses, watched as the fire consumed over a year's worth of Will's work. No one spoke until nothing but ashes remained.

Will stepped in front of the camera. "This has not been a hoax. Everything you saw was real. The following witnesses are here to attest to the authenticity of the event." He named each one in attendance as Jake slowly panned to include the solemn group in the video document. When he'd completed the task, he turned the camera on himself and added his statement of authenticity for the record before ending the recording.

Jake stepped forward. "At Will's request, there's champagne poolside. Shall we go toast to my brother's future?" His statement broke everyone out of the trance they'd been in. Suddenly, everyone was talking at once as they made their way along the new stone pathway to the expansive pool deck where buckets held bottles of bubbly on ice.

Corks flew. Glasses bubbled over with the golden liquid as they toasted to Will's new direction in life. Inside Jake's house, easels bore several paintings bearing the signature of William H. Ingram—proof the artist had moved on from the crime that nearly destroyed him.

Jake found Will staring at a nude he'd done of MacKenzie. As stunning as her body was, strategically draped with a swath of white fabric, it was the emotion in her eyes, the hint of a smile on her lips that truly caught Jake's attention. He'd once thought he'd seen the same expression on Sunny's face after he'd made love to her, but he'd been wrong. He hoped Will wasn't seeing what he wanted to see instead of what was actually there. He rested a hand on his brother's shoulder. "You okay?"

"Yeah. I thought it would be harder to let them go. I don't think I realized how far I've come since all this happened until they went up in flames. It was like a giant weight lifted off my shoulders. A fresh start."

"I spent some time looking at them this week."

Will cut his gaze to Jake. "You did?"

Jake shrugged. "They were in my garage. Figured you wouldn't mind too much if I checked them out."

"No. I don't mind. What did you think?"

"I'm not an art critic, but having seen your earlier work, and now, seeing your more recent paintings, I have to agree with you. They were good, but they weren't you. I don't know how to explain it, but they lacked something…"

"Heart. Soul," his brother supplied.

"Yeah, I think you summed it up." They stared at the painting of MacKenzie for a few minutes. "This is extraordinary. You poured your heart into it."

"I did. I'm in love with her, Jake."

"She loves you?"

"What do you think?" He nodded at the canvas. "Or did I fail to convey her emotions?"

"No, you nailed it, Bro. Just hoping you aren't imagining things."

"You sound like you're doubting yourself. You think Sunny lied to you?"

Jake ground his molars and rocked back on his heels. He hadn't gone into detail about the time he'd spent with Sunny in New York, but Will seemed to have come to some very accurate conclusions all on his own. He'd always possessed a knack for reading Jake's mind and his moods. It could be damn irritating sometimes. Like now. Jake drew a deep breath, let it out. "I know she lied to me. She's had your paintings all along."

"I don't think so." Will faced him. "I'm convinced she didn't have anything to do with the theft." He tapped Jake's chest. "And deep in your heart, you know she didn't."

Maybe, but admitting it would mean he couldn't ignore what had happened between them, and he wasn't ready to go there. Not yet. "I was surprised you invited Hank and Melody to this little burn party." The couple were friends with Sunny. Their connection with the gallery owner brought MacKenzie to Willowbrook.

"You think they knew something?" Will's hostile stance, hands fisted on his hips, called Jake on his inference. "You've known Hank Travis since you were both in diapers. He's a world-famous musician. He's worth millions. You can't really believe he or his wife had anything to do with this."

Jake sipped from the flute he held. God, he hated champagne. He downed the remaining liquid in one gulp, silently vowing to hit the liquor cabinet for a proper drink as soon as possible. Right now, his brother demanded an answer. "No, I don't think Hank had anything to do with stealing your paintings." At his brother's raised eyebrow, he added, "Melody didn't, either." Will made a *come on, you aren't done yet* sign with his hand. Jake shook his head. "I'll take your word when it comes to MacKenzie, but you have to admit, this entire thing looks fishy."

"Damn right it does. I know I won't convince you tonight, but mark my words, Bro, Sunny is innocent. The sooner you get your head out of your ass and admit it, the sooner you'll find the assholes who ripped me off and set her up to take the fall." He poked Jake in the chest then delivered his parting shot. "I hope you yank your head out before you suffocate on your own shit."

He didn't bother to stop Will, though the urge to punch his lights out was strong. The man had a romantic streak a mile wide. It served him well as an artist, but he stuck his nose in other people's business. Like the time he'd tried to set Rick up with a cheerleader. She'd been mildly interested but failed to mention she'd been secretly dating the quarterback at a rival high school for several months. The jock took exception to Rick asking her out. All three brothers ended up in the principal's office over the ensuing fistfight. Jake, quarterback for Willowbrook High, had been forced to sit out an important game, which the home team lost. Will and Rick both served a week in detention.

Perhaps Will had lost his romantic tendencies for a while and ended up in the clutches of Jessica Blackwell and company, but along with his money and the paintings, he'd also recovered his romantic heart.

Just my luck.

Jake took one last look at the painting of MacKenzie. "I hope it's not all an act, Bro," he muttered to himself then stalked off to find something with a lot more kick than champagne.

***

Sunny tucked her hands into the pockets of the old sweater she'd found in the closet at her dad's South Hampton house then set off along the beach. The summer heat had broken, and the leaves were turning. Most of the neighbors had returned to the city to enjoy the upcoming holidays, leaving the beach deserted — just the way Sunny liked it.

She'd come to her dad's place in the Hamptons the same day they released her on bail with only the clothes on her back and a new appreciation for privacy. Over the past few months, she'd taken to online shopping to curate a wardrobe to replace the one she'd left behind. She'd gotten a glimpse at what the police had done to her home before they arrested her, and she never wanted to touch any of her possessions again. They'd gone through everything from her kitchen cabinets to her most intimate clothes to the box of tampons she kept in the cabinet beneath the bathroom sink.

Her dad's assistant coordinated the cleanup efforts. With her dad's help, he'd boxed up her photos and other personal mementos. Those went into storage. They'd tossed or donated everything else to local charities, including all her clothing and furniture. She'd rented the brownstone out to a couple with two small children. When this was over, she'd find another place to live. Maybe a chicken farm upstate.

A brisk wind lifted her overlong hair, swirled it around her face. She stopped, looked out to sea as she attempted to tame the wayward strands. The gray sky matched her mood. Not a good sign. She'd spent enough time on the tip of Long Island to know storms could brew up in a matter of minutes and wreak havoc almost without warning. Like life, she mused, drawing the fresh, salty air into her lungs. Unlike the storm making its way ashore now, she hadn't seen the one coming that destroyed her career and her life. One minute she was sipping coffee, wondering if she'd like living in Texas because Jake would be miserable in New York—and the next, she'd been in handcuffs, facing a judge and pleading not guilty to a slew of charges she still couldn't wrap her head around.

And the man she'd fallen in love with disappeared. Left her to face the worst days of her life all alone.

She rubbed at the ache lodged deep inside her chest—a raw wound where her heart had once been. Jake's defection hurt more than she'd believed possible. She'd expected him to at least want to hear her side of the story, but he'd passed judgment, even played the role of her own, personal Judas, delivering her home so they could arrest her. It took her a while to put the events leading up to her arrest all together, but once she did, her lawyer confirmed her suspicions. Jake had known about the painting they'd accused her of selling even before she did. That explained his behavior on the ride from Scranton to Manhattan.

If he'd only asked, she could have told him she'd been set up. Somehow. By someone.

Sunny couldn't remember the last time she'd been in the brownstone's basement. Perhaps when the boiler needed repair? That had been last winter. But she visited the gallery storeroom, almost daily. Every item stored there had been meticulously documented, both for inventory and for insurance. Nothing went in or came out without the movement being noted in the logbook she kept in her office. According to her lawyer, the paintings hadn't been entered into the logbook. She'd pointed that out as a plus on her side, but he'd been quick to point out a thief would hardly keep an official record of the stolen items they had on the premises.

The real kicker was, she'd seen the photos the police department's hired art expert had taken of the paintings and knew she never would have consigned them, much less risked everything to steal them. Jake's brother was right. They weren't the quality product W.H. Ingram was capable of.

She'd thought not finding her fingerprints on any of the canvases was another chink in the case, but as her lawyer pointed out, she kept a supply of cotton gloves handy and donned them anytime she handled the artwork in her gallery. The police hadn't been able to explain how she'd broken into Hawthorne's gallery and made off with the paintings in the first place. They never would because She. Hadn't. Done. It.

A wave washed over her toes as another gust of frigid air lashed at the lapels of her sweater. Sunny jumped back from the icy water and, crossing her arms over her midsection, turned for her temporary home. At the end of the wooden walkway leading from the beach to her dad's house, she picked up the canvas sneakers she'd left there then hurried past the pool, closed for the winter, and onto the covered deck. A wall of wind-driven rain drove her inside.

She cleaned her feet then flicked the switch to turn on the gas fireplace. After fixing herself a mug of hot chocolate, complete with mini marshmallows, she curled on the sofa facing the fire. She'd never minded being alone until she'd spent most of a week with Jake Ingram. Now, she couldn't seem to settle. She tried reading but gave up after staring at the same page for untold minutes. Even her favorite TV shows didn't hold her attention. She was contemplating the movie offerings on a satellite subscription service when her cell phone rang.

Her best friend, Melody Travis, called her frequently since Sunny's arrest and release on bail. Apparently, the fiasco made national news. Mel and her husband, rock star Hank Travis, coincidentally, an old friend of Jake's, offered their support from the get-go. They'd even suggested she come stay with them but apologized when they realized what they'd offered. No way could she hide out in the man's hometown they'd accused her of stealing from. And she especially couldn't hide out in the home of one of his friends.

Sunny picked up on the second ring.

"Melody, hi. How are things in Texas?"

Mel filled Sunny in on her perfect husband and her more perfect daughter, Gloria. Sunny didn't mind. It did more to take her mind off her troubles than anything else she'd tried lately.

"How are things with you? Any news?" Mel asked when she wound down.

"No. I'm still the prime suspect. I don't think the police are looking for the actual culprits."

"They can't convict you without proof, can they?"

"My lawyer seems to think otherwise. I don't have an alibi for the day they stole the paintings. Apparently, being sick as a dog and spending the day at home alone isn't considered an alibi."

"But there's no motive!" Mel cried over the line. "Why would you steal awful paintings?"

Suddenly, she had Sunny's full attention. "You've seen them?"

"Yeah." Sunny thought she could have heard her friend's sigh all the way from Texas without aid of a phone. "Will invited us to his bonfire last night. I got a good look at them before he torched them."

Sunny gasped. "He really burned them?"

"To cinders. There's a video. I sent you a copy. Watch it then call me."

"Okay. I'll call you right back."

Her phone dinged, showing she'd received a text message. She opened it and waited for the extensive video file to download.

CHAPTER SEVENTEEN

Before she finished watching the video, several more text messages arrived from her dad and her lawyer. She ignored them, mesmerized by the flames and hoping desperately to get a glimpse of Jake. When nothing but embers remained, Will made another statement then the camera panned over the small group gathered to witness the destruction of the paintings. When Jake's face filled the frame, Sunny paused the video, staring at the man who owned her heart.

Tears streamed down her cheeks. She wiped them away with the flat of her hand. He was still as handsome as ever, but there was a tension in his features she didn't recall. He looked…tired. Stressed. Like he hadn't been sleeping well. "Welcome to the crowd," she mumbled, pressing the button to restart the video.

As she'd promised, she placed a call to Melody Travis. "Hey, it's me."

"Did you watch it?"

"From start to finish," she confirmed. "It was hard to watch."

"Tell me about it. It's something I'll never forget."

"Will seemed determined. How was he off camera?"

"For someone who torched over a year of his own work, worth an estimated cool million? He seemed relieved. He served champagne and had some of his recent work on display. Based on what I saw before he burned them, I can tell you, they weren't anything like the ones I bought from you a few years ago. Those are masterpieces. The burned ones? Not so much. I'm no art critic, so I'm probably using the wrong words, but I'd say they had no soul."

"What about the new ones he displayed?"

"Is magnificent a word you use in the art world? Is there something more descriptive? I'd trade my husband for one of them, and you know how I feel about Hank. They're that good."

"You didn't take any pictures, did you?"

"What kind of idiot do you think I am? Of course I did. I'm sending them now."

Sunny's phone vibrated. She opened the text app and pulled up the photos. "Wow. They're stunning."

"Stunning. Magnificent. Museum quality."

"I'm so glad he's painting again, and his work is even better than before." She'd love to get her hands on one of them for her own collection. "What does he plan to do with them?"

"He said they aren't for sale. But he mentioned he was working on another one he planned to put up for auction. Sotheby's offered to handle the sale without taking their cut."

Sunny's head spun. "Can you let me know when that happens?"

"I told him to give me a heads-up. Are you going to bid against me?"

"Probably." Given her infamous connection to the artist, she'd need to have her lawyer bid on her behalf.

"Be prepared to pay up then because, sight unseen, I want whatever he's painting."

"With the notoriety around his name, lots of art collectors are going to be interested. The price will skyrocket."

"I figured as much. I'll have to determine how high I'm willing to go and maybe enter a maximum bid beforehand."

A maximum bid would keep a bidder in the running up until the bids exceeded the predetermined ceiling. It was a safeguard used by many collectors to keep from getting caught up in the excitement and paying too much for a single item. She'd used the strategy before but knew she'd do no such thing for this auction. "That's an excellent idea. I've got a feeling this one will be wild."

"Speaking of wild, how are you *really* doing? Don't bullshit me, girlfriend. I can tell when you are.

Sunny closed her eyes. The concern in her friend's voice brought fresh tears to the surface which only added to her frustration. "The truth is, I'm a basket case. I can't sleep. I can't eat. All I do is cry. The police aren't even looking for anyone else!" She broke down and sobbed. "How is this my life?"

"Oh, honey, I'm so sorry. What about the PI you hired?"

"He hasn't had any luck, either. It's like Cecil and Jessica dropped off the face of the earth. How is that even possible?"

"I have no idea. New identities, maybe? I've hidden behind a different name before, remember? I used my mom's family name most of my life. I bought my house here in Willowbrook through a corporation I set up to hide my involvement. What did they do with the money they stole from Will's bank accounts? They didn't give it back, so it must be somewhere. Did they get it in cash? Or was it transferred to another account?"

Sunny's ears perked. Melody's father was a legendary rock star who died when she was young. To avoid the spotlight, she'd claimed her mother's family name as her own until a few years ago when her identity became public. Sunny's dad used a fake name to check into hotels all the time. "You're right. They're probably using fake names, and the money has to be somewhere. I wonder if Jake's PI tried to trace it. I wonder if mine has?"

"Ask, girlfriend. There's a lot on the line here. You need to clear your name."

"I don't want to go to jail."

"That's the spirit. Hey, if you need me to come hold your hand, just say the word. Gloria and I will fire up the jet and be there in a few hours."

Smiling for the first time since her arrest, she laughed. Her friend would use any excuse to bring her toddler daughter to New York for a shopping trip. "I appreciate your willingness to leave your hunky husband, but I'm fine. I need to be proactive. Get the charges dropped and clear my name, once and for all. Then we'll shop until our credit cards cry, Uncle! Deal?"

"Deal, girlfriend. But the offer still stands. Anytime."

***

They'd become a tabloid sensation.

Will's video, despite its extended length, went viral. Even though MacKenzie offered to handle PR for him in her spare time, he'd hired a firm out of Dallas to deal with requests for interviews and to monitor his social media accounts.

Jake dropped a copy of a national scandal sheet on his desk. Ever since it hit the newsstands, his phones, business and personal, had been ringing constantly. He'd silenced his cell phone and blocked dozens of numbers in a matter of hours, and he'd instructed his admin not to answer the office line unless she knew the person calling in.

He should sue the rag for the story they'd printed about him and Sunny. However, most of what they'd printed was true. They'd done their research and come up with a detailed timeline for the days he and the gallery owner, now the prime suspect in the theft of his brother's paintings, spent in upstate New York. They'd even interviewed the chicken farmers!

The reporter drew some accurate conclusions about what the two of them had been up to during the times they couldn't be accounted for and the night they'd spent at the bed-and-breakfast. The one thing they hadn't uncovered was the night they'd spent at Ross McClelland's house or why they'd been in Scranton, the morning before Sunny's arrest at her

Manhattan brownstone. It was only a matter of time, Jake concluded, before they came up with the rest of the story.

Jake picked up the phone to warn Ross what was headed his way. The old man answered on the third ring.

"Jake. Hey, I heard the news about Ms. Sheldon. It's bullshit, of course."

He wasn't so sure, but he hadn't called to debate Sunny's guilt or innocence. "A lot has happened since we were at your house. I thought I'd warn you. The tabloids have gotten their hooks into the story. One of them has a reporter tracing every step Sunny and I took the week we came to see you. So far, they've stopped short of calling our relationship a conspiracy to undermine my brother's career, but if they could find a scrap of evidence to support it, I'm sure they would. So…just be aware if someone comes snooping around."

"I get it. You'd rather I not comment."

"That's not what I'm saying. Be straight with them, but you know how those rags are. If a nun says she's married to Christ, they'll drag God and the holy spirit into it and call it an orgy."

The former PR guru laughed. "You're right. I think it's best to stick with no comment. If they find me. I'm far off-the-grid. You didn't tell anyone where you were going or that you'd been here, did you?"

"No, I didn't. But I can't vouch for Sunny. We parted on less-than-friendly terms."

"I'm real sorry to hear that. You don't believe what they're saying about her, do you?"

Jake sighed and scrubbed his free hand over his face. "I don't want to, but the evidence doesn't lie, Ross."

"Fuck the evidence—pardon my French. She loves art. She's devoted her career to helping young artists make a name for themselves. She'd never steal from anyone, let alone an artist with the promise your brother shows." He paused. Jake could hear him coughing in the background. Then he came back on the line. "Don't be stupid, boy. She loves you.

Take it from someone who knows, you only get so many days with the ones you love. Don't waste them."

The line went silent. "Hello? Ross? Are you there?" Jake took the phone from his ear, glared at the words on the screen. Call Ended. "He hung up on me. The old bastard hung up on me." He dropped his phone on top of the tabloid with his picture front and center.

"Shit."

The rest of the day, McClelland's words echoed in his brain. She'd never steal from anyone. *Don't be stupid, boy. She loves you.*

Was she capable of stealing? Even Will didn't think she'd stolen his paintings. Yesterday, Melody Travis called to chastise him for abandoning Sunny to the tabloids, claiming her friend had done nothing but try to help him find the people who wronged his brother. According to her, Sunny was holed up at her dad's house in the Hamptons, afraid to even return to Manhattan. He couldn't reconcile the image with the one he had of the woman. The Sunny Sheldon he knew wasn't afraid of anything.

His body hardened at the thought of all the places and ways they'd made love on their road trip. She'd given herself to him in a clearing in the freakin' woods. Twice. And then there was the time she gave him a blow job in the car, in a restaurant parking lot. Talk about fearless.

But it had all been a distraction. A way to keep him from discovering the truth.

Was he being stupid? Did she love him?

He closed his eyes, recalling his brother's latest painting. The nude of MacKenzie where more than her body was exposed. In fact, her physical nudity was the last thing he noticed. Her expression, the love apparent in the depth of her gaze, had captured his attention first. It drew him in instantly because he'd seen that look before. Sunny gazed at him in the same way, and he'd felt the power of her emotion down to his toes and returned it in equal measure.

Jake's entire body shook as his newfound awareness hit him full force. Sunny loved him. And he loved her. And, he'd left her at the mercy of a rabid press and a police department eager to close a case.

The realization nearly brought him to his knees.

He spun his chair around to peer out the window. Heat shimmered off the earth's surface giving the landscape a surreal presence. Jake narrowed his gaze to a garden gnome, a gift a few years ago from his administrative assistant. A joke gift that appeared in the garden alcove, holding a balloon bouquet on his birthday. The balloons were long since gone, but the statue remained.

He'd screwed up. Let Sunny down and, by extension, his brother. Getting Will's money and paintings back wasn't the end of it. He'd still been wronged, and convicting the wrong person wouldn't serve justice. Wouldn't provide the closure his brother deserved.

And Sunny didn't deserve to suffer for something she didn't do. She was as much a victim as Will. Maybe more so because the actual culprits had targeted her to take the blame for their crimes.

"Why would anyone want to hurt her?" he asked the grinning gnome. "What did she do to them?" He stood to pace the length of his office. "Had destroying her been part of the plan all along? Leave her holding the bag for the art heist while Hawthorne and Blackwell got away with the money?"

"Don't forget Ginger Carpenter, Sunny's part-time salesperson."

Jake glared at his middle brother who lounged in the open doorway. "Eavesdropping, Bro?"

"No. Your door was open." Will strode in like he belonged and took a seat facing Jake's desk. "You talk to yourself often?"

After dropping into his desk chair, Jake propped his feet on his desk. "Sometimes, it's the only way to have an intelligent conversation."

Will shrugged. "As long as you don't answer yourself, I guess it's okay." His mischievous smile reminded Jake of when they were kids. Will was always coming up with a plan guaranteed to get the three of them in trouble. "You don't answer yourself, do you?"

Jake grinned. "Like I said, it's a surefire way to have an intelligent conversation." Placing his elbows on the arms of his chair, he steepled his fingers, studying his nails. "What do you know about Ginger Carpenter?"

"Nope. Not telling you anything until you tell me why you were pacing and asking yourself questions about my case."

He dropped his feet to the floor, leaned into his desk. "Sunny didn't steal your paintings."

"What makes you think so?"

"I know her. She's not a criminal. Think about it. She doesn't need the money from your accounts, and she'd have to be stupid to sell stolen paintings out of her gallery."

"Do you know where the money went? Maybe she was working with Jessica all along and they split the money. Put it in offshore accounts. And someone did sell one of the paintings at her gallery."

Dumbfounded by Will's about-face where Sunny was concerned, he lit into him. "What's gotten into you? Do you know something I don't? If you do, you'd better tell me now before I knock some sense into you."

Will doubled over, laughing. "Oh, man. You've got it bad." He slapped his knee. "Never thought I would see the mighty Jake Ingram fall for a woman, but it's happened. You're in love with her, aren't you?"

"Fuck you." Jake stood, ready to beat the shit out of his brother. "Sunny did nothing wrong, and I intend to prove it. You can help me, or you can go fuck yourself."

"Stand down, Bro." Will raised his hand in surrender. "I was trying to get your goat. See how committed you are to getting answers to the questions you were asking yourself."

"Why the hell didn't you just ask, asswipe?" He sat, picked up a pen, then slid a yellow note pad front and center. "If you have nothing helpful to contribute, get the hell out. I have work to do."

CHAPTER EIGHTEEN

Jake tossed his pen down then rocked back in his chair. Rubbing his eyes with the heels of his hands, he groaned. He brought himself upright and surveyed the damage. Coffee cups and note pads, many sporting brown rings and coffee splatters, littered his desk. "Looks like we pulled an all-nighter," he commented to his brother who'd given up on the uncomfortable visitors' chair hours ago and was now stretched out on the sofa across the room.

Will shifted to a sitting position, resting his elbows on his knees, hands clasped in front. "What time is it?"

"Past time to go home." He consulted his watch. "If we hurry, we can grab a bite at the diner before it closes."

Stretching his arms above his head as he stood, Will replied, "Don't have to tell me twice."

The brothers walked the single block to the local establishment they'd eaten at since they were kids. At this hour, the place was empty, except for a few locals having pie and coffee at the counter. Jake led the way to a booth next to the window, close enough the sole waitress wouldn't have far to walk yet far enough away from the other customers to carry on a conversation without being overheard.

Given the late hour, they both waved off the offered caffeine, choosing large glasses of milk instead to go with the hearty breakfast platters they ordered. "Did we accomplish anything at all?" Will asked when they were alone.

"Maybe." Jake downed half his milk to appease his protesting stomach. He wasn't sure how much of his problem was lack of food and how much resulted from all the coffee he'd consumed. "I'll call Philip in the morning," he said, referencing the PI he'd worked with in New York. "Last time I talked to him I was pissed off and told him to quit looking. I'll see if he can pick up where he left off. If not, I'll find someone who can, or I'll go back and do it myself."

"Maybe you should go back anyway. See Sunny. Try to explain your behavior."

He doubted she wanted to hear anything he had to say. His stomach felt like it was twisting into a knot. He took a tiny sip of his milk. "You think that's wise?"

"Why wouldn't it be?"

"If I were her attorney, I'd tell her to stay the hell away from anyone associated with the case."

"Do your clients listen when you tell them shit like that?"

"No." He drained his glass, setting it on the edge of the table as a silent signal for a refill. "They usually go out and do exactly the opposite."

"There you go." Will saluted with his beverage then took a sip. "If nothing else, she'll want to tell you off for abandoning her to the police."

The server set another glass of milk on the table. "Food's almost ready," she said, taking the empty glass with her as she left.

"You've got a point." He stared at the ancient Formica tabletop. "I really fucked this up."

"She'll understand…eventually."

Jake huffed out a laugh. Glancing up, he caught his brother's smirk. "Asshole."

"Hey, what are brothers for? You don't want me to sugarcoat it, do you? You acted like a jerk, now you're going to have to make amends."

"In other words, I need to clear her name then beg her to listen."

"Beg being the operative word."

"Maybe you can give me pointers on begging. I've never done it before."

"Now who's being an asshole?"

Their food arrived, putting an end to the banter. Once their plates were empty, they relaxed, arms stretched across the back of the booth. Will nudged Jake's foot under the table. "So, when are you leaving?"

"Don't know. Depends on what the PI has, and I have work I need to finish up. Maybe day after tomorrow?"

"I could go with you."

"Nah. No need for you to get tangled up in this mess again." Jake leaned forward, wrapped his hands around his glass. "I'm thinking this never really was about you. If it was, why go after Sunny now?"

"You think they stole my money and my paintings in some sick game to damage Sunny's reputation?"

"I know it sounds nuts, but how is it any crazier than them targeting you in the first place?"

Will picked up his fork, used it to draw lines in the syrup left behind on his plate. When the grooves filled in, he repeated the process. "You could be right, but there must be a reason they chose me and not some other schmuck."

"I can't come up with a reason to target you or Sunny. None of this makes any sense." They'd been over every scrap of information, spouted out every theory and a few impossible ones over the course of the afternoon. As tired as they both were, nothing would be gained by rehashing everything tonight.

Will picked up the check the server had left on the table, examined it. "I appreciate all you've done for me. I was in a bad place when I came home. Broke. Broken. You never questioned how I got myself into such a mess, you just jumped in and worked the problem. Thanks to you, my money was returned and those damn paintings won't be coming back to haunt me years from now." He creased the paper in his hands then smoothed it out. "I'm sorry you got dragged into this but at the same time, I'm grateful you did."

"I probably wouldn't have ever met Sunny if it weren't for you and your screwed-up life, so I should be grateful you let me help you." Jake straightened the flatware dropped haphazardly on his plate. "I love her, Will." He looked up, locked gazes with his brother. "I'll do whatever it takes to get her out of this mess."

"I know you will." He held up the bill. "I've got this, Bro."

Jake nodded. "Tip's on me." He pulled a couple of bills from his wallet, tossed them on the table.

They made the short walk to Jake's office in silence. Will waved as he left the parking lot. Jake returned to his office to turn out lights and secure his files. He crammed the notes he'd scribbled earlier into his briefcase. At home, he poured himself two fingers of his best whiskey and sat down to prioritize the questions they'd come up with.

Top of the list—Who was Ginger Carpenter, and could she be involved with Cecil Hawthorne and Jessica Blackwell?

***

"You sure you don't want me to come with you?" Will asked as he pulled Jake's car to the curb.

"I appreciate the offer, but like I tell all my clients, let me handle it. It's what you pay me for."

"If that's a subtle way of telling me I'm going to have to pay you, think again." His brother shoved the gearshift into Park.

Jake popped the passenger-side door open, slid his right foot to the pavement, ignoring his brother's attempt at humor. "Don't wreck my car on the way home, asshole." He slammed the door shut, opened the rear door, and yanked his carry-on out. He leaned into the car. "I'll call when I have something to report."

Will craned his head around. "Text me when you land. Believe it or not, Rick and I worry about you."

Not as much as I worry about the two of you. "Yes, Mom," he said, slamming the door. Turning his back on his brother, he entered the terminal. He hadn't heard from his PI since yesterday morning when he'd given him another list of things to check out. Waiting at the gate, he phoned the NYPD detective in charge of the case but ended up having to leave a voice message.

Technically, Jake had done his job. He'd made sure Will's funds and property were returned to him. He could walk away now, let the police and prosecutors do their job, but his gut told him Sunny wasn't guilty of anything, except maybe hiring the wrong person to help at her gallery. He'd gone over the original police reports and discovered they'd never interviewed Ginger Carpenter about the heist, leaving her free to carry out the third leg of the crime—frame Sunny Sheldon.

He didn't want to throw shade on any law enforcement, but he suspected they hadn't interviewed her about the sale of the stolen painting, either. When he'd spoken to Detective Reeves outside Sunny's brownstone the day they arrested her, he'd mentioned the buyer's description of the woman who introduced herself as Sunny Sheldon. Called it a slam-dunk. Eager to close the case, he probably hadn't bothered to question the woman's memory. Jake wasn't even sure he'd asked if Sunny could provide an alibi.

As soon as the wheels touched the runway at JFK, Jake checked his messages. There was one from the PI. After texting Will and Rick to let them know he'd landed safely, he listened to his voicemail.

"Good morning, Mr. Ingram. This is Philip Holland. I've got some information for you regarding the person of interest you contacted me about. Please call me." He rattled off his phone number. Jake ended the recitation. He'd rather hear what the man found out in person. Carry-on in hand, he hopped into the first available cab and gave the driver the PI's address.

If the PI was surprised to see Jake, he hid it well. The two men shook hands. "Come on back to my office." The private investigator shut the door then took a seat behind his desk. He opened a folder. "You asked me to find anything I could on a Ginger Carpenter employed by Sunnyside Gallery in Manhattan."

Jake nodded. "What did you find out?"

"Ginger is her stage name. Landed a few bit parts on Broadway, but most of her credits are for off-Broadway productions. Small stuff. Nothing anyone has ever heard of. She auditions for any and everything. Plays, musicals, commercials, TV shows, movies. Her agent says she hasn't found the right vehicle for her brand of talent, which is entertainment speak for she's unmarketable."

Jake nodded his understanding. "She has no talent."

"Exactly."

"Go on."

Philip consulted his report. "To make ends meet, and I use the term loosely, she works multiple part-time retail jobs. The longest, by far, is her time with Sunnyside Gallery. She's been there for several years."

"Do you have an address for her?"

"I do, but she no longer lives there."

"Why not?"

"I spoke to the property owner. Her name wasn't on the lease, but he remembered her. He was about to evict her for nonpayment when she disappeared."

"Whose name was on the lease?"

"Cecil Hawthorne."

Jake stared across the desk at the PI. "Seriously?"

"I have a copy of the lease. Shitty place, too. If she was sleeping with him, she should have demanded better accommodations."

"When did she skip out?"

The PI consulted his papers, named a date.

"That's a few days after the sale of my brother's stolen painting." Jake filled the PI in on the developments regarding the missing paintings on the same day he'd informed him to quit looking for Hawthorne and Blackwell. "Where has she been for the weeks between now and then?"

"I spoke with the building superintendent. Asked if he'd seen anything unusual. He mentioned seeing her and a guy meeting Hawthorne's description hauling a bunch of canvases up the three flights of stairs months ago. Never saw them leave, but he wasn't watching her apartment. It's only luck he was there the day she moved them in. The property owner told me she'd left everything behind, except for her clothes. I asked about the paintings. He assured me there were a few cheap prints on the walls and nothing else. Which bears out since your brother's paintings turned up elsewhere."

Jake slumped in his chair. "Well, now we know where the paintings were all this time."

"The question is, why? If they were worth as much as everyone assumed, why did Hawthorne give them to her?"

"Assuming he did so willingly?"

Philip shrugged. "Or not so willingly." He steepled his fingers in front of his face. "They could have been payment for something. Services rendered or perhaps blackmail. Maybe he gave them to her in exchange for keeping her mouth shut."

"She had to have known stolen paintings weren't worth anything except a prison sentence," Jake surmised.

"Unless you have another use for them." The PI turned a few pages over, scanned the page he'd found. "Here's the interesting part." He smiled a cat-with-a-canary smile. "Care to guess what Ginger Carpenter's actual name is?"

***

"Son of a bitch."

"My thoughts, exactly." Philip scribbled something on a piece of paper, slid it across the desk.

Jake took the note, eyed the address. "Whose place is this?"

"Curtis Sheldon."

Nodding, Jake stood, offered his hand.

The PI did likewise then handed Jake the thick file folder. "Let me know if I can be of any more help."

On the sidewalk, Jake took a minute to get his bearings. Philip saved the best for last. Jake needed a few minutes to wrap his head around the new information and to come up with a plan. Spying a coffee shop down the block, he made his way there and ordered a giant cup of java and a slice of lemon pound cake. Luckily, most of the customers took theirs to go, leaving plenty of seats to choose from. Jake claimed a big leather chair in the corner and sat to enjoy the afternoon treat. While he ate, he read through the report. The PI was right. He needed to visit Mr. Sheldon before he did anything else.

***

Jake dismissed the Uber driver before he could change his mind about the path he'd chosen. The townhouse, not far from Sunny's on the Upper East Side of Manhattan, was impressive. The white marble facade boasted a lot of carved detail. About a dozen steps led up to a glossy black door embellished with a polished brass handle and door knocker. Colorful fall flowers adorned window boxes along the first-floor windows and others in pots lined the staircase. Everything about the place screamed money. With his overnighter still in hand, Jake climbed the steps to Curtis Sheldon's front door. As he pressed the doorbell, it occurred to him he didn't even know if the man was home. He could literally be anywhere in the world.

Hearing footsteps approaching, Jake squared his shoulders and cleared his throat. The door swung open. Jake recognized Sunny's father from the many movies he'd seen the man in over the years. Mr. Sheldon's gaze swept Jake from head to toe, paused a moment on the carry-on sitting next to him on the top step, then swung back to his face. "I don't care what you're selling. I don't want any."

Jake spoke up before the door fully closed in his face. "Mr. Sheldon. I'm here about your daughter, Samantha."

CHAPTER NINETEEN

The door swung wide again. Jake wasn't sure if the actor's expression was shock or anger. Perhaps some of both.

Sunny's father glared at him. "Who the hell are you?"

"Jake Ingram, sir. Your other daughter, Sunny, is accused of stealing my brother's paintings. I don't think she did it."

"Jake Ingram," he mused. "You're the lawyer?"

"Yes, sir."

He stepped back. "Come in before someone sees you."

Jake stepped into the spacious vestibule. From the outside, the place appeared small, but from the entryway, he could see all the way to the kitchen which occupied the back portion of the first floor. Although narrow, the townhouse had plenty of square footage if you considered the two floors above and one below. The modern décor suggested a recent update, but personal touches like family photos on the walls and a well-loved sofa made the home look lived in.

Mr. Sheldon shut and locked the door.

"Nice place," Jake said as he followed his host through to the kitchen where the actor waved him to a barstool at the large kitchen island.

Sunny's dad poured himself a cup of coffee from the pot of an aged coffeemaker out of place in the ultra-modern kitchen. "Coffee?"

Jake nodded. "Thanks." As the actor poured another cup and slid the mug across the counter to him, Jake fought the urge to laugh. Who would have thought Curtis Sheldon would serve him coffee? On what planet did something like this happen?

After ascertaining Jake took his coffee black, the older man leaned back against the counter, facing Jake. "What's this about Samantha?"

"Did you know she's been working as Sunny's assistant at the gallery for several years?"

Mr. Sheldon froze, his coffee almost to his lips. Slowly, he lowered the mug then gripped the edge of the soapstone on either side of him. "No, I didn't." His jaw clenched, and his knuckles grew white as he dug his fingers into the stone. Jake could see the wheels turning behind the man's astute eyes.

"She's been using her stage name, Ginger Carpenter."

"Fuck." Sunny's father spun, braced himself on the counter, his head hanging. Jake sipped his coffee, waiting for the man to regain his composure. His shocked reaction to Jake's statement confirmed his suspicion Sunny didn't know she had a sister. Half sister.

"Sunny doesn't know, does she?"

"No." The actor turned. He'd aged ten years in the last minute. Not a good sign. "I need to sit." He waved Jake to follow him. "Bring your coffee." Sunny's dad left his in the kitchen, opting for a shot of whiskey from the antique sideboard that doubled as a bar in the living area. After downing the shot, he poured two fingers into the cut-crystal tumbler. "Care for something stronger?"

"No, thanks. Coffee's fine."

Mr. Sheldon sat on one end of the sofa, kicked his feet up on the reclaimed wood coffee table. Jake took a seat on the opposite end and kept his feet on the floor. And waited. Curtis Sheldon was a brilliant man who used his intelligence to bring the characters he portrayed to life. He'd won the industry's highest awards on both screen and stage, though you wouldn't know it from looking at this portion of his home. Maybe he kept them in an office or at one of his other homes. Sunny mentioned her father owned a house in upstate New York, one in Los Angeles, and the beach house in the Hamptons.

"Margery and I decided not to tell Sunny about her half sister when they were both infants."

"Margery is Sunny's mother?"

"Yes. My affair with Samantha's mother was the end of our marriage, though Marge is still the love of my life. I fucked it all up, literally. Marge could have forgiven me just about anything, but infidelity wasn't one of them."

"Sunny told me you and her mother were still in love but couldn't live with each other."

He stared at the brown liquid in his glass. "She's right. I've never loved anyone else. I've been with others over the years, but my heart still belongs to Margery. I never questioned why she didn't remarry."

"What about Samantha's mother?"

"Ginger?" Mr. Sheldon's gaze clouded. "She was a one-night stand. I was starring in a Broadway musical. Margery was pregnant with Sunny. Difficult pregnancy. On bedrest for months. Ginger was there. Part of the dance company—you know—extras that fill in the non-speaking parts. She was beautiful and spirited. Most of the extras were afraid to talk to the stars." He put the last word in air quotes. "But not Ginger. She was always hanging around. Learning from us, she said. I was lonely. That's not an excuse, just a fact. Margery was in California, and I was in New York. We talked on the phone, and I went to see her every chance I got, but my schedule didn't allow it often. Broadway is grueling. Eight live shows a week. The only way to get a night off is to be sick or pay the stand-in to go on for you. The show had just opened, and the producers frowned on the stars taking time off. People payed to see the big names, not the stand-ins."

The actor stood, refilled his glass, then paced to gaze out the window. "We'd accomplished a rare, perfect night on stage. Everyone was on. No one missed a line or a cue. The audience ate it up. I'd never taken as many curtain calls as I did that night. We threw a cast party afterward to celebrate. I drank too much. Might have been feeling sorry for myself because I didn't have anyone to celebrate with, if you get my meaning." He sipped his drink. "Ginger was there. Telling me everything I wanted Margery to be there telling me. Next thing I knew, we were in the prop room and my pants were around my ankles. I backed her up against the wall and fucked her. It was over in minutes. We straightened our clothes and went back to the party. Didn't talk about it again until a few weeks later when she told me she was pregnant.

"I almost had a heart attack. I knew I couldn't tell Margery, not until after she delivered. I agreed to pay all of Ginger's medical expenses. Set up a trust fund for the baby even before Samantha was born.

"Hardest thing I ever had to do was tell Margery what I'd done. Sunny was a year old, Samantha about six months old. Margery told me to get out. She never wanted to see me again. We've shared custody of Sunny from then on. Never disagreed about how to raise her."

"But you never told Sunny about her half sister."

"No. Margery and I decided she didn't need to know."

"What about Samantha? Obviously, she has known for a while."

Sunny's dad ran his free hand through his hair. "Ginger died about five years ago. Breast cancer. Her attorney notified me since I'd been financially supporting them for years. Samantha wasn't supposed to be told about me until she turned twenty-five and her trust fund was turned over to her. She was only about a year from reaching her majority, so I amended the trust to let her have access. I met with her a few times after that, always with our lawyers present. She wanted nothing to do with me, and I didn't try to convince her otherwise. I didn't want to rub Margie's face in my mistake, and I wasn't keen on telling Sunny how I'd screwed up."

"You haven't heard from Samantha in all this time?"

"No. Not a word. Occasionally, I'll see her stage name listed in the supporting cast, mostly off-Broadway productions or mentioned in *Variety*. It always gives me a jolt, since she uses her mother's name. Seeing it brings back unpleasant memories. Anyway, Samantha made no attempt to contact me, and God forgive me, I didn't contact her, either. If what you say is true, my cowardice has come around to bite me in the ass."

"I have documentation of her employment at Sunnyside Gallery. The private investigator I hired spoke to her landlord and her building superintendent. The property owner confirmed Cecil Hawthorne paid her rent until he disappeared. They'd given her multiple eviction notices in the last few months. The building super said he saw her lugging a bunch of paintings up the stairs to her apartment about the time my brother's paintings went missing from Hawthorne's gallery."

"Yet, they turned up in the basement of Sunny's brownstone and the storeroom at the gallery."

Jake nodded. "Do you think Sunny would have given Ginger, I mean, Samantha, access to her home? I know she had a key to the gallery. Sunny mentioned calling her to have her open a few hours a day while the two of us were upstate."

Mr. Sheldon settled back on the sofa, placing his empty tumbler on the coffee table. "Let me guess. Samantha sold the painting, the one that led to Sunny's arrest? And now she's disappeared."

"Sounds like the plot of a really bad movie, but yeah, I think she pretended to be Sunny when she sold the painting. The PI gave me a picture of her. It wouldn't take much to pass herself off as Sunny, especially to someone who didn't know her. Side by side, I think I'd notice the resemblance, though, not knowing their actual relationship, I doubt I'd make the connection."

"I need to tell Sunny."

"And the cops."

Sunny's dad rested his forearms on his thighs, clasped his hands in front. His head hung between his shoulders. "One stupid mistake three decades ago. I need to call Margery. Give her a heads-up. This will cause a media frenzy. My agent is going to kill me."

Jake ignored his self-pity party. He couldn't count how many times he'd heard similar laments, minus the PR nightmare, from his clients, both male and female. Marital mistakes were a dime a dozen no matter what your profession. Still, he found it difficult to feel sorry for the man. If he'd come clean from the beginning, told Sunny and Samantha, perhaps built a genuine relationship with both, fostered one between the sisters, things would have turned out differently.

Jake stood, helped himself to two fingers of the man's excellent bourbon. He fortified himself with a sip before making his request. "I want to be there when you tell Sunny."

The declaration brought the actor's head up. He studied Jake like he was memorizing everything about him in order to play him onstage. "You broke her heart."

The older man's barb hit him hard, buried under his skin. "I made a mistake. I'm willing to admit it and live with the consequences."

"Why didn't you leave this alone? As I understand it, your brother got his money and his paintings back. Why not let the NYPD think they'd solved the case?"

"I thought about it, sir. I thought your daughter lied to me. Betrayed my family. It took me a while, but I came to my senses and realized Sunny isn't stupid. She'd never sell a stolen painting, much less one she knew everyone in the art world would be on the lookout for."

"The police think differently."

"I know her better than they do."

Mr. Sheldon stood. "How well do you know her?"

The weight of the concerned father's stare made him feel like a bug under a microscope. Jake took another sip from his mug. The cooled tea tasted bitter, as bitter as the words he refused to hold back. "I know her well enough. Better than you knew Ginger Carpenter." He drew a fortifying breath and spoke from his heart. "I'm in love with her, sir. If she's anything like her mother, she probably won't forgive me, but if she will, I'll do whatever it takes to make her happy for the rest of her life."

CHAPTER TWENTY

"Wait here while I make a few phone calls. This might take a while, so make yourself at home. Rec room's in the basement."

Jake let out a pent-up breath as Curtis Sheldon, possibly his future father-in-law, disappeared up the staircase, leaving him to his own devices. At least he hadn't punched him for the veiled reference he'd made to the older man's decades-old fuckup, or to the inference of an intimate relationship with the man's daughter. Jake's statement of intent where Sunny was concerned gained him a grudging smile from her father. Facing off with the famous actor felt surreal. Jake could admit to himself he'd been a little intimidated by the man, not because of his fame but because of the influence he held over his daughter. One word from him, and Sunny might never forgive him.

With an unknown amount of time to kill, Jake made his way around the room, checking out the framed photos. Most were casual snapshots of him and Sunny taken at recognizable tourist spots around the world. A few were of him and other easily recognizable actors on a boat, showing off their catch. He couldn't believe these were the people Sunny and her dad called friends. Surreal. If Sunny forgave him, he hoped to become a permanent part of her world—a world he knew nothing about.

Having examined everything on public display, he ventured down the stairs to see what passed for a rec room in the world of the rich and famous. He stopped on the last stair tread and stared. Talk about a man cave. A giant screen TV occupied an entire wall, while a giant trophy fish claimed another. A grouping of overstuffed sofas and chairs provided enough lounge space for a football team. A pool table and various electronic games occupied one corner, and a massive wet bar completed the dream space. Jake expected the basement to be dark and cramped, but this one was bright as day, lit with subtle lighting that bounced off walls painted off-white to match the rugs scattered over the hardwood floors.

He forced his feet to move. Found a massive remote on the coffee table. After spending a few minutes guessing at which button to push first, he found one that looked promising. The giant screen came to life with a menu. From there, it was easy enough to maneuver through the channels to find a baseball game already in progress. Didn't matter who was playing. Even when he'd been playing football in high school, he'd preferred to watch baseball. Turned out, he didn't have the hand/eye coordination to play the game at anything beyond a rec level, but the complexity of it appealed to him.

Jake muted the game then grabbed a soda from the well-stocked bar. After settling into the inviting sofa, he placed a call to Will.

"Hey. You'll never guess where I am." He spent the next half hour catching his brother up on everything he'd found out since arriving in New York. "He's making some phone calls. His ex and Sunny. Don't know if he'll get her to come here or if we're going out to the Hamptons to talk to her. I'll keep you informed." He shifted into big brother mode. "How's everything there?"

"I finished the painting I was working on. Might start another one tomorrow if I don't have to finish up work on Rick's latest project."

Their youngest brother's home remodel business had taken off in the last few months. Last Jake heard, Rick was booked up through the new year with jobs both big and small. "What do you mean? Why can't Rick finish it up?"

"He's not here." Until Will found a place of his own, he was still bunking with Rick at the house they'd grown up in.

"What do you mean, not here? Where is he?"

"He left right after I got home from dropping you at the airport. Said his Marine buddy was in Dallas again and he was going to go see him. I thought he'd be home by now, that's all. I'm sure he'll realize it's getting late and drag his ass home soon."

Rick had mentioned this friend several times, but Jake couldn't recall hearing the guy's name. His brother had been in such a funk when he left the Marines and returned home, Jake hadn't pressed him for details about his service. Now, he wished he had. "If you don't hear from him soon, let me know. Okay?"

"Okay, but what are you going to do about it from New York?"

Will had a point. Jake sighed and rubbed at the knot forming at the back of his neck. "I don't know, Will. One problem at a time, Brother."

"Don't worry about Rick. He's a grown man. He can take care of himself. Probably a hell of a lot better than either of us. Focus on getting Sunny to forgive you. You deserve some happiness, Jake."

"Yeah, well, even if she forgives me and we get her name cleared, I don't know how a relationship with her would work. We live in two different worlds."

"Call me a romantic, but I'm a firm believer love always finds a way."

"You've let your happiness with MacKenzie go to your head." Footsteps on the stairs reminded him why he was here. He rubbed at his neck again. The pain crept up the back of his skull. "Gotta go. I'll keep you informed."

***

Sunny was used to her dad's unexpected visits. Given his celebrity status, he preferred to be spontaneous, rarely announcing his plans to anyone ahead of time. Since this was his house, he didn't bother to knock, just walked right in, as usual. At least this time, probably because of the late hour, he announced his presence immediately instead of scaring the bejesus out of her. Hearing him call her name, she grabbed a sweater off the chair next to the bed and bounded down the stairs to meet him.

"Hey, Dad," she called out, "what are you…?" The sight of the man standing behind her father robbed her of speech. The last time she'd seen Jake Ingram had been the day of her arrest. She'd found out later he'd known what was about to happen and been a willing participant in the day's festivities. His betrayal was still a boiling cauldron making her sick to her stomach and keeping her awake nights.

"Sunny." Her dad drew her attention. "We need to talk."

His words and solemn demeanor helped her find her voice. "I have nothing to say to him." She nodded at Jake.

"He might have something to say to you later on, but first, you need to hear what I have to say."

The sadness in his voice broke through the anguish squeezing her heart. She turned her gaze to her dad, only then noticing the red rims around his eyes and the deep lines formed around his mouth. She took the last few steps, stopping to embrace her dad. "What's wrong? Is Mom okay?"

"Your mom is fine. I spoke to her before I left to come see you. She sends her love and said to expect a call from her in the morning. She also said you can call her anytime if you want to talk."

Despite his reassurances, she couldn't help feeling like he was about to yank the rug out from under her feet. Dread gripped her in a cold vise. She wrapped her arms around her midsection, willing the bad mojo to go away. "I could use some hot tea. Let's go into the kitchen."

She led the way. The two men took seats at the island. While the kettle heated, she put out a plate of cookies she'd made earlier, for lack of something better to do. For the life of her, she couldn't imagine why Jake was here, with her father, no less. How did that happen? The more she thought about it, the more she became convinced this had to do with her arrest. From the expression on both their faces, it couldn't be good. Even more reason to postpone this talk as long as possible.

When they all had cups of tea, and there wasn't anything more she could do to stall the inevitable, she dragged a stool around the corner of the island where she could see them and sat. "Okay. What's this all about?"

"I understand you have an assistant by the name of Ginger Carpenter."

Sunny wrapped her chilled hands around her mug. The heat helped thaw her fingers and her nerves. "Yes. She's been with me as a part-time employee for about five years now. Why? Did something happen to her?" Suddenly, her hands were cold again.

"She's fine. As far as I know. But Jake here" — he hitched a thumb at the silent man beside him — "uncovered something that might clear you of all charges."

Sunny snapped her gaze to Jake. His eyes locked with hers, and, for a brief second, she was back in the clearing with him, their bodies moving as one, with so many unspoken words between them. Shaking her head, she broke the connection, giving her dad her full attention once again. "What did he find, and what does it have to do with Ginger?"

Her dad's gaze drifted to the steaming mug in his hands. "Maybe I should start at the beginning."

She nodded. "Okay."

"Your mom and I broke up because I had an affair. A one-night stand, actually."

Sunny listened to her dad's recitation of the events leading up to the demise of his marriage. What this had to do with Ginger or anything else, besides the fact both her parents lied to her for her entire life, she didn't know. Eventually, he got around to mentioning the woman's name.

"Wait a minute. Her name was Ginger Carpenter?"

"Yes. It was once, Sunny. We had no feelings for each other, not like your mom and I did before I ruined it."

"Mom wouldn't forgive you?"

"She might have if it ended there, but Ginger became pregnant. With my child."

"Oh. My. God." The puzzle pieces fell into place creating an awful picture she didn't want to see. "My assistant, Ginger Carpenter, is my sister?"

Her dad nodded once and, with a shaking hand, raised his mug to his lips. He took a sip then raised his eyes to hers once again. "Ginger Carpenter is her stage name, an homage to her mother, I guess. The name on her birth certificate is Samantha Sheldon."

It was almost too much to comprehend. She'd known Ginger for years, and they'd often joked about their uncanny resemblance. Had Ginger known all along they were related? "How long has she known we were sisters?"

"She found out about five years ago, when her mother died."

"Why wouldn't she say something?"

"I don't know. But Jake here found out some things. I'll let him tell you."

She still didn't see what any of this had anything to do with her being suspected of selling stolen property, but she was curious enough to hear what Jake had to say. She turned her attention to the man who, despite his betrayal, owned her heart. "I'm listening."

"Ginger is nowhere to be found. Disappeared when you and I were upstate looking for answers. Turns out, the answers were back in Manhattan. The PI I hired tracked down her landlord, found out he'd been trying to evict her for months for nonpayment. The apartment she occupied was leased to Cecil Hawthorne. He quit paying rent the same month Jessica disappeared."

Sunny held her hand up like a stop sign. She closed her eyes and shook her head. "Wait a second." She popped her eyes open, stared at Jake. "Ginger and Cecil? Are you kidding me?"

"No. There's more if you're ready to hear it."

She huffed out a laugh. "By all means, continue."

"The PI also talked to the building super. He said he helped Ginger carry a bunch of paintings up the stairs to her apartment about the time Will's paintings went missing from Hawthorne's gallery."

She didn't know what to say. She'd known and trusted Ginger for years. It was beyond comprehension the woman could be involved with something like this.

Jake grabbed one of her homemade cookies and bit into it. He washed the bite down with a swig of his tea. "We think Ginger pretended to be you when she sold Will's stolen painting. The two of you look enough alike, a stranger, someone who'd only met one of you, would months later provide a vague enough description to the police to make them think she'd interacted with you. And since Ginger is MIA, a side-by-side comparison is impossible."

"We joked about our resemblance. I thought it was funny, you know? We were rarely in the gallery at the same time, and when we were, I was usually in my office doing paperwork while she covered the sales floor. A time or two, customers would see us both and ask if we were sisters. We both laughed it off. Now, you're telling me she knew we were related and said nothing?"

"It looks that way," Jake confirmed. "Did you ever give her a key to your house, or could she have made a copy of your key?"

Sunny sipped her tea, giving the question time to sink in. "I didn't give her a key, but there was a day last year… We were crazy busy. We had a big shipment going out the next day, so I took some shipping orders home the night before to finish up and forgot to bring them in. To save time, Ginger offered to go get them while I finished the other paperwork. I gave her my keys and wrote the alarm code down for her."

"That answers the question of how the paintings ended up in your basement. She must have made a duplicate key, and you'd handed her the alarm code."

"And she already had access to the gallery. I know every inch of the storeroom there. Those paintings were not there the day you and I left on our trip. I'm certain. She had to have brought them in while we were away." She folded her arms on the island and dropped her forehead to her crossed arms. "I can't believe this."

The sound of chair legs scraping on the floor had her sitting up. Her dad stood beside the island. "I don't care how late it is, I'll call Detective Reeves. Now that we know how she got into your house, we need to turn this all over to him. This should be enough to clear your name."

That was the best news she'd heard in months. "God, I hope so." Relieved her ordeal might end soon, she waited until her dad turned down the hallway, out of sight. Feeling the heat of Jake's gaze on her back, she faced him. "You didn't have to follow up on this, but I'm grateful you did."

CHAPTER TWENTY-ONE

Jake dropped his gaze to his now-disgustingly cool tea. The last few months had taken a toll on Sunny, but she was still the most beautiful woman he'd ever seen. Always would be. He hoped she could forgive him for doubting her, for believing she could have done the things they accused her of. Glancing up, he met her gaze head-on. "I'm sorry, Sunny. I never should have doubted you. Not even for a second. I knew I'd made a mistake before my plane landed in Dallas. Hell, I knew it before the plane was in the air. I just couldn't admit it to myself."

"Why did you get involved again? Will has his money and his paintings back. You'd done what you promised you would do for him."

"Truthfully?"

"Please, Jake."

"Will pushed me to keep looking. He never believed you were guilty, and I think he knew I didn't believe it, either. He finally pushed hard enough. Siblings can be a pain in the ass."

"I'm beginning to see that."

"Oh shit." He rubbed a hand over his face. "I'm sorry. See, I can't think straight when you're around. Maybe that's why I needed to go home to figure this out."

She dropped her gaze to her mug then used both hands to spin it in place. "You hurt me, Jake. I thought we had something."

"You weren't wrong," he said, consulting his mug. "I felt it, too. Something." He tipped the mug, examined its contents—like he'd find answers or the right words there. "Did I fuck it up beyond repair, Sunny? Can you forgive me for not believing in you? For not sticking by you?"

"I want to. I really do, but I need time, Jake. This entire thing has made me question everything in my life. And now, I have a sister who apparently hates me and has for some time. It's a lot to process, and until they drop the charges, I'm still the alleged perpetrator of several major crimes."

Hearing the despair in her voice and knowing he was partly responsible for it, twisted his gut up in knots. He'd do anything in his power to bring sunshine back into her life. Rising, he rounded the island. As if her body remembered his, she turned to face him. He stepped into the V of her legs. She tilted her face up, and he gave in to temptation, cradling her cheek with his palm. The pain and uncertainty in her eyes were like arrows to his heart, wounding him.

"I'm so sorry, sweetheart. I never meant for you to get hurt." He stroked her soft skin with his thumb, memorizing the curve of her cheek, then the softness of her lips. "I love you, Sunny. More than you can ever know. I hope you can find it in your heart to forgive me, but if you can't, I'll understand. You deserve a man who won't ever doubt you, one who'll cherish you forever. One who would walk through Hell to protect you." He kissed her forehead then met her gaze. "I want to be that man, Sunny. I swear to God, if you can forgive me, I'll be that man for you."

Footsteps sounded from the hallway. Jake reluctantly stepped away. He caught the sheen of tears in her eyes and cursed himself anew for making her cry.

Her father stepped into the room. "Woke the son of a bitch up. He'll meet us tomorrow morning at my house, look over this new evidence."

The news eased some of Jake's anxiety. "He's willing to listen, so that's good." Once a cop made up his mind, it wasn't easy to convince him he might be wrong. Jake hoped Detective Reeves was different.

"If he doesn't see what's obvious, we'll go over his head." Mr. Sheldon gave his daughter a hug. "We'll get this cleared up tomorrow. I promise."

"Thanks, Dad. I appreciate you standing by me."

Jake didn't think she meant the comment to be a jab at his lack of faith, but it hit him hard anyway. He turned his back on them while he tried to get his emotions under control. He'd bared his soul, pleaded his case. It was up to Sunny to either forgive him or not. Jake took another sip from his glass. The aged bourbon burned a trail all the way to his stomach.

"I know you, Sunshine. You don't have a dishonest bone in your body, and with your acting skills, you'd never pull off that kind of deceit."

"Hey." Her laugh was sweet music to Jake's ears. "I'm not so bad. Ask Jake. I pulled off quite the performance with the real estate agent we questioned. Tell him, Jake."

Stunned at the easy banter and teasing lilt in her voice, Jake spun around. Her eyes were still bright with unshed tears, but her smile was that of an angel. "Yeah," he croaked. He cleared his throat, shifting his gaze away from her before he forgot he had no right to touch her. "You should have seen her. She pretended to be interested in moving out of the city, got the woman to show us pictures of the place my brother and Jessica asked about. Because she played her part so well, we were able to get the address and verify the new owners weren't Cecil and Jessica."

Mr. Sheldon raised an eyebrow. "Well, well. I guess the apple doesn't fall far from the old tree."

Sunny shook her head. "Old tree? Dad, you aren't very old." Then she shifted her gaze to Jake. "And who says I'm not interested in moving out of the city?"

"Speaking of the city," her dad interrupted before Jake could press Sunny regarding her statement, "it's a lengthy drive. If we want to get any sleep at all tonight, we need to get moving."

Sunny hopped off her barstool. "I'll pack a bag."

Jake's gaze followed her out of the room. When she was gone, he started grabbing mugs. Her dad's voice gave him pause. "Leave them. We have staff who'll come in tomorrow and clean up."

"Okay. I'll put them in the sink." He also turned off the burner beneath the teakettle.

"I've got plenty of room. You'll stay with us?"

His every thought centered on clearing Sunny's name, and he hadn't even thought of making a hotel reservation. He nodded. "Okay, but you'd better check with Sunny first. I don't want her to be uncomfortable."

The actor clapped him on the back. "Are you blind, son? She's in love with you."

"Oh, no, sir. You're mistaken. I betrayed her." He was rambling but couldn't seem to stop himself. "She has every right to hate me."

"But she doesn't. She was mad at you. Wanted to throw you to the sharks a couple of times, but she doesn't hate you. But make no mistake, if you hurt her again, I'll turn you into fish bait myself." He squeezed Jake's shoulder hard enough to make the younger man wince. "Am I making myself clear?"

Jake swallowed hard. "Yes, sir. Crystal."

He eased up on Jake's shoulder—patted him on the back. "I'm glad we got everything cleared up. Do you like to fish, Jake?" He steered Jake toward the front door where they waited for Sunny. "I've got a boat. She's a beaut. A thirty-seven-footer. Twin inboard motors. We should take her out sometime, you and me. Get to know each other. You ever caught a striped bass?"

"Dad." Sunny came down the stairs, carrying a small overnight bag. "Jake doesn't want to hear your fish stories." She handed Jake her bag then slid her arms into a puffy jacket she'd brought down with her. "If you haven't figured out by now, Dad loves to fish. If you aren't interested, better tell him now, or you'll never shut him up."

"Uh, no, I mean, I like to fish." Leaving her dad to set the alarm and lock up, he followed Sunny out. He dropped her bag next to his in the trunk of her dad's Bentley then climbed into the backseat behind Sunny. He didn't mind riding in the back. This way, he'd have several hours to stare at her. Mr. Sheldon slid behind the wheel. "Did Sunny tell you I live on a lake? I keep a boat at a nearby marina. It's only a twenty-footer, but it's plenty big enough for me. Maybe you could come down sometime. You ever do any lake fishing?"

He talked fishing with her dad until Sunny gave up trying to get a word in and drifted off to sleep. From then on, their conversation revolved around more practical matters.

"How long can you stay?" Mr. Sheldon asked.

Jake didn't take his eyes off the woman sleeping in the front passenger seat. "A few days. I left in a hurry. I'll need to do some work while I'm here then I've got a couple of court cases coming up next week. I have to be back for those."

"Her life is here," her dad stated, unnecessarily.

"I'm aware of the geographical problem. I don't know how we'll make this work, but if it matters as much to her as it does to me, we'll figure it out."

"The media frenzy died down some over the last few weeks. After this news breaks, it'll pick up again. Can you handle the scrutiny?"

Jake caught her dad's gaze on him in the rearview mirror. "I can handle anything your daughter needs me to, sir. I let her down once, I won't do it again."

The actor nodded. "You'll do, Ingram. I think you'll do."

A sleepy voice made them both smile. "Leave him alone, Dad. I'm a grown woman. I can take care of myself."

"Never said you couldn't, Sunshine. Never said you couldn't."

"Her name's Sunshine?"

"Sunshine Margery Sheldon. Margie said Sunny was a ray of sunshine after all the months she'd spent on bedrest. When they brought around the papers to fill out for her birth certificate, we looked at each other and we both said Sunshine at the same time." He smiled at the memory. "She's been Sunny ever since."

"That's a nice story. They named me after my father. Jacob Tyler Ingram. Tyler was my mother's family name. I've got two younger brothers. We all got the same middle name. They're named after my mother's brothers, William and Richard Tyler." Talking about them reminded him he needed to call Will, fill him in on everything happening here, and to see if Rick had shown up. He checked his phone for the time and decided it was too late to call. He'd check in first thing in the morning. He'd rather wake them both up early than roust them out of a sound sleep in the middle of the night.

"Will is the artist, right? What does Richard do?"

"Rick," Jake corrected then explained about his brother's stint in the Marines before returning home to open his own home remodeling business. By the time he'd finished, they were entering the city. He shut up to let the man concentrate on driving.

Her dad dropped them off in front of his house then parked his car in the garage a few blocks away where he rented space for several vehicles. Sunny unlocked the door then led him inside.

"My room and Dad's room are on the second floor. Guest rooms are on the third floor. Pick whichever you want." She shed her coat, hanging it on a hook on the hall tree behind the door. "Help yourself to anything in the kitchen. Dad's casual about guests. His house is your house." She waved her hand around. "You get the idea." She made for the stairs, overnight bag in hand.

Jake caught up easily, taking her bag in his free hand. "I'll get it." He could see she wanted to argue, but fatigue, or maybe something else, made her reconsider.

"Okay, but, Jake, I haven't made up my mind yet about you. About us. Just so you know."

He nodded. "I know. I won't pressure you, Sunshine."

Using her full name earned him a smile. "Don't call me that. I hate it."

"Why?" He trailed her up the stairs and to a room a much younger Sunny had decorated, judging by the pink frilly curtains and matching comforter that set off the white furniture. Pink flowered wallpaper adorned the walls. Jake's eyes crossed at the overpowering floral pattern.

Sunny stood in the doorway, blocking him from entering, thank God. He didn't know how anyone could spend ten minutes, let alone an entire night, in her room. "Sunshine is a hippy name. Like Moon or River. Clearly, my parents were out of their minds with joy or something else I don't want to think about when they came up with my name."

"Your dad has a perfectly reasonable explanation for your name."

"Yeah, I've heard it. Bullshit, I tell you." She pulled the door halfway closed. "Upstairs, Jake. Take your pick. I'll see you in the morning." She shut the door in his face.

CHAPTER TWENTY-TWO

Sunny clasped her hands in her lap to keep them from shaking. Detective Reeves had been there almost two hours, listening and asking questions, and she'd been a nervous wreck the entire time. She hated someone she'd called a friend for the last five years or so could be so devious. Finding out the person was her half sister only made the deception worse. Sunny didn't want to see her sister go to prison for the possession and sale of stolen merchandise, but she had no intention of serving a sentence for something she didn't do, either.

Her dad called his team, and they were working on a way to spin the story so it didn't sound as bad as it really was. Talk about a Hollywood-style scandal. This took the cake. It was the kind of story even the legitimate news outlets couldn't ignore. She'd lived most of her life in the shadows of the spotlight trained on her dad. Since her arrest, she'd been the one under scrutiny. Once the latest became public, her entire family would be held up to public scorn. A marital affair. An illegitimate child. A high-profile crime. A sibling framing another for said crime. Her mother would be the object of pity. Until they found Ginger/Samantha and got a confession out of her, Sunny would forever be under suspicion by the public, if not the police.

Then there was Jake. Keeping his name out of it would be impossible. The tabloids already linked him to her and ran with the story of their trip upstate, turning it into something lurid, if not illegal. He said he could deal with the fallout, but could he really? Sunny'd seen others who were used to the public scrutiny buckle under the pressure. And what about his law practice? Would his notoriety, even if short-lived, influence his livelihood?

Everywhere she looked, her life spilled over onto those she loved, and not in a good way. Her mom and dad had to put up with her, but Jake didn't. If it all became too much, he could walk away. He'd done it once, and it hurt more than she ever imagined. The man held her heart in his hands, and the thought of him crushing it a second time was the only thing she feared more than going to jail.

Detective Reeves shuffled the pages Jake's PI had provided and stuffed them back in the folder. "Mind if I take these?"

The question jerked Sunny out of her maudlin thoughts.

Jake made a dismissive gesture. "Help yourself."

Everyone stood when the detective did. "Ms. Sheldon, I'll let you know if this information checks out, but Mr. Ingram has put forth a logical scenario to explain many of the unanswered questions in your case."

"So, I'm not off the hook yet?" God, she hated the way her voice shook, but she couldn't help it. She was so cold inside, her whole body trembled with it.

"No, ma'am. Not until I can verify the latest information. Given the photograph of your sister, I can see how she could pass herself off as you. It would be best if we could find her, but if her connection to Cecil Hawthorne checks out, and what her building super said holds, those facts would cast a different light on the investigation but not necessarily rule out your involvement."

Disappointment felt like a giant stone hanging around her neck. The news Jake brought last night gave her hope. Too much hope, according to the detective. Without the confession of one of the real culprits, everything the police had still pointed to Sunny's involvement in some way. All she had in her favor was the testimony of a building superintendent who couldn't say for sure if the paintings he'd helped tote up the stairs were the ones stolen from Hawthorne's gallery.

Even she had to admit, the story about a sister she hadn't known she had, who, for reasons unknown, happened to have it out for her, sounded a bit too convenient. Until the missing sister was found and her motives uncovered, a cloud of suspicion would hover over Sunny's head. Another reason Jake should stay far away from her.

Her dad spoke up. "Samantha has access to her trust fund. Maybe she's using it to fund this caper. She's got to be living on something."

Detective Reeves tucked the folder under his arm. "I'll try to get a warrant for her financials and her phone records. Based on all this"—he tapped the folder—"I would expect the judge to sign off on the warrant. But remember, Hawthorne was paying her rent. If she had the kind of money you say she has, then why wasn't she paying her own rent? I know that neighborhood. No one with a trust fund would live there unless they didn't have a choice."

"You think she's depleted her trust fund?" Mr. Sheldon sounded horrified at the thought.

"Happens more often than you think," the detective said as he ambled toward the front door.

"You'll keep Ms. Sheldon informed?" Jake asked.

The detective opened the door. "Of course, and thanks for running down this new information."

Jake banged a fist on the closed door. "Fuck!"

Sunny sank to the sofa, exhausted from the strain of keeping it together in the presence of the detective, when she wanted to shout and cry, and possibly throw something. She clenched her fists as frustration boiled to the surface, spilling down her cheeks in a torrent. "He doesn't believe me. He thinks Ginger and I did this together and we had a falling out and she left me holding the bag."

Suddenly, Jake was there, wrapping her in his arms, providing a bulwark to protect and support her. "Shh," he whispered as he cradled her head against his shoulder. "It's going to be alright. He'll follow the evidence. Those three must be living on something. It wouldn't take long for three people to blow through the money they stole from Will's accounts, especially if they're still in Manhattan."

"You think they're still in the city?" Glass clinked on glass as Sunny's dad poured himself a drink at the sideboard.

Jake's hands felt wonderful on her, one stroking her hair, the other firm on her back. "I do. At least Samantha is. She went to a lot of trouble to frame Sunny. Stands to reason she'd hang around close enough to watch it all unfold."

"Do you trust the PI you hired?"

Jake shrugged. "A friend I attended law school with recommended him. So far, he's been professional and discreet. Why?"

"Because I have information on Samantha's trust fund. Maybe he could at least tell us if the principle is still intact. I can't believe she could have blown through it in the few years since she gained control of it."

"I take it the principle was substantial." Jake held her tight, his warmth slowly battling the pervasive cold inside.

"If she managed it even halfway right, she could have lived comfortably the rest of her life, even in New York."

Jake whistled low. "Then we need to find out what she's done with it." He bent his head so he could see her face. "You okay?"

Sunny nodded and sniffed as she swiped her damp cheeks with her fingers. "Better." She pushed away from him, instantly regretting the loss of his heat and his strength. "Everything came crashing in all of a sudden." She patted the giant wet spot on his shirt. "Thanks for letting me lean on you."

His smile was like a ray of sunshine aimed right at her heart. "Anytime, sweetheart. Anytime." He used a thumb to brush away an errant tear from her cheek then he looked past her to her dad. "I'll call him. You got the information handy?"

***

Jake didn't want to leave her, but he had obligations back home he couldn't shirk, not if he wanted to keep his license to practice law. Sunny sat in the back of the limo her dad hired to take Jake to the airport, looking a little lost and not at all the spirited woman he knew and loved.

He was still getting used to the idea of being in love. It no longer scared him the way it did at first. He didn't have a clue how they could manage to be together, but he was dedicated to finding a way. But first, he needed to take care of things at home, and they had to get the charges dropped against her. Completely clearing her name would be nice, but as long as the real culprits remained at large, she'd remain under suspicion. He didn't want her to live with a dark cloud hanging over her. He vowed to do all he could to change her situation. His PI was working on the information Sunny's dad provided. Hopefully, he'd come up with a solid lead soon. Every day suspicion lay on her shoulders killed a little more of Sunny's spirit.

Framing her face with his hands, he looked deep into her eyes. "I love you. No matter what, don't forget you mean the world to me."

"I love you, too, Jake." Tears, almost ever-present now, leaked from the corner of her eyes. "Do you have to go?"

"Yes, but I'll be back." He thumbed her tears away. "If this doesn't get cleared up soon, you should come stay with me. If Detective Reeves knows where you are, he shouldn't care if you get away for a while."

She sniffed back more tears and a hint of a smile broke across her face. "I'd like to see where you live. And I could see Hank and Melody, too."

"They'd love to have you come visit, but, call me selfish, I want you all to myself — in my bed."

Instead of tears, her eyes sparkled then with the same want he felt to his core. "I can't think of anywhere else I want to be." She dipped her head, resting her forehead on his chest. "I need you. I want this all to go away so we can be together."

He held her tight, memorizing the feel of her soft body next to his hard one. He'd never felt this all-encompassing love for another person before. He loved his brothers, would do anything for them, but being physically distant from them didn't make him feel like a part of him was missing. "We're going to be together; I promise. We just have a few things to work out first." Like where they would live. What he would do for a living if he left Texas behind to be with her.

A horn honked as a car sped around them, protesting their prolonged curbside goodbye.

"I've got to go, sweetheart." He kissed her, pouring the cocktail of emotions swirling inside him into the connection. Showing her without words how she affected him, how much he hated to leave her. When he broke away, he captured her gaze with his. "I'm leaving my heart in your hands. Take care of it until I get back."

Her bottom lip trembled, and the tears he hated so much were back. Before he changed his mind and tossed his career away, he climbed from the car, carry-on in hand, and walked inside the terminal.

***

Jake had never spent a more hellish week. Not even when Rick had been in Afghanistan and they hadn't heard from him following an attack on his forward base. Somehow, call it a brother's intuition, he'd known Rick was okay. The tremble in Sunny's voice, the longing in her tone, however, gutted him every damn time. He placed a call to Detective Reeves.

"Mr. Ingram," the detective said. "If you're calling for an update, I'm sorry to disappoint you. I'm still waiting on the warrant for Samantha Sheldon's financials and phone records."

Jake shook his head at the delay. He understood the crime they were talking about wasn't murder, but someone's life was still fucked up. A little expediency would be appreciated. He kept his impatience to himself, though, and got to the point of his call. "I'd like Sunny Sheldon to come stay with me in Texas until this is over."

"Does she want to go to Texas?"

"I believe she does. Look, I'm an officer of the court. I'll take full responsibility for her while she's here. I'll even come to New York and escort her to Texas. If you need her back there for anything at any time, I'll escort her home."

Jake listened to the sound of papers shuffling on the other end as the detective considered his request. "Okay, but I want her to surrender her passport, and I'll expect her to report in weekly. She's still a suspect in a high-profile crime, Mr. Ingram."

"I understand, and your terms are fair. Will it be okay if she leaves her passport with her lawyer?"

"That's fine. Have him call me when he has it in hand." A long sigh sounded over the phone. "Between you, me, and a stump, Mr. Ingram, I don't think Sunny had anything to do with any of this. However, the evidence says she's complicit, and I have to follow the evidence."

Jake was thankful the detective shared his thoughts. They went a long way to relieving his fear Sunny would be held responsible for something she didn't do. "I appreciate your candor, Detective. Keep following the evidence, and eventually it will lead you to the truth. Sunny Sheldon is innocent. I wouldn't bring her to the same town my brother lives in if I thought, for a second, she had anything to do with the crime committed against him. And for the record, he doesn't believe she was involved, either. He's the one who has pushed me to investigate on my own. That's how much he believes in her innocence."

"Victims of crimes often see what they want to see, but I'll take your brother's support for Ms. Sheldon under advisement. She's fortunate to have the kind of support she has."

Jake ended the call with a promise to stay in touch then he called Sunny to give her the good news.

CHAPTER TWENTY-THREE

Sunny clasped her hands in her lap to keep them from shaking. Detective Reeves had been there almost two hours, listening and asking questions, and she'd been a nervous wreck the entire time. She hated someone she'd called a friend for the last five years or so could be so devious. Finding out the person was her half sister only made the deception worse. Sunny didn't want to see her sister go to prison for the possession and sale of stolen merchandise, but she had no intention of serving a sentence for something she didn't do, either.

Her dad called his team, and they were working on a way to spin the story so it didn't sound as bad as it really was. Talk about a Hollywood-style scandal. This took the cake. It was the kind of story even the legitimate news outlets couldn't ignore. She'd lived most of her life in the shadows of the spotlight trained on her dad. Since her arrest, she'd been the one under scrutiny. Once the latest became public, her entire family would be held up to public scorn. A marital affair. An illegitimate child. A high-profile crime. A sibling framing another for said crime. Her mother would be the object of pity. Until they found Ginger/Samantha and got a confession out of her, Sunny would forever be under suspicion by the public, if not the police.

Then there was Jake. Keeping his name out of it would be impossible. The tabloids already linked him to her and ran with the story of their trip upstate, turning it into something lurid, if not illegal. He said he could deal with the fallout, but could he really? Sunny'd seen others who were used to the public scrutiny buckle under the pressure. And what about his law practice? Would his notoriety, even if short-lived, influence his livelihood?

Everywhere she looked, her life spilled over onto those she loved, and not in a good way. Her mom and dad had to put up with her, but Jake didn't. If it all became too much, he could walk away. He'd done it once, and it hurt more than she ever imagined. The man held her heart in his hands, and the thought of him crushing it a second time was the only thing she feared more than going to jail.

Detective Reeves shuffled the pages Jake's PI had provided and stuffed them back in the folder. "Mind if I take these?"

The question jerked Sunny out of her maudlin thoughts.

Jake made a dismissive gesture. "Help yourself."

Everyone stood when the detective did. "Ms. Sheldon, I'll let you know if this information checks out, but Mr. Ingram has put forth a logical scenario to explain many of the unanswered questions in your case."

"So, I'm not off the hook yet?" God, she hated the way her voice shook, but she couldn't help it. She was so cold inside, her whole body trembled with it.

"No, ma'am. Not until I can verify the latest information. Given the photograph of your sister, I can see how she could pass herself off as you. It would be best if we could find her, but if her connection to Cecil Hawthorne checks out, and what her building super said holds, those facts would cast a different light on the investigation but not necessarily rule out your involvement."

Disappointment felt like a giant stone hanging around her neck. The news Jake brought last night gave her hope. Too much hope, according to the detective. Without the confession of one of the real culprits, everything the police had still pointed to Sunny's involvement in some way. All she had in her favor was the testimony of a building superintendent who couldn't say for sure if the paintings he'd helped tote up the stairs were the ones stolen from Hawthorne's gallery.

Even she had to admit, the story about a sister she hadn't known she had, who, for reasons unknown, happened to have it out for her, sounded a bit too convenient. Until the missing sister was found and her motives uncovered, a cloud of suspicion would hover over Sunny's head. Another reason Jake should stay far away from her.

Her dad spoke up. "Samantha has access to her trust fund. Maybe she's using it to fund this caper. She's got to be living on something."

Detective Reeves tucked the folder under his arm. "I'll try to get a warrant for her financials and her phone records. Based on all this" — he tapped the folder — "I would expect the judge to sign off on the warrant. But remember, Hawthorne was paying her rent. If she had the kind of money you say she has, then why wasn't she paying her own rent? I know that neighborhood. No one with a trust fund would live there unless they didn't have a choice."

"You think she's depleted her trust fund?" Mr. Sheldon sounded horrified at the thought.

"Happens more often than you think," the detective said as he ambled toward the front door.

"You'll keep Ms. Sheldon informed?" Jake asked.

The detective opened the door. "Of course, and thanks for running down this new information."

Jake banged a fist on the closed door. "Fuck!"

Sunny sank to the sofa, exhausted from the strain of keeping it together in the presence of the detective, when she wanted to shout and cry, and possibly throw something. She clenched her fists as frustration boiled to the surface, spilling down her cheeks in a torrent. "He doesn't believe me. He thinks Ginger and I did this together and we had a falling out and she left me holding the bag."

Suddenly, Jake was there, wrapping her in his arms, providing a bulwark to protect and support her. "Shh," he whispered as he cradled her head against his shoulder. "It's going to be alright. He'll follow the evidence. Those three must be living on something. It wouldn't take long for three people to blow through the money they stole from Will's accounts, especially if they're still in Manhattan."

"You think they're still in the city?" Glass clinked on glass as Sunny's dad poured himself a drink at the sideboard.

Jake's hands felt wonderful on her, one stroking her hair, the other firm on her back. "I do. At least Samantha is. She went to a lot of trouble to frame Sunny. Stands to reason she'd hang around close enough to watch it all unfold."

"Do you trust the PI you hired?"

Jake shrugged. "A friend I attended law school with recommended him. So far, he's been professional and discreet. Why?"

"Because I have information on Samantha's trust fund. Maybe he could at least tell us if the principle is still intact. I can't believe she could have blown through it in the few years since she gained control of it."

"I take it the principle was substantial." Jake held her tight, his warmth slowly battling the pervasive cold inside.

"If she managed it even halfway right, she could have lived comfortably the rest of her life, even in New York."

Jake whistled low. "Then we need to find out what she's done with it." He bent his head so he could see her face. "You okay?"

Sunny nodded and sniffed as she swiped her damp cheeks with her fingers. "Better." She pushed away from him, instantly regretting the loss of his heat and his strength. "Everything came crashing in all of a sudden." She patted the giant wet spot on his shirt. "Thanks for letting me lean on you."

His smile was like a ray of sunshine aimed right at her heart. "Anytime, sweetheart. Anytime." He used a thumb to brush away an errant tear from her cheek then he looked past her to her dad. "I'll call him. You got the information handy?"

***

Jake didn't want to leave her, but he had obligations back home he couldn't shirk, not if he wanted to keep his license to practice law. Sunny sat in the back of the limo her dad hired to take Jake to the airport, looking a little lost and not at all the spirited woman he knew and loved.

He was still getting used to the idea of being in love. It no longer scared him the way it did at first. He didn't have a clue how they could manage to be together, but he was dedicated to finding a way. But first, he needed to take care of things at home, and they had to get the charges dropped against her. Completely clearing her name would be nice, but as long as the real culprits remained at large, she'd remain under suspicion. He didn't want her to live with a dark cloud hanging over her. He vowed to do all he could to change her situation. His PI was working on the information Sunny's dad provided. Hopefully, he'd come up with a solid lead soon. Every day suspicion lay on her shoulders killed a little more of Sunny's spirit.

Framing her face with his hands, he looked deep into her eyes. "I love you. No matter what, don't forget you mean the world to me."

"I love you, too, Jake." Tears, almost ever-present now, leaked from the corner of her eyes. "Do you have to go?"

"Yes, but I'll be back." He thumbed her tears away. "If this doesn't get cleared up soon, you should come stay with me. If Detective Reeves knows where you are, he shouldn't care if you get away for a while."

She sniffed back more tears and a hint of a smile broke across her face. "I'd like to see where you live. And I could see Hank and Melody, too."

"They'd love to have you come visit, but, call me selfish, I want you all to myself—in my bed."

Instead of tears, her eyes sparkled then with the same want he felt to his core. "I can't think of anywhere else I want to be." She dipped her head, resting her forehead on his chest. "I need you. I want this all to go away so we can be together."

He held her tight, memorizing the feel of her soft body next to his hard one. He'd never felt this all-encompassing love for another person before. He loved his brothers, would do anything for them, but being physically distant from them didn't make him feel like a part of him was missing. "We're going to be together; I promise. We just have a few things to work out first." Like where they would live. What he would do for a living if he left Texas behind to be with her.

A horn honked as a car sped around them, protesting their prolonged curbside goodbye.

"I've got to go, sweetheart." He kissed her, pouring the cocktail of emotions swirling inside him into the connection. Showing her without words how she affected him, how much he hated to leave her. When he broke away, he captured her gaze with his. "I'm leaving my heart in your hands. Take care of it until I get back."

Her bottom lip trembled, and the tears he hated so much were back. Before he changed his mind and tossed his career away, he climbed from the car, carry-on in hand, and walked inside the terminal.

***

Jake had never spent a more hellish week. Not even when Rick had been in Afghanistan and they hadn't heard from him following an attack on his forward base. Somehow, call it a brother's intuition, he'd known Rick was okay. The tremble in Sunny's voice, the longing in her tone, however, gutted him every damn time. He placed a call to Detective Reeves.

"Mr. Ingram," the detective said. "If you're calling for an update, I'm sorry to disappoint you. I'm still waiting on the warrant for Samantha Sheldon's financials and phone records."

Jake shook his head at the delay. He understood the crime they were talking about wasn't murder, but someone's life was still fucked up. A little expediency would be appreciated. He kept his impatience to himself, though, and got to the point of his call. "I'd like Sunny Sheldon to come stay with me in Texas until this is over."

"Does she want to go to Texas?"

"I believe she does. Look, I'm an officer of the court. I'll take full responsibility for her while she's here. I'll even come to New York and escort her to Texas. If you need her back there for anything at any time, I'll escort her home."

Jake listened to the sound of papers shuffling on the other end as the detective considered his request. "Okay, but I want her to surrender her passport, and I'll expect her to report in weekly. She's still a suspect in a high-profile crime, Mr. Ingram."

"I understand, and your terms are fair. Will it be okay if she leaves her passport with her lawyer?"

"That's fine. Have him call me when he has it in hand." A long sigh sounded over the phone. "Between you, me, and a stump, Mr. Ingram, I don't think Sunny had anything to do with any of this. However, the evidence says she's complicit, and I have to follow the evidence."

Jake was thankful the detective shared his thoughts. They went a long way to relieving his fear Sunny would be held responsible for something she didn't do. "I appreciate your candor, Detective. Keep following the evidence, and eventually it will lead you to the truth. Sunny Sheldon is innocent. I wouldn't bring her to the same town my brother lives in if I thought, for a second, she had anything to do with the crime committed against him. And for the record, he doesn't believe she was involved, either. He's the one who has pushed me to investigate on my own. That's how much he believes in her innocence."

"Victims of crimes often see what they want to see, but I'll take your brother's support for Ms. Sheldon under advisement. She's fortunate to have the kind of support she has."

Jake ended the call with a promise to stay in touch then he called Sunny to give her the good news.

EPILOGUE

Three months later…

Sunny stood before the full-length mirror in the bride's chamber of the church the Ingram's had belonged to for as long as anyone could recall. "I can't believe this is finally happening."

Melody, her closest friend and Matron of Honor, sighed. "Believe it, girlfriend. Hank came up a few minutes ago to tell me Jake is pacing a bare spot in the carpet, waiting for you."

"Oh no!"

"No worries. He's a nervous groom, is all. Hank said he was afraid you'd come to your senses and run."

"I came to my senses when I agreed to marry him. Best decision of my life."

Mel flounced the cathedral-length veil, allowing it to float to the floor in a wide arc of lace-edged tulle. "You're gorgeous, Sunny. Your mother's dress is timeless and stunning."

"I'm so happy." She used the blue antique hanky Melody had loaned her for the occasion to dab at the tears that lurked right below the surface these days. "I don't deserve a man like Jake."

"Shut up." Mel grabbed a tissue and helped dry her friend's tears. "He's a lucky man to be getting a woman like you, and he knows it. Now, take a deep breath, and let's get this show on the road."

Sunny laughed through the relentless tears. At least they were happy tears. She had so much to be grateful for. She'd been all set to marry Jake, had been on the way to see the Justice of the Peace three months ago when the call came for her to return to New York. They'd found her sister and her two cohorts in a rented house in Brooklyn. Cecil Hawthorne and Jessica Blackwell had covered their tracks well, but Samantha had left a paper trail leading directly to the place where the threesome, yes, threesome, had been living since they'd pulled off the caper. The money they'd stolen had run out fast, and they'd begun dipping into Samantha's trust fund.

Her sister admitted to planting the paintings and selling the one to a customer who had no prior purchase record with the gallery. All because she believed Sunny had the life she should have had. Sunny still didn't understand why her father hadn't played a part in Samantha's life. Seemed to her, once the secret was out and his marriage over, there was no reason not to acknowledge his other daughter. But it wasn't her problem to figure out.

"My dad's down there?"

"He is, and your mother. I think it's special to have both walk you down the aisle."

Sunny spun on her heels. "Oh, Melody, I'm so sorry. This must be so hard for you." Melody's father, Earl Ravenswood, a legendary rock star, had died on her tenth birthday. Since the circumstances of his death came to light, Melody had a rocky relationship with her mother. "I didn't think…"

"No worries. I'm over it. Hank and I had a beautiful wedding, and you will, too. So, dry those eyes, that's an order, and let's get out there before Jake comes barreling in here and drags you to the altar himself."

"He'd do it, too. You should have seen how upset he was when we didn't make it to the JP as planned. Getting him to wait, given the circumstances"—she placed a loving hand over her belly—"was nearly impossible."

"I heard all about it, multiple times." Mel gathered up the train and veil worthy of a Hollywood wedding, which it had starred in once upon a time. "Jake has made no secret of his impatience. I really think he's afraid you'll wise up and run."

"Never. Jake is all I've ever wanted, and more. I can't wait to be his wife, and the mother of his children. Nothing has ever felt more right."

MacKenzie barreled in carrying three bouquets. "You'd better hurry. Jake is not a patient groom. If you don't show soon, we'll have to sedate him." She passed out the flowers, one for Sunny, one for Melody, and kept one for herself. She held Sunny's billowing skirt to one side so Melody could get past. "Everybody ready?"

"Ready," Melody said.

"Ready," Sunny chimed in.

"Okay, let's get you married." Kenzie practically shoved the Matron of Honor out the door then followed, turning halfway down the hallway to make sure Sunny hadn't bolted.

Sunny paused in the doorway leading to the narthex. Her mother, looking radiant in a blue gown in a color similar to the bride's maids' dresses, rushed forward. "Sunshine, you are breathtaking. My dress looks better on you than it did on me."

"Oh, I wouldn't say that." Her dad, looking like the dazzling star he was in his custom tuxedo, beamed at his ex-wife, the woman he still claimed to be the love of his life. "You took my breath away on our wedding day, and you still do." Sunny noted the wistful look in his eyes just before he turned to watch her enter the room. "You're glowing, Sunshine. Jake's knees are going to buckle when he sees you."

She took his arm then her mother's. "You think so, Dad?"

"If they don't, I'll knock them out from under him myself."

"Dad," she mock scolded. "Be nice."

"Hey, he's marrying my daughter. I have every right to question his worthiness."

"No need to worry," Sunny said as they reached the door, and she caught sight of Jake and his brothers waiting at the front of the church.

Melody had let her in on a secret. Around town, the Ingram brothers were known as the brothers grim as in ghastly, gloomy, and glum. Many single women over the years had tried unsuccessfully to crack through the hard shells. Then MacKenzie had won Will's heart. And now, Sunny was about to marry the eldest of the bunch, leaving the youngest, Rick, the last single brother. She'd gotten to know him since she'd moved to Willowbrook, and she had a hunch he might not be as available as everyone thought. Only time would tell. Until then…

"Jake's a wonderful man, Dad." It was a truth written on her heart. He was loyal to those he loved. He hadn't betrayed her. He'd been showing his loyalty to his brother. The man who now had a steadying hand on Jake's shoulder. Alone, each of the brothers turned heads, but together, lord have mercy. They were a sight to behold.

She felt for those who'd tried and failed to capture the attention of one of the brothers. They were a brooding lot, but once they gave their heart, they did it without reservation.

Melody wished her luck then walked regally down the aisle to an original tune composed by her husband and played softly by his band, BlackWing. They'd taken several weeks off from their American tour around the holidays and had insisted on being a part of the ceremony. Sunny would have been happy with piped-in music as long as she was marrying Jake today, but they'd offered, and she'd accepted. Who could say they'd had a world-famous rock band play them down the aisle at their wedding?

Next in line, MacKenzie gave her one last, *don't you dare run* look then followed Melody to the altar.

The music shifted to the traditional "Here Comes the Bride," and Jake turned to face the back of the church. Their gazes met over the sea of heads, and his smile nearly knocked her over with its intensity. His body swayed, and he gripped the altar rail to steady himself.

"Guess I won't have to knock him on his ass after all." Curtis smiled at his daughter then, with his ex-wife, led Sunny down the aisle where her future awaited her.

***

Jake Ingram tugged at the collar of his tuxedo shirt, silently praying his bride hadn't come to her senses and run. He wouldn't blame her if she had, but God, how he hoped she hadn't. As glad as he was to have her name cleared and all charges against her dropped, the timing couldn't have been worse. They'd been minutes from the JP's office where he planned to seal the deal before she could change her mind. Then the call had come, and he'd had to wait three interminably long months to make her his.

In the meantime, he'd learned he was going to be a father. Talk about a sledgehammer to the frontal lobe. Who knew stress could mess with a woman's hormones and screw with the effectiveness of the pill? He couldn't have cared less about how the pregnancy came about. The baby only tied her closer to him, a lifetime bond even more sacred than the one they would make today. He didn't know squat about being a husband or a father. His only role model, his own dad, had been abysmal at both. A good thing, Sunny insisted. All he had to do was ask himself what his dad would have done then do the opposite. *Not terrible advice.*

He was about a breath away from going in search of her when Will placed a hand on his shoulder. He looked up in time to see Melody Travis make her way down the aisle. Will's girlfriend, MacKenzie Carlysle followed. Then the love of his life stood at the back of the church, her father on one side, her mother on the other.

God, she was beautiful. Radiant. Glowing from within. Her dress was pretty, too. Her mother's, he recalled her saying. But who the hell cared? He would have married her even if she'd worn a tote-sack.

Relief, pride, and the ever-present desire where she was concerned coursed through his body like a potent cocktail. One second, he was smiling at her then, the next, his knees turned to jelly. He reached for the altar rail at the same time Will and Rick grabbed his arms, setting him upright. He shrugged the laughing loons off and straightened. Determined to make it through the ceremony with as much dignity as he could muster. She deserved her special day. Deserved a hell of a lot more than him, but in a few minutes, provided she didn't bolt, she'd be stuck with him for life.

What a life it would be. Once she saw the town, she'd fallen in love with Willowbrook and decided right away it was missing one thing—an art gallery. After their honeymoon, she planned to open the new Sunnyside Gallery in a vacant storefront on Main Street. She'd already convinced Will to let her be the exclusive purveyor of original William H. Ingram paintings and planned to comb the region for other local artists to showcase.

While moving in, she'd found his stash of manuscripts beneath the bed, and, being the nosy person she was, she'd read them then convinced him to let her dad read them. When Jake returned from the honeymoon, he'd be turning over most of his law practice to a junior lawyer he'd hired out of his old firm in Houston. Jake would keep a few clients, like his brothers, then spend the rest of his time writing.

She'd walked into his life, tossed it upside down, shook it a couple of times, and set him on a new path. One he'd gladly walk with her by his side.

She paused briefly at the last row of pews. Raised her gaze to his. And he knew the only place she was going was with him. Hank and his band, BlackWing, struck up Wagner's "Bridal Chorus." The audience rose to watch the bride come down the aisle. Jake couldn't wait another second. Wedding etiquette be damned. He walked to the front row of seats and held out his hand. If he had hold of her hand, he'd have a fighting chance of stopping her before she could get away.

The next few minutes were a blur of promises and declarations. Nothing they hadn't said to each other in private, except, this time, with a lot less clothes between them. He placed a ring on her finger, repeating the words that, until this day, had meant little to him, officially claiming her as his. Then she slid a simple gold band on his finger, and once again, his knees failed him. He reached for her, and she grasped his arm to steady him.

Her words rang in his ears like the clearest bell. "With this ring, I thee wed. For better or for worse. For richer or poorer. In sickness and in health. Until death we do part."

Needing to see her, he lifted his gaze to hers and said the first thing that came to mind. "Yours."

Her cheeks bloomed prettier than cherry blossoms. She dipped her chin, glanced up at him through her lashes, and gave him the vow he'd treasure the most. "Yours."

THE END

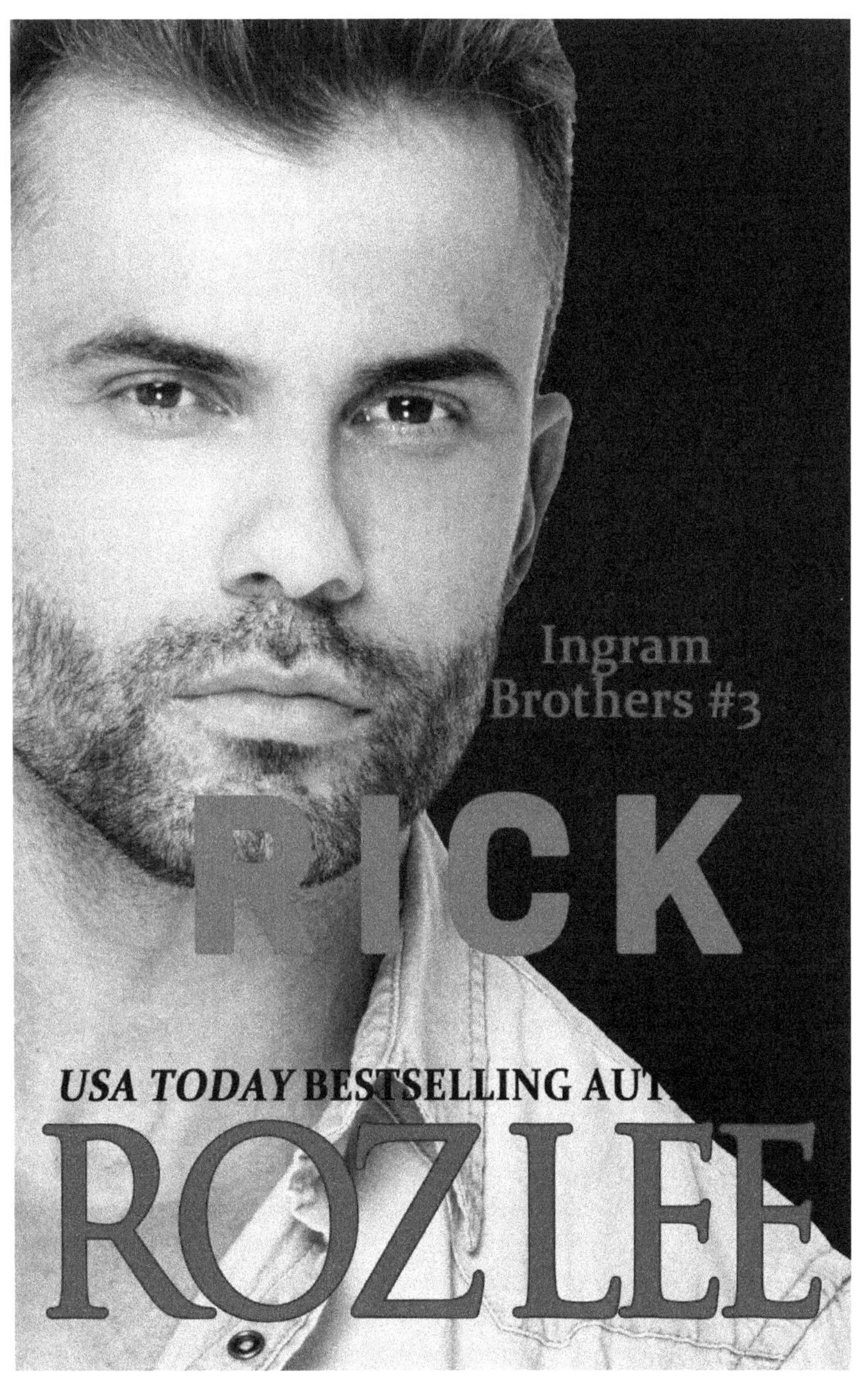

Ingram
Brothers #3
RICK
USA TODAY BESTSELLING AUT
ROZLEE

<h1 style="text-align:center">PROLOGUE</h1>

Six years ago…

Rick thanked the Uber driver then stepped out onto the sidewalk in front of the bar. He'd been here a couple of times. It had become his go-to place the night before shipping out. The place had a good reputation for discretion and safety. And, it was clear across town from the military base he called home when he wasn't in some hellhole overseas. The Marines had been good to him, providing him with the discipline and structure he'd needed in his life. He wasn't ready to make the Corps his career, but he wasn't ready to give it up, either, though he didn't know how much longer he could hide his sexual orientation. He wasn't keen on coming out to his brothers, and he sure as hell wasn't going to tell the Corps. There was some shit better kept in the closet. Preferring dick to pussy was one of them.

He'd be shipping out Monday for a year-long deployment to Iraq, his second deployment to the war-torn region. In honor of the occasion, his entire unit had been given the weekend off to say their goodbyes and to get their shit together. Those with families nearby had gone home. The rest had hightailed it off base to the nearest watering hole to get shitfaced and find some pussy.

This place guaranteed he could have a couple of beers and not be hit on by sword bunnies—desperate women with dreams of a military wedding. They'd settle for becoming some Marine's baby momma, laying claim to the guy's paycheck for the next eighteen years. In his time with the Corps, he'd seen more good men make bad decisions than he cared to think about. He prided himself on not being one of them. He wouldn't rule out a chance encounter with a hot guy though. Someone to dream of in the desert. Someone to replace the fantasies he harbored in regard to a certain corporal who had recently been assigned to his unit.

When it came to David Turner, Rick's thoughts didn't border on inappropriate. They 100 percent crossed the line into enemy territory—without backup. Not that he'd ever, in a million years, do anything about the attraction. The last thing he wanted was anyone in the unit to feel uncomfortable around him, so he'd keep his crazy fantasies to himself. And he'd stay the fuck as far away from Cpl Turner as circumstances allowed.

Rick took a seat at the bar and ordered a beer. It had been so fucking long since he'd had one, he held the bottle, savoring the cold weight of it before lifting it to his lips. The first long draw sent his taste buds into orgasm, so he did it again, draining the bottle. He signaled for another. This time, he let the flavor linger before swallowing. The process brought to mind one of his favorite fantasies—him, on his knees, taking a slow taste of a certain Marine's cock.

Fuck. This wasn't working. The whole reason for coming to this particular bar had been to find some eye candy. Cultivate some new fantasies to override the ones he, in no way, could take with him to Iraq.

Rick twisted his stool around, checked out the mass of bodies packing every inch of the space allotted. The place had really filled up since he'd arrived. Music, courtesy of a DJ atop a raised platform in the back, pounded through the speakers, inviting patrons to dance. Quite a few had succumbed to the offer, making the dance floor into a writhing pit of indecency. Rick sipped his beer, admiring a cute ass here and there when one swung toward him. The place attracted an eclectic group, which was fine by him. His daily world thrived on conformity in everything. It was nice to be surrounded by guys in civilian clothes and with actual hair on their heads. Thank fuck, he didn't see a military high-and-tight haircut anywhere until he swung back around and caught a glimpse of himself in the mirrored barback.

Yeah, that right there probably accounted for the empty stools on either side of him. Nothing screamed military like a Marine haircut. Among the gay community, military types often received a cold shoulder. He couldn't blame them. Historically, the armed forces hadn't welcomed alternative lifestyles with open arms, and despite advances in that area, most gay service members preferred to remain in the closet with the door firmly shut. Rick congratulated himself on at least cracking the door every once in a while, to take a peek at the outside world. Like tonight.

He'd have a few more beers. Maybe find someone to dance with. Haircut aside, guys rarely refused a little no-strings grope and grind. And if things went well, perhaps he'd spend a few hours creating some memories to take to the desert.

He was working on his third beer when someone claimed the stool next to him. Rick lifted his gaze to the mirror and damn near choked on his drink.

Shit. Fuck. God-blessed-damn.

What was *he* doing there?

Rick ducked his head, knowing full well it was way too late to yell *incoming!* The fucking bomb had already landed. All that was left to do was pray and prepare to be blown to bits.

Corporal David Turner signaled the bartender, inquired about the quality of the local brews then proceeded to down one — all without acknowledging Rick's presence. Like it was a coincidence he'd sat next to the only other Marine in the bar. But it had to be a coincidence, didn't it? No way was the man gay.

Rick had been trained to assess situations quickly — to calculate the odds and make decisions based on his best judgement. It was a good thing his enemy wasn't armed because Rick would be a dead man. Hell, maybe the bomb had already exploded. Didn't the experts say you'd never know? One minute you were breathing and cracking jokes with your buddies, and the next you were standing in line at the pearly gates? Rick closed his eyes and prayed that to be the case. Death had to be better than spending the next year in close quarters with a man who knew his deepest, darkest secret — a man Rick couldn't stop fantasizing about.

Rick finished his beer then dug a twenty out of his pocket to cover his tab. Just as he placed his hands on the polished wood to push himself away from the bar, the man beside him clamped a paw around Rick's wrist hard enough to spike his temper. Rick jerked his arm, and Dave let him go. He was about to give the corporal shit when the man slid off his stool, crooked his head toward a hallway marked bathrooms, and started walking.

The darkened hallway swallowed the man whole while Rick remained glued to the barstool. He'd been in enough life-or-death situations to recognize the adrenaline rush brought on by fear. Some guys lived for the rush; Rick wasn't one of them. He welcomed the extra energy and the heightened awareness that had saved his ass more than once, but in this instance, the urge to flee, to get the hell out of here while he still could, almost overwhelmed him.

Shit, the man looked fucking fuckable in civilian clothes. The starched button-down dress shirt stretched across broad shoulders and did nothing to hide the hard body beneath. Hard because that was the only option in the Corps. Tight jeans with a dark wash molded to a backside meant to be fucked. Goddamn, the strength evident in his swagger was a turn-on. Rick resisted the urge to massage the massive erection he'd sported ever since the lethal bomb named David Turner sat down beside him.

Fuck me.

Rick stood.

He'd had more confidence storming buildings in search of terrorists than he had following his fellow Marine in a crowded bar. He went into combat with his armor and a small arsenal strapped to his body—and he never went in alone. Wearing only jeans and a stupid fucking BlackWing concert T-shirt, he'd never been more vulnerable. Yet his feet still propelled him toward the unknown. Was he in for an ass-kicking, or did Turner have something else in mind?

Whatever it was, he would find out soon enough.

At the end of the dimly lit hallway, Corporal Turner held a door open for him. Rick brushed past him into the alley only to have his face shoved against a brick wall. Turner breathed in his ear. "Don't say a fuckin' word, Lance Corporal Ingram, you fuckin' cock tease. Do not turn around. Do not fuckin' look at me. Do exactly as I say, and no one will ever know your secret. Nod if you hear me."

Rick nodded.

"Pants down, Marine. Spread 'em and fuckin' show me your hole."

Rick's hands shook like he'd been too fucking close to an incoming mortar round, but he managed to unbuckle his belt and shove his jeans and boxers to his knees. Then, like a good Marine, he followed orders. Bent at the waist, he used one hand to brace against the wall and the other to expose himself.

Turner hocked up a loogy and spit it out. The wad of saliva hit the bullseye and slid along Rick's crack, sending a shudder of desire up his spine to his nape. From there, it ricocheted straight to his already hard as fuck dick. A single digit worked the lubricant past the tight muscles. "Fuck. Goddamnit, Lance Corporal, your ass is fine."

Trembling like a fucking virgin, Rick swallowed a curse and scrunched his eyes shut, envisioning the scene. He hoped to god there weren't any cameras nearby, but who the fuck was he kidding? He'd give anything to see David Turner's cock. To see the look on his face when he came. To witness the man's surrender to his basest desires. God, that would be hot as fuck.

Rick gasped as a second finger joined the first, scissoring to stretch him.

Do it. Fuck the preliminaries. Breech the goddamn door!

He no longer cared about the consequences. Fuck the Marines. Fuck the whole Corps. His cock throbbed. Need held his balls in a vise.

"Gonna tap it, Marine. Gonna tap it hard."

In the distant recesses of his mind, Rick registered the sound of a wrapper ripping, the rattle of a belt buckle, and the rasp of a zipper. Fabric sliding against flesh. Then big, hot, callused hands gripped his ass cheeks—forced them wide.

"Brace yourself. Easy ain't in my vocabulary."

More than ready to be fucked, Rick flattened both palms on the brick wall. The rough baked clay scraped his palms, but he couldn't have cared less as Turner's cock pressed against his tight entrance. A moment of pressure then he tunneled in like a goddamn bunker buster. Fast. Hard. A huge motherfucker meant to destroy on impact.

He might have blacked out. Pain. So much goddamn pain. Followed by pleasure. White. Hot. A fucking heat-seeking missile streaking from his balls through his cock. He came hard, embarrassingly fast, shooting his wad onto his shirt, the fucking wall, every goddamn place imaginable. So much cum he'd need a goddamn IV to replace the lost fluids. Yet Turner kept on. Driving into him like a battering ram. Cursing every time he bottomed out, his bull balls slapping against Rick's shriveled ones.

Turner dug his fingers into Rick's hips hard enough to bruise. His thrusts became erratic. Rick's entire being focused on the pole up his ass. The fucking amazing pleasure/pain. The eroticism of the moment. He'd give anything to see Turner's face. To see what he did to the man. A primal cry burst from the big man's chest. He hammered in again. A string of curses filled the dank air in the alley as Turner emptied himself into the condom.

Still impaled, Rick fought the urge to cry. Because it happened or because it was over? Both? He didn't know, but Marines didn't fuckin' cry. Even when they'd been fucked to within an inch of their life. His fuckin' hole would never be the same, yet he couldn't help thinking that was a good thing.

Hands gripping his hips eased. Slid beneath his shirt to soothe his back muscles then down to caress the crest of his ass. Heartbreakingly tender after such a brutal assault.

"Best goddamn fuck, ever." The breathless words penetrated Rick's post-orgasmic haze, sent a shiver along his spine. Turner retreated, leaving a gaping hole to mark where he'd been.

Rick kept his face to the wall, listened as the corporal righted his clothes. Waited for more orders.

A slap to his ass. "You all packed, Marine?"

Rick nodded.

"No, you're fuckin' not. Lube and condoms. Lots of them. I'm not finished with your ass." Cpl. Turner exited the alley, leaving Rick there to assess the damage.

CHAPTER ONE

Rick exited the church behind the bride and groom with Melody Travis on his arm. "I'm glad that's over," he confessed as they cleared the last pew. He wouldn't have put on a monkey suit and stood in front of a packed church for anyone other than Jake or Will. His older brothers were all the family he had, and he'd do anything for them.

Mel's laughter rang out in the vestibule. "Poor thing. Was it that bad?"

Hell, yes. "I've been through worse." No lie there. At least no one had shot at him, and nothing had blown up. Yet.

They hurried out the front door. Limos waited at the curb to carry the guests to the reception being held in a giant tent out at Melody and Hank's place. The wedding party made an abrupt turn at the foot of the steps, making their way around the corner of the building where they would reenter through a side door to take pictures in the empty church.

Melody tightened her grip on his arm. "Thank you for your service."

Rick nodded, uneasy accepting gratitude for his stint in the Marines. He was proud of the years he'd served his country, would always be a Marine at heart, but those days were behind him. He'd fulfilled a dream and come back a different man. Older. Wiser. Changed in fundamental ways he didn't discuss with anyone. The Marine Corps had taken a green recruit and forced him into their mold, and in doing so, compelled him to grow up, to accept things about himself no amount of discipline or routine could alter.

"Jake said you were in the Marines?"

"Yes, ma'am."

"I bet you turned heads in your uniform."

If you only knew. He held the door for her then followed her inside the small office space off the sanctuary. "I wouldn't know, ma'am."

The woman whirled on him, the skirt of her blue bridesmaid's dress caressing his calf before settling. She fingered the lapel of his tux. "He's modest, too."

The mischief in her smile set him on edge. He knew what was coming next and was powerless to stop it. Why did every married woman think it was their god-given duty to fix up every single man?

"Have you met Sunny's cousin, Amanda? She's about your age and single." She adjusted his boutonniere. "I'll introduce you at the reception. She's got the same blonde hair as Sunny. God," she gushed, "you two will look splendid together."

He would have told her she needn't bother with an introduction since Sunny had thrown her cousin at him the minute the girl arrived in town, but was saved from replying when the bride's parents entered behind them. Apparently, that was the signal the photographer had been waiting for. He ushered everyone into the sanctuary. Rick stood where he was told. Smiled on command. If the Marines had taught him anything, it was that a well-planned mission was a successful one, so he spent every interminable second of the photo shoot planning his next mission — Operation Avoid Matchmaker Melody. He'd prefer to skip the reception altogether, but Jake would murder him, so the best plan he could come up with relied on avoiding Melody Travis as much as possible.

Just because he hadn't brought a date to Jake's wedding didn't mean he needed help getting one. He'd never been short on companionship, but he wasn't going to stand by and let some busybody fix him up at a wedding reception. Even if this Amanda person were interested, nothing could come of them meeting. Looking for the one person he had no business seeking out, Rick swept his gaze over the round tables set with silver, crystal, and fancy china, settling on a table in the back. The stray singles, he surmised. Made sense they'd all be seated together. Avoid-at-all-cost Amanda was one of them, along with a couple of Jake's lawyer friends, including the one his brother had recently hired to take on his workload.

Rick allowed his gaze to linger on the man. A few years younger than Rick, the junior lawyer looked fine in a dark three-piece suit that set off his pale skin and blond hair styled to within an inch of its life — probably with some fancy product with a French name. His trendy glasses screamed designer label.

The only designer duds Rick had ever worn had been provided by Uncle Sam and came in two color-distinctive patterns — woodland and desert. These days he preferred discount store T-shirts, sturdy denim jeans, and steel-toed boots. Stan, Willowbrook's only barber, cut his hair but only when needed — like for a wedding. Jake had threatened to kick his ass if he didn't get a haircut in time for the wedding. Poor Brent was in for a rude awakening. Willowbrook wasn't his kind of town.

One of the Houston lawyers held everyone's attention at the table then, as if on cue, they all burst out laughing. Brent turned toward the infamous Amanda, said something to her, then the two of them weaved their way through the tables to the dance floor. From the looks of things, those two would keep each other occupied for the remainder of the evening. Just as well. Rick didn't hit on heterosexuals. Hell, he didn't hit on anyone. Never had. His one relationship had developed all on its own. A real magnets-and-steel cliché. As the couple danced to a sappy ballad, Rick drained the last of his champagne and silently congratulated himself on a narrow escape. He stuck it out to the end, but as soon as the lights of the limo carrying the newlyweds to the airport disappeared, he loosened his bow tie and made for the car his brother had left for him the night before. It saved Rick hunting up a ride home, and he'd need it to pick up the honeymooners when they returned in a couple of weeks. Even if there had been room in the old pickup Rick used for work, Jake refused to ride in it.

Having said goodbye to those who mattered, he didn't think twice about skirting the crowded tent. He'd successfully avoided Melody's matchmaking, so now it was time to get the hell out of here. If his luck held, he'd make it to Dallas in time to share a couple of drinks with his buddy from the Marines. David's new job, working for a firm that installed security systems for businesses, often brought him to the area. Rick's body hummed with excitement at the opportunity to spend time with Dave. They'd met six years ago when Dave had been assigned to Rick's unit. Prior to their first deployment together, things had turned personal between them—a secret they kept over multiple deployments. Rick had separated from the military first, having had enough of risking his life in the desert. Dave had followed almost a year later when his contract ran out. Rick would be lying if he said he didn't hold out hope of something more than the occasional hookup when Dave's job brought him to Dallas, but neither of them was ready to open the closet door.

Rick stopped at home long enough to change into his best jeans, the ones with a dark wash, and a long-sleeved Henley. Anticipating spending the night, he shoved a clean pair of underwear and his toiletry kit into a backpack. At the last minute, he chucked a box of condoms in on top then he texted his longtime lover to let him know he was on the way. He smiled when Dave responded with his hotel and room number. His luck was definitely holding. No clubbing tonight. A few drinks from the minibar then a night of private debauchery suited him just fine. Tomorrow was Sunday, and with Jake on his honeymoon and Will cozying up with MacKenzie, no one would be expecting to see his face until Monday morning. Life was good.

Until it wasn't.

The instant Dave opened the door, Rick knew something was wrong. He stepped inside, dropped his backpack, and wrapped his arms around Dave's waist, dragging his hard body tight against him. When Dave didn't return the hug, Rick's heart dropped to his toes. He stepped back, taking in the red eyes, the deep lines etched into the beloved face. "What's wrong? Did someone die?"

Dave shook his head. His lower lip trembled, and damn if that didn't shoot a lightning bolt of fear down Rick's spine. "Are you sick?" He cradled his lover's face in his palms. "I'm imagining all kinds of scary shit here, babe. Tell me."

"I can't."

In all the years he'd known David, he'd never heard him utter those words. There wasn't *anything* Staff Sergeant Turner couldn't or wouldn't do. If you looked up the word badass in the dictionary, you'd find a picture of Dave. No mission was too dangerous or impossible. Rick still had nightmares about the shit his best friend and lover had done with him at his side. That they were both alive and still had all their body parts was nothing short of a miracle Rick thanked the universe for every day.

Rick grasped the broadest shoulders he'd ever seen then let his hands fall to lace his fingers with his lover's. "Come." He tugged the big man from the alcove to bed. "Sit the fuck down and tell me what's going on." He was going for tender, but his words came out sounding more like an order. Whatever.

The former Marine dropped to the mattress. He leaned forward, braced his elbows on his knees, and cradled his head in his upturned hands. Rick dragged the desk chair over and sat. Offering support, he wrapped his fingers around the other man's wrists and squeezed.

Dave wasn't a cologne sort of guy, the lack of artifice making his natural musk all the more potent. Despite the fear clawing at Rick's innards, his dick responded to the earthiness of the man. "There isn't anything we can't face together, babe. So, spit it out."

Dave shook his head, and his back heaved as great, gulping sobs ravaged his body.

"Did you kill somebody? What the fuck, man? Talk to me."

"No. No. No."

Rick sat back, observing the broken man before him. "No, you didn't kill somebody, or no, you won't tell me?"

"Both." The usually verbose man couldn't seem to come up with a full sentence.

Gentle wasn't working. Time to try a different tactic. "Fuck you, Staff Sergeant." Rick lunged, catching the larger man off guard, and flattened him on the bed. Climbing astride, one of their favorite positions, he pinned Dave's wrists to the mattress. He leaned over, getting right in his face. "We're a team, fuckwad. Tell me what the fuck is going on. Do I need to kick somebody's ass? What?" Yeah, there was nothing tender about that. The hard ridge of the man's cock lined up with his own burgeoning erection. Whatever was going on, it hadn't affected Dave's libido. Nothing ever had.

Rick shifted gears again, pressing soft kisses to tear-ravaged cheeks. "It's okay, babe. I'm here. You can tell me."

The tender words only made the man blubber harder.

What. The. Ever-loving. Fuck?

Rick trailed kisses along the strong jaw, down the corded neck then back up to the sensitive spot behind his ear—the one that never failed to get Dave's motor running full throttle. "Babe," he whispered then flicked his tongue out to tickle that one special spot.

That was all it took. The beast beneath him growled, reared up, and tossed Rick over onto the bed, pinning him in a grip he had no chance of overcoming. The man may have been a civilian now, but he kept in shape. His muscles had muscles—one of the things Rick admired most about the body pressing him into the comforter.

No words were spoken. None were needed. Sex was a language they both spoke fluently. Dave straddled him. His hot breath fanning Rick's face. His red eyes searching, not for permission, that was a given, but for something else Rick couldn't name. Didn't want to name because his gut told him it would shatter him just as it had shattered the man he loved.

CHAPTER TWO

Clothes vanished like the sex fairy had waved a magic wand. Dave positioned Rick where he wanted him, on his back, his knees wide and at his shoulders, then he shoved his dick up Rick's ass like a battering ram to a fortified door. No condom. No lube. No preliminaries. Rick refused to wince at the pain in his ass or his heart. This was too much like their first time. The night before their first deployment together, Dave had taken out months of frustration on Rick's ass in the alley behind a bar. The encounter had left Rick shaken, embarrassed, and after the shock wore off, determined to get to know the then corporal better.

Over multiple deployments, the two became inseparable. Best friends, teammates, secret lovers. They'd seen shit. Done shit. And fucked each other's brains out. They talked about their families, their hometowns, growing up, any and everything save one. Dave Turner didn't talk about his feelings. He fucked them out. Rick had been the recipient of every fuck Dave could give.

The *fuck that was good* fuck.

The *fuck I'm the best motherfucker on the planet* fuck.

The *fuck that image out of my brain* fuck.

The *fuck you* fuck.

The *fuck the Marines* fuck.

The *fuck the desert* fuck.

The *fuck I miss my family* fuck.

The *fuck I hate you* fuck.

The *fuck I need you* fuck.

The *fuck I love you* fuck.

The *fuck I hate myself* fuck.

The list was endless. As his lover powered into him with mindless brutality, Rick called upon everything he knew about the man and came to one conclusion. If their first fuck had been a *fuck you're mine* fuck, then this one had to be a *fuck I don't want to let you go* fuck.

But he *would* let Rick go. The tears were the key. David Turner didn't cry. Whatever had brought Dave to this point, it was eating him up inside, yet the decision had been made. Once committed to a mission plan, David didn't change his mind.

Tamping down the need to scream, the need to rage against an outcome he had no say in, Rick stroked his aching dick and stared into his lover's eyes. The pain harbored there only served to harden Rick against the inevitable. No way in hell was he letting the bastard off easy. Holding his gaze captive, Rick let him see the suffering already brewing deep in his gut. He let him see his heart shattering into a million pieces. He let him see the gaping wound opening in his chest. He let him see the disappointment.

I loved you, asshole.

I gave you everything.

And this is how you repay me.

A goodbye fuck in a hotel room.

Fuck you.

When Dave succumbed and released his self-loathing in hot spurts, Rick came, fiery ribbons of emotion directed at his lover's chest and abdomen. Marking him one final time.

Dave wiped tears from his cheeks, glanced at the streaks of white jizz on his torso. With a silent nod of acceptance, he withdrew and flopped to his back beside Rick.

The scent of sex and their mingled sweat hung heavy in the atmosphere. Heart racing, Rick focused on his survival training. *Breathe. In. Out. Remain still. Breathe. In. Out. Wait. Wait. Wait until the enemy makes the first move. Breathe. In. Out.*

Beside him, the enemy lay still, his arms folded to shield his eyes from whatever harsh reality he was trying to come to terms with. Rick waited, his heart breaking more with each passing minute, until Dave delivered the kill shot.

"I'm engaged. To the girl from my parents' church."

CHAPTER THREE

Rick stumbled into the bar, not entirely sure how he'd gotten there. Everything between David's confession and this moment was a blur. He vaguely recalled getting dressed while Dave cried and pleaded with him to understand. The pressure was too much. It was easier to give in than to stand up for himself. For *them*. It would be alright. They could continue to meet like they had been. She wouldn't change anything. There'd been more, but he'd successfully tuned most of it out, but his parting shot rang like an air-raid siren in his ears. "Don't act like the scorned lover, Rick. It's not like you were going to come out of the closet for me."

The concussive force of that direct hit followed Rick out of the room, to the elevator, and out to the street where he'd somehow summoned an Uber. He'd given the address of the first place that came to mind.

Nothing said *leave me the fuck alone* like claiming the stool situated next to the wall on the end of the bar. The barkeep wandered over. Rick ordered two fingers of Jack Black, downed the whole thing with one swallow then signaled for a refill while the whiskey seared the lining of his esophagus.

"Bad day?" the affable bartender asked as he poured the refill.

"Don't want to talk about it."

"Don't have to. Just letting you know I'll cut you off when you've had enough. You drive yourself here?"

He shook his head. At least he'd had the foresight to leave Jake's car in the hotel parking garage.

The barkeep slid a piece of paper and a pen across the polished wood. "Write down where you want to go when you leave here. I'll hand it to the cab driver when the time comes."

Rick nodded. "Okay. Okay. Sounds good." He scribbled the name of a hotel chain, pushed the paper away. "Closest one will do." He dug out his credit card, handed it over. "Just stick it in my pocket when you cart me out of here."

The credit card and slip of paper disappeared into the register drawer. He hoped the guy would add a generous tip for himself. Then he shot back half of drink number two.

He might have been on his third or fourth and no closer to obliterating the night's events from his memory when his friendly keeper plopped a hamburger and fries in front of him. He didn't ask questions, just ate it, washing the food down with the Daniels family's finest. He should have chosen a different bar. Memories of evenings spent here with Dave crept out of hiding to torment his already tortured soul.

He poured liquor on the flames of his life—to no avail. There wasn't enough liquor in Texas to drown out Dave's last words.

Rick had known about the girl. Dave's ultra-religious parents had been nagging him for years to leave the Corps. They'd encouraged the girl to write to him. Sappy letters the two of them laughed about. As religious as his folks, she was saving herself for her husband—on her wedding night. God, they'd laughed themselves silly over that one. She had no idea the kind of man she was writing to. Debauched Dave. He sucked cock like a Hoover and fucked ass like a demon. Under the right circumstances, he begged Rick to fuck him hard enough to make him forget whatever deviled him at the time. Dave couldn't see himself tied down, and he damn sure wasn't going to marry some skirt-wearing, Bible-thumping, woman.

His parents didn't know, and he wasn't going to tell them. On the few occasions he went home, he'd played the happy bachelor and kept the closet door locked tight.

Rick couldn't imagine what kind of pressure had compelled Dave to propose. It had to be some deep shit to make a guy like him denounce everything he was and veer down a road lined with misery and discontent. Unwilling to admit his own refusal to open the closet door in any way justified Dave's actions, and Rick raised his glass in a mock toast. "Fuck you, Dave." As he downed the last drops in his glass, a familiar silhouette across the room caught his attention.

He squinted to get a better look. Blond hair. Glasses. Fancy duds. *Sin-in-a-suit*. Where did that thought come from, and where had he seen the man before? If his present was looking fuzzy around the edges, his past, at least the immediate past, thankfully, was shrouded in dense fog. Fuck! Why couldn't he remember? If he hadn't been plastered, he'd go over, ask the guy to dance. Maybe end the night in the back alley. A new beginning.

Vague images of the man dancing — with a woman — peeked through the alcohol haze. A name popped into his head. Cousin Amanda. Yeah. Sin-in-a-suit had danced with Amanda.

Where?

"Last one." The barkeep's baritone broke through the haze. Rick shook his head, jerking his much-used tumbler out of reach before the man could provide another refill. Time to cut himself off. Somewhere amid the pain lurked something important. He clenched his jaw tight. Resting his elbows on the bar, he linked his fingers and used his thumbs like a vise on his temples.

Think. Think. Think.

"You okay?"

"Coffee. Water. Something." Rick barked the order, waving the bartender away. Something deep in his gut, besides the fine whiskey he'd consumed, told him the lost memory was important. The rich scent of coffee wafted beneath his nose. He grabbed the cup like a drowning man grasping for a lifeline and sipped. Once. Twice. Again. When he chanced a glance at the man, he'd turned, and their gazes locked. As he peered into the most intense green eyes he'd ever seen, the elusive memory surged out of the blasted haze in all its gut-clenching Technicolor glory. Jake's wedding. A sea of people. Crystal. Silver. Flowers every fucking where. Matchmaking Melody. Cousin Amanda to be avoided at all costs dancing with *him*. Brent something or other. The junior attorney Jake hired to take over most of his brother's accounts.

Rick froze like a deer in the headlights. Blinded.

Oh fuck.

He vaulted off the stool, threading his way through tables and chairs that fucking wavered on a floor that bucked and shifted beneath him. Patrons cursed his stumbling gait, shoved at him.

Fuck. Fuck. Fuck.

He had to get to him. Explain.

He stood face-to-face with Sin-in-a-suit. Up close, he was even sexier than he'd been from a distance. Drunk or not, his body responded in the most primal way possible. Impossible, his brain argued. He loved David. Impossible, beyond his reach, David. The fucking asshole who'd dumped him for a life he couldn't live. Fuck him.

Rick teetered. Sin-in-a-suit reached out, splayed his hands on his chest. "Whoa. Steady." A sympathetic smile graced the younger man's lips and his green eyes behind stylish glasses sparkled with mischief…and recognition. "Hey, you're Jake's brother. Right? William?"

"Richard. Rick," he corrected.

"That's right. Hey, fancy meeting you here. Nice wedding."

Rick leaned in. Last thing he needed was everyone hearing their conversation. "We need to talk," he whispered. At least, he thought it was a whisper. Maybe not.

The guy standing way too close to Sin glanced at Rick then back to Sin. "I'll let you two catch up. Save me a dance?"

Sin nodded. "Later." He turned his less-than-joyful countenance on Rick. "This better be good. I was going to get laid. Like, sure thing. If you screwed that up, you're going to have to make it up to me."

Fuck. Was he implying what Rick thought he was? God, he wished he'd limited himself to two drinks. Nothing like going into battle fucked up. God, he was fucked up. He didn't know which one of them was swaying. He grabbed at Sin, clamped a hand around his bicep. Best to get this over with as soon as possible. He tried for another whisper. "You can't tell anyone."

Those sinful green eyes narrowed. "Tell anyone what?"

Confused, Rick spelled it out. "That you saw me here. Dude. You gotta keep your mouth shut."

A shit-ton of emotions paraded across Sin's face. Understanding. Pity. Regret. Maybe Rick imagined that last one.

What did Sin have to regret? Rick had enough regrets to fill a fucking dump truck. "You curious, or is this your thing?"

"Curious?" What the hell was he talking about? "Fuck, no."

Sin nodded. "Then your secret is safe with me." He made a show of zipping his lips shut and throwing away the key. "Richard Ingram was not shit-faced in a gay bar a few hours after his brother's wedding."

"That's right." Rick smiled so hard his face hurt. "Thanks, man. Your secret is safe with me, too." The room spun. He stumbled, would have smashed into a table full of people if Sin hadn't caught him in time.

"How much did you have to drink?"

"Not enough." He clamped a hand to the top of his head to keep it from exploding. "Not nearly enough if I can still feel this shitty."

"Fuck. This is not how I wanted this night to end." He shoved Rick backward and into a chair. "Sit the fuck down. You got a tab at the bar?"

"Yeah. Why? You want a drink?"

"No, I don't want a drink." He blew out a breath. "Stay here. Don't move an inch. I'll be right back."

CHAPTER FOUR

Brent drew the bartender's attention. "You got a tab for Richard Ingram? Says he gave you his credit card."

"Yeah. I got it. Why?"

"He's had enough." He gestured to the corner table where Rick slumped, his forehead resting on crossed arms. "I'm taking him home. Can you close it out?"

"You a friend of his?"

"Sort of. Don't worry. I'll take care of him."

"What's your name?"

"Brent Whitehall. I'm an attorney. I'm in the process of moving here from Houston. I'll be working with his brother Jake over in Willowbrook as soon as I get settled. We were both at Jake's wedding a few hours ago. Don't know why Rick is here and skunk drunk, but I'll see he gets home safe."

"You got some ID?"

What was with this guy? He'd never envisioned handing the first of his new business cards to a nosy, overprotective bartender, but he slid the fancy embossed rectangle across the polished wood anyway. "You his keeper or something?"

"Nah. Just looking out for him. Do it for all my regulars."

Brent hoped his lawyer face hid his surprise at the unexpected bit of news. He'd assumed Rick to be homo-curious or maybe bi.

Being a regular at one of Dallas's well-known gay bars suggested something else entirely. "Does he always come in alone?"

"Nah. Usually meets some big guy. Ex-military type. Bookends. A matching pair, those two."

Another piece of the puzzle. Brent added a generous tip to the total then signed the charge slip. "He got stood up tonight?"

The bartender took the signed ticket, slid it into a slot beneath the register. "Don't know. Figured something was going on. He was hell-bent on getting plastered from the get-go. I asked if he drove himself here, and he said he hadn't, so I had him write down where he wanted to go when he left. Told him I'd pour him into a cab. Looks like you're going to save me the trouble." He slapped two pieces of paper on the bar then pointed to the stool Rick recently vacated. "Don't forget his jacket."

Brent picked up the bar receipt and the accompanying scrap of paper containing the name of a popular mid-priced hotel chain sans specific location. "Thank you. You're a good man…"

"Benjamin. This is my place. I take care of my boys."

Brent smiled and tapped the bar. "Nice to meet you, Benjamin. If you need any legal services, give me a call. I'll do right by you." He grabbed Rick's coat then threaded his way through the maze of tables to where the youngest of the Ingram brothers dozed. He shook him awake. "On your feet, soldier. It's time to go."

Rick raised his head. "Marine. Noz a fuc-fuckin' solzier."

He mentally snapped another piece of the Rick Ingram puzzle into place. "Whatever. Can you stand?"

"Fuck, yez."

He did, but it wasn't pretty. Brent wrestled him into his coat then shrugged on his own. He wrapped an arm around his waist to steady him then Rick slung an arm over Brent's shoulder, and the two of them stumbled into the night. Brent had parked his car down the block. If he could get the idiot there, he stood a decent chance of dropping him off somewhere and still having enough time to return to the bar and pick up where he'd left off.

Getting the drunk into the passenger seat of his Corvette took longer than he'd anticipated. He kept trying to go in headfirst, and no amount of reasoning could convince him it was a bad idea. Giving up, Brent let him do it his way, failing to rein in his amusement as the man squirmed and twisted his large frame until he settled into the seat, exhausted from his efforts.

Brent settled into the driver's seat. He buckled his passenger in first then secured his own seat belt. "You have a hotel room? Some place you can sleep this off?"

Rick gave an exaggerated head shake. "Nah. Dis izgood." He dropped his head against the headrest and closed his eyes.

Brent elbowed him. "You are not sleeping in my car."

He cranked the engine, turned up the heat then got out his phone and looked up the nearest location for the chain hotel Rick had given Benjamin. There was one two blocks over. A phone call ascertained they had a room available.

"You're in luck, buddy," he muttered as he pulled away from the curb. "Gonna get you settled then I'm out."

Brent declined the fancy suite in favor of a standard room without a view. If they'd had a bed in a broom closet, he would have taken that. Rick wasn't going to know one way or the other. All he needed was a safe place to sleep it off. He handed over Rick's credit card then returned to the parking garage to collect his charge. He'd gone to sleep in the few minutes it had taken to secure a room.

When nothing he did rousted the inebriated man, Brent grabbed a half-empty water bottle from the console and splashed it in the man's face. "Wake the fuck up. It's time to go to bed."

"Fuck!" Rick came up swinging. His wrist connected with the car frame with a sickening thud.

"Serves you right." Brent grabbed him by the neck of his shirt and yanked him out of the vehicle. Rick stumbled but righted himself with the aid of the car door.

"Whatz dis?" he asked as they drunk walked to the elevator that would take them to the lobby level.

"Hotel." Brent leaned his charge against the back wall of the paneled car then punched the "L" button.

He wagged a pointer finger in Brent's face. "Nasleeingwizyoudude."

Brent rolled his eyes. "Wouldn't sleep with you if you were the last drunk on the planet."

They reached the lobby and successfully switched elevators to the upper floors.

"Whazwrongwizme?" The insult in his voice would have been comical under different circumstances. The former Marine was so far from Brent's type, he might as well have been a Martian.

Brent dragged him out on the fifth floor, consulted the arrow boards then turned left, hoping Rick would follow. The man weighed a fucking ton, and, from what he could tell, it was all muscle. If the lug collapsed in the hallway, he'd have to spend the night there. No way Brent could pick him up on his own. He located the room number written on the sleeve for the keycard and was grateful when Rick stumbled up next to him and successfully followed him inside.

The door closed behind them.

Brent tossed the keycard on the dresser. "I'm done here." He motioned to the bed. "Get some sleep, buddy."

In a blink, he was up against the wall, breathing in Rick's alcohol-tainted breath and, beneath it, the pure scent of sexy-as-hell male.

"Whazwrongwhifme, pwittyboy?"

His vision clouded. Ugh. How could he have forgotten who this guy was? "Pretty boy?" he ground out. Placing both hands on Rick's chest, he shoved as hard as he could. If he'd been sober, Brent couldn't have moved him an inch, but because he was inebriated, the asshole stumbled, ricocheted off the dresser before he fell, landing flat on his back on the end of the bed. Time to set Rick Ingram straight. "I'll tell you what's wrong with you, Jarhead. All you military types are the same. You're self-centered, egotistical assholes with a god complex. Get over yourself."

"Tellmewhazyouwillythink." His eyes rolled back in his head then he passed out cold.

Brent shook him. No response. He tried again. "Shit." Even if he wasn't his new boss's brother, he couldn't leave him like this. Drunks were known to choke on their own vomit if they slept on their back.

Half an hour later, he collapsed in the desk chair. His shirt had come untucked from his trousers and the sweat stains under his pits looked like he'd run a marathon. Wasn't far from the truth. He'd started by removing Rick's shoes. When he still couldn't wake him enough to get him to assist in his own comfort and safety, he dragged and tugged until he'd maneuvered Rick fully onto the bed. In the process, Rick's coat became twisted, so he'd worked that off. The Henley underneath was just as bad, so he'd removed it as well.

Taking a breather, he glared down at the drunken fool. He'd never seen a more perfect human specimen than the one before him. Acres of tanned skin flowed over a sculpted landscape meant to be explored—slowly, reverently. Strong shoulders gave way to defined pecs sprinkled liberally with dark hair. Below that were the rolling hills of his abs. Another spattering of hair around his navel formed an arrow and disappeared below the waistband of his low-slung jeans.

"Lord, have mercy," he whispered. "That's got to be illegal." If he'd taken his shirt off in the bar, the patrons would have eaten him alive. Some out of desire, others out of jealousy.

Shaking off his ridiculous thoughts, Brent consulted his watch. *Shit.* By now the Adonis he'd planned to fuck the rest of the night away with had probably left with someone else. Brent plucked at his shirt. Nobody in his right mind would find him attractive in his current condition. Wrestling with Rick's dead weight had him sweaty and his shirt wrinkled beyond repair.

He rubbed a hand over his face. He'd envisioned a night of hot, no-strings-attached sex before he drove all the way to Houston tomorrow to supervise the packing of his belongings. Nothing about this trip had gone as planned. He still didn't have a place to live in Willowbrook, which, besides the wedding, had been his primary reason for the visit. He'd planned to spend the two weeks of Jake's vacation settling into his new place and reading over current files in his new office.

So much for plans.

Rick groaned, grabbed at his stomach. Afraid the drunk was about to spew his guts up, Brent hooked a finger in a beltloop and tugged the man over onto his side. He piled all the pillows on the bed behind him to keep him from rolling to his back then placed a wastebasket next to the bed.

Exhausted, Brent sank into the desk chair to keep vigil. He couldn't fuckin' sit up all night long, and he didn't feel right leaving him here alone. The wall of pillows wasn't a match for a guy that size. If he rolled, he'd squish them flat, putting himself in danger.

"Fuck me sideways," he growled. He slid his coat on, grabbed the room key, and stomped out the door to get his suitcase. If he was going to spend the night, he'd at least get a shower and have fresh clothes in the morning.

CHAPTER FIVE

The pounding in his head woke Rick. He rolled over and cursed as he landed on a pile of pillows. *What the fuck?* He tossed the offending bedding then cracked one eye open. Light shown through a gap between the drapes, providing enough illumination for a one-eyed inspection. Hotel room. He wracked his brain, trying to recall checking in and coming up blank.

Mentally searching for a place to start, his brain clicked on a solid memory—Jake's wedding. His sappy-in-love brother going weak in the knees at the sight of his bride. A funny-as-hell moment, but no explanation for his present whereabouts or the entire Marine Corps band marching around in his skull. Had he overindulged at the reception?

Memories flooded his brain. Food, champagne toasts, the private, kickass, BlackWing concert for the newlyweds. Celebrities everywhere—friends and relatives of the bride. A bunch of unfamiliar faces—his brother's friends from law school and the firm he'd worked at in Houston for several years. Rick had left there sober with plans to see Dave.

Shit.

Dave.

The same memories he'd tried to drown in a sea of booze rushed to the forefront. Dave's tear-ravaged face as they fucked.

His bullshit confession. His excuse for cutting Rick out of his life. His accusations.

The unthinkable popped into his head. His heart skipped a beat. Had he gone back to Dave's room and begged? *Fuck, no. I. Do. Not. Beg.* He *did*, however, drink to forget.

Yeah. He'd gone to the bar, where he and Dave had spent many hours over the last year, with every intention of getting wasted.

Mission accomplished.

He swallowed the bile rising to his throat and searched his pickled memory banks for anything to explain how he'd ended up here. A vague recollection pierced through the haze—a dude pressed against the wall. Eyes as green as winter wheat. His glasses askew and his full, kissable lips saying…something.

Damn. Had he picked somebody up last night? Were they still here?

Shit!

He sat up, knocking something off the nightstand as he groped for the light switch. He flicked the bedside lamp on then immediately wished he hadn't. The soft glow momentarily blinded him. He slapped a hand over his eyes. His eyes slowly adjusted, and he risked a glance at the other side of the bed.

Empty. *Thank, god.* But slept in. *Jesus, what did I do?*

He scrubbed at his face with both hands, trying to recall anything beyond getting shitfaced at the bar. Nothing. Nada. Zip. Damn, he'd fucked up. Perhaps, literally. Tossing the covers aside, he swung his feet to the floor where they landed atop his discarded clothes. All of them. Ahh, shit! He must have been beyond drunk to not remember taking his clothes off—or doing…whatever he'd done.

Naked, he gingerly made his way to the bathroom. He took a piss, washed his hands, and splashed cold water on his face. A glance in the mirror revealed bloodshot eyes complete with dark baggage, sallow skin, and a hairstyle he couldn't pass off as artfully disheveled. In other words, he looked like hell.

And felt like it, too.

He switched on the water in the shower then looked around for the little wrapped bar of soap. Something in the wastebasket caught his eye.

Fuck. Fuck. Double fuck!

Someone, presumably the guy who had shared his bed, had taken the time to shower before leaving. A closer inspection of the small enclosure revealed the used bar of soap resting on the ledge provided for such things. His gaze landed on a damp towel hanging from a wall hook, partially obscured by the open bathroom door.

What. Did. I. Do?

He'd never been so drunk he couldn't recall sleeping with someone. Never. *Oh, Christ! Condom!*

He grabbed the wastebasket beneath the bathroom counter, dumped it out in the sink. Nothing but the soap wrapper.

Shit.

He scurried into the main room, located the waste and recycle bins underneath the desk. Empty.

Shit. Shit. Double shit.

He checked both nightstands.

Picked his clothes up off the floor.

Crawled on his hands and knees to look under the bed.

Tossed all the bedding to the floor.

Nothing. No used condom. No empty wrapper.

He sat on the mattress, rested his elbows on his knees, and cradled his aching head in his upturned hands. Either he hadn't had sex with the person he'd shared the room with, or he'd had unprotected sex.

Another thought made his blood run cold. He grabbed his jeans, fished around for his wallet and keys, sighing in relief when he found them right where they were supposed to be. And in his wallet—the exact amount of cash he expected to see and the emergency condom he was never without even though he hadn't been with anyone other than Dave in years. Still, the *be prepared* lesson his older brothers had practically beat into him when he reached puberty was one he'd taken to heart.

Christ, why can't I remember?

He needed to get home. Forget last night even happened and hope his actions didn't come back to bite him in the ass.

Freshly showered, he pulled on his jeans then yanked his wrinkled shirt over his head. A whiff of a vaguely familiar scent teased his nostrils. He brought the collar to his nose and sniffed. Not his cologne or aftershave. Not Dave's. He drew the scent in again, let it linger on his consciousness. The same obscure memory he'd experienced earlier flashed through his brain—a dude pressed against the wall, glasses askew, kissable lips set in a sinfully handsome face he couldn't for the life of him assign a name to.

He glanced at the entry alcove. He could feel the ugly, textured wallpaper imprinting his palms as he held the guy captive for the span of a heartbeat. Had he kissed him? Dragged him to bed and had his way with him?

Everything he'd seen pointed in that direction.

He brought his shirt to his nose, inhaling the fading evidence. The scent stirred a hazy memory of want and need. His cock, ever its own master, responded.

This was so far from good, it bordered on disaster.

Not having any clue where he actually was, Rick ordered an Uber to take him to the hotel garage where he'd left Jake's car the night before. Waiting at the valet stand for his ride, he fingered the scrap of paper he'd found on the dresser next to the keycard.

The bold scrawl imparted a simple message that was both reassuring and frightening at the same time.

Rick,
Your secret is safe with me.
Brent

Whoever Brent was, he knew Rick's name. Knew he was in the closet. Agreeing to keep Rick's secret meant he knew someone who might find the information interesting. Which meant, they had friends or acquaintances in common.

At least he had a name to go with the face now.

He gave the driver the name and address of the other hotel then closed his eyes against the bright Texas sun. Who the hell was this Brent person? He couldn't recall knowing anyone by that name. Yet, every time the man's visage popped into his mind, Rick's dick stood at attention like it knew the man.

Rick asked to be dropped off at the garage entrance. He didn't know if Dave was still around and didn't want to know. On the drive home, he tried to reconcile himself to the choice Dave had made. He understood, he really did, but he'd believed the man was stronger than to let himself be railroaded into a loveless, passionless, lie of a marriage. No matter how hard Dave tried to push his guilt off on Rick, he liked to think he'd say the hell with what anyone thought before he'd marry a woman he wasn't attracted to, but he couldn't be sure. If Dave had told his parents the truth and asked Rick to be his life partner, would he have come out of the closet?

Yesterday, he probably would have said yes, but today, he wasn't convinced. He chalked his reasoning up to the fuzzy memory of a face, glasses askew, and an enticing scent growing fainter with every passing minute.

There'd been no formal agreement between him and Dave, but he had left the Marines based on Dave's faithless promises to find a way for the two of them to be together in the civilian world. A few hours after learning fearless Dave was more afraid of what his parents thought of him than dying in a godforsaken desert halfway around the globe, Rick had been lusting after another man. Didn't matter he couldn't remember everything that happened. What he did recall was enough to poke holes in the fabric of what he'd thought was the solid cloth of his life.

He loved Dave. Would most certainly have outed himself in order to be with him, if only his lover for the last six years would have done the same.

Six fucking years of sneaking around. Six fucking years of promises and lies.

Rolling the window down, he let the frigid January air whip through the car. The icy blast helped clear away the last vestiges of his hangover. The fog gradually lifted from his brain, revealing the previous night in unrelenting clarity. As before, memories of the wedding were mostly amusing. Seeing his older brother in a panic, worrying his bride would come to her senses and leave him at the altar. The sappy look on Jake's face when he pledged his love for all eternity. Yeah, that right there was funny shit, and he was damn glad he hadn't erased the memories with alcohol. They were prime teasing material not to be messed with.

Knowing he'd be driving to Dallas following the reception, he'd gone easy on the champagne that flowed freely. He'd danced with the bride, and briefly with the groom—a silly moment between brothers that made him smile recalling it. Jake had hugged him tight on the dance floor, rocking side-to-side while whispering insults laced with sentimental I love you's in his ear. He didn't know if Jake had been drunk on happiness or bubbly. Probably a little of both.

After their brothers' dance, Rick returned to his seat on the raised dais where he could keep an eye on things. They'd done a good job of faking out the paparazzi, but with the number of celebrities on hand, anything was possible. All it would take was one social media post to bring the media down on them. So Rick kept watch.

As the miles sped past, he racked his brain for details. His gaze had touched on everyone in the tent at one point or another as they ate, mingled, danced, and toasted the happy couple. He'd known nearly everyone there either in person or by reputation, save the ones seated at a table far in the back. Jake's single friends from his law school days and some colleagues from the firm he'd worked for in Houston right after receiving his law degree. A few had come in the night before for the bachelor party held in Hank's barn turned recording studio. Others had arrived in time for the wedding, and most of them had stopped by the preacher's office where Jake and his groomsmen awaited the nuptials.

A face blasted to the forefront, shaking Rick to the core. His palms grew damp on the steering wheel as he scanned the road for a place to pull over. He'd left the wide freeways behind a while ago for two-lane roads, some with shoulders, others without. A bank of mailboxes up ahead set far enough off the road to be safe. Rick signaled then pulled to the shoulder, kicking up a cloud of dust and debris as he skidded to a halt. He slammed the transmission in to Park then dropped his forehead to the steering wheel, letting the disturbing memories flow like sewage from a burst pipe.

One face. One name stood out from all the sea of people he'd met at the wedding. *Brent.* The fucking junior lawyer Jake hired to take over most of his caseload so he could concentrate on his new bride and the box of unfinished manuscripts under his bed.

Brent. Hauling his drunk ass out of the bar.

Brent. Pressed against the wall, his glasses askew, his kissable lips inches away. His enticing scent weaving a spell past the alcohol-induced haze to set Rick's libido ablaze.

Brent. Pushing him down on the bed. Undressing him.

Rick sat up, stared unseeing into the distance.

"God almighty. Tell me I didn't fuck Jake's new employee."

He bounced his head off the headrest several times in an attempt to shake more memories loose, but there was nothing there. No answer for the questions making him sick to his stomach. If he'd fucked the man, he had no recollection. He fished the handwritten note from his pocket. Read the condemning words again.

Your secret is safe with me.

He crumpled the paper into a ball then flung it across the car. It bounced off the windshield, coming to rest in the passenger seat like a lethal hitchhiker.

Fuck.

Avoiding Brent shouldn't be too difficult, if he put his mind to it. He rarely saw Jake unless they had something planned. Brent would be working in Jake's downtown office. No reason for Rick to go that way other than to visit The Donut Hole or the diner. It was time to change his eating habits anyway. Despite the physical labor required for his job, he'd gained a few pounds since he'd left the Marines. If he kept eating the way he had been, he'd be big as a barn in a couple of years. Better to nip that shit in the bud now while he still had the discipline to stick to a regime.

He took a few more minutes to calm his racing heart before he pulled onto the road. He'd stop at the grocery store, stock up on the essentials. Lots of lean meats to grill. High protein. Low carbs. Maybe he'd take up running in the evenings or early mornings. Or both. Burn off energy and calories. Keep him from thinking about Brent, obsessing about what he had or hadn't done with the man. And, no matter what, he wouldn't seek him out to ask.

Some things were better left in the vast unknown.

CHAPTER SIX

Brent dropped the nearly empty packing tape dispenser on top of the last box then plopped his tired ass onto a barstool at the counter that separated the tiny kitchen of his Houston apartment from equally tiny living space. The movers were due any minute. Everything he owned, save his work clothes and a few casual outfits, would go into storage until he could find a permanent place in Willowbrook. He'd packed everything himself. Not because he couldn't afford to pay someone to do it, but because he needed the physical exertion to keep his mind off things it had no business thinking about. Like his new boss's baby brother.

Stretching sore muscles, Brent limped to the refrigerator. He stared at the meager contents. He'd dumped everything, except a modest supply of beer and water. The beer practically called his name, but he reached for a water bottle instead. Beer made him maudlin, and the last thing he needed right then was to romanticize his situation.

He was moving, goddamnit. Alone. When he'd landed the job in Willowbrook, he'd pictured himself and Kenneth living the small-town life. They'd buy a house with a white picket fence. During the day, Kenn would have all the peace and quiet he needed to draw his comic book characters, and, on the weekends, Brent would mow the lawn. The two of them would tend the flowerbeds then sit on the wide porch and sip cold beers and talk about their week. Maybe they'd have the herb garden they both wanted. And a dog. He'd always wanted a dog, but the nomadic life he'd led growing up hadn't allowed for pets.

He'd envisioned a picture-perfect life. But when he'd asked Kenn to marry him and make his dreams come true, he'd gotten the shock of his life. With a look of horror contorting his beautiful features, his lover of two years turned him down flat. Not just no, but hell, no.

Brent rubbed his chest where the sharp barb of Kenn's arrow still stung. Kenn had begged him to turn the job down, to stay in Houston, but the damage to their relationship had been done. They wanted different things. Brent wanted roots. A home. A family. He'd thought Kenn wanted the same things, but he'd been wrong. So, Brent had taken the job and had been eager to settle into his solo existence in Willowbrook.

Then Rick Ingram happened.

Every cell in his body had taken notice of the ex-Marine when they'd been briefly introduced prior to Jake's wedding. Rick had hardly paid him any mind. At least, that was what anyone else who'd been there would say, but Brent knew better. He'd caught the guy checking him out, his gaze raking him from head to toe, assessing. He'd wondered at the scrutiny, but then he saw that Rick gave every newcomer the same treatment, as if cataloging details in the event they needed to be repeated back to law enforcement later on. He'd chalked it up to the number of celebrities attending on the bride's behalf.

Jake's father-in-law was a well-known Hollywood and Broadway actor, and his friends had turned out for the wedding. Everyone had been a little on edge about strangers. Photo ID that matched the name on the invitation had to be presented in order to get near the church. They weren't taking any chances on paparazzi crashing the nuptials.

Still, he'd been hyperaware of Rick Ingram throughout the ceremony and reception. The man was a god. Dressed in a tux, he had the look of a barely tamed wild man, except when he looked at Jake. Then he resembled a cheerful teddy bear. For as long as he lived, he'd never forget the way Rick had danced with Jake at the reception. With both their parents gone, the Ingram brothers stuck together, as evidenced by the dance. It had been corny as hell, the brothers laughing at each other, Rick playing the stooge, snuggling up to Jake, resting his head on his shoulder, and nibbling at his brother's ear. It had been both hilarious and tender. And all the while, Brent had been hard as stone, imagining Rick holding him on the dance floor. Nuzzling his neck. Whispering sweet nothings in his ear.

Later in the evening, he'd sensed someone's gaze on him, glancing up in time to see Rick's eyes dart away. The man had been watching him from his place on the dais. Brent told himself it was a passing glance. Rick was just being vigilant. Keeping an eye on all the guests. To cover his mounting interest in the man, he'd asked the bride's cousin to dance.

Amanda was a sweet girl. She had a bit part on a TV sitcom and was auditioning for movie roles while trying to earn her place in Hollywood rather than ride the coattails of her famous uncle. She'd pegged him as gay immediately and latched on to him as protection from the groom's bachelor friends. She had plenty of Hollywood stories to tell and a sweet, bubbly personality that entertained him and kept his eyes and mind from roving to a certain member of the wedding party he had no business fantasizing about. Rick Ingram wasn't gay, which made his thoughts about the man ridiculous *and* inappropriate. He'd left the reception with several needs. He needed a place to spend the night. He needed a drink in the worst way. And, he needed to get laid so he could quit obsessing about his new boss's youngest brother.

He'd put off finding a hotel room, planning to get a drink first and hoping he'd satisfy the need to get laid at the same time. A room might not even be necessary if he hooked up with a local. He'd driven straight to the bar his friends in Houston had assured him was the place to go in Dallas if he was looking for companionship. They'd been right. He'd danced with several prospects and flirted with a few more by the time he'd settled on one Adonis who fit what he was looking for. He was tall, had shoulders broad enough to carry the world, and eyes that hinted at a little mystery hidden behind them. All the while he flirted with the guy, he told himself it was a coincidence he resembled Rick Ingram.

A familiar tingle on the back of his neck had him turning to scan the room. Rick Ingram sat at the bar, staring at him.

Everything had gone downhill from that point on. Rick had drunk stumbled in between Brent and the guy he'd been flirting with. At the time, Brent told himself he was doing a good deed. Making sure his boss's brother didn't spend the night in a gutter, or worse, the drunk tank at the local precinct. He told himself the lie as he took care of the man's bar tab. As he poured him into his car. As he undressed him and put him to bed. As he lay awake on the other side of the bed, watching him sleep off what had to be an unhealthy amount of alcohol. He stuck to the story as the man rose in the wee hours of the morning, shucked the remainder of his clothes then fell back, oblivious to Brent's presence, into his drunken stupor. He clung to the story as he showered the following morning then slipped from the room, leaving behind nothing but a note meant to reassure.

He'd just passed the last exit for Waco when his carefully crafted story gave way to reality. Rick Ingram was the sexiest man he'd ever laid eyes on. He'd taken care of him that night, not for the altruistic reasons he'd told himself but because he wanted the man. Rick had made it clear he was in the closet with the door firmly closed, which made him completely off-limits. Despite Kenn's defection, Brent hadn't given up hope of finding a partner who wanted the same things he did. The Adonis in the bar had been a short-term distraction. Someone to make him forget, if only for a few hours, the loneliness stretching out ahead of him. Someone to satisfy a physical need. Instead, he'd spent the loneliest night of his life lying next to a man with hairy toe knuckles, lips that begged to be kissed, and the ability to destroy him.

CHAPTER SEVEN

"Fuck! This stuff makes Super Glue look like kids' paste." Rick dropped the dirty plate into the hot, soapy water to soak then grabbed another one from the stack in the other side of the divided sink. He made a mental note to rinse the egg off next time — before it dried to a baked-on finish. Avoiding the downtown area forced him to eat every meal at home, which created lots of dishes. Worth the headache if it kept him from running into Brent whatever his name was.

Thanks to the job he'd done on the house Will's girlfriend rented, his remodeling business had shot through the roof. In the last week, he'd given out countless bids for new work and split his time between two ongoing projects. He'd barely had time to eat, much less clean up after himself. He rinsed the plate in his hand and stuffed it in the already packed dishwasher.

Note to self: Turn the dishwasher on occasionally.

If he'd done that simple task a few days ago, his sink wouldn't be piled high with dirty dishes, and he wouldn't be up to his elbows in suds, trying to salvage what he could.

Another note to self: Buy frozen dinners so I don't have to do this crap.

That would solve the problem.

He fished the soaking plate out and resumed scrubbing. If nothing else, the mindless chore gave him time to think. If his business grew at the rate it was, he'd have to hire help. He didn't know the first thing about being an employer, but like everything in his life, he'd learn.

Where do you go to find experienced help?

That was another thing he'd have to figure out. He didn't have the time to train someone. Whoever he hired had to be able to work independently and be dependable. He wasn't going to fucking babysit a grown-ass adult.

He contemplated the other things that came with being an employer like insurance, workman's comp, and payroll taxes when the front door opened, followed by the slap of the screen door hitting the jamb. His heartrate spiked as adrenaline shot through his system. He dropped the plate into the sink and spun, his wet, soapsuds-coated hands ready to do battle.

"Yo! Rick? You home?"

Shit.

It's only Will.

He turned around, gripped the rim of the sink, and willed his hands to quit shaking.

"Rick?"

"In here." He picked up the plate, placed it into the last available spot in the dishwasher then shoved the rack hard, rattling the dishes. He opened the cabinet door beneath the sink and crouched, scanning the interior for the dishwasher detergent.

"There you are." Will leaned a hip against the counter on the other side of the dishwasher. "Whatcha doing down there?"

"Looking for the dishwasher detergent. Where the hell is it?"

His brother skirted the open appliance door and leaned over his shoulder to grab a plastic bucket. "Right here. Can't you read?"

Rick stood, yanked the container from his brother's hands. "What the fuck is this?"

"Pods." Will pointed to a picture on the front that looked more like a throat lozenge than detergent. "Don't tell me you haven't used the dishwasher since I bought this new stuff."

Pods. What the hell? Ignoring his brother's snide question, Rick tried to pry the lid off the container. Like the dried-on egg, it wouldn't budge. "What the fuck?" He shoved it into Will's midsection. Instinct had his brother reaching for the box. "You bought it. You figure out how to get it open."

Needing a minute to get himself under control, Rick stomped to the refrigerator for a cold soda. He popped the pull tab and guzzled half the can in one long pull. A plastic *pop* from the other side of the room drew his attention. Will had the container open. He pinched a pod between his thumb and forefinger, held it up.

"This is a detergent pod." He placed it in the dispenser then slid the lid closed. "So easy, even a Marine can do it."

"Fuck you." Rick downed the remainder of his soda, crushed the can in his fist then barked out a satisfying belch.

"Who pissed on your Corn Flakes?" Will snapped the lid shut on the detergent and placed it beneath the sink. Using the toe of his boot, he lifted the dishwasher door. When it was high enough to reach without bending over, he gave it a shove to shut it. "Stuck-on shit cycle?"

Rick shrugged.

"I'll take that as a yes." He pushed a couple of buttons. Lights lit up the control panel, and the sound of running water could be heard. Will grabbed a dish towel and wiped the counter before leaning against it. Arms crossed, he eyed his brother in an all-too-familiar stare-down.

Rick didn't have time to wait Will out. He broke within seconds. "Don't you ever knock?"

The brothers had grown up in this house, and though it was Rick's official residence now, Jake and Will thought nothing of walking in uninvited whenever they wanted. He'd lock the door, but they all had keys. *Should have changed the locks when I remodeled the place.* Hindsight was 20/20.

"Why would I do that?" Will's head swiveled as he took in as much of the living space as he could without moving. "Unless you're not alone." He raised an eyebrow in question.

"That's not the point. This is my house now. I'm entitled to a little privacy, don't you think?"

"Nope." Will pushed away from the counter, helped himself to a soda from the fridge.

While he was pouring it down his gullet, Rick asked, "What are you here for anyway? I thought you moved out." Will had been gradually moving in with his girlfriend over the last few weeks. Since all he owned were clothes and a few art supplies, he'd been carrying a box at a time down the block to her house when the mood struck him or he needed something he'd left behind.

"Jake called, wants us both to come down to his office. I figured since I was here, I'd get some more of my stuff."

"What's big brother want?"

Will finished his soda and chucked the empty can at the recycling bin in the corner. It hit the rim then teetered over, landing atop a beer bottle from the sound of it. "Don't know. He said he wanted both of us, so I'm guessing it has something to do with the estate? Can't think of anything else it could be. You?"

He shook his head. "I got nothing."

"Let me grab one of my boxes then let's see what Jake wants so I can get back home to my woman."

Since Will still hadn't purchased a car of his own, he put his box in the bed of Rick's truck. "You going to be okay here alone?"

A sound, part growl, part laugh, came from Rick's lips. "Seriously? I survived the Marines and multiple trips to the sandbox. I don't need a babysitter."

"Didn't think you did, bro. I just feel bad about leaving you on your own. Thought I'd be here for a while longer."

"I know you did. Glad you got your shit together, and glad you found your woman. Kenzie's great." Just because his own life sucked swamp water didn't mean he wasn't happy for Will and Jake. They'd both found their cliché. The woman to complete them. They were happy as pigs in mud, and he was happy for them. Really. He was.

~ ~ ~

There were only two cars in the parking lot in front of Jake's office. Rick steered clear of the cherry-red Corvette and parked next to his brother's boring sedan instead. Even though it was after-hours, the front door was unlocked. The younger Ingram brothers filed inside like they'd done thousands of times before.

The reception desk was empty, though Jean, the legal secretary Jake had inherited along with the business, had left a lamp on. Up until a few months ago, the smaller office closest to the front door had been used as a storage room, but tonight, the door stood open, the faint glow of a desk lamp visible beyond the otherwise dark portal. Rick's heartbeat sped up, and as much as he told himself not to, he still swiveled his head, hoping for a glimpse of his brother's new employee.

Brent sat at his desk, his focus entirely on a document he held, a pencil threaded through the fingers of his right hand. His discarded suit coat hung over the back of his executive chair. He'd loosened his tie and rolled the cuffs of his shirt up to expose his forearms. The glimpse made Rick's mouth dry and his step falter. He'd thought the man attractive even when he'd believed him to be heterosexual. Now that he knew otherwise, he couldn't stop thinking about him, wanting him.

The man was sexy as shit. He'd done Rick a solid the night of Jake's wedding and he'd yet to thank him for getting him out of the bar safely. He'd also like to know what, exactly, he'd done once they left the bar, but he wasn't sure he was ready to hear the details. Maybe one of these days, when Dave's betrayal didn't feel like someone had taken 80 grit sandpaper to his heart. In the meantime, he'd keep his distance from the man.

Rick stepped into his brother's office and, at his nonverbal command, closed the door behind him and took the only unoccupied chair in the room. "You should let me redo this place. It gives me the heebie-jeebies."

It didn't look like Jake had changed a thing since inheriting their father's law practice nearly five years ago. The desk was the same. The ugly carpet was the same. Hell, even the books and knickknacks on the built-in shelves along one wall appeared to be the same.

"Yeah. I should." Jake rubbed a hand over his face bringing Rick's attention to the dark circles under his eyes and the slack muscles around his mouth. "One of these days, I promise. I've got a shit-ton of other stuff to worry about right now."

Will sat forward. "Shit. Did Sunny figure out you're an asshole and leave?"

Jake shot their middle brother a death stare that reminded Rick way too much of their father, who had been an asshole. Jake physically resembled the man, but beneath the outer shell, the two were nothing alike. Thank god. "No, butt face. Everything is fine. Sunny isn't going anywhere."

"Then what's this about?"

The oldest of the brothers rocked back in his chair, his gaze on the ceiling as he blew out a breath fraught with tension. When he brought his weight forward again, he rested his forearms on the desk and laced his fingers together. "I got a call from the D.A. up in New York this afternoon."

In his peripheral vision, he saw Will straighten, his full attention on their brother. "What did he want?"

"He said Jessica made bail."

"How?"

"He didn't know. He was apologetic, said he called as soon as he heard the news. The problem is, this happened nearly two weeks ago. She was supposed to meet with her lawyer earlier this week. When she didn't, and he couldn't locate her, he reported her missing. That's how the D.A. found out she'd been released in the first place."

Will jumped up like a spring from the ancient, upholstered chair had poked him in the ass and stomped over to the plate-glass window behind Jake's desk. At the best of times, the small garden beyond wasn't much to look at. In the dark, he would only see a reflection of himself in the heavy glass.

Rick hated that Will's past wouldn't let him alone. After his fiancée had betrayed him with the help of a gallery owner and, ironically, an employee of Sunny's gallery, he'd come home a mess. Since Rick had been a mess himself, missing Dave, and the Marine Corps, he knew what a mess looked like. The two of them, living in the same house, had been a mopey shitshow until Kenzie had given his brother a reason to live. It broke his fucking heart to see this shit come back on his brother again, after all this time. "What does that mean for Will? And MacKenzie?"

Kenzie's career had been collateral damage in Jessica's scheme to ruin Will. Thanks to Sunny's friendship with Hank and Melody Travis, Kenzie had come to work for Hank in Willowbrook. He wasn't exactly sure how the two had met, but once they did, it was like watching a spark grow into a wildfire.

"It means, we all need to be extra vigilant. There's no reason to believe she'd come here, but we need to be careful, just in case."

"You've told Sunny?" Will spoke, his back still to them and the room.

Jake's wife had been framed by Jessica and her cohorts for the theft of Will's paintings. The private detective Jake hired had found the evidence needed to clear Sunny, and that had ultimately led to the arrest of the culprits and the return of the stolen paintings to Will. "Not yet. I'm going to though. She won't be going anywhere alone until we know where Jessica is. Same goes for MacKenzie."

"I'll see to it," Will said, his shoulders slumping. "I thought this would be over when I burned the paintings. I'm beginning to think it'll never be over. I'm going to have to carry this shit with me the rest of my life."

Jake swiveled his chair to face Will. "She couldn't have gone far. Not without financial assistance. She'll be behind bars again soon."

Will spun around, leaned his shoulders against the glass. "Someone gave her bail money. Who would do that?"

Jake shrugged. "The D.A. said he was looking into that. I'm sure he'll question the person as to her whereabouts."

"I don't like it." Will shook his head. "She's a master manipulator. She must have some other poor soul on the hook, someone she's convinced of her innocence. Where else would she get bail? With a financial backer, she could be anywhere."

"Let's not borrow trouble, Will." Jake stood, clapped a hand on their middle brother's shoulder. "I know this dredges up bad memories, and I wouldn't have told you she'd made bail if they knew where she was. Since they don't, I'd be remiss in not warning you to be vigilant until she's located."

Will nodded. "You're just doing your job, and I appreciate it. I'd never forgive myself if my past mistakes put Kenzie or Sunny in harm's way."

Rick stood and stretched. "We'll keep our eyes peeled for anything out of the ordinary. Maybe we should give the staff at the diner a heads-up. If Jessica comes to town, chances are she'd stop in there or at The Donut Hole. Everybody else does."

"That's a great idea, Rick." Jake scribbled something on a notepad on his desk. "I'll talk to Marge at the diner. You're still friends with Cathy at The Donut Hole, aren't you?"

He'd dated her all through high school. Everyone thought they'd get married. Everyone but him. They hadn't exactly parted on good terms, but since his return to Willowbrook, the owner of the local donut hot spot had been nothing but cordial to him. Still single, maybe she thought she had another chance with him. He'd do anything for his brother, so he answered the only way he could. "Yeah. I'll stop in tomorrow morning and give her a heads-up."

Jake grabbed his suit coat off the back of his chair. "I'll touch base with the local PD tomorrow, too. Give them a heads-up." He shrugged his coat on. "Let's get out of here. I'm tired. It's been a long fucking day."

The three brothers filed out of the office, Jake in the lead, Rick bringing up the rear. As he passed Brent's office, Jake raised his hand in farewell and called out, "Don't stay too late."

"I won't, boss."

The sound of the man's voice sent a shiver of awareness down Rick's spine. *Shit.* Even his deep voice was sexy. Calling it self-preservation, he kept his gaze forward as he passed Brent's office and followed his brothers out into the frigid night.

CHAPTER EIGHT

Shit.

Brent grabbed his jacket and briefcase from the passenger seat, breaking into a run as he neared the courthouse. He was fucking late. Again. Stuck in traffic on the interstate, he'd made the difficult decision to call his boss and ask him to cover for him for the second time in the first month of his employ. The first time he'd been late to a court appearance, there'd been an accident on the freeway and traffic had been at a standstill for hours. He'd had no choice but to alert Jake and have him stand in for him. Today's delay was due to construction on the same stretch of highway. He'd made his way past the section of lane closure, but the damage had been done. He was due in court half an hour ago.

His anxiety at his boss's reaction to his tardiness earned him a thorough search at the security checkpoint—making him even later than he already was. Great. Just fucking great. He took an extra second to adjust his tie and suitcoat, and to wipe a bead of sweat from his brow, before opening the courtroom door.

Jake had texted him that the judge had her own delays, and the proceedings had been pushed back a few minutes. He breathed a sigh of relief to see the judge's bench still empty. He hurried to the front of the room where Jake sat with the nervous couple eager to finalize the adoption of their first child.

"Sorry I'm late," he said, taking the chair between Jake and the couple. "Construction on the highway." He shook hands with his clients, bumped knuckles with the pint-sized adoptee, then retrieved a file from his briefcase then turned to his boss. "Jake, I can't thank you enough."

His boss held up a hand to stop him. "No thanks needed. However, we've got to get you a place in town. You're running yourself ragged commuting from Dallas, not to mention the cost of gas and your hotel room."

Brent nodded. "Jean has kept her eye on the real estate market for me. There's nothing available to rent or buy in Willowbrook." Truth. In their legal secretary's words, he'd better hope for someone to die. That was the only way something was going to come on the market. He wasn't that desperate. Yet. Though today's delay might push him over the edge. It was one thing to keep a client waiting in the office, another to be a no-show in court. Thank god, Jake was an understanding boss, but how much longer would his goodwill last?

"It's a tough market, that's for sure. We need some new construction in this town." Jake stood then nodded to the still-empty bench. "Since you're here now, I'll get on back to what I was doing." He congratulated the clients on what was a certain outcome of their petition to adopt then turned his attention back to Brent. "Can you meet me at the office Sunday around one? I think I might have a solution to your problem."

"Sure." Brent bobbed his head. "You got a spare closet I can put a cot in?"

Jake smiled. "No, but I might know someone who does."

With that, his boss strode confidently out of the courtroom, leaving Brent with a strange sense of foreboding. What the hell did he have in mind? There were literally no rooms available in Willowbrook.

The courtroom door closed behind his boss just as the judge entered at the other end, putting the kibosh on the questions running through Brent's mind. The entire proceeding took less than fifteen minutes then he was congratulating the new family. As he followed them out of the courthouse, he couldn't help but think how much better this job was, commute aside, than the one he'd had in Houston. When all you dealt with were corporations, you rarely saw how your work affected anyone. The new family walking ahead of him was visible proof his job had meaning.

Later today, he had a meeting with a young couple who were writing their first wills and wanted to establish trusts for their children. His expertise would help them provide for their children in the event something happened to one or both of them. No one liked to think in those terms, but planning for the unimaginable was wise. He liked being a part of the process, helping them to choose the right path for their family. The work wasn't as lucrative as being a corporate attorney, but it was a lot more satisfying. Since money wasn't one of his primary concerns, he welcomed the satisfaction his new job brought to his life.

Houston was in his rearview mirror, and, hopefully, Dallas soon would follow. He hadn't had much time to hang out in Willowbrook, given his commute and the demands of his job, but what he had seen, he liked. The pace was slower. The people genuine and hardworking. The majority of the population had lived there all their lives. Some had spent time away but returned, like his boss. Jake had lived the big city corporate attorney life for several years before coming home to Willowbrook to take over his dad's law practice. Jake's brother, William, had lived the life of a celebrity artist in New York for years before moving back home. He'd come to the office a time or two to see Jake. Apparently, there were some unresolved legal issues from his time in New York. Jake had his hand in a few accounts, his brother's being top on his list. Thinking of his boss's family brought to mind the one Ingram brother Brent needed to stay far, far away from. Richard. The baby of the family but by no means a child. His brain, as it did anytime he thought of Rick Ingram, burst to life with images of the man.

His laugh when his brother's knees gave way when he saw his bride at the back of the church. His smile when he danced with his brother at the reception. The anguish in his voice when he implored Brent to keep his secret. The desire in his eyes when he pressed Brent against the hotel room wall. His sculpted torso when Brent wrestled his drunk body into bed. His naked ass when he drunkenly undressed in the middle of the night. His face relaxed in slumber the next morning.

The slideshow played on an endless loop, tormenting Brent in his loneliest moments. He'd gone back to the bar in Dallas several times, but the Adonis he'd flirted with that night must have been an out-of-towner. Other guys had flirted with him, but Brent wasn't interested. None of them looked like Rick Ingram. None of them were Rick Ingram.

And that was the crux of his current problem.

Only Rick Ingram would do.

~ ~ ~

As agreed, Brent met Jake on Sunday afternoon in the small parking lot behind Jake's law office in downtown Willowbrook. He'd spent the last few days wondering what his boss had up his sleeve. Their shared legal secretary, Jean, remained adamant there wasn't anything available for rent, not a house, not an apartment, not even a single room, in Willowbrook. Either Jake was a miracle worker, or he was full of shit. He hoped for miracle worker but was prepared for full of shit.

He waved as Jake pulled into the lot, came to a stop next to him, and rolled down the passenger side window. He leaned in. "Hey."

"Sorry to keep you waiting," Jake said, sweeping a leather portfolio off the passenger seat. "Hop in."

Brent dropped into the seat and reached for his seat belt. "I'm usually the one apologizing for being late."

His boss handed him the leather folder. "Sunny and I were going over some ideas. Lost track of time."

The slight color on his boss's cheeks led Brent to conclusions of his own about how Jake had lost track of time. He and Sunny were so newlywed, they were practically still on their honeymoon. "Not a problem, boss."

Jake shifted the car into gear and pulled out of the parking lot. He stopped at the stop sign marking the intersection half a block down. "I want you to do me a favor."

"What's that?"

A car crossed in the opposite direction then Jake accelerated through the intersection. "Keep an open mind today. And remember, if this works out, it's temporary."

Brent wanted something permanent, but for now, he'd take temporary. "How temporary?"

"Not sure. Six months, maybe? I'll know more in a bit."

It was on the tip of his tongue to ask what a bit was when Jake pulled to the curb in front of a small bungalow on a tree-shaded street within walking distance of everything downtown, including the law office. Brent's heart hammered. The white house resembled the others on the block but stood out because of the blue shutters. A wide walkway led from the sidewalk to a set of equally wide steps. Rocking chairs, abandoned for the winter, stood sentinel on a porch that spanned the front of the residence. He eyed the bushes across the front of the porch. Azaleas. He'd stake his life on it. Come spring, they'd put on a show with their bright blooms.

The house was exactly what he wanted for himself. "Is this place for sale?"

Jake grabbed the portfolio from Brent's lap then opened his door. "Nope."

He joined his boss on the sidewalk. "Rent?"

"Not the entire place."

He didn't care if the owner/occupant was a crazy cat lady/hoarder. He wanted to live there. Saw himself pushing a lawn mower over the lawn that would be green in a few more weeks. An empty flower bed bordering the driveway suggested bright annuals in springtime and through the summer months. His fingers itched to dig into the soil.

"You know the owner?" He followed Jake up to the porch.

Jake opened the screen door, placed his hand on the doorknob, and turned it. "You could say that."

What. The. Fuck?

Brent caught the screen before it hit him. Jake stepped inside. "Yo. Bro. What's up?"

Bro? Brent closed his eyes and prayed this was the home of the middle brother, Will. A familiar baritone met his ears. "Jesus, Jake. You scared the shit out of me. One of these days one of my idiot brothers is going to walk in on something you don't want to see."

"If only." Jake stepped aside, waving Brent into the room. "Since you're dressed and I don't see any sign of a woman, I think it's safe. I brought you some company."

"The Drillers are playing, Jake! This is my first day off since your wedding. Is it too much to ask to have a little privacy?"

Remaining mostly on the porch and out of sight, Brent tugged on Jake's jacket sleeve. Hoping to avoid detection, he pitched his voice low. "This isn't a good idea. I'm going to…go."

Jake whirled on him. "No. You need a place to live, and my dickhead brother has an extra room. So get your ass in here and let's talk." He tossed the portfolio on the coffee table, picked up the remote, and muted the television.

Brent reluctantly stepped over the threshold, keeping his eyes fixed on his feet, postponing a confrontation as long as possible. When he looked up and met Rick's gaze head-on, something sparked within him and grew into an all-consuming blaze in a matter of seconds. *Fuck!* He was in so much trouble.

"Jake?" Rick's voice sliced the air like a Marine Corps sword wielded by a master. "What's he doing here?"

God, that voice. Brent fought off the shiver racing down his spine. How would he ever survive hearing it on a daily basis?

"He needs a place to stay in town. The commute from Dallas is unacceptable. It's impacting his ability to do the job I hired him to do. There's nothing else available in this town or I wouldn't put you on the spot, but since Will moved in with Kenzie, you have an empty room."

Rick stood, walked away. Brent took the opportunity to admire his firm ass. He returned a moment later, a fresh beer in hand.

Jake paced around the room like he owned the place. "You work long hours. So does Brent. You'll hardly see each other. Did I mention it's a temporary situation?"

"How temporary?"

"Depends on how long it takes you to renovate his new apartment."

"What new apartment?" Brent and Rick asked at the same time.

Jake took a seat on the sofa, opened the portfolio. "The one above Sunny's new gallery, downtown."

Rick sat on one side of Jake. Curious, Brent sat on the opposite side. Jake twirled an architectural drawing around so they could all see it. "Sunny drew this up. It's not to scale or anything, just an artist's vision of the place. She needs some of the upstairs square footage for storage, but the rest we decided to convert into an apartment. We figured Brent could use it until something more to his liking comes on the market. After that, we'll use it as incentive to hire someone to operate the gallery so Sunny can spend more time with the baby."

Rick used a pointer finger to pull the rendering closer. "What about permits?"

"I've got friends at the planning commission. They're excited about bringing residential units to downtown. They're going to talk to some of the other building owners about converting their upper floors to rental units. If you can get this one done in a reasonable amount of time, it could generate a lot more business for you."

Rick lifted his chin at the stack of papers Jake had brought. "What else you got there?"

Jake fanned several sheets across the table. "Again, these aren't to scale, but you can see what Sunny has in mind. The actual apartment would be about twelve-hundred square feet. She envisions two bedrooms, two bathrooms, and a galley kitchen." He pointed to a sketch of the living space. "She figures anyone she'd hire to run the gallery would probably be an artist themselves, so she wants to put in skylights and expand the windows on the front of the building to let in more light in case they want to use it as a studio."

"It's open concept. Have you had an engineer look at the structure to see if the existing walls can be taken down?"

Brent pulled one of the sketches closer while Jake and Rick talked engineering specs. Damn. Sunny had an eye for interior design. The place would be modern yet incorporated what he assumed was the existing charm of the old building. Anyone would be lucky to live there.

"Brent?" Jake elbowed him in the ribs. "What do you think? Can you put up with my brother for a few months while he builds an apartment for you?"

"Well." He swallowed hard then looked past his boss to meet the gaze of his potential landlord. "It would be temporary. Right?"

"It might be more than six months. Jake forgets I've got other obligations. Jobs I've already committed to, including his wife's gallery on the first floor of that building."

"Sunny's dealing with morning sickness, so putting the gallery renovation off is fine with her. Money's no object," Jake interjected. "Hire as many people as you need. Just get the job done. The sooner you do, the sooner Brent is out of your hair."

"I don't want to be a bother." Lord. He didn't want to live in the same house with Rick Ingram. But what choice did he have? Hoping for someone to die so he'd have a chance at a place to live wasn't just gruesome, it was unrealistic. About as unrealistic as keeping his hands off Rick. *But I will. I swear, I will.*

"It's no bother," Jake answered confidently for his brother. "Besides, one-third of this house belongs to me. As of right this minute, I'm claiming the spare bedroom and half the bathroom as mine and loaning it to Brent."

Rick jerked to his feet and paced away, his sexy-as-hell hand wrapped around his nape. He'd let his hair grow out some since the wedding. Brent longed to run his fingers through the too-long strands to see if they felt as soft as they looked.

Rick abruptly spun on his heel to face them. "He's paying rent. Enough to cover his share of the utilities, and he buys his own groceries." His gaze bored into Brent. "This isn't a social club. No dates. No sleepovers."

"Whoa." Jake stood to face off with his brother. "Just because you're antisocial doesn't mean your tenant has to be. He can bring anyone he wants over, and they can stay as long as they like."

Even though their arguing had an underlying tone of brotherly affection and hinted at years of similar negotiations, it was time to put an end to it. Brent stood. "I agree to Rick's terms. I don't have time for a social life anyway." The only person he wanted in his bed was Rick Ingram, and that wasn't going to happen, so no problem.

Rick glared at him. "Fuck." He shook his head then switched his gaze to Jake. "Okay. Okay, big brother. You win. I'll renovate the space, but you better clear the way with the permits. I want half up front to cover materials and hiring extra hands." He pointed a finger at Brent. "Stay the hell out of my way. You clean up your own messes." He named a reasonable rent.

Brent nodded. "Okay. First and last up front? I can draw up a rental agreement if you like."

"You lawyer types are fond of paper, so yeah, you write it up. I'll sign it. After my lawyer"—he cast a knowing glace at his brother—"reads it."

"Fuck, Rick." Jake shook his head. "I'll read the agreement, but I'm taking my fee out of your first payment."

"The fuck you are. You don't charge Will for legal services."

"Will *needs* a lawyer to look out for his interests. You don't."

It was a backhanded compliment—of sorts. The brothers stared at each other for the span of a couple of heartbeats then Rick found the remote under the scattered drawings. He resumed his place on the sofa and unmuted the game. "Fuck. The Drillers gave up two touchdowns. So much for making it to the championship game."

"That's our cue to leave." Jake gathered up his drawings then left without saying goodbye. Brent followed him out.

~~~
~~~

Rick kicked back in his new reclining sofa as the door closed behind his uninvited guests. What the fuck had he just agreed to? He'd just gotten Will out of his hair, and now that Brent guy was moving in?

He'd worked extra hours the day before to finish one job so he'd have one measly day off before starting the next job in the queue. Keeping busy had sustained him the three weeks since Jake's wedding, leaving him too exhausted to think about Dave's defection or the stupid mistake he'd made afterward. Working himself half to death had also kept him away from downtown Willowbrook, reducing the possibility of him running into Jake's new junior attorney—the keeper of Rick's secret. Now the fucker was going to be his roommate. Slash that. Tenant. A paying guest. Nothing more.

A drop of cold water fell from the bottle he'd forgotten he still held. Since his drunken mishap after his brother's wedding, he hadn't allowed himself more than one bottle each night. This was what? His second today? He couldn't afford any more fuckups like that one. However, sobriety came with problems of its own, so he'd loaded his days to the max with work, hoping exhaustion would chase his demons away. When that didn't work, he invested in a set of weights and spent the restless hours in the middle of the night in the garage, lifting until his muscles screamed loud enough to drown out the memories. Surprisingly, it wasn't memories of Dave or of the way the man had broken his heart that kept him awake at night. The memory of emerald eyes behind nerd glasses fueled his late-night weightlifting sessions. Eyes filled with pity. Maybe a hint of amusement. Perhaps regret. Definitely hunger. He'd been drunk as the proverbial skunk that night, but he knew desire when he saw it. When he'd had Mr. Sin-in-a-suit pinned to the wall of that hotel room, glasses askew, he'd seen the flash of desire in his green eyes.

Bringing the bottle to his lips, he savored the cold, bitter taste. He'd discovered the Lucky Lady microbrewery a few towns over soon after his return to Willowbrook. The brewmaster had a sense of humor, assigning unique names to the brews in a way that reminded him of fortune cookies, and changing their flavors often. He had yet to find one he didn't like. This was the first from the six-pack he'd picked up last night, and from the taste of it, one he hadn't had before. He tilted the bottle so he could read the label. The emerald-green background reminded him of Brent's eyes. He shook off the ridiculous comparison and focused on the name of this particular brew. *Mistakes Make the Best Lovers.*

The laugh began as a chuckle deep in his gut, gained momentum the longer he looked at the label then burst forth in waves of mirth he couldn't contain.

Shit. I'm fucking doomed.

CHAPTER TEN

The following evening, Rick pinched the edges of a plastic tray, lifting the nuked meal from the microwave. "Shit. Fuck." He dropped the steaming TV dinner on the countertop with a *plop* then sucked the tip of his right pointer finger into his mouth. *Damn.* There had to be a better way to eat. He'd scalded the thumbs and forefingers on both hands on supposedly sealed entrees.

He'd just plunged his singed fingers under the cold tap when the doorbell rang. "Fuck." Shutting off the water, he hastily dried his hand, tossed the towel over the lip of the sink. The bell rang again just as he reached for the door handle. He yanked the door open, prepared to give whoever the hell it was a boot in the ass for interrupting his supper.

His new tenant, dressed to the nines in a tailored suit, stood on the porch surrounded by a shit-ton of suitcases. Rick's first thought was, *Fuck. I'd buy anything he's selling.* His second thought was, *Where the hell does he think all those clothes are going to go?*

Before he could voice either thought, Sin-in-a-suit grabbed the handle on the nearest roller bag with one hand and the screen door with the other. "You didn't give me a key."

Rick stepped back. "Don't need one. This is Willowbrook. I don't lock the door."

The newcomer dragged the first suitcase in then returned to the porch for another. Rick made no attempt to help him. Concierge wasn't part of his job description.

Brent retrieved the third case, an overstuffed garment bag, setting it on the floor at Rick's feet. "I've got expensive shit. Electronics, and sometimes I bring client files home. I'd appreciate it if we could lock up."

Rick shrugged. "There's a spare key in the bowl." He pointed to a green depression glass serving dish resting on a gateleg table behind the door. "Fits front and back locks. Just so you know, my brothers have keys, and, locked or not, they come and go as they please."

Brent huffed. "Yeah. Saw that for myself yesterday." He hefted a heavy case over the threshold. "Ever think of changing the locks?"

He had but didn't see the point. If Jake or Will wanted in, they knew all the secret ways to accomplish a break-in. Like the fact the window in what would be Brent's room wouldn't lock. "Nope," he said instead. "I repeat. This is Willowbrook. Crime rate — zero." He had cautioned Will and Kenzie to lock their doors. If Will's former fiancée came to town, they were more at risk there than anywhere else in town.

With the last of his wardrobe inside, Brent shut the door. Fuck, he was sexy as hell, even with his nose turned up, sniffing like a goddamn hunting dog.

"What's that smell?" He scrunched his face up like he was going to puke. "Tell me that's not something I'm going to have to get used to."

"Fuck you and the horse you rode in on." Rick left him standing in the living room. He called out from the kitchen, "Last door on the left is your room. Bottom drawer in the bathroom is yours."

He peeled the cellophane film off the top of his meal, grabbed a fork from the dish drainer, and dug in. A spewing sound, followed by a sickeningly overpowering floral smell made him forget all about the last of his meal, a brown brick that in no way resembled the brownie advertised on the meal's packaging. Rick spun around just as Brent entered the kitchen, what looked like a bug-bomb can held aloft as he sprayed chemicals into the air.

"What the fuck are you doing? Cut that shit out!"

Green eyes blinked behind those goddamn sexy glasses. He lowered his arm. He'd taken off his suit coat, rolled the sleeves of his white dress shirt halfway up his forearms, and loosened his tie. Rick's dick twitched to life. He did not want to be attracted to the guy, but fuck, he rocked the casual executive look.

"I will not live in a house that smells like a fart."

It was amazing the things grown men could find to amuse themselves at a remote desert outpost. Rick braced a hand on the counter, bent slightly at the waist, and squeezed out a fart guaranteed to startle any enemy combatants within a quarter mile radius. A championship winner if he ever heard one.

Brent stumbled back. "Oh, gross!" He waved a sheaf of papers in front of his face while directing a stream of flowery chemicals in Rick's general direction.

"Get used to it or get out. And for the love of god, quit spraying that shit everywhere."

"I'm not going anywhere, and I'll quit spraying when you quit fouling the air." He thrust the papers forward. "Here's the rental agreement. Sign it."

Rick lamented that his fart hadn't stunk. Just his luck. But he did get the satisfaction of rattling the lawyer, and damn, if that wasn't fun. He snatched the papers then sat at the small table where he'd eaten meals for most of his life. With just him living here, he rarely bothered to sit, preferring to eat at the counter. Looking at empty chairs around the table while he ate brought home just how much he missed having someone around. In the Marines, he'd never been alone.

Brent ventured closer until he stood over Rick's shoulder. "Just sign the last page. It's a standard rental agreement. Month to month since I don't know how long I'll need the room."

A check for the agreed-upon first and last month's rent was paperclipped to the top of the stack. Rick hesitated. This was his last chance to kick the man out and preserve his sanity. Once he signed the papers, lawyer in the family or not, he'd be stuck for at least six months with a tempting stranger who already knew too much about him. Probably longer.

"Jake looked it over. Call him if you don't believe me."

He'd already peeked at the last page and saw the Post-it Note from Jake that simply read, "Sign it." An arrow pointed to the line for his signature, like he was an idiot or something. Fuck Jake.

"Here. I brought a pen, just in case." Hot breath brushed his ear. A hand holding an expensive gold pen and a surprisingly muscular, masculine forearm appeared in his line of sight. Rick closed his eyes and stifled a groan as he imagined the sexy lawyer naked, strong arms encircling him from behind. This was exactly why he shouldn't sign the document. The man had been in the house, what, ten minutes? And already Rick was thinking inappropriate thoughts. This was never going to work. Absolutely nothing good could come of touching the man. He had to make that clear.

The man behind him straightened. "Is that where the smell is coming from?"

Rick's gaze followed Brent's outstretched arm pointing to the frozen meal he'd almost finished eating. It did smell like shit and tasted little better, but it was fast and easy. He'd worked like the devil was on his heels today, cognizant that every minute wasted was another he'd have to endure this man's presence in his house. He'd been too tired to fix anything better for supper and too sweaty to pick anything up from the diner. Drive-thru fast-food joints had yet to find Willowbrook. "That smell was my supper. I know you're envious, but the frozen dinners in the freezer are mine. You want some, you buy your own."

Brent approached the counter like he expected the plastic tray to attack at any moment. He picked up Rick's abandoned fork and poked at the brownie brick. "You ate this? Man, you must have a cast-iron stomach."

Truth. Anyone who survived on MRE's for more than a day or two developed a thick stomach lining. He'd gone weeks with nothing but the Meals Ready to Eat for sustenance. "We've got more important things to discuss than my eating habits." He tapped the contract lying on the table.

"Like what?" His new tenant busied himself opening cabinets and drawers like he owned the place.

God, did he have to spell it out? "Like what happened after my brother's wedding."

Brent gently closed the cabinet beneath the sink before straightening to his full height. "What, exactly happened?"

Rick ran a hand over his jaw as he considered how much he wanted to tell this man. "Nothing," he said in conclusion. "You didn't see me after you left the reception. Period."

The man leaned his hips against the counter, arms crossed, eyes narrowed. "Okay. If that's what you want. How much do you remember about that night?"

"Not much."

"But you remember seeing me at the bar."

"Yeah. I vaguely remember you in my hotel room. Don't remember how we got there." He closed his eyes, briefly, as flashes of memory blasted through his brain. "You spent the night."

Brent nodded. "You were plastered. It wasn't safe to leave you alone."

"I didn't see any evidence of a condom." Heat rushed up his neck at the admission of just how plastered he'd been.

"That's because we didn't use one."

Rick groaned. His head dipped forward, too heavy for his neck. He rested an elbow on the table then dropped his forehead to his upturned palm. Laughter from across the room jolted him upright. Brent held his glasses in one hand while he dried his eyes with the other.

"You think we fucked?" He replaced his glasses. "Boy, you are so wrong." He chuckled. Pushing away from the counter, he opened the fridge, peered inside for a minute then helped himself to a beer. "Hope you don't mind. I'll replace it as soon as I can get to the store." He popped the top, took a long pull on the bottle then held it out to read the label. "This is some good shit. Where did you get it?"

"There's only one liquor store in town, dickwad. Where do you think I got it?"

Brent nodded then took another swig. "Okay. I'll buy you a six-pack. It was worth it to see the look on your face when you admitted you'd looked for a condom wrapper. You were too shitfaced to undress yourself, much less fuck." He relaxed against the counter. "I got most of your clothes off of you. Put you to bed then I made myself comfortable while you slept it off. I couldn't have lived with myself if I'd walked away then found out you'd choked on your own puke."

"I woke up naked."

"Not my fault. You woke up once. Enough to kick off your jeans and briefs then you went right back to sleep. I kinda thought for a minute you'd see me, maybe jump my bones, but you never even knew I was there."

Christ! Brent's words put more images in Rick's head, ones he now knew were pure fiction. Erotic fiction.

"You can thank me now."

Rick growled. Fuck. He did owe the man. God only knows what would have happened to him if someone else had coaxed him out of that bar. He hadn't been in any shape to say no or defend himself. He'd never been that fucked up in his life, and he never wanted to be again. He opened his mouth, but Brent cut him off before he could thank him.

"Nope. Don't bother. I don't need your thanks. How about you pay it forward? Help someone else out sometime. As for you and me, we met briefly at Jake's wedding and didn't see each other until yesterday when your brother sprang his downtown redevelopment plan on both of us."

Yeah. Rick nodded. "Okay." He half wished Brent wasn't such a decent guy. Maybe then he wouldn't entertain fantasies of unfastening those sexy trousers and sucking the man's cock between his lips — right here in the kitchen. "Pay it forward. I can do that." He picked up the pen he'd dropped and scribbled his name on the rental contract.

CHAPTER ELEVEN

It's self-preservation, Brent told himself as he stuffed papers into his briefcase in preparation for leaving the office earlier than usual. It was Friday night, and he'd have all weekend to read the pages Jean had typed up. He was tired of arriving home to find the entire house smelling like shit, thanks to Rick's obsession with frozen dinners. Tonight, he planned to beat his landlord home and prepare supper for both of them. He'd need to go to the grocery store first. Then make a stop at the liquor store for some wine and the six-pack he'd promised to purchase.

He couldn't understand why the man couldn't fix himself a decent meal. Brent loved the newly refurbished kitchen and couldn't wait to prepare an actual meal in it. So far, he'd existed on lunch meat, chips, and soda since he hadn't had time to shop for anything more elaborate. Tonight, he'd change that. He had a grocery list as long as his arm, and instead of walking to work, he'd driven so he could fill the trunk of his car with enough supplies to last the week. Since the rent he was paying was ridiculously cheap, he could afford to share a few meals with his landlord. Anything to keep those god-awful smells from permeating every room in the house.

He yanked the list from the inside pocket of his suit coat and added spray-on fabric deodorizer to the bottom. Jean had recommended the stuff. If it didn't work as advertised, he was going to have to have every one of his suits, ties, and dress shirts dry-cleaned to get the odors out. As an afterthought, he added plug-in air freshener to the list.

Outside, what had begun as a gloomy day had turned into a nightmare of freezing rain and slick streets, making him doubly glad he'd left the office early. The grocery store had been crazy crowded with people stocking up for a snowstorm rumored to be on the horizon, and since Brent didn't know his way around the aisles yet, the shopping had taken a lot longer than expected. To save time, he nixed the roast he'd planned on making, going with chicken alfredo, garlic bread, and a side salad instead. He'd just finished making the alfredo sauce from scratch when the back door swung open, letting in a blast of frigid air, followed by his sawdust-covered landlord.

"Whoa!" Brent held a hand up to stop the man from shedding his coat inches away from the pot of simmering sauce. "What do you think you're doing?" He shooed Rick back the way he'd come. "Shake that off outside, you moron. You'll ruin our dinner."

Rick glanced at the stovetop then his eyes traveled to the table set for two then back to Brent. "What the fuck?"

"Relax, macho man. It's not a date. It's food. You need it. I need it. Now get out of here until you're not a walking pigpen. Strip down outside then come in and get cleaned up. By the time you finish your shower, the pasta will be ready."

"You expect me to strip outside? It's fucking freezing!"

"At least shake all that…wait. Is that sawdust or snow?"

"It's snow, you idiot. Haven't you heard? They said to expect up to eight inches tonight."

Brent's gaze involuntarily dropped to Rick's crotch. Eight inches? Yeah. He'd caught a glimpse of the man's flaccid cock when he'd drunkenly shed his jeans and briefs that night. Aroused, he'd be every bit of eight inches. Brent swallowed hard and forced his gaze up to his pissed-off landlord's face. "Eight inches?" He turned to stir the sauce. "If you say so."

In his peripheral vision, he saw the man shed his coat and run a hand through his hair. He stomped his boots on the mat. "I was talking about snow, but as for my dick, you'll have to take my word for it, because I wouldn't show it to you if you were the last person on the planet and fucking you would bring back the species."

An image of the unlikely scenario bloomed in his brain. A shiver raced down his spine and straight to his balls. His dick rose to attention. *Shit.* He couldn't let Rick see how his words affected him. He was Jake's brother, for crying out loud. Not to mention, he didn't want to be thrown out on his ass for sexually harassing his landlord—especially when he was at the mercy of said landlord to finish his new apartment. He gave the sauce another stir then because it allowed him to keep his back to his landlord, he crossed to the retro refrigerator for the butter and fresh herbs he planned to spread on the Italian baguette he'd picked up in the bakery department.

"Ditto, macho man." He didn't know what made him say it, but the words were out of his mouth before he could stop them. "You had your chance, but you were too shitfaced to follow through. Your loss."

The air stirred behind him as Rick clomped through the kitchen. Brent inhaled deeply, taking in the fresh scent of the outdoors, and the heady musk of sexy male the man left behind. His cock pressed insistently against the zipper of his jeans. Brent closed the fridge door then leaned his forehead against it. *I'm soooo fucked.*

~ ~ ~

Rick couldn't get out of the kitchen fast enough. Despite the threat of snow and ice, or maybe because of it, he'd put in extra hours on his current project and had anticipated coming home to an empty house as he'd done all week long. He thought he put in long hours, but Brent surpassed him, leaving early in the morning, and not returning until Rick was in bed. He'd hear the man in the kitchen, fixing himself something to eat before he, too, went to bed, but not once had the man actually *cooked* anything.

The cozy scene, complete with delicious smells wafting from pots on the stove, nearly knocked him on his ass. Then he'd caught sight of Brent, and he'd lost the ability to breathe. The man oozed sex appeal in his lawyer gear, but put the man in jeans, a Henley, and an apron, and fuck! Thank god, Brent had lit into him because he had been ten seconds or less from pushing the man up against the refrigerator and kissing the fuck out of him.

He cranked the shower all the way to hot, stripped down then stepped under the spray. The new heating system for the house he was working on wouldn't be installed until next week and the old one barely worked. He'd been fucking freezing his ass off all day long. Then he'd walked in, and his internal temperature had spiked, and his frozen dick had surged to life. Why couldn't the bastard have worked late tonight? Gotten snowed in at the office? Left him the fuck alone?

Rick lifted his face to the hot spray and willed his erection to go the fuck away. Like everyone else in his life, it refused to listen to reason. Brent wasn't his. Wasn't going to be his. Wasn't even his type. If he had a type.

He'd only had one serious relationship in his entire adult life, and he could count the number of sexual partners he'd had on one hand. The only one he'd known well enough to classify as a type had been Dave, and he qualified as the polar opposite of the man standing in Rick's kitchen looking like a fucking celebrity chef in his designer jeans and cashmere sweater.

It was like zero-fucking degrees outside, and the man was barefoot. Barefoot! Why he'd noticed the man's feet, and why their state of undress bothered him, he didn't want to examine. Just another fucking reason he had to get Brent out of his house sooner rather than later. Get him out before he drove him stark, fucking mad.

Willing his mind to focus on something else, Rick took a deep breath. His lungs filled with warm, moist air heavily laden with the scent of Brent's high-end body wash that smelled nothing like his plain-label discount store brand. His abdominal muscles clenched, and his balls drew up tight. Bracing one hand on the tiles he'd installed last summer, he grabbed his straining dick with his free hand and stroked. Once. Twice. He didn't even try to fight the fantasy brought on, apparently, by lack of oxygen to his brain, for there could be no other reason for imagining his roommate, bare-assed and bent over the kitchen table while Rick fucked him into next week.

He took his time dressing. The images his addled brain had conjured up in the shower had yet to fully dissipate. Christ, he had no business fantasizing about the man. Under no circumstances would he become sexually involved with Brent.

He didn't know for sure, but he assumed, since he'd seen him in a gay bar in Dallas, that his brother's new employee wasn't hiding his sexuality in the closet. If he was going to hook up with someone, they'd have to be as circumspect as he. Which meant, if he was going to have sex with anyone other than his own hand, he'd have to go out of town to do it. If an enclave of gay men existed in Willowbrook, he sure as hell hadn't heard about it. Even if he had, he wouldn't trust them to keep his secret. The gossip grapevine in this town worked better than the telephone system. Always had.

When he'd stalled as long as he thought he could without raising suspicion, he pulled on a pair of socks, because there was something about bare feet that suggested a certain level of intimacy, and made his way to the kitchen. Brent, his glasses slightly askew, spun around. He hastily righted the eyewear then wiped his palms on the front of his apron.

"There you are." His smile reminded Rick of the way the Afghani villagers smiled at his team when they walked through their towns, weapons at the ready and in full battle gear. Their smiles would be strained, cautious, as if they weren't sure if they should welcome the newcomers or not. "I was afraid I was going to have to mount a search party." Brent lifted a giant saucepan from the stove. "Much longer and the pasta would be paste." He dumped the creamy sauce over an enormous platter of noodles.

"Have a seat." He rinsed the saucepan in the sink. "I didn't know what kind of salad dressing you liked, so I got a couple of different kinds."

Rick eyed the row of bottles on the table. "You didn't have to do this." But, damn, the kitchen smelled amazing, and after eating nothing but frozen meals for weeks, the fresh salad greens were tempting. He picked up the bottle of creamy ranch dressing.

Brent hefted the platter of sauce and noodles into the center of the table. Before taking his seat at the opposite end of the small table, he removed the apron and hung it from one of the cabinet knobs. "It wasn't any trouble." He poured a vinaigrette over his own salad. "I would have done it sooner, but I needed to take off work early to go to the store. He tossed his head toward the door. "Good thing I made the effort today, or we'd be stuck here all weekend with nothing but a dwindling supply of frozen meals and a stale jar of peanut butter."

Rick glanced out the window over the sink as he munched on a bite of crisp greens. The snow was coming down hard, creating a veil of white outside. "I usually stock up on Saturday. Looks like that'll have to wait this week."

"I bought plenty of food. It should keep starvation from our door until they get the roads cleared or this stuff melts off."

Rick brought his focus to the meal in front of him. "I'll pay you for my share."

He'd never seen the napkin-lined basket Brent held out to him. "Garlic bread. Since we won't be getting physically close, I went heavy on the garlic." Rick selected a perfectly browned slice of bread topped with garlic, butter, and cheese then Brent set the basket in front of his plate. "Consider the groceries, and the meal, a thank-you gift. I can't tell you how much easier my life has been this week. The commute was killing me, and lord, how I hate living out of a suitcase."

Rick scooped a generous helping of pasta onto his plate and dug in. A symphony of flavors burst on his tongue. He hummed his appreciation before swallowing. Shit, the man could cook. Digging his fork in for another bite, Brent's words registered. He recalled the giant suitcases the man had brought with him. "What did you do with all your clothes?"

The closet in that bedroom was tiny. Clothes, shoes, toys, and sporting gear belonging to the three boys who grew up in the room had perpetually tumbled from the sorry excuse for storage. No way would the closet hold even half of Brent's wardrobe.

"Um." His roommate twirled cream-drenched noodles around his fork. "I was going to speak to you about that. Is there another closet I could use? And I could use another dresser, too, though I don't know where I would put it."

Rick had removed the bunk beds they'd slept in as kids and replaced them with a full-sized bedframe. That hadn't left room for anything more than a small dresser and mirror. He probably should have offered to switch rooms with him since everything he owned fit in a couple of drawers, leaving the large closet in his bedroom nearly empty, but this was his house and he hadn't asked for a roommate. Still.

He sighed and dropped his fork. Fuck. The man had cooked for him, and he hadn't uttered a single complaint since he'd moved in. He wasn't even complaining about the lack of storage in his room, he was just pointing it out. Politely.

Rick took a sip of the wine Brent had insisted he try. He preferred beer, but the crisp white tasted pretty damn good. He took another sip then placed his glass on the table, spinning the stem between his thumb and forefinger. The glass itself was a new addition since Rick had never bothered to purchase any, and if his parents had ever owned any, they had long since been broken or perhaps donated to the church rummage sale after their mother's passing.

He cleared his throat. "The closet in my bedroom is a lot bigger, and it's almost empty. You can hang some of your stuff in there if you want. You can store your suitcases in the garage. Since Will moved out, there are a few empty shelves along the back wall."

Brent set his fork on the edge of his plate and reached for his wineglass. "I don't want to inconvenience you. I can make do. I was thinking of getting one of those rolling clothes racks. I could hang my shirts on it and save the sturdier rod in the closet for the heavier suits." He sipped his wine. "I appreciate the offer though." He eyed Rick over the rim of his glass. "This can't be easy for you."

Rich shrugged. "I grew up in this house." Remembering what it was like, he snickered. "I shared the room you're in with two older brothers. I never knew what peace and quiet was until I'd been in the Marines a couple of years and moved off base. Deployment was a lot like three teenagers sharing a tiny room, only we had guns, so we tried to stay in our space and not piss off our roommates." He shoved a forkful of pasta in his mouth and chewed, washing it down with more wine. "You're quieter than Will, and you can cook. My brother *thinks* he can cook, but trust me, he can't, so if you want the closet space, it's yours."

Brent topped off Rick's wineglass. "How about this? I'll accept the closet space, and in return, I'll cook dinner during the week. We can save our eating out for the weekends."

Rick envisioned the crappy frozen dinner he'd be eating tonight if Brent hadn't shared the meal he'd cooked. He didn't relish the idea of the man parading through his room to get to the closet, but damn, he'd be a moron to pass up homecooked meals while the guy was here. He nodded. "Okay, but I'll pay my half of the grocery bill and do the dishes. If something comes up and you can't cook, just let me know and I'll nuke a TV dinner or pick up something at the diner."

Terms agreed upon, they ate in silence. When he was done, Brent took his plate to the sink. "You're sure you're okay doing the dishes?"

Rick eyed the mess and nodded. He'd cleaned up worse. "I'm good." He waved his fork at the remains on the table. "Thanks again."

Brent nodded then pushed away from the counter. "I'm going to sort some clothes. I'll put the things I don't wear as often in your closet. That way I won't be going in and out of your room as often."

Rick finished off the noodles on his plate. "Yeah. That sounds like a good idea."

"I'll leave you to it, then."

Rick remained in his seat after Brent left, willing his dick to behave. Sharing a meal with Brent was pure torture. The man's appreciative sounds when he'd tasted his food were enough to drive a man to drink. Watching his tongue sweep over his lips to capture every stray bit of creamy sauce had Rick so hard, it was a wonder he'd been able to carry on even a half-coherent conversation. Which probably accounted for him offering closet space to the man.

What the hell had he been thinking? The trouble was, he knew exactly what he'd been thinking, and it involved his dick, a different creamy substance on Brent's lips, and that tongue. God almighty, that tongue, licking, teasing, making him see stars. He'd imagined Brent on his knees, wearing his lawyer gear, his glasses magnifying pleading eyes as Rick fucked his mouth.

The sound of a door closing down the hall forced Rick from his X-rated musings. Swiping a sweaty hand over his face, he blew out a frustrated breath. Gathering the bottles of salad dressing, he took them to the refrigerator then stood, letting the chilled air cool his heated skin. This was all Jake's fault. His big brother would pay for putting him through this torture.

CHAPTER TWELVE

Brent collapsed on the bed, face-first, one hand gripping his throbbing erection while he bit down on the other to stifle the frustrated moans burning his throat.

Living in the same house with Rick Ingram was the worst decision he'd ever made in his life. Worse than taking Cynthia Prendergast to the prom and fighting off her wandering hands all night long. Worse than hooking up with that football player his first semester at the University of Texas. Worse than trading a blow job for a well-written paper on *Pride and Prejudice*, even if it did mean the difference between passing or failing Classic Lit. He'd only taken the class because the sexy nerd he was crushing on at the time, ultimately the recipient of the blow job, convinced him he would love the class. Deciding to live with Rick Ingram even topped screwing the proctor of his LSAT session. Granted, he hadn't known the guy would proctor his exam at the time. They'd met at an Austin bar, fucked in the bathroom then, mutually satisfied, parted ways. Brent had been shocked when he'd arrived at the test site the next day and found the guy sitting at the proctor's desk. The tests were all online these days, so there couldn't have been even a hint of fuck-to-pass going on, but still. It wasn't something he wanted anyone to know. Just in case.

He had no one to blame but himself—and maybe Jake Ingram—for his current predicament. Maybe he'd let Jake off the hook. His boss couldn't have predicted Brent would do something so stupid. He'd offered to cook for a man who made him hard just by breathing. And, he'd traded that torture for what was sure to be even more torture.

Walking past Rick's bed. Imagining rumpled sheets that smelled like Rick made his dick even harder. There was no hope for it, he was going to have to ease his own suffering like he'd done every night since he'd moved in, and most mornings, too. He'd spilled more spunk over Rick Ingram in one week than on any man he'd ever been with, including Kenneth. He didn't care to examine what that said about his former relationships. Instead, he rose to his knees and whipped off his shirt. After spreading it on the comforter, he unbuttoned the fly on his jeans and shoved them and his boxers down to mid-thigh. Bracing himself on one outstretched arm, he took his aching cock in hand and, closing his eyes, imagined the shirt beneath him was a certain former Marine. In a matter of minutes, he came, shooting ribbons of hot cum onto his phantom lover.

~ ~ ~

The unnatural silence woke Rick early. He lay in bed for a few minutes listening for the usual sounds that heralded the coming of a new day. Nothing. Not a bird chirping. No cars driving by. Even the house had settled in, refusing to creak its old bones.

He threw the covers off and swung his feet to the floor. "Fuck!"

He really needed to buy a rug for his room. The original hardwood floors in these old pier and beam houses were trendy but cold as fuck in the winter. Grabbing the socks and sweatpants he'd tossed to the end of the bed when he'd crawled beneath the covers the previous night, he hurriedly dressed then eased the door open. He crossed the hall to the shared bathroom, did his business then ambled to the kitchen.

The scene out the living room window stopped him cold. Cold being the operative word. Blinking, he approached the scene with caution. Beyond the plate-glass window, a heavy blanket of snow covered everything like frosting on a fancy cake. A layer of gray clouds filtered the rising sun, adding shadows to the already surreal landscape. *I wonder if Will is seeing this.* His artist brother wasn't a morning person, but for this, he needed to make an exception. Rick extracted his phone from the pocket of his sweatpants, clicked a couple of photos, and sent them in a text message to Will.

"It's beautiful, isn't it?"

The words, spoken softly over his right shoulder, startled him. Rick spun, his fists at the ready. His bare-chested roommate, hands up in surrender, backpedaled.

"Whoa. It's just me, Marine. I heard you moving around. Thought I'd come see what the day has in store for us." He waved at the scene beyond the window. "Didn't expect anything like that."

Rick blew out a breath as his gaze took in the man's disheveled state. His usually impeccably groomed hair looked sinfully mussed. The shadow of a beard, several shades darker than his hair, shadowed his jaw. Rick curled his hands into fists as the need to reach out and touch washed over him. He forced his gaze lower. *Shit.* For a lawyer, Brent was fit as fuck. Defined. That was the word. Every muscle from his shoulders to the carved V disappearing beneath his low-slung pajama pants was delineated to perfection. God. Fucking. Damn.

He faced the winter wonderland, silently cursing Mother Nature's wicked sense of humor. The city of Willowbrook didn't own snow removal equipment. Never had. So, until the sun came out and melted all that fucking snow, he was housebound with a man he wanted more than he wanted his next breath. He'd normally thank the universe for such a problem, but since the man in question was off-limits, he was fucking screwed.

"Well, I didn't hear you. Make some fucking noise in the future." He hoped the emotion in his voice conveyed anger rather than arousal, but he couldn't be sure.

Brent stepped up so they stood facing the window, bare shoulder to bare shoulder. Rick took a slow, deep breath, willing his libido to stand down. His gaze glazed over as Brent's clean scent wafted on the warm air rising from the floor register near their feet.

"How long before they plow the road?"

Rick huffed out a laugh. "The only plows around here are for dirt, city boy."

"Wait. What? You mean no one is going to clear the streets today?"

Rick groaned and rubbed both palms over his face. He needed coffee. Lots of it. He stumbled into the kitchen. "That's what I'm sayin'. Unless you want to walk in that, you're stuck here for a while."

Brent followed him into the kitchen. "How long?" He retrieved a container of cream from the refrigerator while Rick popped a single-serve pod into the coffee maker then slid his favorite mug beneath the spout.

Rick leaned against the counter as the life-giving brew dripped into his mug. "Why? You got someplace to go?"

"No. I was just wondering."

Fuck. He'd hoped Brent had something important to do today. Something that would take him out of the house and keep him out. "Well, to answer your question—how long depends on the weather. I've never seen this much snow before, but if the sun comes out, the roads should be passable tomorrow. If this cloud cover hangs around and the temperature doesn't get above freezing, then the snow isn't going anywhere. There's already a layer of ice beneath all the white stuff. If the snow starts to melt and the temperature drops again, the layer of ice will only get worse."

His roomy rested one hip against the counter, crossed his muscular arms over his chest, his gaze fixed on the brown liquid filling Rick's mug. "They'll treat the ice, right?"

"Eventually. They'll salt and sand the intersections and the main roads." He cocked his head toward the front of the house. "We're not on a main road."

When the coffee maker spit out its last drop, Rick took his mug to the table and sat to savor the first few sips. Brent replaced the spent coffee pod with a new one then slid a fresh mug under the spout. "I guess this means you won't be going to the job site today."

Rick shook his head. "I should, but I'm not." He had no doubt his pickup could handle the snow. It was the layer of ice beneath that made driving tricky. He'd seen it too many times growing up. People didn't see the fluffy white stuff as a threat. They'd get out on the roads and end up in a ditch somewhere because of the hidden ice. He'd just have to work longer hours to make up for the lost time. He took a sip of his coffee. "Don't worry. I'm on track to start work on your apartment week after next, as planned."

Brent added cream to his coffee before joining Rick at the table. "I'm not worried about the apartment. If you need to put it off to take care of your other customers, that's okay with me."

The man's offer brought Rick up short. He locked gazes with his roommate. "I thought you were in a hurry to have your own place."

"I was. I mean, I am." Brent raised his mug to his lips but didn't drink. "I like it here. This kitchen is a dream, and I fell in love with the house before I knew it was yours. It's exactly the kind of place I was hoping to find, but I quickly learned the error of my ways. So"—he sipped his coffee—"the apartment over the gallery will have to do."

Rick dropped his gaze to his almost-empty mug. *Fuck.* He needed something stronger than coffee, but the last thing he needed was alcohol clouding his judgement while he was stuck in the same house with Brent. He still couldn't recall everything that happened after Dave dumped him on the evening of Jake's wedding. Snatches of memory had come back to him, some more clear than others. However, the one he recalled with the most clarity was the one he most wanted to forget. Thank god, he'd been too soused to follow through on his desire, or he would have fucked his brother's new employee up against the hotel room wall then drilled him into the mattress for good measure.

Yeah, the sooner he got Brent out of his house, the better. "I'll get the apartment done for you as soon as possible."

The man nodded then pushed up from the table. "How about pancakes? I've been dying to make them ever since I saw you had a gas range." Without waiting for Rick's reply, he pulled supplies from the cupboards. "They're almost impossible to do on an electric range. Too much temperature variation."

He rambled on, but Rick couldn't hear for the blood rushing past his ears on its way south. He'd never seen a man in pajama pants before. The four males growing up in his household had slept in briefs, and the Marines sure as hell didn't issue sleepwear. Stateside, Dave had slept nude, and Rick had developed the same habit. Made things easier, he figured. He'd pulled on the sweats this morning to keep his dick from shriveling in the cold. He should have known better. Anytime Brent was around, Rick's blood ran hot, and his dick was anything but shriveled.

Damn, cotton plaid should not look sexy, but it fucking did on Brent. Rick couldn't drag his gaze away from the man's ass shifting beneath the thin material or the way the elastic waistband sat low on his hips, revealing two perfect dimples.

Fuck pancakes. Rick desperately wanted to taste those indentations—and more. Stifling a groan, he stood. "I'm going to get dressed." *Right after I strangle the snake.*

"Take your time," Brent singsonged, oblivious, apparently, to Rick's distress.

As soon as Rick's ass disappeared from view, Brent collapsed. Elbows braced on the kitchen counter, he cradled his head in his upturned hands. "Fuck. Fuck. Fuck." He whispered the words to the granite countertop. Two whole days, maybe more, stuck in the house with Rick Ingram. "Just kill me now."

Forcing himself upright, he gripped his raging hard-on through the soft flannel of the pajama pants he'd put on for the sake of decency before joining Rick to survey the snowy landscape. He'd like to pass his erection off as morning wood, but lying to himself wasn't going to help his situation. He'd gone from morning wood to painful steel the second he'd seen Rick standing in the living room, wearing those god-awful white socks, well-worn Marine Corps sweats, and nothing else. It was enough to make a grown man weep with gratitude for being alive. And curse the day he was born.

"Repeat after me. I will not fuck with Rick Ingram." He huffed out a breath then grabbed the wire whisk and took out his frustration on the pancake batter. "I like my job. I like my boss. I like Willowbrook. I will *not* fuck this up." His hand cramped from the strangle hold he had on the whisk. Easing his grip, he tapped the tool on the edge of the bowl to release the batter from the tines. He might have overdone it with the mixing, but he couldn't find it within himself to give a fuck.

Earlier in the week, he'd found a cast-iron griddle in one of the cabinets. He dug it out and placed it on the stovetop. While he waited for it to heat, he opened the new syrup bottle he'd purchased and unwrapped a stick of real butter. None of that fake stuff. Maybe the flavor would make up for overmixing the batter. He turned the first pancake too early then left it too long on the flipside, so it ended up looking like an ink blob. The second one was better, and by the third, he had the timing down and had established a rhythm. Pour. Flip. Scoop. Pour again. He was in the process of pouring batter on the hot griddle when Rick came back in wearing a long-sleeved T-shirt that might have been spray-painted on, faded jeans worn paper thin in all the right places, and paint-splattered work boots. Proving once and for all, it didn't matter what the man did or did not wear, he was sexy as fuck. He hadn't bothered to shave, the thick, dark stubble coupled with his still sleep-tussled hair added a whole new level to his macho-man appearance.

"Whoa." He signaled to the sizzling pan. "Better watch what you're doing."

"Huh?"

"The griddle?"

Yeah. The griddle. Brent snapped his gaze to the iron square. "Shit!" A giant blob of pancake batter oozed toward the edge on all sides. He righted the ladle, but it was too late. If he managed to salvage it, he'd have a pancake the size of a hubcap on a 1950 Cadillac.

Rick chuckled as he reached past Brent to get a plate from an upper cabinet. Using his fingers, he helped himself from the stack warming on the stove. "These look fantastic. Thanks."

Brent kept his back to the man. Rick's chuckle when he'd seen the mess Brent had made suggested he knew he'd caused the mishap to occur. Damn sex bomb. There should be a law against looking as good in clothes as out. Brent concentrated on the mess he'd created and did his best to tune out the sounds of gastronomic pleasure coming from the kitchen table. Bubbles popped in the center of the massive flapjack, and the edges were firming. He'd need to flip it or dump it soon. Dumping it meant admitting, unequivocally, that he'd made a mistake. No way was he acknowledging how much Rick affected him. So, flipping it was.

He dug in the drawer where he'd found the spatula he was using, hoping to find another but came up empty-handed. He could try to toss the cake in the air like he'd seen professional chefs do, but lifting the cast-iron griddle by itself was difficult. Doing it weighted down with a giant glob of batter would be impossible.

"Need help with that?" Rick stood beside him, his gaze fixed on the raw hubcap.

"I need to turn it but can't figure out how," he admitted.

"I've got an idea." His roomy took a plate from the cabinet then returned to stand beside him. "You lift the edge. I'll slip the plate underneath and lift it off the griddle. Then all we have to do is flip it over, and *voila*! Problem solved."

It sounded like it would work. Brent nodded. "Okay. Let's give it a try."

He slid the spatula beneath the front edge and carefully lifted it away from the griddle. He stepped back as far as he could to allow Rick room to edge in and slide the plate underneath the half-baked mess. He got about halfway when the whole thing began to slide. Instead of stopping, he made a last-ditch effort to scoop the mass onto the plate. And it worked.

"Ta-da!" He held the plate aloft, his grin one Brent was sure his brothers had seen many times growing up, one that said *I told you I could do it*. "Now, to flip it onto the griddle."

Immediately realizing Rick's error, Brent cried out, "No!" But it was too late, the plate was already moving, flipping like a flying saucer doing tricks for an alien airshow. The gooey hubcap fell, landing with a sickening splat on the griddle. Raw batter splashed out in every direction, coating everything in its path with sticky goo.

Plate still in hand, Rick's gaze met Brent's then his eyes dropped lower. Brent followed his gaze to the streaks of batter slowly dripping down his bare torso. If a person didn't know it was pancake batter, he might think it was something else. Brent groaned. He lifted his gaze to Rick's. What he saw in the other man's eyes froze the breath in his lungs. Heat. Hot enough to fry brain cells. "Rick." His voice sounded scorched, like he'd downed a bottle of pepper sauce with a vinegar chaser. On the stovetop, batter sizzled, and steam escaped in hiccups from the remains of the hubcap.

Slowly, Rick bent. His tongue darted out, capturing a long, thin line of batter before it slid beneath the waistband of his pajama pants. Brent gasped. A shiver ran down his spine and gooseflesh pebbled his arms where he held them rigid at his sides.

"Mmm." Another tongue swipe. "Tastes good."

"Rick."

Another lick. "Hmm?"

"We…can't." A hand shot to his waist, holding him steady. Another tongue lashing, this one over his right nipple. His eyes rolled back in his head as he fought the urge to wrap his arms around Rick's head and hold him there. Force him to suck his nipple. Beg him to do that and so much more. "We…shouldn't."

Rick straightened, breaking all bodily contact. Brent closed his eyes and bit his lower lip, holding in a plea he had no business uttering. *Good. I got through to him.* He let out a pent-up breath. Recalling his earlier determination to keep his employers' baby brother at arm's length, he mentally congratulated himself on putting a stop to certain disaster. But it had been a close call. One more lick. One more touch, and he wasn't so sure he could or would have said anything.

Click.

Brent popped his eyes open. His gaze flew to the burner control knob, now in the Off position, to the man standing between him and the stove. Okay, he mentally nodded. Safety first. Turning the burner off was a good move. Then both Rick's hands were on his waist, hauling him forward until he collided with a solid wall of muscle. Holy fuckarama. It was like Rick's body was a giant electromagnet and Brent had become steel. He was trapped, immobilized by an attraction as strong as it was invisible.

"Look at me."

CHAPTER THIRTEEN

They were nearly the same height, but the thick soles of his work boots gave him a slight advantage over Brent's bare feet. How he'd ever thought clothes made of ordinary cloth would be sufficient armor against Brent's allure was beyond comprehension. From the moment he'd met him at Jake's wedding, desire for the man had been festering inside him like a fatal disease on the march. He'd kept it at bay with thoughts of Dave. Of being with Dave. But with that barrier shattered, the only thing standing between Rick and his lust was his brother, and he'd be damned if Jake controlled his sex life. As long as Brent was consenting, there wasn't any reason they couldn't fuck themselves into a coma if they wanted. No one outside these walls had to know.

"Look at me," he repeated.

Slowly, Brent lifted his chin. Their gazes locked. "This is insane." The words were nothing more than a whisper.

"Fuck, yeah, it's insane. But I'm tired of fighting it. I want you, and you want me."

Brent remained silent. His eyelids dropped, breaking their connection. His hands fisted at his sides.

"Tell me I'm wrong. Say you don't want me, and I won't touch you again." His patience and his control were slipping. He framed Brent's face with his hands, brushed the man's tight lips with his own. "Maybe you need to hear what I'm going to do to you." Brent's whimper was the cue to proceed Rick needed.

Bending his head, he whispered in his ear. "I'm going to force you to your knees and shove my cock down your throat until your eyes water and you beg me to shove it up your ass. Then I'm going to lay you out on my bed, face-first, and ream your ass so hard, you won't be able to sit for a week." He licked the shell of his ear. Brent shivered but made no effort to move. "Then I'm going to flip you over so I can see your face when I fill you with my cum."

Rick nipped at his earlobe. "And, if you're good and don't come before I tell you, you know what I'll do?"

"What?" If his ear hadn't been an inch from the man's lips, he wouldn't have caught the softly spoken word. But he *had* heard him.

Rick was ready to explode. He'd sped right past the friendly roommates' signpost long ago and had arrived at the final exit on the road to insanity marked, dirty, filthy fuckbuddy. "I'll tell you what," he growled. Speaking low, directly into the man's ear, Rick spelled it out for him. "I'll take your dick in my hot, wet mouth and suck you like a fucking industrial Hoover until you come so hard, they'll see it from the International Space Station and think there's a new geyser on the planet."

He paused to let the man get his breathing under control. "Nod if you want me to do all those things to you or step away now, while I still have the ability to let you go."

Rick had waited hours, sometimes days, for the enemy to make a move, to give away their position, but none of that waiting compared to the excruciatingly long seconds it took for Brent to make up his mind. When the man slowly sank to his knees, it took Rick's brain a moment to catch up. His own words echoed in the space formerly occupied by his brain. *I'm going to force you to your knees and shove my cock down your throat until your eyes water and you beg me to shove it up your ass.*

Grabbing a fistful of the man's hair, Rick dragged his head back. A gasp escaped Brent's parted lips. God, those lips. A fresh supply of blood rushed to Rick's cock in anticipation of fucking that mouth. Orbs as green as spring leaves, clear behind nerdy glasses, peered up at him. Like any enemy combatant facing the reality of failure, Brent's eyes held contempt, for himself, for the overwhelming force—in this case, desire—he couldn't defeat. Deeper still, lay relief. Relief that the battle was over. Won or lost, it didn't matter. War exhausted a man, physically and mentally. Like Rick, Brent had been at war with his desires, his needs. Rick had surrendered to his desires and forced the final battle between them. To the victor goes the spoils. "You agree to my terms of surrender?"

Brent trembled with his answer. "Yes. God damn you, yes."

With his one hand still fisted in Brent's hair, Rick worked his belt loose with the other. In the snow-cloaked silence, the jingle of his belt buckle sounded as loud as mortar rounds. Sucking in his stomach, Rick slid his zipper down. Keeping his gaze locked with Brent's, Rick reached in, dragged his balls and engorged dick through the opening.

"Hands behind your back," he commanded.

With a growl, Brent complied.

Rick fisted his other hand in the man's hair then forced his face down. "Open your mouth."

Brent opened for him.

Rick flexed and shimmied, teasing those perfect lips with the head of his cock. He'd been leaking precum since his first taste of the man's batter-splattered skin. He loved the way his secretions looked slicked over Brent's lips. A mark of possession. When he couldn't stand it any longer, he shoved his cock past Brent's lips until the man gagged on the head of his cock and his balls tapped his chin. Gripping Brent's head tight between his palms, Rick commanded, "Suck me like your life depends on it."

~ ~ ~

Every survival instinct he had urged Brent to fight back. To unclasp his hands and shove the man away. To scramble to his feet and run fast and hard as far away from Rick Ingram as he could get. But he didn't. His eyes watered and his nose ran as he gagged on the man's enormous cock. Another instinct had his lips closing over the wide girth. He forced air in through his nostrils then swallowed. The move earned a curse from his tormentor who pulled his cock almost all the way out then shoved it deep again. And again. And again. Tears ran from Brent's eyes, and he fought for every breath. Spit leaked from his abused lips and coated the steel shaft relentlessly fucking his mouth.

Rick's hands clamped his head like a vise as he grunted and cursed and brutalized his mouth. A hate fuck. Brent hated it almost as much as he loved it. He *hated* that he loved it. Hated that he *wanted* it. Hated that he *needed* it. Hated that Rick knew all those things about him. Yet, Brent loved that Rick felt all those things as well. He loved that Rick had caved to their mutual desire first. The big, bad Marine broke.

Or maybe he was just broken.

A hole opened in Brent's heart at the thought of Rick alone and suffering the way he had been, following his brother's wedding. The man had grown adept at hiding his true self, but that night, and right now, he dropped the walls he'd built and allowed Brent to see him. No doubt, he'd extract another vow of silence when he came to his senses, and Brent would reluctantly grant it. Owning your sexuality was something every person had to come to on their own time in their own way. He'd been lucky. His family loved and accepted him, no matter what. It wasn't that way for everyone, and for whatever reason, Rick didn't want to tell his brothers. Brent had to respect the man's decision.

"Fuck, that feels good, Counselor, but I want more." Rick slid his hands into Brent's hair then tugged his head back. "Stand the fuck up."

Brent braced a hand on the seat of a nearby chair and leveraged himself to his feet. His jaw ached like a son of a bitch. He wiped drool from his chin with the flat of his hand then lifted his gaze to Rick's. The man's eyes were that of a wild animal trained on its next meal.

I'm his next meal.

The thought made every hair on Brent's body stand on end. He could run. Could tell him no and walk away, but Rick would hunt him down. Wear him down until he offered him his throat. The man standing before him, cannon of a cock in hand, wasn't the kind to back down once he'd decided something was his.

I want to be his.

His breath caught in his abused throat. He'd given himself to a lot of men but never in the way this one demanded with just a look. Rick's gaze commanded complete surrender. "Everything," it said.

Others had wanted his body. Wanted his ass. His cock. His mouth. None, not even Kenn, had wanted his heart, his soul. Did Rick know what he wordlessly asked? And would he give half as much in return? Or was this a one-way street?

The man blinked. Brent gasped as he glimpsed something hidden deep within. A pain buried beneath layers of hurt where it silently bled. A pain Rick lived with day in and day out.

Everything. It all made sense now. Rick had given everything and gotten nothing in return, so now he demanded it all up front in exchange for the only part of himself he was willing to give—his body.

The realization was akin to someone driving an invisible knife into his heart. He'd found someone who wanted everything from him, but in an ironic twist of fate, Rick had nothing to give him but a moment's pleasure. A chuckle rose to his throat, a hoarse rumble part tears, part self-deprecating humor. He'd come to Willowbrook looking for everything and had found it in a man who had already given it away.

"Turn around. Shove your pants down and bend over the table."

You want everything? You've got it. Had it since you shoved me up against that hotel room wall.

With nothing left to lose, Brent did as the man said.

CHAPTER FOURTEEN

The old Formica tabletop was as cold as ice beneath Brent's bare chest. Pressing his cheek to the table, he fisted his hands on either side of his head. Behind him, Rick sheathed his cock in preparation for taking what he wanted. Brent had steeled himself to be taken hard, without mercy, so when Rick leaned over him and dragged the butter dish into his line of sight, his heart nearly beat out of his chest.

"Grease yourself up or I'll take you raw. Makes no difference to me."

Thump. Thump. Thump. Brent reached out and curled his fingers into the stick. He'd set the butter out before he'd mixed the pancake batter. It was still cold as fuck but began to soften immediately as he touched it to blazing skin.

"Work it in good."

Thump. Thump. Thump. Brent reached for more. Once he'd coated the outside the best he could, he pushed one butter-coated finger past the initial barrier then withdrew.

"That's enough."

Brent returned his hand to the table and clenched it into a tight fist. At the same moment, Rick scooped up the butter remaining in the dish. *Dear god.* He'd never look at a pat of butter again without hearing the squishing, squashing sounds of the soft condiment being spread over latex sheathing. Never. In. His. Life. The sounds were erotic as hell in a disgustingly fascinating way. His heartbeat sped well past any measure of good health straight into heart-attack zone. Clearly, this man had experience in using whatever lubricant was handy. *What would he have used if the butter hadn't been on the table?*

Rick gripped his ass cheeks and spread him wide. When he notched the head of his cock at Brent's greased hole then slowly pressed forward, all thoughts, save one, left his mind. *I want everything, but I'll take anything.*

Oblivious to the butter on his hand, Brent pressed his forehead against the table, buried both hands in his hair, and tugged his scalp as hard as he could to distract himself from the overwhelming, the *insistent*, pressure against his asshole. Rick advanced like the Marine he was, breaching Brent's tight barrier like a battering ram. Once inside, he paused.

His voice as ragged as Brent's breathing, he whispered, "Fuck, you're tight."

Then he pushed forward in an uninterrupted march that expelled the breath from Brent's lungs and left him weak and limp. A prisoner of a war where he had no weapons. A war he didn't know how to fight.

His head swam from lack of oxygen, causing his involuntary muscles to awaken. He sucked in a breath then let it out on a groan. He was in quicksand and sinking fast. Grasping for purchase, he stretched his arms out and curled his fingers over the opposite edge of the table. His dick, harder than cast iron, hung against the front edge, throbbing with every heartbeat, aching for relief. His asshole was a ring of fire, made worse by the salt in the butter. Why the fuck hadn't he thought about that before? But god, he'd do it all over again to experience the feel, the fullness, the absolute rightness of Rick Ingram buried up inside him.

Two giant, work-worn hands splatted on the table next to his face as Rick curved his rock-hard body over Brent's boneless form.

"That's right, Counselor. Hold on tight because I'm going to ride you so hard, you won't be able to walk." To emphasize his point, he withdrew almost all the way then tunneled back in. The table shook. Brent trembled. "When I'm through with you, I'm going to flip you over and suck you dry."

Then Rick made good on his promise, riding him hard. His balls slapping against Brent's, his carved hip bones digging into Brent's ass, his turgid shaft owning, claiming, with every forward thrust. Nothing had ever felt as good or hurt as bad. He loved that he could give Rick what he needed, but it hurt knowing the man had only this to give. All the while, tears rolled down Brent's cheeks as he told himself the biggest lie ever. *If this is all I ever have, it will be enough.*

His pajama pants had worked their way down to his ankles at some point. Rick's big hand slid the length of Brent's thigh then gripping him hard, lifted his knee to the table, opening him wider. The shift in position allowed Rick to go deeper. Every thrust came harder and deeper until Brent was sure it was Rick's cock shoving his heart into his throat. On the deepest, hardest thrust yet, Rick stopped and let his full weight rest on Brent's back. He nuzzled his ear, his hot breath causing Brent to break out in goose bumps all over. "You like that, Counselor? You like having my pole up your ass?"

"Yes. God, yes." The words came out on a whimper.

"You're so fucking hot and tight. I can feel your balls next to mine. You need to come, don't you?"

"Yes. Please."

"No." He nipped the shell of Brent's ear. "Do. Not. Fucking. Come. Not even when you feel me coming. Do you hear me?"

"Yes."

"If you disobey me, I'll *never* fuck you again. Never." He withdrew partway then barreled back in so hard, his balls slammed Brent's package up against the edge of the table. He cried out but refused to beg for mercy. "Is that what you want?"

"No." *God, no.*

"Good, because I want this ass every day." The words, spoken low and directly into his ear lit him up like a bolt of lightning, sparking every nerve ending in his body. Exhilaration coupled with fear made him tremble. Then Rick pushed himself upright. "I love seeing you this way." A big hand stroked along his spine. Brent groaned. "That's it. Purr for me. It feels so good on my cock." Brent groaned then rocked his hips up against Rick's crotch, silently begging him to move. Much more dirty talk, and he wouldn't be able to stop the orgasm building like a forest fire in his lower back.

Rick stroked Brent from shoulder to ass cheeks, pausing to finger his stretched hole. "Clench for me, baby."

He'd lost all control of his muscles long ago, so it took a few moments to focus on the ones in question and will them to obey Rick's command. A guttural curse, followed by, "Again," was as electrifying as sticking his dick in a light socket. Rick might be calling the shots, but Brent wasn't as helpless as he'd thought. He bore down on Rick's cock, squeezing it as tight as he could. The effort earned a whack to his right butt cheek and a strangled, "Fuck, that's good." So he clenched and released. Over and over. Other than to deliver sharp slaps to Brent's ass, Rick remained perfectly still while Brent massaged his cock. Rick might believe he had nothing left to give, but this one concession wrapped itself around Brent's heart and gave him hope where there had been none before.

"Enough!" Rick withdrew then rammed back in so, hard Brent saw stars. "You're a goddamn tease." The next thrust slapped Brent's dick against the edge of the table. Pain sliced through him, causing his legs to go numb and his knees to buckle. A silent cry fell from his open lips. The thrusts came faster and harder until blinding pain morphed into a need that cut him to the core. He was going to come. No way could he stop it. Then Rick fell atop him, hissed in his ear. "Don't do it. Don't you fuckin' come until you're in my mouth."

Rick leveraged himself up with a hand to the center of Brent's spine. A primal grunt rent the air. The cock impaling him thickened then throbbed inside him. Rick rocked into him, helpless in the face of his release. Brent had never experienced anything as intense as this. He was so fucking hard and on edge himself, but his own pleasure would be nothing in comparison to being on the receiving end of Rick's orgasm. He was going to be sore, but fuck, a little discomfort was a small price to pay for the privilege of experiencing Rick's total surrender to his own pleasure. The man who had let him go, and Brent was certain there was one, was an idiot.

Time seemed to stand still. Brent dragged in a shuddering breath and fought the tears threatening to spill over. The pressure eased as Rick lifted his restraining hand. Brent was trying to muster the energy to move when the two big paws returned, only this time, Rick stroked his back like he had before. Brent sighed and relaxed under the sensual touch. It was one thing to be this exposed in the throes of passion, but, in the aftermath, his skin might as well have been made of glass, brittle and transparent. He was certain Rick could see every emotion written on the walls of his wildly beating heart. A heart he could shatter so easily.

When he spoke, Rick's voice was as thick as the syrup in the container, now teetering on the edge of the table. "I love seeing my dick buried up inside your tight ass."

A hot finger rimmed his stretched hole. Brent squeezed his eyes shut to block the image his words evoked and willed his body not to respond to the intimate touch. He failed on both fronts.

"You like that?" The finger returned, traced the thinned line of sensitive muscle. Brent groaned, clenching his inner muscles around Rick's length. "Keep that up and I'll have another go at you."

Holy moly. "Is that a threat or a promise?" he croaked out.

"What do you want it to be?"

Brent licked his lips and swallowed hard. The answer came out on a whisper. "A promise."

Rick spread his cheeks wide. Brent groaned at the man's obvious perusal of his ass. "I wish I could see what you see."

"It's pretty spectacular," Rick admitted. He held Brent open with one hand while the other returned to a spot between his shoulder blades and pressed him hard against the Formica tabletop.

The man had just erupted like a volcano, yet he remained impossibly hard. Brent had no doubt he could go again, but he wasn't sure his ass was up for it. Rick was bigger than anyone he'd had before. Stronger, too. The way Rick overpowered him took his breath away—in a good way. "Now you're fishing for compliments."

"I was referring to your ass. I could stay here all day. But if I'm going to keep my promise to you and have another go at it, I'm going to have to give it a rest."

Brent's heart rose to his throat at the thought of Rick taking him again.

"I like seeing you this way. Taken. I like seeing my handprints on your skin." Using both hands, he squished Brent's cheeks together then slowly withdrew his cock, leaving Brent aching and emptier than he'd ever been in his life.

Rick covered Brent's hand with his. "Come on. Let me help you up." Brent took his hand and stood, turning so they were eye to eye. "Can you sit?" He indicated one of the kitchen chairs. "Or would you like the bed?"

Still in a brain fog from the thorough fucking coupled with an erection that might need medical attention, Brent replied, "Huh?"

Rick smiled then raised a hand to Brent's face. He tenderly stroked his jaw. Ran a thumb over his dry bottom lip. "I'm going to suck you dry. Remember?"

Later, Brent would wonder if that was the moment he fell in love with Rick Ingram or if it was later when he dropped to his knees between Brent's trembling thighs and made good on his promise.

Brent considered the state of his ass and the choices before him. "Bed," he whispered.

Rick reclaimed his hand and led him to his childhood bedroom, commanded him to sit on the edge of the bed then sank to his knees between Brent's trembling thighs. Rick wrapped one work-worn hand around the base of Brent's dick then bowed over the engorged head. His mouth was Heaven *and* Hell. Blazing hot yet soft and wet. Then he sucked Brent to the back of his throat, and he glimpsed the Pearly Gates.

"I...I can't..." He cradled Rick's head between his hands like a vise. His balls were the devil's hot coals as they drew up so far, they singed his vocal cords. He came on a ragged cry, hot cum searing his cock from the inside out as he spewed buckets of cum down Rick's throat.

Spent and fighting for breath, he released his hold on Rick's head and flopped back on the mattress. Rick licked and swallowed until Brent pleaded with him to stop. Between his ass and his cock, he didn't know which one was more tender. He'd be lucky if his balls descended anytime soon.

Rick hauled Brent fully onto the bed then flopped down beside him. Every muscle in his body ached, his heart most of all. Naked, he pretended to stare at the ceiling while he checked out Rick in his peripheral vision. Still wearing his pancake batter-splattered shirt, his flaccid cock resting in the V of his open jeans, an arm slung over his eyes, Rick looked like he was surrounded by land mines that could go off at the slightest movement.

Brent sighed and waded into the minefield. "I feel like I should say thank you."

"For?" The man's lips barely moved.

"You know. Everything. And I'm eternally grateful you're the kind of man who keeps his promises."

His admission earned him a grunt.

Okay. Sex talk was off the table. Pardon the pun. He searched the ceiling for another topic of conversation. "So…what was it like sharing this tiny room with two brothers?"

A muscle ticked in Rick's jaw. "Hell."

"I can imagine."

Rick tucked himself in and zipped up, leaving the top button of his jeans undone. He sat up then scooted to the edge of the bed. "No, you can't imagine." He ran a hand over his face. His shoulders slumped, but the earlier tension was still there, beneath the surface.

Brent sat up, placed a hand on Rick's shoulder. "Tell me."

"I don't want to talk about it."

Well, okay. "I thought you and your brothers were close." Brent slid to the floor in front of a suitcase that doubled as a makeshift dresser drawer and searched for another pair of pajama bottoms. He found a pair of sweatpants instead and pulled them on. "Jake talks about you and Will all the time."

Rick's eyebrows rose as if Jake mentioning his brothers was news to him. "We were close when we were kids. Had to be to survive."

The admission put every cell in Brent's body on alert. "Survive? What the hell are you talking about?"

Rick sighed and shook his head. "You aren't going to let this go, are you?"

Brent forced a smirk to his lips. "I'm a lawyer. What do you think?"

He patted the bed beside him. Brent sat, hands clasped in his lap. "Just remember, you asked."

"Really, Rick. You don't have to tell me if you don't want to."

"It's not like everyone in town didn't suspect. If you stay here long enough, you're bound to hear about the Brothers Grim."

"Brothers Grimm. As in the fairy tales?"

"Brothers grim, as in ghastly, gloomy, and glum. People don't think we know what they call us, but we've known since we were kids."

Wow, talk about a land mine. Brent had stepped on a doozy. In an effort to defuse the situation, he tried to inject a bit of humor. "Is that a collective description? If not, which one are you? I'd go with glum."

"Glum? Why not ghastly?"

"Honestly, none of you qualify as ghastly. Have you looked in a mirror? Jesus. The Ingram brothers won the genetic lottery for good looks. I could see Will as gloomy. Sometimes, he has that brooding artist look going on. So, that leaves glum, though I don't see it. People in this town must be crazy."

"I think the description is collective. As a unit, it probably fits."

"Explain."

<h1 style="text-align:center">CHAPTER FIFTEEN</h1>

Rick heaved a massive sigh as his gaze swept his childhood bedroom, letting the nightmares flood in. "We had bunk beds on this side of the room. Jake had his own twin bed on the other. Since I was the youngest, I had the lower bunk. I guess we had a pretty good life, even if we had to share a room. But then our mom died, and everything went to shit. Dad became a functioning alcoholic. To everyone outside our house, he was an upstanding citizen. A bastard but an upstanding citizen. Inside these walls, he was a tyrant. We all had chores, responsibilities. Jake had the most, then Will, then me. We had each other's backs, but there were times when it was impossible for us to get everything done, or if we did it get it done, it wasn't to his exacting standards. Thinking back, I'm convinced he set the bar high deliberately so he could punish us when we failed."

"No. Surely not."

Rick shrugged. Brent wrapped an arm around his waist and snuggled close. Odd, how the same body that aroused him like no other could also be comforting.

"Anyway, when we *failed*, he'd come looking for us. Jake took most of it. He'd stand between Dad and me and Will. I'd climb up, and Will and I would huddle in the corner of his bunk, as physically far away from him as we could get, but every blow Jake took hurt us, too. Afterward, he'd lay on his bed and say nothing. Will and I would go to sleep, eventually, but many nights we'd lay awake listening to Jake crying from the pain."

Rick stood, paced away, one hand on the back of his neck. "When Jake left for college, Will and I became the primary targets of Dad's rage. Will did his best to protect me, but there wasn't anywhere for either of us to hide. We spent as much time out of the house as possible, but we eventually had to come home.

Will had always been into art. Drawing and painting. That wasn't a macho enough career choice in Dad's eyes, so he beat Will, even when he was little, for being, in his words, a sissy. He left for New York the day after his high school graduation. I hated Jake for the longest, for leaving us, then I hated Will for leaving. I still had my diploma in my hand when I showed up at the Marine recruiting office. I couldn't get out of here fast enough.

"I didn't know what I was getting myself into. Looking back, I think I was trying to impress Dad. I knew I was gay. Had known since I hit puberty, and I was more fascinated with cock than pussy. If the Marines weren't macho enough for Dad, what was? Because, if Will's career choice disappointed him, god help me if he found out I was gay." He leaned against the far wall, crossed his arms over his chest in an effort to hide his shaking hands. Though his brothers had asked him to explain many times, he'd never told anyone why he'd enlisted. He didn't know why he was telling his brother's lackey now. "A lot of guys washed out in boot camp but not me. There wasn't anything my drill sergeant could do to me that was worse than what my own father had done or what he would do if I failed. So, I stuck. I was still hiding who I was, but I'd learned to fight back. The guys in my unit became my brothers, and, like my flesh-and-blood brothers, they'd risk their life to save mine. The feeling was mutual, but it was a lonely existence—until I met Dave."

Rick studied the toes of his boots. Brent jumped to his feet, took Rick's hand in his, and led him out of the room. "Come on. You can talk while I clean up the mess we made in the kitchen."

"Yeah. Let me change my shirt." Rick disengaged his hand from Brent's. "Then I'll help you clean up."

At Brent's nod, Rick hurried to his room, closed the door, and leaned against it. What the fuck was he doing? He'd broken every rule he'd ever made for himself. He'd screwed a man he had no business wanting, much less touching. Then he'd talked about his childhood and why he'd enlisted. He shook his head. *Fuck.* He was losing his mind. He'd never told Dave about his childhood. Had never told him why he'd joined the Marines. And Dave had never asked. Grabbing fists full of hair, he doubled over, his stomach cramping as the truth hit him. Their relationship had always been about Dave. Every conversation. His Marine fuck buddy hadn't given two shits about Rick's life. All he'd cared about was fucking. Rick sucked in a breath. *He never loved me. And I never loved him.*

Not the way I…

Ah, fuck. He slid down the door till his ass hit the floor. *I'm not in love with Brent.*

Not yet.

Knock. Knock. "You okay in there?"

Shit. Rick scrambled to his feet, yanked off his soiled shirt. "Yeah. Sorry. Just answering a text from Jake." *Liar.* He pulled a clean T-shirt from a drawer and yanked it over his head. "I'll be right there." For good measure, he shot off a preemptive text to Will and Jake letting them know he was fine and inquiring about the snow level at Jake's place out by the lake. He was thumbing a reply to the barrage of text replies when he entered the kitchen a few minutes later.

"There you are." Brent, once again wearing his ridiculous apron, stood at the sink, a soapy sponge in one hand and plate in the other. The scene smacked of domesticity, and fuck, if that wasn't a turn-on. When he turned around, unshed tears shimmered in the man's eyes. "I'm sorry. Didn't mean to rush you. I just thought…"

Rick closed the distance between them, took the bowl and sponge out of the man's hands, and set them in the sink. Then he pulled him in for a hug. No one except his brothers had worried about him the way this man did after only knowing him for a few short weeks. "Shh." He rubbed his hands over the man's bare back in what he hoped was a soothing manner. Brent wound his arms around Rick's waist and tucked his cheek against his chest. Fuck, it felt good to hold him. "I'm fine," he whispered, placing a kiss on the top of his head. "Thanks for coming to check on me."

Brent dug his fingers into Rick's back. "After our talk. I mean, I know it hurt to talk about all that stuff, but I'm glad you told me."

Rick slid the tips of his fingers beneath the waistband of Brent's sweatpants and slowly stroked the skin there. Brent stiffened in his arms. "I need to touch you," he said, dipping his hand lower to cover his cheek. "Are you okay with that?"

"Yeah." His breath hitched. "Totally."

Between them, Rick's erection throbbed to life. With his hand on Brent's ass, he nudged him forward until they were pelvis to pelvis, their boners trapped between them. The man had an impressive cock. It was about the same length as Rick's with enough girth a guy would know he was being fucked. He wasn't ready to go there yet. Wasn't sure he ever would be. Whatever this was with Brent was temporary. Had to be. The longer they lived under the same roof, the more likely someone would find out they'd become fuck buddies. The thought of coming out to his brothers sent a tremor down his spine.

Brent placed a kiss on Rick's neck. "I know how you feel. I'm sore as fuck, but I want you again."

"Jesus!" Rick cupped the man's ass, his fingers searching out the source of Brent's discomfort. "We shouldn't." He dipped his middle finger between his cheeks to stroke the tight pucker.

Brent clenched around his finger. His hot breath fanned the erratic pulse in Rick's neck. "God, that feels good. Inside. Please?"

"Are you sure?"

"Put your fucking finger in me. Now, please."

Rick stifled the laugh rising in his throat. God, Brent was going to be the death of him. He withdrew his hand and stepped back. If he was going to do this, he was going to do it right. No more kitchen table sex. "My room. Take that hideous apron off and lay on the bed."

"Are you always this bossy?"

He hadn't been with Dave, had followed the man's orders in and out of bed. But this was different. Brent was different. He made Rick want things he'd never wanted before. Having this man do his bidding pushed his horny button. "Yes. Do you have a problem with that?"

Brent shook his head. "No. I was just wondering."

"Now you know."

"Yes, I do."

Rick caught the smile on Brent's face as he hurried from the room. Feet braced shoulder width apart, his hands bracketed behind his head, he silently counted to ten before he followed.

~ ~ ~

Rick hadn't specifically said to get naked, but Brent went the extra mile, shucking his sweats along with the apron the second he crossed the threshold into Rick's bedroom. Seeing how neat the room was, bed made, no clothes on the floor, he carefully folded his garments and placed them on the dresser before crawling to the center of the king-sized bed. When Rick appeared in the doorway, Brent was ready for him, one hand behind his neck, the other stroking his cock.

Fuck, the man was gorgeous. The waffle-knit Henley clung to his muscular torso and arms, and lord, jeans like his should be illegal. Eyeing the bulge at his crotch, Brent's mouth watered, and his ass involuntarily clenched at the memory of how well Rick filled him. Yeah, he was sore, and he should have taken the time to clean the salted butter off, but he sort of liked how the slight sting and greasy feel reminded him how it felt to be impaled by Rick's enormous cock. He didn't know what the man had in mind, but he hoped it involved stretching his ass some more.

"Nice." Rick grabbed the hem of his shirt and yanked it over his head. He took the time to fold it then placed it next to Brent's clothes on the dresser. Then he released the button on his jeans and slowly pulled the zipper down.

Brent couldn't take his eyes off the strip of pale skin revealed as the garment parted one slow inch at a time. There was something sexy as fuck about a guy who went commando. Especially in a pair of tight jeans. He licked his lips in anticipation of a glimpse of the man's erection then groaned as he saw it was tucked to one side, safely out of reach of the zipper's teeth. Hell's bells. The man knew how to do a striptease. Strangling his dick to keep from coming, he gritted out, "And you call me a tease."

"You are a tease, and a fucking temptation." Rick kicked his shoes off then hooked his thumbs in the waistband of his jeans. "Did I tell you to take your pants off?"

"No." His confidence slipped a notch. "I assumed…"

"Lucky for you, you assumed right. This time." Rick shoved his jeans past his hips. His impressive erection sprang free. The pearl of precum decorating the tip bolstered Brent's confidence straight to the stratosphere. He hadn't read the situation wrong. This proud, broken warrior wanted him. "Knees up. Spread your legs."

Brent complied. Rick strolled to the end of the bed, affording him an unobstructed view. Brent's thighs trembled under his heated gaze.

"Raise your legs up. Let me see your hole."

Hooking his hands beneath his thighs, he brought his knees up to his shoulders, exposing himself fully. He'd swear hours had passed before the end of the bed dipped under Rick's weight and set Brent's entire body vibrating.

"Stay like that. Let me look at you."

Brent whimpered and called upon the universe to give him strength. His lungs strained, air shuddering in only to be trapped there until being expelled all at once. Rick's gaze raked over him, from his eyes to his leaking cock, to his throbbing balls, then settling on his thoroughly used asshole. The longer Rick stared, the more Brent shook with need for the man to touch him. When he did—a single blunt finger tracing a line of fire around, but not actually touching, his portal—Brent groaned, his butthole clenching in blatant invitation.

"God, that's beautiful." Then his finger was there, pushing, gentle but insistent.

Tears streamed down his temples as he pressed eagerly against the single digit. "I need you."

The words were barely out of his mouth before Rick leaned over him. Braced on one arm, he thumbed Brent's tears with his free hand. "Shh, baby. You're too sore." He made a sound of protest Rick stole from his lips with a kiss so achingly sweet, it cracked something open in his heart. "I'm still going to take care of you." His big hand gently swept hair off Brent's forehead. "Do you *want me* to take care of you?"

Fresh tears blurred his vision, and his arms shook with the need to embrace this incredible man with the heart of gold. He'd been through more than any child should have to endure and came out on the other side a protector. *More than you can know, Marine. More than you can ever know.* "Yes. Please. Please, Rick."

Holding Brent's gaze, Rick snaked his free hand between them. He palmed his erection and balls then slid lower until his middle finger probed the tender ring of muscles. "Relax. Let me in."

Brent emptied his lungs. At the same time, Rick breached his opening, burying his thick finger deep inside him. Brent tensed at the sudden sting. *Ring of fire.* The saying had new meaning. He sucked in a deep breath as his body adjusted and the burn eased.

"Told you you were too sore for my dick."

Nodding, Brent concentrated on breathing. In. Out. "Doesn't make me want you any less."

"Don't say shit like that or I'll forget my manners."

God save me from protective men. "I don't want your manners. I want your cock."

"Put your legs down and take both our cocks in your hand, then."

Brent lowered his shaking legs. His feet hit the mattress then he reached between them and wrapped his hand around both cocks.

Rick sucked in a harsh breath, bowing his head so their foreheads touched. "Fuck, that feels good." Brent tightened his hold, stroking upward then back down. "Do that again." He repeated the move, faster this time. Rick bucked his hips, driving his cock hard against Brent's. "Hold on tight, baby. I'm going to fuck your hand and your ass at the same time." He flexed his hips and his hand at the same time, drilling his finger deep into Brent's ass while his cock thrust hard.

Brent threw his head back and, clamping his jaw tight, lost himself to Rick's ministrations.

"That's it, baby. Lay there and let me make you feel good." Rick placed a kiss on Brent's upturned chin then trailed a line of open-mouth kisses down the slope of his throat.

"So…so good."

"I love the way you taste. I love how tight your ass is. I love your hard cock rubbing against mine." He added a second finger, stretching him wide. The delicious fullness overrode the sting.

I love…you. Brent groaned as the unexpected thought blossomed in his head then spread like an electrical charge throughout his body, lighting up every nerve ending, leaving him teetering on the edge.

"I need you to come, baby." Rick's voice sounded like he'd gargled glass shards. His cock swelled in Brent's grip, signaling his impending release.

"Please," Brent pleaded on a whisper.

"Love. This. Ass." He punctuated each of the first two words with a hard thrust then, on the last one, he added a third digit and buried his fingers so deep, Brent swore the man tapped his heart.

He came, Rick's name stolen from his lips by the man who'd stolen his heart.

CHAPTER SIXTEEN

"Good morning." Brent halted in the doorway. He'd tamed his bedhead hair and shaved the scruff he'd let grow over the weekend. Dressed for work in a navy-blue suit, white shirt, and red tie, he looked like he'd just walked off the cover of GQ. Rick's dick instantly became nuclear hard.

Leaning against the counter, his first cup of coffee in hand, he motioned to the range. "I put water on for your tea."

Brent drank coffee but preferred tea. Just one of the things Rick had learned about the man over the last few days. He'd also discovered his roommate had an insatiable appetite for sex which Rick had taken full advantage of. His ass had to be sore today after all the times they'd fucked. Rick's dick twitched, reminding him he was a little chafed himself. They'd had "the discussion" and thankfully, dispensed with condoms late Saturday afternoon when it became apparent they would soon run out. It was either have the talk or quit fucking. They'd had the talk.

"Thanks." Brent took a mug from the cabinet then selected a tea bag from the box of assorted flavors he'd purchased Friday afternoon before the snowstorm hit. "I guess it's back to work today. At least for me. What about you?"

"As much as I'd like to take you back to bed and keep you there another day, I've got work to do." Rick nodded at the window above the sink. "Roads are mostly clear. If you drive anywhere, be careful. There could still be black ice in places."

"I was going to walk to work, but I think I'll take my car. I took a look out front and the sidewalk's a mess."

Rick's gaze dropped to the floor. "Yeah, the slush and salt would probably ruin those fancy shoes."

Brent shuffled closer so the two men were almost toe-to-toe. "Don't mock my fancy shoes, Marine."

Rick laughed at the man's feigned outrage. "You and your fancy suits." He fingered Brent's silk tie, let it slip through his grasp. "So put together. So fucking uptight. You need to loosen up a bit." He slid his hand down, palmed the hard ridge in his slacks. Brent's groan spurred him on. They'd had good reasons for skipping morning sex, but those reasons weren't sounding so good now. "I should take care of this for you."

Brent shifted his hips away. "We shouldn't."

Rick slipped his fingers beneath Brent's waistband and tugged him closer. He searched the man's face for real resistance and found only need in his eyes. "Maybe not," he conceded, "but it won't take long." He nuzzled the spot beneath his ear he knew made Brent's knees weak. "God, you smell good. Let me have a taste. I'll be quick, I promise."

Brent tilted his head, allowing Rick better access. He took advantage, placing soft kisses on his neck, along his jaw, then up to his lips where he teased the corner with his tongue. He pushed his hand lower, skimming his erection with his fingertips. "Let me fix your little problem."

"Little?" His breathing erratic, his protest was half-hearted at best.

Knowing he would win the round, Rick chuckled. "Then you're admitting you have a big problem and it needs to be addressed."

"Fuck you." Brent pushed him away then fumbled with his zipper. In seconds, he had his shaft out, pumping it with his fist. "This is all your fault, so fix it, asshole."

Rick dropped to his knees. Brushing Brent's hand away, he took over, his grip tight around the velvet-covered steel. "All you had to do was ask," he said, eyeing the magnificent cock in his hand. "You know I'll take care of you."

"Just fucking get on with it. I've got to get to the office."

He'd promised to be quick, but he'd lied. He didn't give a rat's ass if Brent was late for work. With a flick of his tongue, he captured a bead of precum dripping from his slit.

"Fuuuck," Brent cried. "Get on with it. I'm dying here."

Rick smiled then laved the bulbous head with his tongue. Brent hissed and flexed his hips, shoving his dick at Rick's face. The man was too easy to tease. Rick sat back on his heels, his gaze sweeping Brent from head to toe. "I love this look on you. Sexy-as-fuck lawyer, all buttoned-up with your dick hanging out like the horny bitch you are."

Gripping the counter like his life depended on it, Brent responded, "You know what I like better than seeing you on your knees, Marine?"

Rick captured the dick bobbing in front of him and licked the tip. "What's that, Counselor?"

"You, on your knees, sucking my dick." He grabbed Rick's head in both hands. "Open the fuck up and let me in."

Rick obliged, taking Brent to the back of his throat. Then he closed his lips around his girth and sucked.

"Holy fuckin' mother of god, that feels good." Brent grabbed for the countertop as Rick licked and sucked and pumped, driving him to the brink then easing off only to do it all over again. He tasted too good, and the sexy-as-fuck sounds he made were the best kind of aphrodisiac. Rick could suck him off all day long and never grow tired of it. The tea kettle sent up an unholy howl they both ignored.

Then it stopped.

"Good morning, bro," an all-too-familiar voice called.

"Holy shit!" Brent withdrew fast like he'd accidentally stuck his dick in a pencil sharpener. He tucked his withering erection back in his pants, yanking the zipper up lightning fast. With an apologetic glance at Rick, he hurried out of the room.

Rick, eyes closed as his world came crashing down around his ears, blew out a pent-up breath. Refusing to meet his brother's gaze, he slowly regained his feet. He wiped his mouth on his sleeve then placed his coffee mug in the microwave, staring at it as it spun around inside. Behind him, Will popped a pod in the brewer for his own cup of coffee.

Shit. He should have known his nosy-ass brother wouldn't leave until he had an explanation. Like what he'd walked in on needed explaining. Will might be a busybody, all up in his business, but he wasn't stupid. He knew exactly what he'd walked in on.

Nuking the coffee bought him a few seconds to get his shit together. Not nearly enough time, but it was all he was going to get. Mug in hand, he dropped into a chair and took a sip of the steaming liquid, swallowing past the steel band tightening around his chest. He didn't want to have this conversation with Will, or anyone else, for that matter. In all the times he'd imagined coming out to his family, he'd never imagined it happening like this. "I thought I told you to knock."

"I did. You couldn't hear me" — he motioned toward the kettle he'd removed from the burner — "probably because of Mom's old kettle. Thing sounds like a banshee. So, I let myself in." He retrieved his filled cup from the brewer, rummaged in the fridge for milk then added some to his drink before joining Rick at the table, as if he hadn't just turned his life upside down and inside out.

Silence settled between them. When the swish and thud of the front door opening then closing met his ears, Rick raised his gaze to Will's. "It's none of your business."

His brother sipped then carefully set his mug on the table. "I know it isn't, but I still want to know why you hid this from us."

"What makes you think I've been hiding something? Maybe this was a one-time thing."

"Don't bullshit me, baby brother. Unlike you, I didn't fall off a turnip truck."

"Fuck you." Rick jerked to his feet, giving his brother his back.

"Whoa. Hold it right there. First, that would be incest, and second, I don't swing that way."

Rick groaned. "Can you at least try to be serious here?" He stomped to the sink, braced his hands on either side, and stared out the window at the bleak winter landscape. "This is my life we're talking about."

"You're right, bro. It's your life, and as you pointed out, your sexual orientation isn't any of my business. But *you* are my business."

Water dripped from the eaves like a cold heartbeat. "How do you figure that?"

"You're my brother. I've got your back, always. No matter what." He paused to sip his drink. "Let me ask you something. Does it matter to you that *I'm* not gay?"

He shook his head. "No."

"Then why the fuck would it matter to me if *you* are?"

Rick shrugged, letting Will's question sink in. Could it be that simple? Would his brothers accept his being gay so easily? Taking a deep breath and letting it out, he blinked away the tears threatening to fall and faced his brother. "You really don't care?"

"Fuck, no, I don't care."

"I used to wonder if you were gay."

"Me? Why the fuck would you think that? Oh! Because I'm an artist?" Will laughed. "Stereotyping much, baby brother?"

Relieved the conversation hadn't gone the way he'd feared, Rick smiled. "Maybe."

"And I never suspected you were. Probably because you joined the Marines. The biggest, baddest motherfuckers on the planet. How did that work out for you?"

Rick turned back to the window. "I got fucked."

CHAPTER SEVENTEEN

"Want to explain?"

Rick shook his head. "Look, Will. I don't want to talk about any of this, and I especially don't want to talk about my time in the Corps. Why don't you tell me why you came by, and let's forget this ever happened?"

"You've been fucked up since you came home. I know I wasn't here when your enlistment was up, but I am now. Jake and I thought you were in for the long haul. You were a Marine for eight fucking years."

"I'm still a Marine."

"I get it, *Semper fi*, and all that shit, but Jake and I both knew something happened or you would have re-upped. Did someone give you shit because you're gay? Is that it?"

God, both his brothers could be a pain in the ass, but Will, especially, was like a dog with a bone. He didn't know when to let something go. "Forget it, Will. I don't want to talk about the Corps."

"Fine." Will raised his hands in surrender. "Then let's talk about your roommate."

Hands clenched into fists; Rick spun around. "I don't want to talk about him, either. Leave it alone."

"Why?" His brother stood. "Why won't you talk about him?"

"Because he's none of your fucking business. It was a one-time thing. Over."

"Who are you trying to convince? Me? Or yourself?" Will poured the rest of his coffee in the sink, rinsed the cup, and placed it in the dishwasher. "You've been living a lie long enough, don't you think? No one who loves you will give a shit about your sexual orientation."

Rick huffed out a breath. "That's a short list in this town, brother."

"The rest of them don't matter…brother." He paused in the doorway. "For what it's worth, I'm sorry I interrupted." A smile broke across his face. "It looked like both of you were enjoying the blow job. *Oorah!* brother."

Rick listened for the front door to shut before collapsing to the floor, his back to the range, his knees drawn up. "Shit."

He raked a hand through his hair, his heart pounding like a racehorse out of the starting gate. Will hadn't said so, but he would tell Jake. They'd both tell their women. He kicked out at the nearest chair leg, slamming the chair against a nearby cabinet. His days in the closet were over. Give it twenty-four hours, forty-eight tops, and everyone in Willowbrook would know. "Fuck!"

So much for his fledgling business. Who the hell in this town would hire him now? He squeezed his eyes shut as reality sliced him in half. The fuck of it was, they *had* been enjoying the blow job, and no matter how much he wished Will hadn't walked in on them, he couldn't wish the interlude away, and he hoped to fuck Brent felt the same way. But after that scene? All bets were off.

Rising to his feet, he washed out his coffee mug and set it in the drainer to dry. If he worked through lunch and skipped dinner, he might be able to finish the job he was on today. Tomorrow, he'd start work on the apartment above Sunny's gallery downtown. The sooner he got that done, the sooner Brent would move out and talk would die down. In the meantime, he had no choice but to act like nothing had happened. He grabbed the lunch box he'd packed earlier, slamming the back door behind him on his way out.

He finished the last coat of paint on the Riverton's living room wall and sat down to eat his lunch when the doorbell rang. The homeowners were away on a Caribbean cruise while Rick worked on their house. He opened the door, sandwich in hand. "Well, shit." Shaking his head, he stood back, holding the door open so his oldest brother could step inside. "Wipe your damn feet. They had the hardwood floors refinished last week." Appetite lost, he tossed the sandwich in his soft-sided cooler then stood, arms crossed and feet braced apart. Jake shut the door behind him then wiped his feet on the old towel Rick had left by the door. "Fucking Will and his big mouth."

Jake fixed him with a glare. "Don't blame this on Will. I asked him to stop by your place this morning. It's not his fault you had a mouth full of dick at the time."

Heart pounding, jaw clenching, Rick flexed the fingers on both hands, prepared to beat the ever-loving shit out of his brother if he went down the homophobe road. "He should have fucking knocked."

Jake shrugged. "He said he did. That's neither here nor there. The fact remains, you've been lying to us." He raked a hand through his hair. "What the fuck, Rick? We're your family. Both of us stood up for you until you were big enough to stand up for yourself. You're a fucking Marine, for god's sake. I can't even imagine the shit you've seen and done, but you didn't have the guts to tell your flesh and blood that you're gay? I tell you, brother, that hurts." He placed a fist over his heart.

Rick blinked. "I didn't think it was any of your business."

"Fuck you." Jake crossed the room, got up in his face. "You. Are. My. Business. I went through hell to protect you and Will, and this is the way you repay me?"

"I didn't ask to be gay."

Jake snarled, grabbed the neck of Rick's shirt, and dragged him close so they were nose to nose. "Get this through your thick skull. I. Don't. Care if you like dick or not. But I do care that you didn't think you could confide in me." He released his hold, shoved Rick back a step. "Don't ever fucking keep things like that from me again. Do you hear me?"

Rick choked back tears. "Yeah. I hear you."

Jake paced away, rubbing the back of his neck. "How long have you known?"

Rick shrugged. "Since I was a kid. Puberty, I guess."

His brother spun around. "You wound me, brother."

"I wanted to tell you, but I hardly knew what it meant myself. You and Will dated. You talked about pussy and tits and"—he shrugged self-consciously—"I thought I'd eventually grow up enough to appreciate girls, but it never happened. I dated girls. You know I did. I kissed 'em and made out. Felt 'em up, but in the back of my mind, I was wishing I was pawing the quarterback instead of the cheerleader. My thoughts and desires went against everything I was taught to expect from my body—yet, there I was, having wet dreams about guys." Rick sank to the floor, his back to the wall. "Then there was Dad. He hated Will for being an artist. Can you imagine what he would have done if he'd found out I was gay?"

Jake sat on a capped five-gallon paint can. "You're absolutely right. Dad would have shit a brick."

"Or thrown one at me."

His brother nodded. "Yeah. I'm sorry, Rick. You shouldn't have had to go through that alone."

"It would have been nice to have someone to talk to, I suppose, but honestly, I'm not sure I would have said anything even if Dad had been the opposite of what he was. I was scared to act on my desires. Thought if I tried hard enough, I could be like everyone else, but it wasn't something I could change. It was just me."

"So, why the fuck did you enlist?"

Rick rubbed a hand over his face. "At the time, I just wanted to get the fuck out of this town, like you and Will. But in hindsight, I think I was trying to prove to myself that I wasn't gay and at the same time, make sure Dad never suspected."

"Fucking Marines," Jake muttered. "You took decades off my life. I worried about you every fucking day."

"I'm sorry. I was only in real danger a couple of times, and I had a lot of good men at my back."

"Will said when he asked you about the Marines you said you got fucked. What did you mean by that?"

"Will has a big fucking mouth."

"He loves you as much as I do. When you came home, you were, for lack of a better phrase, fucked up. Will and I came up with the idea of you renovating the house to get you out of your own head." He surveyed the newly painted room. "Never thought you'd turn it into a business, but we're proud of you anyway."

"Let's just say, I left something behind, and I wasn't happy about it."

"Something or someone?"

"Both?" He stood. "The Corps was more than a job. It was a family. A brotherhood. I missed it when I came home, more than I thought I would."

Jake got to his feet. "I'm sorry you miss it, but I'm not sorry you're home." He crossed to the front door. "I asked Will to walk down and talk to you before you went to work this morning. I'd been trying to reach you, but your phone must have been off."

He'd been preoccupied with Brent and had completely forgotten about his phone. "I forgot to plug it in. I didn't notice it was dead until this morning." He cocked his head toward an outlet on the far end of the room. "I plugged it in as soon as I got here."

"I thought you were just ignoring me."

"Nah. I'd never do that." He cracked his first smile since he'd opened the door to find Jake on the porch. "So, what did you want?"

"We're having a little thing tonight. Wanted to do it Saturday, but the weather fucked up our plans."

"What kind of thing?"

"They call it a gender reveal. It's something new, I guess. At least, I'd never heard of it. Come. Have dinner with us. For dessert we've got a cake. It's either pink or blue inside. When we cut it, we'll know if we're having a girl or a boy."

"Why don't you just tell me now?"

"Because we don't know. Sunny's doctor put it in a sealed envelope. We took it straight to the bakery, so only the baker and her doctor know." He rolled his eyes. "Sounds stupid to me, but whatever my wife wants, she gets."

"And she wants to torture everyone she knows with a gender reveal party."

Jake pointed a finger at him. "You got it." He opened the door then turned back. "Six o'clock. Bring Brent."

CHAPTER EIGHTEEN

Brent ignored the call from his sister and yanked open the door to his place of employment. Jean, Jake's legal secretary, and by extension his, sat at her desk, a steaming cup of coffee resting on a coaster next to her keyboard. She was hard at work. On what, he didn't know or care.

With the hem of his pants damp and muddy, his shoes squeaking with every step, he stopped in front of her desk and tried for a pleasant smile but knew he failed miserably. "Good morning."

He hated to interrupt her workflow, but shit happened. Like being interrupted in the middle of a blow job by a family member. Jean would get over it. He wasn't so sure about Rick. Will's interruption had ruined Brent's day, and possibly his lover's life, and he felt guilty as hell about that. He should have refused Rick's advances this morning. They'd existed in a snow globe environment the last few days, but he'd known as soon as he saw the sun streaming through Rick's bedroom window this morning, their time was up. Boy, how right he'd been.

Jean smiled up at him. "Good…lord. What happened to you?" Her gaze raked his soiled suit and ruined shoes.

"I walked to work." He'd done it nearly every day since moving into Rick's house, but today, he should have gone back into the house when he'd realized he'd left without his keys, coat, or briefcase. Warmer temperatures had turned the snow to slush with icy patches underneath in places. More than once he'd narrowly escaped ending up on his ass. Then he'd been on the receiving end of a muddy shower, courtesy of a trash truck that had barreled through a puddle.

"Why in heaven's name would you walk on a day like today? Is there something wrong with your car?"

"Nah. I just wasn't thinking." Truth. His mind had been on Rick, and how he'd left him to face his brother alone. It was a chicken-shit thing to do but when he'd left the room, Rick hadn't called him back. Call him a coward, but he didn't want to get in the middle of whatever was going to transpire once he left. He'd been caught with his dick in his boss's brother's mouth by another of his boss's brothers.

"Well, there are some towels in the cabinet next to the sink in the bathroom. You should take your socks and shoes off and let them dry. You don't have any appointments this morning, but you have two this afternoon."

Brent nodded as she rambled on. When she ran out of sage advice, he said what had been on his mind when he stopped at her desk. "Can you take another look at the real estate market in town? See if something had come on the market recently? Sale or rental, I don't care. I'll take anything."

Jean's eyes narrowed, and her lips pursed. "Something wrong with where you're at?"

After this morning, Rick is going to toss me out on my ass. Brent lied through his teeth. "I'd really like to have my own place."

The woman's eyes softened, and her lips curved up on the corners. "Oh, I get it. Need your privacy?" She chuckled. "Grown man. Single. I get it." She winked and waved him away. "I'll see what I can do."

Christ on a cracker. He kicked his shoes off, picked them up then padded in his wet socks to his office and shut the door. Leaning against the closed portal, he sighed. What was it with middle-aged women and their need to see everyone paired off for a cruise on Noah's Ark? He hadn't told her he was gay, not because he was hiding it but because he didn't think it should matter to anyone but him. Thank god, Jean only had boys or she probably would have tried to fix him up the first week he was here.

He tossed his shoes behind his desk. Settling into his desk chair, he removed his socks and spread them out on the floor next to his shoes. At lunch he'd go back to the house, change clothes, and get the car and briefcase he'd left behind. He'd completely forgotten about the papers he'd taken home on Friday. After asking Jean to print another copy for him, he forced himself to concentrate on work instead of the man he'd inadvertently outed to his family in the worst possible way.

The morning passed slower than molasses in winter. As soon as Brent could reasonably consider taking a lunch break, he put his soggy socks and shoes back on and hurried to Rick's cozy bungalow for a change of clothes. He tossed his soiled suit in the bag he kept for his dry cleaning then donned clean slacks and a shirt.

He'd skipped breakfast in favor of other things and, after the interruption, never got around to eating. Stepping into the kitchen, he closed his eyes. The earlier scene, permanently embedded in his reel of all-time worst moments, played on a continuous loop. He could still see Rick leaning against the counter, coffee mug in hand, dressed in paint-splattered jeans, plaid shirt layered over a long-sleeved T-shirt, and work-worn boots. The scruff shading his jaw and sexy mussed hair had added to his barely tamed appearance. Despite being sore from the man's attentions the last few days, he'd wanted him more than he could recall ever wanting someone. The offer of a blow job had been too good to refuse. Breakfast was overrated anyway.

Shaking the memory loose, he crossed to the refrigerator. Coming up with a container of leftover pasta from Friday night, he popped it in the microwave. He'd no sooner settled in to eat than his phone dinged with an incoming message.

Rick: *Don't cook for me tonight. I'll be out late.*

Brent stared at the message, wondering if Rick needed to work late or if he was avoiding him because of what had happened earlier. If it was the latter, discussing it over text message wasn't a good idea, and if it was the former, he'd just have to accept that Rick had deadlines to meet and sometimes would miss supper. Either way, there wasn't anything he could do about it, so he replied with a thumbs-up emoji and resumed his meal.

Jean greeted him with a wide smile upon his return. He smiled back, because it was impossible not to, and stopped at her desk. "What's got you so happy? Did Bill Gates call and say he's fed up with his current slate of attorneys and wants to hire us?"

"Nope. I just got off the phone with Jake. He and Sunny are having a gender reveal tonight."

It was all he could do to keep a smile on his face. Rick wasn't working late. He was going to a party at his brother's house and didn't want Brent to know. *Maybe he didn't know if I was invited and was protecting my feelings.*

"I asked him if you knew how to get to his house and he said not to worry, that you were coming with Rick." As if she hadn't just shattered all his illusions, she prattled on, "I never thought I'd see the day Jake Ingram settled down, much less became a father, but here we are. I wonder what if it will be, a boy or a girl? What are the odds?"

"Fifty-fifty," he answered robotically. Did Jake know about what Will had walked in on this morning, or had he told Rick to bring his tenant along?

Jean giggled. Lord, he didn't know women her age still did that. The weirdness of it shook his feet loose from the floor. He purposely strode toward his office. Jean called out to him, "Your first appointment is in fifteen minutes. I'll give you a holler when they get here."

He raised his hand, signaling he'd heard her then shut his door and leaned against it. What the hell was he supposed to do now? If he didn't go, would his employer be offended? If he did go, would Rick be pissed? Yes, was the answer to both questions, so his decision came down to which Ingram brother he wanted to offend the least. One could fire him. The other could render him homeless.

The intercom buzzed, forcing him over to his desk. He pressed the button and the secretary's voice filled the room. "I have a call for you on line one. A Kenneth Westinghouse. He says it's important."

And the hits keep on comin'. He sat in his chair, dropped his elbows to the desk, and his head into his upturned palms. *I never should have gotten out of bed this morning.*

"Mr. Whitehall?"

"Brent? What should I tell him?"

Holding the button down, he replied, "Thanks, Jean. I'll take the call."

Heart pounding, he picked up the receiver and punched the blinking button indicating an incoming call. "Hey, Kenn."

"Brent. It's good to hear your voice."

At the sound of the deep voice he'd loved so much, his racing heart shifted into overdrive. "What's up?" It was a lame question considering this was a man he'd asked to make a life with him just a few short weeks ago.

There was a long silence then a heavy sigh came over the line. "I want you to come back. I'm miserable without you. We'll get a house in the burbs, if that's what you want. A picket fence. A dog. I talked to Everett at your old office. He said he'd take you back. They miss you, too."

Of all the things Kenn said, his brain stuck on the last one. "You called Everett?" Everett was another attorney at Brent's former firm, and he was flamboyantly gay.

"I saw him at a party, and we got to talking. You know how it is."

He knew exactly how it was. Kenn had always had a thing for Everett. They'd met socially on numerous occasions, and, oblivious to Brent's embarrassment, his former lover had flirted with Everett shamelessly.

"You slept with him, didn't you?" The silence on the other end was all the answer he needed. "Why did you call me, Kenn?" He now knew the call had nothing to do with wanting him back.

"I told you. I miss you. Everett misses you." More silence. The kind Brent didn't feel like filling, so he waited. "Ev has a place at the lake. It's a big house. Plenty of room for the three of us. Room to party. Entertain."

Ev? He was calling him Ev now? Jesus, the man had nerve. The nickname was a spear to his heart and proof he'd done the right thing when he'd left, even if he'd chosen the wrong place to go. Squaring his shoulders, he clenched the handset tight. "Let me get this straight. I asked you to move to Willowbrook with me, to make a life with me, and you declined. Then you have the audacity to call me up and tell me you're fucking one of my former coworkers and the two of you want me to move back, shack up with you out at the lake, and resume working side by side with a man I'm living with. Did I get that right?"

"Well…yeah. It'll be great, Brent. You'll see. We can have great parties at the lake house. Just last weekend, Ev and I hosted—"

"No. I don't want to hear about your parties, Kenn. I told you before, I'm through with that life. I want to settle down. Have a home. Maybe kids one day." He rubbed a hand over his face and tried to find words beneath this new heartbreak. "I wanted that with you."

"Wanted. Past tense."

Brent gave him credit for picking up on the important part of what he'd said. "Yes. Past tense."

"You've met someone? Already?" His voice rose to a high pitch. "What. The. Fuck? You've been there, what, six, eight weeks?"

Four. But who was counting? "And you're fucking Everett."

"Yeah, but I've known Ev for, like, forever."

And it felt as if he'd known Rick forever. "I've got to go. I have a client waiting." Brent swallowed hard then pushed the painful words past his lips. "Don't call me again, Kenn." He forced himself to carefully replace the handset in the cradle, when he wanted to slam it down hard enough to break it in half.

Rocking back in his chair, he scrubbed both palms over his face and blew out a heavy breath. Kenn had ruined any chance he had to return to Houston and resume any part of his old life. And he'd blown, pardon the pun, any chance of being happy in Willowbrook. *Fuck!*

Jean's voice came over the intercom. "Mr. Whitehall, the Wilsons are here to see you."

Standing, he smoothed his jacket and straightened his glasses as he mentally went over what he knew about this next appointment. A family trust, if he recalled correctly. The couple had recently inherited some property and wanted to preserve it for their kids. He greeted the couple and, once they were all seated, pulled out a note pad and focused on helping someone else instead of obsessing about the shambles he'd made of his personal life.

The afternoon went by in a flash as he consulted with clients, one after the other. When Jean appeared in his door late in the day, he sighed with relief at her words. "Well, that was the last one. Unless you need something else, I'm going to head home now. I need some time to decompress before Jake's party." He'd forgotten all about it. "So? Do you need anything?"

"Nah. I'm good." He waved her off.

She pushed away from the doorframe where she'd been leaning. "Okeydokey, then. I'll see you there?"

Hell, no. He caught the words before they formed then forced a smile to his lips. "Sure." Any other answer would require an explanation, and he didn't want to get into his personal life with his secretary. It would be easier to make an excuse for not attending after the fact.

"I'm out of here." She wiggled her fingers at him. "Tootles."

As soon as Jean turned her key in the lock on the front door, he tossed his glasses across his desk and let his body go limp in the chair. What a fucking day. It was over, finally. He'd go home, heat some leftovers for dinner, and take a long soak in the tub. With a little luck, he'd be fast asleep before Rick got home from the party. Tomorrow, he'd get up and out of the house before his landlord. The plan would buy him another twenty-four hours before he had to face Rick.

His phone vibrated in his pocket as he wearily dropped into his car. Stifling a groan, he pushed the Accept Call button as he fired the powerful engine to life. "Sis. What's up?"

"I'm sorry, Brent."

He loved his youngest sister, he really did, but Meg had a flare for the dramatic. He rolled his eyes and cranked the heater up to full blast. "What do you have to be sorry for?" A long silence from the other end put him on alert. He straightened his spine. "Megan Renee. You better tell me right now or I'll—"

"Don't you dare tell Mom about my trip to New Orleans. I swear, Brent, I'll kill you if you do."

His sister had trusted him with her shocking secret, and, as her lawyer, he couldn't legally disclose anything she'd told him, but he wasn't going to remind her of that—not when she was withholding something from him. "Spill, Megs."

She sighed loud enough he took the phone from his ear and switched to speaker mode. "Okay. Okay. But promise me you won't be mad at me."

"I'm not promising anything, egg head." He hoped using the nickname he'd given her when he was eleven and her eight would loosen her tongue.

"Jerk."

"Butt fungus."

Another long silence. He could picture her biting her lower lip, her brows knit as she worked up the courage to admit to whatever she'd done. As a child, she'd gotten into more trouble than anyone he knew, and it hadn't stopped once she reached adulthood. Trouble seemed to find her the way tornadoes found trailer parks. Often with similar results. "I called to warn you."

"Of?" He drew out the single syllable.

"I think Kenn is coming to see you."

He closed his eyes, remembering the call from his former lover earlier. "Why would you think that?"

"Because he called me and asked for your address."

"You told him?" He hated how his voice rose there at the end, but he couldn't help it.

"Well, you didn't tell me it was a secret, and he told me how much he missed you. Said he'd made a mistake."

Shit. "What time did this conversation happen?"

"This morning. I tried to call you when I thought you'd be a lunch, but it went straight to voicemail."

"I was with a client," he lied.

"I'm sorry, Brent. I should have asked you before giving out your private information. But it was Kenn. Besides, he knew the name of the hotel you'd been staying in. Even had the room number right. I figured if you'd told him that, then you wouldn't mind him knowing where you were now."

It was sound logic, if he'd told Kenn those details, but he hadn't. *I should have stayed in bed this morning.* "No worries, egg head. I'm not mad at you." Another lie but a little one. He was peeved, and that was at least one step below full-out mad.

A glance up told him the defroster had cleared the windshield. "I gotta go, sis. My boss is having a party tonight." He wasn't going, but she didn't need to know that.

"You're sure you aren't mad at me?"

"Positive." He put the car in gear and checked the rearview mirror. "Now, I really need to go."

"Go," she said, sounding less stressed and more like the bubbly person she was. "Have fun tonight."

The line went dead. He backed out of his parking space and turned the car toward his temporary home. He made a mental note to ask Jean tomorrow if she'd had any luck finding him a new place.

It took longer to warm up the car than to make the drive to Rick's house. As he neared the perfect little cottage, he noted a familiar silhouette sitting on the top step of the porch. Rick's beat-up old truck was gone, giving him a measure of relief, so he pulled into the driveway and got out. Approaching the front door, keys in hand in case his landlord had locked the door for a change, he stopped when his visitor stood.

He let his chin drop to his chest. *Fuck, how is this my life?*

"Brent?"

Clutching the keys in his fist until the sharp edges cut into his skin, he lifted his gaze to the man who had cut his heart out and stomped on it for good measure. He wore his usual work clothes, jeans aged to perfection and a long-sleeved T-shirt beneath a butter-soft leather bomber-style jacket. Years of familiarity allowed him to see the fatigue in his eyes and in the lines of his face. "Kenn. What are you doing here?" *How the hell did he get here so soon? Hadn't he been in Houston when we talked a few hours ago?* "*How* did you get here?"

"I needed to see you." He couldn't say the same, so he didn't. "You look good. Small-town life agrees with you."

That was bullshit if he'd ever heard it. *I look like hell, and Willowbrook is killing me.* He'd caught a glimpse of himself in the rearview mirror. His eyes were red. His hair in disarray from running his fingers through it. He needed a shave and a frown had carved deep brackets around his mouth and between his brows. Choosing to ignore the absurd comment, he stalked past his unwanted guest and tried the doorknob. When it turned easily, he silently cursed Rick Ingram for being such a trusting bastard.

Willowbrook might be relatively crime-free, but you never knew when some asshole from out of town would drop by. Lucky for him, it never would have occurred to this particular asshole to check the door. Where he came from, no one left their doors unlocked.

Standing in the open portal, he half turned to the man standing behind him. "I've got some place to be, and I'm running late." More lies, but he needed Kenn to leave sooner rather than later.

"That's okay. We can talk while you get ready."

Motherfucker. The man couldn't take a hint. Resigned to letting him have his say, he huffed out a breath then invited the man in.

"Shut the door behind you," he said, shedding his overcoat as he stomped down the hall to his room. He tossed the coat on the bed then toed off his dress shoes while he shrugged his suit coat off.

"Nice room." Sarcasm dripped from Kenn's words.

"It's a place to sleep until my new apartment is finished."

"I thought you wanted a house. One like this one." He listed all the things Brent had said he wanted in his new home. Rick's house checked off every box.

Lord, save me. "I do, but there aren't any available at the moment, so I'm renting a room from my boss's brother."

Kenn's posture in the doorway grew rigid. "He's the guy your sleeping with?"

"That's none of your business."

"Are you sure, Brent?"

No matter how bad things seemed at this moment, he hadn't changed his mind about leaving the big city for a small town. It sucked that he hadn't found a house of his own, but he would. Eventually. After what happened that morning, Rick would probably work night and day to get the apartment done and Brent out of his house.

He fixed his gaze on his guest. "I'm sure. I asked you to come with me, to make a life with me, and you declined. I might not be settled yet, but I'm happy here. I like my job. I like this town. It's a community, something a big city can never be."

Kenn's shoulders slumped, and he dropped his gaze to the floor. He was no longer trying to hide his exhaustion. "I came to say I'm sorry, Brent. I made a mistake letting you go. I thought you'd find this place boring and come back in a few weeks, but I got tired of waiting, so I tried to push you."

"That's what all that shit was about, Everett?" He pulled a flannel shirt from the closet, and a pair of jeans from a drawer.

"That was bullshit. I haven't been with anyone since you left. I thought I could make you jealous, but then you said you'd moved on, and…shit…I knew I'd fucked up, big-time."

"So, you aren't sleeping with my former coworker, and you aren't interested in a threesome with him?"

His gaze shot up to Brent's. "No." Hands he'd had tucked in his pockets rose to a defensive position. "I swear. I said that shit to get a reaction out of you."

Brent dropped his trousers, pulled his jeans on then switched his dress shirt and tie for the more casual shirt he'd laid out. It was time to put an end to the conversation. "I'm not going back to Houston, or to you, Kenn."

"I know that now. That's why I'm here. Show me this town you like so much. I'm miserable without you, baby. I think I could be happy anywhere you are."

He tucked his shirt in then bent to find a pair of casual loafers he'd stuffed under the bed for lack of another place to put them. "You aren't listening," he said, leveraging to his feet. "You and I are finished."

"I heard you. Loud and clear, but you aren't hearing me. Houston isn't the same without you. The parties aren't as much fun, and it turns out, most of *our* friends were *your* friends."

Shit. I shouldn't feel sorry for him, but I do. As a military brat, he'd moved around a lot and had learned, out of necessity, to make friends. Kenn was an only child and had never lived anywhere but Houston where his parents were both professors at a prestigious private college. To say his social skills were stunted was an understatement.

"Where you going? Are you meeting your new lover there?"

There is no new lover. Not after what happened this morning. But Kenn didn't need to know the details of his sordid sex life. However, what would it hurt to rub Rick's nose in the shitshow he'd created by staying in the closet until the door hinges were almost too rusty to open? The least the man could have done was call him and let him know how it went with his brother, or brothers, as the case might be. He got the sense the brothers grim were a tight bunch, despite the secret the youngest had been keeping most of his life. He hoped they'd accepted the news with open minds, but he wouldn't know unless he walked into the lion's den on his own since Rick apparently wasn't going to talk about it. Decision made, he slipped a worn leather belt through the loops on his pants. "My boss and his wife are having a gender reveal party tonight. Wanna go?"

Kenn straightened his shoulders. "You want me to go with you?"

Not really, but, "Yeah. Might as well. Knowing Jake, nearly everyone in town will be there."

CHAPTER NINETEEN

Hoping to avoid Brent, Rick knocked off work early, went home, showered, and changed then lit out for Jake's house. His brother, still in jeans and barefoot, met him at the door.

"You're early."

He shrugged and stepped past him into the foyer. "Found a good place to stop, so I thought I'd come see if I could help out, but from the trucks in the driveway, you've got it handled."

"Yeah." Jake glanced at the empty porch before shutting the door. "I didn't want Sunny to overdo, so I had the entire thing catered."

Rick nodded. "I'll be the official taste-tester, then. Wouldn't want to serve something sub-standard to your guests."

"Speaking of guests, where's Brent?"

He didn't want to admit he didn't ask his tenant/lover to come with him, so he lied through his teeth. "Said he had something else tonight."

Jake strode past him, and Rick followed. "What the hell could he have to do in Willowbrook on a weeknight?"

"Work, maybe? You're his boss. You know him better than I do." Jake stopped so fast, Rick almost plowed into him. The look he shot over his shoulder reminded Rick of their father when he had a burr up his butt about something. "Don't fucking look at me that way." He lowered his voice. "We had sex, Jake. Just sex. We don't share our plans with each other." That much was true.

His older brother shook his head then strode off. Rick let out a relieved breath then took off after him. He caught up with him in the kitchen. Jake's wife, Sunny, rose from her spot at the island to give Rick a hug.

"I'm so glad you're here." She smiled up at him. "I know you're busier than a one-armed bartender on ten-cent beer night, but Jake needs help with the nursery. Can you take a look?"

"I've got it," Jake protested.

"No. You don't." Ignoring her husband, she grabbed Rick's wrist and tugged him down the hallway leading to the bedrooms. Jake trailed behind them, grumbling about being underappreciated. Rick smiled to himself knowing his brother's complaints were all for show. The man didn't have a handyman bone in his body. "It doesn't need much. Just some paint and a closet organizer, I think." She dragged him into the bedroom across the hall from the master suite. "What do you think?"

Rick took in the little-used room with its dull beige paint, standard small closet, and unimaginative lighting. "You keeping the carpet?"

Sunny bit her bottom lip and shrugged. "I don't know. Am I?"

Rick laughed. "No. I can match the hardwood in the rest of the house, if you want."

"I want," she replied, a giant smile on her face. "And could we change the overhead light? I saw this really nice chandelier the other day…"

"Honey," Jake interrupted. "Rick has a lot on his plate."

"It's a small room," he countered. Even if he had to do the work after hours, he couldn't disappoint his sister-in-law, not when she gave him that lost puppy dog look. "It won't take long. Why don't you show me the light you want, and I bet you have a closet organizer picked out, too."

"How did you know?"

He shrugged, suppressing the laughter bubbling inside him. "Just a hunch." Jake had stopped by several times in the last few weeks ostensibly to talk about the upcoming apartment renovation when Rick suspected he'd wanted an excuse to get out of working on the nursery. As they filed out of the room, he clapped his brother on the back. "Don't worry. I've got this. It's going to cost you, big-time, but I've got it."

The elbow he received to the ribs was as good a thank you as he was going to get from his big brother. It would do. Guests began arriving shortly after their nursery consultation. The expectant couple had invited a houseful, and Rick found himself relaxing, enjoying catching up with old friends. He was part of a group listening to Hank Travis tell a story from BlackWing's latest European tour when Will pulled him aside. "Where's your boy toy? Kenzie wants to meet him."

Rick's gaze slid from his brother to the woman standing beside him. Will's girlfriend smiled up at him. "I hope you don't mind. Will told me what happened."

He did mind which was the point of keeping his secret in the first place, but his impulsiveness had created a gap in the careful seal he'd placed around his privacy. It was his lousy luck his brother had stumbled his way in. Now, every goddamn person on the planet was going to know his most private business. Still, it wasn't Kenzie's fault, so he reached deep for the patience he'd honed on countless missions overseas and lied through his teeth. "No, I don't mind, but I'd appreciate it if you both" —he shot Will a pointed look—"kept it to yourself."

"Of course we will," Kenzie promised. "It's really none of our business, but we both wanted you to know it makes no difference to us. You're Will's brother. Full stop. But..." She stretched the word out. "I missed meeting him at Jake's wedding. Did he come with you?"

"No. I'm not sure where he is." Truth without admitting anything. He'd learned a few things from his lawyer brother.

Someone touched his elbow. He glanced over his shoulder to see Jake's legal secretary and a familiar older man standing there. *Shit.* "Jean," he greeted her with a hug. He'd known her most of his life. She'd worked for his asshole dad before his death and had always been good to him and his brothers. She baked a mean Snickerdoodle, too. He shook hands with her husband, a retired Air Force pilot who operated the small, local airstrip outside of town. "Lowell. Nice to see you again. It's been a while. You remember my brother, Will?" He brought his middle brother into the conversation then introduced Will's fiancée. Will and Lowell struck up a conversation regarding the airstrip he managed and something about the Yankee billionaire who had purchased it a couple of years ago and put it back on the map. Rick was thanking his lucky stars for the change of topic when Jean drew him aside.

"Where's Brent?"

Why did everyone here expect Brent to be glued to his side? He shot a glare at his chatty middle brother whose disrespect of personal boundaries had started this whole mess then glanced around the room as if looking for the man in question. "Don't know. Did you look outside?"

Jake had heaters set up on the patio for those who wanted to catch some fresh air. The underwater lights and steam rising from the heated pool created a mystical atmosphere that had drawn some of the guests outside.

"No. I thought he'd be with you."

"Why would he be with me?"

"Jake told me he was coming with you, and when I spoke with Brent about the party, he said he'd be here."

Shit. Shit. Shit. He'd known better than to hope Jake hadn't invited his new employee. From the looks of the crowded room, he'd invited everyone in town. Or not. Most folks in Willowbrook didn't think they needed an invitation. If there was a party going on, they considered themselves invited. The only time he could recall security being tight for an event was Jake's wedding, and even then, his brother had provided an extensive list of party crashers who were allowed in without showing an invitation. Almost everyone on the list had attended.

Avoiding eye contact with Jean, he went with a version of the truth. "He didn't come with me." It came out sharper than he intended causing the older woman to take a step back.

"Okay. Sorry I asked." She steered her husband away.

He owed her an apology, but it could wait. Jake and Sunny sidled up next to him. "What did you do to her?"

"Nothing. She was being nosy."

"So you rubbed her nose in it?"

"Something like that." Giving most of the room his back, he addressed his sister-in-law. "Nice party."

Her smile lit their corner of the room, and he didn't miss the way the hand that wasn't clinging to his brother cradled her ever-growing baby bump. "Thanks. Have you had something to eat? The barbequed brisket is to die for."

He returned her smile. Jake was a lucky man. His wife was beyond beautiful, and her name fit her personality to a T. "Is there any left? I've been trying to get to the buffet for a while now and keep getting waylaid."

"There's plenty. Jake ordered enough to feed an army." She uncoupled from her husband and took Rick's arm instead. "Come on. Everyone knows not to get in between a pregnant woman and a buffet table."

As she led him off, the crowd parting like the Red Sea, he glanced over his shoulder at his brother. Jake saluted him with the beer he'd held in his free hand then ambled off to speak with another guest.

"This is my second pass," Sunny confided as they loaded up their plates with brisket, baked beans, potato salad, and cornbread. "But don't tell anybody, okay?"

"Your secret is safe with me."

"I'm sure it is," she deadpanned. "You're like a vault."

He followed her through the kitchen to the laundry/mudroom. "Shut the door, please?"

Rick shut the door, sealing them away from the noise and crowds. "You okay?" She sat on the bench near the door leading to the garage and dug into her food.

"I'm fine. Just wanted a chance to eat before my food gets cold." She practically inhaled half of her slice of cornbread. "This is amazing, don't you think?"

"It sure is," he replied, not bothering to taste it himself. The catering was from a local barbeque place he'd eaten at dozens of times. People came from all around to sample their barbeque.

"I'll give you one thing about Texas. The cuisine here is stupendous. I've gained more weight than I should have, but everything here is so good." The transplant from New York shoveled in a bite of potato salad, humming her enthusiastic approval of the side dish. "So, want to tell me what's going on between you and Brent?"

Her abrupt change of subject caused him to swallow wrong. After nearly coughing up a lung, he washed everything down with a giant gulp of the sweet tea he'd snagged on the way to their hideout. "What?" he croaked.

"Don't pretend ignorance. Jake told me everything."

God, save me from busybodies. "There's nothing going on. It was sex between consenting adults."

She forked up a slice of brisket but didn't immediately eat it. She shook her head. "I don't believe you. You've gone to a lot of trouble to keep your sexuality private. To be caught the way you were…it doesn't make sense."

He'd placed his plate on top of the washing machine. Appetite lost, he shoved it away. "It's not like I was blowing him on the sidewalk. We were in *my* kitchen. In *my* house, where I have every right to expect privacy."

Chewing, Sunny nodded. After taking a sip from the water bottle she'd brought with her, she sliced off another bite of the barbequed meat. "You're absolutely right about the expectation of privacy, but still—you're a Marine. You didn't survive multiple deployments by not being aware of your surroundings and potential threats."

"Your point?"

"You were distracted. I'm thinking the distraction had to be more than sex. You're a grown man, presumably capable of curbing your appetites unless…you couldn't help yourself."

Bracing his hips against the washer, he crossed his arms over his chest and studied the herringbone tile pattern on the floor. "I don't know what you want me to say, Sunny. I wanted to suck his dick, so I did. If Will had respected my privacy, no one but Brent and me would know. I wanted to keep it that way."

"Well, that ship has sailed." She stuffed her face with potato salad, chewed, and swallowed. "I really didn't drag you in here to pry into your private life. What I wanted to say is, we all love you, and if Brent makes you happy, that's great. If not, then that's okay, too. Jake said he'd fire him if he hurt you, but since you're adamant it's only sex, then there isn't much chance of him breaking your heart. Not that Jake would actually fire him. He's too good at his job." Polishing off the last bite on her plate, she stood. As she passed by him, she patted him on the shoulder. "Glad we had this little chat. We'll be cutting the cake soon, so finish up and get out there."

The door shut behind her, leaving Rick alone with his turbulent thoughts. He'd once thought being out of the closet would be so much easier. No more secrets. Nothing to hide. Piece of rainbow-tinted cake. Except it wasn't easier. Now that his siblings and their women knew he *had* a sex life, they felt entitled to the details. Well, fuck them. Maybe it had been the isolation this past weekend, or the loneliness he'd experienced since Dave's defection that had made him think he could have a relationship with Brent. Whatever the cause of his stupid thoughts along those lines, reality set in the second his brother caught him with Brent's dick down his throat. He'd come to his senses. His brothers still loved him, as he knew they would. It was the rest of the world he wasn't ready to face. Brent made no effort to hide his sexual orientation. If he was seen around town with the openly gay man, the news would travel so fast, it would set the grapevine on fire. Everyone would know his private business. He'd be labeled *different*. Some wouldn't care. Others would care too much. He and his brothers had been the source of enough gossip growing up. Giving them more fuel as an adult made him want to vomit.

"It's fucking none of their business," he exclaimed to the ceiling.

A knock sounded on the door a split second before the handle turned and Will peeked inside. "Sunny said for you to get your ass out here so they can cut this fucking cake. Her words, not mine."

He couldn't keep Jake's wife waiting. No telling what she'd do if he didn't join the other guests in time to see if they were having a boy or a girl. He gathered his plate and drink. "I'm coming."

"That's what *he* said." Will winked at him, adding the *cha-ching* to his lame joke.

When Will turned his back, Rick allowed himself a smile. "You're just jealous because *she* never says it."

The guests had gathered in a loose circle around a giant sheet cake that had been set up on a table in the living room. The brothers took up a spot on the outer ring where they could see the happy couple.

Will smirked. "*She* says it *multiple* times every day."

He nudged Will in the ribs. "TMI, brother."

Though his food had grown cold, Rick quickly cleaned his plate anyway then stepped away to toss the soiled paper plate into one of the large trash cans set up in the kitchen for the occasion. He was returning to his spot next to Will when a shiver of awareness caused him to scan the crowd. Like Sunny had said, he hadn't stayed alive by sticking his head in the sand, and he never ignored his gut when it told him something was wrong. He just wished his gut had spoken up this morning. Damned unreliable alarm system.

Still, he hung back, his gaze quickly assessing the gathering for whatever had made his hackles rise.

It didn't take him long to spy Brent among the guests. His breath caught in his lungs, and his dick twitched to life. The last time he'd seen him he'd been tucking his dick back in his pants as he practically ran out of the room, leaving Rick to deal with Will. It was a chickenshit thing to do, but Rick hadn't exactly asked him to stay, either.

His tenant had swapped out his fancy suit for jeans, and the collar of a plaid shirt peeked from the neck of a heavy, cream-colored sweater. There wasn't anything special about the outfit, but Brent wore it like a fashion model. Rick's fingers itched to toss the bulky clothes off to get to the ripped body beneath. To wrap his lips around his cock and finish what he'd started earlier. To hear his name grunted out as the man dropped his civilized veneer and came.

Jean approached Brent, her husband in tow, blocking his sightline and ripping him out of his inappropriate musings. She made the introductions then Brent half turned and, with the familiarity of a longtime friend, took the hand of the dark-haired man on his other side and pulled him front and center.

Rick's feet grew heavy, like he'd stepped in quick-drying cement, and his heart lodged in his throat, blocking his airway. *What. The. Fuck?* He'd brought a date? *What. The.* Ever-loving. *Fuck?*

The sound of silver tapping crystal drew his attention away from Brent and his date to Sunny and Jake who'd gravitated to the center of the circle. Jake cleared his throat. "We'd like to thank you all for coming out tonight on such short notice. After the record snowfall over the weekend, we thought you could all use a night out, so we threw this together on the fly," he said. Sunny elbowed him in the ribs. Jake grunted, a smile coming over his face. "That's a lie. We were going to do this next week, but my lovely wife couldn't wait any longer to find out if she's carrying our son or our daughter. Some nonsense about what color to paint the nursery."

The comment earned him another elbow to the ribs. Sunny gave him a long-suffering look then addressed the gathering. "Don't believe a word out of his mouth. He's the one who can't stand not knowing. He's the one to blame for dragging you out for barbeque and cake on a cold Monday night."

Several comments rose from the crowd. "Anytime."

"Not a problem."

"Cake? Did someone say cake?" Laughter rose from the guests.

Jake raised his hand. "So, without further ado…"

They joined hands like they'd done a few months ago at their wedding and sliced into the cake. Sunny let out a gasp, tears instantly brightening her eyes. Beaming, she turned her face up to Jake's. His brother's smile was as big as Texas as he bent to place a kiss on his wife's lips.

"Well?" some jackass yelled.

"Should we tell them?" Jake asked Sunny.

His sister-in-law nodded. "Yeah, we should."

Together, they grasped the knife, carved out the corner piece, and slid it around, revealing the bright-pink center. "It's a girl!" they said in unison.

Kenzie, Will's fiancée rushed in to slice the cake into serving pieces while Jake and Sunny accepted congratulations and kept the cake line moving.

CHAPTER TWENTY

He sensed Rick's gaze on him but refused to hunt for him in the crowd. As he smiled and introduced Kenn to the few people he knew, he mentally told his landlord to go fuck himself. It was one thing to be caught with his dick down someone's throat before breakfast. It was another to have the owner of said throat project his shame on him. They hadn't been doing anything wrong, and they'd been in their own kitchen, for crying out loud.

He got it. He really did. Rick had been in the closet for a long time, and he'd gone to great lengths to keep the metaphorical door locked tight. It wasn't Brent's fault the ass hadn't laid down the law with his family—or at the very least, changed the locks on his physical doors. That shit landed square on Rick's shoulders.

Was he sorry Rick's brothers had found out the way they had? Yes. But he wasn't sorry Rick's secret was out. He was a grown-ass man. It was about time he owned his sexuality, though, a part of him wished he'd had the chance to tell his family in his own way. Seeing his presumably hetero brother sucking dick had to have been a shock for Will. Which was why he tensed as the other man approached.

"Brent." Will Ingram held out his hand. "Glad you could make it. I know Jake will be happy to see you."

He took the middle Ingram brother's hand in his and shook it. "I wouldn't have missed it for the world. I thought Jake was happy on his wedding day, but the day he told me about the baby, his feet barely touched the ground."

"I know." Will smiled. "The fucker is crazy happy."

The sound of a throat being cleared drew his attention to the man standing beside him. "Will Ingram, this is an old friend of mine, Kenneth Westinghouse. I hope Jake doesn't mind an extra guest. Kenn stopped by for a visit, and I didn't want to disappoint my boss, so I brought him along."

Will's smile froze as he sized Kenn up then, he gave a slight nod and held his hand out in a friendly gesture. The two men shook hands. "Welcome, Kenn. You haven't met my older brother yet, but I can assure you, Jake won't mind another party crasher. Hell, half the people here weren't invited. It's the way things are in Willowbrook. We're all one big, happy family."

"Speaking of Jake," Brent said, "I need to go razz him about having a daughter."

Will pointed over his shoulder. "He and Sunny are still holding court by the cake. Better hurry if you want a piece."

Once they were out of earshot, Kenn grabbed his sleeve and pulled him to a stop. "Was that W.H. Ingram? The artist?" he asked in a near whisper.

"Yeah. I think he signs his latest work as William H. Ingram though. Don't ask me why. Jake handles all his legal affairs. Why?"

"Is he the one you're fucking?"

"What? No. He's engaged. His fiancée is around here somewhere."

"Honest? I wouldn't be all that upset if you were fucking him. That's W.H. Ingram! I'd fuck him in a heartbeat. Lord, that man is sexy. And talented. He's your boss's brother?"

"Middle brother. There's another Ingram. Jake's the oldest of the three."

"Let me guess." His gaze raked the crowd that had dispersed some to enjoy their pink cake. "It's the sexy-as-hell guy over there giving us both the stink-eye, right? He looks like a bigger, badder version of William. Tell me he's gay. Please."

He didn't need to look to know exactly who Kenn referred to. There was only one sexy male in the room who would be giving them the stink-eye. It was petty of him, but a thrill shot through him at the thought of having rattled Rick's cage enough to get a public reaction out of him. Maybe bringing his former lover along hadn't been such a bad idea after all. "Fuck, Kenn. What's the matter with you? The Ingram brothers are off-limits. All of them."

"Then I nailed it. He's the other brother. What's his name? I'd ride that all day long and twice on Sunday."

Kenn's crude remark made Brent think about the various ways Rick had fucked him over the weekend and how twice hadn't been anywhere near the count on Sunday. The memories brought a wave of heat to his cheeks and made his dick throb for a repeat. Or at least a conclusion to what they'd started that morning. "Cut it out, Kenn."

At Brent's sharp reprimand, the cartoonist cut him a glance. "Oh. My. God. It's him, isn't it? He's the one your fucking?" He cocked his head toward the man he'd been ogling. "He's the reason you won't move back to Houston? The reason you won't be with me?"

"No," he lied.

"Then why is he looking at me like he wants to kill me?"

He didn't dare glance Rick's way. And even though he'd brought Kenn to the party as a fuck-you to Rick, he couldn't bear to see the lips that had been wrapped around his cock less than twelve hours ago turned down in disapproval. "It's your imagination. Come on. Let's say hi to Jake and his wife and get the fuck out of here."

~ ~ ~

"That was awkward."

"Do me a favor, Kenn, and shut the fuck up." Brent white-knuckled the Corvette steering wheel. The car seemed to know its way to Dallas without any input from him. A good thing since he was too busy cursing himself, the man in the passenger seat, and Rick Fucking Ingram to pay attention to the road.

"I will if you tell me where we're going."

"Airport."

"My return ticket isn't good until day after tomorrow. Why don't we go back to your place?"

He ground his teeth in an effort to keep from saying something he'd regret later on. Once he gained control of his words, he carefully enunciated his thoughts. "We aren't going back to my place because I don't want you there. There aren't any spare beds and you aren't sleeping with me."

"I could sleep with your roomie."

His molars were going to be dust soon. They were miles from their destination, but he started paying attention to the billboards, looking for the first motel, hotel, or hovel where he could dump his passenger. "Don't even think it," he ground out.

"I knew it."

Kenn's words lacked the teasing tone he'd adopted earlier, causing Brent to glance at him. The light over an exit ramp briefly illuminated the man's features. Where he'd been a bright balloon, trying to tease a positive response out of Brent, he looked spent. Dejected. *Welcome to the crowd.* "Knew what?"

"You're hung up on Rick Ingram. Your landlord." In his periphery, he saw the man shake his head. "How cliché can you get, Brent?"

"Don't say another fucking word or I'll pull over and leave your ass on the side of the road."

"He's a Neanderthal for Christ's sake, Brent! You don't belong with someone like him. Does he even know how to read?"

Before he was through spewing crap from his mouth, Brent pulled the car to a stop on the shoulder of the road. "Out. Get. The. Fuck. *Out!*"

"No. Not until you listen to me."

Short of physically hauling his ass out, there wasn't much he could do but let him have his say. He shoved the transmission into Park and turned on his flashers. "Say what you want to say, Kenn, then I don't want to hear another word out of you. Okay?"

"Okay." His former lover tugged at his jacket, settling into his seat. "I don't know what's going on with you, Brent. We had something good in Houston. We were happy. At least I was, and I thought you were, too. Then this offer came up in Willowbrook and everything changed. You changed. I get it. I do. I've dated military brats before. They either can't settle down or it's all they think about. I thought you were settled. You had a great job and a kick-ass apartment. You had friends. You had me." He sighed.

Brent remained quiet, his gaze focused on a reflective mile marker post in the distance, waiting for his passenger to get everything he wanted to say off his chest.

Kenn shifted in his seat, and Brent could feel the man's gaze on him. "You have nothing in common with him. Can't you see that? I heard someone at the party talking about how he renovated her kitchen. For Christ's sake, Brent, he's a construction worker!"

That was it. Maybe Rick didn't want him enough to be seen with him in public, but he wasn't going to let anyone talk smack about him. "Shut. The. Fuck. Up." He forced his gaze on the man he'd once thought he'd spend the rest of his life with. Light from the dashboard instruments touched on his soft facial features—such a contrast from the way moonlight off the snow had softened Rick's sharp edges. How had he ever thought Kenn was the one for him? "You don't know anything about him. He's a former Marine who survived multiple deployments to war zones and came home to build his own renovation business from scratch. He might not have an Ivy League education, but he's not stupid. And I'd trust him with my life." Unlike you, went unsaid.

They'd been mugged once on vacation in New Orleans, and Brent had done more to fight back than Kenn, who'd cowered on the sidewalk and pissed his pants. Rick Ingram might not want anything to do with him, but he knew down to the marrow of his bones the man would put his own life on the line to protect him.

"He makes me feel safe." He wasn't sure where the thought had come from, but he knew it to be true.

He put the car in Drive and took his foot off the brake. "There's a chain motel at the next exit. We aren't far from the airport. I'm sure they have a shuttle, or you can call a car service to get you there."

To Kenn's credit, he didn't say another word until they pulled up beneath the motel's portico and he'd retrieved his backpack, the only luggage he'd brought with him, from the backseat. "I'm sorry, Brent. I shouldn't have come, but I had to see you…give it one more try."

"I get it, but I hope you understand now. I'm not going back to Houston. Even if things don't work out with Rick, I'm going to stay in Willowbrook. It feels like home." He'd never thought those words about any place he'd ever lived, much less said them aloud. The truth of them warmed a cold place in his heart. It was a night for truths, he supposed.

Kenn nodded then, without a second look, exited the car. The glass doors parted automatically at his approach. Brent waited until he'd checked in and walked toward the elevators before he drove across the street to a similar hotel and booked himself a room for the night.

CHAPTER TWENTY-ONE

Rick's truck was gone when Brent pulled up in front of the house the following morning. He mentally congratulated himself on his timing. He still wasn't ready to face his landlord, and after parading his "date" around at Jake's party, he was sure Rick had plenty to say to him. None of which could be good. He'd be lucky if he still had a place to live this time tomorrow. No, his best plan of action was to avoid Rick Ingram at all costs, for as long as possible. Give him time to cool down. Time to process what it meant to be out of the closet, even if it was only to family members.

He parked in the driveway and cut through the backyard to the kitchen door. He'd skipped the free breakfast at the hotel in favor of getting out of there before Kenn got out of bed. Since his former lover rarely got out of bed before noon, there was little chance of him seeing Brent's car in the lot across the street, but it was a chance he hadn't been willing to take. Better to head home — yeah, Willowbrook was home — as early as possible.

First things first. He popped a pod into the coffee maker, pulled a container of cream from the refrigerator while his first cup brewed. He normally didn't drink more than one cup in the morning, but today was definitely a two-cup day. He was in the process of removing a slice of bread from the wrapper when the back door opened. Certain Rick had returned for some reason, he didn't bother to look up. Even when the door slammed shut, rattling the windows and jump-starting his heart, he refused to look up. If the man wanted to talk, he could talk. Brent was a good listener, had to be in his job. Clients often didn't know how to verbalize what they wanted, so a good lawyer had to listen close and cull out the important parts of what they were saying. He'd let him have his say then he had a few things he wanted to get off his mind.

The fact that Rick hadn't spoken barely registered until he turned to put his bread slices into the toaster. Movement near the door drew his gaze. He gasped. The bread slid from his fingers that had gone numb at the sight of a woman standing there with a wide grin on her face.

"You really should lock your doors." As she spoke, she raised her hand above the level of the counter. A gun. Brent stumbled back.

"Whoa. Whoa. You can have anything you want." He held both hands up, palms out in an effort to placate the intruder. "I've got a little cash in my wallet. You can have it. I'll give you the pin for my debit card. Anything you want. There's stuff here you can pawn." She had to be a drug addict in need of money. Right? What else could this be about? Hell, he'd help her load up her car with shit if she'd just leave him alone.

She took another step into the kitchen, brandishing the weapon in his direction. "I want your worthless brother," she said. "He owes me."

Brother? "Wha-what? Wh-who?"

"William. Your brother. Where is he?"

God, he wished she'd quit waving that thing around. Between the gun and the fact he hadn't had any caffeine yet, he was having a hard time deciphering her words. "He's...not here."

"I heard he was living here."

"Uh. Not anymore?"

"He talked about this shit town all the time. I'd bet he didn't go far. Call him. Get him over here."

"Ca-call him?" If he got out of this alive, he was going to carve Rick Ingram a new asshole for never locking his doors.

"Call him. You've got a phone, don't you?"

He nodded. *I've got a phone. Where is it?* He patted all his pockets and came up empty. Oh, right. The jacket he'd shrugged off as soon as he'd walked in the door. "It's in my coat." He gestured toward the article of clothing draped over the back of a nearby chair.

The woman used her gun hand to wave him toward the garment. "Get it, but if you try anything funny, I'll shoot you and call him myself."

"Okay. No funny stuff." There was nothing funny about this shit.

He hated the way his hands shook as he searched his coat pockets for the slender device. There were any number of things in the kitchen he could use as a weapon. If he could get to his coffee, he could throw that in her face, but she'd stepped between him and the coffee maker. He could toss his coat at her and run, but that would only be a moment's distraction, and she might decide to shoot first and untangle herself second.

As his hand closed around the plastic case, he considered throwing the phone at her. Only he'd never been any good at throwing. He'd been decent with a baseball bat, but he'd been so lousy at throwing, he'd given up on playing the game. Again, if he managed to hit her, it wouldn't buy him enough time to get to the front door, much less out of the house before she shot his ass. Better to play along until help arrived.

"Got it." He held his cell phone up for her to see.

"Call him. Now."

"Okay. Okay." He didn't have William's number, but she didn't need to know that. *She thinks I'm Rick.*

He brought up his contact list. It took two tries to key in Rick's name. When the number came up, he pressed the Call button and hoped to hell his landlord was over being mad at him enough to take the call. If he wasn't, maybe he could hit her over the head with the cast-iron skillet he'd left out on the stove. If he could reach it before she shot him.

"It's ringing." He glanced up at his captor and mentally tabulated a list of all the crimes she was guilty of so far. Trespassing. Kidnapping. He hoped to hell murder didn't get added to the list.

~ ~ ~

Rick slipped his phone from his pocket and sighed. He wasn't in the mood to talk to his tenant. The fucker. Who did he think he was, bringing a date to Jake's party not even twelve hours after Rick had sucked his dick? He hadn't come home last night, and knowing he'd spent the night with another man chapped Rick's butt. If he was calling to apologize, he could save his breath. He didn't want to hear it.

He stuck the phone in his pocket and measured the front window, noting the measurement on his old-fashioned notepad. When his phone vibrated, indicating a message had been left, he let loose a string of profanity harsh enough to peel the paint off the walls of the vacant building, then keyed in his password to retrieve the message.

"Hey, Will. This is Rick." He held the phone away from his ear and stared at the screen as Brent's voice droned on. What the fuck? Had he lost his ever-loving mind? He brought the device back up, catching the tail end of the message. "…need you to come to my place ASAP and take her off my hands. I gotta go to work soon."

Take her off his hands? What the fuck was he talking about? He hit the Replay button and closed his eyes, as he focused on every syllable. "Hey, Will. This is Rick. I've got an unexpected visitor. Lady says she needs to talk to you. I…" He could hear another voice in the background, female, most likely, but her words were unintelligible. Then Brent's voice returned, sounding muffled, like he'd pulled the phone away from his mouth. "I won't say anything. I know. You can put that thing down. I promise I won't say anything." Then more clearly, "I need you to come to my place, ASAP and take her off my hands. I gotta go to work soon."

Brent was a lot of things, but an actor he was not. Judging from the tremor in his voice, and the fact he'd been pretending to be *him*, calling *Will*, told him something was terribly wrong at his house. He dropped his tool belt where he stood, and as he took the stairs down to what would eventually be Sunny's new gallery, he placed a call to his oldest brother.

"Jake. We've got a problem." He relayed the bizarre message Brent had left. "Could it be Jessica?"

"Could be. Don't go in guns blazing." His brother knew him well. He kept a shotgun under the seat of his truck and a handgun attached to the underside of the dashboard via a heavy-duty magnet. Just in case. There were several other firearms stashed around the house, but they wouldn't do Brent any good since he didn't know about them. "I'll call a friend of mine on the police force. Wait for backup, Rick. If it is Jessica, she's batshit crazy."

He'd make no promises about waiting for backup. If Will's crazy ex was holding Brent at gunpoint, he wasn't going to sit on his hands and wait to see what she'd do when Will didn't show up. "Do not call Will. Keep him out of this."

Jake didn't make any promises, either, as he warned Rick again to wait for the police then hung up to make his call. Rick's truck was parked behind the store. Before getting in, he reached under the dashboard and released the Sig Sauer P226 from its hiding place. In a move he'd done thousands of times, he released the magazine, verified it was full, and shoved it back in before racking the slide to drop a round into the chamber. A quick look under the seat assured him the Henry 410 shotgun was still there. He hoped to hell he didn't need it.

As he turned the corner onto his street, he saw a familiar figure running down the walk. He pulled over and shoved the passenger side door open. "Get the fuck in here before she sees you, asshole."

His brother grabbed the door and hopped in, dragging ragged breaths in. "Is it Jessica?"

"You tell me." He pulled his phone out of his pocket. "Listen to my voicemail. See if you can identify her voice in the background."

He played the message on speaker. Brent's shaky voice was like a spear to his gut. He'd never forgive himself if something happened to him. The last time he'd spoken to the man was seconds before he'd taken his dick to the back of his throat. A lot of shit had gone down since then. Shit they needed to discuss. Shit Rick needed to apologize for. No way was he going to sit on his ass and let some crazy fucker take him away. Not on his watch.

"That's her." Will pointed to the phone. "That's Jessica." He braced an elbow on the passenger door and rubbed his upturned hand over his face. "What the fuck is she doing here?"

"Don't know. Don't care. But that's my guy in there. I'm not going to let her hurt him." He held the Sig close to his thigh. "You understand?"

"I understand." A muscle ticked in Will's jaw. "Let me go in and talk to her. See what she wants."

"Hell, no. I'm not letting you anywhere near her."

His brother faced him, his eyes burning with determination. "That's not for you to decide, asswipe. She's here because of me. I'll talk to her. Get her to let Brent out of there then I'll find out what she wants."

"No." He couldn't say it any plainer. "I spent eight fucking years busting down doors for a living. I can take her out."

"I know you can, but let me try talking to her first. It's me she wants, not Brent, or you, since she thinks he's you."

"She's armed," he reminded his brother. "You heard Brent. She's got a knife or a gun. She came here to kill you, bro. I'm not letting that happen."

"She won't kill me."

"What makes you so certain?"

"Because I'm going to buy you and the cops time to get in a position to stop her. If I don't show up soon, she'll get impatient, and she might harm Brent in retaliation. Remember, she thinks he has me in his phone contacts. She doesn't need him to get to me now."

The fucker was right. Who knew how long she'd wait for Will to respond to the voicemail Brent had left? His phone was the connection she needed. She might not kill Brent, but she could make him suffer as a means to encourage Will to meet with her. "Okay, but don't get anywhere near her. You hear me? Or I'll kill you myself when this is over."

His brother nodded. "I won't get close to her."

"If she has a handgun, you don't need to be close for her to make a lucky shot, but the farther you are away, the less accurate the firearm will be."

"Got it. Anything else?"

"Tell her you won't talk in front of me. Get Brent out of there then keep her talking. Provided she wants to talk. She might just want to kill you, so don't be a putz. Once Brent is out of there, try to get her to put her weapon down as a condition of talking."

"Is that all?"

"You got your phone on you?"

"Yeah. Why?"

"Put everything on silent then call me."

Will changed his phone sound settings to silent then placed a call to Rick.

He answered, put his phone on Mute, then instructed his brother to put his phone back in his pocket. "I'll be able to hear everything, I hope."

Will nodded.

"Okay. Let's do this."

Rick eased the pickup to the curb one house down from his and killed the engine. Before his brother stepped out, he cautioned him one more time. "Be careful, and if she starts shooting, run like hell."

Will raised an eyebrow. "Is that what the Marines do?"

"Fuck, no. But you aren't a Marine."

"Gotcha. I'll be careful. I know her. Or I did. She might be here to kill me, but she won't do it before she gives me an earful. If I'm right, I'm about to find out why she stole from me. I've always wondered. It never made any sense." He opened the door and put one foot on the ground. Halfway across the neighbor's lawn, he stopped and turned to face Rick who was still in the truck. "Nod if you can hear me."

Rick nodded.

"I'll try to get your boyfriend out in one piece, but in case things go wrong in there, I love you, bro. Tell Jake and Kenzie I love them, too."

Rick nodded.

Will resumed his casual stroll across the lawn as if there weren't a lunatic waiting for him. He didn't know if his brother was crazy or brave. Probably a little of both. He'd met Marines who would balk at walking into a situation like this with little to no backup.

He waited until Will let himself in the front door then he slipped out of the cab and made his way to the side of the house, stepping carefully to avoid alerting the intruder to his presence.

CHAPTER TWENTY-TWO

Will rapped his knuckles on Rick's front door, something he'd never do under normal circumstances, then turned the handle. The door opened on silent hinges, thanks to Rick's excellent maintenance of the aging abode. He poked his head inside. Seeing no one in the living room, he called out, "Rick! Hey, man. What's going on?" as he stepped inside like nothing was wrong. "Where the fuck are you?"

"In here." Brent's voice shook, but he was alive. He hoped Rick heard that. If it had been Kenzie in the same situation, he'd be a basket case, wondering if she was okay. Rick tried to play off his relationship with Brent as no big deal, but he'd seen more than Rick thought he had the morning he'd walked in on them. He'd seen enough to know the two men had feelings for each other. Feelings that found expression through a physical connection. Rick could protest all he wanted, but Brent wasn't a meaningless hookup. Which meant Will had to do whatever it took to keep the man safe. He'd never be able to look his brother in the eye again if he let his past interfere with Rick's future.

He crossed the room to the door leading to the tiny, eat-in kitchen. He paused in the doorway, taking in the scene. His former fiancée stood near the sink, a small revolver in her hand which she had pointed at Brent, who sat at the table, his face pale, his eyes wide behind his designer glasses. "You okay, Rick?"

His brother's boyfriend nodded which wouldn't do. Will had waited a long time to find out why Jessica had made off with his paintings and his money. The last thing he needed was Rick barreling in here, guns blazing, before he had a chance to talk to her. "Why don't you run along then, bro? Jessica and I need to talk." He cocked his head toward the door leading to the backyard. "Go on. This is none of your business."

Brent placed his hands on the table to leverage himself up. "Sit your ass back down." Jessica stepped closer, pressing the muzzle of the gun to his temple. Brent, trembling like a leaf in the wind, dropped his butt back to the chair.

"Okay. Okay. I'm not going anywhere."

"You can put the gun down, Jess. At least point it at me. I'm the one you came here for, not my brother."

"Don't flatter yourself, asshole." Jessica spat the words out. "You'd rather die than watch your brother die, so don't think I'll make this easy on you."

Shit. He hadn't known her at all, but apparently, she knew him too well. Rick's reminder to stall, rang in his ears. If he was going to get anything out of her, now was the time. "What do you want, Jess? You took everything I had. Left me practically destitute. Why'd you do that anyway? I thought we had a good life. I was painting the commercial crap you wanted me to paint."

Her lips twisted in a sinister sneer. "I see you're still the arrogant prick you were when we first met." That stung, but he kept his thoughts from showing on his face. "You were a means to an end, asshole."

"To what end? Prison?"

"Fuck you!" She turned the pistol on him. Hands raised, palms out, he took a step back. "If everything had gone as planned, you'd be dead by now and I'd be a fucking millionaire."

I'd be dead? What. The. Fuck? "You were going to kill me?"

"I sure as hell wasn't going to spend the rest of my life married to you."

"I don't understand." Truer words had never been spoken.

"Of course you don't. You never did see anything but the canvas in front of you. People didn't exist in your world unless they were there to satisfy your needs. You never gave a fuck about anyone but yourself." She waved the pistol toward Brent. "And your idiot brothers. You deserved everything I had planned for you."

The shit of it was, he couldn't argue with her. She'd nailed him. He'd always been more focused on his art than on the world around him. Achieving a measure of success had only made him narrow his focus more in an effort to propel his career forward. He'd seen Jessica as a tool he needed in his box to help him. It had taken her betrayal to open his eyes to his personal failings, and MacKenzie's love to show him what a relationship was supposed to look like. In a twisted sort of way, he owed Jessica for the life he had now. For the future he had with Kenzie. "What, exactly, did you have planned? I kind of thought you'd done enough."

"God, you didn't learn anything, did you?"

He'd learned plenty, but she didn't need to know that. "Guess not."

"I should have killed you when I had the chance, just on principal, but Cecil and Ginger told me to wait."

Does she know Ginger Carpenter is really Samantha Sheldon, Sunny's half-sister? It didn't seem like she knew, and he damn sure wasn't going to be the one to tell her. "Wait for what?"

"God, you are dense, aren't you?" She shifted so she faced him head-on. "I was supposed to wait until we were married, you idiot. As your grieving widow, I'd inherit the missing paintings."

"Which weren't missing because you knew where they were."

"Did that light bulb just flash on in your pea brain?"

"No. Ginger tried to frame Sunny Sheldon for the theft, but she screwed up and got caught. I got all my paintings back."

"Another pea brain." She shook her head. "Her and Cecil both."

"So, let me get this straight." His brother had granted him the opportunity to get the answers he wanted, but he wasn't stupid enough to think Rick was going to stand around twiddling his thumbs, hoping the she-bitch was going to let her hostages go. Keeping her talking would allow Rick and the cops time to get in place. "You were going to marry me. Then you were going to kill me. After my death, the stolen paintings would miraculously be found, and because they'd gone up in value following my death, you'd sell them and make millions. Do I have that right?"

"It was a sound plan."

"Only we didn't get married."

"You wouldn't set the date! I kept nagging you to, but you had your head in your paintings!"

Thank god he had. At least one good thing came out of his tunnel vision. MacKenzie would get a kick out of that since he was still guilty of getting lost in his work at times. He made a mental note to set a wedding date—the sooner, the better—if Jessica didn't kill him first.

"So you just decided to rob me blind instead?"

"That was Cecil's decision. He let that airhead actress of his convince him to go ahead with the plan, sans the wedding and killing you. We'd have to hold on to the paintings a lot longer, but we were eventually going to sell them on the black market. We still would have made a fortune, but that bimbo pushed her own agenda and got caught."

He'd thought he'd lost everything when he'd raised his head up long enough to realize Jess was gone and she'd taken everything with her, but in reality, she'd done him a solid. The least he could do was return the favor. "Jess, give me the gun." He held his hand out, palm up. "If you don't, you aren't going to get out of here alive."

"You're the one who's going to die, asshole. You think I came all this way to reminisce?"

"No, I think you came here to kill me, but that isn't going to happen. If you try, they'll kill you."

"Who? What are you talking about?"

She'd been so focused on telling her story and berating him, she'd failed to see the officer signaling him through the kitchen window. "The house is surrounded, Jess. At the very least, let this guy go. He's not my brother."

Her eyes widened. "What? Who the hell is he?"

"Just a guy who rents a room from Rick. No one important. He's certainly not worth the death penalty."

"You're lying."

He shook his head. "No, I'm not." He glanced at Brent. "Tell her who you are."

His brother's boyfriend opened his mouth. Closed it then tried again. "My name is Brent. I'm not related to Will or Rick in any way."

"See? I didn't lie about him, and I'm not lying about the house being surrounded." He raised his voice. "Rick! Show her that big-ass gun you have in your hands."

The barrel of a gun came into sight in the window.

"Jess, look." He nodded toward the window. "Rick's a Marine. He won't miss, and even if he did, the entire Willowbrook PD is out there now. You might get off a shot. Maybe two, before someone takes you out. Think about it, Jess. So far, you're only charged with theft, and since I got all the paintings and my money back, I'm willing to put in a good word for you. But you have to let Brent go, and give me the gun."

She glanced at the window then her gaze darted to Brent then him. She chewed on her bottom lip, a habit he recalled her doing when she was trying to work something out in her mind. He'd thought it cute, once upon a time. Not so much when he knew she was contemplating who to kill first, him or Brent. "Stop this before you get in so deep you can't get out, Jess."

"Did you ever love me? Even just a little?"

Her questions, asked with a little bit of a pout in her voice, cut him to the quick. He'd come to terms with the shitty way he'd treated her, and he understood how his actions had played a part in what she and the others had done to him. He'd hurt her, and she'd hurt him right back.

"I did," he lied. Now that he knew what real love felt like, he could see he'd never loved Jessica, not in the way she meant. This wasn't the time to confess that, either. "I was devastated when you left me." That much was true, though he'd mourned the loss of his paintings and his cash more than he'd missed her. Another thing she didn't need to know.

Her lips lifted in a weak smile, and her gaze softened. Thinking he'd convinced her, he held out his hand for the gun. She swayed toward him then she blinked, twice. A grimace replaced the smile on her face, and her gaze hardened. Another blink, and Will's heart vaulted to his throat as she lifted her arm and pointed the gun at his chest.

~ ~ ~

Considering he had more experience facing off with armed gunmen than all three of Willowbrook's police officers combined, it didn't take much to convince them to let him enter the house while they waited outside both exits, in case Jessica decided to make a run for it.

Rick eased the window in Brent's room open and crawled through. Lowering himself to the floor, Sig in hand, he belly-crawled to the door and down the short hallway to the kitchen. Rick had swapped phones with the senior officer in charge so they could listen in on Will's conversation while he got closer. With his front-row seat, he could hear everything being said, and it made his blood run cold. The bitch had planned to murder his brother in order to drive up the prices of the missing paintings that would mysteriously be found in Sunny's gallery after his death. Will's tunnel vision when it came to his work had saved his life.

As his brother kept his former fiancée talking, Rick eased the camera aperture on the borrowed phone past the doorframe until he had a visual on what was going on in the kitchen. Rick stood with his back to the interior door. Jessica, gun in her unsteady hand, stood with her back to the window above the sink. He adjusted the camera angle, caught a glimpse of Brent sitting at the table. Still wearing the clothes he'd worn to Jake's party the previous evening; a day's worth of stubble roughened his clenched jaw. Under normal circumstances, Rick would have thought the look to be sexy as hell, but closer examination revealed bags beneath terror-filled eyes. *Hang in there, baby. I'll get you out of there.*

He forced his attention away from Brent and onto the woman who had put that look in his lover's eyes. With every word out of Jessica's mouth, he mentally charted her downward spiral. She'd come with an agenda, and Will's trip down memory lane was only serving to reinforce the fucked-up reasons she'd come up with this plan in the first place. She'd meant to kill him before, and cheated of that opportunity, she wasn't about to let another get away. With no way to communicate his thoughts to his brother, he had no choice but to stand by and let the situation unfold and hope to hell his reflexes were still quick enough to react once she lost her shit. Because he had no doubt she was going to. Her intent was in her erratic gestures and every quavering word from her lips.

"Stop this before you get in so deep you can't get out, Jess."
Keep her talking, Will.

"Did you ever love me? Even just a little?"

Shit. Judging by the way her voice wavered, things were quickly going to hell in a handbasket. He adjusted his grip on the only weapon he'd brought with him, the 9mm Sig, and prepared to do whatever needed to be done to protect the people he loved.

His heart tripped over itself. *The people I love.* No question, he loved his brother, would do anything for him, but Brent? Taking a deep breath in through his nose, he let the thought of loving Brent settle. *Do I love him?* He winced recalling the tight band around his chest and the pain of betrayal when Brent had arrived at Jake's party with another man. Seeing Brent's bravery in the face of a madwoman made him face the truth his heart had known for some time. *I love him. I really fucking love him.* And there wasn't anything he wouldn't do for the people he loved.

"I did," Will told her. "I was devastated when you left me."

Rick didn't know if Will had ever really loved Jessica, but he wasn't lying about the devastation she'd left in her wake. His brother had been a shell of a man when he'd returned home to Willowbrook. It had taken him months, and the love of a good woman, to come out of the funk he'd been in. Rick had been as bad as Will when he'd come home. Renovating the house he'd grown up in and starting his own construction business had gone a long way to lifting him out of his own personal pit of self-pity, but Brent had stolen his heart and given him a reason to want to live.

I love him. God, how I love him.

He forced himself to concentrate on the gun-wielding woman standing in his kitchen. Her lips lifted in a weak smile, and her gaze softened.

Ask her for the gun, bro. Ask her now.

As if he'd heard Rick's thoughts, his brother extended his hand—a silent invitation for her to hand the weapon over.

Do it. Do it. Do it.

She swayed toward his brother, blinked twice, then her pseudo-smile turned to a grimace and her gaze hardened. Another blink.

Oh shit.

Rick dropped the phone and stepped into the open doorway, drawing the woman's attention away from her two hostages. Time slowed as it had many times when he'd been in the middle of a firefight.

Jessica raised her arm.

Will dove.

Rick stared down the barrel of her gun.

Two shots rang out simultaneously, deafening in the confined space.

A searing pain in his abdomen doubled him over.

He raised his weapon and fired again as Will tackled the assailant to the floor.

Another shot rent the air. More pain, this time in his right shoulder. He dropped to his knees.

Eight fucking years with the Marines, been in more gun battles than I can count, and I get shot in my own home.

I love you, Brent.

His world faded to black.

CHAPTER TWENTY-THREE

Silence. Deafening silence followed the split second of terror-inducing, ear-splitting, gunfire. Beneath the table where he'd taken cover the second the crazy woman had pointed her gun at Will, Brent slowly uncoiled. Nearby, Will lay motionless atop their assailant. The gun she'd pointed at him lay on the floor near her limp hand. Blood was everywhere. On the floor. The chair he'd been sitting in. Splattered on the legs of the table. Bile rose in his throat, but he swallowed it back down.

Will. He had to help him. *Oh god! The man in the doorway!* The one he'd caught the barest glimpse of as he dove beneath the table. He swung his gaze away from Will. All he could see of the man was from the thighs down, but it was enough. *Rick.* Will hadn't lied to the woman. *Rick is here!* Had come to save them.

Tears of gratitude and love welled in his eyes. On his hands and knees, he crawled out of his hiding place when Rick's knees bent. And the man who owned his heart crashed to the floor, terror like nothing he'd ever known in his life seized him.

"Rick!" He scrambled, pushing empty chairs aside in a desperate attempt to get to the man's side. "Rick! Somebody! Help!" He felt, more than heard, heavy footsteps approaching, seemingly from every direction as he knelt beside the inert figure. "Rick!" he wailed. "Rick!"

"Brent. Brent!" A firm hand on his shoulder. He looked up and met Will's gaze. "You gotta move, man. Let the EMTs take over."

EMTs? A trio of uniformed men and a woman loaded down with equipment bags crowded the hallway. Reining in his fear, he allowed Will to help him to his feet, giving the team room to work. The first of the bunch brushed past them. Brent followed his progress and was stunned to see the small room filled with police.

"Pulse is weak." The comment drew his attention to the paramedic attending to Rick. "Let's roll him over and see what we've got."

"Come on." Will wrapped a hand around the back of Brent's neck and pulled him face-first into his chest and held him there while Brent bawled his eyes out. "He's going to be okay. He won't leave us like this."

"He saved us." He hiccupped the words out.

Will stroked the back of his head. "He's a hero. Got a chest full of medals hidden under his bed. It'll take more than this to take him away from us."

"We're going to transport him now." The woman's voice over his shoulder had him pulling out of Will's embrace. "We've got a chopper waiting at the football field to take him to a trauma unit in Dallas." She named the hospital.

"We'll follow." He pointed to one of the officers occupying the kitchen. "Steve has my phone number. Call if there's any news?"

The woman nodded. Behind her, the three men she'd come in with lifted Rick's still body to a gurney and strapped him in. "I'll get the info from Steve. Drive safe. He'll need you when he wakes up."

It was Will's turn to nod then he took Brent's hand in his and they followed the team out the door. They were on the lawn, watching them load Rick into the ambulance when Jake ran up the street. "What the hell happened?"

Will faced his brother. "The bitch shot him. Twice, I think."

His boss's face turned white. "Sonofabitch. I'm going to kill her with my bare hands."

"Not necessary." Will shook his head. "Rick beat you to it."

"She's dead?"

"Yeah." Will held up his hands. Brent shivered at the dried blood in the creases of his knuckles and rimming his fingernails. "He saved our lives."

"Fucking hero," Jake muttered. He dragged Will into a hug. "You okay?"

"Fine."

Jake let Will go then pulled Brent in for a hug. "You okay?"

"Physically, yeah."

His boss drew back and, hands on Brent's shoulders, looked him over. "Have a little faith in him, Brent. He's going to be okay."

"You don't know that."

"Yes, I do." He glanced at Will then to Brent. "Because we won't let him be anything else."

Will nodded. "They're life-flighting him to Dallas. We need to go."

"My car's down the street." Jake took off at a brisk clip. Brent fell into step with Will as they followed the oldest Ingram brother to where he'd left his car.

He'd made the long drive to and from Dallas more times than he wanted to think about. Jake had a steady hand on the wheel and a heavy foot on the gas pedal, but still, the miles crept by as Brent stared, unseeing, at the passing scenery. He tried closing his eyes, but that only made the images burned onto his brain more vivid. For as long as he lived, he'd never forget Rick laying lifeless on the floor or the scent of blood permeating the air.

Rick had saved his and Will's lives. If he hadn't been there, Jessica would have killed Will then, he had no doubt, she would have turned the gun on him. He'd seen the desperation in her eyes when she'd confronted him in the kitchen. He still wasn't sure exactly what she'd done to Rick's brother in the past, only what he'd spoken of to try to talk her off the ledge, and he didn't care. She was, make that *had been*, off her rocker.

"You okay back there?"

He met Jake's gaze in the rearview mirror. "Can you drive any faster?"

"I could," his boss replied. "But Rick's going to need us to be all in one piece to help him recover."

Not trusting his voice, Brent nodded.

Will glanced over his shoulder. "He's going to be okay. The two of you will have a lifetime together."

Guilt was a lead weight anchoring his heart to his toes. He hoped Will was right, but he'd fucked up, big-time. The moment he'd spotted Kenn sitting on the front porch, he should have called a car service to pick him up and return him to whatever hole he'd crawled out of. Instead, he'd taken him to Jake's party just to spite Rick.

Fresh tears pricked his eyes. Facing the window, he swiped at them with the palm of his hand. He'd been an ass to Rick, and the man had still come to his rescue. He'd taken a bullet, maybe two.

He sucked in a deep breath. "I don't deserve your brother."

"What's that you say?" Will gave him the stink-eye over the seat.

"It's true. I don't deserve him."

"Did you fuck that guy you were with last night?" Jake's glare in the mirror matched Will's tight inquiry.

Brent shook his head then focused on the old-fashioned map book peeking out of the seat back pocket. "No, but I used him to make Rick jealous, so I might as well have. The result's the same."

"How do you figure?" Being on the receiving end of Jake's questioning reminded Brent why the man was such a good lawyer. He could slice a witness in half with his voice alone.

"He sent my call to voicemail this morning. I'm surprised he listened to the message I left." He dropped his voice to a whisper. "He had no reason to."

"Bringing that guy to the party was a shitty thing to do. Rick hid it well, but he was hurt."

Brent glanced at the back of Will's head. "I shouldn't have done it. I regretted it as soon as we got there. I should have stayed away, like Rick wanted me to."

"What?" Jake glanced over his shoulder then focused on the road ahead. "Rick didn't want you there?"

"He didn't. Rick sent me a text earlier saying he would be working late and not to expect him home for dinner. I only knew about the party because Jean mentioned she'd see me there. I put two and two together. He didn't want to be seen with me."

"That's bullshit." Will shook his head.

Jake spoke to his brother. "He told me Brent was working late."

"Yeah. He told me something like that, too," Will confirmed.

After that, they made the rest of the trip in silence. By the time they'd parked and found out Rick was in surgery, Brent had made up his mind. He couldn't stay in Willowbrook. Couldn't work for Rick's brother and live in his house any longer.

They'd been in the designated waiting room for less than half an hour when Sunny and MacKenzie arrived. Brent's heart ached as he sat alone, watching as whispered words and hugs were exchanged. He recalled the way Will had embraced him at the house. The way his strong arms had reminded him so much of his brother's. Unable to sit and watch, he walked away. Surely, there had to be a drink machine somewhere.

A kind nurse pointed him toward the cafeteria where he purchased a cup of tea and found a seat in a back corner, away from prying eyes. He didn't know how long he sat there, but by the time he wandered into the waiting room, it was filled with people he recognized from Willowbrook.

Jake pushed his way through the crowd. "Where the fuck have you been? We've been looking all over for you!"

"I went to the cafeteria. Why? Is Rick out of surgery?"

"Over an hour ago. He's in recovery, and they said the only person he wants to see is you."

His heart lodged in his throat. "Me?" he croaked.

"Told you so." Will joined them, clapping Brent on the back. "My brother's crazy about you."

Ignoring Will's optimism, he asked, "He's going to be okay?"

Jake ran a hand through his hair. "Doctor said he's got a long road ahead, but he's going to be okay. Go see him. They'll only let one person at a time in, so let him see your face then come out so we can have a chance at him."

Will put a hand on his brother's chest. "Jake's going to rip him a new one for getting himself shot then he's probably going to finish the job Jessica started." He was all smiles as he said it, but from the look on Jake's face, it wasn't far from the truth. They'd almost lost their brother today. Hero or not, Jake wasn't going to let it rest.

"Are you sure?" Brent massaged his nape. "Family should probably go first."

Jake pinned him with a look. "I would have been in there an hour ago, but the doc said Rick wanted you and nobody else. The fucker."

"So go, would you?" Will shoved him toward the door. "Apologize or whatever it is you need to do to make him happy. There are a lot of people out here who want to see him."

"You must be Brent." A nurse greeted him at the door leading to the recovery wing.

"Yes, ma'am. I'm here to see Rick Ingram."

She gave him a bright smile. "Thank god you're here. Mr. Ingram has asked about you every few minutes. I thought we were going to have to put out an APB to locate you."

"I'm sorry. I went to the cafeteria, and I guess the time got away from me."

She stopped in front of a closed door. "No worries. You're here now. Just let me peek inside to make sure he's awake. Don't stay too long. He needs his rest, and I'm sure there are other family members anxious to see him."

"I'm sorry if they've been giving you a hard time."

"We're used to it, but I have to say, his brothers have been persistent."

"I won't stay long. They told me Rick's only allowed one visitor at a time, but it might be in everyone's best interest if you let both his brothers in together. Jake's a little worked up right now."

She held his gaze while she digested what he was saying. "I'll take your recommendation under advisement." Then she pushed the door open just enough to peek in.

Rick's voice bellowed through the crack. "Did you fucking find him yet?"

The nurse, Karen, her badge said, glanced back at Brent. "He's all yours." She pushed the door wide.

"It's about fucking time!" Rick grimaced as he tried to shift his weight. "Where the hell have you been?"

Needing a moment to collect himself, Brent focused his gaze on Nurse Karen. "Thank you."

"You're welcome." She winked at him. "See if you can get him to calm down."

"I'll do my best." The door shut behind him, leaving them alone. "You wanted to see me?"

"Where the fuck were you?"

"The cafeteria. Their tea sucks, by the way."

CHAPTER TWENTY-FOUR

Rick had never been so happy to see anyone in his entire life as he was to see Brent standing there, hale and hearty. Not a scratch on him. Nurse Karen told him both his brothers were in the waiting room, and, according to her, "in perfect health and mad as hornets" over his refusal to see them. The fuckers could wait. No one had been able or willing to tell him where Brent had disappeared to, and, in his mind, that meant they were keeping something from him. Had he screwed up? Had the bitch shot Brent? He wasn't going to quit until he knew for certain, one way or the other. Now that he knew Brent was safe, anger, at himself, replaced the fear he'd been living with since he'd woken up in the hospital.

He'd been such a fucking fool. This morning was a reminder of how short life could be, and he'd wasted enough of his hiding who he was and denying himself happiness because he worried about what other people would think. Fuck them. He didn't give a shit what anyone thought anymore. No one, except Brent. He blew out a cleansing breath. "I'm sorry, baby. I should have been there when you got home this morning."

Brent sniffed. "It's okay. I should have come home last night. I deliberately waited until I knew you'd be at work before I came home this morning." His lover dissolved into a puddle of tears. "This is all my fault," he wailed.

He had a lot to say to the man, and he wasn't going to do it from across the room. His right arm was in a sling, so he wiggled the fingers of his left hand. "Come here." When Brent didn't budge, he dropped his voice an octave. "Come here, Brent. I need to fucking touch you."

Brent swiped at the tears tracking down his cheeks as he shuffled to the bedside. Rick reached for his hand. His skin was warm and reassuring. He hadn't realized what he had until he'd almost lost it. "Never should have let you leave the house yesterday. I'm fucking never letting you out of my sight again."

The lawyer sobbed harder, if that was possible.

"When they wouldn't tell me where you were, I thought the bitch had shot you or something, and they didn't want to tell me. Christ, I was going out of my mind, worrying about you."

His gorgeous lips formed a shocked O. "They didn't tell you I rode here with Jake and Will?"

"They did, but when they didn't or wouldn't say where you were, I thought they were lying to me."

Brent shook his head. "I'm so sorry. I just needed some time to myself to think. I wandered around the hospital for a while then some nurse pointed me to the cafeteria. That place is creepy. Lots of dark corners."

"You were in one of them?"

He nodded.

"What were you thinking about?"

Brent sucked in a shaky breath then let it out. "You. Me. Us."

"I've been thinking about us, too." The events of the previous day were branded on his memory as some of the worst moments of his life. Getting caught with his dick down another man's throat wasn't the way he'd pictured his brothers finding out he was gay, but that was the way it happened, and he hadn't dealt with it well. He stroked the back of Brent's hand with his thumb. "I can't apologize enough for yesterday, baby. I wanted to stop you from leaving the house so bad, but I was afraid you'd tell me no."

Brent squeezed his fingers. "I wanted to stay, to let you know I wasn't ashamed of what we were doing, but that moment belonged to you. You needed to deal with your brother on your own terms." He let out a long sigh, his gaze focused on something across the room. "It hurt to walk out the door and leave you there, and I'll admit, it hurt worse that you let me. I thought you were ashamed to admit you had feelings for me."

Rick dropped his head to the pillow and groaned. "I'm so fucking sorry. I don't want you to ever feel that way again." He raised his head. "Look at me." When Brent's gaze locked with his, he said the words he'd never said to anyone other than his brothers. "I love you. I'm not ashamed to admit that, and I'm not ashamed I want you more than I've ever wanted anyone in my life. I'm a stupid fuck for letting you think for a minute you don't mean the world to me, but if you'll give me another chance, I promise I'll make it up to you. I'll never let you out of my sight again."

Brent squeezed his hand, giving him courage "I understand if you don't want to be with me." His voice sounded like he'd gargled with gravel as he brought up the subject that had left a hole in his heart. "The guy you were with last night. He means something to you?"

He wasn't sure if the sound Brent made was a laugh or a cry. "He's nothing, Rick. Nothing at all."

God, it hurt to say the words. "But you spent the night with him."

"No. I dropped him off at a hotel and got myself a room at a different hotel." Brent flipped their linked hands over, caressing the back of Rick's with his thumb. "Kenn's my ex. I asked him to move to Willowbrook with me, but he declined. He was sitting on our porch when I got home from work yesterday. He said all the right things, but seeing him, I realized he wasn't what I wanted anymore."

"When I saw the two of you together, I don't know who I wanted to murder more, you or him."

"I'm so sorry. I was hurt and pissed at you for what happened that morning. Jean spilled the beans about the party, and that pissed me off even more. Kenn was spouting off about wanting to give Willowbrook a chance, so I figured I could kill two birds with one stone. I'd show you I didn't need you and get Kenn off my back at the same time."

"Did it work? Did you get him off your back?"

Brent smiled. "Is that what you picked up on?"

"Yeah." He grinned. "Sue me, lawyer. I *know* you need me, so tell me the fucker isn't coming back."

His gaze was tender, his voice soft. "He's not, Rick. And if he did, I'd tell him the same thing I told him last night."

The beeping of his heart monitor took off like a racehorse out of the chute. Nurse Brenda would be rushing in any second now to see what the heck was going on. "What's that?"

"That I've given my heart to someone else." He brought Rick's hand up to his lips and placed a kiss on his knuckles. "I hope he doesn't crush it."

"I won't." Christ, he was going to cry. Maybe it was the pain meds. It *had to be* the pain meds. "I won't, Brent. I promise." He inhaled a ragged breath. Shit, it even hurt to breathe. "I thought I was in love once, and when he left, it nearly killed me. But what I felt for him was nothing compared to what I feel for you. I love you, and it took seeing you held at gunpoint to get me to admit it. For a second there, I thought I might not get the chance to tell you."

"The night I put your drunk ass to bed…"

Rick forced a smile to his lips. "I bare my heart to you, and *that's* what you ask about?"

"Yeah. Tell me, baby. I want to know everything about you."

He nodded. "We'd been together for six years." The words came easier than he'd imagined they would. He told Brent everything, from the way he'd met Dave to the fucked-up way their relationship had ended. "I thought he was the love of my life. I was wrong. If we'd loved each other enough, we would have done anything to be together. He wasn't willing to come out of the closet for me, and I wasn't willing to come out for him."

"Would you have come out for me if Will hadn't walked in on us?"

"Truth?"

Brent nodded.

"Not right away, but I would have, eventually. I was already thinking about telling my brothers, but what happened this morning made me realize how short life is, and that I don't want to waste another minute pretending *you* aren't my life." He shook his head. "I understand Will came out of this unscathed. I should kill him for putting you in danger."

"It wasn't his fault. I heard everything she said. She was deranged. Probably has been for a long time but hid it well. He was taken in by her, so don't blame him."

His brother had admitted as much when they'd talked about his time in New York, but if he'd never gotten involved with the woman in the first place, none of this would have happened.

"Besides, if she hadn't shown up here, who knows how long it would have taken you to see the error of your ways."

Grinning, Rick shook his head. "Fuck off, asshole."

"Hmm. Sounds like a plan, dickwad."

Rick squeezed his hand. "You like my dick."

"I do. Very much." His gaze smoldered. "You know what else I like?"

Breathless, his heart tripping all over itself again, he asked, "What?"

"Your lips. I need to feel them on me. Can I kiss you?"

"If you don't, I'm going to get out of this bed and kick your ass."

Brent's smile was pure evil as he bent, bringing his lips to within an inch of where Rick wanted them to be. His breath brushed Rick's cheek, his comment for Rick's ears only. "There are lots of things I want you to do to my ass. Kicking isn't one of them."

Then he stole the breath from his lungs with a kiss that promised more carnal things to come. He didn't know how long they kissed before a familiar voice interrupted them.

"Jesus, Brent," Jake said. "At least wait until he's had a chance to recover before you molest him."

They both groaned. Gazes locked; Brent placed one last peck on his lips then straightened to face his boss. "I thought they said only one visitor at a time."

Jake looked worse than a mile of bad road. His hair stood on end, his skin was pale, and his face had acquired a whole new set of deeply etched lines. "They did, but you were taking so fucking long, I threatened to sue them if they didn't let me see my brother."

Rick smiled. "Throwing your weight around, big brother?"

"Just wanted to see for myself that you were going to be okay." His voice was thick with emotion. "It's not every day one of my brothers gets shot in his own home." He cleared his throat. "How are you feeling?"

"Better, now that Brent's here." He tried to shift to a more comfortable position but every time he moved, it felt like someone stabbed him with a white-hot poker. He clenched his jaw hard enough to break molars. No way was he letting Jake know how bad he hurt.

Jake nodded. "You look like shit. Don't know what he sees in you." He addressed both of them. "Sunny wants you both to stay at our house, at least until the police release the property. Right now, it's a crime scene. The investigation could take a while."

Rick had seen more than his share of crime scenes. He'd have to hire someone to clean the place. Even though he'd recently remodeled the kitchen, he'd probably want to do it all over again. Give it a fresh look to erase the bad memories associated with its present décor.

"It's an open invitation. You can stay with us as long as you want. We didn't know if you'd want to go back there anytime soon."

Brent squeezed his hand. "I appreciate the offer, Jake, and maybe we'll take you up on it when Rick is released, but for now, I'm planning on staying here."

"Jake makes a good point," Rick said. "Staying at his place, at least for a while, makes a lot of sense."

Jake's gaze darted between him and Brent then landed on Rick. "Nothing has to be decided today, so think about it, okay?" He cleared his throat again. "Sorry about the interruption, but now that I've seen you for myself, I can relax a little." His gaze swung to Brent. "Kenzie offered to go get coffee and snacks. Can we get anything for you?"

"Thanks, but I'm good."

Jake paused in the doorway. "The police want to talk to both of you. I told them I'd let them know when Rick was up to talking. As your lawyer, I'm advising both of you to not say anything to anyone about what happened unless I'm present. Understood?" They both nodded. "Okay, then."

The door closed behind him. *Thank god.* "Push that for me?" He pointed to the button the nurse had shown him earlier. If the pain got too bad, all he had to do was push it and he'd get another shot of the good stuff.

"You're hurting. I won't stay much longer. You need your rest."

"I'm fine. I could use a nap though." He reached for Brent's hand. "You really want to go back to our house? After everything that happened?"

"Your brother is a great boss, and Sunny is about the nicest person I've ever met."

"But?"

"It's one thing for my boss to know I'm fucking his brother. It's another for me to do it in his home."

Rick smiled so hard, it was a wonder his cheekbones didn't shatter. The meds were kicking in and he was drifting, so his smile might have looked a little goofy. Fuck, if he cared. All that mattered was that he hadn't lost Brent. "I gotcha. Our place it is." His head lolled on the pillow and his eyelids slid shut. He couldn't wait to take Brent home and start their life together.

EPILOGUE

Two years later…

What passed for the spring season in Texas was in full swing as Rick followed his brothers down the aisle between rows of white folding chairs set up on Jake's lawn. The sun would soon set on a picture-perfect day, the majesty of it framed by an arch covered in Texas wildflowers. Taking his place beneath the vibrant floral display, Rick faced away from the stunning show on the horizon and toward the brilliance of his future. In a few short minutes, he'd formally pledge his love and his life to the man who had taught him the meaning of love.

Brent had come into his life when Rick had been at his lowest. He'd left a career he loved on the faithless promises of another man and had his heart shattered. He'd found some peace in the business he'd created with a little help from his brothers, but it was Brent's love that had mended his heart. It was Brent who gave him the courage to own his truth and to live his truth.

Patience was a virtue he'd learned while in the Marines, and it served him well as he waited for his groom to make an appearance. He wasn't sure anyone would come, besides immediate family, but he should have known better. Every seat had been taken, and several members of the community stood along the back rows. Like every other event in Willowbrook, no invitation was needed. If you wanted to go, you went. Some, he knew, were there to witness a spectacle—a same-sex marriage—but most were there because they loved and supported one or both of the men pledging themselves today.

On his side, he acknowledged several people with a chin nod or a smile, or both. Cathy, who he'd dated in high school had been one of the first of his childhood friends to voice her support for his choice in life partners, claiming she'd suspected back then that he batted for the other team—her words, not his. If anyone would have suspected, it would have been her. He'd tried with her, but the depth of feeling she'd expected and the depth he'd been capable of had been two different things. In hindsight, he should have been more forthright with her. At the very least, he should have told her about his plan to enlist right after graduation. In his own defense, though, he hadn't told anyone. Not even his brothers and especially not his dad.

Several of his teachers were in attendance, and a bunch of kids he'd grown up with. He hadn't kept in touch with any of them while he was away, but in a small community like Willowbrook, it was hard to maintain any kind of distance. Over time, he'd run into one, then another, then another, until, slowly, he'd been pulled back into the social fabric of his small town. A few had turned their backs on him, but most had accepted Brent as his partner without question or censure. He shouldn't have kept his secret so long, but that was water under the proverbial bridge. He had Brent to thank for giving him the courage to live the life he deserved.

Speaking of…where the hell was he? He checked his watch, his gut clenching when he saw the time. Two minutes late. *What. The. Fuck?* He was going to kill him, right after he fucked him silly for making him wait.

Jake, his co-best man along with Will, leaned in. "He's coming. Nothing to worry about."

He wasn't worried, just pissed. He hated being the center of attention, and standing here with nearly everyone he knew wondering if he'd been stood up, made his skin crawl. Brent was going to pay for his tardiness but in a way they would both enjoy.

Returning his gaze to the crowd, he smiled at Jake's wife, Sunny, who bounced their baby girl, Amy, on her lap. Beside her, Will's wife, MacKenzie, cradled her baby bump with a loving hand as she winked at him. He winked back then his gaze briefly locked with that of his former lover, Dave Turner, who knew him well enough to crack a smile at his discomfort. The fucker. He'd shown up over a year ago, having left his fiancée at the altar. He said he hadn't expected Rick to pine away for him, and with Brent by his side, Rick had spent hours talking to Dave about the past and what they both wanted in the future. He'd told his fiancée the truth before leaving town, and with his and Brent's encouragement, he'd broken the news to his immediate family. They'd responded by cutting off all communication with him, so he'd moved into the apartment over Sunny's gallery and had rented another vacant storefront on Main Street and opened a gym that offered the usual fitness machines; plus, Dave acted as a personal trainer for those who needed a little extra push.

With a chin nod, Rick let his gaze wander to Brent's side of the aisle. He recognized several locals who were also Brent's clients at the law office. Then there was Jean and her husband who could have sat on either side of the aisle. Brent's large family had turned out for the occasion. All three of his younger sisters were seated in the front row. Aunts, uncles, and cousins filled up most of the next several rows. His dad and mom were to walk him down the aisle, preceded by his two brothers, who would stand up for him.

Shortly after he and Brent had officially announced they were a couple, they'd traveled to Houston to meet his family. To say he'd been surprised would be the understatement of the century. Brent had failed to mention his father was the commanding general of the largest Army base in Texas and that both his brothers were Army Rangers. Rick had nearly shit his pants when his father had answered the door in his full dress uniform. When they'd returned to their hotel room, Brent had paid for not warning him in advance.

After a smile and finger wave to Brent's sisters, his gaze wandered toward the rear of the seating arrangement where he found another face that had become familiar to him. Kenneth Westinghouse. The famous cartoonist, and Brent's former lover, sat on the back row. Kenn had been a pain in Rick's ass since the day they'd met, but once he'd made it clear Brent was his, and always would be, Kenn had come around. He'd recently moved to Dallas, partly to be closer to Brent, but mainly to get his life in order. He'd grown tired of the shallow party scene he'd been a part of in Houston and was looking for a deeper, more satisfying life now. Brent had plans to introduce their former lovers to each other at the reception later today. Rick wasn't sure it was a good idea, but they were grown men. They could decide for themselves.

Just as Kenn acknowledged him with a wide grin, movement near the pool house drew Rick's attention. Over the shoulders of the standing-room-only crowd, he caught a glimpse of a tan beret. Then another, advancing on his position. The hummingbirds in his stomach took flight, and his heart lodged in his throat as the men wearing the headgear drew closer.

It was hard to believe Brent and these men were related. His groom shared a lot of the same facial features, and he equaled them in height, but that was where the similarities ended. Brent kept in shape, but the two military men had the physique to go with their elite warrior status. Rick had worked with several Army Rangers overseas and had nothing but respect for the men who wore those berets.

The two men paused at the back of the makeshift aisle, allowing time for Brent and their parents to catch up. The moment the music began and his soon-to-be brothers-in-law stepped down the aisle, Rick got his first glimpse of his groom.

Flanked by his father, wearing his dress uniform, on one side, and his mother on the other, Brent looked like a million bucks in his tuxedo. Their gazes locked, and Rick's knees gave out. He was sinking like a rock, but before he hit the ground, strong arms lifted him to a standing position. Jake, the fucker, laughed in his left ear, while Brent's brother, Bryce, whispered, none to softly, "Stand the fuck up, Marine, before I whoop your ass."

Rick brushed both their well-meaning hands away. "I'm standing." He glared at Bryce who smirked at him before taking his place on the opposite side of the archway. They'd given him shit for being a Marine since the day they'd met, but it was all in fun…so they claimed. He wasn't so sure, but for the sake of familial peace, he held his tongue. What mattered was the way they supported their kid brother, and for that, Rick would take whatever shit they shoveled his way and do it with a smile on his face.

Jake elbowed him in the ribs. "Buck it up, brother. You're about to get hitched."

He jerked his attention away from Bryce. Brent and his parents had stopped two steps away. His mother broke ranks first, coming to place a kiss on Rick's cheek, whispering in his ear before she stepped back, "Take care of my baby."

Taking her hands in his, Rick nodded. "I will. I promise."

Brent's dad took her place, offering his hand. His grip was firm, as were his words of advice, given with the kind of smile he bet made hardened warriors piss their pants. "Hurt him and you'll wish you were never born."

Rick nodded, offering his truth in return for the man's honesty. "I used to wish that, sir, but your son gave me a reason to live. I won't hurt him. You have my word."

He patted their joined hands with his free one then released his hold. Brent's father acknowledged his other sons then he and his wife took the front row seats reserved for them. As soon as they were seated, Rick turned his gaze to the man he would spend the rest of his life with. Brent remained there, two steps away, his eyes shining with love and maybe an unshed tear or two. Rick held out his hand, palm up. When Brent took it, he closed his fingers and drew the man closer.

Before he and his brothers had left Jake's house to walk the hundred yards or so to the archway erected especially for his wedding, Will had asked if he was sure. He'd assured his brother that he was, but looking into Brent's eyes, he knew for certain. He'd been attracted to him from the first moment he'd laid eyes on him, but that was nothing compared to the overwhelming, all-encompassing, knee-weakening love he held for the man now.

He'd gotten to know the man behind the awesome body and nerd glasses and found him to have a heart of gold. He'd helped countless people in their small town and had been instrumental in encouraging acceptance for all. By some miracle, he'd looked at Rick and seen past the broken man he'd been on the night they met. He'd told Brent's father his son had given him a reason to live, but it was more than that. He'd taught him how to live.

~ ~ ~

Brent held his husband's hand tight as they navigated through the guests enjoying the poolside reception. *His husband.* Thinking those two words was like swallowing a rainbow. It filled him with light and love and most of all, promise. The promise of a lifetime of love and companionship with a man who made his blood run hot with a single touch. A man whose heart was as beautiful as the outside packaging. Growing up in a military household, he'd always sworn he wouldn't fall in love with a soldier, and he hadn't. He'd fallen for a Marine! His brothers gave him a lot of shit about his choice in men, but they did it out of love.

Rick lived the Marine Corps motto—*Semper Fidelis*—always faithful—in his civilian life. Anyone who knew him knew that about him, so Brent wasn't surprised in the least when the love of his life steered them toward his Marine buddy, and former lover, who was carrying on a conversation with Hank Travis, one of Jake's oldest friends and the drummer for BlackWing. The world renowned rock band had recently returned from an extended tour to promote their latest album, and the man knew how to tell a good story. A small crowd had gathered to listen.

"You don't mind, do you?" Rick asked.

"No, but do you think you'll be able to pull him away from Hank?"

"Won't know until I try." He squeezed Brent's hand. "Why don't you see if you can find Kenn? I'll drag Dave away if I have to then we can all meet up at the bar in a few."

He returned the hand squeeze adding a little tug. "I don't want to let go of you."

Rick thumbed the titanium band on Brent's ring finger. "We have the rest of our lives, baby. We can spare a few minutes to introduce our guys, can't we? I think they'll be good together."

"Or they'll hate each other then they'll hate us."

"Nah." His husband bent to place a gentle kiss on his lips. "Run along, now. Find Kenn and convince him he needs a beer. I'll get Dave."

Brent sighed and wrapped his arms around his husband's waist. Rick's arms surrounded him with love. "When did you become a matchmaker?"

"When I met you and realized what I'd been missing." His next kiss was more than a peck and a smidge less than an invitation to get naked. "I love you. I never knew true happiness until I met you. It hurts me to see Kenn and Dave alone. They're good men. They deserve to find their happy ever after."

"Like you found yours?"

His lips brushed lightly over Brent's. "Like *we* found *ours*." Brent's lips parted—an invitation Rick took advantage of. His mouth plundered. His tongue thrust in and out, mimicking the thrust and parry of their lower bodies. He didn't know how long they'd been locked in a carnal embrace when someone clapped him on the shoulder.

"Save that for the honeymoon, would ya?" His oldest brother, Bryce, the motherfucker.

Brent dropped his forehead to Rick's shoulder which shook with laughter. "Not funny. They're all looking at us, aren't they?"

"Pretty much," Rick confirmed. "Why don't we say the hell with our exes and get the fuck out of here?"

They'd long since cut the cake and listened to the requisite speeches. They'd only been hanging around out of courtesy, but fuck courtesy. "I think that's an excellent idea."

"Show's over, folks." Rick held him tight as he addressed the crowd. "Thanks for coming, now if you'll give us a minute to change out of these monkey suits, we'll be out to say goodbye."

Brent's cheeks were on fire as they made their way to the pool house. Once the door was locked behind them and Rick made sure the drapes were closed, it took only a minute for them to shed their wedding finery and come together heated flesh to heated flesh.

"They'll know," Brent cautioned.

"Do you care? Because I don't." Rick closed a hand around Brent's dick. "I'll never make it to the hotel. I need to be inside you. Now." They'd booked the honeymoon suite at one of Dallas's most prestigious hotels for the weekend. Monday, they'd fly to Alaska for a two-week outdoor adventure with a side of luxury accommodations Brent had insisted on as payment for camping on his honeymoon.

At Rick's touch, Brent's heart raced. He'd follow this man, *his husband,* to the ends of the earth. He palmed Rick's erection. God, he'd never get enough of him. He slid his free hand to the back of Rick's neck and pulled him in until their lips were almost touching. "Are you forgetting what today is?"

"If you're asking if I've forgotten the promise I made to you when I asked you to marry me, the answer is no. I haven't forgotten."

Brent stroked Rick's cock. "I held up my end of the bargain. I married you. You're mine, Rick. Forever and always. And I want what's mine."

Rick cradled his head in both hands, tilted his head so he could nibble on his earlobe. "I thought you'd rather wait until we got to the hotel so you could take your time."

Brent stroked Rick's cock harder. Damn, the man knew how to get his way, but he wasn't going to get it this time. "I've waited two years to make you mine. I'm not waiting a second longer. You aren't going to renege on our deal, are you, Marine?"

"No."

~ ~ ~

Brent pressed his lips to Rick's in a tender kiss that quickly burst into flames. Lips melded together; Brent walked him backward until his calves met the sofa then, hand on his chest, pushed him to his back on the plush cushions.

He'd really hoped Brent would forget about the deal they'd made or at least wait until they were somewhere more private, but the determination on his groom's face suggested the time for negotiations was over. He'd given Brent everything, except this one thing. He'd held back his submission, at first for selfish reasons, but as time went on, his motivations had changed. They'd done everything together but this, and he'd wanted to keep it that way until their wedding night. He'd saved his ass as a wedding present for Brent. Giving it to him now would have more meaning than anything else he could give him. It would mean more than the words they'd exchanged, the love they'd publicly declared, the rings they'd given each other. Submitting to Brent was the ultimate expression of his love for the man. If he wanted to claim his gift now, Rick wouldn't argue. "Wouldn't this be easier if I'm on my hands and knees?"

Brent shook his head. "I want to see your face when I shove my dick in you for the first time. I want to see your face when I make you mine."

Rick smiled to himself. *Right answer.* He wanted to see Brent's face, too. Wanted him to see the love, the trust in his eyes. "Whatever you want," he said, meaning every word. "There should be lube in the drawer over there." He pointed to an end table. If he knew his brother, there'd be lube and condoms in every room of the little love shack he fondly called a pool house.

"Remind me to thank Jake." Brent held up a small squeeze bottle.

"Over my dead body," he growled. The last thing he needed was Jake knowing for certain what they'd done in his guest accommodations. "This is none of his business."

Brent knelt on the sofa between Rick's legs. "Everyone is going to know anyway."

"Why do you say that?" He gripped his thighs and brought his knees up to his chest, his legs spread wide in invitation.

He squirted a generous amount of lube between Rick's cheeks. "Because I'm going to fuck you so damn hard, you'll need help walking out of here."

Rick groaned at his husband's declaration accompanied by two fingers spreading the cold liquid around his hole. It had been nearly three years since he'd allowed anyone the kind of intimacy he was granting Brent today, and he was loathe to admit he needed it every bit as much as Brent did. "Fuck, that feels good."

He applied more lube, working it inside with one finger, then another, stretching him a little at a time. "I've wanted to fuck you for so long, baby. I'm not going to last long."

"I don't care." He bucked his hips, silently begging for more. "We've got the rest of our lives, B., so quit fucking around and just do it."

"Someone's impatient."

Rick groaned at the teasing tone in his voice. Propping one leg up on the back of the sofa, he grabbed his dick and stroked. He was so fucking hard, he hurt. "Much more of that, and I'm going to blow without you. Is that what you want?"

Brent withdrew his fingers, making Rick moan and his hips rise…seeking. "Are you ready for me?"

He'd been ready for what seemed like forever. Taking Brent inside his body would be the final commitment between them. They'd truly belong to each other, partners for life. Taking Brent's cock in hand, he guided the head to his entrance. "Always ready, baby. Always."

Brent braced himself with one hand on the back of the sofa while the other cradled the back of Rick's neck, supporting him so he could watch their joining. "Watch, baby. Watch me claim what's mine." He flexed his hips and ever so slowly pushed his way in. Balls deep, his dick pulsing against Rick's walls. He held perfectly still, his gaze fixed on the point of their joining. Rick's rigid cock twitched. A bead of precum glistened on the tip.

"Fuuuck." Rick sucked in a breath and let it out. "Fuck, Brent. You feel so fuckin' good."

"I know." His husband's chest heaved above him. "You're so fucking beautiful. So fucking hot. I want to stay like this forever. Just you and me. Tell the rest of the world to go fuck themselves. Look at me."

Rick forced his gaze away from the miracle of their joining. Brent's eyes blazed with need, and an emotion deeper than anything Rick had ever experienced before. "I fucking love you, Rick Ingram. Now and forever. Your ass is mine. You're mine."

Rick swallowed hard. If he'd had any doubts about saving this part of himself for this moment, Brent's words and the emotion behind them, vanquished them. He'd done the right thing.

He dropped his arms, his hands on the cushion above his head in total surrender. "I love you, Brent Ingram. Everything I am belongs to you. I'm yours, now and forever."

Brent slowly withdrew then tunneled back in. Over and over as they gazed into each other's eyes, expressing their love in the most primal and physical way possible. Brent came first, emptying himself into Rick's tight channel. Afterward, he withdrew then took Rick into his mouth, ultimately taking the only gift he had left to give.

ABOUT THE AUTHOR

USA Today Best-Selling author Roz Lee is the author of over thirty romances. The first, The Lust Boat, was born of an idea acquired while on a Caribbean cruise with her family, and soon blossomed into a five-book series originally published by Red Sage. Following her love of baseball, Roz turned her attention to sexy athletes in tight pants, writing the critically acclaimed Mustangs Baseball series.

Roz has been married to her best friend, and high school sweetheart, for over four decades. They have two daughters and are the proud grandparents of three adorable grandkids. Roz and her husband live in the wilds of New Jersey with their Labrador Retriever, Bud which is code for Big Unruly Dog.

Even though Roz has lived on both coasts, her heart lies in between, in Texas. A Texan by birth, she can trace her family back to the Republic of Texas. With roots that deep, she says, "You can't ever really leave."

When Roz isn't writing, she's reading or traipsing around the country on one adventure or another. No trip is too small, no tourist trap too cheesy, and no road unworthy of travel.

Learn more at: www.RozLee.net